D0593966

MARGARET ATWOOD

MARGARET ATWOOD

THE EDIBLE WOMAN

·

SURFACING

·

LADY ORACLE

The Edible Woman first published in 1969 by McClelland and Stewart
Surfacing first published in 1972 by McClelland and Stewart
Lady Oracle first published in 1976 by McClelland and Stewart

This edition first published in 1987
by arrangement with McClelland and Stewart by

Treasure Press
59 Grosvenor Street
London W1

ISBN 0 7064 3188 X

Printed and bound in Great Britain by William Clowes Limited, Beccles

CONTENTS

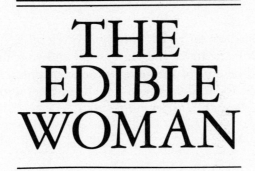

THE EDIBLE WOMAN

For J.

'The surface on which you work (preferably marble), the tools, the ingredients and your fingers should be chilled throughout the operation. . . .' (Recipe for Puff Pastry in I. S. Rombauer and M. R. Becker, *The Joy of Cooking*.)

Introduction

I wrote *The Edible Woman* in the spring and summer of 1965, on empty examination booklets filched from the University of British Columbia, where I had been teaching freshman English for the previous eight months. The title scene dates from a year earlier; I'd thought it up while gazing, as I recall, at a confectioner's display window full of marzipan pigs. It may have been a Woolworth's window full of Mickey Mouse cakes, but in any case I'd been speculating for some time about symbolic cannibalism. Wedding cakes with sugar brides and grooms were at that time of particular interest to me. *The Edible Woman*, then, was conceived by a twenty-three-year-old and written by a twenty-four-year-old, and its more self-indulgent grotesqueries are perhaps attributable to the youth of the author, though I would prefer to think that they derive instead from the society by which she found herself surrounded.

(*The Edible Woman* was not my first novel. The first one had been composed in a rentable broom closet in Toronto, but it had been rejected by all three of the then-existent Canadian publishers for being too gloomy. It ended with the heroine deciding whether or not to push the male protagonist off a roof, a conclusion that was well ahead of its time in 1963 and probably too indecisive now.)

I finished *The Edible Woman* in November of 1965 and sent it to a publisher who'd displayed some interest in my previous book. After an initial positive letter, I heard nothing. I was too busy worrying about my PhD Orals to follow up at that point, but after a year and a half I began probing and discovered that the publisher had lost the manuscript. By this time I was marginally visible, having won an award for poetry, so the publisher took me out to lunch. 'We'll publish your book,' he said, not looking me in the eye. 'Have you read it?' I said. 'No, but I'm going to,' he said. It was probably not the first book he'd published out of sheer embarrassment.

The Edible Woman appeared finally in 1969, four years after it was written and just in time to coincide with the rise of feminism in North America. Some immediately assumed that it was a product of the movement. I myself see the book as protofeminist rather than feminist: there was no women's movement in sight when I was composing the book in 1965, and I'm not gifted with clairvoyance, though like many at the time I'd read Betty Friedan and Simone de Beauvoir behind locked doors. It's noteworthy that my heroine's choices remain much the same at the end of the book as they are at the beginning: a career going nowhere, or marriage as an exit from it. But these were the options for a young woman, even a young educated woman, in Canada in the early sixties. It would be a mistake to assume that everything has changed. In fact, the tone of the book seems more contemporary now than it did in, say, 1971, when it was believed that society could change itself a good deal faster than presently appears likely. The goals of the feminist movement have not been achieved, and those who claim we're living in a post-feminist era are either sadly mistaken or tired of thinking about the whole subject.

The Edible Woman has been in print continuously in North America, in one form or another, since its publication. I'm grateful to Virago for bringing to it life again in England.

Margaret Atwood, Edinburgh, 1979

PART ONE

Chapter One

I know I was all right on Friday when I got up; if anything I was feeling more stolid than usual. When I went out to the kitchen to get breakfast Ainsley was there, moping: she said she had been to a bad party the night before. She swore there had been nothing but dentistry students, which depressed her so much she had consoled herself by getting drunk.

'You have no idea how soggy it is,' she said, 'having to go through twenty conversations about the insides of peoples' mouths. The most reaction I got out of them was when I described an abscess I once had. They positively drooled. And most men look at something besides your *teeth*, for god's sake.'

She had a hangover, which put me in a cheerful mood – it made me feel so healthy – and I poured her a glass of tomato juice and briskly fixed her an alka-seltzer, listening and making sympathetic noises while she complained.

'As if I didn't get enough of that at work,' she said. Ainsley has a job as a tester of defective electric toothbrushes for an electric toothbrush company: a temporary job. What she is waiting for is an opening in one of those little art galleries, even though they don't pay well: she wants to meet the artists. Last year, she told me, it was actors, but then she actually met some. 'It's an absolute fixation. I expect they all carry those bent mirrors around in their coat pockets and peer into their own mouths every time they go to the john to make sure they're still cavity-free.' She ran one hand reflectively through her hair, which is long and red, or rather auburn. 'Could you imagine kissing one? He'd say "Open wide" beforehand. They're so bloody one-track.'

'It must have been awful,' I said, refilling her glass. 'Couldn't you have changed the topic?'

Ainsley raised her almost non-existent eyebrows, which hadn't been coloured in yet that morning. 'Of course not,' she said. 'I pretended to be terribly interested. And naturally I didn't let on what my job was: those professional men get so huffy if you know anything about their subject. You know, like Peter.'

Ainsley tends to make jabs at Peter, especially when she isn't feeling well. I was magnanimous and didn't respond. 'You'd better eat something before you go to work,' I said, 'it's better when you've got something on your stomach.'

'Oh god,' said Ainsley, 'I can't face it. Another day of machines and mouths. I haven't had an interesting one since last month, when that lady sent back her toothbrush because the bristles were falling off. We found out she'd been using Ajax.'

I got so caught up in being efficient for Ainsley's benefit while complimenting myself on my moral superiority to her that I didn't realize how late it was until she reminded me. At the electric toothbrush company they don't care what time you breeze in, but my company thinks of itself as punctual. I had to skip the egg and wash down a glass of milk and a bowl of cold cereal which I knew would leave me hungry long before lunchtime. I chewed through a piece of bread while Ainsley watched me in nauseated silence and grabbed up my purse, leaving Ainsley to close the apartment door behind me.

We live on the top floor of a large house in one of the older and more genteel districts, in what I suppose used to be the servants' quarters. This means there are two flights of stairs between us and the front door, the higher flight narrow and slippery, the lower one wide and carpeted but with stair-rods that come loose. In the high heels expected by the office I have to go down sideways, clutching the bannister. That morning I made it safely past the line of pioneer brass warming-pans strung on the wall of our stairway, avoided catching myself on the many-pronged spinning-wheel on the second-floor landing, and sidestepped quickly down past the ragged regimental flag behind glass and the row of oval-framed ancestors that guard the first stairway. I was relieved to see there was no one in the downstairs hall. On level ground I strode towards the door, swerving to avoid the rubber-plant on one side and the hall table with the écru doily and the round brass tray on the other. Behind the velvet curtain to the right I could hear the child performing her morning penance at the piano. I thought I was safe.

But before I reached the door it swung silently inward upon its hinges, and I knew I was trapped. It was the lady down below. She was wearing a pair of spotless gardening gloves and carrying a trowel. I wondered who she'd been burying in the garden.

'Good morning, Miss MacAlpin,' she said.

'Good morning.' I nodded and smiled. I can never remember her name, and neither can Ainsley; I suppose we have what they call a mental block about it. I looked past her towards the street, but she didn't move out of the doorway.

'I was out last night,' she said. 'At a meeting.' She has an indirect way of going about things. I shifted from one foot to the other and smiled again, hoping she would realize I was in a hurry. 'The child tells me there was another fire.'

'Well, it wasn't exactly a fire,' I said. The child had taken this mention of her name as an excuse to stop practising, and was standing now in the velvet doorway of the parlour, staring at me. She is a hulking creature of fifteen or so who is being sent to an exclusive private girls' school, and she has to wear a green tunic with knee-socks to match. I'm sure she's really quite normal, but there's something cretinous about the hair-ribbon perched up on top of her gigantic body.

The lady down below took off one of her gloves and patted her chignon. 'Ah,' she said sweetly. 'The child says there was a lot of smoke.'

'Everything was under control,' I said, not smiling this time. 'It was just the pork chops.'

'Oh, I see,' she said. 'Well, I do wish you would tell Miss Tewce to try not to make quite so much smoke in future. I'm afraid it upsets the child.' She holds Ainsley alone responsible for the smoke, and seems to think she sends it out of her nostrils like a dragon. But she never stops Ainsley in the hall to talk about it: only me. I suspect she's decided Ainsley isn't respectable, whereas I am. It's probably the way we dress: Ainsley says I choose clothes as though they're a camouflage or a protective colouration, though I can't see anything wrong with that. She herself goes in for neon pink.

Of course I missed the bus: as I crossed the lawn I could see it disappearing across the bridge in a cloud of air pollution. While I was standing under the tree – our street has many trees, all of them enormous – waiting for the next bus, Ainsley came out of the house and joined me. She's a quick-change artist; I could never put myself together in such a short time. She was looking a lot healthier – possibly the effects of makeup, though you can never tell with Ainsley – and she had her red hair piled up on top of her head, as she always does when she goes to work. The rest of the time she wears it down in straggles. She had on her orange and pink sleeveless dress, which I judged was too tight across the hips. The day was going to be hot and humid; already I could feel a private atmosphere condensing around me like a plastic bag. Maybe I should have worn a sleeveless dress too.

'She got me in the hall,' I said. 'About the smoke.'

'The old bitch,' said Ainsley. 'Why can't she mind her own business?' Ainsley doesn't come from a small town as I do, so she's not as used to people being snoopy; on the other hand she's not as afraid of it either. She has no idea about the consequences.

'She's not that old,' I said, glancing over at the curtained windows of the house; though I knew she couldn't hear us. 'Besides, it wasn't her who noticed the smoke, it was the child. She was at a meeting.'

'Probably the WCTU,' Ainsley said. 'Or the IODE. I'll bet she wasn't at a meeting at all; she was hiding behind that damn velvet curtain, wanting us to think she was at a meeting so we'd *really* do something. What she wants is an orgy.'

'Now Ainsley,' I said, 'you're being paranoid.' Ainsley is convinced that the lady down below comes upstairs when we aren't there and looks round our apartment and is silently horrified, and even suspects her of ruminating over our mail, though not of going so far as to open it. It's a fact that she sometimes answers the front door for our visitors before they ring the bell. She must think she's within her rights to take precautions: when we first considered renting the apartment she made it clear to us, by discreet allusions to previous tenants, that whatever happened the child's innocence must not be corrupted, and that two young ladies were surely more to be depended upon than two young men.

'I'm doing my best,' she had said, sighing and shaking her head. She had intimated that her husband, whose portrait in oils hung above the piano, had not left as much money as he should have. 'Of course you realize your apartment has no private entrance?' She had been stressing the drawbacks rather than the advantages, almost as though she didn't want us to rent. I said we did realize it;

Ainsley said nothing. We had agreed I would do the talking and Ainsley would sit and look innocent, something she can do very well when she wants to – she has a pink-and-white blunt baby's face, a bump for a nose, and large blue eyes she can make as round as ping-pong balls. On this occasion I had even got her to wear gloves.

The lady down below shook her head again. 'If it weren't for the child,' she said, 'I would sell the house. But I want the child to grow up in a good district.'

I said I understood, and she said that of course the district wasn't as good as it used to be: some of the larger houses were too expensive to keep up and the owners had been forced to sell them to immigrants (the corners of her mouth turned gently down) who had divided them up into rooming houses. 'But that hasn't reached our street yet,' she said. 'And I tell the child exactly which streets she can walk on and which she can't.' I said I thought that was wise. She had seemed much easier to deal with before we had signed the lease. And the rent was so low, and the house was so close to the bus stop. For this city it was a real find.

'Besides,' I added to Ainsley, 'they have a right to be worried about the smoke. What if the house was on fire? And she's never mentioned the other things.'

'What other things? We've never *done* any other things.'

'Well . . .' I said. I suspected the lady down below had taken note of all the bottle-shaped objects we had carried upstairs, though I tried my best to disguise them as groceries. It was true she had never specifically forbidden us to do anything – that would be too crude a violation of her law of nuance – but this only makes me feel I am actually forbidden to do everything.

'On still nights,' said Ainsley as the bus drew up, 'I can hear her burrowing through the woodwork.'

We didn't talk on the bus; I don't like talking on buses, I would rather look at the advertisements. Besides, Ainsley and I don't have much in common except the lady down below. I've only known her since just before we moved in: she was a friend of a friend, looking for a room-mate at the same time I was, which is the way these things are usually done. Maybe I should have tried a computer; though on the whole it's worked out fairly well. We get along by a symbiotic adjustment of habits and with a minimum of that pale-mauve hostility you often find among women. Our apartment is never exactly clean, but we keep it from gathering more than a fine plum-bloom of dust by an unspoken agreement: if I do the breakfast dishes, Ainsley does the supper ones; if I sweep the living-room floor, Ainsley wipes the kitchen table. It's a see-saw arrangement and we both know that if one beat is missed the whole thing will collapse. Of course we each have our own bedroom and what goes on in there is strictly the owner's concern. For instance Ainsley's floor is covered by a treacherous muskeg of used clothes with ashtrays scattered here and there on it like stepping-stones, but though I consider it a fire-hazard I never speak to her about it. By such mutual refrainings – I assume they are mutual since there must be things I do that she doesn't like – we manage to preserve a reasonably frictionless equilibrium.

We reached the subway station, where I bought a package of peanuts. I was beginning to feel hungry already. I offered some to Ainsley, but she refused, so I ate them all on the way downtown.

We got off at the second-last stop south and walked a block together; our office buildings are in the same district.

'By the way,' said Ainsley as I was turning off at my street, 'have you got three dollars? We're out of scotch.' I rummaged in my purse and handed over, not without a sense of injustice: we split the cost but rarely the contents. At the age of ten I wrote a temperance essay for a United Church Sunday-school competition, illustrating it with pictures of car-crashes, diagrams of diseased livers, and charts showing the effects of alcohol upon the circulatory system; I expect that's why I can never take a second drink without a mental image of a warning sign printed in coloured crayons and connected with the taste of tepid communion grape-juice. This puts me at a disadvantage with Peter; he likes me to try and keep up with him.

As I hurried towards my office building, I found myself envying Ainsley her job. Though mine was better-paying and more interesting, hers was more temporary: she had an idea of what she wanted to do next. She could work in a shiny new air-conditioned office-building, whereas mine was dingy brick with small windows. Also, her job was unusual. When she meets people at parties they are always surprised when she tells them she's a tester of defective electric toothbrushes, and she always says, 'What else do you do with a BA these days?' Whereas my kind of job is only to be expected. I was thinking too that really I was better equipped to handle her job than she is. From what I see around the apartment, I'm sure I have much more mechanical ability than Ainsley.

By the time I finally reached the office I was three-quarters of an hour late. None commented but all took note.

Chapter Two

The humidity was worse inside. I waded among the ladies' desks to my own corner and had scarcely settled in behind the typewriter before the backs of my legs were stuck to the black leatherette of the chair. The air-conditioning system, I saw, had failed again, though since it is merely a fan which revolves in the centre of the ceiling, stirring the air around like a spoon in soup, it makes little difference whether it is going or not. But it was evidently bad for the ladies' morale to see the blades dangling up there unmoving: it created the impression that nothing was being done, spurring their inertia on to even greater stasis. They squatted at their desks, toad-like and sluggish, blinking and opening and closing their mouths. Friday is always a bad day at the office.

I had begun to peck languidly at my damp typewriter when Mrs Withers, the dietician, marched in through the back door, drew up, and scanned the room. She wore her usual Betty Grable hairdo and open-toed pumps, and her shoulders had an aura of shoulder pads even in a sleeveless dress. 'Ah, Marian,' she said, 'you're just in time. I need another pre-test taster for the canned rice pudding study, and none of the ladies seem very hungry this morning.'

She wheeled and headed briskly for the kitchen. There is something unwiltable about dieticians. I unstuck myself from my chair, feeling like a volunteer singled out from the ranks; but I reminded myself that my stomach could use the extra breakfast.

In the tiny immaculate kitchen she explained her problem while spooning equal portions of canned rice pudding into three glass bowls. 'You work on questionnaires, Marian, maybe you can help us. We can't decide whether to have them taste all three flavours at the same meal, or each flavour separately at subsequent meals. Or perhaps we could have them taste in pairs – say, Vanilla and Orange at one meal, and Vanilla and Caramel at another. Of course we want to get as unbiased a sampling as possible, and so much depends on what else has been served – the colours of the vegetables for instance, and the tablecloth.'

I sampled the Vanilla.

'How would you rate the colour on that?' she asked anxiously, pencil poised. 'Natural, Somewhat Artificial, or Definitely Unnatural?'

'Have you thought about putting raisins in it?' I said, turning to the Caramel. I didn't wish to offend her.

'Raisins are too risky,' she said. 'Many don't like them.'

I set down the Caramel and tried the Orange. 'Are you going to have them serve it hot?' I asked. 'Or maybe with cream?'

'Well, it's intended primarily for the time-saver market,' she said. 'They naturally would want to serve it cold. They can add cream if they like, later, I mean we've nothing really against it though it's not nutritionally necessary, it's fortified with vitamins already, but right now we want a *pure* taste-test.'

'I think subsequent meals would be best,' I said.

'If we could only do it in the middle of the afternoon. But we need a family reaction. . . .' She tapped her pencil thoughtfully on the edge of the stainless steel sink.

'Yes, well,' I said, 'I'd better be getting back.' Deciding for them what they wanted to know wasn't part of my job.

Sometimes I wonder just which things are part of my job, especially when I find myself calling up garage mechanics to ask them about their pistons and gaskets or handing out pretzels to suspicious old ladies on street corners. I know what Seymour Surveys hired me as – I'm supposed to spend my time revising the questionnaires, turning the convoluted and overly-subtle prose of the psychologists who write them into simple questions which can be understood by the people who ask them as well as the people who answer them. A question like 'In what percentile would you place the visual impact value?' is not useful. When I got the job after graduation I considered myself lucky – it was better than many – but after four months its limits are still vaguely defined.

At times I'm certain I'm being groomed for something higher

up, but as I have only hazy notions of the organizational structure of Seymour Surveys I can't imagine what. The company is layered like an ice-cream sandwich, with three floors: the upper crust, the lower crust, and our department, the gooey layer in the middle. On the floor above are the executives and the psychologists – referred to as the men upstairs, since they are all men – who arrange things with the clients; I've caught glimpses of their offices, which have carpets and expensive furniture and silk-screen reprints of Group of Seven paintings on the walls. Below us are the machines – mimeo machines, IBM machines for counting and sorting and tabulating the information; I've been down there too, into that factory-like clatter where the operatives seem frayed and overworked and have ink on their fingers. Our department is the link between the two: we are supposed to take care of the human element, the interviewers themselves. As market research is a sort of cottage industry, like a hand-knit sock company, these are all housewives working in their spare time and paid by the piece. They don't make much, but they like to get out of the house. Those who answer the questions don't get paid at all; I often wonder why they do it. Perhaps it's the come-on blurb in which they're told they can help to improve the products they use right in their own homes, something like a scientist. Or maybe they like to have someone to talk to. But I suppose most people are flattered by having their opinions asked.

Because our department deals primarily with housewives, everyone in it, except the unfortunate office-boy, is female. We are spread out in a large institutional-green room with an opaque glassed cubicle at one end for Mrs Bogue, the head of the department, and a number of wooden tables at the other end for the motherly-looking women who sit deciphering the interviewers' handwriting and making crosses and checkmarks on the completed questionnaires with coloured crayons, looking with their scissors and glue and stacks of paper like a superannuated kindergarten class. The rest of us in the department sit at miscellaneous desks in the space between. We have a comfortable chintz-curtained lunchroom for those who bring paper-bags, and a tea and coffee machine, though some of the ladies have their own teapots; we also have a pink washroom with a sign over the mirrors asking us not to leave our hairs or tea leaves in the sink.

What, then, could I expect to turn into at Seymour Surveys? I couldn't become one of the men upstairs; I couldn't become a machine person or one of the questionnaire-marking ladies, as that would be a step down. I might conceivably turn into Mrs Bogue or her assistant, but as far as I could see that would take a long time, and I wasn't sure I would like it anyway.

I was just finishing the scouring-pad questionnaire, a rush job, when Mrs Grot of Accounting came through the door. Her business was with Mrs Bogue, but on her way out she stopped at my desk. She's a short tight woman with hair the colour of a metal refrigerator-tray.

'Well, Miss MacAlpin,' she grated, 'you've been with us four months now, and that means you're eligible for the Pension Plan.'

'Pension Plan?' I had been told about the Pension Plan when I joined the company but I had forgotten about it. 'Isn't it too soon for me to join the Pension Plan? I mean – don't you think I'm too young?'

'Well, it's just as well to start early, isn't it,' Mrs Grot said. Her eyes behind their rimless spectacles were glittering: she would relish the chance of making yet another deduction from my paycheque.

'I don't think I'd like to join the Pension Plan,' I said. 'Thank you anyway.'

'Yes, well, but it's obligatory, you see,' she said in a matter-of-fact voice.

'Obligatory? You mean even if I don't want it?'

'Yes, you see if nobody paid into it, nobody would be able to get anything out of it, would they? Now I've brought the necessary documents; all you have to do is sign here.'

I signed, but after Mrs Grot had left I was suddenly quite depressed; it bothered me more than it should have. It wasn't only the feeling of being subject to rules I had no interest in and no part in making: you get adjusted to that at school. It was a kind of superstitious panic about the fact that I had actually signed my name, had put my signature to a magic document which seemed to bind me to a future so far ahead I couldn't think about it. Somewhere in front of me a self was waiting, pre-formed, a self who had worked during innumerable years for Seymour Surveys and was now receiving her reward. A pension. I foresaw a bleak room with a plug-in electric heater. Perhaps I would have a hearing aid, like one of my great-aunts who had never married. I would talk to myself; children would throw snowballs at me. I told myself not to be silly, the world would probably blow up between now and then; I reminded myself I could walk out of there the next day and get a different job if I wanted to, but that didn't help. I thought of my signature going into a file and the file going into a cabinet and the cabinet being shut away in a vault somewhere and locked.

I welcomed the coffee break at ten-thirty. I knew I ought to have skipped it and stayed to expiate my morning's lateness, but I needed the distraction.

I go for coffee with the only three people in the department who are almost my own age. Sometimes Ainsley walks over from her office to join us, when she is tired of the other toothbrush-testers. Not that she's especially fond of the three from my office, whom she calls collectively the office virgins. They aren't really very much alike, except that they are all artificial blondes – Emmy, the typist, whisk-tinted and straggly; Lucy, who has a kind of public-relations job, platinum and elegantly coiffured, and Millie, Mrs Bogue's Australian assistant, brassy from the sun and cropped – and, as they have confessed at various times over coffee-grounds and the gnawed crusts of toasted Danishes, all virgins – Millie from a solid girl-guide practicality ('I think in the long run it's better to wait until you're married, don't you? Less bother.'), Lucy from social quailing ('What would people *say*?'), which seems to be rooted in a conviction that all bedrooms are wired for sound, with society gathered at the other end tuning its earphones; and Emmy, who is the office hypochondriac, from the belief that it would make her sick, which it probably would. They are all interested in travelling: Millie has lived in England, Lucy has been twice to New York, and Emmy wants to go to Florida. After they have travelled enough they would like to get married and settle down.

'Did you hear the laxative survey in Quebec has been cancelled?' Millie said when we were seated at our usual table at the wretched, but closest, restaurant across the street. 'Great big job it was going to be, too – a product test in their own home and thirty-two pages of questions.' Millie always gets the news first.

'Well I must say that's a good thing,' Emmy sniffed. 'I don't see how they could ask anybody thirty-two pages about *that*.' She went back to peeling the nailpolish off her thumbnail. Emmy always looks as though she is coming unravelled. Stray threads trail from her hems, her lipstick sloughs off in dry scales, she sheds wispy blonde hairs and flakes of scalp on her shoulders and back; everywhere she goes she leaves a trail of assorted shreds.

I saw Ainsley come in and waved to her. She squeezed into the booth, saying 'Hi' all round, then pinned up a strand of hair that had come down. The office virgins responded, but without marked enthusiasm.

'They've done it before,' Millie said. She's been at the company longer than any of us. 'And it works. They figure anybody you could take past page three would be a sort of laxative addict, if you see what I mean, and they'd go right on through.'

'Done what before?' said Ainsley.

'What do you want to bet she doesn't wipe the table?' Lucy said, loudly enough so the waitress would overhear. She carries on a running battle with the waitress, who wears Woolworth earrings and a sullen scowl and is blatantly not an office virgin.

'The laxative study in Quebec,' I said privately to Ainsley.

The waitress arrived, wiped the table savagely, and took our orders. Lucy made an issue of the toasted Danish – she definitely wanted one without raisins this time. 'Last time she brought me one *with* raisins,' she informed us, and I told her I just couldn't stand them. I've never been able to stand raisins. Ugh.'

'Why only Quebec?' Ainsley said, breathing smoke out through her nostrils. 'Is there some psychological reason?' Ainsley majored in psychology at college.

'Gosh, I don't know,' said Millie, 'I guess people are just more constipated there. Don't they eat a lot of potatoes?'

'Would potatoes make you *that* constipated?' asked Emmy, leaning forward across the table. She pushed several straws of hair back from her forehead and a cloud of tiny motes detached themselves from her and settled gently down through the air.

'It can't be only the potatoes,' Ainsley pronounced. 'It must be their collective guilt-complex. Or maybe the strain of the language-problem; they must be horribly repressed.'

The others looked at her with hostility: I could tell they thought she was showing off. 'It's awfully hot out today,' said Millie, 'the office is like a furnace.'

'Anything happening at your office?' I asked Ainsley, to break the tension.

Ainsley ground out her cigarette. 'Oh yes, we've had quite a bit of excitement,' she said. 'Some woman tried to bump off her husband by short-circuiting his electric toothbrush, and one of our boys has to be at the trial as a witness; testify that the thing couldn't possibly short-circuit under normal circumstances. He wants me to go along as a sort of special assistant, but he's such a bore. I can tell he'd be rotten in bed.'

I suspected Ainsley of making this story up, but her eyes were at their bluest and roundest. The office virgins squirmed. Ainsley has an offhand way of alluding to the various men in her life that makes them uncomfortable.

Luckily our orders arrived. 'That bitch brought me one *with* raisins again,' Lucy wailed, and began picking them out with her long perfectly-shaped irridescent fingernails and piling them at the side of her plate.

As we were walking back to the office I complained to Millie about the Pension Plan. 'I didn't realize it was obligatory,' I said. 'I don't see why I should have to pay into their Pension Plan and have all those old crones like Mrs Grot retire and feed off my salary.'

'Oh yes, it bothered me too at first,' Millie said without interest. 'You'll get over it. Gosh, I hope they've fixed the air conditioning.'

Chapter Three

I had returned from lunch and was licking and stamping envelopes for the coast-to-coast instant pudding-sauce study, behind schedule because someone in mimeo had run one of the question sheets backwards, when Mrs Bogue came out of her cubicle.

'Marian,' she said with a sigh of resignation, 'I'm afraid Mrs Dodge in Kamloops will have to be removed. She's pregnant.' Mrs Bogue frowned slightly: she regards pregnancy as an act of disloyalty to the company.

'That's too bad,' I said. The huge wall-map of the country, sprinkled with red thumbtacks like measles, is directly above my desk, which means that the subtraction and addition of interviewers seems to have become part of my job. I climbed up on the desk, located Kamloops, and took out the thumbtack with the paper flag marked DODGE.

'While you're up there,' Mrs Bogue said, 'could you just take off Mrs Ellis in Blind River? I hope it's only temporary, she's always done good work, but she writes that some lady chased her out of the house with a meat cleaver and she fell on the steps and broke her leg. Oh, and add this new one – a Mrs Gauthier in Charlottetown. I certainly hope she's better than the last one there; Charlottetown is always so difficult.'

When I had climbed down she smiled at me pleasantly, which put me on guard. Mrs Bogue has a friendly, almost cosy manner that equips her perfectly for dealing with the interviewers, and she is at her most genial when she wants something. 'Marian,' she said, 'we have a little problem. We're running a beer study next week – you know which one, it's the telephone-thing one – and they've decided upstairs that we need to do a pre-test this weekend. They're worried about the questionnaire. Now, we could get Mrs Pilcher, she's a dependable interviewer, but it *is* the long weekend and we don't like to ask her. You're going to be in town, aren't you?'

'Does it have to be this weekend?' I asked, somewhat pointlessly.

'Well, we absolutely have to have the results Tuesday. You only need to get seven or eight men.'

My lateness that morning had given her leverage. 'Fine,' I said, 'I'll do them tomorrow.'

'You'll get overtime, of course,' Mrs Bogue said as she walked away, leaving me wondering whether that had been a snide remark. Her voice is always so bland it's hard to tell.

I finished licking the envelopes, then got the beer questionnaires from Millie and went through the questions, looking for trouble-spots. The initial selection questions were standard enough. After that, the questions were designed to test listener response to a radio jingle, part of the advertising campaign for a new brand of beer one of the large companies was about to launch on the market. At a certain point the interviewer had to ask the respondent to pick up the telephone and dial a given number, whereupon the jingle would play itself to him over the phone. Then there were a number of questions asking the man how he liked the commercial, whether he thought it might influence his buying habits, and so on.

I dialled the phone number. Since the survey wasn't actually being conducted till the next week, someone might have forgotten to hook up the record, and I didn't want to make an idiot of myself.

After a preliminary ringing, buzzing and clicking a deep bass voice, accompanied by what sounded like an electric guitar, sang:

Moose, Moose,
From the land of pine and spruce,
Tingly, heady, rough-and-ready. . . .

Then a speaking voice, almost as deep as the singer's, intoned persuasively to background music,

Any real man, on a real man's holiday – hunting, fishing, or just plain old-fashioned relaxing – needs a beer with a healthy, hearty taste, a deep-down flavour. The first long cool swallow will tell you that Moose Beer is just what you've always wanted for true beer enjoyment. Put the tang of the wilderness in YOUR life today with a big satisfying glass of sturdy Moose Beer.

The singer resumed:

Tingly, heady,
Rough-and-ready,
Moose, Moose, Moose, Moose, BEER!!!

and after a climax of sound the record clicked off. It was in satisfactory working order.

I remembered the sketches I'd seen of the visual presentation, scheduled to appear in magazines and on posters: the label was to have a pair of antlers with a gun and a fishing-rod crossed beneath them. The singing commercial was a reinforcement of this theme; I didn't think it was very original but I admired the subtlety of 'just plain old-fashioned relaxing.' That was so the average beer-drinker, the slope-shouldered pot-bellied kind, would be able to feel a mystical identity with the plaid-jacketed sportsman shown in the pictures with his foot on a deer or scooping a trout into his net.

I had got to the last page when the telephone rang. It was Peter. I could tell from the sound of his voice that something was wrong.

'Listen, Marian, I can't make it for dinner tonight.'

'Oh?' I said, wanting further explanation. I was disappointed, I had been looking forward to dinner with Peter to cheer me up. Also I was hungry again. I had been eating in bits and pieces all day and I had been counting on something nourishing and substantial. This meant another of the TV dinners Ainsley and I kept for emergencies. 'Has something happened?'

'I know you'll understand. Trigger' – his voice choked – 'Trigger's getting married.'

'Oh,' I said. I thought of saying 'That's too bad,' but it didn't seem adequate. There was no use in sympathizing as though for a minor mishap when it was really a national disaster. 'Would you like me to come with you?' I asked, offering support.

'God no,' he said, 'that would be even worse. I'll see you tomorrow. Okay?'

When he had hung up I reflected upon the consequences. The most obvious one was that Peter would need careful handling the next evening. Trigger was one of Peter's oldest friends; in fact, he had been the last of Peter's group of oldest friends still left unmarried. It had been like an epidemic. Just before I'd met him two had succumbed, and in the four months since that another two had gone under without much warning. He and Trigger had found themselves more and more alone on their bachelor drinking sessions during the summer, and when the others did take an evening off from their wives to go along, I gathered from Peter's gloomy accounts that the flavour of the evening was a synthetic substitute for the irresponsible gaiety of the past. He and Trigger had clutched each other like drowning men, each trying to make the other the reassuring reflection of himself that he needed. Now Trigger had sunk and the mirror would be empty. There were the other law students of course, but most of them were married too. Besides, they belonged to Peter's post-university silver age rather than to his earlier golden one.

I felt sorry for him, but I knew I would have to be wary. If the other two marriages had been any indication, he'd start seeing me after two or three drinks as a version of the designing siren who had carried off Trigger. I didn't dare ask how she had done it: he might think I was getting ideas. The best plan would be to distract him.

While I was meditating Lucy came over to my desk. 'Do you think you can write a letter to this lady for me?' she asked. 'I'm getting a splitting headache and I really can't think of a thing to say.' She pressed one elegant hand to her forehead; with the other she handed me a note written in pencil on a piece of cardboard. I read it:

> *Dear Sir, The cereal was fine but I found this in with the raisins. Yours Truly, (Mrs) Ramona Baldwin.*

A squashed housefly was scotch-taped to the bottom of the letter.

'It was that raisin-cereal study,' Lucy said faintly. She was playing on my sympathies.

'Oh, all right,' I said; 'have you got her address?'

I made several trial drafts:

> *Dear Mrs Baldwin; We are extremely sorry about the object in your cereal but these little mistakes will happen. Dear Mrs Baldwin; We are so sorry to have inconvenienced you; we assure you however that the entire contents of the package was absolutely sterile. Dear Mrs Baldwin; We are grateful to you for calling this matter to our attention as we always like to know about any errors we may have made.*

The main thing, I knew, was to avoid calling the housefly by its actual name.

The phone rang again; this time it was an unexpected voice.

'Clara!' I exclaimed, conscious of having neglected her. 'How *are* you?'

'Shitty, thanks,' Clara said. 'But I wonder if you can come to dinner. I'd really like to see an outside face.'

'I'd love to,' I said, my enthusiasm half-genuine: it would be better than a TV dinner. 'About what time?'

'Oh, you know,' Clara said. 'Whenever you come. We aren't what you'd call punctual around here.' She sounded bitter.

Now I was committed I was thinking rapidly of what this would involve: I was being invited as an entertainer and confidante, someone who would listen to a recital of Clara's problems, and I didn't feel like it. 'Do you think I could bring Ainsley too?' I said. 'That is, if she isn't doing anything.' I told myself it would be good for Ainsley to have a wholesome dinner – she had only had a coffee at the coffee-break – but secretly I wanted her along to take off a bit of the pressure. She and Clara could talk about child psychology.

'Sure, why not?' Clara said. 'The more the merrier, that's our motto.'

I called Ainsley at work, carefully asking her whether she was doing anything for dinner and listening to her accounts of the two invitations she had received and turned down – one from the toothbrush murder trial witness, the other from the dentistry student of the night before. To the latter she had been quite rude: she was never going out with him again. She claimed he had told her there would be artists at the party.

'So you aren't doing anything then,' I said, establishing the fact.

'Well, no,' said Ainsley, 'unless something comes along.'

'Then why don't you come with me to Clara's for dinner?' I was expecting a protest, but she accepted calmly. I arranged to meet her at the subway station.

I left the desk at five and headed for the cool pink Ladies' Room. I wanted a few minutes of isolation to prepare myself for coping before I set out for Clara's. But Emmy, Lucy and Millie were all there, combing their yellow hair and retouching their makeup. Their six eyes glittered in the mirrors.

'Going out tonight, Marian?' Lucy asked, too casually. She shared my telephone line and naturally knew about Peter.

'Yes,' I said, without volunteering information. Their wistful curiosity made me nervous.

Chapter Four

I walked down towards the subway station along the late-afternoon sidewalk through a thick golden haze of heat and dust. It was almost like moving underwater. From a distance I saw Ainsley shimmering beside a telephone pole, and when I had reached her she turned and we joined the lines of office workers who were funnelling down the stairs into the cool underground caverns below. By quick manoeuvring we got seats, though on the opposite sides of the car, and I sat reading the advertisements as well as I could through the screen of lurching bodies. When we got off again and went out through the pastel corridors the air felt less humid.

Clara's house was a few blocks further north. We walked in silence; I thought about mentioning the Pension Plan, but decided not to. Ainsley wouldn't understand why I found it disturbing: she'd see no reason why I couldn't leave my job and get another one, and why this wouldn't be a final solution. Then I thought about Peter and what had happened to him; Ainsley, however, would only be amused if I told her. Finally I asked her if she was feeling better.

'Don't be so concerned, Marian,' she said, 'you make me feel like an invalid.'

I was hurt and didn't answer.

We were going uphill at a slight angle. The city slopes upwards from the lake in a series of gentle undulations, though at any given point it seems flat. This accounted for the cooler air. It was quieter here too; I thought Clara was lucky, especially in her condition, to be living so far away from the heat and noise of downtown. Though she herself thought of it as a kind of exile: they had started out in an apartment near the university, but the need for space had forced them further north, although they had not yet reached the real suburbia of modern bungalows and station-wagons. The street itself was old but not as attractive as our street: the houses were duplexes, long and narrow, with wooden porches and thin back gardens.

'Christ it's hot,' Ainsley said as we turned up the walk that led to Clara's house. The grass on the doormat-sized lawn had not been cut for some time. On the steps lay a nearly-decapitated doll and inside the baby-carriage was a large teddy-bear with the stuffing coming out. I knocked, and after several minutes Joe appeared behind the screen door, harried and uncombed, doing up the buttons on his shirt.

'Hi Joe,' I said 'here we are. How's Clara feeling?'

'Hi, come on through,' he said, stepping aside to let us past. 'Clara's out back.'

We walked the length of the house, which was arranged in the way such houses usually are – living-room in front, then dining-room with doors that can be slid shut, then kitchen – stepping over some of the scattered obstacles and around the others. We negotiated the stairs of the back porch, which were overgrown with empty bottles of all kinds, beer bottles, milk bottles, wine and scotch bottles, and baby bottles, and found Clara in the garden, sitting in a round wicker basket-chair with metal legs. She had her feet up on another chair and was holding her latest baby somewhere in the vicinity of what had once been her lap. Clara's body is so thin that her pregnancies are always bulgingly obvious, and now in her seventh month she looked like a boa-constrictor that has swallowed a watermelon. Her head, with its aureole of pale hair, was made to seem smaller and even more fragile by the contrast.

'Oh hi,' she said wearily as we came down the back steps. 'Hello Ainsley, nice to see you again. Christ it's hot.'

We agreed, and sat down on the grass near her, since there were no chairs. Ainsley and I took off our shoes; Clara was already barefoot. We found it difficult to talk: everyone's attention was necessarily focussed on the baby, which was whimpering, and for some time it was the only person who said anything.

When she telephoned Clara had seemed to be calling me to some sort of rescue, but I felt now that there was nothing much I could do, and nothing she had even expected me to do. I was to be only a witness, or perhaps a kind of blotter, my mere physical presence absorbing a little of the boredom.

The baby had ceased to whine and was now gurgling. Ainsley was plucking bits of grass.

'Marian,' Clara said at last, 'could you take Elaine for a while? She doesn't like going on the ground and my arms are just about falling off.'

'I'll take her,' said Ainsley unexpectedly.

Clara pried the baby away from her body and transferred it to Ainsley, saying 'Come on, you little leech. I sometimes think she's all covered with suckers, like an octopus.' She lay back in her chair and closed her eyes, looking like a strange vegetable growth, a bulbous tuber that had sent out four thin white roots and a tiny pale-yellow flower. A cicada was singing in a tree nearby, its monotonous vibration like a hot needle of sunlight between the ears.

Ainsley held the baby awkwardly, gazing with curiosity into its face. I thought how closely the two faces resembled each other. The baby stared back up with eyes as round and blue as Ainsley's own; the pink mouth was drooling slightly.

Clara raised her head and opened her eyes. 'Is there anything I can get you?' she asked, remembering she was the hostess.

'Oh no, we're fine,' I said hastily, alarmed by the image of her struggling up out of the chair. 'Is there anything I can get you?' I would have felt better doing something positive.

'Joe will come out soon,' she said as if explaining. 'Well, talk to me. What's new?'

'Nothing much,' I said. I sat trying to think of things that would entertain her, but anything I could mention, the office or places I had been or the furnishings of the apartment, would only remind Clara of her own inertia, her lack of room and time, her days made claustrophobic with small necessary details.

'Are you still going out with that nice boy? The good-looking one. What's-his-name. I remember he came by once to get you.'

'You mean Peter?'

'Yes she is,' said Ainsley, with a hint of disapproval. 'He's monopolized her.' She was sitting cross-legged, and now she put the baby down in her lap so she could light a cigarette.

'That sounds hopeful,' Clara said gloomily. 'By the way, guess who's back in town? Len Slank. He called up the other day.'

'Oh really? When did he get in?' I was annoyed that he hadn't called me too.

'About a week ago, he said. He said he'd tried to phone you but couldn't get hold of your number.'

'He might have tried Information,' I said drily. 'But I'd love to see him. How did he seem? How long is he staying?'

'Who is he?' Ainsley asked.

'Oh, no-one you'd be interested in,' I said quickly. I couldn't think of two people who would be worse for each other. 'He's just an old friend of ours from college.'

'He went to England and got into television,' said Clara. 'I'm not just sure what he does. A nice type though, but he's horrible with women, sort of a seducer of young girls. He says anything over seventeen is too old.'

'Oh, one of those,' Ainsley said. 'They're such a bore.' She stubbed out her cigarette in the grass.

'You know, I got the feeling that's why he's back,' Clara said, with something like vivacity. 'Some kind of a mess with a girl; like the one that made him go over in the first place.'

'Ah,' I said, not surprised.

Ainsley gave a little cry and deposited the baby on the lawn. 'It's wet on my dress,' she said accusingly.

'Well, they do, you know,' said Clara. The baby began to howl, and I picked her up gingerly and handed her over to Clara. I was prepared to be helpful, but only up to a point.

Clara joggled the baby. 'Well, you goddamned fire-hydrant,' she said soothingly. 'You spouted on mummy's friend, didn't you? It'll wash out, Ainsley. But we didn't want to put rubber pants on you in all this heat, did we, you stinking little geyser? Never believe what they tell you about maternal instinct,' she added grimly to us. 'I don't see how anyone can love their children till they start to be human beings.'

Joe appeared on the back porch, a dishtowel tucked apron-like into the belt of his trousers. 'Anybody for a beer before dinner?'

Ainsley and I said Yes eagerly, and Clara said, 'A little vermouth for me, darling. I can't drink anything else these days, it upsets my bloody stomach. Joe, can you just take Elaine in and change her?'

Joe came down the steps and picked up the baby. 'By the way,' he said, 'you haven't seen Arthur around anywhere, have you?'

'Oh god, now where has the little bugger got to now?' Clara asked as Joe disappeared into the house; it seemed a rhetorical question. 'I think he's found out how to open the back gate. The little bastard. Arthur! Come here, darling,' she called languidly.

Down at the end of the narrow garden the line of washing that hung almost brushing the ground was parted by two small grubby hands, and Clara's firstborn emerged. Like the baby he was naked except for a pair of diapers. He hesitated, peering at us dubiously.

'Come here love, and let mummy see what you've been up to,' Clara said. 'Take your hands off the clean sheets,' she added without conviction.

Arthur picked his way over the grass towards us, lifting his bare feet high with every step. The grass must have been ticklish. His diaper was loose, suspended as though by will-power alone below the bulge of his stomach with its protruding navel. His face was puckered in a serious frown.

Joe returned carrying a tray. 'I stuck her in the laundry basket,' he said. 'She's playing with the clothes pins.'

Arthur had reached us and stood beside his mother's chair, still frowning, and Clara said to him, 'Why have you got that funny look, you little demon?' She reached down behind him and felt his diaper. 'I should have known,' she sighed, 'he was so quiet. Husband, your son has shat again. I don't know where, it isn't in his diaper.'

Joe handed round the drinks, then knelt and said to Arthur firmly but kindly, 'Show Daddy where you put it.' Arthur gazed up at him, not sure whether to whimper or smile. Finally he stalked portentously to the side of the garden, where he squatted down near a clump of dusty red chrysanthemums and stared with concentration at a patch of ground.

'That's a good boy,' Joe said, and went back into the house.

'He's a real nature-child, he just loves to shit in the garden,' Clara said to us. 'He thinks he's a fertility-god. If we didn't clean it up this place would be one big manure field. I don't know what he's going to do when it snows.' She closed her eyes. 'We've been trying to toilet-train him, though according to some of the books it's too early, and we got him one of those plastic potties. He hasn't the least idea what it's for; he goes around wearing it on his head. I guess he thinks it's a crash-helmet.'

We watched, sipping our beer, as Joe crossed the garden and returned with a folded piece of newspaper. 'After this one I'm going on the pill,' said Clara.

When Joe had finally finished cooking the dinner we went into the house and ate it, seated around the heavy table in the dining-room. The baby had been fed and exiled to the carriage on the front porch, but Arthur sat in a highchair, where he evaded with spastic contortions of his body the spoonfuls of food Clara poked in the direction of his mouth. Dinner was wizened meat balls and noodles from a noodle mix, with lettuce. For dessert we had something I recognized.

'This is that new canned rice pudding; it saves a lot of time,' Clara said defensively. 'It's not too bad with cream, and Arthur loves it.'

'Yes,' I said. 'Pretty soon they'll be having Orange and Caramel too.'

'Oh?' Clara deftly intercepted a long drool of pudding and returned it to Arthur's mouth.

Ainsley got out a cigarette and held it for Joe to light. 'Tell me,' she said to him, 'do you know this friend of theirs – Leonard Slank? They're being so mysterious about him.'

Joe had been up and down all during the meal, taking off the plates and tending things in the kitchen. He looked dizzy. 'Oh yes, I remember him,' he said, 'though he's really a friend of Clara's.' He finished his pudding quickly and asked Clara whether she needed any help, but she didn't hear him. Arthur had just thrown his bowl on the floor.

'But what do *you* think of him?' Ainsley asked, as though appealing to his superior intelligence.

Joe stared at the wall, thinking. He didn't like giving negative judgements, I knew, but I also knew he wasn't fond of Len. 'He's not ethical,' he said at last. Joe is an Instructor in Philosophy.

'Oh, that's not quite fair,' I said. Len had never been unethical towards me.

Joe frowned at me. He doesn't know Ainsley very well, and tends anyway to think of all unmarried girls as easily victimized and needing protection. He had several times volunteered fatherly advice to me, and now he emphasized his point. 'He's not someone to get ... mixed up with,' he said sternly. Ainsley gave a short laugh and blew out smoke, unperturbed.

'That reminds me,' I said, 'you'd better give me his phone number.'

After dinner we went to sit in the littered living-room while Joe cleared the table. I offered to help, but Joe said that was all right, he would rather I talked to Clara. Clara had settled herself on the chesterfield in a nest of crumpled newspapers with her eyes closed; again I could think of little to say. I sat staring up at the centre of the ceiling where there was an elaborately-scrolled plaster decoration, once perhaps the setting for a chandelier, remembering Clara at highschool: a tall fragile girl who was always getting exempted from Physical Education. She'd sit on the sidelines watching the rest of us in our blue-bloomered gymsuits as though anything so sweaty and ungainly was foreign enough to her to be a mildly-amusing entertainment. In that classroom full of oily potato-chip-fattened adolescents she was everyone's ideal of translucent perfume-advertisement femininity. At university she had been a little healthier, but had grown her blonde hair long, which made her look more medieval than ever: I had thought of her in connection with the ladies sitting in rose-gardens on tapestries. Of course her mind wasn't like that, but I've always been influenced by appearances.

She married Joe Bates in May at the end of our second year, and at first I thought it was an ideal match. Joe was then a graduate student, almost seven years older than she was, a tall shaggy man with a slight stoop and a protective attitude towards Clara. Their worship of each other before the wedding was sometimes ridiculously idealistic; one kept expecting Joe to spread his overcoat on mud puddles or drop to his knees to kiss Clara's rubber boots. The babies had been unplanned: Clara greeted her first pregnancy with astonishment that such a thing could happen to her, and her second with dismay; now, during her third, she had subsided into a grim but inert fatalism. Her metaphors for her children included barnacles encrusting a ship and limpets clinging to a rock.

I looked at her, feeling a wave of embarrassed pity sweep over me; what could I do? Perhaps I could offer to come over some day and clean up the house. Clara simply had no practicality, she wasn't able to control the more mundane aspects of life, like money or getting to lectures on time. When we lived in residence together she used to become hopelessly entangled in her room at intervals, unable to find matching shoes or enough clean clothes to wear, and I would have to dig her out of the junk pile she had allowed to accumulate around her. Her messiness wasn't actively creative like Ainsley's, who could devastate a room in five minutes if she was feeling chaotic; it was passive. She simply stood helpless while the tide of dirt rose round her, unable to stop it or evade it. The babies were like that too; her own body seemed somehow beyond her, going its own way without reference to any directions of hers. I studied the pattern of bright flowers on the maternity smock she was wearing; the stylized petals and tendrils moved with her breathing, as though they were coming alive.

We left early, after Arthur had been carried off to bed screaming after what Joe called 'an accident' behind the living-room door.

'It was no accident,' Clara remarked, opening her eyes. 'He just loves peeing behind doors. I wonder what it is. He's going to be secretive when he grows up, an undercover agent or a diplomat or something. The furtive little bastard.'

Joe saw us to the door, a pile of dirty laundry in his arms. 'You must come and see us again soon,' he said, 'Clara has so few people she can really talk to.'

Chapter Five

We walked down towards the subway in the semi-dusk, through the sound of crickets and muffled television sets (in some of the houses we could see them flickering blue through the open windows) and a smell of warm tar. My skin felt stifled, as though I was enclosed in a layer of moist dough. I was afraid Ainsley hadn't enjoyed herself: her silence was negative.

'Dinner wasn't bad,' I said, wanting to be loyal to Clara, who was after all an older friend than Ainsley; 'Joe's turning into quite a good cook.'

'How can she stand it?' Ainsley said with more vehemence than usual. 'She just lies there and that man does all the work! She lets herself be treated like a *thing*!'

'Well, she is seven months pregnant,' I said. 'And she's never been well.'

'*She's* not well!' Ainsley said indignantly. 'She's flourishing; it's him that's not well. He's aged even since I've known him and that's less than four months. She's draining all his energy.'

'What do you suggest?' I said. I was annoyed with Ainsley: she couldn't see Clara's position.

'Well, she should *do* something; if only a token gesture. She never finished her degree, did she? Wouldn't this be a perfect time for her to work on it? Lots of pregnant women finish their degrees.'

I remembered poor Clara's resolutions after the first baby: she had thought of it as only a temporary absence. After the second she had wailed, 'I don't know what we're doing wrong! I always try to be so careful'. She had always been against the pill – she thought it might change her personality – but gradually she had become less adamant. She had read a French novel (in translation) and a book about archaeological expeditions in Peru and had talked about night school. Lately she had taken to making bitter remarks about being 'just a housewife'. 'But Ainsley,' I said, 'you're always saying that a degree is no real indication of anything.'

'Of course the degree in itself isn't,' Ainsley said, 'it's what it stands for. She should get organized,'

When we were back at the apartment I thought of Len, and decided it wasn't too late to call him. He was in, and after we'd exchanged greetings I told him I would love to see him.

'Great,' he said, 'when and where? Make it some place cool. I didn't remember it was so bloody hot in the summers over here.'

'Then you shouldn't have come back,' I said, hinting that I knew why he had and giving him an opening.

'It was safer,' he said with a touch of smugness. 'Give them an inch and they'll take a mile.' He had acquired a slight English accent. 'By the way, Clara tells me you've got a new roommate.'

'She isn't your type,' I said. Ainsley had gone into the living-room and was sitting on the chesterfield with her back to me.

'Oh, you mean too old, like you, eh?' My being too old was one of his jokes.

I laughed. 'Let's say tomorrow night,' I said. It had suddenly struck me that Len would be a perfect distraction for Peter. 'About eight-thirty at the Park Plaza. I'll bring a friend along to meet you.'

'Aha,' said Len, 'this fellow Clara told me about. Not serious, are you?'

'Oh no, not at all,' I said to reassure him.

When I had hung up Ainsley said, 'Was that Len Slank you were talking to?'

I said yes.

'What does he look like?' she asked casually.

I couldn't refuse to tell her. 'Oh, sort of ordinary. I don't think you'd find him attractive. He has blond curly hair and horn-rimmed glasses. Why?'

'I just wondered.' She got up and went into the kitchen. 'Want a drink?' she called.

'No thanks,' I said, 'but you could bring me a glass of water.' I moved into the living-room and went to the window seat where there was a breeze.

She came back in with a scotch on the rocks for herself and handed me my glass of water. Then she sat down on the floor. 'Marian,' she said, 'I have something I need to tell you.'

Her voice was so serious that I was immediately worried. 'What's wrong?'

'I'm going to have a baby,' she said quietly.

I took a quick drink of water. I couldn't imagine Ainsley making a miscalculation like that. 'I don't believe you.'

She laughed. 'Oh, I don't mean I'm already pregnant. I mean I'm going to get pregnant.'

I was relieved, but puzzled. 'You mean you're going to get married?' I asked, thinking of Trigger's misfortune. I tried to guess which of them Ainsley could be interested in, without success; ever since I'd known her she had been decidedly anti-marriage.

'I knew you'd say that,' she said with amused contempt. 'No, I'm not going to get married. That's what's wrong with most children, they have too many parents. You can't say the sort of household Clara and Joe are running is an ideal situation for a child. Think of how confused their mother-image and their father-image will be; they're riddled with complexes already. And it's mostly because of the father.'

'But Joe is marvellous!' I cried. 'He does just about everything for her! Where would Clara be without him?'

'Precisely,' said Ainsley. 'She would have to cope by herself. And she would cope, and their total upbringing would be much more consistent. The thing that ruins families these days is the husbands. Have you noticed she isn't even breast-feeding the baby?'

'But it's got teeth,' I protested. 'Most people wean them when they get teeth.'

'Nonsense,' Ainsley said darkly, 'I bet Joe put her up to it. In South America they breast-feed them much longer than that. North American men hate watching the basic mother-child unit functioning naturally, it makes them feel not needed. This way Joe can give it the bottle just as easily. Any woman left to her own devices would automatically breast-feed as long as possible: I'm certainly going to.'

It seemed to me that the discussion had got off the track: we were talking theory about a practical matter. I tried a personal attack: 'Ainsley, you don't know anything at all about babies. You don't even like them much, I've heard you say they're too dirty and noisy.'

'Not liking other people's babies,' said Ainsley, 'isn't the same as not liking your own.'

I couldn't deny this. I was baffled: I didn't even know how to justify my own opposition to her plan. The worst of it was that she would probably do it. She can go about getting what she wants with a great deal of efficiency, though in my opinion some of the things she wants – and this was a case in point – are unreasonable. I decided to take a down-to-earth approach.

'All right,' I said. 'Granted. Buy why do you want a baby, Ainsley? What are you going to *do* with it?'

She gave me a disgusted look. 'Every woman should have at least one baby.' She sounded like a voice on the radio saying that every woman should have at least one electric hair-dryer. 'It's even more important than sex. It fulfills your deepest femininity.' Ainsley is fond of paper-back books by anthropologists about primitive cultures: there are several of them bogged down among the clothes on her floor. At her college they make you take courses in it.

'But why now?' I said, searching my mind for objections. 'What about the job at the art gallery? And meeting the artists?' I held them out to her like a carrot to a donkey.

Ainsley widened her eyes at me. 'What has having a baby got to do with getting a job at an art gallery? You're always thinking in terms of either/or. The thing is *wholeness*. As for why now, well, I've been considering this for some time. Don't you feel you need a sense of purpose? And wouldn't you rather have your children while you're young? While you can enjoy them. Besides, they've proved they're likely to be healthier if you have them between twenty and thirty.'

'And you're going to keep it,' I said. I looked around the living-room, calculating already how much time, energy and money it would take to pack and move the furniture. I had contributed most of the solider items: the heavy round coffee table donated from a relative's attic back home, the walnut drop-leaf we used for company, also a donation, the stuffed easy-chair and the chesterfield I had picked up at the Salvation Army and re-covered. The outsize poster of Theda Bara and the bright paper flowers were Ainsley's; so were the ash trays and the inflatable plastic cushions with geometric designs. Peter said our living-room lacked unity. I had never thought of it as a permanent arrangement, but now it was threatened it took on a desirable stability for me. The tables planted their legs more firmly on the floor; it was inconceivable that the round coffee table could ever be manipulated down those narrow stairs, that the poster of Theda Bara could be rolled up, revealing the crack in the plaster, that the plastic cushions could allow themselves to be deflated and stowed away in a trunk. I wondered whether the lady down below would consider Ainsley's pregnancy a breach of contract and take legal action.

Ainsley was getting sulky. 'Of course I'm going to keep it. What's the good of going through all that trouble if you don't keep it?'

'So what it boils down to,' I said, finishing my water, 'is that you've decided to have an illegitimate child in cold blood and bring it up yourself.'

'Oh, it's such a bore to *explain*. Why use that horrible bourgeois word? Birth is legitimate, isn't it? You're a prude, Marian, and that's what's wrong with this whole society.'

'Okay, I'm a prude,' I said, secretly hurt: I thought I was being more understanding than most. 'But since the society is the way it is, aren't you being selfish? Won't the child suffer? How are you going to support it and deal with other people's prejudices and so on?'

'How is the society ever going to change,' said Ainsley with the dignity of a crusader, 'if some individuals in it don't lead the way? I will simply tell the truth. I know I'll have trouble here and there, but some people will be quite tolerant about it, I'm sure, even here. I mean, it won't be as though I've gotten pregnant by accident or anything.'

We sat in silence for several minutes. The main point seemed to have been established. 'All right,' I said finally, 'I see you've thought of everything. But what about a father for it? I know it's a small technical detail, but you will need one of those, you know, if only for a short time. You can't just send out a bud.'

'Well,' she said, taking me seriously, 'actually I have been thinking about it. He'll have to have a decent heredity and be fairly good-looking; and it will help if I can get someone co-operative who will understand and not make a fuss about marrying me.'

She reminded me more than I liked of a farmer discussing cattle-breeding. 'Anyone in mind? What about that dentistry student?'

'Good god no,' she said, 'he has a receding chin.'

'Or the electric toothbrush murder-witness man?'

She puckered her brow. 'I don't think he's very bright. I'd prefer an artist of course, but that's too risky genetically; by this time they must all have chromosome breaks from LSD. I suppose I could unearth Freddy from last year, he wouldn't mind in the least, though he's too fat and he has an awfully stubbly five o'clock shadow. I wouldn't want a fat child.'

'Nor one with heavy stubble either,' I said, trying to be helpful.

Ainsley looked at me with annoyance. 'You're being sarcastic,' she said. 'But if only people would give more thought to the characteristics they pass on to their children maybe they wouldn't rush blindly into things. We know the human race is degenerating and it's all because people pass on their weak genes without thinking about it, and medical science means they aren't naturally selected out the way they used to be.'

I was beginning to feel fuzzy in the brain. I knew Ainsley was wrong, but she sounded so rational. I thought I'd better go to bed before she had convinced me against my better judgement.

In my room, I sat on the bed with my back against the wall, thinking. At first I tried to concentrate on ways to stop her, but then I became resigned. Her mind was made up, and though I could hope this was just a whim she would get over, was it any of my business? I would simply have to adjust to the situation. Perhaps when we had to move I should get another room-mate; but would it be right to leave Ainsley on her own? I didn't want to behave irresponsibly.

I got into bed, feeling unsettled.

Chapter Six

The alarm clock startled me out of a dream in which I had looked down and seen my feet beginning to dissolve, like melting jelly, and had put on a pair of rubber boots just in time only to find that the ends of my fingers were turning transparent. I had started towards the mirror to see what was happening to my face, but at that point I woke up, I don't usually remember my dreams.

Ainsley was still asleep, so I boiled my egg and drank my tomato juice and coffee alone. Then I dressed in an outfit suitable for interviewing, an official-looking skirt, a blouse with sleeves, and a pair of low-heeled walking shoes. I intended to get an early start, but I couldn't be too early or the men, who would want to sleep in on the holiday, wouldn't be up yet. I got out my map of the city and studied it, mentally crossing off the areas I knew had been selected for the actual survey. I had some toast and a second cup of coffee, and traced out several possible routes for myself.

What I needed was seven or eight men with a certain minimum average beer consumption per week, who would be willing to answer the questions. Locating them might be more difficult than usual, because of the long weekend. I knew from experience that men were usually more unwilling than women to play the questionnaire game. The streets near the apartment were out: word might get back to the lady down below that I had been asking the neighbours how much beer they drank. Also, I suspected that it was a scotch area rather than a beer one; with a sprinkling of teetotalling widows. The rooming-house district further west was out, too: I had tried it once for a potato-chip taste-test and found the landladies very hostile. They seemed to think I was a government agent in disguise, trying to raise their tax by discovering they had more lodgers than they claimed. I considered the fraternity houses near the university, but remembered the study demanded answerers over the age-limit.

I took the bus, got off at the subway station, paused to note down my fare as 'Transportation' on my expenses time-sheet, and crossed the street. Then I went down a slope into the flat treeless park spread out opposite the station. There was a baseball diamond in one corner, but nobody was playing on it. The rest of the park was plain grass, which had turned yellow; it crackled underfoot. This day was going to be like the one before, windless and oppressive. The sky was cloudless but not clear: the air hung heavily, like invisible steam, so that the colours and outlines of objects in the distance were blurred.

At the far side of the park was a sloping asphalt ramp, which I climbed. It led to a residential street lined with small, rather shabby houses set close together, the two-storey shoe-box kind with wooden trim round the windows and eaves. Some of the houses had freshly-painted trimmings, which merely accentuated the weatherbeaten surfaces of the shingled fronts. The district was the sort that had been going downhill for some decades but had been pushed uphill again in the past few years. Several refugees from the suburbs had bought these city houses and completely refinished them, painting them a sophisticated white and adding flagstone walks and evergreens in cement planters and coachlamps by the doors. The re-done houses looked flippant beside the others, as though they had chosen to turn their backs with an irresponsible light-heartedness upon the problems of time and shabbiness and puritan weather. I resolved to avoid the transformed houses when I began to interview. I wouldn't find the right sort of people there: they would be the martini set.

There is something intimidating about a row of closed doors if you know you have to go up and knock on them and ask what amounts to a favour. I straightened my dress and my shoulders and assumed what I hoped was an official but friendly expression, and walked as far as the next block practising it before I had worked up resolution enough to begin. At the end of the block I could see what looked like a fairly new apartment-building. I made it my goal: it would be cool inside, and might supply me with any missing interviews.

I rang the first doorbell. Someone scrutinized me briefly through the white semi-transparent curtains of the front window; then the door was opened by a sharp-featured woman in a print apron with a bib. Her face had not a vestige of makeup on it, not even lipstick, and she was wearing those black shoes with laces and thick heels that make me think of the word 'orthopaedic' and that I associate with the bargain-basements of department stores.

'Good morning, I represent Seymour Surveys,' I said, smiling falsely. 'We're doing a little survey and I wonder if your husband would be kind enough to answer a few questions for me?'

'You selling anything?' she asked, glancing at my papers and pencil.

'Oh, no! We have nothing to do with selling. We're a market research company, we merely ask questions. It helps improve the products,' I added lamely. I didn't think I was going to find what I was looking for.

'What's it about? she asked, the corners of her mouth tightening with suspicion.

'Well, actually it's about beer,' I said in a tinsel-bright voice, trying to make the word sound as skim-milk-like as possible.

Her face changed expression. She was going to refuse, I thought. But she hesitated, then stepped aside and said in a voice that reminded me of cold oatmeal porridge, 'Come in.'

I stood in the spotless tiled hallway, inhaling the smell of furniture-polish and bleach, while she disappeared through a door farther on, closing it behind her. There was a murmured conversation; then the door opened again and a tall man with grey hair and a severe frown came through it, followed by the woman. The man wore a black coat even though the day was so warm.

'Now young lady,' he said to me, 'I'm not going to chastize you personally because I can see you are a nice girl and only the innocent means to this abominable end. But you will be so kind as to give these tracts to your employers. Who can tell but that their hearts may yet be softened? The propagation of drink and of drunkenness to excess is an iniquity, a sin against the Lord.'

I took the pamphlets he handed me, but felt enough loyalty to Seymour Surveys to say, 'Our company doesn't have anything to do with *selling* the beer, you know.'

'It is the same thing,' he said sternly, 'it is all the same thing, "Those who are not with me are against me, saith the Lord." Do not try to whiten the sepulchres of those traffickers in human misery and degradation.' He was about to turn away, but said to me as an afterthought, 'You might read those yourself, young lady. Of course you never pollute your lips with alcohol, but no soul is utterly pure and proof against temptation. Perhaps the seed will not fall by the wayside, nor yet on stony ground.'

I said a faint 'Thank you,' and the man extended the edges of his mouth in a smile. His wife, who had been watching the small sermon with frugal satisfaction, stepped forward and opened the door for me, and I went out, resisting the reflex urge to shake both of them by the hand as though I was coming out of church.

It was a bad beginning. I looked at the tracts as I walked to the next house. 'TEMPERANCE,' commanded one. The other was titled, more stirringly, 'DRINK AND THE DEVIL'. He must be a minister, I thought, though certainly not Anglican, and probably not even United. One of those obscure sects.

No-one was at home in the next house, and at the one after that the door was opened by a chocolate-smeared urchin who informed me that her daddy was still in bed. At the next one though I soon knew that I had come at last to a good place for head-hunting. The main door was standing open, and the man I could see coming towards me several moments after I had rung was of medium height but very thickly built, almost fat. When he opened the screen door I could see that he had only his socks on his feet, no shoes; he was wearing an undershirt and a pair of bermuda shorts. His face was brick-red.

I explained my errand and showed him the card with the average-beer-consumption-per-week scale on it. Each average is numbered, and the scale runs from 0 to 10. The company does it that way because some men are shy about naming their consumption in so many words. This man picked No. 9, the second from the top. Hardly anybody chooses No. 10: everyone likes to think there's a chance that somebody else drinks more than he does.

When we had got that far the man said, 'Come on into the living room and sit down. You must be tired walking around in all that heat. My wife's just gone to do the shopping,' he added irrelevantly.

I sat down in one of the easy-chairs and he turned down the sound on the TV set. I saw a bottle of one of Moose Beer's competitors standing on the floor by his chair, half-empty. He sat down opposite me, smiling and mopping his forehead with his handkerchief, and answered the preliminary questions with the air of an expert delivering a professional verdict. After he had listened to the telephone commercial he scratched the hair on his chest thoughtfully and gave the sort of enthusiastic response for which a whole seminary of admen had no doubt been offering daily prayers. When we finished and I had written down the name and address, which the company needs so it won't re-interview the same people, got up, and began to thank him, I saw him lurching out of his chair towards me with a beery leer. 'Now what's a nice little girl like you doing walking around asking men all about their beer?' he said moistly. 'You ought to be at home with some big strong man to take care of you.'

I pressed the two Temperance pamphlets into his damp outstretched hand and fled.

I shuffled through four more complete interviews without much incident, discovering in the process that the questionnaire needed the addition of a 'Does not have phone . . . End interview' box and a 'Does not listen to radio' one, and that men who approved of the chest-thumping sentiments of the commercial tended to object to the word 'Tingly' as being 'Too light,' or, as one of them put it, 'Too fruity'. The fifth interview was with a spindly balding man who was so afraid of expressing any opinions at all that getting words out of him was like pulling teeth with a monkey-wrench. Every time I asked him a new question he flushed, bobbed his Adam's apple, and contorted his face in a wince of agony. He was speechless for several minutes after he had listened to the commercial and I had asked him, 'How did you like the commercial? Very Much; Only Moderately; or Not Very Much?' At last he managed to whisper, feebly, 'Yes.'

I had now only two more interviews to get. I decided to skip the next few houses and go to the square apartment-building. I got in by the usual method, pressing all the buttons at once until some deluded soul released the inner door.

The coolness was a relief. I went up a short flight of stairs whose carpeting was just beginning to wear thin, and knocked at the first door, which was numbered Six. I found this curious because from its position it should have been numbered *One*.

Nothing happened when I knocked. I knocked again more loudly, waited, and was about to go on to the next apartment when the door swung inward noiselessly and I found myself being looked at by a young boy whom I judged to be about fifteen.

He rubbed one of his eyes with a finger, as if he had just got up. He was cadaverously thin; he had no shirt on, and the ribs stuck out like those of an emaciated figure in a medieval woodcut. The skin stretched over them was nearly colourless, not white but closer to the sallow tone of old linen. His feet were bare; he was wearing only a pair of khaki pants. The eyes, partly hidden by a rumpled mass of straight black hair that came down over the forehead, were obstinately melancholy, as though he was assuming the expression on purpose.

We stared at each other. He was evidently not going to say anything, and I could not quite begin. The questionnaires I was carrying had suddenly become unrelated to anything at all, and at the same time obscurely threatening. Finally I managed to say, feeling very synthetic as I did so, 'Hello there, is your father in?'

He continued to stare at me without a tremor of expression. 'No. He's dead,' he said.

'Oh.' I stood, swaying a little; the contrast with the heat outside had made me dizzy. Time seemed to have shifted into slow-motion;

there seemed to be nothing to say; but I couldn't leave or move. He continued to stand in the doorway.

Then after what seemed hours it occurred to me that he might not actually be as young as he looked. There were dark circles under his eyes, and some fine thin lines at the outer corners. 'Are you really only fifteen?' I asked, as though he had told me he was.

'I'm twenty-six,' he said dolefully.

I gave a visible start, and as if the answer had stepped on some hidden accelerator in me I babbled out a high-speed version of the blurb about being from Seymour Surveys and not selling anything and improving products and wanting to ask a few simple questions about how much beer he drank in an average week, thinking while I did so that he didn't look as though he ever drank anything but water, with the crust of bread they tossed him as he lay chained in the dungeon. He seemed gloomily interested, much as one would be interested (if at all) in a dead dog, so I extended the average-weekly-consumption card towards him and asked him to pick his number. He looked at it a minute, turned it over and looked at the back, which was blank, closed his eyes, and said 'Number six.'

That was seven to ten bottles per week, high enough to qualify him for the questionnaire, and I told him so. 'Come in then,' he said. I felt a slight sensation of alarm as I stepped over the threshold and the door closed woodenly behind me.

We were in a living room of medium size, perfectly square, with a kitchenette opening off it on one side and the hallway to the bedrooms on the other. The slats of the venetian blind on the one small window were closed, making the room dim as twilight. The walls, as far as I could tell in the semi-darkness, were a flat white; there were no pictures on them. The floor was covered by a very good Persian carpet with an ornate design of maroon and green and purple scrolls and flowers, even better, I thought, than the one in the lady down below's parlour which had been left her by her paternal grandfather. One wall had a bookcase running its whole length, the kind people make themselves out of boards and bricks. The only other pieces of furniture were three huge, ancient and overstuffed easy chairs, one red plush, one a worn greenish-blue brocade, and one a faded purple, each with a floor-lamp beside it. All exposed surfaces of the room were littered with loose papers, notebooks, books opened face-down and other books bristling with pencils and torn slips of paper stuck in them as markers.

'Do you live here alone?' I asked.

He fixed me with his lugubrious eyes. 'It depends what you mean,' he intoned, 'by "alone".'

'Oh, I see,' I said politely. I walked across the room, trying to preserve my air of cheerful briskness while picking my way unsteadily over and around the objects on the floor. I was heading towards the purple chair, which was the only one that didn't have a rat's-nest of papers in it.

'You can't sit there,' he said behind me in a tone of slight admonishment, 'that's Trevor's chair. He wouldn't like you sitting in his chair.'

'Oh. Is the red one all right then?'

'Well,' he said, 'that's Fish's, and he wouldn't mind if you sat in it; at least I don't think he would. But he's got his papers in it and you might mess them up.' I didn't see how by merely sitting on them I could possibly disorganize them any more, but I didn't say so. I was wondering whether Trevor and Fish were two imaginary playmates that this boy had made up, and also whether he had lied about his age. In this light his face could have been of a ten-year-old. He stood gazing at me solemnly, shoulders hunched, arms folded across his torso, holding his own elbows.

'And I suppose yours is the green one then.'

'Yes,' he said, 'but I haven't sat in it myself for a couple of weeks. I've got everything all arranged in it.'

I wanted to go over and see exactly what he had got all arranged in it, but I reminded myself that I was there on business. 'Where are we going to sit then?'

'The floor,' he said, 'Or the kitchen, or my bedroom.'

'Oh, not the bedroom,' I said hurriedly. I made my way back across the expanse of paper and peered around the corner into the kitchenette. A peculiar odour greeted me – there seemed to be garbage bags in every corner, and the rest of the space was taken up by large pots and kettles, some clean, others not. 'I don't think there's room in the kitchen,' I said. I stooped and began to skim the papers off the surface of the carpet, much as one would skim scum from a pond.

'I don't think you'd better do that,' he said. 'Some of them aren't mine. You might get them mixed up. We'd better go into the bedroom.' He slouched across to the hall and through an open doorway. Of necessity I followed him.

The room was a white-walled oblong box, dark as the living room: the venetian blind was down here too. It was bare of furniture except for an ironing-board with an iron on it, a chess set with a few scattered pieces in a corner of the room, a typewriter sitting on the floor, a cardboard carton which seemed to have dirty laundry in it and which he kicked into the closet as I came in, and a narrow bed. He pulled a grey army-blanket over the tangle of sheets on the bed and crawled onto it, where he settled himself crosslegged, backed into the corner formed by the two walls. he switched on the reading-lamp over the bed, took a cigarette from a pack which he replaced in his back pocket, lit it, and sat holding the cigarette before him, his hands cupped, like a starved buddha burning incense to itself.

'All right,' he said.

I sat down on the edge of the bed – there were no chairs – and began to go through the questionnaire with him. After I had asked each question he would lean his head back against the wall, close his eyes, and give the answer; then he would open his eyes again and watch me with barely-perceptible signs of concentration while I asked the next.

When we got to the telephone commercial he went to the phone in the kitchen to dial the number. He stayed out there for what seemed to me a long time. I went to check, and found him listening with the receiver pressed to his ear and his mouth twisted in something that was almost a smile.

'You're only supposed to listen once,' I said reproachfully.

He put down the receiver with reluctance. 'Can I phone it after you go and listen some more?' he asked in the diffident but wheedling voice of a small child begging an extra cookie.

'Yes,' I said, 'but not next week, okay?' I didn't want him blocking the line for the interviewers.

We went back to the bedroom and resumed our respective postures. 'Now I'm going to repeat some of the phrases from the commercial to you, and for each one I would like you to tell me what it makes you think of,' I said. This was the free-association part of the questionnaire, meant to test immediate responses to certain key phrases. 'First, what about "Deep-down manly flavour?"'

He threw his head back and closed his eyes. 'Sweat,' he said, considering. 'Canvas gym shoes. Underground locker-rooms and jock-straps.'

An interviewer is always supposed to write down the exact words of the answer, so I did. I thought about slipping this interview into the stack of real ones, to vary the monotony for one of the women with the crayons – Mrs Weemers, perhaps, or Mrs Gundridge. She'd read it out loud to the others, and they would remark that it took all kinds; the topic would be good for at least three coffee-breaks.

'Now what about "Long cool swallow?"'

'Not much. Oh, wait a moment. It's a bird, white, falling from a great height. Shot through the heart, in winter; the feathers coming off, drifting down. ... This is just like those word-game tests the shrink gives you,' he said with his eyes open. 'I always liked doing them. They're better than the ones with pictures.'

I said, 'I expect they use the same principle. What about "Healthy hearty taste?"'

He meditated for several minutes. 'It's heartburn,' he said. 'Or no, that can't be right.' His forehead wrinkled. 'Now I see. It's one of those cannibal stories.' For the first time he seemed upset. 'I know the pattern, there's one of them in the Decameron and a couple in Grimm's; the husband kills the wife's lover, or vice versa, and cuts out the heart and makes it into a stew or a pie and serves it up in a silver dish, and the other one eats it. Though that doesn't account for the Healthy very well, does it? Shakespeare,' he said in a less agitated voice, 'Shakespeare has something like that too. There's a scene in *Titus Andronicus*, though it's debatable whether Shakespeare really wrote it, or ...'

'Thank you,' I wrote busily. By this time I was convinced that he was a compulsive neurotic of some sort and that I'd better remain calm and not display any fear. I wasn't frightened exactly – he didn't look like the violent type – but these questions definitely made him tense. He might be tottering on an emotional brink, one of the phrases might be enough to push him over. Those people are like that I thought, remembering certain case histories Ainsley had told me; little things like words can really bother them.

'Now, "Tingly, heady, rough-and-ready?"'

He contemplated that one at length. 'Doesn't do a thing for me,' he said, 'it doesn't fit together. The first bit gives me an image of someone with a head made out of glass being hit with a stick: like musical glasses. But rough-and-ready doesn't do anything. I suppose,' he said sadly, 'that one's not much use to you.'

'You're doing fine,' I said, thinking of what would happen to the IBM machine if they ever tried to run this thing through it. 'Now the last one: "Tang of the wilderness."'

'Oh,' he said, his voice approaching enthusiasm, 'that one's easy; it struck me at once when I heard it. It's one of those technicolour movies about dogs or horses. "Tang of the Wilderness" is obviously a dog, part wolf, part husky, who saves his master three times, once from fire, once from flood and once from wicked humans, more likely to be white hunters than Indians these days, and finally gets blasted by a cruel trapper with a .22 and wept over. Buried, probably in the snow. Panoramic shot of trees and lake. Sunset. Fade-out.'

'Fine,' I said, scribbling madly to get it all down. There was silence while we both listened to the scratching of my pencil. 'Now, I hate to ask you, but you're supposed to say how well you think each of those five phrases applies to a beer – Very Well, Medium Well, or Not Very Well At All?'

'I couldn't tell you,' he said, losing interest completely. 'I never drink the stuff. Only scotch. None of them are any good for scotch.'

'But,' I protested, astonished, 'you picked Number Six on the card. The one that said seven to ten bottles per week.'

'You wanted me to pick a number,' he said with patience, 'and six is my lucky number. I even got them to change the numbers on the apartments; this is really Number One, you know. Besides, I was bored; I felt like talking to someone.'

'That means I won't be able to count your interview,' I said severely. I had forgotten for the moment that it wasn't real.

'Oh, you enjoyed it,' he said, smiling his half-smile again. 'You know all the other answers you've been getting are totally dull. You have to admit I've livened up your day considerably.'

I had a twinge of irritation. I had been feeling compassion for him as a sufferer on the verge of mental collapse, and now he had revealed the whole thing as a self-conscious performance. I could either get up and leave at once, showing my displeasure, or admit that he was right. I frowned at him, trying to decide what to do; but just then I heard the front door opening and the sound of voices.

He jerked forward and listened tensely, then leaned back against the wall. 'It's only Fish and Trevor. They're my room-mates,' he said, 'the other two bores. Trevor's the mother bore: he's going to be shocked when finds me with my shirt off and a capital-G girl in the room.'

There was a brown-paper crunkle of grocery-bags being set down in the kitchen, and a deep voice said, 'Christ, it's hot out there!'

'I think I'd better go now,' I said. If the others were at all like this one I didn't think I would be able to cope. I gathered my questionnaires together and stood up, at the same time as the voice said 'Hey Duncan, want a beer?' and a furry bearded head appeared in the doorway.

I gasped. 'So you do drink beer after all!'

'Yes, I'm afraid so. Sorry. I didn't want to finish, that's all. The rest of it sounded like a drag, and I'd said all I wanted to say about it anyway. Fish,' he said to the beard, 'this is Goldilocks.' I smiled rigidly. I am not a blonde.

Another head now appeared above the first: a white-skinned face with receding lightish hair, skyblue eyes, and an admirably-chiselled nose. His jaw dropped when he saw me.

It was time to leave. 'Thank you,' I said coolly but graciously to the one on the bed. 'You've been most helpful.'

He actually grinned as I marched to the doorway and as the heads retreated in alarm to let me pass he called, 'Hey, why do you have a crummy job like this? I thought only fat sloppy housewives did that sort of thing.'

'Oh,' I said with as much dignity as I could muster, and not intending to justify myself by explaining the high – well, higher – status of my real job, 'we all have to eat. Besides, what else can you do with a BA these days?'

When I was outside I looked at the questionnaire. The notes I had made of his answers were almost indecipherable in the glare of the sunlight; all I could see on the page was a blur of grey scribbling.

Chapter Seven

Technically I was still one and a half interviews short, but I had enough for the necessary report and the questionnaire changes. Besides, I wanted to have a bath and change before going to Peter's and the interviewing had taken longer than I expected.

I got back to the apartment and threw the questionnaires on the bed. Then I looked around for Ainsley, but she was out. I gathered together my washcloth, soap, toothbrush and toothpaste, put on my dressing gown, and went downstairs. Our apartment has no bathroom of its own, which helps to account for the low rent. Perhaps the house was built before they had them, or perhaps it was felt that servants didn't need bathrooms; at any rate, we have to use the second floor bathroom, which makes life difficult at times. Ainsley is always leaving rings, which the lady down below regards as a violation of her shrine. She leaves deodorants and cleansers and brushes and sponges in conspicuous places, which has no effect on Ainsley but makes me feel uneasy. Sometimes I go downstairs after Ainsley has taken a bath and clean out the tub.

I had wanted to soak for a while, but I had barely scrubbed away the afternoon's film of dust and bus fumes when the lady down below began making rustling and throat-clearing noises outside the door. This is her way of suggesting that she wants to get in: she never knocks and asks. I clambered upstairs again, dressed, had a cup of tea, and set out for Peter's. The ancestors watched me with their fading daguerrotyped eyes as I went down the stairs, their mouths bleak above their stiff collars.

Usually we went out for dinner, but when we didn't the pattern was that I would walk over to Peter's and get something to cook at a store on the way – one of those small grubby stores you sometimes find in the older residential districts. Of course he could have picked me up at the house in his Volkswagen, but he is made irritable by errands; also I don't like to give the lady down below too much food for speculation. I didn't know whether we were going out for dinner or not – Peter had said nothing about it – so I dropped in at the store just to be on the safe side. He would probably have a hangover from the celebration of the night before and wouldn't feel like a full-scale dinner.

Peter's apartment-building is just far enough away to make getting there by transportation-system more bother than it's worth. It's south of our district and east of the university, in a rundown area, nearly a slum, that is scheduled to be transformed over the next few years by high-rise apartments. Several have been completed but Peter's is still under construction. Peter is the only person who lives there; he does so temporarily, at only a third of the price they'll charge when the building is finished. He was able to make this deal through a connection he acquired during a piece of contract manipulating. Peter's in his articling year as a lawyer and doesn't have extravagant amounts of money yet – for instance he couldn't have afforded the apartment at its list price – but his is a small firm and he's rising in it like a balloon.

All summer whenever I went to the apartment I had to thread my way through piles of concrete blocks near the entrance to the lobby, around shapes covered with dusty tarpaulins on the floor inside, and sometimes over troughs for plaster and ladders and stacks of pipes on the stairway going up; the elevators aren't in working order yet. Occasionally I would be stopped by workmen who didn't know about Peter and who would insist that I couldn't go in because nobody lived there. We would then have arguments about the existence or non-existence of Mr Wollander, and once I'd had to take some of them up to the seventh floor with me and produce Peter in the flesh. I knew there wouldn't be any men working as late as five on Saturday though; and they probably had the whole long weekend off anyway. Generally they seem to go about things in a leisurely manner, which suits Peter. There's been a strike or a layoff too which has held things up. Peter hopes it will go on: the longer they take, the longer his rent will be low.

Structurally the building was complete, except for the finishing touches. They had all the windows in and had scrawled them with white soap hieroglyphics to keep people from walking through them. The glass doors had been installed several weeks before, and Peter had got an extra set of keys made for me: a necessity rather than just a convenience, since the buzzer-system for letting people in had not yet been connected. Inside, the shiny surfaces – tiled floors, painted walls, mirrors, light-fixtures – which would later give the building its expensive gloss, its beetle-hard internal shell, had not yet begun to secrete themselves. The rough grey underskin of subflooring and unplastered wall-surface was still showing, and raw wires dangled like loose nerves from most of the sockets. I went up the stairs carefully, avoiding the dirty bannister, thinking how much I had come to associate weekends with this new-building smell of sawn boards and cement-dust. On the floors I passed, the doorways of the future apartments gaped emptily, their doors as yet unhung. It was a long climb up; as I reached Peter's floor I was breathing hard. I would be glad when the elevators were running.

Peter's apartment, of course, has been largely finished; he'd never live in a place without proper floors and electricity, no matter how low the rent. His connection uses it as a model of what the rest of the apartments will be like, and shows it to the occasional prospective tenant, always phoning Peter before he arrives. It doesn't inconvenience Peter much: he's out a lot and doesn't mind people looking through his place.

I opened the door, went in, and took the groceries to the refrigerator in the kitchenette. I could tell by the sound of running water that Peter was taking a shower: he often is. I strolled into the living room and looked out of the window. The apartment isn't far enough up for a good view of the lake or the city – you can only see a mosaic of dingy little streets and narrow backyards, and you aren't low enough to see clearly what the people are doing in them. Peter hasn't put much in the living room yet. He's got a Danish-modern sofa and a chair to match and a hi-fi set, but nothing else. He says he'd rather wait and get good things than clutter the place up with cheap things he doesn't like. I suppose he is right, but still it will help when he gets more: his two pieces of furniture are made to look very spindly and isolated by the large empty space that surrounds them.

I get restless when I'm waiting for anyone, I tend to pace. I wandered into the bedroom and looked out the window there, though it's much the same view. Peter has the bedroom nearly done, he's told me, though for some tastes it might be slightly sparse. He has a good-sized sheepskin on the floor and a plain, solid bed, also good sized, second-hand but in perfect condition, which is always neatly made. Then an austere square desk, dark wood, and one of those leather-cushioned office swivel-chairs that he picked up second-hand too; he says it's very comfortable for working. The desk has a reading lamp on it, a blotter, an assortment of pens and pencils, and Peter's graduation portrait in a stand-up frame. On the wall above there's a small bookcase – his law books on the bottom shelf, his hoard of paperback detective novels on the top shelf, and miscellaneous books and magazines in between. To one side of the bookcase is a pegboard with hooks that holds Peter's collection of weapons: two rifles, a pistol, and several wicked-looking knives. I've been told all the names, but I can never remember them. I've never seen Peter use any of them, though of course in the city he wouldn't have many opportunities. apparently he used to go hunting a lot with his oldest friends. Peter's cameras hang there too, their glass eyes covered by leather cases. There's a full-length mirror on the outside of the cupboard door, and inside the cupboard are all of Peter's clothes.

Peter must have heard me prowling. He called from inside the bathroom, 'Marian? That you?'

'I'm here,' I called back. 'Hi.'

'Hi. Fix yourself a drink. And one for me too – gin and tonic, okay? I'll be out in a minute.'

I knew where everything was. Peter has a cupboard shelf well-stocked with liquor, and he never forgets to re-fill the ice-cube trays. I went to the kitchen, and carefully assembled the drinks, remembering not to leave out the twist of lemon-peel Peter likes. It takes me longer than average to make drinks: I have to measure.

I heard the shower stop and the sound of feet, and when I turned around Peter was standing in the kitchen doorway, dripping wet, wearing a tasteful navy-blue towel.

'Hi,' I said. 'Your drink's on the counter.'

He stepped forward silently, took my glass from my hand, swallowed a third of its contents and set it on the table behind me. Then he put both of his arms round me.

'You're getting me all wet,' I said softly. I put my hand, cold from holding the icy glass, on the small of his back, but he didn't flinch. His flesh was warm and resilient after the shower.

He kissed my ear. 'Come into the bathroom,' he said.

I gazed up at Peter's shower-curtain, a silver plastic ground covered with curve-necked swans in pink swimming in groups of three among albino lily-pads; it wasn't Peter's taste at all, he'd bought it in a hurry because the water kept running over the floor when he showered, he hadn't had time to look properly and this one had been the least garish. I was wondering why he had insisted that we get into the bathtub. I hadn't thought it was a good idea, I much prefer the bed and I knew the tub would be too small and uncomfortably hard and ridgey, but I hadn't objected: I felt I should be sympathetic because of Trigger. However I had taken the bath mat in with me, which softened the ridges.

I had expected Peter to be depressed, but though he wasn't his usual self he certainly wasn't depressed. I couldn't quite figure out the bathtub. I thought back to the other two unfortunate marriages. After the first, it had been the sheepskin on his bedroom floor, and after the second a scratchy blanket in a field we'd driven four hours to get to, and where I was made uneasy by thoughts of farmers and cows. I supposed this was part of the same pattern, whatever the pattern was. Perhaps an attempt to assert youthfulness and spontaneity, a revolt against the stale doom of stockings in the sink and bacon fat congealed in pans evoked for him by his friends' marriages. Peter's abstraction on these occasions gave me the feeling that he liked doing them because he had read about them somewhere, but I could never locate the quotations. The field was, I guessed, a hunting story from one of the outdoorsy male magazines; I remembered he had worn a plaid jacket. The sheepskin I placed in one of the men's glossies, the kind with lust in penthouses. But the bathtub? Possibly one of the murder mysteries he read as what he called 'escape literature'; but wouldn't that rather be someone drowned in the bathtub? A woman. That would give them a perfect bit to illustrate on the cover: a completely naked woman with a thin covering of water and maybe a bar of soap or a rubber duck or a blood-stain to get her past the censors, floating with her hair spread out on the water, the cold purity of the bathtub surrounding her body, chaste as ice only because dead, her open eyes staring up into those of the reader. The bathtub as a coffin. I had a fleeting vision: what if we both fell asleep and the tap got turned on accidentally, lukewarm so we wouldn't notice, and the water slowly rose and killed us? That would be a surprise for the connection when he came to show his next batch of apartment-renters around: water all over the floor and two naked corpses clasped in a last embrace. 'Suicide,' they'd all say. 'Died for love.'

And on summer nights our ghosts would be seen gliding along the halls of the Brentview Apartments, Bachelor, Two-Bedroom and Luxury, clad only in bath towels. . . .

I shifted my head, tired of the swans, and looked instead at the curving silver nozzle of the shower. I could smell Peter's hair, a clean soap smell. He smelled of soap all the time, not only when he had recently taken a shower. It was a smell I associated with dentists' chairs and medicine, but on him I found it attractive. He never wore sickly-sweet shaving lotion or the other male substitutes for perfume.

I could see his arm where it lay across me, the hairs arranged in rows. The arm was like the bathroom: clean and white and new, the skin unusually smooth for a man's. I couldn't see his face, which was resting against my shoulder, but I tried to visualize it. He was, as Clara had said, 'good-looking'; that was probably what had first attracted me to him. People noticed him, not because he had forceful or peculiar features, but because he was ordinariness raised to perfection, like the youngish well-groomed faces of cigarette ads. But sometimes I wanted a reassuring wart or mole, or patch of roughness, something the touch could fix on instead of gliding over.

We had met at a garden party following my graduation; he was a friend of a friend, and we had eaten ice-cream in the shade together. He had been quite formal and had asked me what I planned to do. I had talked about a career, making it sound much less vague than it was in my own mind, and he told me later that it was my aura of independence and common sense he had liked: he saw me as the kind of girl who wouldn't try to take over his life. He had recently had an unpleasant experience with what he called 'the other kind'. That was the assumption we had been working on, and it had suited me. We had been taking each other at our face values, which meant we had got on very well. Of course I had to adjust to his moods, but that's true of any man, and his were too obvious to cause much difficulty. Over the summer he had become a pleasant habit, and as we had been seeing each other only on weekends the veneer hadn't had a chance to wear off.

However the first time I had gone to his apartment had almost been the last. He had plied me with hi-fi music and brandy, thinking he was crafty and suave, and I had allowed myself to be manipulated into the bedroom. We had set our brandy snifters down on the desk, when Peter, being acrobatic, had knocked one of the glasses to the floor where it smashed.

'Oh leave the damn thing,' I said, perhaps undiplomatically; but Peter had turned on the light, gone for the broom and dustpan, and swept up all the bits of glass, picking the larger ones up carefully and accurately like a pigeon pecking crumbs. The mood had been shattered. We had said goodnight soon afterwards, rather snappishly, and I hadn't heard from him after that for over a week. Of course things were much better now.

Peter stretched and yawned beside me, grinding my arm against the porcelain. I winced and withdrew it gently from beneath him.

'How was it for you?' he asked casually, his mouth against my shoulder. He always asked me that.

'Marvellous,' I murmured; why couldn't he tell? One of these days I should say 'Rotten,' just to see what he would do; but I knew in advance he wouldn't believe me. I reached up and stroked his damp hair, scratching the back of his neck; he liked that, in moderation.

Maybe he had intended the bathtub as an expression of his personality. I tried thinking of ways to make that fit. Asceticism? A modern version of hair shirts or sitting on spikes? Mortification of the flesh? But surely nothing about Peter suggested that; he liked his comforts, and besides it wasn't his flesh that was being mortified: he had been on top. Or maybe it had been a reckless young-man gesture, like jumping into the swimming pool with your clothes on, or putting things on your head at parties. But this image didn't suit Peter either. I was glad there were no more of his group of old friends left to be married: next time he might have tried cramming us into a clothes closet, or an exotic posture in the kitchen sink.

Or maybe – and the thought was chilling – he had intended it as an expression of *my* personality. A new corridor of possibilities extended itself before me: did he really think of me as a lavatory fixture. What kind of a girl did he think I was?

He was twining his fingers in the hair at the nape of my neck. 'I bet you'd look great in a kimono,' he whispered. He bit my shoulder, and I recognized this as a signal for irresponsible gaiety: Peter doesn't usually bite.

I bit his shoulder in return, then, making sure the shower lever was still up, I reached out my right foot – I have agile feet – and turned on the COLD tap.

Chapter Eight

By eight-thirty we were on our way to meet Len. Peter's mood, whatever it had been, had changed to one which I hadn't yet interpreted, so I didn't attempt conversation as we drove along. Peter kept his eyes on the road, turning corners too quickly and muttering under his breath at the other drivers. He hadn't fastened his seat belt.

He had not been pleased at first when I told him about the arrangements I'd made with Len, even when I said, 'I'm sure you'll like him.'

'Who is he?' he had asked suspiciously. If it wasn't Peter I would have suspected jealousy. Peter isn't the jealous type.

'He's an old friend,' I said, 'from college. He's just got back from England; I think he's a TV producer or something,' I knew Len wasn't that high on the scale, but Peter is impressed by people's jobs. Since I had intended Len as a distraction for Peter I wanted the evening to be pleasant.

'Oh,' said Peter, 'one of those arts-crafts types. Probably queer.'

We were sitting at the kitchen table, eating frozen peas and smoked meat, the kind you boil for three minutes in the plastic packages. Peter had decided against going out for dinner.

'Oh no,' I said, eager to defend Len, 'quite the opposite.'

Peter pushed his plate away. 'Why can't you ever *cook* anything?' he said petulantly.

I was hurt: I considered this unfair. I like to cook, but I had been deliberately refraining at Peter's for fear he would feel threatened. Besides, he had always liked smoked meat before, and it was perfectly nourishing. I was about to make a sharp comment, but repressed it. Peter after all was suffering. Instead I asked, 'How was the wedding?'

Peter groaned, leaned back in his chair, lit a cigarette, and gazed inscrutably at the far wall. Then he got up and poured himself another gin-and-tonic. He tried pacing up and down in the kitchen, but it was too narrow, so he sat down again.

'God,' he said, 'poor Trigger. He looked terrible. How could he let himself be taken in like that?' He continued in a disjointed monologue in which Trigger was made to sound like the last of the Mohicans, noble and free, the last of the dinosaurs, destroyed by fate and lesser species, and the last of the dodos, too dumb to get away. Then he attacked the bride, accusing her of being predatory and malicious and of sucking poor Trigger into the domestic void (making me picture her as a vacuum-cleaner), and finally ground to a halt with several funereal predictions about his own solitary future. By solitary he meant without other single men.

I swallowed the last of my frozen peas. I had heard this speech twice before, or something like it, and I knew there was nothing I could say. If I agreed with him it would only intensify his depression, and if I disagreed he would suspect me of siding with the bride. The first time I had been cheerful and maxim-like, and had attempted consolation. 'Well, it's done now,' I had said, 'and maybe it'll turn out to be a good thing in the end. After all, it isn't as though she's robbing the cradle. Isn't he twenty-six?'

'*I'm* twenty-six,' Peter had said moodily.

So this time I said nothing, remarking to myself that it was a good thing Peter had got this speech over with early in the evening. I got up and dished him out some ice-cream, which he took as a sympathetic gesture, putting his arm round my waist and giving me a gloomy hug.

'God, Marian,' he said, 'I don't know what I'd do if you didn't understand. Most women wouldn't, but you're so sensible.'

I leaned against him, stroking his hair while he ate his ice-cream.

We left the car in one of the usual places, on a side-street behind the Park Plaza. As we started to walk along I put my hand through Peter's arm and he smiled down at me abstractedly. I smiled back at him – I was glad he was out of the teeth-gritting mood he had been in while driving – and he brought his other hand over and placed it on top of mine. I was going to bring my other hand up and place it on top of his, but I thought if I did then mine would be on top and he'd have to take his arm out from underneath so he'd have another hand to put on top of the heap, like those games at recess. I squeezed his arm affectionately instead.

We reached the Park Plaza and Peter opened the plate glass door for me as he always does. Peter is scrupulous about things like that; he opens car doors too. Sometimes I expect him to click his heels.

While we waited for the elevator I watched our double image in the floor-to-ceiling mirror by the elevator doors. Peter was wearing one of his more subdued costumes, a brownish-green summer suit whose cut emphasized the functional spareness of his body. All his accessories matched.

'I wonder if Len's up there yet,' I said to him, keeping an eye on myself and talking to him in the mirror. I was thinking I was just about the right height for him.

The elevator came and Peter said 'Roof, please,' to the white-gloved elevator girl, and we moved smoothly upwards. The Park Plaza is a hotel really, but they have a bar at the top, one of Peter's favourite places for a quiet drink, which was why I had suggested it to Len. Being up that high gives you a sense of the vertical which is rare in the city. The room itself is well-lit, not dark as a drain like many others, and it's clean. No one ever seems to get offensively drunk there, and you can hear yourself talk: there's no band or singer. The chairs are comfortable, the décor is reminiscent of the eighteenth century, and the bartenders all know Peter. Ainsley told me once that she had been there when someone threatened to commit suicide by jumping off the wall of the patio outside, but it may have been one of her stories.

We walked in; there weren't many people, so I immediately spotted Len, sitting at one of the black-topped tables. We went over and I introduced Peter to him; they shook hands, Peter abruptly, Len affably. The waiter appeared promptly at our table and Peter ordered two more gin-and-tonics.

'Marian, it's good to see you!' Len said, leaning across the corner of the table to kiss my cheek; a habit, I reflected, he must have picked up in England, as he never used to do it. He had put on a little weight.

'And how was England?' I asked him. I wanted him to talk and entertain Peter, who was looking grumpy.

'All right, I guess; crowded, though. Every time you turn around you bump into somebody from here. It's getting so you might as well not go there at all, the place is so cluttered up with bloody tourists. I was sorry, though,' he said, turning to Peter, 'that I had to leave; I had a good job going for me and some other good things too. But you've got to watch these women when they start pursuing you. They're always after you to *marry* them. You've got to hit and run. Get them before they get you and then get out.' He smiled, showing his brilliantly-polished white teeth.

Peter brightened perceptibly. 'Marian tells me you're in television,' he said.

'Yes,' Len said, examining the squarish nails of his disproportionately large hands; 'I haven't got anything at the moment but I ought to be able to pick up something here. They need people with my experience. News reports. I'd like to see a good commentary programme in this country, I mean a really good one, though god knows how much red tape you have to go through to get anything done around here.'

Peter relaxed; anyone interested in news reports, he was probably thinking, couldn't be queer.

I felt a hand touch my shoulder, and looked around. A young girl I'd never seen before was standing there. I opened my mouth to ask her what she wanted, when Peter said, 'Oh. It's Ainsley. You didn't tell me she was coming along.' I looked again: it *was* Ainsley.

'Gosh, Marian,' she said in a breathless semi-whisper, 'you didn't tell me this was a *bar*. I sure hope they don't ask me for my birth certificate.'

Len and Peter had risen. I introduced Ainsley to Len, much against my better judgement, and she sat down in the fourth chair. Peter's face had a puzzled expression. He had met Ainsley before and hadn't liked her, suspecting her of holding what he called 'wishy-washy radical' views because she had favoured him with a theoretical speech about liberating the Id. Politically Peter is conservative. She had offended him too by calling one of his opinions 'conventional', and he had retaliated by calling one of hers 'uncivilized'. Right now, I guessed, he could tell she was up to something but was unwilling to rock her boat until he knew what it was. He required evidence.

The waiter appeared and Len asked Ainsley what she would have. She hesitated, then said timidly, 'Oh, could I have just a – just a glass of gingerale?'

Len beamed at her. 'I knew you had a new room-mate, Marian,' he said, 'but you didn't tell me she was so young!'

'I'm sort of keeping an eye on her,' I said sourly, 'for the folks back home.' I was furious with Ainsley. She had put me in a very awkward position. I could either give the game away by revealing she had been to college and was in fact several months older than me, or I could keep silent and participate in what amounted to a fraud. I knew perfectly well why she had come: Len was a potential candidate, and she had chosen to inspect him this way because she had sensed she'd have difficulty forcing me to introduce them otherwise.

The waiter returned with gingerale. I was amazed that he hadn't asked for her birth-certificate, but upon reflection I decided that any experienced waiter would assume that no girl who seemed so young would dare to walk into a bar dressed like that and order gingerale unless she was in reality safely over-age. It's the adolescents who overdress that they suspect, and Ainsley was not overdressed. She had dug out from somewhere a cotton summer creation I'd never seen before, a pink and light-blue gingham check on white with a ruffle around the neck. Her hair was tied behind her head with a pink bow and on one of her wrists she had a tinkly silver charm-bracelet. Her makeup was understated, her eyes carefully but not noticeably shadowed to make them twice as large and round and blue, and she had sacrificed her long oval fingernails, biting them nearly to the quick so that they had a jagged schoolgirlish quality. I could see she was determined.

Len was talking to her, asking her questions, trying to draw her out. She sipped at her gingerale, giving short, shy answers. She was evidently afraid of saying too much, aware of Peter as a threat. When Len asked her what she did, however, she could give a truthful answer. 'I work at an electric toothbrush company,' she said, and blushed a warm and genuine-looking pink. I almost choked.

'Excuse me,' I said, 'I'm just going out on the patio for a breath of air.' Actually I wanted to decide what I should do – surely it was unethical of me to let Len be deceived – and Ainsley must have sensed this, for she gave me a quick warning look as I got up.

Outside, I leaned my arms against the top of the wall, which came almost to my collarbone, and gazed out over the city. A moving line of lights ran straight in front of me till it hit and broke against and flowed around a blob of darkness, the park; and another line went at right-angles, disappearing on both sides into the distance. What could I do? Was it any of my business? I knew that if I interfered I would be breaking an unspoken code, and that Ainsley was sure to get back at me some way through Peter. She was clever at such things.

Far off on the eastern horizon I saw a flicker of lightning. We were going to have a storm. 'Good,' I said out loud, 'it'll clear the air.' If I wasn't going to take deliberate steps, I'd have to be sure of my self-control so I wouldn't say something by accident. I paced the terrace a couple of times till I felt I was ready to go back in, noting with a faint surprise that I was wobbling slightly.

The waiter must have been around again: there was a fresh gin-and-tonic in my place. Peter was deep in a conversation with Len and scarcely acknowledged my return. Ainsley sat silent, her eyes lowered, jiggling her icecube around in her gingerale glass. I studied her latest version of herself, thinking that it was like one of the large plump dolls in the stores at Christmas-time, with washable rubber-smooth skin and glassy eyes and gleaming artificial hair. Pink and white.

I attuned myself to Peter's voice; it sounded as though it was coming from a distance. He was telling Len a story, which seemed to be about hunting. I knew Peter used to go hunting, especially with his group of old friends, but he had never told me much about it. He had said once that they never killed anything but crows, groundhogs and other small vermin.

'So I let her off and Wham. One shot, right through the heart. The rest of them got away. I picked it up and Trigger said, "You know how to gut them, you just slit her down the belly and give her a good hard shake and all the guts'll fall out." So I whipped out my knife, good knife, German steel, and slit the belly and took her by the hind legs and gave her one hell of a crack, like a whip you see, and the next thing you know there was blood and guts all over the place. All over me, what a mess, rabbit guts dangling from the trees, god the trees were red for yards. . . .'

He paused to laugh. Len bared his teeth. The quality of Peter's voice had changed; it was a voice I didn't recognize. The sign saying TEMPERANCE flashed in my mind: I couldn't let my perceptions about Peter be distorted by the effects of alcohol, I warned myself.

'God it was funny. Lucky thing Trigger and me had the old cameras along, we got some good shots of the whole mess. I've been meaning to ask you, in your business you must know quite a bit about cameras ...' and they were off on a discussion of Japanese lenses.

Peter's voice seemed to be getting louder and faster – the stream of words was impossible to follow, and my mind withdrew, concentrating instead on the picture of the scene in the forest. I saw it as though it was a slide projected on a screen in a dark room, the colours luminous, green, brown, blue for the sky, red. Peter stood with his back to me in a plaid shirt, his rifle slung on his shoulder. A group of friends, those friends whom I had never met, were gathered around him, their faces clearly visible in the sunlight that fell in shafts down through the anonymous trees, splashed with blood, the mouths wrenched with laughter. I couldn't see the rabbit.

I leaned forward, my arms on the black table-top. I wanted Peter to turn and talk to me, I wanted to hear his normal voice, but he wouldn't; I studied the reflections of the other three as they lay and moved beneath the polished black surface as in a pool of water; they were all chin and no eyes, except for Ainsley's eyes, their gaze resting gently on her glass. After a while I noticed with mild curiosity that a large drop of something wet had materialized on the table near my hand. I poked it with my finger and smudged it around a little before I realized with horror that it was a tear. I must be crying then! Something inside me started to dash about in dithering mazes of panic, as though I had swallowed a tadpole. I was going to break down and make a scene, and I couldn't.

I slid out of my chair, trying to be as inconspicuous as possible, walked across the room avoiding the other tables with great care, and went out to the Ladies' Powder Room. Checking first to make sure no one else was in there – I couldn't have witnesses – I locked myself into one of the plushy-pink cubicles and wept for several minutes. I couldn't understand what was happening, why I was doing this; I had never done anything like it before and it seemed to me absurd. 'Get a grip on yourself,' I whispered. 'Don't make a fool of yourself.' The roll of toilet paper crouched in there with me, helpless and white and furry, waiting passively for the end. I tore some of it off and blew my nose.

Some shoes appeared. I watched them carefully from under the door of my cell. They were, I decided, Ainsley's shoes.

'Marian!' she called, 'Are you all right?'

'Yes,' I said. I wiped my eyes and came out.

'Well,' I said, trying to sound controlled, 'getting your sights set?'

'We'll see,' she said coolly. 'I have to find out more about him first. Of course you won't say anything.'

'I suppose not,' I said, 'though it doesn't seem ethical. It's like bird-liming, or spearing fish by lantern or something.'

'I'm not going to *do* anything to him,' she protested. 'It won't hurt.' She took off her pink bow and combed her hair. 'But what's wrong? I saw you start to cry at the table.'

'Nothing,' I said. 'You know I can't drink very much. It's probably the humidity.' By now I was perfectly under control.

We walked back to our chairs. Peter was talking at full speed to Len about the different methods of taking self-portraits: with reflecting images in mirrors, self-timers that let you press the shutter-release and then run to position and pose, and long cable-releases with triggers and air-type releases with bulbs. Len was contributing some information about the correct focussing of the image, but several minutes after I had sat down he gave me a quick peculiar look, as though he was disappointed with me. Then he switched back to the conversation.

What had he meant? I glanced from one to the other. Peter smiled at me in the middle of one of his sentences, fondly but from a distance, and then I thought I knew. He was treating me as a stage-prop; silent but solid, a two-dimensional outline. He wasn't ignoring me, as perhaps I had felt (did that account for the ridiculous flight?) – he was depending on me! And Len had looked at me that way because he thought I was being self-effacing on purpose, and that if so the relationship was more serious than I had said it was. Len never wished matrimony on anyone, especially anyone he liked. But he didn't know the situation; he had misinterpreted.

Suddenly the panic swept back over me. I gripped the edge of the table. The square elegant room with its looped curtains and muted carpet and crystal chandeliers was concealing things; the murmuring air was filled with a soft menace. 'Hang on,' I told myself. 'Don't move,' I eyed the doors and windows, calculating distances. I had to get out.

The lights flicked off and on and one of the waiters called 'Time, gentlemen.' There was a pushing back of chairs.

We descended in the elevator. Len said as we stepped off, 'The evening's young, why don't you all come over to my place for another drink? You can take a look at my teleconverter,' and Peter said 'Great. Love to.'

We went out through the glass doors. I took Peter's arm and we walked on ahead. Ainsley had cut Len out from the herd and was allowing him to keep her safely behind.

On the street the air was cooler; there was a slight breeze. I let go of Peter's arm and began to run.

Chapter Nine

I was running along the sidewalk. After the first minute I was surprised to find my feet moving, wondering how they had begun, but I didn't stop.

The rest of them were so astonished they didn't do anything at all for a moment. Then Peter yelled, 'Marian! Where the hell do you think you're going?'

I could hear the fury in his voice: this was the unforgivable sin, because it was public. I didn't answer, but I looked back over my shoulder as I ran. Both Peter and Len had started to run after me. Then they both stopped and I heard Peter call, 'I'll go get the car and head her off, you try to keep her out of the main drag,' and he turned around and sprinted off in the other direction. This disturbed me – I must have been expecting Peter to chase me, but instead it was Len who was galloping heavily along behind me. I turned my head to the front just in time to avoid collision with an old man who was shambling out of a restaurant, then glanced back again. Ainsley had hesitated, not knowing which of them to follow, but now she was bouncing off in the direction Peter had taken. I saw her wobble in a flounce of pink and white around the corner.

I was out of breath already, but I had a good head start on them. I could afford to slow down. Each lamp post as I passed it became a distance-marker on my course: it seemed an achievement, and accomplishment of some kind to put them one by one behind me. Since it was bar-closing time there were quite a few people on the street. I grinned at them and waved at some as I went by, almost laughing at the surprise on their faces. I was filled with the exhilaration of speed; it was like a game of tag. 'Hey! Marian! Stop!' Len called behind me at intervals.

Then Peter's car turned the corner in front of me on to the main street. He must have driven around the block. That's all right, I thought, he's got to go across to the other lane, he won't be able to reach me.

The car was on the far side of the road, coming towards me; but there was a gap in the line of traffic, and it spurted forward and swivelled into a reckless U-turn. It was parallel to me now, slowing down. I could see Ainsley's round expressionless face peering at me through the back window like a moon.

All at once it was no longer a game. The blunt tank-shape was threatening. It was threatening that Peter had not given chase on foot but had enclosed himself in the armour of the car; though of course that was the logical thing to do. In a minute the car would stop, the door would swing open ... where was there to go?

By this time I had passed the stores and restaurants and had come to a stretch of large old houses set well back from the street, most of which, I knew, were no longer lived in but had been converted into dentists' offices and dress-making establishments. There was an open wrought-iron gateway. I plunged through it and ran up the gravel drive.

It must have been some sort of private club. The front door of the house had an awning over it, and the windows were lit up. As I hesitated, hearing Len's footsteps pounding nearer along the sidewalk, the front door started to open.

I couldn't be caught there; I knew it was private property. I leapt the small hedge by the side of the driveway and skittered diagonally across the lawn into the shadows. I visualized Len pelting up the driveway and colliding with the outraged forces of society, which I pictured as a group of middle-aged ladies in evening dress, and was momentarily conscience-stricken. He was my friend. But he had taken sides against me and would have to pay the price.

In the darkness at the side of the house I paused to consider.

Behind me was Len; on one side was the house, and on the other two sides I could see something that was more solid than the darkness, blocking my way. It was the brick wall attached to the iron gate at the front; it seemed to go all the way around the house. I would have to climb it.

I pushed my way through a mass of prickly shrubberies. The wall was only shoulder high; I took off my shoes and threw them over, then scrambled up, using branches and the uneven bricking of the wall as toe-holds. Something ripped. The blood was throbbing in my ears.

I closed my eyes, knelt for a moment on the top of the wall, swaying dizzily, and dropped backwards.

I felt myself caught, set down and shaken. It was Peter, who must have stalked me and waited there on the side-street, knowing I would come over the wall. 'What the hell got into you?' he said, his voice stern. His face in the light of the streetlamps was partly angry, partly alarmed. 'Are you all right?'

I leaned against him and put my hand up to touch his neck. The relief of being stopped and held, of hearing Peter's normal voice again and knowing he was real, was so great I started to laugh helplessly.

'I'm fine,' I said, 'of course I'm all right. I don't know what got into me.'

'Put on your shoes then,' Peter said, holding them out to me. He was annoyed but he wasn't going to make a fuss.

Len heaved himself over the wall and landed on the earth with a thunk. He was breathing heavily. 'Got her? Good. Let's get out of here before those people get the police after us.'

The car was right there. Peter opened the front door for me and I slid in. Len got into the back seat with Ainsley. All he said to me was, 'Didn't think you were the hysterical type.' Ainsley said nothing. We pulled away from the curb and rounded the corner, Len giving directions. I would rather have gone home, but I didn't want to cause Peter any more trouble that night. I sat up straight and folded my hands in my lap.

We parked beside Len's apartment building, which as far as I could tell at night was of the collapsing brown-brick ramshackle variety, with fire-escapes down the outside. There was no elevator, just creaky stairs with dark wooden railings. We ascended in decorous couples.

The apartment itself was tiny, only one main room with a bathroom opening to one side and a kitchen to the other. It was somewhat disarranged, with suitcases on the floor and books and clothes strewn about: Len evidently hadn't finished moving into it yet. The bed was immediately to the left of the door, doubling as a chesterfield, and I kicked off my shoes and subsided onto it. My muscles had caught up with me and were beginning to ache with fatigue.

Len poured the three of us generous shots of cognac, rummaged in the kitchen and managed to find some coke for Ainsley, and put on a record. Then he and Peter began to fiddle with a couple of cameras, screwing various lenses onto them and peering through them and exchanging information about exposure times. I felt deflated. I was filled with penitence, but there was no outlet for it. If I could be alone with Peter it would be different, I thought: he could forgive me.

Ainsley was no help. I saw she was going to keep up her little-girls-should-be-seen-and-not-heard act, as the safest course to follow. She had settled into a round wicker basket-chair, like the one in Clara's back yard except that this one had a quilted corduroy cover in egg-yolk yellow. I'd experienced those covers before. They're kept on by elastic, and they have a habit of slipping off the edges of the chair if you wiggle around too much and closing up around you. Ainsley sat quite still though, holding her coca cola glass in her lap and contemplating her own reflection on the brown surface inside it. She registered neither pleasure nor boredom; her inert patience was that of a pitcher-plant in a swamp with its hollow bulbous leaves half-filled with water, waiting for some insect to be attracted, drowned, and digested.

I was leaning back against the wall, sipping at my cognac, the noise of voices and music slapping against me like waves. I suppose the pressure of my body had pushed the bed out a little; at any rate, without thinking much about anything I turned my head away from the room and looked down. I began to find something very attractive about the dark cool space between the bed and the wall.

It would be quiet down there, I thought; and less humid. I set my glass down on the telephone-table beside the bed and glanced quickly around the room. They were all engrossed: no one would notice.

A minute later I was wedged sideways between the bed and the wall, out of sight but not at all comfortable. This will never do, I thought; I'll have to go right underneath. It will be like a tent. It didn't occur to me to scramble back up. I eased the bed out from the wall as noiselessly as I could, using my whole body as a lever, lifted the fringed border of the bedspread, and slid myself in like a letter through a slot. It was a tight fit: the slats were unusually low for a bed, and I was forced to lie absolutely flat against the floor. I inched the bed back flush with the wall.

It was quite cramped. Also, there were large rolls and clusters of dust strewn thickly over the floor like chunks of mouldy bread (I thought indignantly, What a pig Len is! Doesn't sweep under his bed, then re-considered: he hadn't been living there long and some of the dust may have been left over from whoever lived there before). But the semi-darkness, tinted orange by the filter of the bedspread that curtained me on all four sides, and the coolness and the solitude were pleasant. The raucous music and staccato laughter and the droning voices reached me muffled by the mattress. In spite of the narrowness and dust I was glad I didn't have to sit up there in the reverberating hot glare of the room. Though I was only two or three feet lower than the rest of them, I was thinking of the room as 'up there'. I myself was underground, I had dug myself a private burrow. I felt smug.

One male voice, Peter's I think, said loudly, 'Hey, where's Marian'? and the other one answered, 'Oh, probably in the can.' I smiled to myself. It was satisfying to be the only one who knew where I really was.

The position, however, was becoming more and more of a strain. The muscles in my neck were hurting; I wanted to stretch; I was going to sneeze. I began to wish they would hurry up and realize I had disappeared, so they could search for me. I could no longer recall what good reasons had led me to cram myself under Len's bed in the first place. It was ridiculous: I would be all covered with fluff when I came out.

But having taken the step I refused to turn back. There would be no dignity at all in crawling out from under the bedspread, trailing dust, like a weevil coming out of a flour-barrel. It would be admitting I had done the wrong thing. There I was, and there I would stay until forcibly removed.

My resentment at Peter for letting me remain crushed under the bed while he moved up there in the open, in the free air, jabbering away about exposure times, started me thinking about the past four months. All summer we had been moving in a certain direction, though it hadn't felt like movement: we had deluded ourselves into thinking we were static. Ainsley had warned me that Peter was monopolizing me; she saw no reason why I shouldn't, as she termed it, 'branch out'. This was all very well for her but I couldn't get over the subjective feeling that more than one at a time was unethical. However it had left me in a sort of vacuum. Peter and I had avoided talking about the future because we knew it didn't matter: we weren't really involved. Now, though, something in me had decided we were involved: surely that was the explanation for the powder-room collapse and the flight. I was evading reality. Now, this very moment, I would have to face it. I would have to decide what I wanted to do.

Someone sat down heavily on the bed, mashing me against the floor. I gave a dusty squawk.

'What-the-hell!' whoever it was exclaimed, and stood up. 'Someone's under the bed.'

I could hear them conferring in low tones, and then Peter called, much louder than necessary, 'Marian, are you under the bed?'

'Yes,' I answered in a neutral voice. I had decided to be noncommittal about the whole thing.

'Well, you'd better come out now,' he said carefully. 'I think it's time for us to go home.'

They were treating me like a sulking child who has locked itself in a cupboard and has to be coaxed. I was amused, and indignant. I considered saying, 'I don't want to,' but decided that it might be the last straw for Peter, and Len was quite capable of saying, 'Aw, let her stay under there all night, Christ *I* don't mind. That's the way to handle them. Whatever's eating her, that'll cool her off.' So instead I said, 'I can't I'm stuck!'

I tried to move: I *was* stuck.

Up above, they had another policy-meeting. 'We're going to lift up the bed,' Peter called, 'and then you come out, got that?' I heard them giving orders to each other. It was going to be a major feat of engineering skill. There was a scuffling of shoes as they took their positions and got purchase. Then Peter said 'Hike!' and the bed rose into the air, and I scuttled out backwards like a crayfish when its rock has been upset.

Peter stood me up. Every inch of my dress was furred and tufted with dust. They both started to brush me off, laughing.

'What the hell were you doing under there?' Peter asked. I could tell by the way they were picking off the larger pieces of dust, slowly and making an effort to concentrate, that they'd put away a lot of brandy while I was below ground.

'It was quieter,' I said sullenly.

'You should have told me you were stuck!' he said with magnanimous gallantry. 'Then I would have got you out. You look a sight.' He was superior and amused.

'Oh,' I said, 'I didn't want to interrupt you.' I had realized by this time what my prevailing emotion was: it was rage.

The hot needle of anger in my voice must have penetrated the cuticle of Peter's euphoria. He stepped back a pace; his eyes seemed to measure me coldly. He took me by the upper arm as though he was arresting me for jaywalking, and turned to Len. 'I really think we'd better be pushing along now,' he said. 'It's been awfully pleasant. I hope we can get together again sometime soon. I'd really like to see what you think of my tripod.' Across the room Ainsley disengaged herself from the corduroy chair-cover and stood up.

I wrenched my arm away from Peter's hand. I said frigidly, 'I'm not going back with you. I'll walk home,' and bolted out the door.

'Do whatever the hell you like,' Peter said; but he began to stride after me, abandoning Ainsley to her fate. As I pelted down the narrow stairs I could hear Len saying, 'Why don't we have another drink, Ainsley? I'll see that you get home safely; better let the two love-birds settle their own affairs,' and Ainsley protesting with alarm, 'Oh, I don't think I should. . . .'

Once I was outside I felt considerably better. I had broken out; from what, or into what, I didn't know. Though I wasn't at all certain why I had been acting this way, I had at least acted. Some kind of decision had been made, something had been finished. After that violence, that overt and suddenly to me embarrassing display, there could be no reconciliation; though now that I was moving away I felt no irritation at all towards Peter. It crossed my mind, absurdly, that it had been such a peaceful relationship: until that day we had never fought. There had been nothing to fight about.

I looked behind me: Peter was nowhere in sight. I walked along the deserted streets, past the rows of old apartment buildings, towards the nearest main street where I could get a bus. At this hour though (what hour was it?) I'd have to wait a long time. The thought made me uneasy: the wind was now stronger and colder and the lightning seemed to be moving closer by the minute. In the distance the thunder was beginning. I was wearing only a flimsy summer dress. I wondered whether I had enough money to take a taxi, stopped to count it, and found I hadn't.

I had been walking north for about ten minutes, past the closed icily-lighted stores, when I saw Peter's car draw up to the curb about a hundred yards ahead of me. He got out and stood on the empty sidewalk, waiting. I walked on steadily, neither slackening my pace nor changing direction. Surely there was no longer any reason to run. I was no longer involved.

When I was level with him he stepped in front of me. 'Would you kindly permit me,' he said with iron-clad politeness, 'to drive you home? I wouldn't want to see you get drenched to the skin.' As he spoke, a few heavy preliminary drops were already coming down.

I hesitated. Why was he doing this? It might be only the same formal motive that prompted him to open car doors – almost an automatic reflex – in which case I could accept the favour just as formally, with no danger; but what would it really involve if I got into the car? I studied him: he had clearly had too much to drink, though clearly also he was in near-perfect control of himself. His eyes were a little glazed, it was true, but he was holding his body stiffly upright.

'Well,' I said doubtfully, 'really I'd rather walk. Though thank you just the same.'

'Oh come along Marian, don't be childish,' he said brusquely, and took my arm.

I allowed myself to be led to the car and inserted into the front seat. I was, I think, reluctant; but I did not particularly want to get wet.

He got in and slammed his own door and started the motor. 'Now perhaps you'll tell me what all that nonsense was about,' he said angrily.

We turned a corner and the rain hit, blown against the windshield by sharp gusts of wind. At any moment we were going to have, as one of my great-aunts used to say, a trash-mover and a gully-washer.

'I didn't request to be driven home,' I said, hedging. I was convinced that it hadn't been nonsense, but also acutely aware that it would look very much like nonsense to any outside observer. I didn't want to discuss it; in that direction there could only be a dead end. I sat up straight in the front seat, staring through a window out of which I could see little or nothing.

'Why the hell you had to ruin a perfectly good evening I'll never know,' he said, ignoring my remark. There was a crack of thunder.

'I don't seem to have ruined it much for you,' I said. 'You were enjoying *your*self enough.'

'Oh so that's it. We weren't entertaining you enough. Our conversation bored you, we weren't paying enough attention to you. Well, next time we'll know enough to save you the trouble of coming with us.'

This seemed to me quite unfair. After all, Len was my friend. 'Len's *my* friend, you know,' I said. My voice was beginning to quaver. 'I don't see why I shouldn't want to talk with him a little myself when he's just got back from England.' I knew even as I said it that Len was quite beside the point.

'Ainsley behaved herself properly, why couldn't you? The trouble with *you* is,' he said savagely, 'you're just rejecting your femininity.'

His approval of Ainsley was a vicious goad. 'Oh, SCREW my femininity,' I shouted. 'Femininity has nothing to do with it. You were just being plain ordinary *rude*!' Unintentional bad manners was something Peter couldn't stand to be accused of, and I knew it. It put him in the class of the people in the deodorant ads.

He glanced quickly over at me, his eyes narrowed as though he was taking aim. Then he gritted his teeth together and stepped murderously hard on the accelerator. By that time the rain was coming down in torrents: the road ahead, when it could be seen at all, looked like a solid sheet of water. When I made my thrust we'd been going down a hill, and at the suddenly-increased speed the car skidded, turned two-and-a-quarter times round, slithered backwards down over someone's inclined lawn, and came to a bone-jolting stop. I heard something snap.

'You maniac!' I wailed, when I had ricochetted off the glove-compartment and realized I wasn't dead. 'You'll get us all killed!' I must have been thinking of myself as plural.

Peter rolled down the window and stuck his head out. Then he began to laugh. 'I've trimmed their hedge a bit for them,' he said. He stepped on the gas. The wheels spun for an instant, churning up the mud of the lawn and leaving (as I later saw) two deep gouges, and with a grinding of gears we moved up over the edge of the lawn and back onto the road.

I was trembling now from a combination of fright, cold, and fury. 'First you drag me into your car,' I chittered, 'and brow-beat me because of your own feelings of guilt, and then you try to *kill* me!'

Peter was still laughing. His head was soaking wet, even from that brief exposure to the rain, and the hair was plastered down on his head, the water trickling from it over his face. 'They're going to see an alteration in their landscape gardening when they get up in the morning,' he chuckled. He seemed to find wilfully ruining other people's property immensely funny.

'You seem to find wilfully ruining other people's property immensely funny,' I said, with sarcasm.

'Oh, don't be such a killjoy,' he replied pleasantly. His satisfaction with what he considered a forceful display of muscle was obvious. It irritated me that he should appropriate as his own the credit due to the back wheels of his car.

'Peter, why can't you be *serious*? You're just an overgrown adolescent.'

This he chose to disregard.

The car stopped jerkily. 'Here we are,' he said.

I took hold of the doorhandle, intending, I think, to make a final unanswerable remark and dash for the house; but he put his hand on my arm. 'Better wait until it lets up a bit.'

He turned the ignition key and the heartbeats of the windshield-wipers stopped. We sat silently, listening to the storm. It must have been right overhead; the lightning was dazzling and continuous, and each probing jagged fork was followed almost at once by a rending crash, like the trees of a whole forest splitting and falling. In the intervals of darkness we heard the rain pounding against the car; water was coming through in a fine spray around the edges of the closed windows.

'It's a good thing I didn't let you walk home,' Peter said in the tone of a man who has made a firm and proper decision. I could only agree.

During a long flickering moment of light I turned and saw him watching me, his face strangely shadowed, his eyes gleaming like an animal's in the beam from a car headlight. His stare was intent, faintly ominous. Then he leaned towards me and said, 'You've got some fluff. Hold still.' His hands fumbled against my head: he was awkwardly but with gentleness untangling a piece of dust that was caught in my hair.

I suddenly felt limp as a damp kleenex. I leaned my forehead against his and closed my eyes. His skin was cold and wet and his breath smelled of cognac.

'Open your eyes,' he said. I did: we still had our foreheads pressed together, and I found myself at the next bright instant gazing into a multitude of eyes.

'You've got eight eyes,' I said softly. We both laughed and he pulled me against him and kissed me. I put my arms around his back.

We rested quietly like that for some time in the centre of the storm. I was conscious only that I was very tired and that my body would not stop shivering. 'I don't know what I was doing tonight,' I murmured. He stroked my hair, forgiving, understanding, a little patronizing.

'Marian,' I could feel his neck swallow. I couldn't tell now whether it was his body or my own that was shuddering; he tightened his arms around me. 'How do you think we'd get on as . . . how do you think we'd be, married?'

I drew back from him.

A tremendous electric blue flash, very near, illuminated the inside of the car. As we stared at each other in that brief light I could see myself, small and oval mirrored in his eyes.

Chapter Ten

When I woke up on Sunday morning – it was closer to Sunday afternoon – my mind was at first as empty as though someone had scooped out the inside of my skull like a cantaloupe and left me only the rind to think with. I looked around the room, scarcely recognizing it as a place I had ever been before. My clothes were scattered over the floor and draped and crumpled on the chairback like fragments left over from the explosion of some life-sized female scarecrow, and the inside of my mouth felt like a piece of cotton wool stuffing. I got up and wavered out to the kitchen.

Clear sunshine and fresh air were shimmering in through the open kitchen window. Ainsley was up before me. She was leaning forward, concentrating on something that was spread out in front of her, her legs drawn up and tucked under her on the chair, her hair cascading over her shoulders. From the back she looked like a mermaid perched on a rock: a mermaid in a grubby green terry-cloth robe. Around her on a table-top pebbled with crumbs lay the remnants of her breakfast – a limp starfish of a banana peel, some bits of shell, and brown crusts of toast beached here and there, random as driftwood.

I went to the refrigerator and got out the tomato juice. 'Hi,' I said to Ainsley's back. I was wondering whether I could face an egg.

She turned around. 'Well,' she said.

'Did you get home okay?' I asked. 'That was quite a storm.' I poured myself a large glassful of tomato juice and drank it blood-thirstily.

'Of course,' she said. 'I made him call a taxi. I got home just before the storm broke and had a cigarette and a double scotch and went straight to bed; god, I was absolutely exhausted. Just sitting still like that takes a lot out of you, and then after you'd gone I didn't know how I was going to get away. It was like escaping from a giant squid, but I did it, mostly by acting dumb and scared. That's very necessary at this stage, you know.'

I looked into the saucepan that was sitting, still hot, on one of the burners. 'You through with the egg water?' I switched the stove on.

'Well, what about you? I was quite worried, I thought maybe you were really drunk or something; if you don't mind my saying so you were behaving like a real idiot.'

'We got engaged,' I said, a little reluctantly. I knew she would disapprove. I manoeuvred the egg into the saucepan; it cracked immediately. It was straight out of the refrigerator and too cold.

Ainsley lifted her barely-nubile eyebrows; she didn't seem surprised. 'Well, if I were you I'd get married in the States, it'll be so much easier to get a divorce when you need one. I mean, you don't really know him, do you? But at least,' she continued more cheerfully, 'Peter will soon be making enough money so you can live separately when you have a baby, even if you don't get a divorce. But I hope you aren't getting married right away. I don't think you know what you're doing.'

'Subconsciously,' I said, 'I probably wanted to marry Peter all along.' That silenced her. It was like invoking a deity.

I inspected my egg, which was sending out a white semi-congealed feeler like an exploring oyster. It's probably done, I thought, and fished it out. I turned on the coffee and cleared a space for myself on the oilcloth. Now I could see what Ainsley was busy with. She had taken the calendar down from the kitchen wall – it had a picture of a little girl in an old-fashioned dress sitting on a swing with a basket of cherries and a white puppy – I get one every year from a third cousin who runs a service station back home – and was making cryptic marks on it with a pencil.

'What're you doing?' I asked. I whacked my egg against the side of my dish and got my thumb stuck in it. It wasn't done after all. I poured it into the dish and stirred it up.

'I'm figuring out my strategy,' she said in a matter-of-fact voice.

'Really Ainsley, I don't see how you can be so cold-blooded about it,' I said, eyeing the black numbers in their ordered rows.

'But I need a father for my child!' Her tone implied I was trying to snatch bread from the mouths of all the world's widows and orphans, incarnate for the moment in her.

'Okay, granted, but why Len? I mean it could get complicated with him, after all he *is* my friend and he's had a bad time lately; I wouldn't want to see him upset. Aren't there lots of others around?'

'Not right now; or at least nobody who's such a good specimen,' she said reasonably, 'and I'd sort of like the baby in the spring. I'd like a spring baby; or early summer. That means he can have his birthday parties outside in the back yard instead of in the house, it'll be less noisy . . .'

'Have you investigated his ancestors?' I asked acidly, spooning up the last strand of egg.

'Oh yes,' said Ainsley with enthusiasm, 'we had a short conversation just before he made his pass. I found out his father went to college. At least there don't seem to be any morons on his side of the family, and he doesn't have any allergies either. I wanted to find out whether he was Rh Negative but that would have been a little pointed, don't you think? And he *is* in television, that means he must have something artistic in him somewhere. I couldn't find out much about the grandparents, but you can't be too selective about heredity or you'd have to wait around forever. Genetics are deceptive anyway,' she went on; 'some real geniuses have children that aren't bright at all.'

She put a decisive-looking checkmark on the calendar and frowned at it. She bore a chilling resemblance to a general plotting a major campaign.

'Ainsley, what you really need is a blueprint of your bedroom,' I said, 'or no, a contour map. Or an aerial photograph. Then you could draw little arrows and dotted lines on it, and an X at the point of conjunction.'

'Please don't be frivolous,' she said. Now she was counting under her breath.

'When's it going to be? Tomorrow?'

'Wait a sec,' she said, and counted some more. 'No. It can't be for a while. At least a month anyway. You see, I've got to make sure that the first time will do it; or the second.'

'The first time?'

'Yes,' she said, 'I've got it all worked out. It's going to be a problem though, you see it all depends on his psychology. I can tell he's the sort that'll get scared off if I act too eager. I've got to give him lots of rope. Because as soon as he gets anywhere, I can just hear it, he'll go into the old song-and-dance about maybe we'd better not see each other any more, wouldn't want this to get too serious, neither of us should get tied down and so on. And he'll evaporate. I won't be able to call him up when it's really essential, he'd accuse me of trying to monopolize his time or of making *demands* on him or something. But as long as he hasn't got me,' she said, 'I can have him whenever I need him.'

We ruminated together for some moments.

'The place is going to be a problem too,' she said. 'It's all got to seem accidental. A moment of passion. My resistance overcome, swept off my feet and so forth.' She smiled briefly. 'Anything prearranged, meeting him at the motel for instance, wouldn't do at all. So it's either got to be his place, or here.'

'Here?'

'If necessary,' she said firmly, sliding off her chair. I was silent: the thought of Leonard Slank being undone beneath the same roof that also sheltered the lady down below and her framed family-tree was disturbing to me; it would almost be a sacrilege.

Ainsley went into her bedroom, humming busily to herself, taking the calendar with her. I sat thinking about Len. I was again having stirrings of conscience about allowing him to be led flower-garlanded to his doom without even so much as a word of warning. Of course he had asked for it, in a way, I suppose, and Ainsley seemed determined not to make any further claims on whoever she singled out for this somewhat dubious, because anonymous, honour. If Leonard had been merely the standardized ladies'-man I wouldn't have worried. But surely he was, I reflected as I sipped my coffee, a more complex and delicately-adjusted creature. He was a self-consciously-lecherous skirt-chaser, granted; but it wasn't true as Joe had said, that he had no ethical sense. In his own warped way he was a kind of inverted moralist. He liked to talk as though everyone was out for nothing but sex and money, but when anyone provided a demonstration of his theories in real life, he reacted with scalding critical invective. His blend of cynicism and idealism had a lot to do with his preference for 'corrupting', as he called it, greenish girls, as opposed to the more vine-ripened variety. The supposedly pure, the unobtainable, was attractive to the idealist in him; but as soon as it had been obtained, the cynic viewed it as spoiled and threw it away. 'She turned out to be just the same as all the rest of them,' he would remark sourly. Women whom he thought of as truly out of his reach, such as the wives of his friends, he treated with devotion. He trusted them to an unrealistic degree simply because he would never be compelled by his own cynicism to put them to the test: they were not only unassailable but too old for him anyway. Clara, for instance, he idolized. At times he showed a peculiar tenderness, almost a sloppy sentimentality, towards the people he liked, who were few in number; but in spite of this he was constantly accused by women of being a misogynist and by men of being a misanthropist, and perhaps he was both.

However, I could think of no specific way in which Ainsley's making use of him as she had planned could damage him irreparably, or even much at all, so I consigned him to whatever tough-minded, horn-rimmed guardian angels he might possess, finished the granular dregs of my coffee, and went to dress. After that I phoned Clara to tell her the news; Ainsley's reaction had not been very satisfying.

Clara sounded pleased, but her response was ambiguous. 'Oh, good,' she said, 'Joe will be delighted. He's been saying lately that it's about time you settled down.' I was slightly irritated: after all, I wasn't thirty-five and desperate. She was talking as though I was simply taking a prudent step. But I reflected that people on the outside of a relationship couldn't be expected to understand it. The rest of the conversation was about her digestive upsets.

As I was washing the breakfast dishes I heard footsteps coming up our stairs. That was another variation of the door-opening gambit employed by the lady down below: she would let people in quietly without announcing them, usually at times of disintegration like Sunday afternoons, doubtless hoping that we'd be caught in some awkward state, with our hair up in curlers or down in wisps, or lolling about in our bathrobes.

'Hi!' a voice said, halfway up. It was Peter's. He had already assumed impromptu visiting privileges.

'Oh *hi*,' I answered, making my voice casual but welcoming. 'I was just doing the dishes,' I added inanely as his head emerged from the stairwell. I left the rest of the dishes in the sink and dried my hands on my apron.

He came into the kitchen, 'Boy,' he said, 'judging from the hangover I had when I woke up, I must've been pie-eyed last night. I guess I really tied one on. This morning my mouth tasted like the inside of a tennis-shoe.' His tone was half-proud, half-apologetic.

We scanned each other warily. If there was going to be a retraction from either side, this was the moment for it; the whole thing could be blamed on organic chemistry. But neither of us backed down. Finally Peter grinned at me, a pleased though nervous grin.

I said, solicitously, 'Oh that's too bad. You *were* drinking quite a lot. Like a cup of coffee?'

'Love one,' he said, and came over and pecked me on the cheek, then collapsed on one of the kitchen chairs. 'By the way, sorry I didn't phone first – I just felt like seeing you.'

'That's okay,' I said. He did look hung-over. He was carelessly dressed, but it's impossible for Peter to dress with genuine carelessness. This was an arranged carelessness; he was meticulously unshaven, and his socks matched the colour of the paint-stains on his sports-shirt. I turned on the coffee.

'Well!' he said, just as Ainsley had but with a very different emphasis. He sounded as though he'd just bought a shiny new car. I gave him a tender chrome-plated smile; that is, I meant the smile to express tenderness, but my mouth felt stiff and bright and somehow expensive.

I poured two cups of coffee, got out the milk and sat down in the other kitchen chair. He put one of his hands over mine.

'You know,' he said, 'I didn't think I was intending – what happened last night – at all.' I nodded: I hadn't thought I was, either.

'I guess I've been running away from it.'

I had been, too.

'But I guess you were right about Trigger. And maybe I was intending it, without knowing it. A man's got to settle down sometime, and I am twenty-six.'

I was seeing him in a new light: he was changing form in the kitchen, turning from a reckless young bachelor into a rescuer from chaos, a provider of stability. Somewhere in the vaults of Seymour Surveys an invisible hand was wiping away my signature.

'And now things are settled I feel I'm going to be much happier. A fellow can't keep running around indefinitely. It'll be a lot better in the long run for my practice too, the clients like to know you've got a wife; people get suspicious of a single man after a certain age, they start thinking you're a queer or something.' He paused, then continued, 'And there's one thing about you, Marian, I know I can always depend on you. Most women are pretty scatterbrained but you're such a sensible girl. You may not have known this but I've always thought that's the first thing to look for when it comes to choosing a wife.'

I didn't feel very sensible. I lowered my eyes modestly and fixed them upon a toast crumb that had eluded me when I wiped the table. I wasn't sure what to say – 'You're very sensible too' didn't seem appropriate.

'I'm very happy too,' I said. 'Let's take our coffee into the living room.'

He followed me in; we set our cups on the round coffee table and sat down on the chesterfield.

'I like this room,' he said, glancing over it. 'It's so homey.' He put his arm around my shoulders, and we sat in what I hoped was a blissful silence. We were awkward with each other. We no longer had the assumptions, the tracks and paths of our former relationship to guide us. Until we'd established the new assumptions we wouldn't know quite what to do or say.

Peter chuckled to himself.

'What's funny?' I asked.

'Oh, not much. When I went out to get the car I found three shrubs caught underneath it; so I just took a drive past that lawn. We made a neat little hole in their hedge.' He was still pleased with himself about that.

'You big silly idiot,' I said fondly. I could feel the stirrings of the proprietary instinct. So this object, then, belonged to *me*. I leaned my head against his shoulder.

'When do you want to get married?' he asked, almost gruffly.

My first impulse was to answer, with the evasive flippancy I'd always used before when he'd asked me serious questions about myself, 'What about Groundhog Day?' But instead I heard a soft flannelly voice I barely recognized, saying, 'I'd rather have you decide that. I'd rather leave the big decisions up to you.' I was astounded at myself. I'd never said anything remotely like that to him before. The funny thing was I really meant it.

Chapter Eleven

Peter left early. He said he needed to get some more sleep and he advised me to do the same. However I wasn't at all tired. I was filled with a nervous energy which refused to dissipate itself in the restless forages I made through the apartment. This afternoon held that special quaity of mournful emptiness I've connected with late Sunday afternoons ever since childhood: the feeling of having nothing to do.

I finished the dishes, sorted the knives and forks and spoons into their compartments in the kitchen drawer, though I knew they wouldn't stay put for long, scanned the magazines in the living room for the seventh time, my attention snagging briefly but with new significance on such titles as 'ADOPTION: YES OR NO?' 'YOU'RE IN LOVE – IS IT REAL? A TWENTY-QUESTION QUIZ,' and 'HONEYMOON TENSIONS,' and fiddled with the controls of the toaster, which had been burning things. When the telephone rang I jumped for it eagerly: it was a wrong number. I suppose I could have talked with Ainsley, who was still in her bedroom; but somehow I didn't think it would be much help. I wanted to do something that could be finished, accomplished, though I didn't know what. Finally I resolved to spend the evening at the laundromat.

We do not, of course, use the lady down below's laundry facilities. If she has any. She never allows anything as plebeian as washing to desecrate the well-kept expanse of her back lawn. Maybe it's that she and the child just never get their clothes dirty; perhaps they have an invisible plastic coating. Neither of us has been in her cellar or even heard her acknowledge the existence of one. It's possible that washing is, in her hierarchy of the proprieties, one of those things that everyone knows about but nobody who is at all respectable discusses.

So when the mounds of unwearable clothes become intolerable and the drawersful of wearable ones are all but empty, we go to the laundromat. Or, usually, I go alone: I can't hold out as long as Ainsley can. Sunday evening is a better time to go than any of the rest of the weekend. There are fewer elderly gentlemen tying up and de-aphidizing their rose-bushes, and fewer elderly ladies, flowery-hatted and white-gloved, driving or being driven up to the houses of other elderly ladies for tea. The nearest laundromat is a subway-stop away, and Saturdays are bad because of the shoppers on the bus, again elderly ladies hatted and gloved, though not as immaculately; and Saturday evenings bring out the young moviegoers. I prefer Sunday evenings; they are emptier. I don't like being stared at, and my laundry bag is too obviously a laundry bag.

That evening I looked forward to the trip. I was anxious to get out of the apartment. I warmed up and ate a frozen dinner, then changed to my laundromat clothes – denims, sweatshirt, and a pair of plaid running-shoes I'd picked up once on impulse and never wore anywhere else – and checked my purse for quarters. I was stuffing the pertinent garments into my laundry bag when Ainsley wandered in. She'd been closeted in her bedroom most of the day, engaging in heaven-knows-what black magic practices: brewing up an aphrodisiac, no doubt, or making wax dolls of Leonard and transfixing them with hatpins at the appropriate points. Now some intuition had alerted her.

'Hi, going to the laundromat?' she said with careful nonchalance.

'No,' I said, 'I've chopped Peter up into little bits. I'm camouflaging him as laundry and taking him down to bury him in the ravine.'

She must have thought this remark in bad taste. She did not smile. 'Look, would you mind very much throwing in a few of my things while you're there? Just essentials.'

'Fine,' I said, resigned. 'Bring them along.' This is standard procedure. It's one of the reasons Ainsley never has to go to the laundromat.

She disappeared, and came back in a few minutes with both arms around a huge heap of multicoloured lingerie.

'Ainsley. Just essentials,'

'They're all essentials,' she said sulkily; but when I insisted I couldn't get it all into the bag she divided the pile in half.

'Thanks a lot, that's a real lifesaver,' she said. 'See you later.'

I trailed the sack behind me down the stairs, picked it up, slung it over my shoulder and staggered out the door, intercepting a frigid look in passing from the lady down below as she glided out from behind one of the velvet curtains that hung at the entrance to the parlour. She meant, I knew, to convey her disapproval of this flagrant exhibition of soilage. We are all, I silently quoted at her, utterly unclean.

Once I had settled myself on the bus I propped the laundry bag beside me on the seat, hoping it looked from a distance enough like a small child to fend off the righteous indignation of those who might object to working on the Lord's Day. I was remembering a previous incident, a black-silk-swathed old lady with a mauve hat who had clutched at me one Sunday as I was getting off the bus. She was disturbed not only because I was breaking the fourth commandment, but also because of the impious way I had dressed in order to do it: Jesus, she implied, would never forgive my plaid running-shoes. Then I concentrated on one of the posters above the windows, a colourful one of a young woman with three pairs of legs skipping about in her girdle. I must admit to being, against my will, slightly scandalized by those advertisements. They are so public. I wondered for the first few blocks what sort of person would have enough response to that advertisement to go and buy the object in question, and whether there had ever been a survey done on it. The female form, I thought, is supposed to appeal to men, not to women, and men don't usually buy girdles. Though perhaps the lithe young woman was a self-image; perhaps the purchasers thought they were getting their own youth and slenderness back in the package. For the next few blocks I thought about the dictum I'd read somewhere that no well-dressed woman is ever without her girdle. I considered the possibilities suggested by the word 'ever'. Then for the rest of the journey I thought about middle-aged spread: when would I get it? – maybe I already had it. You have to be careful about things like that, I reflected; they have a way of creeping up on you before you know it.

The laundromat was just along the street from the entrance to the subway station. When I was actually standing in front of one of the large machines I discovered I had forgotten the soap.

'Oh fiddlesticks!' I said out loud.

The person stuffing clothes into the machine next to mine turned towards me.

He looked at me without expression. 'You can have some of mine,' he said, handing me the box.

'Thank you. I wish they'd put in a vending machine, you'd think they'd have the sense to.' Then I recognized him: it was the young man from the beer interview. I stood there holding the box. How had he known I'd forgotten my soap? I hadn't said it out loud.

He was scrutinizing me more closely. 'Oh,' he said, 'now I know who you are. I didn't place you at first. Without that official shell you look sort of – exposed.' He bent over his machine again.

Exposed. Was that good or bad? I checked quickly to make sure no seams were split or zippers undone; then I began to cram the clothes hastily into the machines, putting darks in one and lights in the other. I didn't want him to be finished before I was so that he would be able to watch me, but he was done in time to observe several of Ainsley's lacy frivolities being flung through the door.

'Those yours?' he asked with interest.

'No,' I said, flushing.

'Didn't think so. They didn't look like you.'

Had that been a compliment or an insult? Judging by his uninflected voice it had been merely a comment; and as a comment it was accurate enough, I thought wryly.

I shut the two thick glass doors and put the quarters in the slots, paused till the familiar sloshing sound informed me that all was well, then went over to the line of chairs provided by the management and sat down in one of them. I'd have to wait it out, I realized; there was nothing else to do in that area on Sundays. I could have gone to a movie, but I didn't have enough money with me. I'd even forgoten to bring a paperback to read. What could I have been thinking of when I left the apartment? I don't usually forget things.

He sat down next to me. 'The only thing about laundromats,' he said, 'is that you're always finding other people's pubic hairs in the washers. Not that I mind particularly. I'm not picky about germs or anything. It's just rather gross. Have some chocolate?'

I glanced around to see if anyone had heard, but we were alone in the laundromat. 'No thanks.' I said.

'I don't like it much either but I'm trying to quit smoking.' He peeled the chocolate bar and slowly devoured it. We both stared at the long line of gleaming white machines, and especially at those three glass windows, like portholes or aquaria, where our clothes were going round and around, different shapes and colours appearing, mingling, disappearing, appearing again out of a fog of suds. He finished his chocolate bar, licked his fingers, smoothed and folded the silver wrapper neatly and put it in one of his pockets, and took out a cigarette.

'I sort of like watching them,' he said; 'I watch laundromat washers the way other people watch television, it's soothing because you always know what to expect and you don't have to think about it. Except I can vary my programmes a little; if I get tired of watching the same stuff I can always put in a pair of green socks or something colourful like that.' He was talking in a monotone, sitting hunched forward, his elbows on his knees, his head drawn down into the neck of his dark sweater like a turtle's into its shell. 'I come here quite a lot; sometimes I just have to get out of that apartment. It's all right as long as I have something to iron; I like flattening things out, getting rid of the wrinkles, it gives me something to do with my hands, but when I run out of things to iron, well, I have to come here. To get some more.'

He wasn't even looking at me. He might have been talking to himself. I leaned forward too, so I could see his face. In the blue-tinged fluorescent lighting of the laundromat, a light that seems to allow no tones and no shadows, his skin was even more unearthly. 'I have to get out, it's that apartment. In the summer it's like a hot, dark oven, and when it's that hot you don't even want to turn on the iron. There isn't enough space anyway but the heat makes it shrink, the others get too close. I can feel them even in my own room with the door closed; I can tell what they're doing. Fish barricades himself into that chair and hardly moves, even when he's writing, and then he tears it all up and says it's no good and sits there for days staring at the pieces of paper on the floor; once he got down on his hands and knees and tried to put them together again with scotch-tape, and failed of course, and threw a real scene and accused both of us of trying to use his ideas to publish first and stealing some of the pieces. And Trevor, when he isn't away at summer school or heating the apartment up cooking twelve-course dinners, I'd just as soon eat canned salmon, practises his fifteenth-century Italian calligraphy, scrollwork and flourishes, and goes on and on about the quattrocento. He has an amazing memory for detail. I guess it's interesting but somehow it isn't the answer, at least not for me, and I don't think it really is for him either. The thing is, they repeat themselves and repeat themselves but they never get anywhere, they never seem to finish anything. Of course I'm no better, I'm just the same, I'm stuck on that wretched term paper. Once I went to the zoo and there was a cage with a frenzied armadillo in it going around in figure-eights, just around and around in the same path. I can still remember the funny metallic sound its feet made on the bottom of the cage. They say all caged animals get that way when they're caged, it's a form of psychosis, and even if you set the animals free after they go like that they'll just run around in the same pattern. You read and read the material and after you've read the twentieth article you can't make any sense out of it anymore, and then you start thinking about the number of books that are published in any given year, in any given month, in any given week, and that's just too much. Words,' he said, looking in my direction finally but with his eyes strangely unfocussed, as though he was really looking at a point several inches beneath my skin, 'are beginning to lose their meanings.'

The machines were switching into one of their rinsing cycles, whirling the clothes around faster and faster; then there was more running water, and more churning and sloshing. He lit another cigarette.

'I gather you're all students, then,' I said.

'Of course,' he said mournfully, 'couldn't you tell? We're all graduate students. In English. All of us. I thought everyone in the whole city was; we're so totally inbred that we never see anyone else. It was quite strange when you walked in the other day and turned out not to be.'

'I always thought that would be sort of exciting.' I didn't really, I was trying to be responsive, but I was conscious as soon as I'd closed my mouth of the schoolgirl gushiness of the remark.

'Exciting.' He snickered briefly. 'I used to think that. It looks exciting when you're an eager brilliant undergraduate. They all say, Go on to graduate studies, and they give you a bit of money; and so you do, and you think, Now I'm going to find out the real truth. But you don't find out, exactly, and things get pickier and pickier and more and more stale, and it all collapses in a welter of commas and shredded footnotes, and after a while it's like anything else: you've got stuck in it and you can't get out, and you wonder how you got there in the first place. If this were the States I could excuse myself by saying I'm avoiding the draft, but, as it is, there's no good reason. And besides that, everything's being done, it's been done already, fished out, and you yourself wallowing around in the dregs at the bottom of the barrel, one of those ninth-year graduate students, poor bastards, scrabbling through manuscripts for new material or slaving away on the definitive edition of Ruskin's dinner-invitations and theatre-stubs or trying to squeeze the last pimple of significance out of some fraudulent literary nonenity they dug up somewhere. Poor old Fischer is writing his thesis now, he wanted to do it on Womb Symbols in D. H. Lawrence but they all told him that had been done. So now he's got some impossible theory that gets more and more incoherent as he goes along.' He stopped.

'Oh, what is it?' I said, to joggle him out of silence.

'I don't really know. He won't even talk about it anymore except when he's loaded, and then no one can understand him. That's why he keeps tearing it up – he reads it over and he can't understand any of it himself.'

'And what are you doing yours on?' I couldn't quite imagine.

'I haven't got to that point yet. I don't know when I ever will or what will happen then. I try not to think about it. Right now I'm supposed to be writing an overdue term paper from the year before last. I write a sentence a day. On good days, that is.' The machines clicked into their spin-dry cycle. He stared at them, morosely.

'Well, what's your term-paper on then?' I was intrigued; as much, I decided, by the changing contours of his face as by what he was saying. At any rate I didn't want him to stop talking.

'You don't really want to know,' he said. 'Pre-Raphaelite pornography. I'm trying to do something with Beardsley, too.'

'Oh.' We both considered in silence the possible hopelessness of this task. 'Maybe,' I suggested somewhat hesitantly, 'you're in the wrong business. Maybe you might be happier doing something else.'

He snickered again, then coughed. 'I should stop smoking,' he said. 'What else *can* I do? Once you've gone this far you aren't fit for anything else. Something happens to your mind. You're overqualified, overspecialized, and everybody knows it. Nobody in any other game would be crazy enough to hire me. I wouldn't even make a good ditch-digger, I'd start tearing apart the sewer-system, trying to pick-axe and unearth all those chthonic symbols – pipes, valves, cloacal conduits ... No, no. I'll have to be a slave in the paper-mines for all time.'

I had no answer. I looked at him and tried to picture him working at a place like Seymour Surveys; even upstairs with the intelligence men; but without success. He definitely wouldn't fit.

'Are you from out of town?' I asked finally. The subject of graduate school seemed to have been exhausted.

'Of course, we all are; nobody really comes from here, do they? That's why we've got that apartment, god knows we can't afford it but there aren't any graduate residences. Unless you count that new pseudo-British joint with the coat of arms and the monastery wall. But they'd never let *me* in and it would be just as bad as living with Trevor anyway. Trevor's from Montreal, the family is sort of Westmount and well-off; but they had to go into trade after the war. They own a coconut-cookie factory but we aren't supposed to refer to it around the apartment; it's awkward though, these mounds of coconut cookies keep appearing and you have to eat them while pretending you don't know where they come from. I don't like coconut. Fish was from Vancouver, he keeps missing the sea. He goes down to the lakeshore and wades through the pollution and tries to turn himself on with seagulls and floating grapefruit peels, but it doesn't work. Both of them used to have accents but now you can't tell anything from listening to them; after you've been in that braingrinder for a while you don't sound as though you're from anywhere.'

'Where are you from?'

'You've never heard of it,' he said curtly.

The machines clicked off. We both got wire laundry-carts and transferred our clothes to the dryers. Then we sat down in the chairs again. Now there wasn't anything to watch; just the humming and thumping of the dryers to listen to. He lit another cigarette.

A seedy old man shuffled through the door, saw us, and shuffled out again. He was probably looking for a place to sleep.

'The thing is,' he said at last, 'it's the inertia. You never feel you're getting anywhere; you get bogged down in things, waterlogged. Last week I set fire to the apartment, partly on purpose. I think I wanted to see what they would do. Maybe I wanted to see what *I* would do. Mostly though I just got interested in seeing a few flames and some smoke, for a change. But they just put it out, and then they ran around in frenzied figure-eights like a couple of armadilloes, talking about how I was 'sick' and why did I do it, and maybe my inner tensions were getting too much for me and I'd better go see a shrink. That wouldn't do any good. I know about all of that and none of it does any good. Those types can't *convince* me anymore, I know too much about it, I've been through that already, I'm immune. Setting fire to the apartment didn't change anything, except now I can't flex my nostrils without having Trevor squeal and leap a yard and Fischer look me up in his leftover freshman Psych. textbook. They think I'm mad.' He dropped his cigarette stub on the floor and ground it underfoot. 'I think they're mad,' he added.

'Maybe,' I said cautiously, 'you should move out.'

He smiled his crooked smile.

'Where could I go? I couldn't afford it. I'm stuck. Besides, they sort of take care of me, you know.' He hunched his shoulders further up around his neck.

I looked at the side of his thin face, the high stark ridge of his cheekbone, the dark hollow of his eye, marvelling: all this talking, this rather liquid confessing, was something I didn't think I could ever bring myself to do. It seemed foolhardy to me, like an uncooked egg deciding to come out of its shell: there would be a risk of spreading out too far, turning into a formless puddle. But sitting there with the plug of a fresh cigarette stoppering his mouth he didn't appear to be sensing any danger of that kind.

Thinking about it later, I'm surprised at my own detachment. My restlessness of the afternoon had vanished; I felt calm, serene as a stone moon, in control of the whole white space of the laundromat. I could have reached out effortlessly and put my arms around that huddled awkward body and consoled it, rocked it gently. Still, there was something most unchildlike about him, something that suggested rather an unnaturally old man, old far beyond consolation. I thought too, remembering his duplicity about the beer-interview, that he was no doubt capable of making it all up. It may have been real enough; but then again, it may have been calculated to evoke just such a mothering reaction, so that he could smile cleverly at the gesture and retreat further into the sanctuary of his sweater, refusing to be reached or touched.

He must have been equipped with a kind of science-fiction extra sense, a third eye or an antenna. Although his face was turned away so that he couldn't see mine, he said in a soft dry voice, 'I can tell you're admiring my febrility. I know it's appealing, I practise at it; every woman loves an invalid. I bring out the Florence Nightingale in them. But be careful.' He was looking at me now, cunningly, sideways. 'You might do something destructive. Hunger is more basic than love. Florence Nightingale was a cannibal, you know.'

My calmness was shattered. I felt mice-feet of apprehension scurrying over my skin. What exactly was I being accused of? Was I exposed?

I could think of nothing to say.

The dryers whirred to a standstill. I got up. 'Thanks for the soap,' I said with formal politeness.

He got up too. He seemed again quite indifferent to my presence. 'That's all right,' he said.

We stood side by side without speaking, pulling the clothes out of the dryers and wadding them into our laundry bags. We shouldered our laundry and walked to the door together, I a little ahead. I paused for an instant at the entrance, but he made no move to open the door for me so I opened it myself.

When we were outside the laundromat we turned, both at once so that we almost collided. We stood facing each other irresolutely for a minute; we both started to say something, and both stopped. Then, as though someone had pulled a switch, we dropped our laundry bags to the sidewalk and took a step forward. I found myself kissing him, or being kissed by him, I still don't know which. His mouth tasted like cigarettes. Apart from that taste, and an impression of thinness and dryness, as though the body I had my arms around and the face touching mine were really made of tissue paper or parchment stretched on a frame of wire coat-hangers, I can remember no sensation at all.

We both stopped kissing at the same time, and stepped back. We looked at each other for another minute. Then we picked up our laundry bags, slung them over our shoulders, turned around, and marched away in opposite directions. The whole incident had been ridiculously like the jerky attractions and repulsions of those plastic dogs with magnets on the bottoms I remembered getting as prizes at birthday parties.

I can't recall anything about the trip back to the apartment, except that on the bus I stared for a long time at an advertisement with a picture of a nurse in a white cap and dress. She had a wholesome, competent face and she was holding a bottle and smiling. The caption said: GIVE THE GIFT OF LIFE

Chapter Twelve

So here I am.

I'm sitting on my bed in my room with the door shut and the window open. It's Labour Day, a fine cool sunny day like yesterday. I found it strange not to have to go to the office this morning. The highways outside the city will be coagulating with traffic even this early, people already beginning to come back from their week-ends at summer cottages, trying to beat the rush. At five o'clock everything will have slowed down to an ooze out there and the air will be filled with the shimmer of sun on miles of metal and the whining of idling motors and bored children. But here, as usual, it's quiet.

Ainsley is in the kitchen. I've hardly seen her today. I can hear her walking about on the other side of the door, humming intermittently. I feel hesitant about opening the door. Our positions have shifted in some way I haven't yet assessed, and I know I would find it difficult to talk with her.

Friday seems a long time ago, so much has happened since then, but now I've gone over it all in my mind I see that my actions were really more sensible than I thought at the time. It was my subconscious getting ahead of my conscious self, and the subconscious has its own logic. The way I went about doing things may have been a little inconsistent with my true personality, but are the results that inconsistent? The decision was a little sudden, but now I've had time to think about it I realize it is actually a very good step to take. Of course I'd always assumed through highschool and college that I was going to marry someone eventually and have children, everyone does. Either two or four, three is a bad number and I don't approve of only children, they get spoiled too easily. I've never been silly about marriage the way Ainsley is. She's against it on principle, and life isn't run by principles but by adjustments. As Peter says, you can't continue to run around indefinitely; people who aren't married get funny in middle age, embittered or addled or something, I've seen enough of them around the office to realize that. But although I'm sure it was in the back of my mind I hadn't consciously expected it to happen so soon or quite the way it did. Of course I was more involved with Peter all along than I wanted to admit.

And there's no reason why our marriage should turn out like Clara's . Those two aren't practical enough, they have no sense at all of how to manage, how to run a well-organized marriage. So much of it is a matter of elementary mechanical detail, such as furniture and meals and keeping things in order. But Peter and I should be able to set up a very reasonable arrangement. Though of course we still have a lot of the details to work out. Peter is an ideal choice when you come to think of it. He's attractive and he's bound to be successful, and also he's neat, which is a major point when you're going to be living with someone.

I can imagine the expressions on their faces at the office when they hear. But I can't tell them yet, I'll have to keep my job there for a while longer. Till Peter is finished articling we'll need the money. We'll probably have to live in an apartment at first, but later we can have a real house, a permanent place; it will be worth the trouble to keep clean.

Meanwhile I should be doing something constructive instead of sitting around like this. First I should revise the beer questionnaire and make out a report on my findings so I can type it up first thing tomorrow and get it out of the way.

Then perhaps I'll wash my hair. And my room needs a general clean-up. I should go through the dresser-drawers and throw out whatever has accumulated in them, and there are some dresses hanging in the closet I don't wear enough to keep. I'll give them to the Salvation Army. Also a lot of costume jewellery, the kind you get from relatives at Christmas: imitation gold pins in the shapes of poodle dogs and bunches of flowers with pieces of cut-glass for petals and eyes. There's a cardboard box full of books, textbooks mostly, and letters from home I know I'll never look at again, and a couple of ancient dolls I've kept for sentimental reasons. The older doll has a cloth body stuffed with sawdust (I know that because I once performed an operation on it with a pair of nail scissors) and hands, feet and head made of a hard woody material. The fingers and toes have been almost chewed off; the hair is black and short, a few frizzy wisps attached to a piece of netting which is coming unglued from the skull. The face is almost eroded but still has its open mouth with the red felt tongue inside and two china teeth, its chief fascination as I remember. It's dressed in a strip of old sheet. I used to leave food in front of it overnight and was always disappointed when it wasn't gone in the morning. The other doll is newer and has long washable hair and a rubbery skin. I asked for her one Christmas because you could give her baths. Neither of them is very attractive any longer; I might as well throw them out with the rest of the junk.

I still can't quite fit in the man at the laundromat or account for my own behaviour. Maybe it was a kind of lapse, a blank in the ego, like amnesia. But there's little chance of my ever running into him again – I don't even know his name – and anyway he has nothing at all to do with Peter.

After I finish cleaning my room I should write a letter home.

They will all be pleased, this is surely what they've been waiting for. They'll want us to come down for the weekend as soon as possible. I've never met Peter's parents either.

In a minute I'll get off the bed and walk through the pool of sunshine on the floor. I can't let my whole afternoon dribble away, relaxing though it is to sit in this quiet room gazing up at the empty ceiling with my back against the cool wall, dangling my feet over the edge of the bed. It's almost like being on a rubber raft, drifting, looking up into a clear sky.

I must get organized. I have a lot to do.

PART TWO

Chapter Thirteen

Marian was sitting listlessly at her desk. She was doodling on the pad for telephone messages. She drew an arrow with many intricate feathers, then a cross-hatch of intersecting lines. She was supposed to be working on a questionnaire, something about stainless-steel razorblades; she had got as far as the question that directed the interviewer to ask the victim for the used razorblade currently in his razor and offer him a new one in exchange. This had stalled her. She was thinking now that it must be an elaborate plot: the president of the razorblade company had possessed a miraculous razorblade which had been in his family for generations and which not only renewed its sharpness every time it was used but also granted the shaver anything he wished for after every thirteenth shave ... the president, however, had not guarded his treasure carefully enough. One day he had forgotten to replace it in its velvet-lined case and had left it lying around in the bathroom, and one of the maids, trying to be useful, had ... (the story was unclear at this point, but it was very complicated. The razorblade had somehow managed to make its way into a store, a second-hand store where it had been bought by an unsuspecting customer and ...). The president had that very day needed some money in a hurry. He had shaved frantically every three hours to make up the number 13, scraping his face raw; what was his surprise and dismay when. ... So he had found out what had happened, commanded the offending maid to be tossed into a pit full of used razorblades, and had covered the city with a dragnet of middle-aged female private detectives posing as Seymour Surveys interviewers, their eagle-eyes trained to ferret out everyone, male or female, with the least trace of a beard, crying 'New Razorblades For Old,' in a desperate attempt to recover the priceless lost. ...

Marian sighed, drew a small spider in one corner of the maze of lines, and turned to her typewriter. She typed the section intact from the rough questionnaire – 'We would like to examine the condition of your razorblade. Would you give me the razorblade that is *now* in your razor? Here is a new one in return for it,' – adding a 'please' before the 'give'. There was no way of rewording the question that would make it sound less eccentric, but at least it could be made more polite.

Around her the office was in a turmoil. It was always either in a turmoil or in a dead flat calm, and on the whole she preferred the turmoils. She could get away with doing less, everyone else was in such a state, skittering about and screeching, that they didn't have time to lounge around and peer over her shoulder and wonder what was taking her so long or what exactly she was doing anyway. She used to feel a sense of participation in the turmoils themselves; once or twice she had even allowed herself to become frenzied in sympathy, and had been surprised at how much fun it was; but ever since she had become engaged and had known she wasn't going to be there forever (they'd talked about it, Peter said of course she could keep working after the wedding if she wanted to, for a while at least, though she didn't need to financially – he considered it unfair to marry, he said, if you couldn't afford to support your wife, but she had decided against it), she had been able to lean back and view them all with detachment. In fact, she found that she couldn't become involved even when she wanted to. They had taken lately to complimenting her on her calmness in emergencies. 'Well, thank goodness for Marian,' they'd say, as they soothed themselves with cups of tea and patted their overwrought foreheads with pieces of kleenex, breathing hard. '*She* never lets herself get out of control. Do you, dear?'

At the moment they were running around, she thought, like a herd of armadilloes at the zoo. Armadilloes recalled briefly to her mind the man in the laundromat, who had never reappeared, though she had been to the laundromat several times and had always half-expected to see him there. But that wasn't surprising, he was obviously unstable; he had probably vanished down some drain or other a long time ago. . . .

She watched Emmy as she darted to the filing cabinet and rummaged feverishly among the files. This time it was the coast-to-coast sanitary-napkin survey: something had gone embarrassingly wrong in the West. It was supposed to have been what they called a 'three-wave' survey: the first wave surging out through the mails, locating and bringing back on its returning crest a shoal of eligible and willing answerers, and the second and third waves following up with interviews of greater depth, done in person. And, Marian hoped, behind closed doors. The whole business, especially some of the questions that were to be asked, had rather shocked her sense of fitness, though Lucy had pointed out over a coffee-break that it was most proper these days, after all it was a respectable product, you could buy it in the supermarket and it had full-page advertisements in some of the best magazines, and wasn't it nice they were getting it out in the open and not being so Victorian and repressed about it. Millie had said of course that was the enlightened view but these surveys were always a pain, not only did you have trouble with people at the doors but you couldn't get the interviewers to do them anyway, lots of them were quite old-fashioned, especially the ones in small towns, some of them even resigned if you asked them to do it (that was the worst of using housewives, they didn't really *need* the money, they were always getting bored with it or fed up or pregnant and resigning and then you had to get new ones and train them up from scratch), the best thing was to send them out a form letter telling them how they must all do their best to better the lot of Womankind – an attempt to appeal, Marian reflected, to the embryonic noble nurse that is supposed to be curled, efficient and self-sacrificing, in the heart of every true woman.

This time something worse had happened. In the West, whoever had been in charge of selecting from the local phone books the names of the women who were to be hit by the first wave (who *had* been in charge out there? Mrs Lietch in Foam River? Mrs Hatcher in Watrous? No one could remember, and Emmy said they seemed to have misplaced the file) had not been overly meticulous. Instead of the expected flood of responses, only a mere trickle of filled-in questionnaires had been coming through the mail. Millie and Lucy were scrutinizing these now at the desk opposite Marian's, trying to figure out what had gone wrong.

'Well, some of them obviously went out to men,' Millie snorted. 'Here's one with "Tee Hee" written on it, from a Mr Leslie Andrewes.'

'What I can't understand is the ones that come back from women with NO checked in *all* the boxes. What on earth *do* they use then?' said Lucy peevishly.

'Well this lady's over eighty.'

'Here's one who says she's been pregnant for seven years straight.'

'Oh, *no*, poor thing,' gasped Emmy, who was listening. 'Why she'll ruin her health.'

'I bet that dumb cluck Mrs Lietch – or Mrs Hatcher, whoever it was – sent them to Indian reservations again. I specifically *told* her not to. The lord knows what *they* use,' sniffed Lucy.

'Moss,' Millie said decisively. This wasn't the first time something had gone wrong in the West. She counted once more through the stack of questionnaires. 'We're going to have to start it all over again and the client will be furious. All our quotas are thrown off and I hate to think what'll happen to our deadlines.'

Marian looked at the clock. It was almost time for lunch. She drew a row of moons across her page: crescent moons, full moons, then crescent moons pointing the other way, then nothing: a black moon. For good measure she drew a star inside one of the crescents. She set her watch, the one Peter had given her for her birthday, though it was only two minutes off by the office clock, and wound it. She typed another question. She was aware of being hungry, and wondered whether her hunger had been produced by her knowledge of the time. She got out of her chair, spun it round a couple of times to raise the height, sat down again and typed another question; she was tired, tired, tired of being a manipulator of words. At last, unable to remain sitting in her chair at her desk in front of her typewriter a moment longer, she said 'Let's go have lunch now.'

'Well . . .' Millie hesitated, and looked at the clock. She was still semi-held by the illusion that there was something she could *do* about the mess.

'Yes, let's,' said Lucy, 'this is driving me bats, I've just got to get out of here.' She walked towards the coat-rack, and Emmy followed her. When Millie saw the others putting on their coats she reluctantly abandoned the questionnaires.

On the street the wind was cold. They turned their collars up, holding the fronts of their coats together near the neck with gloved hands, threading two by two among the other lunchtime scurriers, their heels clicking and grating on the bare sidewalk: it had not yet snowed. They had further to walk than usual. Lucy had suggested that they go to a more expensive restaurant than the ones they normally frequented, and in the state of heightened metabolism created by the sanitary-napkin turmoil they had agreed.

'OOoo,' Emmy wailed as they leaned into the gritty wind. 'In this dry weather I just don't know what I'll do. My skin's just all drying up and flaking away.' When it rained she got terrible pains in her feet and when it was sunny she got eye-strain, headaches and freckles and dizzy spells. When the weather was neutral, grey and lukewarm, she got hot flushes and coughs.

'Cold cream's the best,' Millie said. 'My gran had dry skin too and that's what she used.'

'But I've heard it gives you pimples,' Emmy said dubiously.

The restaurant was one with old-world English pretensions and stuffed leather chairs and Tudor beams. After a short wait they were led to a table by a black-silk hostess; they settled themselves and slipped off their coats. Marian noticed that Lucy was wearing a new dress, a stately dark-mauve laminated jersey with a chaste silver pin at the neckline. So that's why she wanted to come here today, Marian thought.

Lucy's long-lashed gaze was brushing over the other lunchers – stolid breadfaced businessmen most of them, gobbling their food and swilling a few drinks to get the interruptions of lunch over with as soon and as numbly as possible so they could get back to the office and make some money and get that over with as soon as possible and get back through the rush hour traffic to their homes and wives and dinners and to get those over with as soon as possible too. Lucy had mauve eye-shadow to match her dress, and lipstick with a pale mauve tinge. She was, as always, elegant. She had been lunching out expensively more and more in the last two months (though Marian wondered how she could afford it), trailing herself like a many-plumed fish-lure with glass beads and three spinners and seventeen hooks through the likely-looking places, good restaurants and cocktail bars with their lush weed-beds of potted philodendrons, where the right kind of men might be expected to be lurking, ravenous as pike, though more maritally inclined. But those men, the right kind, weren't biting, or had left for other depths, or were snapping at a different sort of bait – some inconspicuous brown-plastic minnow or tarnished simple brass spoon, or something with even more feathers and hooks than Lucy could manage. And in this restaurant, and similar ones, it was in vain that Lucy displayed her delicious dresses and confectionery eyes to the tubfulls of pudgy guppies who had no time for mauve.

The waitress came. Millie ordered steak-and-kidney pie, a good substantial lunch. Emmy chose a salad with cottage cheese, to go with her three kinds of pills, the pink, the white, and the orange, which were lined up on the table beside her water glass. Lucy fussed and fretted and changed her mind several times and finally asked for an omelette. Marian was surprised at herself. She had been dying to go for lunch, she had been starving, and now she wasn't even hungry. She had a cheese sandwich.

'How's Peter?' Lucy asked after she had fiddled with her omelette and accused it of being leathery. She took an interest in Peter. He had got into the habit of phoning Marian at the office to tell her what he had done that day and what he was going to do that evening, and when Marian wasn't there he left messages with Lucy, who shared Marian's phone. Lucy thought him most polite, and found his voice intriguing.

Marian was watching Millie as she stowed away her steak-and-kidney pie, methodically, like putting things in a trunk. 'There,' she'd say, or ought to, when it was finished: 'All stored neatly away.' And her mouth would close like a lid.

'Just fine,' Marian said. She and Peter had decided she shouldn't tell them at the office quite yet. She had been holding out therefore, day after day, but now the question caught her desire to announce off-guard, and she couldn't resist. They might as well know there's hope in the world yet, she rationalized. 'I have something to tell you all,' she said, 'but it isn't to go any further just now.' She waited until the three pairs of eyes had transferred their attention from the plates to her, then said, 'We're engaged.'

She smiled glowingly at them, watching the expression in their eyes change from expectation to dismay. Lucy dropped her fork and gasped, 'No!' adding, 'how wonderful!' Millie said, 'Oh. Jolly good.' Emmy hurriedly took another pill.

Then there were flurried questions, which Marian dealt with calmly, doling out the information like candies to small children: one at a time, and not too much: it might make them sick. The triumphant elation she had assumed would follow the announcement, for her at least, was only momentary. As soon as the surprise-effect had worn off, the conversation became as remote and impersonal, on both sides, as the razorblade questionnaires;

enquiries about the wedding, the future apartment, the possible china and glassware, what would be bought and worn.

Lucy asked finally, 'I always thought he was the confirmed bachelor type, that's what you said. How on earth did you ever catch him?'

Marian looked away from the suddenly pathetic too-eager faces poised to snatch at her answer, down at the knives and forks on the plates. 'I honestly don't know,' she said, trying to convey a becoming bridal modesty. She really didn't know. She was sorry now that she had told them, dangled the effect in front of them that way without being able to offer them a reproducible cause.

Peter phoned almost as soon as they got back to the office. Lucy handed the phone to Marian with a whispered 'It's the man!', a little awed by the presence of an actual prospective groom at the other end of the line. Marian felt through the air the tensing of three pairs of ear-muscles, the swivelling of three blonde heads, as she spoke into the phone.

Peter's voice was terse. 'Hi honey how are you? Listen, I really can't make it tonight. A case came up suddenly, something big, and I've just got to do some work on it.'

He sounded as though he was accusing her of trying to interfere with his work, and she resented this. She hadn't even been expecting to see him in mid-week like that until he'd called the day before and asked her to have dinner; since then she'd been looking forward to it. She said rather sharply. 'That's all right, darling. But it would be nice if we could get these things straight before the last minute.'

'I told you it came up *suddenly*,' he said with irritation.

'Well you needn't bite my head off.'

'I wasn't,' he said, exasperated. 'You know I'd much rather see you, of course, only you've got to understand. . . .' The rest of the conversation was a tangle of retractions and conciliations. Well, we have to learn to compromise, Marian thought, and we might as well begin working at it now. She concluded, 'Tomorrow then?'

'Look darling,' he said, 'I really don't know. It'll really all depend, you know how these things are, I'll let you know, okay?'

When Marian had said good-bye sweetly for the benefit of her audience and had put down the phone she felt exhausted. She must watch how she spoke to Peter, she would have to handle him more carefully, there was evidently a good deal of pressure on him at his office. . . . 'I wonder if I'm getting anaemia?' she said to herself as she turned back to the typewriter.

After she had finished the razorblade questionnaire and had begun to work on a different one, the instructions for a product-test of a new dehydrated dog-food, the phone rang again. It was Joe Bates. She had been half-expecting the call. She greeted Joe with false enthusiasm: she knew she had been shirking her responsibilities lately, avoiding the Bates' dinner-invitations even though Clara had been wanting to see her. The pregnancy had gone first one week, then two weeks longer than it was supposed to, and Clara had sounded over the phone as though she herself was being dragged slowly down into the gigantic pumpkin-like growth that was enveloping her body. 'I can hardly stand up,' she had groaned. But Marian had not been able to face another evening of contemplating Clara's belly and speculating with her on the mysterious behaviour of its contents. She had responded the last time only with cheerful but notably uncheering remarks intended to lighten the atmosphere, such as 'Maybe it's got three heads,' and 'Maybe it isn't a baby at all but a kind of parasitic growth, like galls on trees, or elephantiasis of the navel, or a huge bunion. . . .' After that evening she had rationalized that she would do Clara more harm by going to see her than by staying away. In a spurt of solicitude catalysed by guilt, though, she had made Joe promise as she was leaving to let her know as soon as anything happened, even offering heroically to babysit for the others if absolutely necessary; and now his voice was saying, 'Well thank god it's all over. It's another girl, ten pounds seven ounces, and she only went into the hospital at two last night. We were afraid she was going to have it in the taxi.'

'Well that's marvellous,' Marian exclaimed, and added various inquiries and congratulations. She got the visiting hours and the room-number from Joe and wrote them down on her telephone-messages pad. 'Tell her I'll come down and see her tomorrow,' she said. She was thinking that now Clara was deflating toward her normal size again she would be able to talk with her more freely: she would no longer feel as though she was addressing a swollen mass of flesh with a tiny pinhead, a shape that had made her think of a queen-ant, bulging with the burden of an entire society, a semi-person – or sometimes, she thought, several people, a cluster of hidden personalities that she didn't know at all. She decided on impulse to buy her some roses: a welcoming-back gift for the real Clara, once more in uncontended possession of her own frail body.

She settled the phone in its black cradle and leaned back in her chair. The second-hand on the clock was sweeping around, accompanied by the ticking of typewriters and the click-clack of high-heeled shoes on the hard floor. She could feel time eddying and curling almost visibly around her feet, rising around her, lifting her body in the office-chair and bearing her, slowly and circuitously but with the inevitability of water moving downhill, towards the distant, not-so-distant-anymore day they had agreed on – in late March? – that would end this phase and begin another. Somewhere else, arrangements were being gradually made; the relatives were beginning to organise their forces and energies, it was all being taken care of, there was nothing for her to do. She was floating, letting the current hold her up, trusting to it to take her where she was going. Now there was this day to get through: a landmark to be passed on the shore, a tree not much different from any of the others that could be distinguished from the rest only by being here rather than further back or further on, with no other purpose than to measure the distance travelled. She wanted to get it behind her. To help the propelling second hand she typed out the rest of the dog-food questionnaire.

Towards the end of the afternoon Mrs Bogue sauntered out of her cubicle. The upwardly-arranged lines on her brow expressed consternation, but her eyes were level as ever.

'Oh dear,' she said to the office at large – it was part of her human-relations policy to let them in on minor managerial crises – 'what a day. Not only that disturbance in the West, but there's been some trouble with that horrible Underwear Man again.'

'Not that filthy man!' Lucy said, wrinkling her opalescently-powdered nose in disgust.

'Yes,' said Mrs Bogue, 'it's so upsetting.' She wrung her hands together in feminine despair. She was evidently not at all upset. 'He seems to have shifted his field of operations to the suburbs, to Etobicoke as a matter of fact. I've had two ladies from Etobicoke on the phone this afternoon complaining. Of course he's probably some nice ordinary man, perfectly harmless, but it's so nasty for the company's image.'

'What does he do?' asked Marian. She had never heard about the Underwear Man before.

'Oh,' said Lucy, 'he's one of those dirty men who phone women and say filthy things to them. He was doing it last year too.'

'The trouble is,' Mrs Bogue lamented, still clasping her hands in front of her, 'he tells them he's from our company. Apparently he has a very convincing voice. Very official. He says he's doing a survey on underwear, and I guess the first questions he asks must sound genuine. Brands and types and sizes and things. Then he gets more and more personal until the ladies get annoyed and hang up. Of course then they phone the company to complain, and sometimes they've accused us of all sorts of indecent things before I can explain that he's not one of our interviewers and our company would never ask questions like that. I wish they'd catch him and ask him to stop, he's such a nuisance, but of course he's almost impossible to trace.'

'I wonder why he does it?' Marian speculated.

'Oh, he's probably one of those sex-fiends,' Lucy said with a delicate mauve shiver.

Mrs Bogue puckered her brow again and shook her head. 'But they all say he sounds so *nice*. So normal and even intelligent. Not at all like those awful people who call you up and breathe at you.'

'Maybe it all proves that some sex-fiends are very nice normal people,' Marian said to Lucy when Mrs Bogue had gone back to her cubicle.

As she put on her coat and drifted out of the office and down the hall and let herself be floated down in the decompression chamber of the elevator, she was still thinking about the Underwear Man. She pictured his intelligent face, his polite, attentive manner, something like that of an insurance salesman; or an undertaker. She wondered what sort of personal questions he asked, and what she would say if he were ever to phone *her* (Oh, you must be the Underwear Man. I've heard *so* much about you. ... I think we must have some friends in common). She saw him as wearing a business suit and a fairly conservative tie, diagonal stripes in brown and maroon; shoes well-shined. Perhaps his otherwise normal mind had been crazed into frenzy by the girdle advertisements on the buses: he was a victim of society. Society flaunted these slender laughing rubberized women before his eyes, urging, practically forcing upon him their flexible blandishments, and then refused to supply him with any. He had found when he had tried to buy the garment in question at store counters that it came empty of the promised contents. But instead of raging and fuming and getting nowhere he had borne his disappointment quietly and maturely, and had decided, like the sensible man he was, to go systematically in search of the underwear-clad image he so ardently desired, using for his purposes the handy telecommunications network provided by society. A just exchange: they owed it to him.

As she stepped onto the street a new thought came to her. Maybe it was really Peter. Slipping out from his law office into the nearest phone booth to dial the numbers of housewives in Etobicoke. His protest against something or other – surveys? housewives in Etobicoke? vulcanization? – or his only way of striking back at a cruel world that saddled him with crushing legal duties and prevented him from taking her to dinner. And he had got the company name and the knowledge of official interviewing procedures, of course, from her! Perhaps this was his true self, the core of his personality, the central Peter who had been occupying her mind more and more lately. Perhaps this was what lay hidden under the surface, under the other surfaces, that secret identity which in spite of her many guesses and attempts and half-successes she was aware she had still not uncovered; he was really the Underwear Man.

Chapter Fourteen

The first thing Marian's eyes encountered as her head emerged periscope-like through the stairwell was a pair of naked legs. They were topped by Ainsley, who was standing half-dressed in the small vestibule, gazing down upon her, the usual blankness of her face tinged almost imperceptibly here and there with shades of surprise and annoyance.

'Hi,' she said. 'I thought you were going out for dinner tonight.' She fastened her eyes accusingly upon the small bag of groceries Marian was carrying.

Marian's legs pushed the rest of her body up the remaining stairs before she answered. 'I was, but I'm not. Something came up at Peter's office.' She went into the kitchen and deposited the paper bag on the table. Ainsley followed her in and sat down on one of the chairs.

'Marian,' she said dramatically, 'it has to be tonight!'

'What does?' Marian asked vaguely, putting her carton of milk into the refrigerator. She wasn't really listening.

'It. Leonard. You know.'

Marian had been so occupied with her own thoughts that it was a moment before she remembered what Ainsley was talking about. 'Oh. That,' she said. She took off her coat, reflectively.

She hadn't been paying close attention to the progress of Ainsley's campaign (or was it Leonard's?) over the past two months – she'd wanted to keep her hands clean of the whole thing – but she had been force-fed enough with Ainsley's own accounts and analyses and complaints to be able to deduce what had been happening; after all, however clean one's hands, one's ears were of necessity open. Things hadn't gone according to schedule. It appeared that Ainsley had overshot the mark. At the first encounter she had made herself into an image of such pink-gingham purity that Len had decided, after her strategic repulse of him that evening, that she would require an extra-long and careful siege. Anything too abrupt, too muscular, would frighten her away; she would have to be trapped with gentleness and caution. Consequently he had begun by asking her to lunch several times, and had progressed, at intervals of medium length, to dinners out and finally to foreign films, in one of which he had gone so far as to hold her hand. He had even invited her to his apartment once, for afternoon tea. Ainsley said later with several vigorous oaths that he had been on this occasion a model of propriety. Since by her own admission she didn't drink, she could not even pretend to permit him to get her drunk. In conversation he treated her as though she was a little girl, patiently explaining things to her and impressing her with stories about the television studio and assuring her that his interest in her was strictly that of a well-wishing older friend until she wanted to scream. And she couldn't even talk back: it was necessary for her mind to appear as vacant as her face. Her hands were tied. She had constructed her image and now she had to maintain it. To make any advances herself, or to let slip a flicker of anything resembling intelligence, would have been so out of character as to give her dumb-show irrevocably away. So she had been stewing and fussing in private, suffering Len's overly-subtle manoeuvrings with suppressed impatience and watching the all-important calendar days slide uneventfully by.

'If it isn't tonight,' Ainsley said, 'I don't know what I'll do. I can't stand it much longer – I'll have to get another one. But I've wasted so much *time*.' She frowned, as much as she was able to with her embryonic eyebrows.

'And where ...?' Marian asked, beginning to see why Ainsley had been annoyed at her unexpected return.

'Well he's obviously not going to ask me up to see his camera-lenses,' Ainsley said petulantly. 'And anyway if I said Yes he'd get suspicious as hell. We're going out to dinner though, and I thought maybe if I invited him up for coffee afterwards. ...'

'So you'd rather I went out,' Marian said, her voice heavy with disapproval.

'Well, it would be an awful help. Ordinarily I wouldn't give a damn if there was a whole camp meeting in the next room, or under the bed for that matter, and I bet he wouldn't either, but you see, he'll think I ought to care. I've got to let myself be backed slowly into the bedroom. Inch by inch.'

'Yes, I can see that.' Marian sighed. Censure was, at this point, none of her business. 'I'm just wondering where I can go.'

Ainsley's face brightened. Her main objective had been gained; the rest of the details were secondary. 'Well, do you think maybe you could just phone up Peter and tell him you're coming over? He shouldn't mind, he's engaged to you.'

Marian considered. Previously, in some area of time she could not at the moment remember clearly, she would have been able to; it wouldn't have mattered if he had got peeved. But these days, and especially after their conversation in the afternoon, it would not be a good idea. No matter how unobtrusive she made herself with a book in the living room, he would silently accuse her of being overpossessive, or of being jealous and interfering about his work. Even if she explained the real situation. And she didn't want to do that: though Peter had seen almost nothing of Len since the first evening, having exchanged the free-bachelor image for the mature-fiancé one and adjusted his responses and acquaintances accordingly, there would still be a kind of clan-loyalty that might cause trouble, if not for Ainsley, at least for her. It would give him ammunition. 'I don't think I'd better,' she said. 'He's working awfully hard.' There was really no place she could go. Clara's was out. It was getting too cold for sitting in parks or for prolonged walking. She might call one of the office virgins. ... 'I'll see a movie,' she said at last.

Ainsley smiled with relief. 'Fabulous,' she said, and went into her bedroom to finish dressing. She stuck her head out a few minutes later to ask, 'Can I use that bottle of scotch if I need it? I'll say it's yours but that you won't mind.'

'Sure, go ahead,' Marian said. The scotch was mutually owned. Ainsley, she knew, would pay her back out of the next bottle. Even if she forgot to, a half-bottle of scotch would be a small enough sacrifice to get the thing decisively over and done with. This vicariously nervewracking delay and shilly-shally had gone on far too long. She remained in the kitchen, leaning against the counter and gazing with pensive interest into the sink, which contained four glasses partly filled with opaque water, a fragment of eggshell, and a pot that had recently been used for cooking macaroni and cheese. She decided not to wash the dishes, but as a token gesture of cleanliness she picked out the eggshell and put it in the garbage. She disliked remnants.

When Ainsley reappeared, in a blouse and jumper outfit set off by earrings in the shape of tiny daisies and an extra good eye-job, Marian said to her, 'That movie isn't going to last all night, you know. I'll have to come back around twelve-thirty.' Even if she expects me to sleep in the gutter, she thought.

'I imagine the situation will be well under control by then,' Ainsley said with determination. 'If it isn't, neither of us will be there anyway: I'll have thrown him out of the window. And leaped out myself. But just in case, don't go charging through any closed doors without knocking.'

Marian's mind selected the most ominous word. *Any* closed doors. 'Now look,' she said, 'I draw the line at my own bedroom.'

'Well, it *is* neater,' Ainsley said reasonably, 'and if I'm being overwhelmed in a moment of passion and swept off my feet I can't very well interrupt and say "You've got the wrong bedroom," can I?'

'No, I guess not,' said Marian. She was beginning to feel homeless and dispossessed. 'I just don't like the thought of stumbling into my bed and finding that there are people in it already.'

'Tell you what,' said Ainsley, 'if we do happen to end up in your room I'll hang a tie on the doorknob, okay?'

'Whose tie?' Marian asked. She knew Ainsley collected things – among the objects covering the floor of her room were several photographs, some letters, and a half-dozen dried out flowers – but didn't know she had collected any ties.

'Why his, of course,' said Ainsley.

Marian had a disturbing vision of a trophy room with stuffed and antlered heads nailed to the walls. 'Why not just use his scalp?' she asked. Leonard, after all, was supposed to be her friend.

She pondered the situation while she ate her TV dinner and drank her tea in solitude, Ainsley having departed, and while she dawdled around the apartment waiting for it to be the right time for the late show. All the way to the nearest movie theatre district she was still pondering it. She had felt for some time, in one of the smaller and more obscure crevices of her mind, that she ought to do something to warn Len, but she didn't know what, or, more importantly, why. She knew he would not readily believe that Ainsley, who seemed as young and inexperienced as a button mushroom, was in reality a scheming superfemale carrying out a foul plot against him, using him in effect as in inexpensive substitute for artificial insemination with a devastating lack of concern for his individuality. And there was no convincing evidence as yet; Ainsley had been most discreet. Marian had thought several times of calling him up in the middle of the night with a nylon stocking over the telephone mouthpiece and whispering 'Beware!'; but that would do no good. He would never guess what he was supposed to beware of. Anonymous letters . . . he'd think it was some crank; or a jealous former girlfriend trying to foil his own fiendish plans, which would only make his pursuit more eager. Besides, ever since she had become engaged there had been a tacit agreement with Ainsley: neither was to interfere with the other's strategy, though it was apparent that each disapproved of the other's course of action on moral grounds. If she said anything to Len she knew that Ainsley would be perfectly capable of carrying out a successful, or at any rate an unsettling, counter-attack. No, Len must be abandoned to his fate, which he would no doubt embrace with glee. Marian was further confused by the fact that she didn't exactly know whether an early Christian was being thrown to the lions, or an early lion to the Christians. Was she, as Ainsley had asked her during one of their Sunday discussions, on the side of the Creative Life Force, or wasn't she?

There was also the lady down below to be considered. Even if she wasn't peering out a window or standing in ambush behind one of the velvet curtains when Leonard arrived, she would almost certainly be aware that a pair of masculine feet had ascended the stairs; and in her mind, that despotic empire where the properties had the rigidity and force of the law of gravity, what went up must come down, preferably before eleven-thirty at night. Though she had never said so: it was merely something one took into account. Marian hoped Ainsley would have the sense either to get him over with and get him out before twelve at the latest, or, if the worst came to the worst, to keep him there, and keep him quiet, all night; what they would do with him the next morning, in that case, she was not sure. He would probably have to be smuggled out in the laundry bag. Even if he was in any condition to walk by himself. Oh, well; they could always find another apartment. But she hated scenes.

Marian got off the subway at the station near the laundromat. There were two movie-theatres close by, across the street from each other. She inspected them. One was offering a foreign film with subtitles, advertised outside by black-and-white fuzzy reproductions of ecstatic newspaper reviews and much use of the words 'adult' and 'mature'. It had won several awards. The other had a low-budget American Western and technicolour posters of horsemen and dying Indians. In her present state she did not feel like writhing through intensities and pauses and long artistic closeups of expressively-twitched skin-pores. She was looking only for warmth, shelter, and something resembling oblivion, so she chose the Western. When she groped her way to a seat in the half-empty theatre the movie had already begun.

She slouched her body down, resting her head on the back of the seat and her knees against the seat in front and half-closing her eyes. Not a lady-like position, but nobody could see in the dark; and the seats on either side of her were empty. She had made sure of that: she didn't want any trouble with furtive old men. She recalled such encounters from early school days, before she had learned about movie theatres. Hands squeezing against knees and similar bits of shuffling pathos, although not frightening (one should just move quietly away), were painfully embarrassing to her simply because they were sincere. The attempt at contact, even slight contact, was crucial for the fumblers in the dark.

The coloured pictures succeeded each other in front of her: gigantic stetsoned men stretched across the screen on their even more gigantic horses, trees and cactus-plants rose in the foreground or faded in the background as the landscape flowed along; smoke and dust and galloping. She didn't attempt to decide what the cryptic speeches meant or to follow the plot. She knew there must be bad people who were trying to do something evil and good people who were trying to stop them, probably by getting to the money first (as well as Indians who were numerous as buffalo and fair game for everyone), but it didn't matter to her which of these moral qualities was incarnate in any given figure presented to her. At least it wasn't one of the new Westerns in which people had psychoses. She amused herself by concentrating on the secondary actors, the bit players, wondering what they did in their no doubt copious spare time and whether any of them still had illusions of future stardom.

It was night, the purplish-blue translucent night that descends only on the technicolour screen. Someone was sneaking through a meadow towards someone else; all was quiet except for the rustling of the grass and the chirping of several mechanical crickets. Close beside her, to the left, she heard a small cracking noise, then the sound of something hard hitting the floor. A gun went off, there was a struggle, and it was day. She heard the cracking noise again.

She turned her head to the left. In the faint reflection from the glare of sunlight on the screen she could barely make out who was sitting beside her, two places away. It was the man from the laundromat. He was slumped in the seat, staring glassily in front of him. Every half-minute or so he would lift his hand to his mouth from a bag he was holding in his other hand, and there would be the small crack and then the sound from the floor. He must be eating something with shells, but they weren't peanuts. That would make a softer noise. She studied his dim profile, the nose and one eye and the shadowed hunch of one shoulder.

She turned her head to the front again and tried to concentrate all her attention on the screen. Although she found herself being glad that he had suddenly materialized in that seat, it was an irrational gladness: she didn't intend to speak to him, in fact she was hoping very much that he had not seen her, would not see her sitting alone there in the movie-theatre. He seemed entranced by the screen, almost totally absorbed in it, and in whatever he was eating – what could possibly make that exasperating thin cracking sound? – and he might not notice her if she kept quite still. But she had the disquieting sense that he knew perfectly well who she was and had been aware of her presence for some time before she had recognized his. She gazed at the vast featureless expanse of prairie before her. At her side the cracking went on, irritatingly regular.

They were fording a river, men and horses together and one blonde woman in a dishevelled dress, when she noticed a peculiar sensation in her left hand. It wanted to reach across and touch him on the shoulder. Its will seemed independent of her own: surely she herself wanted nothing of the kind. She made its fingers grip the arm of her seat. 'That would never do,' she admonished it silently, 'he might scream.' But she was also afraid, now that she wasn't looking at him any more, that if she did reach across, her hand would encounter only darkness and emptiness or the plush surface of movie-theatre upholstery.

The sound-track exploded, spattering the air with yelps and whoops, as a band of Indians swept from their hiding-place for the attack. After they had been demolished and listening was possible again she could no longer hear the small clock-like sound he had been making. She jerked her head round to the side: nobody. Well, he had gone then, or perhaps he had never been there in the first place; or maybe it had been somebody else.

On the screen a gargantuan cowboy was pressing his lips chastely to those of the blonde woman. 'Hank, does this mean . . .?' she was whispering. Shortly there would be a sunset.

Then, so close to her ear that she could feel the breath stirring her hair, a voice spoke. 'Pumpkin seeds,' it said.

Her mind accepted the information calmly. 'Pumpkin seeds,' it replied in silence, 'of course, why not?' But her body was startled, and froze momentarily. When she had overcome its purely muscular surprise enough to turn around, there wasn't anybody behind her.

She sat through the closing scene of the movie, beginning to be convinced that she was the victim of a complicated hallucination. 'So I'm finally going mad,' she thought, 'like everybody else. What a nuisance. Though I suppose it will be a change.' But when the lights went on after a brief shot of a waving flag and some tinny music, she took the trouble to examine the floor beneath the seat where he had (possibly) been sitting. She found a little pile of white shells. They were like some primitive signal, a heap of rocks or a sign made with sticks or notches cut in trees, marking a path or indicating something ahead, but though she stared down at them for several minutes while the handful of moviegoers straggled past her up the aisle, she could not interpret them. At any rate, she thought as she left the theatre, this time he left a visible trail.

She took as much time as she could getting home; she did not wish to walk in on the middle of anything. The house, as far as she could tell from the outside, was in darkness, but when she stepped through the door and switched on the hall light, an intercepting form glided out from the dining-room. It was the lady down below, still managing to look dignified even in pincurls and a purple viyella-flannel dressing-gown.

'Miss McAlpin,' she said, her eyebrows severe, 'I have been so upset. I'm sure I heard a – some man went upstairs earlier this evening with Miss Tewce, and I'm positive I haven't heard him come down yet. Of course, I don't mean to imply that – I know that you are *both* very nice girls, but still, the child. . . .'

Marian looked at her watch. 'Well, I don't know,' she said doubtfully, 'I don't *think* anything like that would happen. Perhaps you were mistaken. After all it's past one, and when she isn't out somewhere Ainsley usually goes to bed before that.'

'Well, that's what I thought, I mean I haven't heard any conversation from up there . . . not that I mean to say. . . .'

The mangy old eavesdropper, she's perfectly avid, Marian thought. 'Then she *must* have gone to bed,' she said cheerfully. 'And whoever it was probably came downstairs very quietly so as not to disturb you. But I'll speak to her about it in the morning for you.' She smiled with what she intended to be a reassuring efficiency, and escaped up the stairs.

Ainsley is a whited sepulchre, she thought as she climbed, and I've just applied another coat of whitewash. But remember the mote in thy neighbour's eye and the beam in thine own, etcetera. How on earth are we going to convey him, whatever is left of him, down past that old vulture in the morning?

On the kitchen table she found the scotch bottle, three-quarters empty. A tie with green and blue stripes was dangling victoriously on the closed door of her own room.

That meant she'd have to clear some place that could be slept in, more or less, from the tangled crow's-nest of sheets, clothing, blankets and paperback books that was Ainsley's bed.

'Oh rats!' she said to herself as she flung off her coat.

Chapter Fifteen

At four-thirty the next day Marian was walking along a hospital corridor searching for the right room. She had skipped her lunch-hour, substituting a cheese-and-lettuce sandwich – a slice of plastic cheese between two pieces of solidified bubble-bath with several flaps of pallid greenery, brought in a cardboard carton by the restaurant take-out-order boy – for real food, so that she could leave the office an hour early, and had already spent half-an-hour buying roses and getting to the hospital. Now she had only thirty minutes of visiting time in which to talk with Clara; she wondered whether they would be able to produce, between them, thirty minutes' worth of conversation.

The doors of the rooms were standing open, and she had to pause in front of them and step almost into the rooms to read the numbers. From within each came the high-pitched bibblebobble of women talking together. At last she reached the right number, close to the end of the corridor.

Clara was lying diaphanously on a high white hospital bed, its raised back propping her in a half-sitting position. She was wearing a flannelette hospital gown. Her body under the sheet looked to Marian unnaturally thin; her pale hair was falling loosely over her shoulders.

'Well hi,' she said. 'Come down to see the old mum at last, eh?'

Marian thrust her flowers forward in place of the guilty apologetic remark she should have made. Clara's fragile fingers unwrapped the cornucopia of green paper from around them. 'They're lovely,' she said. 'I'll have to get that damn nurse to put them in some decent water. She's just as likely to stick them in the bedpan if you don't watch her.'

When selecting them, Marian had been uncertain whether to get deep red ones, or salmon pink, or white; she was a little sorry now that she had chosen white. In some ways they went almost too well with Clara; in other ways not at all.

'Draw the curtains a bit,' Clara said in a low voice. There were three other women in the room and private conversation was obviously difficult.

When Marian had pulled the heavy canvas curtains that were attached by rings to a curved metal rod suspended like a large oval halo above the bed and had sat down on the visitor's chair she asked, 'Well, how do you feel?'

'Oh marvellous; really marvellous. I watched the whole thing, it's messy, all that blood and junk, but I've got to admit it's sort of fascinating. Especially when the little bugger sticks its head out, and you finally know after carrying the damn thing around all that time what it *looks* like; I get so excited waiting to see, it's like when you were little and you waited and waited and finally got to open your Christmas presents. Sometimes when I was pregnant I wished like hell we could just hatch them out of eggs, like the birds and so on; but there's really something to be said for this method.' She picked up one of the white roses, and sniffed at it. 'You really ought to try it sometime.'

Marian wondered how she could be so casual about it, as if she was recommending a handy trick for making fluffier pie-crust or a new detergent. Of course it was something she had always planned to do, eventually; and Peter had begun to make remarks with paternal undertones. But in this room with these white-sheeted outstretched women the possibility was suddenly much too close. And then there was Ainsley. 'Don't rush me,' she said, smiling.

'Of course it hurts like hell,' Clara said smugly, 'and they won't give you anything till quite far along, because of the baby; but that's the funny thing about pain. You can never remember it afterwards. I feel just marvellous now – I keep thinking I'll get post-puerperal depression, like a lot of women do, but I never seem to; I save that till I have to get up and go home. It's so nice just to lie here; I really feel marvellous.' She hitched herself up a little against the pillows.

Marian sat and smiled at her. She couldn't think of anything to say in reply. More and more, Clara's life seemed cut off from her, set apart, something she could only gaze at through a window. 'What are you going to call her?' she asked, repressing a desire to shout, not quite sure whether Clara would be able to hear her through the glass.

'We don't really know yet. We're sort of considering Vivian Lynn, after my grandmother and Joe's grandmother. Joe wanted to call her after me but I've never liked my own name much. It's really marvellous though to have a man who's just as pleased with a daughter as a son, so many men aren't, you know, though maybe Joe wouldn't be if he didn't have one son already.'

Marian stared at the wall above Clara's head, thinking that it was painted the same colour as the office. She almost expected to hear the sound of typewriters from beyond the curtains, but instead there were only the murmuring voices of the three other women and their visitors. When she came in she had noticed that one of them, the young one in the pink-lace bedjacket, had been sitting up working at a paint-by-numbers picture. Maybe she should have brought Clara something to do, instead of just flowers: it must be very tiresome lying around like that all day.

'Would you like me to bring you anything to read?' she asked, thinking as she did so how much she was sounding like the kind of ladies'-club member who makes a part-time career out of visiting the sick.

'Now that's a kind thought. But really I don't think I could concentrate enough, not for a while. I'll either be sleeping, or,' she said in a lower voice, 'listening to those other women. Maybe it's the hospital atmosphere, but all they ever talk about are their miscarriages and their diseases. It makes you feel very sickly after a while: you start wondering when it'll be *your* turn to get cancer of the breast or a ruptured tube, or miscarry quadruplets at half-weekly intervals; no kidding, that's what happened to Mrs Moase, the big one over there in the far corner. And christ they're so *calm* about it, and they seem to think that each of their grisly little episodes is some kind of service medal: they haul them out and compare them and pile on the gory details, they're really *proud* of them. It's a positive gloating about pain. I even find myself producing a few of my own ailments, as though I have to compete. I wonder why women are so morbid?'

'Oh, some men are morbid too, I guess,' Marian said. Clara was talking a lot more, and a lot more quickly, than she usually did, and Marian found herself being surprised. During the later, more vegetable stage of Clara's pregnancy she had tended to forget that Clara had a mind at all or any perceptive faculties above the merely sentient and sponge-like, since she had spent most of her time being absorbed in, or absorbed by, her tuberous abdomen. To have her observing, commenting like this, was a slight shock. It might be some kind of reaction, but it certainly wasn't hysteria: she seemed throroughly in control. Something to do with hormones maybe.

'Well, Joe certainly isn't,' Clara said happily. 'If he weren't so un-morbid I don't know how I'd ever manage. He's so good about the children and the washing and everything. I don't feel at all uneasy about leaving everything up to him at a time like this. I know he manages just as well as I would if I were there, though we're having a bit of trouble with poor Arthur. He's beautifully toilet-trained now, he uses his plastic potty almost every time, but he's become a hoarder. He rolls the shit into little pellets and hides them places – like cupboards and bottom drawers. You have to watch him like a hawk. Once I found some in the refrigerator, and Joe tells me he just discovered a whole row of them hardening on the bathroom window-sill behind the curtain. He gets very upset when we throw them out. I can't imagine why he does it; maybe he'll grow up to be a banker.'

'Do you think it has anything to do with the new baby?' Marian said. 'Jealousy perhaps?'

'Oh, probably,' Clara said, smiling serenely. She was twirling one of the white roses between her fingers. 'But here I am running on about myself,' she said, turning herself on the bed so she was facing more directly towards Marian. 'I haven't really had a chance to talk to you about your engagement. We both think it's wonderful, of course, although we don't really *know* Peter.'

Marian said, 'We must all get together sometime, after you're home and have got yourself organized again. I'm sure you'll like him.'

'Well he *looks* awfully nice. Of course you never really know someone till you've been married to them for a while and discover some of their scruffier habits. I remember how upset I was when I realized for the first time that after all Joe wasn't Jesus Christ. I don't know what it was, probably some silly thing like finding out he's crazy about Audrey Hepburn. Or that he's a secret philatelist.'

'A what?' asked Marian. She didn't know what it was but it sounded perverted.

'Stamp collecting. Not a real one of course, he tears them off the mail. Anyway it takes adjustment. Now,' she said, 'I just think he's one of the minor saints.'

Marian didn't know what to say. She found Clara's attitude towards Joe both complacent and embarrassing: it was sentimental, like the love stories in the back numbers of women's magazines. Also she felt Clara was trying to give her some kind of oblique advice, and this was even more embarrassing. Poor Clara, she was the last person whose advice would be worth anything. Look at the mess she had blundered into: three children at her age. Peter and she were going into it with far fewer illusions. If Clara had slept with Joe before marriage she would have been much better able to cope afterwards.

'I think Joe's a wonderful husband,' she said generously.

Clara gave a snort of laughter, then winced. 'Oh. Screw. It hurts in the most ungodly places. No you don't; you think we're both shiftless and disorganized and you'd go bats if you lived in all that chaos; you can't understand how we've survived without hating each other.' Her voice was perfectly good-natured.

Marian started to protest, thinking it was unfair of Clara to force the conversation out into the open like that; but a nurse popped her head through the doorway long enough to announce that visiting time was up.

'If you want to see the baby,' Clara said as Marian was leaving, 'you can probably get someone to tell you where they've stowed it. You can see them through a plate-glass window somewhere; they all look alike, but they'll point out mine if you ask. If I were you I wouldn't bother though, they aren't very interesting at this stage. They look like shrivelled prunes.'

'Maybe I'll wait then,' said Marian.

It struck her as she went out the door that there had been something in Clara's manner, especially in the slightly worried twist of her eyebrows once or twice, that had expressed concern; but concern about what, exactly, she didn't know and couldn't stop to puzzle over. She had the sense of having escaped, as if from a culvert or cave. She was glad she wasn't Clara.

Now there was the rest of the day to unravel. She would eat quickly at the nearest restaurant she could find and by the time she was finished the traffic would have cleared somewhat, and she could rush home and grab some laundry. What on earth did she have that was fit to take? Perhaps a couple of blouses. She wondered whether a pleated skirt would do, that would keep him busy and she had one that needed pressing, but on second thought it was the wrong sort of thing, and surely too complicated anyway.

The hours before her were going to be, she felt, as convoluted as that hour in the afternoon during which Peter had called to arrange dinner and they had discussed at length – too great a length, she was afraid – where they were going to eat; and then after all that she had had to call him back and say, 'I'm terribly sorry darling, but something really unavoidable has come up; can we put it off? Tomorrow maybe?' He had been peevish, but he couldn't say much about it because he had just finished doing the same thing to her the day before.

There had been a difference, of course, in what had come up. In her case it had been another telephone call.

The voice at the other end had said 'This is Duncan.'

'Who?'

'The guy at the laundromat.'

'Oh. Yes.' Now she recognized the voice, though it sounded more nervous than usual.

'I'm sorry I startled you in the movie, but I knew you were dying to know what I was eating.'

'Yes, I was actually,' she said, glancing at the clock and then at the open door of Mrs Bogue's cubicle. She had already spent far too much time on the phone that afternoon.

'They were pumpkin seeds. I'm trying to stop smoking, you know, and I find them very helpful. There's a lot of oral satisfaction in cracking them open. I get them at the pet store, they're supposed to be for birds, really.'

'Yes,' she said, to fill up the pause that followed.

'It was a crummy movie.'

Marian wondered whether the switchboard girl downstairs was listening in on the conversation, as she had been known to do, and if so, what was she thinking about it; she must have realized by now that it was not a business call. 'Mr . . . Duncan,' she said in her most official voice, 'I'm sort of at the office, and we aren't supposed to take much time for outside calls; I mean from friends and so on.'

'Oh,' he said. He sounded discouraged, but he made no attempt to clarify the situation.

She pictured him at the other end of the line, morose, hollow-eyed, waiting for the sound of her voice. She had no idea why he had called. Perhaps he needed her, needed to talk to her. 'But I *would* like to talk to you,' she said encouragingly. 'Some more convenient time?'

'Well,' he said, 'as a matter of fact I sort of need you; right now. I mean I need – what I need is some ironing. I've just got to iron something and I've already ironed everything in the house, even the dishtowels, and I sort of wondered whether maybe I could come over to your house and maybe iron some of your things.'

Mrs Bogue's eye was now definitely upon her. 'Why, of course,' she said crisply. Then she suddenly decided that it would be, for some as yet unexamined reason, disastrous if this man were to encounter either Peter or Ainsley. Besides, who could tell what variety of turmoil had broken loose after she had tiptoed out of the house that morning, leaving Len still caught in the toils of vice behind the door ornamented with his own tie? She hadn't heard from Ainsley all day, which might be either a good or an evil omen. And even if Len had managed to escape safely, the wrath of the lady down below, foiled of its proper object, might very well descend on the head of the harmless ironer as a representative of the whole male species. 'Maybe I'd better bring some things to your house,' she said.

'Actually I'd prefer that. It means I can use my own iron; I'm used to it. It makes me uncomfortable to iron with other people's irons. But please hurry, I really do need it. Desperately.'

'Yes, as soon as I can after work,' she said, trying both to reassure him and to sound, for the benefit of the office, as though she was making a dentist appointment. 'About seven.' She realised as soon as she had hung up that this would mean postponing dinner with Peter yet again; but then she could see him any night. The other thing was an emergency.

By the time she had got matters straightened out with Peter she had felt as though she had been trying to unsnarl herself from all the telephone lines in the city. They were prehensile, they were like snakes, they had a way of coiling back on you and getting you all wrapped up.

A nurse was coming towards her, pushing a rubber-wheeled

wagon loaded with trays of food. Although her mind was occupied with other things, Marian's eyes registered the white shape and found it out of place. She stopped and looked around. Wherever else she was going it was not towards the main exit. She had been so involved in the threads of her own plans and reflections that she must have got off the elevator on the wrong floor. She was in a corridor exactly similar to the one she had just come from, except that all the room-doors were closed. She looked for a number: 273. Well, that was simple: she had got off a floor too soon.

She turned and walked back, trying to remember where the elevator was supposed to be; she seemed to recall having gone around several corners. The nurse had disappeared. Coming towards her now from the far end of the hallway was a figure, a man wearing a green smock, with a white mask over the lower part of his face. She was aware for the first time of the hospital smell, antiseptic, severe.

It must be one of the doctors. She could see now that he had a thin black thing, a stethoscope, around his neck. As he came nearer she looked at him more closely. In spite of the mask there was something familiar about him; it bothered her that she could not tell what it was. But he passed her, staring straight ahead, his eyes expressionless, and opened one of the doors to the right and went in. When he turned she could see that he had a bald spot on the back of his head.

'Well, nobody I know is going bald, at any rate,' she said to herself. She was relieved.

Chapter Sixteen

She remembered the way to his apartment perfectly, although she couldn't recall either the number or the street name. She hadn't been in that district for a long time, in fact ever since the day of the beer interviews. She took the right directions and turnings almost automatically, as though she was trailing somebody by an instinct that was connected not with sight or smell but with a vaguer sense that had to do with locations. But it wasn't a complicated route: just across the baseball park, up the asphalt ramp and along a couple of blocks; though the way seemed longer now that she was walking in a darkness illuminated only by the dim street lamps rather than the former searing light of the sun. She walked quickly: already her legs were cold. The grass on the baseball park had been grey with frost.

The few times she had thought about the apartment, in idle moments at the office when she had had nothing but a blank sheet of paper in front of her or at other times when she was bending to pick some piece of clutter off the floor, she had never given it any specific place in the city. She had an image in her mind of the inside, the appearance of the rooms, but not of the building itself. Now it was disconcerting to have the street produce it, square and ordinary and anonymous, more or less exactly where it had been before.

She pushed the buzzer of Number Six and slipped through the inside glass door as soon as the mechanism started its chain-saw noise. Duncan opened the door part-way. He stared at her suspiciously; in the semi-darkness his eyes gleamed behind his hair. He had a cigarette stub in his mouth, burning dangerously close to his lips.

'Got the stuff?' he asked.

Mutely she held towards him the small cloth bundle she had been carrying under her arm, and he stepped aside to let her come in.

'It's not very much,' he said, undoing the clothes. There were only two white cotton blouses, recently washed, a pillowcase, and a few guest towels embroidered with flowers, donated by a great-aunt, that were wrinkled from lying underneath everything else on the linen shelf.

'I'm sorry,' she said, 'it was really all I had.'

'Well, it's better than nothing,' he said grudgingly. He turned and walked towards his bedroom.

Marian wasn't certain whether she was supposed to follow him or whether he expected her to go away now that she had made the delivery. 'Can I watch?' she asked, hoping he wouldn't consider it an invasion of privacy. She didn't feel like going back to her own apartment right away. There would be nothing to do and she had, after all, sacrificed an evening with Peter.

'Sure, if you want to; though there isn't much to see.'

She made her way towards the hall. The living room had not been altered since her former visit, except that there were if possible more stray papers lying about. The three chairs were still in the same positions; a slab of board was leaning against an arm of the red plush one. Only one of the lamps, the one by the blue chair, was turned on. Marian inferred that both of the room-mates were out.

Duncan's room too was much the same as she remembered it. The ironing-board was nearer the centre of the room and the chessmen had been set up in their two opposing rows; the black-and-white chequered board was resting now on top of a stack of books. On the bed were several freshly-ironed white shirts on coathangers. Duncan hung them up in the closet before going over to plug in the iron. Marian took off her coat and sat down on the bed.

He threw his cigarette into one of the crowded ashtrays on the floor, waited for the iron to heat, testing it at intervals on the board, and then began to iron one of the blouses, with slow concentration and systematic attention to collar corners. Marian watched him silently; he obviously didn't want to be interrupted. She found it strange to see someone else ironing her clothes.

Ainsley had given her a peculiar look when she had come out of her bedroom with her coat on and the bundle under her arm. 'Where are you going with those?' she had asked. It was too small a lot for the laundromat.

'Oh, just out.'

'What'll I say if Peter calls?'

'He won't call. But just say I'm out.' She had plunged down the stairs then, not wishing to explain anything at all about Duncan or even to reveal his existance. She felt it might upset the balance of power. But Ainsley had no time at the moment for anything more than a tepid curiosity: she was too elated by the probable success of her own campaign, and also by what she had called 'a stroke of luck'.

Marian had asked, when she had reached the apartment and had found Ainsley in the living room with a paperback on Baby and Child Care, 'Well, how did you get the poor thing out of here this morning?'

Ainsley laughed. 'Great stroke of luck,' she said. 'I was sure the old fossil down there would be lying in wait for us at the bottom of the stairs. I really didn't know what I'd do. I was trying to think of some bluff, like saying he was the telephone man. . . .'

'She tried to pin me down about it last night,' Marian interjected. 'She knew perfectly well he was up there.'

'Well for some reason she actually went *out*. I saw her go from the living room window; just by chance really. Can you imagine? I didn't think she ever went out, not in the mornings. I skipped work today of course and I was just wandering around having a cigarette. But when I saw her go I got Len up and stuck his clothes on him and hustled him down the stairs and out of there before he was quite awake. He had a terrible hangover too, he just about killed that bottle. All by himself. I don't think he's too sure yet exactly what happened.' She smiled with her small pink mouth.

'Ainsley, you're immoral.'

'Why? He seemed to enjoy it. Though he was terribly apologetic and anxious this morning when we were out having breakfast, and then sort of soothing, as though he was trying to console me or something. Really it was embarrassing. And then, you know, as he got wider and wider awake and soberer and soberer, he couldn't wait to get away from me. But now,' she said, hugging herself with both arms, 'we'll have to wait and see. Whether it was all worth it.'

'Yes, well,' Marian said, 'would you mind fixing the bed?'

Thinking back on it, she found something ominous about the fact that the lady down below had gone out. It wasn't like her at all. She'd be much more likely to lurk behind the piano or the velvet curtains while they were creeping down the stairs and spring out upon them just as they had reached the threshold of safety.

He was starting on the second blouse. He seemed to be unaware of everything but the wrinkled white material spread on the board in front of him, poring over it as though it was an ancient and very fragile manuscript that he couldn't quite translate. Before, she had thought of him as being short, perhaps because of the shrunken child's-face, or because she had mostly seen him sitting down; but now she thought, actually he would be quite tall if he didn't slouch like that.

As she sat watching him she recognized in herself a desire to say something to him, to intrude, to break through the white cloth surface of his absorption: she did not like being so totally closed out. To avoid the emotion she picked up her purse and went into the bathroom, intending to comb her hair, not because it needed combing but as what Ainsley called a substitution-activity; like a squirrel scratching itself when confronted by hazardous or unobtainable breadcrumbs. She wanted to talk to him, but talking to him now, she thought, might cancel out any therapeutic effects the ironing was having.

The bathroom was ordinary enough. Damp towels were mounded on the racks and a clutter of shaving things and men's cosmetics covered the various porcelain ledges and surfaces. But the mirror over the basin had been broken. There were only a few jagged pieces of glass left sticking around the edges of the wooden frame. She tried peering into one of them but it wasn't large enough to be of much use.

When she went back into the room he was doing the pillowcase. He seemed more relaxed: he was ironing with a long easy sweeping motion instead of the exact staccato strokes he had been using on the blouse. He looked up at her as she came in.

'I suppose you're wondering what happened to the mirror,' he said.

'Well . . .'

'I smashed it. Last week. With the frying-pan.'

'Oh,' she said.

'I got tired of being afraid I'd walk in there some morning and wouldn't be able to see my own reflection in it. So I went and grabbed the frying-pan out of the kitchen and gave it a whack. They both got very upset,' he said meditatively, 'particularly Trevor, he was cooking an omelette at the time and I guess I sort of ruined it. Got it all full of broken glass. But I don't really see why it should disturb them, it was a perfectly understandable symbolic narcissistic gesture, and it wasn't a good mirror anyway. But they've been jittery ever since. Especially Trevor, subconsciously he thinks he's my mother; it's rather hard on him. It doesn't bother me that much, I'm used to it, I've been running away from understudy mothers ever since I can remember, there's a whole herd of them behind me trying to catch up and rescue me, god knows what from, and give me warmth and comfort and nourishment and make me quit smoking, that's what you get for being an orphan. And they're quoting things at me: Trevor quotes T. S. Eliot these days and Fish quotes the Oxford English Dictionary.'

'How do you shave then?' Marian asked. She could not quite imagine life without a mirror in the bathroom. She speculated, while she spoke, about whether he even shaved at all. She had never examined him for bristles.

'What?'

'I mean with no mirror.'

'Oh,' he said, grinning, 'I've got my own private mirror. One I can trust, I know what's in it. It's just the public ones that I don't like.' He seemed to lose interest in the subject, and ironed in silence for a minute. 'What grisly things,' he said at last; he was doing one of the guest towels. 'I can't stand things with flowers embroidered on them.'

'I know. We never use them.'

He folded the towel, then looked up at her gloomily. 'I suppose you believed all that.'

'Well . . . all what?' she answered cautiously.

'About why I broke the mirror and my reflection and so on. Really I broke it because I felt like breaking something. That's the trouble with people, they always believe me. It's too much of an encouragement, I can never resist the temptation. And those brilliant insights about Trevor, how do *I* know whether they're true? Maybe the real truth is that I want to think that he wants to think he's my mother. Actually I'm not an orphan anyway, I do have some parents, back there somewhere. Can you believe that?'

'Should I?' She couldn't tell whether or not he was being serious; his expression revealed nothing. Perhaps this was another labyrinth of words, and if she said the wrong thing, took the wrong turning, she would suddenly find herself face to face with something she could not cope with.

'If you like. But the real truth is, of course' – he waved the iron in the air for emphasis, watching the movement of his hand as he did so – 'that I'm a changeling. I got switched for a real baby when young and my parents never discovered the fraud, though I must admit they suspected something.' He closed his eyes, smiling faintly. 'They kept telling me my ears were too big; but really I'm not human at all, I come from the underground. . . .' He opened his eyes and began to iron again, but his attention had wandered away from the ironing-board. He brought the iron too close to his other hand, and gave a yelp of pain. 'Damn,' he said. He set the iron down and stuck his fingers in his mouth.

Marian's first impulse was to go over and see whether it was a bad burn, and suggest remedies, butter or baking-soda; but she decided against it. Instead she sat unmoving and said nothing.

He was looking at her now, expectantly but with a trace of hostility. 'Aren't you going to comfort me?' he asked.

'I don't think,' she said, 'that it's really needed.'

'You're right; I enjoy it though,' he said sadly. 'And it does hurt.' He picked up the iron again.

When he had folded the last towel and pulled the plug out of the wall-socket he said, 'That was a vigorous session, thanks for the clothes, but it wasn't really enough. I'll have to think of something else to do with the rest of the tension. I'm not a chronic ironer you know, I'm not hooked, it's not one of the habits I ought to kick, but I go on these binges.' He came over and sat gingerly down beside her on the bed, and lit a cigarette. 'This one started the day before yesterday when I dropped my term-paper in a puddle on the kitchen floor and I had to dry it out and iron it. It was all typed and I couldn't face typing it over again, plowing through all that verbiage, I'd start wanting to change everything. It came out okay, nothing blurred, but you could tell it had been ironed, I scorched one of the pages. But they can't reasonably object, it would sound pretty silly to say, "We can't accept a term-paper that's been ironed." So I turned it in and then of course I had to get rid of all that frenzy, so I ironed everything in the house that was clean. Then I had to go to the laundromat and wash some dirty things, that's why I was sitting in that wretched movie, I was waiting for the clothes to get done. I got bored watching them churning around in there, that's a bad sign, if I get bored with the laundromat even, what the hell am I going to do when I get bored with everything else? Then I ironed all the things I'd washed, and then I'd run out.'

'And then you phoned me,' Marian said. It irritated her slightly that he went on talking to himself, about himself, without giving much evidence that he even knew she was there.

'Oh. You. Yes. Then I phoned you. At least, I phoned your company. I remembered the name, I guess it was the switchboard girl I got, and I sort of described you to whoever it was for a while, I said you didn't look like the usual kind of interviewer; and then they figured out who you were. You never told me your name.'

It had not occurred to Marian that she hadn't told him her name. She had taken it for granted that he knew it all along.

Her introduction of a new subject seemed to have brought him to a standstill. He stared down at the floor, sucking on the end of his cigarette.

She found the silence disconcerting. 'Why do you like ironing so much?' she asked. 'I mean, apart from relieving tension and all that; but why ironing? Instead of maybe bowling, for instance?'

He drew his thin legs up and clasped his arms around his knees. 'Ironing's nice and simple,' he said. 'I get all tangled up in words when I'm putting together those interminable papers, I'm on another one by the way, "Sado-Masochistic Patterns in Trollope," and ironing – well, you straighten things out and get them flat. God knows it isn't because I'm neat and tidy; but there's something about a flat surface. . . .' He had shifted his position and was contemplating her now. 'Why don't you let me touch up that blouse for you a bit while the iron's still hot?' he said. 'I'll just do the sleeves and the collar. It looks like you missed a few places.'

'You mean the one I have on?'

'That's the one,' he said. He unwound his arm from around his knees and stood up. 'Here, you can wear my dressing-gown. Don't worry, I won't peek.' He took a grey object out of the closet, handed it to her, and turned his back.

Marian stood for a moment, clutching the grey bundle, uncertain how to act. Doing as he suggested, she knew, was going to make her feel both uneasy and silly; but to say at this point, 'No thank you, I'd rather not,' when the request was obviously harmless, would have made her feel even sillier. After a minute she found herself undoing the buttons, then slipping on the dressing-gown. It was much too large for her: the sleeves came down over her hands and the bottom edge trailed along the floor.

'Here you are then,' she said.

She watched with slight anxiety as he wielded the iron. This time the activity seemed more crucial, it was like a dangerous hand moving back and forth slowly an inch away, the cloth had been so recently next to her skin. If he burns it or anything though, she thought, I can always put on one of the others.

'There,' he said, 'all done.' He unplugged the iron again and draped the blouse over the small end of the ironing-board; he seemed to have forgotten that she was supposed to be wearing it. Then, unexpectedly, he came over to the bed, crawled onto it beside her, and stretched himself out on his back with his eyes closed and his arms behind his head.

'God,' he said, 'all these distractions. How does one go on? It's like term-papers, you produce all that stuff and nothing is ever done with it, you just get a grade for it and heave it in the trash, you know that some other poor comma-counter is going to come along the year after you and have to do the same thing over again, it's a treadmill, even ironing, you iron the damn things and then you wear them and they get all wrinkled again.'

'Well, and then you can iron them again, can't you?' Marian said soothingly. 'If they stayed neat you wouldn't have anything to do.'

'Maybe I'd do something worthwhile for a change,' he said. His eyes were still closed. 'Production-consumption. You begin to wonder whether it isn't just a question of making one kind of garbage into another kind. The human mind was the last thing to be commercialized but they're doing a good job of it now; what *is* the difference between the library stacks and one of those used-car graveyards? What bothers me though is that none of it is ever final; you can't ever finish anything. I have this great plan for permanent leaves on trees, it's a waste for them having to produce a new lot each year; and come to think of it there's no reason at all why they have to be green, either; I'd have them white. Black trunks and white leaves. I can hardly wait till it snows, this city in the summer has altogether too much vegetation, it's stifling, and then it all falls off and lies around in the gutter. The thing I like about the place I came from, it's a mining town, there isn't much of anything in it but at least it has no vegetation. A lot of people wouldn't like it. It's the smelting plants that do it, tall smokestacks reaching up into the sky and the smoke glows red at night, and the chemical fumes have burnt the trees for miles around, it's barren, nothing but the barren rock, even grass won't grow on most of it, and there are the slag-heaps too; where the water collects on the rock it's a yellowish-brown from the chemicals. Nothing would grow there even if you planted it, I used to go out of the town and sit on the rocks, about this time of year, waiting for the snow. . . .'

Marian was sitting on the edge of the bed, bending slightly down towards his talking face, only half-listening to the monotonous voice. She was studying the contours of his skull under the papery skin, wondering how anyone could be that thin and still remain alive. She did not want to touch him now, she was even slightly repelled by the hollowness of the eye-sockets, the angular hinge of the jawbone moving up and down in front of the ear.

Suddenly he opened his eyes. He stared at her for a minute as though he couldn't remember who she was and how she happened to be in his bedroom. 'Hey,' he said finally in a different voice, 'you look sort of like me in that.' He reached out a hand and tugged at the shoulder of the dressing-gown, pulling her down. She let herself sink.

The transition from the flat hypnotic voice, and then the realization that he had actual flesh, a body like most other people, startled her at first. She felt her own body stiffen in resistance, begin to draw away; but he had both arms around her now. He was stronger than she had thought. She was not sure what was happening: there was an uneasy suspicion in one corner of her mind that what he was really caressing was his own dressing-gown, and that she merely happened to be inside it.

She pulled her face away and gazed down at him. His eyes were closed. She kissed the end of his nose. 'I think I ought to tell you something,' she said softly; 'I'm engaged.' At that moment she could not recall exactly what Peter looked like, but the memory of his name was accusing her.

His dark eyes opened and looked up at her vacantly. 'That's your problem, then,' he said. 'It's like me telling you I got an A on my Pre-Raphaelite Pornography paper – interesting, but it doesn't have much of anything to do with anything. Does it?'

'Well, but it does,' she said. The situation was rapidly becoming a matter of conscience. 'I'm going to get married, you know. I shouldn't be here.'

'But you are here.' He smiled. 'Actually I'm glad you told me. It makes me feel a lot safer. Because really,' he said earnestly, 'I don't want you to think that all this means anything. It never sort of does, for me. It's all happening really to somebody else.' He kissed the end of her nose. 'You're just another substitute for the laundromat.'

Marian wondered whether her feelings ought to be hurt, but decided that they weren't: instead she was faintly relieved. 'I wonder what you're a substitute for, then,' she said.

'That's the nice thing about me. I'm very flexible, I'm the universal substitute.' He reached up over her head and turned off the light.

Not very much later the front door was opened and closed, admitting a number of heavy footsteps. 'Oh, shit,' he said from somewhere inside his dressing-gown. 'They're back.' He pushed her upright, turned the light back on, yanked the dressing-gown closed around her and slithered off the bed, smoothing his hair down over his forehead with both hands, then straightening his sweater. He stood in the middle of the room for an instant, glaring wildly at the bedroom doorway, then dashed across the room, seized the chessboard, dropped it onto the bed, and sat down facing her. He quickly began to set the toppled pieces upright.

'Hi,' he said calmly a moment later, to someone who had presumably appeared in the doorway. Marian was feeling too dishevelled to look around. 'We were just having a game of chess.'

'Oh, good show,' said a dubious voice.

'Why get all upset about it?' Marian said, when whoever it was had gone into the bathroom and shut the door. 'It's nothing to be disturbed about, it's all perfectly natural, you know. If anything it's their fault for barging in like that.' She herself was feeling extraordinarily guilty.

'Well, I told you,' he said, staring down at the orderly pattern of chessmen on the board. 'They think they're my parents. You know parents never understand about things like that. They'd think you were corrupting me. They have to be protected from reality.' He reached across the chessboard and took hold of her hand. His fingers were dry and rather cold.

Chapter Seventeen

Marian gazed down at the small silvery image reflected in the bowl of the spoon: herself upside down, with a huge torso narrowing to a pinhead at the handle end. She tilted the spoon and her forehead swelled, then receded. She felt serene.

She looked fondly across the white tablecloth and the intervening plates and the basket of rolls at Peter, who smiled back at her.

The angles and curves of his face were highlighted by the orange glow from the shaded candle at the side of the table; in the shadow his chin was stronger, his features not so smooth. Really, she thought, anyone seeing him would find him exceptionally handsome. He was wearing one of his suave winter costumes – dark suit, sombrely-opulent tie – not as jaunty as some of his young-man-about-town suits, but more quietly impressive. Ainsley had once called him 'nicely packaged', but now Marian decided that she found this quality attractive. He knew how to blend in and stand out at the same time. Some men could never wear dark suits properly, they got flaky on the shoulders and shiny at the back, but Peter never shed and never shone in the wrong places. The sense of proud ownership she felt at being with him there in that more or less public way caused her to reach across the table and take his hand. He put his own hand on top of hers in answer.

The waiter appeared with the wine, and Peter tasted it and nodded. The waiter poured and stepped back into the darkness.

That was another nice thing about Peter. He could make that kind of decision so effortlessly. She had fallen into the habit in the last month or so of letting him choose for her. It got rid of the vacillation she had found herself displaying when confronted with a menu: she never knew what she wanted to have. But Peter could make up their minds right away. His taste ran towards steak and roast beef: he did not care for peculiar things like sweetbreads, and he didn't like fish at all. Tonight they were having Filet Mignon. Already it was fairly late, they had spent the earlier hours of the evening at Peter's apartment, and they were both, they had told each other, ravenous.

Waiting for their food, they resumed the conversation they had begun earlier, while they were getting dressed again, about the proper education of children. Peter talked theoretically, about children as a category, carefully avoiding any application. But she knew perfectly well that it was their own future children they were really discussing: that was why it was so important. Peter thought that all children ought to be punished for breaches of discipline; even physically. Of course no one should ever strike a child in anger; the main thing was to be consistent. Marian was afraid of warping their emotions.

'Darling, you don't understand these things,' Peter said; 'you've led a sheltered life.' He squeezed her hand. 'But I've seen the results, the courts are full of them, juvenile delinquents, and a lot of them from good homes too. It's a complex problem.' He compressed his lips.

Marian was secretly convinced she was right and resented being told she had led a sheltered life. 'But shouldn't they be given understanding, instead of... ?'

He smiled indulgently. 'Try giving understanding to some of those little punks: the motorcycle boys and the dope addicts and the draft dodgers up from the States. You've never even seen one up close, I bet; some of them have lice. You think you can solve everything by good will, Marian, but it doesn't work; they have no sense of responsibility at all, they run around smashing things up just because they feel like it. That's how they were brought up, nobody kicked hell out of them when they deserved it. They think the world owes them a living.'

'Perhaps,' Marian said primly, 'somebody kicked hell out of them when they didn't deserve it. Children are very sensitive to injustice, you know.'

'Oh, I'm all in favour of justice,' Peter said. 'What about justice for the people whose property they destroy?'

'You'd teach them not to drive around mowing down other people's hedges, I suppose.'

Peter chuckled warmly. Her disapproval of that incident and his laughter at her for it had become one of the reference points in their new pattern. But Marian's serenity had vanished with her own remark. She looked intently at Peter, trying to see his eyes, but he was glancing down at his wineglass, admiring perhaps the liquid richness of the red against the white of the tablecloth. He had leaned back a little in his chair and his face was now in shadow.

She wondered why restaurants like this one were kept so dark. Probably to keep people from seeing each other very clearly while they were eating. After all, chewing and swallowing are pleasanter for those doing them than for those watching, she thought, and observing one's partner too closely might dispel the aura of romance that the restaurant was trying to maintain. Or create. She examined the blade of her knife.

The waiter stepped forward from somewhere, soft and deft as a cat on the carpeted floor, and set her order before her: the filet on a wooden platter, oozing juicily within its perimeter of bacon. They both liked it rare: synchronizing the cooking times would never be a problem at any rate. Marian was so hungry she would have liked to devour the steak at one gulp.

She began slicing and chewing, conveying the food to her grateful stomach. She was reconsidering the conversation, trying to get a clearer image of what she had meant by 'justice'. She thought that it ought to mean being fair, but even her notion of that became hazy around the edges as she looked at it. Did it mean an eye for an eye? And what good did it do anyway to destroy someone else's eye if you had lost your own? What about compensation? It seemed to be a matter of money in things like car accidents; you could even be awarded money for having suffered emotional distress. Once on a streetcar she had seen a mother bite a small child because it had bitten her. She gnawed thoughtfully through a tough piece, and swallowed.

Peter, she decided, wasn't himself today. He had had a difficult case, one that involved a lot of intricate research; he had gone through precedent after precedent only to find that they all favoured the opposition. That was why he was making stern pronouncements: he was frustrated by complications, he wanted simplicity. He should realize though that if the laws weren't complicated he would never make any money.

She reached for her wine glass, and looked up. Peter was watching her. He was three-quarters finished and she wasn't even half.

'Thoughtful?' he said mellowly.

'Not really. Just absent-minded.' She smiled at him and returned her attention to the platter.

Lately he had been watching her more and more.

Before, in the summer, she used to think he didn't often look at her, didn't often really see her; in bed afterwards he would stretch out beside her and press his face against her shoulder, and sometimes he would go to sleep. These days however he would focus his eyes on her face, concentrating on her as though if he looked hard enough he would be able to see through her flesh and her skull and into the workings of her brain. She couldn't tell what he was searching for when he looked at her like that. It made her uneasy. Frequently when they were lying side by side exhausted on the bed she would open her eyes and realize that he had been watching her like that, hoping perhaps to surprise a secret expression on that face. Then he would run his hand gently over her skin, without passion, almost clinically, as if he could learn by touch whatever it was that had escaped the probing of his eyes. Or as if he was trying to memorize her. It was when she would begin feeling that she was on a doctor's examination table that she would take hold of his hand to make him stop.

She picked at her salad, turning the various objects in the wooden bowl over with her fork: she wanted a piece of tomato. Maybe he had got hold of one of those marriage-manuals; maybe that was why. It would be just like Peter, she thought with fondness. If you got something new you went out and bought a book that told you how to work it. She thought of the books and magazines on cameras that were part of the collection on the middle shelf in his room, between law books and the detective novels. And he always kept the car manual in the glove compartment. So it would be according to his brand of logic to go out and buy a book on marriage, now that he was going to get married; one with easy-to-follow diagrams. She was amused.

She spiked and devoured a black olive from her salad. That must be it. He was sizing her up as he would a new camera, trying to find the central complex of wheels and tiny mechanisms, the possible weak points, the kind of future performance to be expected: the springs of the machine. He wanted to know what made her tick. If that was what he was looking for. . . .

She smiled to herself. Now I'm making things up, she thought.

He was almost finished. She watched the capable hands holding the knife and fork, slicing precisely with an exact adjustment of pressures. How skilfully he did it: no tearing, no ragged edges. And yet it was a violent action, cutting; and violence in connection with Peter seemed incongruous to her. Like the Moose Beer commercials, which had begun to appear everywhere, in the subway trains, on hoardings, in magazines. Because she had worked on the pre-marketing survey she felt partially responsible for them; not that they were doing any harm. The fisherman wading in the stream, scooping the trout into his net, was too tidy: he looked as though his hair had just been combed, a few strands glued neatly to his forehead to show he was windblown. And the fish also was unreal; it had no slime, no teeth, no smell; it was a clever toy, metal and enamel. The hunter who had killed a deer stood posed and urbane, no twigs in his hair, his hands bloodless. Of course you didn't want anything in an advertisement to be ugly or upsetting; it wouldn't do, for instance, to have a deer with its tongue sticking out.

She was reminded of the newspaper that morning, the front page story she had skimmed over without paying much attention. The young boy who had gone berserk with a rifle and killed nine people before he was cornered by the police. Shooting out of an upstairs window. She remembered him now, grey and white, gripped by two darker policemen, the eyes remote, guarded. He wasn't the kind who would hit anyone with his fist or even use a knife. When he chose violence it was a removed violence, a manipulation of specialized instruments, the finger guiding but never touching, he himself watching the explosion from a distance; the explosion of flesh and blood. It was a violence of the mind, almost like magic: you thought it and it happened.

Watching him operating on the steak like that, carving a straight slice and then dividing it into neat cubes, made her think of the diagram of the planned cow at the front of one of her cookbooks: the cow with lines on it and labels to show you from which part of the cow all the different cuts were taken. What they were eating now was from some part of the back, she thought: cut on the dotted line. She could see rows of butchers somewhere in a large room, a butcher school, sitting at tables, clothed in spotless white, each with a pair of kindergarten scissors, cutting out steaks and ribs and roasts from the stacks of brown-paper cow-shapes before them. The cow in the book, she recalled, was drawn with eyes and horns and an udder. It stood there quite naturally, not at all disturbed by the peculiar markings painted on its hide. Maybe with lots of careful research they'll eventually be able to breed them, she thought, so that they're born already ruled and measured.

She looked down at her own half-eaten steak and suddenly saw it as a hunk of muscle. Blood red. Part of a real cow that once moved and ate and was killed, knocked on the head as it stood in a queue like someone waiting for a streetcar. Of course everyone knew that. But most of the time you never thought about it. In the supermarket they had it all pre-packaged in cellophane, with name-labels and price-labels stuck on it, and it was just like buying a jar of peanut-butter or a can of beans, and even when you went into a butcher shop they wrapped it up so efficiently and quickly that it was made clean, official. But now it was suddenly there in front of her with no intervening paper, it was flesh and blood, rare, and she had been devouring it. Gorging herself on it.

She set down her knife and fork. She felt that she had turned rather pale, and hoped that Peter wouldn't notice. 'This is ridiculous,' she lectured herself. 'Everyone eats cows, it's natural; you have to eat to stay alive, meat is good for you, it has lots of proteins and minerals.' She picked up her fork, speared a piece, lifted it, and set it down again.

Peter raised his head, smiling. 'Christ I was hungry,' he said, 'I sure was glad to get that steak inside. A good meal always makes you feel a little more human.'

She nodded, and smiled back limply. He shifted his glance to her platter. 'What's the matter, darling? You aren't finished.'

'No,' she said, 'I don't seem to be hungry any more. I guess I'm full.' She meant to indicate by her tone of voice that her stomach was too tiny and helpless to cope with that vast quantity of food. Peter smiled and chewed, pleasantly conscious of his own superior capacity. 'God,' she thought to herself, 'I hope it's not permanent; I'll starve to death!'

She sat twisting her napkin unhappily between her fingers, watching the last of Peter's steak disappear into his mouth.

Chapter Eighteen

Marian was sitting at the kitchen table, disconsolately eating a jar of peanut butter and turning over the pages of her largest cookbook. The day after the filet, she had been unable to eat a pork chop, and since then, for several weeks, she had been making experiments. She had discovered that not only were things too obviously cut from the Planned Cow inedible for her, but that the Planned Pig and the Planned Sheep were similarly forbidden. Whatever it was that had been making these decisions, not her mind certainly, rejected anything that had an indication of bone or tendon or fibre. Things that had been ground up and re-shaped, hot-dogs and hamburgers for instance, or lamb patties or pork sausages, were all right as long as she didn't look at them too closely, and fish was still permitted. She had been afraid to try chicken: she had been fond of it once, but it came with an unpleasantly complete skeletal structure, and the skin, she predicted, would be too much like an arm with goose bumps. For protein variety she had been eating omelettes and peanuts and quantities of cheese. The quiet fear, that came nearer to the surface now as she scanned the pages – she was in the 'Salads' section – was that this thing, this refusal of her mouth to eat, was malignant; that it would spread; that slowly the circle now dividing the non-devourable from the devourable would become smaller and smaller, that the objects available to her would be excluded one by one. 'I'm turning into a vegetarian,' she was thinking sadly, 'one of those cranks; I'll have to start eating lunch at Health Bars.' She read, with distaste, a column headed *Hints For Serving Yoghurt*. 'For a taste sensation, sprinkle it with chopped nuts!' the editress suggested with glee.

The telephone rang. She let it ring a couple of times before getting up to answer it. She didn't feel like talking to anyone and it was an effort to pull herself up out of the gentle realm of lettuce and watercress and piquant herb dressings.

'Marian?' It was Leonard Slank's voice. 'Is that you?'

'Yes, hi Len,' she said. 'How are you?' She hadn't seen him or even spoken to him for quite a long time.

He sounded urgent. 'Are you alone? I mean is Ainsley there?'

'No; she isn't back from work yet. She said she was going to do some shopping.' It was the Christmas season; had been, it seemed, for several months; and the stores were staying open till nine. 'But I can get her to call you when she comes in.'

'No no,' he said hastily. 'It's you I want to talk to. Can I come over?'

Peter was working on a case that night, so technically she wasn't busy; and her brain did not provide her with any excuse. 'Sure, of course Len,' she said. So she's told him, she thought as she put down the phone. The idiot. I wonder what she did that for.

Ainsley had been in the highest of spirits for the past few weeks. She had been certain from the beginning that she was pregnant, and her mind had hovered over the activities of her body with the solicitous attention of a scientist towards a crucial test-tube, waiting for the definitive change. She spent more time than usual in the kitchen, trying to decide whether or not she had strange cravings and sampling a multitude of foods to see if they tasted at all different, reporting her findings to Marian: tea, she said, was more bitter, eggs were sulphury. She stood on Marian's bed to examine the profile of her belly in Marian's dresser-mirror, which was bigger than her own. When she wandered around the apartment she hummed to herself, constantly, intolerably; and finally one morning she had retched in the kitchen sink, to her immense satisfaction. At last it had been time to go and see the gynaecologist, and just yesterday she had bounced up the stairs, her face radiant, waving an envelope: the result was Positive.

Marian congratulated her, but not as dourly as she would have done if it had happened several months earlier. At that time she would have had to cope with the resulting problems, such as where Ainsley would live – the lady down below would certainly not tolerate her once she became rotund – and whether she herself should get another room-mate, and if so, whether she would feel guilty about deserting Ainsley, and if not, whether she could face all the intricacies and tensions that would result from living with an unmarried mother and a newborn baby. But now it wasn't her concern, and she could afford to sound genuinely pleased for Ainsley's sake. After all, she herself was getting married; she had contracted out.

It was because she didn't want to be involved that she resented Len's phone call. From the tone of his voice she guessed Ainsley had told him something, but it hadn't been clear from the conversation exactly what he knew. She was already resolved to be as passive as possible. She would listen, of course – she had ears, she couldn't help it – to whatever he had to say (what was there for him to say, anyway? His function, such as it had been, was over); but beyond that there was nothing she could do. She felt incapable of handling the situation, and irritated too: if Len wanted to talk to anyone he should talk to Ainsley. She was the one with the answers.

Marian ate another spoonful of peanut butter, disliking the way it cleaved to the roof of her mouth, and to pass the time turned to the shellfish chapter and read the part about de-veining shrimps (who, she wondered, still bought real shrimps?) and then the instructions for turtles, which she had recently begun to find of interest: precisely what kind of interest, she was not certain. You were supposed to keep your live turtle in a cardboard box or other cage for about a week, loving it and feeding it hamburger to rid it of its impurities. Then just as it was beginning to trust you and perhaps follow you around the kitchen like a sluggish but devoted hard-shelled spaniel, you put it one day into a cauldron of cold water (where no doubt it would swim and dive happily, at first) and then brought it slowly to the boil. The whole procedure was reminiscent of the deaths of early Christian martyrs. What fiendishness went on in kitchens across the country, in the name of providing food! But the only alternative for that sort of thing seemed to be the cellowrapped and plasticoated and cardboard-cartoned surrogates. Substitutes, or merely disguises? At any rate, whatever killing had gone on had been done efficiently, by somebody else, beforehand.

Down below the doorbell rang. Marian tensed, listening: she didn't want to start down the stairs if it wasn't necessary. She heard a mumble of voices and the reverberation of the closing door. The lady down below had been on the alert. She sighed, closed the cookbook, tossed her spoon into the sink after giving it one last lick, and screwed the top on the peanut butter jar.

'Hi,' she said to Len as he rose, white-faced and out of breath, from the stairwell. He looked ill. 'Come on in and sit down.' Then, because it was only six-thirty, she asked, 'Have you had dinner? Can I get you anything?' She wanted to prepare something for him, if only a bacon-and-tomato sandwich. Ever since her own relation to food had become ambiguous she found she took a perverse delight in watching other people eat.

'No thanks,' he said, 'I'm not hungry. But I could use a drink if you've got one.' He walked into the living room and plopped himself onto the chesterfield as though his body was a sack that he was too tired to carry around any longer.

'I've only got beer – that okay?' She went into the kitchen, opened two bottles, and carried them into the living room. With good friends like Len she didn't bother with the formality of glasses.

'Thanks,' he said. He upended the squat brown bottle. His mouth, pursed budlike around the bottleneck, was for a moment strangely infantile. 'Christ, do I need this,' he said, putting the bottle down on the coffee table. 'I guess she must've told you.'

Marian sipped at her beer before replying. It was Moose Beer; she had bought some out of curiosity. It tasted just like all the other brands.

'You mean that she's pregnant,' she said in a neutral conversational tone. 'Yes, of course.'

Len groaned. He took off his hornrimmed glasses and pressed one hand over his eyes. 'God, I feel just sick about it,' he said. 'I was so shocked when she told me, god I'd just called her up to see if she'd have coffee with me, she's been sort of avoiding me ever since that night, I guess all that really shook her up, and then to have *that* hit you over the phone. I haven't been able to work all afternoon. I hung up right in the middle of the conversation, I don't know what she thought about that but I couldn't help it. She's such a little *girl*, Marian, I mean most women you'd feel what the hell, they probably deserved it, rotten bitches anyway, not that anything like that has ever happened to me before. But she's so *young*. The damn thing is, I can't really remember what happened that evening. We came back for coffee, and I was feeling sort of rotten and that bottle of scotch was sitting on the table and I started in on it. Of course I won't deny that I'd been angling for her, but, well, I wasn't expecting it, I mean I wasn't ready, I mean I would have been a lot more careful. What a mess. What'm I going to *do*?'

Marian sat watching him silently. Ainsley, then, hadn't had a chance to explain her motives. She wondered whether she should attempt to unsnarl, for Len's benefit, that rather improbable tangle, or wait and let Ainsley do it herself, as by right she ought to.

'I mean I can't *marry* her,' Len said miserably. 'Being a husband would be bad enough, I'm too *young* to get married, but can you imagine me as a husband and *father*?' He gave a small gurgle and upended his beer bottle again. 'Birth,' he said, his voice higher and more distraught, 'birth terrifies me. It's revolting. I can't stand the thought of having' – he shuddered – 'a baby.'

'Well, it isn't you who's going to have it, you know,' Marian said reasonably.

Len turned to her, his face contorted, pleading. The contrast between this man, his eyes exposed and weak without their usual fence of glass and tortoise-shell, and the glib, clever, slightly leering Len she had always known was painful. 'Marian,' he said, 'please, can't you try to reason with her? If she'd only decide to have an abortion, of course I'll pay for it.' He swallowed; she watched his Adam's apple go up and down. She hadn't known anything could make him this unhappy.

'I'm afraid she won't,' she said gently. 'You see, the whole point of it was that she *wanted* to get pregnant.'

'She what?'

'She did it on purpose. She wanted to get pregnant.'

'That's ridiculous!' Len said. 'Nobody *wants* to get pregnant. Nobody would deliberately do a thing like that!'

Marian smiled; he was being simple-minded, which she found sweet, in a sticky sort of way. She felt as though she should take him upon her knee and say, 'Now Leonard, it's high time I told you about the Facts of Life.'

'You'd be surprised,' she said, 'a lot of people do. It's fashionable these days, you know; and Ainsley reads a lot; she was particularly fond of anthropology at college, and she's convinced that no woman has fulfilled her feminity unless she's had a baby. But don't worry, you won't have to be involved any further. She doesn't want a husband, just a baby. So you've already done your bit.'

Len was having trouble believing her. He put on his glasses, stared at her through them, and took them off again. There was a pause while he drank more beer. 'So she's been to college, too. I should have known. That's what we get then,' he said nastily, 'for educating women. They get all kinds of ridiculous ideas.'

'Oh, I don't know,' Marian said with a touch of sharpness, 'there's some men it doesn't do much good for either.'

Len winced. 'Meaning me, I suppose. But how was I to know? *You* certainly didn't tell me. What a friend.'

'Why, I'd never presume to try and tell you how to run your life,' Marian said indignantly. 'But why should you be upset, now that you know? You don't have to *do* anything. She'll take care of the whole business. Believe me, Ainsley's quite capable of looking after herself.'

Leonard's mood seemed to be changing rapidly from despair to anger. 'The little slut,' he muttered. 'Getting me into something like this. . . .'

There were footsteps on the stairs.

'Shhh,' Marian said, 'here she is. Now keep calm.' She went out into the small vestibule to greet Ainsley.

'Hi, just wait till you see what I *got*,' Ainsley called, lilting up the stairs. She bustled into the kitchen, setting her parcels on the table and taking off her coat and talking breathlessly. 'It was such a jam down there but besides the groceries – have to eat enough for two now, you know – oh, and I got my vitamin pills – and I got the darlingest little patterns, just wait till you see.' She produced a knitting book, then some blue baby-wool.

'So it's going to be a boy,' Marian said.

Ainsley's eyes widened. 'Well of course. I mean, I thought it might be better. . . .'

'Well, maybe you should have discussed it with the prospective father before you took the necessary steps. He's in the living room, and he seems rather annoyed at not being consulted. You see,' Marian said maliciously, 'he may have wanted a girl.'

Ainsley pushed back a strand of auburn hair that had fallen over her forehead. 'Oh. Len's here, is he?' she said, with pronounced coolness. 'Yes. He sounded a little upset on the phone.' She walked into the living room. Marian did not know which of them needed her support more or which she would give it to if forced to choose between them. She followed Ainsley, aware that she should extricate herself before the thing got much messier, but not knowing how.

'Hi Len,' Ainsley said lightly. 'You hung up on me before I had a chance to explain.'

Len wouldn't look at her. 'Marian has already explained, thanks.'

Ainsley pouted reproachfully. She had evidently wanted to do it herself.

'Well, it was somebody's duty to,' Marian said, compressing her lips in a slightly presbyterian manner. 'He was suffering.'

'Maybe I shouldn't have told you at all,' Ainsley said, 'but I really couldn't keep it to myself. Just think, I'm going to be a mother! I'm really so happy about it.'

Len had been gradually bristling and swelling. 'Well I'm not so damn happy about it,' he burst out. 'All along you've only been *using* me. What a moron I was to think you were sweet and innocent, when it turns out you were actually college-educated the whole time! Oh, they're all the same. You weren't interested in *me* at all. The only thing you wanted from me was my body!'

'What did you want,' Ainsley asked sweetly, 'from me? Anyway, that's all I took. You can have the rest. And you can keep your peace of mind, I'm not threatening you with a paternity suit.'

Len had stood up and was pacing the floor, at a safe distance from Ainsley. 'Peace of mind. Hah. Oh no, you've involved me. You involved me psychologically. I'll have to think of myself as a father now, it's indecent, and all because you' – he gasped: the idea was a novel one for him – '*you* seduced *me*!' He waved his beer-bottle at her. 'Now I'm going to be all mentally tangled up in Birth. Fecundity. Gestation. Don't you realize what that will do to me? It's obscene, that horrible oozy. . . .'

'Don't be idiotic,' Ainsley said. 'It's perfectly natural and beautiful. The relationship between mother and unborn child is the loveliest and closest in the world.' She was leaning in the doorway, gazing towards the window. 'The most mutually balanced. . . .'

'Nauseating!' interjected Len.

Ainsley turned on him angrily. 'You're displaying the classic symptoms of uterus envy. Where the hell do you think *you* came from, anyway? You're not from Mars, you know, and it may be news but your mother didn't find you under a cabbage-plant in the garden either. You were all curled up inside somebody's *womb* for nine months just like everybody else, and. . . .'

Len's face cringed. 'Stop!' he cried. 'Don't remind me. I really can't stand it, you'll make me sick. Don't come near me!' he yelped, as Ainsley took a step towards him. 'You're unclean!'

Marian decided he was becoming hysterical. He sat down on the arm of the chesterfield and covered his face with his hands. 'She made me do it,' he muttered. 'My own mother. We were having eggs for breakfast and I opened mine and there was, I swear there was a little chicken inside it, it wasn't born yet, I didn't want to touch it but she didn't *see*, she didn't see what was really there, she said Don't be silly, it looks like an ordinary egg to me, but it wasn't, it wasn't and she made me eat it. And I know, I know there was a little beak and little claws and everything. . . .' He shuddered violently. 'Horrible. Horrible, I can't stand it,' he moaned, and his shoulders began to heave convulsively.

Marian blushed with embarrassment, but Ainsley gave a maternal coo of concern and hurried to the chesterfield. She sat down beside Len and put her arms around him, pulling him down so that he was resting half across her lap with his head against her shoulder. 'There, there,' she soothed. Her hair fell down around their two faces like a veil, or, Marian thought, a web. She rocked her body gently. 'There, there. It's not going to be a little chicken anyway, it's going to be a lovely nice baby. Nice baby.'

Marian walked out to the kitchen. She was coldly revolted: they were acting like a couple of infants. Ainsley was getting a layer of blubber on her soul already, she thought; aren't hormones wonderful. Soon she would be fat all over. And Len had displayed something hidden, something she had never seen in him before. He had behaved like a white grub suddenly unearthed from its burrow and exposed to the light of day. A repulsive blinded writhing. It amazed her though that it had taken so little, really, to reduce him to that state. His shell had not been as thick and calloused as she had imagined. It was like that parlour trick they used to play with eggs: you put the egg endwise between your locked hands and squeezed it with all your might, and the egg wouldn't break; it was so well-balanced that you were exerting your force against yourself. But with only a slight shift, an angle, a re-adjustment of the pressure, the egg would crack, and skoosh, there you were with your shoes full of albumin.

Now Len's delicate adjustment had been upset and he was being crushed. She wondered how he had ever managed to avoid the issue for so long, to persuade himself that his own much-vaunted sexual activities could have nothing whatever to do with the manufacture of children. What would he have done then if the situation had been as he first imagined it, and he *had* got Ainsley pregnant by accident? Would he have been able to play guilt off against a blamelessness based on no-intent-to-injure, have let them cancel each other out and escaped unscathed? Ainsley couldn't have foreseen his reaction. But it was her decision that was responsible for this crisis. What was she going to do with him now? What *should* she do?

Oh well, she thought, it's their problem, let them solve it; I'm well out of it anyway. She went into her bedroom and closed the door.

The next morning, however, when she opened her soft-boiled egg and saw the yolk looking up at her with its one significant and accusing yellow eye, she found her mouth closing together like a frightened sea-anemone. It's living; it's alive, the muscles in her throat said, and tightened. She pushed the dish away. Her conscious mind was used to the procedure by now. She sighed with resignation and crossed one more item off the list.

Chapter Nineteen

'There's jelly, salmon, peanut butter and honey, and egg salad,' Mrs Grot said, shoving the platter under Marian's nose – not because she was being rude but because Marian was sitting on the chesterfield and Mrs Grot was standing up, and the assemblage of vertebrae, inflexible corsetry, and desk-oriented musculature that provided Mrs Grot with her vertical structure would not allow her to bend very far over.

Marian drew herself back into the soft chintz cushions. 'Jelly, thanks,' she said, taking one.

It was the office Christmas party, which was being held in the ladies' lunchroom where they could be, as Mrs Gundridge had put it, 'more comfy.' So far their comfiness, all-permeating as it was in these close quarters, had been tampered by a certain amount of suppressed resentment. Christmas fell on a Wednesday this year, which meant that they all had to come back to work on Friday, missing by a single day the chance of a gloriously long weekend. It was the knowledge of this fact however that had, Marian was sure, put the twinkle in Mrs Grot's spectacles and even infused her with gaiety enough to sustain this unprecedentedly-social sandwich-passing. It's because she wants to take a good close look at our sufferings, Marian thought, watching the rigid figure as it progressed around the room.

The office party seemed to consist largely of the consumption of food and the discussion of ailments and bargains. The food had all been brought by the ladies themselves: each of them had agreed to provide a certain item. Even Marian had been pressured into promising some chocolate brownies, which she had actually bought at a bakery and switched to a different bag. She had not felt much like cooking lately. The food was heaped on the table that stood at one end of the lunchroom – much more food than they needed really, salads and sandwiches and fancy breads and desserts and cookies and cakes. But since everyone had brought something, everyone had to eat at least some of everything, or else the contributor would feel slighted. From time to time one or another of the ladies would shriek, 'Oh Dorothy, I just *have* to try some of your Orange-Pineapple Delight!' or 'Lena, your Luscious Fruit Sponge looks just scrummy!' and heave to her feet and trundle to the table to re-fill her paper plate.

Marian gathered that it had not always been like this. For some of the older girls, there was a memory, fast fading to legend, of a time when the office party had been a company-wide event; that was when the company had been much smaller. In those far-off days, Mrs Bogue said mistily, the men from upstairs had come down, and they even had drinks. But the office had expanded, finally things reached a stage at which nobody knew everybody any longer, and the parties started to get out of hand. Small ink-stained girls from Mimeo were pursued by wandering executives, there were untimely revelations of smouldering lust and concealed resentments, and elderly ladies had a papercupful too much and hysterics. Now, in the interests of allover office morale, each department had its own office party; and Mrs Gundridge had volunteered earlier that afternoon that it was a lot comfier this way anyhow, just all us girls here together, a comment which had produced glutinous murmurs of assent.

Marian was sitting wedged between two of the office virgins; the third was perched on the arm of the chesterfield. In situations like this, the three of them huddled together for self-protection: they had no children whose cutenesses could be compared, no homes whose furnishings were of much importance, and no husbands, details of whose eccentricities and nasty habits could be exchanged. Their concerns were other, though Emmy occasionally contributed an anecdote about one of her illnesses to the general conversation. Marian was aware that her own status among them was doubtful – they knew that she was on the fringe of matrimony and therefore regarded her as no longer genuinely single, no longer able to empathize with their problems – but in spite of their slight coolness towards her she still preferred being with them to joining any of the other groups. There was little movement in the room. Apart from the platter-passers, most of the ladies remained seated, in various clusters and semi-circles, re-clumping themselves every now and then by an exchange of chairs. Mrs Bogue alone circulated, bestowing a sociable smile here, a mark of attention or a cookie there. It was her duty.

She was working at it the more assiduously because of the cataclysm that had taken place earlier in the day. The giant city-wide instant tomato juice taste-test, in the offing since October but constantly delayed for further refinements, had been due to go out that morning. A record number of interviewers, almost the whole available crew, were to have descended on the unwary front porches of the housewives with cardboard trays on strings around their necks, like cigarette girls (privately, to Lucy, Marian had suggested bleaching them all and dressing them up in feathers and net stockings), carrying small paper cups of real canned tomato juice and small paper cups of Instant tomato juice powder and small pitchers of water. The housewife was to take a sip of the real juice, watch the interviewer mix the Instant right before her astounded eyes, and then try the result, impressed, possibly, by its quickness and ease: 'One Stir and you're Sure!' said the tentative advertisement sketches. If they'd done it in October it might have worked.

Unfortunately the snow that had been withholding itself during five uniformly overclouded grey days had chosen that morning at ten o'clock to begin to fall, not in soft drifting flakes or even intermittent flurries, but in a regular driving blizzard. Mrs Bogue had tried to get the higher-ups to postpone the test, but in vain. 'We're working with humans, not with machines,' she had said on the phone, her voice loud enough so that they could hear it through the closed door of her cubicle. 'It's utterly impossible out there!' But there was a deadline to be met. The thing had already been postponed for so long that it could be kept back no longer, and furthermore a delay of one day at this point would mean an actual delay of three because of the major inconvenience of Christmas. So Mrs Bogue's flock had been driven, bleating faintly, out into the storm.

For the rest of the morning the office had resembled the base of a mercy-mission in a disaster-area. Phone-calls flooded in from the hapless interviewers. Their cars, anti-freeze and snow-tireless, balked and stalled, stranded themselves in blowing drifts, and slammed their doors on hands and their trunk-lids on heads. The paper cups were far too light to withstand the force of the gale, and whirled away over the lanes and hedges, emptying their blood-red contents on the snow, on the interviewers, and, if the interviewers had actually made it as far as a front door, on the housewife herself. One interviewer had her whole tray ripped from her neck and lifted into the air like a kite; another had tried to shelter hers inside her coat, only to have it tipped and spewn against her body by the wind. From eleven o'clock on, the interviewers themselves had come straggling in, wild-haired and smeared with red, to resign or explain or have their faith in themselves as scientific and efficient measurers of public opinion restored, depending on temperament; and Mrs Bogue had had to cope in addition with the howls of rage from the broadloomed Olympics above who refused to recognize the existence of any storm not of their own making. The traces of the fray were still evident on her face as she moved among the eating women. When she was pretending to be flustered and upset, she was really serene; but now, attempting serenity, she reminded Marian of a club-lady in a flowered hat making a gracious speech of thanks, who has just felt a small many-legged creature scamper up her leg.

Marian gave up half listening to several conversations at once and let the sound of voices filling the room wash across her ears in a blur of meaningless syllables. She finished her jelly sandwich and went for a piece of cake. The loaded table made her feel gluttonous: all that abundance, all those meringues and icings and glazes, those coagulations of fats and sweets, that proliferation of rich glossy food. When she returned with a piece of spongecake Lucy, who had been talking with Emmy, had turned and was now talking with Millie, so that after she had taken her place again Marian found herself in the middle of their conversation.

'Well naturally they just didn't know what to do about it,' Lucy was saying. 'You just don't ask someone would they please take a bath. I mean it's not very polite.'

'And London's so dirty too,' Millie said sympathetically. 'You see the men in the evenings, the collars of their white shirts are black, just black. It's all the soot.'

'Yes well, and this went on and it got worse and worse, it was getting so bad they were ashamed to even ask their friends in. ...'

'Who's this?' Marian asked.

'Oh this *girl* who was living with some friend of mine in England and she just stopped *washing*. Nothing else was wrong with her, she just didn't wash, even her *hair* even, or change her clothes or anything, for the longest time, and they didn't want to say anything because she seemed perfectly *normal* in every other way, but obviously underneath it she must have been really *sick*.'

Emmy's narrow peaked face swung round at the word 'sick', and the story was repeated to her.

'So what happened, then?' Millie asked, licking chocolate icing from her fingers.

'Well,' said Lucy, nibbling daintily at a morsel of shortcake, 'it got pretty horrible. I mean, she was wearing the same *clothes*, you can imagine. And I guess it must have been three or four months.'

There was a murmur of 'Oh no's,' and she said, 'Well, at least two. And they were just about to ask her for god's sake either take a bath or move out. I mean, wouldn't you? But one day she came home and just took off those clothes and burnt them, and had a bath and everything, and she's been perfectly normal ever since. Just like that.'

'Well that *is* queer!' Emmy said in a disappointed voice. She had been expecting a severe illness, or perhaps even an operation.

'Of course they're all a lot dirtier Over There, you know,' Millie said in a woman-of-the-world tone.

'But *she* was from Over Here!' Lucy exclaimed. 'I mean she'd been brought up the right way, she was from a good family and all; it wasn't as if they didn't have a *bath*room, *they* were always perfectly clean!'

'Maybe it was one of those things we sort of all go through,' said Millie philosophically. 'Maybe she was just immature, and being away from home like that and all. . . .'

'I think she was *sick*,' Lucy said. She was picking the raisins out of a piece of Christmas-cake, preparatory to eating it.

Marian's mind had grasped at the word 'immature', turning it over like a curious pebble found on a beach. It suggested an unripe ear of corn, and other things of a vegetable or fruitlike nature. You were green and then you ripened: became mature. Dresses for the mature figure. In other words, fat.

She looked around the room at all the women there, at the mouths opening and shutting, to talk or to eat. Here, sitting like any other group of women at an afternoon feast, they no longer had the varnish of officialdom that separated them, during regular office hours, from the vast anonymous ocean of housewives whose minds they were employed to explore. They could have been wearing housecoats and curlers. As it was, they all wore dresses for the mature figure. They were ripe, some rapidly becoming over-ripe, some already beginning to shrivel; she thought of them as attached by stems at the tops of their heads to an invisible vine, hanging there in various stages of growth and decay ... in that case, thin elegant Lucy, sitting beside her, was merely at an earlier stage, a springtime green bump or nodule forming beneath the careful golden calyx of her hair. ...

She examined the women's bodies with interest, critically, as though she had never seen them before. And in a way she hadn't, they had just been there like everything else, desks, telephones, chairs, in the space of the office: objects viewed as outline and surface only. But now she could see the roll of fat pushed up across Mrs Gundridge's back at the top of her corset, the ham-like bulge of thigh, the creases round the neck, the large porous cheeks; the blotch of varicose veins glimpsed at the back of one plump crossed leg, the way her jowls jellied when she chewed, her sweater a woolly teacosy over those rounded shoulders; and the others too, similar in structure but with varying proportions and textures of bumpy permanents and dune-like contours of breast and waist and hip; their fluidity sustained somewhere within by bones, without by a carapace of clothing and makeup. What peculiar creatures they were; and the continual flux between the outside and the inside, taking things in, giving them out, chewing, words, potato-chips, burps, grease, hair, babies, milk, excrement, cookies, vomit, coffee, tomato juice, blood, tea, sweat, liquor, tears, and garbage. ...

For an instant she felt them, their identities, almost their substance, pass over her head like a wave. At some time she would be – or no, already she was like that too; she was one of them, her body the same, identical, merged with that other flesh that choked the air in the flowered room with its sweet organic scent; she felt suffocated by this thick sargasso-sea of femininity. She drew a deep breath, clenching her body and her mind back into her self like some tactile sea-creature withdrawing its tentacles; she wanted something solid, clear: a man; she wanted Peter in the room so that she could put her hand out and hold on to him to keep from being sucked down. Lucy had a gold bangle on one arm. Marian focussed her eyes on it, concentrating on it as though she was drawing its hard gold circle around herself, a fixed barrier between herself and that liquid amorphous other.

She became aware of a silence in the room. The hen-yard gabble had ceased. She lifted her head: Mrs Bogue was standing at the end of the room near the table, holding up her hand.

'Now that we're all gathered together here in this unofficial way,' she said, smiling benignly, 'I'd like to take this opportunity to make a very pleasant announcement. I've learned recently through the grapevine that one of our girls will soon be getting married. I'm sure we'll all wish Marian McAlpin the very best in her new life.'

There were preliminary squeals and chirps and burbles of excitement; then the whole mass rose up and descended upon her, deluging her with moist congratulations and chocolate-crumbed inquiries and little powdery initiatory kisses. Marian stood up, and was immediately pressed against the more-than-ample bosom of Mrs Gundridge. She unstuck herself and backed against the wall; she was blushing, but more from anger than from modesty. Someone had let it slip; one of them had told on her; Millie, it must have been.

She said 'Thank you' and 'September' and 'March,' the only three words necessary for the questions they were asking. 'Wonderful!' and 'Marvellous!' cried the chorus. The office virgins remained aloof, smiling wistfully. Mrs Bogue also stood aside. She had, by the tone of her speech, and by the mere fact of this public announcement coming without warning or prior consultation, made it clear to Marian that she would be expecting her to leave her job whether she wanted to or not. Marian knew, from the rumour and from the banishment of a typist just after she had begun to work at the office, that Mrs Bogue preferred her girls to be either unmarried or seasoned veterans with their liability to unpredictable pregnancies well in the past. Newly-weds, she had been heard to say, were inclined to be unstable. Mrs Grot from Accounting kept at the rim of the circle too, her smile tight-lipped and acid. I bet her festive mood is quite spoiled now, Marian thought; I'm lost to the Pension Plan forever.

To emerge from the building and walk along the street in the cold air was like throwing open the window of an overheated and stuffy room. The wind had subsided. It was already dark, but the jangling light from the store windows and the Christmas decorations overhead, festoons and stars, made the snow that was falling, softly now, glow like the spray from a gigantic and artificially-lit waterfall. Underfoot, there was less snow than she had anticipated. It was wet, trodden to a brown slush by the pedestrians. The blizzard had not started until after Marian had left for work that morning, and she wasn't wearing boots. Her shoes were soaked through by the time she had reached the subway station.

But in spite of her wet feet she got off the subway a stop before the right one. After that tea-party she could not possibly confront the apartment yet. Ainsley would come in and take up her infernal knitting, and there was the Christmas-tree, a plastic table-model in silver and azure. There were still the presents to be wrapped, lying on her bed; and her suitcase to be packed: early the next morning she had to leave on the bus for a two-day visit with her parents and their town and their relatives. When she thought of them at all, they no longer seemed to belong to her. The town and the people waited for her on some horizon, somewhere, unchanging, monolithic and grey, like the weathered stone ruins of an extinct civilization. She had bought all the presents last weekend, shoving her way through the crowds that clamoured and shouted at the store-counters, but she no longer felt like giving anybody anything. She felt even less like receiving, having to thank them all for things she didn't need and would never use; and it was no use telling herself, as she had been told all her life, that it was the spirit of the giver and not the value of the gift that counted. That was worse: all the paper tags with Love on them. The kind of love they were given with was also by now something she didn't need and would never use. It was archaic, sadly ornate, kept for some obscure nostalgic reason, like the photograph of a dead person.

She had been walking west but with little sense of direction along a street walled with stores and with elegant mannequins posturing in their bright glass cages. Now she had passed the final store and was walking in a darker space. As she approached the corner, she realized she had been heading toward the Park. She crossed the street and turned south, following the stream of cars. The Museum was on her left, its frieze of stone figures thrown into relief by the garish orange floodlights they seemed to be using more and more for night-lighting.

Peter had been a problem. She hadn't known what she ought to buy him. Clothes were out of the question, she had decided: he would always want to choose his own. What else was there? Something for the apartment, some household object, would be like making a gift to herself. She had finally settled on a handsome expensive technical book about cameras. She knew nothing about the subject but she had taken the word of the salesman, hoping that the book was one he didn't already have. She was glad he had hobbies: he would be less likely to get heart failure after retiring.

She was passing under the arching branches of the trees that grew within these nearby fences and seclusions of the university. The sidewalk was less trampled here, and the snow was deeper, above her ankles in some places. Her feet were aching with the cold. Just as she was beginning to wonder why she kept on walking, she had crossed the street again and was standing in the Park.

It was a huge dimly-white island in the darkness of the night. The cars flowed around it, counter clockwise; on the further side lay the buildings of the university, those places she thought she had known so well only half a year ago but which now radiated a faint hostility towards her through the cold air, a hostility she recognized as coming from herself: in some obscure way she was jealous of them. She would have liked them to have vanished when she left, but they had remained standing, kept going on, as indifferent to her absence as they had actually been, she supposed, to her presence.

She walked further into the Park through the soft ankle-deep snow. Here and there it was criss-crossed by random trails of footprints, already silting over, but mostly it was smooth, untouched, the trunks of the bare trees coming straight up out of the snow as though it was seven feet deep and the trees had been stuck there like candles in the icing of a cake. Black candles.

She was near the round concrete pool that had a fountain in the summers but would be empty of water now, gradually filling instead with snow. She stopped to listen to the distant sounds of the city, which seemed to be moving in a circle around her; she felt quite safe. 'You have to watch it,' she said to herself, 'you don't want to end up not taking baths.' In the lunchroom she had felt for a moment dangerously close to some edge; now she found her own reactions rather silly. An office party was merely an office party. There were certain things that had to be got through between now and then, that was all: details, people, necessary events. After that it would be all right. She was almost ready to go back and wrap the presents; she was even hungry enough now to devour half a cow, dotted lines and all. But she wanted to stand for only one more minute with the snow sifting down here in this island, this calm open eye of silence. . . .

'Hello,' a voice said.

Marian was hardly startled. She turned: there was a figure seated on the far end of a bench in the darker shadow of some evergreen trees. She walked towards it.

It was Duncan, sitting hunched over, a cigarette glowing between his fingers. He must have been there for some time. The snow had settled on his hair and on the shoulders of his coat. His hand, when she took off her glove to touch it, was cold and wet.

She sat down beside him on the snow-covered bench. He flicked away his cigarette and turned towards her, and she undid the buttons of his overcoat and huddled herself inside it, in a space that smelled of damp cloth and stale cigarettes. He closed his arms around her back.

He was wearing a shaggy sweater. She stroked it with one of her hands as though it was a furry skin. Beneath it she could feel his spare body, the gaunt shape of a starved animal in time of famine. He nuzzled his wet face under her scarf and hair and coat collar, against her neck.

They sat without moving. The city, the time outside the white circle of the Park, had almost vanished. Marian felt her flesh gradually numbing; her feet had even ceased to ache. She pressed herself deeper into the furry surface; outside, the snow was falling. She could not begin the effort of getting up. . . .

'You took a long time,' he said quietly at last. 'I've been expecting you.'

Her body was beginning to shiver. 'I have to go now,' she said.

Against her neck she felt a convulsive movement of the muscles beneath his face.

Chapter Twenty

Marian was walking slowly down the aisle, keeping pace with the gentle music that swelled and rippled around her. 'Beans,' she said. She found the kind marked 'Vegetarian' and tossed two cans into her wire cart.

The music swung into a tinkly waltz; she proceeded down the aisle, trying to concentrate on her list. She resented the music because she knew why it was there: it was supposed to lull you into a euphoric trance, lower your sales resistance to the point at which all things are desirable. Every time she walked into the supermarket and heard the lilting sounds coming from the concealed loudspeakers she remembered an article she had read about cows who gave more milk when sweet music was played to them. But just because she knew what they were up to didn't mean she was immune. These days, if she wasn't careful, she found herself pushing the cart like a somnambulist, eyes fixed, swaying slightly, her hands twitching with the impulse to reach out and grab anything with a bright label. She had begun to defend herself with lists, which she printed in block letters before setting out, willing herself to buy nothing, however deceptively-priced or subliminally-packaged, except what was written there. When she was feeling unusually susceptible she would tick the things off the list with a pencil as an additional counter-alarm.

But in some ways they would always be successful: they couldn't miss. You had to buy something sometime. She knew enough about it from the office to realize that the choice between, for instance, two brands of soap or two cans of tomato juice was not what could be called a rational one. In the products, the things themselves, there was no real difference. How did you choose then? You could only abandon yourself to the soothing music and make a random snatch. You let the thing in you that was supposed to respond to the labels just respond, whatever it was; maybe it had something to do with the pituitary gland. Which detergent had the best power-symbol? Which tomato juice can had the sexiest-looking tomato on it, and did she care? Something in her must care; after all, she did choose eventually, doing precisely what some planner in a broadloomed office had hoped and predicted she would do. She had caught herself lately watching herself with an abstracted curiosity, to see what she would do.

'Noodles,' she said. She glanced up from her list just in time to avoid a collision with the plump lady in frazzled muskrat. 'Oh no, they've put another brand on the market.' She knew the noodle business: several of her afternoons had been spent in stores in the Italian section, counting the endless varieties and brands of *pasta*. She glared at the noodles, stacks of them, identical in their cello-paks, then shut her eyes, shot out her hand and closed her fingers on a package. Any package.

'Lettuce, radishes, carrots, onions, tomatoes, parsley,' she read from her list. Those would be easy: at least you could tell by looking at them, though some things came in bags or rubber-banded bunches arranged with some good and some bad in each, and the tomatoes, hothouse-pink and tasteless at this time of year, were prepackaged in cardboard and cellophane boxes of four. She steered her cart towards the vegetable area, where a slickly-finished rustic wooden sign hung on the wall: 'The Market Garden.'

She picked listlessy through the vegetables. She used to be fond of a good salad but now she had to eat so many of them she was beginning to find them tiresome. She felt like a rabbit, crunching all the time on mounds of leafy greenery. How she longed to become again a carnivore, to gnaw on a good bone! Christmas dinner had been difficult. 'Why Marian, you're not eating!' her mother had fussed when she had left the turkey untouched on her plate. She had said she wasn't hungry, and had eaten huge quantities of cranberry sauce and mashed potatoes and mince pie when no one was looking. Her mother had set her strange loss of appetite down to overexcitement. She had thought of saying she had taken up a new religion that forbade her to eat meat, Yoga or Doukhobor or something, but it wouldn't have been a good idea: they had been pathetically eager to have the wedding in the family church. Their reaction though, as far as she could estimate the reactions of people who were now so remote from her, was less elated glee than a quiet, rather smug satisfaction, as though their fears about the effects of her university education, never stated but always apparent, had been calmed at last. They had probably been worried she would turn into a high-school teacher or a maiden aunt or a dope addict or a female executive, or that she would undergo some shocking physical transformation, like developing muscles and a deep voice or growing moss. She could picture the anxious consultations over cups of tea. But now, their approving eyes said, she was turning out all right after all. They had not met Peter, but for them he seemed to be merely the necessary X-factor. They were curious though: they continued to urge her to bring him home for the weekend soon. As she had moved around the town during those two cold days, visiting relatives, answering questions, she could not convince herself that she was actually back in it.

'Kleenex,' she said. She glanced with distaste at the different brands and colours offered – what difference did it make what you blew your nose on? – and at the fancy printed toilet-paper – flowers and scrolls and polka-dots. Pretty soon they would have it in gold, as though they wanted to pretend it was used for something quite different, like wrapping Christmas presents. There really wasn't a single human unpleasantness left that they had not managed to turn to their uses. What on earth was wrong with plain white? At least it looked clean.

Her mother and her aunts of course had been interested in the wedding dress and the invitations and things like that. At the moment, listening to the electric violins and hesitating between two flavours of canned rice pudding – she had no reservations about eating that, it tasted so synthetic – she couldn't remember what they had all decided.

She looked at her watch: she didn't have much time. Luckily they were playing a tango. She wheeled rapidly towards the canned soup section, trying to shake the glaze out of her eyes. It was dangerous to stay in the supermarket too long. One of these days it would get her. She would be trapped past closing time, and they would find her in the morning propped against one of the shelves in an unbreakable coma, surrounded by all the pushcarts in the place heaped to overflowing with merchandise. . . .

She steered towards the checkout counters. They were having another of their sales-promoting special programmes, some sort of contest that would send the winner on a three-day trip to Hawaii. There was a big poster over the front window, a semi-nude girl in a grass skirt and flowers, and beside it a small sign: PINEAPPLES, Three Cans 65¢. The cashier behind the counter had a paper garland around her neck; her orange mouth was chewing gum. Marian watched the mouth, the hypnotic movements of the jaws, the bumpy flesh of the cheeks with their surface of dark pink makeup, the scaling lips through which glinted several rodent-yellow teeth working as with a life of their own. The cash register totalled her groceries.

The orange mouth opened. 'Five twenty-nine,' it said. 'Just write your name and address on the receipt.'

'No thanks,' Marian said, 'I don't want to go.'

The girl shrugged her shoulders and turned away. 'Excuse me, you forgot to give me my stamps,' Marian said.

That was another thing, she thought as she hoisted the grocery bag and went through the electric-eye door into the slushy grey twilight. For a while she had refused them: it was another hidden way for them to make money. But they still made the money anyway, more of it; so she had begun accepting them and hiding them in kitchen drawers. Now, however, Ainsley was saving for a baby-carrier, so she made a point of getting them. It was the least she could do for Ainsley. The flowery cardboard Hawaiian smiled at her as she trudged off towards the subway station.

Flowers. They had all wanted to know what kind of flowers she was going to carry. Marian herself was in favour of lilies; Lucy had suggested a cascade of pink tea-roses and baby's-breath. Ainsley had been scornful. 'Well, I suppose you have to have a traditional wedding, since it's Peter,' she had said. 'But people are so hypocritical about flowers at weddings. Nobody wants to admit they're really fertility symbols. What about a giant sunflower or a sheaf of wheat? Or a cascade of mushrooms and cactuses, that would be quite genital, don't you think?' Peter didn't want to be involved in such decisions. 'I'll leave all that sort of thing up to you,' he would say with fondness when questioned seriously.

Lately she had been seeing more and more of Peter, but less and less of Peter alone. Now that she had been ringed he took pride in displaying her. He said he wanted her to really get to know some of his friends, and he had been taking her around with him to cocktail parties with the more official ones and to dinners and evening get-togethers with the intimates. She had even been to lunch with some lawyers, during which she had sat the whole time silent and smiling. The friends collectively were all well-dressed and on the verge of being successful, and they all had wives who were also well-dressed and on the verge of being successful. They were all anxious; they were all polite to her. Marian found it difficult to connect these sleek men with the happy hunters and champion beer-drinkers that lived in Peter's memories of the past, but some of them were the same people. Ainsley referred to them as 'the soap men', because once when Peter had come to pick Marian up he brought with him a friend who worked for a soap company. Marian's greatest apprehension about them was that she would get their names mixed up.

She wanted to be nice to them for Peter's sake; however, she had been feeling somewhat bombarded with them, and she had decided it was time for Peter to start really getting to know some of *her* friends. This was why she had asked Clara and Joe to dinner. She had been guilty of neglecting them anyway; though it was curious, she thought, how married people always assumed they were being neglected when you didn't phone them, even when they themselves had been too dug under to even think about phoning you. Peter had been recalcitrant; he had seen the inside of Clara's living room once.

As soon as she had issued the invitations she realized that the menu would be a major problem. She couldn't feed them milk and peanut butter and vitamin pills, or a salad with cottage cheese, she couldn't have fish because Peter didn't like it, but she couldn't serve meat either – because what would they all think when they saw her not eating any of it? She couldn't possibly explain; if she didn't understand it herself, how could she expect them to? In the past month a few forms that had been available to her had ex luded themselves from her diet: hamburger after a funny story of Peter's about a friend of his who had got some analysed just for a joke and had discovered it contained ground-up mouse hairs; pork because Emmy during a coffee break had entertained them with an account of trichinosis and a lady she knew who got it – she mentioned the name with almost religious awe ('She ate it too pink in a restaurant, I'd never dare eat anything like that in a restaurant, just *think*, all those little things curled up in her muscles and they can't ever get them out'); and mutton and lamb because

Duncan had told her the etymology of the word 'giddy': it came, he said, from 'gid', which was a loss of equilibrium in sheep caused by large white worms in their brains. Even hot dogs had been ruled out; after all, her stomach reasoned, they could mash up any old thing and stick it in there. In restaurants she could always hedge by ordering a salad, but that would never do for guests, not for dinner. And she couldn't serve them Vegetarian Baked Beans.

She had fallen back on a casserole, a mushroom-and-meatballs affair of her mother's which would disguise things effectively. 'I'll turn off the lights and have candles,' she thought, 'and get them drunk on sherry first so they won't notice.' She could dish herself a very small helping, eat the mushrooms, and roll the meatballs under one of the lettuce leaves from the accompanying salad. It wasn't an elegant solution but it was the best she could do.

Now, hurriedly slicing up the radishes for the salad, she was grateful for several things: that she had made the casserole the night before so all she had to do was stick it in the oven; that Clara and Joe were coming late, after they had put the children to bed; and that she could still eat the salad. She was becoming more and more irritated by her body's decision to reject certain foods. She had tried to reason with it, had accused it of having frivolous whims, had coaxed it and tempted it, but it was adamant; and if she used force it rebelled. One incident like that in a restaurant had been enough. Peter had been terribly nice about it, of course; he'd driven her straight home and helped her up the stairs as though she was an invalid and insisted she must have the stomach-flu; but also he had been embarrassed and (understandably) annoyed. From then on she had resolved to humour it. She had done everything it wanted, and even had bought it some vitamin pills to keep its proteins and minerals balanced. There was no sense in getting malnutrition. 'The thing to do,' she had told herself, 'is to keep calm.' At times when she had meditated on the question she had concluded that the stand it had taken was an ethical one: it simply refused to eat anything that had once been, or (like oysters on the half-shell) might still be living. But she faced each day with the forlorn hope that her body might change its mind.

She rubbed the wooden bowl with a half-clove of garlic and threw in the onion rings and sliced radishes and the tomatoes, and tore up the lettuce. At the last minute she thought of adding a grated carrot to give it more colour. She took one from the refrigerator, located the peeler finally in the bread-box, and began to peel off the skin, holding the carrot by its leafy top.

She was watching her own hands and the peeler and the curl of the crisp orange skin. She became aware of the carrot. It's a root, she thought, it grows in the ground and sends up leaves. Then they come along and dig it up, maybe it even makes a sound, a scream too low for us to hear, but it doesn't die right away, it keeps on living, right now it's still alive. . . .

She thought she felt it twist in her hands. She dropped it on the table. 'Oh no,' she said, almost crying. 'Not this too!'

When they had finally gone, even Peter, who had kissed her on the cheek and said jokingly, 'Darling, we're never going to be like *that*.' Marian went out to the kitchen and scraped the plates into the garbage pail and stacked them in the sink. The dinner had not been a good idea. Clara and Joe hadn't been able to get a baby-sitter so they had brought the children, lugging them up the stairs and putting them to bed, two in Marian's room and one in Ainsley's. The children had wept and excreted, and the fact that the bathroom was down a flight of stairs didn't help. Clara carted them out to the living room to reassure them and change them; she had no qualms. Conversation had ceased. Marian hovered about, handing diaper pins and pretending to be helpful, but secretly wondering whether it would be bad taste to go down and get one of the many odour-killing devices from the lady down below's bathroom. Joe bustled about, whistling and bringing fresh supplies; Clara made apologetic remarks in Peter's direction. 'Small children are like this, it's only shit. Perfectly natural, we all do it. Only,' she said, joggling the youngest on her knee, 'some of us have a sense of timing. Don't we, you little turd?'

Peter had pointedly opened a window; the room became ice-cold. Marian served the sherry, despairingly. Peter was not getting the right impression, but she didn't know what could be done. She found herself wishing that Clara had a few more inhibitions. Clara didn't deny that her children stank, but neither did she take any pains to conceal it. She admitted it, she almost affirmed it; it was as though she wanted it to be appreciated.

When the children had been swathed and pacified and arranged, two on the chesterfield and one in its carrier on the floor, they sat down to dinner. Now, Marian hoped, they will all have a conversation. She was concentrating on how to conceal her meatballs and didn't want the position of referee: she just couldn't think up any bright topical remarks. 'Clara tells me you're a philatelist,' she had ventured, but for some reason Joe didn't hear her; at least he didn't answer. Peter gave her a quick inquisitive look. She sat fidgeting with a piece of roll, feeling as though she had made an indecent joke and nobody had laughed.

Peter and Joe had started talking about the international situation, but Peter had tactfully changed the subject when it became obvious they would disagree. He said he had once had to take a philosophy course at university and had never been able to understand Plato; perhaps Joe could explain? Joe said he thought not, as he himself specialized in Kant, and asked Peter a technical question about inheritance taxes. He and Clara, he added, belonged to a co-operative burial society.

'I didn't know that,' Marian said in an undertone to Clara as she dished herself a second helping of noodles. She felt as though her plate was exposed, all eyes fixed upon it, the hidden meatballs showing up from beneath the lettuce leaves like bones in an X-ray; she wished she had used one candle instead of two.

'Oh yes,' said Clara briskly, 'Joe doesn't believe in embalming.'

Marian was afraid Peter might find this a little too radical. The trouble was, she sighed inwardly, that Joe was idealistic and Peter was pragmatic. You could tell by their ties: Peter's was paisley and dark-green, elegant, functional; while Joe's was – well, it wasn't exactly a tie any more; it was the abstract idea of a tie. They themselves must have realized the difference: she caught them separately eyeing each others' ties, each probably thinking he would never wear a tie like that.

She began putting the glasses into the sink. It bothered her that things hadn't gone well; it made her feel responsible, like being It in a game of tag at recess. 'Oh well,' she remembered, 'he got on with Len.' It didn't really matter anyway: Clara and Joe were from her past, and Peter shouldn't be expected to adjust to her past; it was the future that mattered. She shivered slightly; the house was still chilly from when Peter had opened the window. She would smell maroon velvet and furniture polish, behind her there would be rustlings and coughings, then she would turn and there would be a crowd of watching faces, they would move forward and step through a doorway and there would be a flurry of white, the bits of paper blowing against their faces and settling on their hair and shoulders like snow.

She took a vitamin pill and opened the refrigerator door to get herself a glass of milk. Either she or Ainsley should really do something about the refrigerator. In the past couple of weeks their interdependent cleaning cycle had begun to break down. She had tidied up the living room for this evening, but she knew she was going to leave the dishes unwashed in the sink, which meant Ainsley would leave hers, and they would go on like that until they had used up all the dishes. Then they would start washing the top plate when they needed one and the others would sit there undisturbed. And the refrigerator: not only did it need defrosting, but its shelves were getting cluttered up with odds and ends, scraps of food in little jars, things in tinfoil and brown paper bags. . . . Soon it would begin to smell. She hoped that whatever was going on in there wouldn't spread too quickly to the rest of the house, at least not down the stairs. Maybe she would be married before it became epidemic.

Ainsley had not been at dinner; she had gone to the Pre-Natal Clinic, as she did every Friday evening. While Marian was folding the tablecloth, she heard her come upstairs and go into her room, and shortly afterwards her tremulous voice called, 'Marian? Could you please come here?'

She went to Ainsley's room, picking her way over the boggy surface of clothes that covered the floor towards the bed where Ainsley had thrown herself. 'What's the matter?' she asked. Ainsley looked dismayed.

'Oh Marian,' she quavered, 'it's too awful. I went to the Clinic tonight. And I was so happy, and I was doing my knitting and everything during the first speaker – he talked about The Advantages of Breast Feeding. They even have an Association for it now. But then they had this psy-psy-psychologist, and he talked about the Father Image.' She was on the verge of tears, and Marian got up and rooted around on the dresser until she unearthed a grubby piece of kleenex, just in case. She was concerned: it wasn't like Ainsley to cry.

'He says they ought to grow up with a strong Father Image in the home,' she said when she had composed herself. 'It's good for them, it makes them *normal*, especially if they're boys.'

'Well, but you sort of knew that before, didn't you?' Marian asked.

'Oh no Marian, it's really a lot more drastic. He has all kinds of statistics and everything. They've proved it scientifically.' She gulped. 'If I have a little boy, he's absolutely *certain* to turn into a ho-ho-ho-homosexual!' At this mention of the one category of man who had never shown the slightest interest in her, Ainsley's large blue eyes filled with tears. Marian extended the kleenex, but Ainsley waved it away. She sat up and pushed back her hair.

'There's got to be a way,' she said; her chin lifted, courageously.

Chapter Twenty-one

They were holding hands as they went up the wide stone stairway and through the heavy doors, but they had to let go to pass through the turnstile. Once they were inside it didn't seem right to take hands again. The church-like atmosphere created by the high gold-mosaicked dome under which they were standing discouraged any such fleshly attempts, even if they involved only fingers, and the blue-uniformed and white-haired guard had frowned at them as he took her money. Marian connected the frown with dim recollections of two previous visits during all-day educational bus excursions to the city when she was in elementary school: perhaps it came with the price of admission.

'Come on,' Duncan said, almost in a whisper. 'I'll show you my favourite things.'

They climbed the spiral staircase, round and around the incongruous totem-pole, up towards the geometrical curved ceiling. Marian had not been in this part of the Museum for so long that it seemed like something remembered from a not altogether pleasant dream, the kind you had when recovering from ether after having your tonsils out. When at university she had attended one class on the basement floor (Geology; it had been the only way to avoid

Religious Knowledge, and she had felt surly towards rock-specimens ever since), and occasionally she had gone to the Museum Coffee Shop on the main floor. But not up these marble stairs again, into the bowl-shaped space of air that looked almost solid now, shafted with dustmotes whenever the weak winter sunlight became positive enough through the narrow windows high above.

They paused for a minute to look over the balustrade. Down below a batch of schoolchildren was filing through the turnstile and going to pick up folding canvas chairs from the stack at the side of the rotunda, their bodies foreshortened by perspective. The shrill edges of their voices were dulled by the thick encircling space, so that they seemed even further away than they actually were.

'I hope they don't come up here,' Duncan said as he pushed himself away from the marble railing. He tugged at her coatsleeve, turning and drawing her with him into one of the branching galleries. They walked slowly along the creaking parquet floor past the rows of glass cases.

She had been seeing Duncan frequently during the past three weeks, by collusion rather than by coincidence, as formerly. He was writing another term-paper, he had told her, called 'Monosyllables in Milton,' which was to be an intensive stylistic analysis done from a radical angle. He had been stuck on the opening sentence, 'It is indeed highly significant that . . .' for two and a half weeks and, having exhausted the possibilities of the laundromat, he had felt a need for frequent escapes.

'Why don't you find a *female* graduate student in English?' she had asked once when their two faces, reflected in a store window, had struck her as particularly ill-matched. She looked like someone who was hired to take him out for walks.

'That wouldn't be an escape,' he said, 'they're all writing term-papers too; we'd have to discuss them. Besides,' he added morosely, 'they don't have enough breasts. Or,' he qualified after a pause, 'some of them have too many.'

Marian was being, she supposed, what they called 'used', but she didn't at all mind being used, as long as she knew what for: she liked these things to take place on as conscious a level as possible. Of course Duncan was making what they called 'demands', if only on her time and attention; but at least he wasn't threatening her with some intangible gift in return. His complete self-centredness was reassuring in a peculiar way. Thus, when he would murmur, with his lips touching her cheek, 'You know, I don't even really *like* you very much,' it didn't disturb her at all because she didn't have to answer. But when Peter, with his mouth in approximately the same position, would whisper 'I love you' and wait for the echo, she had to exert herself.

She guessed that she was using Duncan too, although her motives eluded her; as all her motives tended to these days. The long time she had been moving through (and it was strange to realize that she had after all been moving: she was due to leave for home in another two weeks, the day after a party Peter was going to give, and two, or was it three, weeks after that she would be married) had been merely a period of waiting, drifting with the current, an endurance of time marked by no real event; waiting for an event in the future that had been determined by an event in the past; whereas when she was with Duncan she was caught in an eddy of present time: they had virtually no past and certainly no future.

Duncan was irritatingly unconcerned about her marriage. He would listen to the few things she had to say about it, grin slightly when she would say she thought it was a good idea, then shrug and tell her neutrally that it sounded evil to him but that she seemed to be managing perfectly well and that anyway it was her problem. Then he would direct the conversation towards the complex and ever-fascinating subject of himself. He didn't seem to care about what would happen to her after she passed out of the range of his perpetual present: the only comment he had ever made about the time after her marriage implied that he supposed he would have to dig up another substitute. She found his lack of interest comforting, though she didn't want to know why.

They were passing through the Oriental section. There were many pale vases and glazed and lacquered dishes. Marian glanced at an immense wall-screen that was covered with small golden images of the gods and goddesses, arranged around a gigantic central figure: an obese Buddha-like creature, smiling like Mrs Bogue controlling by divine will her vast army of dwarfed housewives, serenely, inscrutably.

Whatever the reasons though she was always glad when he telephoned, urgent and distraught, and asked her to meet him. They had to arrange out-of-the-way places – snowy parks, art galleries, the occasional bar (though never the Park Plaza) – which meant that their few embraces had been unpremeditated, furtive, gelid, and much hampered by muffling layers of winter clothing. That morning he had phoned her at work and suggested, or rather demanded, the Museum: 'I crave the Museum,' he had said. She had fled the office early, pleading a dental appointment. It didn't matter anyway, she was leaving at last in a week and her successor was already training for the job.

The Museum was a good place: Peter would never go there. She dreaded having Peter and Duncan encounter each other. An irrational dread because for one thing there was no reason, she told herself, why Peter should be upset – it had nothing to do with him, there was obviously no question of competition or anything silly like that – and, for another, even if they did collide she could always explain Duncan as an old friend from college or something of the sort. She would be safe; but what she really seemed to fear was the destruction, not of anything in her relationship with Peter, but of one of the two by the other; though who would be destroyed by whom, or why, she couldn't tell, and most of the time she was surprised at herself for having such vague premonitions.

Nevertheless it was for this reason that she couldn't let him come to her apartment. It would be too great a risk. She had gone to his place several times, but one or both of the roommates had always been there, suspicious and awkwardly resentful. That would make Duncan more nervous than ever and they would leave quickly.

'Why don't they like me?' she asked. They had paused to look at a suit of intricately embossed Chinese armour.

'Who?'

'Them. They always act as though they think I'm trying to gobble you up.'

'Well actually it isn't that they don't like you. As a matter of fact, they've said that you seem like a nice girl and why don't I ask you home to dinner sometime, so they can really get to know you. I haven't told them,' he said, suppressing a smile, 'that you're getting married. So they want a closer look at you to see if you're acceptable to the family. They're trying to protect me. They're worried about me, it's how they get their emotional vitamins, they don't want me to get corrupted. They think I'm too young.'

'But why am I such a threat? What are they protecting you from?'

'Well, you see, you're not in graduate English. And you're a girl.'

'Well, haven't they ever seen a girl before?' she asked indignantly.

Duncan considered. 'I don't think so. Not exactly. Oh I don't know, what do you ever know about your parents? You always think they live in some kind of primal innocence. But I get the impression that Trevor believes in a version of Mediaeval Chastitie, sort of Spenserian you know. As for Fish, well, I guess he thinks it's all right in theory, he's always talking about it and you ought to hear his thesis-topic, it's all about sex, but he thinks you've got to wait for the right person and then it will be like an electric shock. I think he picked it up from Some Enchanted Evening or D. H. Lawrence or something. God, he's been waiting long enough, he's almost thirty. . . .'

Marian felt compassion; she started to make a mental list of ageing single girls she knew who might be suitable for Fish. Millie? Lucy?

They walked on, turned another corner, and found themselves in yet another room full of glass cases. By this time she was thoroughly lost. The labyrinthine corridors and large halls and turnings had confused her sense of direction. There seemed to be no one else in this part of the Museum.

'Do you know where we are?' she asked, a little anxiously.

'Yes,' he said. 'We're almost there.'

They went under another archway. In contrast to the crowded and gilded oriental rooms they had been passing through, this one was comparatively grey and empty. Marian realized, from the murals on the walls, that they were in the Ancient Egyptian section.

'I come up here occasionally,' Duncan said, almost to himself, 'to meditate on immortality. This is my favourite mummy-case.'

Marian looked down through the glass at the painted golden face. The stylized eyes, edged with dark-blue lines, were wide open. They gazed up at her with an expression of serene vacancy. Across the front of the figure, at chest-level, was a painted bird with outstretched wings, each feather separately defined; a similar bird was painted across the thighs, and another one at the feet. The rest of the decorations were smaller: several orange suns, gilded figures with crowns on their heads, seated on thrones or being ferried in boats; and a repeated design of odd symbols that were like eyes.

'She's beautiful,' Marian said. She wondered whether she really thought so. Under the surface of the glass the form had a peculiar floating drowned look; the golden skin was rippling. . . .

'I think it's supposed to be a man,' Duncan said. He had wandered over to the next case. 'Sometimes I think I'd like to live forever. Then you wouldn't have to worry about Time anymore. Ah, Mutabilitie; I wonder why trying to transcend time never even succeeds in stopping it. . . .'

She went to see what he was looking at. It was another mummy-case, opened so that the shrivelled figure inside could be seen. The yellowed linen wrappings had been removed from the head, and the skull with its dried grey skin and wisps of black hair and curiously perfect teeth was exposed. 'Very well preserved,' Duncan commented, in a tone that implied he knew something about the subject. 'They could never do a job like that now, though a lot of those commercial body-snatchers pretend they can.'

Marian shuddered and turned away. She was intrigued, not by the mummy itself – she didn't enjoy looking at things like that – but by Duncan's evident fascination with it. From somewhere the thought drifted into her mind that if she were to reach out and touch him at that moment he would begin to crumble. 'You're being morbid,' she said.

'What's wrong with death?' Duncan said, his voice suddenly loud in the empty room. 'There's nothing morbid about it; we all do it, you know, it's perfectly natural.'

'It's not natural to like it,' she protested, turning toward him. He was grinning at her.

'Don't take me seriously,' he said. 'I've warned you about that. Now come on and I'll show you my womb-symbol. I'm going to show it to Fish pretty soon. He's threatening to write a short monograph for *Victorian Studies* called "Womb-Symbols in Beatrix Potter." He has to be stopped.'

He led her to the far corner of the room. At first in the rapidly fading light she couldn't make out what was inside the case. It looked like a heap of rubble. Then she saw that it was a skeleton, still covered in places with skin, lying on its side with its knees drawn up. There were some clay pots and a necklace lying beside it. The body was so small it looked like that of a child.

'It's sort of pre-pyramid,' Duncan said. 'Preserved by the sands of the desert. When I get really fed up with this place I'm going to go and dig myself in. Maybe the library would serve the purpose just as well; except this city is kind of damp. Things would rot.'

Marian leaned further over the glass case. She found the stunted figure pathetic: with its jutting ribs and frail legs and starved shoulder-blades it looked like the photographs of people from underprivileged countries or concentration camps. She didn't exactly want to gather it up in her arms, but she felt helplessly sorry for it.

When she moved away and glanced up at Duncan, she realized with an infinitesimal shiver of horror that he was reaching out for her. Under the circumstances, his thinness was not reassuring, and she drew back slightly.

'Don't worry,' he said. 'I'm not going to return from the tomb.' He passed his hand over the curve of her cheek, smiling down at her sadly. 'The trouble is, especially with people and when I'm touching them and so on, I can't concentrate on the surface. As long as you only think about the surface I suppose it's all right, and real enough; but once you start thinking about what's inside. . . .'

He bent to kiss her. She swerved, rested her head against his winter-coated shoulder, and closed her eyes. He felt more fragile than usual against her: she was afraid of holding him too tightly.

She heard a creaking of the parquet floor, opened her eyes, and found herself confronted by a pair of austere grey scrutinizing eyes. They belonged to a blue-uniformed guard, who had come up behind them. He tapped Duncan on the shoulder.

'Pardon me, sir,' he said, politely though firmly, 'but – ah – kissing in the Mummy Room is not permitted.'

'Oh,' said Duncan. 'Sorry.'

They wound their way back through the maze of rooms and reached the main staircase. A stream of schoolchildren carrying folding stools was coming out of the gallery opposite, and they were caught up by the current of small moving feet and swept down the marble stairs in a waterfall of strident laughter.

Duncan had suggested that they go for coffee, so they were sitting at a square grubby-surfaced table in the Museum Coffee Shop, surrounded by groups of selfconsciously disconsolate students. Marian had for so long associated having coffee in a restaurant with the office and morning coffee breaks that she kept expecting the three office virgins to materialize across the table from her, beside Duncan.

Duncan stirred his coffee. 'Cream?' he asked.

'No thanks,' she said, but changed her mind and took some after she had reflected that it was nourishing.

'You know, I think it might be a good idea if we went to bed,' Duncan said conversationally, putting his spoon down on the table.

Marian blenched inwardly. She had been justifying whatever had been happening with Duncan (whatever *had* been happening?) on the grounds that it was, according to her standards, perfectly innocent. It had seemed to her lately that innocence had some imperfectly-defined connection with clothing: the lines were drawn by collars and long sleeves. Her justifications always took the form of an imagined conversation with Peter. Peter would say, jealously, 'What's this I hear about you seeing a lot of some scrawny academic type?' And she would reply, 'Don't be silly Peter, it's perfectly innocent. After all, we're getting married in two months.' Or a month and a half. Or a month.

'Don't be silly Duncan,' she said, 'that's impossible. After all, I'm getting married in a month.'

'That's your problem,' he said, 'it has nothing to do with me. And it's me I thought it would be a good idea for.'

'Why?' she asked, smiling in spite of herself. The extent to which he could ignore her point of view was amazing.

'Well of course it's not you. It's just it. I mean you personally don't arouse exactly a raging lust in me or anything. But I thought you would know how, and you'd be competent and sensible about it, sort of calm. Unlike some. I think it would be a good thing if I could get over this thing I have about sex.' He poured some of the sugar out onto the table and started tracing designs in it with his index-finger.

'What thing?'

'Well, maybe I'm a latent homosexual.' He considered that for a moment. 'Or maybe I'm a latent heterosexual. Anyway I'm pretty latent. I don't know why, really. Of course I've taken a number of stabs at it, but then I start thinking about the futility of it all and I give up. Maybe it's because you're expected to do something and after a certain point all I want to do is lie there and stare at the ceiling. When I'm supposed to be writing term-papers I think about sex, but when I've finally got some willing lovely backed into a corner or we're thrashing about under hedges and so on and everybody is supposed to be all set for the *coup de grace*, I start thinking about term-papers. I know it's an alternation of distractions, both of those things are basically distractions you know, but what am I really being distracted from? Anyway they're all too literary, it's because they haven't read enough books. If they'd read more they'd realize that all those scenes have been done already. I mean *ad nauseum*. How can they be so trite? They sort of get limp and sinuous and passionate, they try so hard, and I start thinking oh god it's yet another bad imitation of whoever it happens to be a bad imitation of, and I lose interest. Or worse, I start to laugh. Then they get hysterical.' He licked the sugar from his fingers, thoughtfully.

'What makes you think it would be any different with me?' She was beginning to feel very experienced and professional: almost matronly. The situation, she thought, called for stout shoes and starched cuffs and a leather bag full of hypodermic needles.

'Well,' he said, 'it probably wouldn't be. But now that I've told you at least you wouldn't get hysterical.'

They sat in silence. Marian was thinking about what he had said. She supposed that the impersonality of his request was quite insulting. Why didn't she feel insulted then? Instead she felt she ought to do something helpful and clinical, like taking his pulse.

'Well ...' she said, deliberating. Then she wondered whether anyone had been listening. She glanced around the coffee shop, and her eyes met those of a large man with a beard who was sitting at a table near the door, looking in her direction. She thought he might be an anthropology professor. It was a moment before she recognized him as one of Duncan's room-mates. The blond man with him, sitting with his back to her, must be the other one.

'That's one of your parents over there,' she said.

Duncan swivelled round. 'Oh,' he said. 'I'd better go say hello.' He got up, walked over to their table, and sat down. There was a huddled conversation and he got up and came back. 'Trevor wants to know if you'd like to come to dinner,' he said in the tone of a small child delivering a memorized message.

'Do you want me to?' she asked.

'Me? Oh, sure. I guess so. Why not?'

'Tell him then,' she said, 'that I'd be delighted.' Peter was working on a case and it was Ainsley's night at the clinic.

He went to convey her acceptance. After a minute the two roommates got up and went out, and Duncan slouched back and sat down. 'Trevor said that's thrilling,' he reported, 'and he'll just rush off and pop a few things in the oven. Nothing fancy, he says. We're expected in an hour.'

Marian started to smile, then put her hand over her mouth: she had suddenly remembered all the things she couldn't eat. 'What do you think he'll have?' she asked faintly.

Duncan shrugged. 'Oh, I don't know. He likes skewering things and setting fire to them. Why?'

'Well,' she said, 'there are a lot of things I can't eat; I mean, I haven't been eating them lately. Meat, for instance, and eggs and certain vegetables.'

Duncan did not seem in the least surprised. 'Well, okay,' he said, 'but Trevor's very proud of his cooking. I mean I don't care, I'd just as soon eat hamburger any day, but he'll be insulted if you don't eat at least some of what's on your plate.'

'He'll be even more insulted if I throw it all up,' she said grimly. 'Maybe I'd better not come.'

'Oh, come along, we'll work something out.' His voice had a hint of malicious curiosity.

'I'm sorry, I don't know why I do it, but I can't seem to help it.' She was thinking, maybe I can say I'm on a diet.

'Oh,' said Duncan, 'you're probably representative of modern youth, rebelling against the system; though it isn't considered orthodox to begin with the digestive system. But why not?' he mused. 'I've always thought eating was a ridiculous activity anyway. I'd get out of it myself if I could, though you've got to do it to stay alive, they tell me.'

They stood up and put on their coats.

'Personally,' he said as they went out the door. 'I'd prefer to be fed through the main artery. If I only knew the right people I'm sure it could be arranged. . . .'

Chapter Twenty-two

As they entered the vestibule of the apartment building Marian, who had taken off her gloves, slipped her hand into her coat pocket and turned her engagement ring halfway around on her finger. She did not think it would be courteous to the room-mates, who had misunderstood with such touching concern, to flaunt the enlightening diamond too ostentatiously. Then she took the ring off altogether. Then she thought, 'What am I doing? I'm getting married in a month. Why shouldn't they find out?' and put it back on. Then she thought, 'But I'll never see them again. Why complicate things at this point?' and took it off for the second time and deposited it for safe-keeping in her change-purse.

By now they had gone up the stairs and were at the door of the apartment, which was opened before Duncan had touched the handle by Trevor. He was wearing an apron and was surrounded by a delicate aroma of spices.

'I thought I heard you two out there,' he said. 'Do come in. Dinner'll be a few more minutes, I'm afraid. I'm so glad you could come, ah. . . .' He fixed his pale blue eyes enquiringly on Marian.

'Marian,' Duncan said.

'Oh yes,' said Trevor, 'I don't think we've really met – formally.' He smiled, and a dimple appeared in each cheek. 'You're just getting pot-luck tonight – nothing fancy.' He frowned, sniffed the air, gave a shriek of alarm, and scuttled sideways into the kitchenette.

Marian left her boots on the newspapers outside the door and Duncan took her coat into the bedroom. She walked into the living room, searching for a place to sit down. She didn't want to sit in Trevor's purple chair, nor in Duncan's green one – that would create a problem for Duncan when he came out of the bedroom – nor on the floor among the papers: she might be disarranging someone's thesis; and Fish was barricaded into the red chair with the slab of board across its arms in front of him, writing with great concentration on yet another piece of paper. There was an almost-empty glass by his elbow. Finally she balanced herself on one of the arms of Duncan's chair, folding her hands in her lap.

Trevor warbled out of the kitchenette, bearing a tray with crystal sherry glasses. 'Thank you, this is very nice,' Marian said politely as he dispensed hers. 'What a beautiful glass!'

'Yes, isn't it elegant? It's been in the family for years. There's so little elegance left,' he said, gazing at her right ear as though he could see inside it a vista of an immemorially-ancient but fast-vanishing history. 'Especially in this country. I think we all ought to do our bit to preserve some of it, don't you?'

With the arrival of the sherry Fish had put down his pen. He was now staring fixedly at Marian, not at her face but at her abdomen, somewhere in the vicinity of the navel. She found it disconcerting, and said, to distract him, 'Duncan tells me you've been doing some work on Beatrix Potter. That sounds exciting.'

'Huh? Oh yeah. I was contemplating it, but I've got into Lewis Carroll, that's really more profound. The nineteenth century is very hot property these days, you know.' He threw his head back against the chair and closed his eyes; his words rose in a monotonously-intoned chant through the black thicket of his beard. 'Of course everybody knows *Alice* is a sexual-identity-crisis book, that's old stuff, it's been around for a long time, I'd like to go into it a little deeper though. What we have here, if you only look at it closely, this is the little girl descending into the very suggestive rabbit-burrow, becoming as it were pre-natal, trying to find her role,' he licked his lips, 'her role as a Woman. Yes, well that's clear enough. These patterns emerge. Patterns emerge. One sexual role after another is presented to her but she seems unable to accept any of them, I mean she's really blocked. She rejects Maternity when the baby she's been nursing turns into a pig, nor does she respond positively to the dominating-female role of the Queen and her castration cries of "Off with his head!" And when the Duchess makes a cleverly concealed lesbian pass at her, sometimes you wonder how *conscious* old Lewis was, anyway she's neither aware nor interested; and right after that you'll recall she goes to talk with the Mock-Turtle, enclosed in his shell and his self-pity, a definitely pre-adolescent character; then there are those most suggestive scenes, most suggestive, the one where her neck becomes elongated and she is accused of being a serpent, hostile to eggs, you'll remember, a rather destructively-phallic identity she indignantly rejects; and her negative reaction to the dictatorial Caterpillar, just six inches high, importantly perched on the all-too-female mushroom which is perfectly round but which has the power to make you either smaller or larger than normal, I find that particularly interesting. And of course there's the obsession with time, clearly a cyclical rather than a linear obsession. So anyway she makes a lot of attempts but she refuses to commit herself, you can't say that by the end of the book she has reached anything that can be definitely called maturity. She does much better though in *Through The Looking Glass*, where, as you'll remember. . . .'

There was a smothered but audible snicker. Marian jumped. Duncan must have been standing in the doorway: she hadn't noticed him come in.

Fish opened his eyes, blinked, and frowned at Duncan, but before he could make any comment Trevor bustled into the room.

'Has he been going on about those horrid symbols and things again? I don't approve of that kind of criticism myself, I think *style's* so much more important, and Fischer gets much too Viennese, especially when he drinks. He's very wicked. Besides, he's so out of *date*,' he said cattily. 'The very latest approach to *Alice* is just to dismiss it as a rather charming children's book. I'm almost ready, Duncan could you just help me set the table?'

Fischer sat watching them, sunk in the depths of his chair. They were putting up two card tables, placing the legs carefully in the gaps between the piles of paper, shifting the papers when necessary. Then Trevor spread a white cloth over the two tables and Duncan started to arrange the silverware and dishes. Fish picked up his sherry glass from his board and swallowed the contents at one gulp. He noticed the other glass that was standing there, and emptied that one also.

'There now!' Trevor cried. 'Dinner will be served!'

Marian stood up. Trevor's eyes were glittering and a round red spot of excitement had appeared in the centre of each of his flour-white cheeks. A strand of blond hair had come detached and was hanging limply across his high forehead. He lit the candles on the table, and went around the living room turning off the floorlamps. Finally he removed the board from in front of Fish.

'You sit here, ah, Marian,' he said, and disappeared into the kitchen. She sat down in the card table chair indicated. She could not get as close to the table as she would have liked, because of the legs. She ran her eyes over the dishes, checking: they were to begin with shrimp cocktail. That was all right. She wondered apprehensively what else would be produced for her body's consumption. Evidently there would be many more objects: the table bristled with silverware. She noted with curiosity the ornately-garlanded silver Victorian salt-cellar and the tasteful flower-decoration which stood between the two candles. They were real flowers too, chrysanthemums in an oblong silver dish.

Trevor returned and sat down in the chair nearest the kitchen and they began to eat. Duncan was seated opposite, and Fish to her left, at what she supposed was the foot of the table, or possibly the head. She was glad they were dining by candlelight: it would be easier to dispose of things if necessary. She hadn't as yet the least idea of how she was going to cope, if coping was going to be required, and it did not look as though Duncan would be much help. He seemed to have retreated into himself; he ate mechanically, and while chewing fixed his gaze on the candle flames, which made his eyes appear to be slightly crossed.

'Your silverware is beautiful,' she said to Trevor.

'Yes, isn't it,' he smiled. 'It's been in the family for ages. The china too, I think it's rather heavenly, so much nicer than those stark Danish things everybody is using nowadays.'

Marian inspected the pattern. It was a burgeoning floral design with many scallops, flutings and scrolls. 'Lovely,' she said. 'I'm afraid you've taken too much trouble.'

Trevor beamed. She was obviously saying the right things. 'Oh, no trouble at all. I think eating *well* is awfully important, why eat just to stay alive as most people do? The sauce is my own, do you like it?' He went on without waiting for an answer. 'I can't stand these bottled things, they're so standardized; I can get real horse-radish at the Market down near the waterfront but of course it's so difficult to get fresh shrimp in this city. . . .' He cocked his head to one side as though listening, then sprang out of his chair and pivoted round the corner into the kitchenette.

Fischer, who had not said anything since they had sat down, now opened his mouth and began to speak. Since he continued to eat at the same time, the intake of food and the output of words made a rhythm, Marian commented to herself, much like breathing, and he seemed to be able to handle the alternation quite as automatically; which was a good thing because she was sure that if he paused to think about it something would go down the wrong way. It would be more than painful to have a shrimp caught in one's windpipe; especially with horse-radish sauce. She watched him, fascinated. She was able to stare openly because he had his eyes shut most of the time. His fork found its way to his mouth by some mechanism or sense peculiar to himself, she couldn't imagine how: perhaps batlike supersonic radar-waves bounced back from the fork; or perhaps his individual whiskers functioned like antennae. He didn't break his pace even when Trevor, who had been busily removing the shrimp-cocktail dishes, set his soup plate in front of him, though he opened his eyes long enough to pick up his soup-spoon after a preliminary trial with his fork.

'Now my proposed thesis-topic,' he had begun. 'They may not approve of it, they're very conservative around here, but even if they turn it down I can always write it up for one of the journals, no human thought is ever wasted; anyway it's publish or perish these days, if I can't do it here I can always do it in the States. What I have in mind is something quite revolutionary, "Malthus and the Creative Metaphor," Malthus being of course merely a symbol for what I want to get at, that's the inescapable connection between the rise of the birth-rate in modern times, say the past two or three centuries, especially the eighteenth to the middle of the nineteenth, and the change in the way the critics have been thinking about poetry, with the consequent change in the way poets have been writing it, and oh I could safely extend the thing to cover all of the creative arts. It'll be an interdisciplinary study, a crossing over the presently much too rigid field-lines, a blend of say economics, biology, and literary criticism. People get much too narrow, too narrow, they're specializing too much, that makes you lose sight of a lot of things. Of course I'll have to get some statistics and draw some graphs: thus far I've merely been doing the groundwork thinking, the primary research, the necessary examination of the works of ancient and modern authors. . . .'

They were having sherry with the soup. Fish groped for his sherry glass, almost upsetting it.

Marian was now under cross-fire, since as soon as Trevor had sat down again he had begun to talk at her from the other side, telling her about the soup, which was clear and subtly flavoured: how he had extracted its essences, painstakingly, moment by moment, at a very low heat; and since he was the only person at the table who was looking more or less at her she felt obliged to look at him in return. Duncan wasn't paying any attention to anyone and neither Fish nor Trevor seemed at all disconcerted by the fact that both of them were talking at once. They were evidently used to it. She found however that she could manage by nodding and smiling from time to time and keeping her eyes riveted on Trevor and her ears on Fish, who was continuing, 'You see as long as the population, per square mile especially, was low and the infant mortality rate and the death-rate in general was high, there was a premium on Birth. Man was in harmony with the purposes, the cyclical rhythms of Nature, and the earth said, Produce, Produce. Be fruitful and multiply, if you'll recall. . . .'

Trevor sprang up and dashed around the table, removing the soup plates. His voice and his gestures were becoming more and more accelerated; he was popping in and out of the kitchen like the cuckoo in a cuckoo-clock. Marian glanced at Fish. Apparently he had missed several times with the soup: his beard was becoming glutinous with spilled food. He looked like a highchaired and bewhiskered baby; Marian wished someone would tie a bib around his neck.

Trevor made an entrance with clean plates, and another exit. She could hear him fidgeting about the kitchen, in the background of Fish's voice: 'And so then consequently the poet also thought of himself as the same kind of natural producer; his poem was something begotten so to speak on him by the Muses, or let's say maybe Apollo, hence the term "inspiration," the instilling of breath as it were into; the poet was pregnant with his work, the poem went through a period of gestation, often a long one, and when it was finally ready to see the light of day the poet was delivered of it often with much painful labour. In this way the very process of artistic creation was itself an imitation of Nature, of the thing in nature that was most important to the survival of Mankind. I mean birth; birth. But what do we have nowadays?'

There was a fizzling sound, and Trevor appeared dramatically in the doorway, holding a flaming blue sword in either hand. Marian was the only person who even looked at him.

'Oh my goodness,' she said appreciatively. 'That's quite an effect!'

'Yes, isn't it? I just love things flambé. It's not really shishkebab of course, its a little more French, not so blatant as the Greek kind. ...'

When he dexterously slid whatever was impaled on the skewers onto her plate, she could see that most of it was meat. Well, now her back was to the wall. She would have to think of something. Trevor poured the wine, explaining how hard it was to find really fresh tarragon in this city.

'What we have now, I say, is a society in which all the values are anti-birth. Birth control, they all say, and, It's the population explosion not the atomic explosion that we must all worry about. Malthus, you see, except that war no longer exists as a means of seriously diminishing the population. It's easy to see in this context that the rise of Romanticism ...'

The other dishes contained rice with something in it, an aromatic sauce which went on the meat, and an unidentifiable vegetable. Trevor passed them round. Marian put some of the dark green vegetable substance into her mouth, tentatively, as one would make an offering to a possibly angry god. It was accepted.

'... coincides most informatively with the population increase which had started of course some time earlier but which was reaching almost epidemic proportions. The poet could no longer see himself with any self-congratulation as a surrogate mother-figure, giving birth to his works, delivering as it were another child to society. He had to become a something else, and what really is this emphasis on individual expression, notice it's expression, a pressing out, this emphasis on spontaneity, the instantaneous creation? Not only does the twentieth century have ...'

Trevor was in the kitchen again. Marian surveyed the chunks of meat on her plate with growing desperation. She thought of sliding them under the tablecloth – but they would be discovered. She would have been able to put them into her purse if only she hadn't left it over by the chair. Perhaps she could slip them down the front of her blouse or up her sleeves. ...

'... painters who splatter the paint all over the canvas in practically an orgasm of energy but we have writers thinking the same way about themselves ...'

She reached under the table with her foot and prodded Duncan gently on the shin. He started, and looked across at her. For a moment his eyes held no recognition whatsoever; but then he watched, curious.

She scraped most of the sauce from one of the hunks of meat, picked it up between thumb and finger, and tossed it to him over the candles. He caught it, put it on his plate, and began to cut it up. She started to scrape another piece.

'... no longer as giving birth however; no, long meditation and bringing forth are things of the past. The act of Nature that Art now chooses to imitate, yes is *forced* to imitate, is the very act of copulation. ...'

Marian flung the second chunk, which was also neatly caught. Maybe they should quickly exchange plates, she thought; but no, that would be noticed, he had finished his before Trevor left the room.

'What we need is a cataclysm,' Fish was saying. His voice had become almost a chant, and was swelling in volume; he seemed to be building up to some kind of crescendo. 'A cataclysm. Another Black Death, a vast explosion, millions wiped from the face of the earth, civilization as we know it all but obliterated, then Birth would be essential again, then we could return to the tribe, the old gods, the dark earthgods, the earth goddess, the goddess of waters, the goddess of birth and growth and death. We need a new Venus, a lush Venus of warmth and vegetation and generation, a new Venus, a big-bellied, teeming with life, potential, about to give birth to a new world in all its plenitude, a new Venus rising from the sea. ...'

Fischer decided to stand up, perhaps to give rhetorical emphasis to his last words. To lift himself he placed his hands on the card table, two of whose legs jacknifed, sending Fish's plate slithering into his lap. At that moment the chunk of meat which Marian had just hurled was in mid-air; it caught Duncan squarely in the side of the head, then deflected, bounced across the floor, and landed on a pile of term-papers.

Trevor, a small salad dish in either hand, had stepped through the doorway just in time to witness both events. His jaw dropped.

'At last I know what I really want to be,' Duncan said into the suddenly quiet room. He was gazing serenely at the ceiling, a whitish-grey trace of sauce in his hair. 'An amoeba.'

Duncan had said he would walk her part way home: he needed a breath of fresh air.

Luckily none of Trevor's dishes had been broken, although

several things had been spilled; and when the table had been straightened and Fischer had subsided, muttering to himself, Trevor had gracefully dismissed the whole incident, though for the remainder of the meal, through the salad and the *pêches flambées* and the coconut cookies and the coffee and liqueurs, his manner to Marian had been cooler.

Now, crunching along the snowy street, they were discussing the fact that Fischer had eaten the slice of lemon out of his fingerbowl. 'Trevor doesn't like it, of course,' Duncan said, 'and I told him once that if he doesn't like Fish eating it he shouldn't put one in. But he insists on doing these things properly, though as he says, nobody appreciates his efforts much. I generally eat mine, too, but I didn't today: we had company.'

'It was all very ... interesting,' Marian said. She was considering the total absence all evening of any reference to or question about herself, though she had assumed she was invited because the two room-mates wanted to know more about her. Now, however, she thought it more than likely that they were merely desperate for new audiences.

Duncan looked at her with a sardonic smile. 'Well, now you know what it's like for me at home.'

'You might move out,' she suggested.

'Oh no. Actually I sort of like it. Besides, who else would take such good care of me? And worry about me so much? They do, you know, when they aren't engrossed in their hobbies or off on some other tangent. They spend so much time fussing about my identity that I really shouldn't have to bother with it myself at all. In the long run they ought to make it a lot easier for me to turn into an amoeba.'

'Why are you so interested in amoebas?'

'Oh, they're immortal,' he said, 'and sort of shapeless and flexible. Being a person is getting too complicated.'

They had reached the top of the asphalt ramp that led down to the baseball park. Duncan sat down on the snow bank at one side and lit a cigarette; he never seemed to mind the cold. After a moment she sat down beside him. Since he made no attempt to put his arm around her, she put hers around him.

'The thing is,' he said after a while, 'I'd like something to be real. Not everything, that's impossible, but maybe one or two things. I mean Dr Johnson refuted the theory of the unreality of matter by kicking a stone, but I can't go around kicking my roommates. Or my professors. Besides, maybe my foot's unreal anyway.' He threw the stub of his cigarette into the snow and lit another. 'I thought maybe you would be. I mean if we went to bed, god knows you're unreal enough now, all I can think of is those layers and layers of woolly clothes you wear, coats and sweaters and so on. Sometimes I wonder whether it goes on and on, maybe you're woollen all the way through. It would be sort of nice if you weren't. . . .'

Marian couldn't resist this appeal. She knew she wasn't woollen. 'All right, suppose we did,' she said, speculating. 'We can't go to my place though.'

'And we can't go to mine,' Duncan said, showing neither surprise nor glee at her implied acceptance.

'I guess we'd have to go to a hotel,' she said, 'as married people.'

'They'd never believe it,' he said sadly. 'I don't look married. They're still asking me in bars whether I'm sixteen yet.'

'Don't you have a birth certificate?'

'I did once, but I lost it.' He turned his head and kissed her on the nose. 'I suppose we could go to the kind of hotel where you don't have to be married.'

'You mean ... you'd want me to pose as a – some kind of prostitute?'

'Well? Why not?'

'No,' she said, a little indignantly. 'I couldn't do that.'

'I probably couldn't either,' he said in a gloomy voice. 'And motels are out, I can't drive. Well I guess that's that.' He lit another cigarette. 'Oh well, it's true anyway; doubtless you would be corrupting me. But then again,' he said with mild bitterness, 'maybe I'm incorruptible.'

Marian was looking out over the baseball park. The night was clear and crisp, and the stars in the black sky burnt coldly. It had snowed earlier, fine powdery snow, and the park was a white blank space, untracked. Suddenly she wanted to go down and run and jump in it, making footmarks and mazes and irregular paths. But she knew that in a minute she would be walking sedately as ever across it towards the station.

She stood up, brushing the snow from her coat. 'Coming any further?' she asked.

Duncan stood up too and put his hands into his pockets. His face was shadowed in places and yellowed by the light from the feeble street lamp. 'Nope,' he said. 'See you, maybe.' He turned away, his retreating figure blurring almost noiselessly into the blue darkness.

When she had reached the bright pastel oblong of the subway station, Marian took out her change purse and retrieved her engagement ring from among the pennies, nickels and dimes.

Chapter Twenty-three

Marian was resting on her stomach, eyes closed, an ashtray balanced in the hollow of her bare back where Peter had set it. He was laying beside her, having a cigarette and finishing his double scotch. In the living room the hi-fi set was playing cocktail music.

Although she was keeping her forehead purposefully unwrinkled, she was worrying. That morning her body had finally put its foot down on canned rice pudding, after accepting it with scarcely a tremor for weeks. It had been such a comfort knowing she could rely on it: it provided bulk, and as Mrs Withers the dietician had said, it was fortified. But all at once as she had poured the cream over it her eyes had seen it as a collection of small cocoons. Cocoons with miniature living creatures inside.

Ever since this thing had started she had been trying to pretend there was nothing really wrong with her, it was a superficial ailment, like a rash: it would go away. But now she had to face up to it; she had wondered whether she ought to talk to someone about it. She had already told Duncan, but that was no good; he seemed to find it normal, and what was essentially bothering her was the thought that she might not be normal. This was why she was afraid to tell Peter: he might think she was some kind of freak, or neurotic. Naturally he would have second thoughts about getting married; he might say they should postpone the wedding until she got over it. She would say that, too, if it was him. What she would do after they were married and she couldn't conceal it from him any longer, she couldn't imagine. Perhaps they could have separate meals.

She was drinking her coffee and staring at her uneaten rice pudding when Ainsley came in, wearing her dingy green robe. These days she no longer hummed and knitted; instead she had been reading a lot of books, trying, she said, to nip the problem in the bud.

She assembled her ironized yeast, her wheat-germ, her orange juice, her special laxative and her enriched cereal on the table before sitting down.

'Ainsley,' Marian said, 'do you think I'm normal?'

'Normal isn't the same as average,' Ainsley said cryptically. 'Nobody is normal.' She opened a paperback book and began to read, underlining with a red pencil.

Ainsley wouldn't have been much help anyway. A couple of months ago she would have said it was something wrong with Marian's sex life, which would have been ridiculous. Or some traumatic experience in her childhood, like finding a centipede in the salad or like Len and the baby chicken; but as far as Marian knew there wasn't anything like that in her past. She had never been a picky eater, she had been brought up to eat whatever was on the plate; she hadn't even balked at such things as olives and asparagus and clams, that people say you have to *learn* to like. Lately though Ainsley had been talking a lot about Behaviourism. Behaviourists, she said, could cure diseases like alcoholism and homosexuality, if the patients really wanted to be cured, by showing them images associated with their sickness and then giving them a drug that stopped their breathing.

'They say whatever causes the behaviour, it's the behaviour itself that becomes the problem,' Ainsley had told her. 'Of course there are still a few hitches. If the cause is deep-rooted enough, they simply switch their addiction, like from alcohol to dope; or they commit suicide. And what I need is not a cure but a prevention. Even if they can cure him – if he *wants* to be cured,' she said darkly, 'he'll still blame me for causing it in the first place.'

But Behaviourism, Marian thought, wouldn't be much use in her case. How could it work on any condition so negative? If she were a glutton it would be different; but they couldn't very well show her images of *non*-eating and then stop her breathing.

She had gone over in her mind the other people she might talk to. The office virgins would be intrigued and would want to hear all about it, but she didn't think they would be able to give her any constructive advice. Besides, if she told one they'd all know and soon everyone they knew would know: you could never tell how it might get back to Peter. Her other friends were elsewhere, in other towns, other cities, other countries, and writing it in a letter would make it too final. The lady down below . . . that was the bottom of the barrel; she would be like the relatives, she would be dismayed without understanding. They would all think it in bad taste for Marian to have anything wrong with what they would call her natural functions.

She decided to go and see Clara. It was a faint hope – surely Clara wouldn't be able to offer any concrete suggestions – but at least she would listen. Marian telephoned her to make certain she would be in, and left work early.

She found Clara in the play-pen with her second youngest child. The youngest was asleep in its carrier on the dining room table, and Arthur was nowhere to be seen.

'I'm so glad you came,' she said, 'Joe's down at the university. I'll get out in a minute and make the tea. Elaine doesn't like the play-pen,' she explained, 'and I'm helping her get used to it.'

'I'll make the tea,' Marian said; she thought of Clara as a perpetual invalid and connected her with meals carried on trays. 'You stay where you are.'

It took her some time to find everything but at last she had the tray arranged, with tea and lemon and some digestive biscuits she had discovered in the laundry basket, and she carried it in and set it on the floor. She handed Clara her cup over the bars.

'Well,' said Clara when Marian had settled herself on the rug, so as to be on the same level, 'how's everything? I bet you're busy these days, getting ready and all.'

Looking at her sitting in there with the baby chewing on the buttons of her blouse, Marian found herself being envious of Clara for the first time in three years. Whatever was going to happen to Clara had already happened: she had turned into what she was going to be. It wasn't that she wanted to change places with Clara; she only wanted to know what she was becoming, what direction she was taking, so she could be prepared. It was waking up in the morning one day and finding she had already changed without being aware of it that she dreaded.

'Clara,' she said, 'do you think I'm normal?' Clara had known her a long time; her opinion would be worth something.

Clara considered. 'Yes, I would say you're normal,' she said, removing a button from Elaine's mouth. 'I'd say you're almost abnormally normal, if you know what I mean. Why?'

Marian was reassured. That was what she herself would have said. But if she was so normal, why had this thing chosen to attack *her*?

'Something's been happening to me lately,' she said. 'I don't know what to do about it.'

'Oh, what's that? No, you little pig, that's mummy's.'

'I can't eat certain things; I get this awful feeling.' She wondered whether Clara was paying as much attention as she ought to.

'I know what you mean,' said Clara, 'I've always felt that way about liver.'

'But these are things I used to be able to eat. It isn't that I don't like the taste; it's the whole. . . .' It was difficult to explain.

'I expect it's bridal nerves,' Clara said, 'I threw up every morning for a week before my wedding. So did Joe,' she added. 'You'll get over it. Did you want to know anything about ... sex?' she asked, with a delicacy Marian found ludicrous, coming from Clara.

'No, not really thanks,' she had said. Though she was sure Clara's explanation wasn't the right one she had felt better.

The record had begun to play from the middle again. She opened her eyes; from where she was lying she could see a green plastic aircraft carrier floating in the circle of light from Peter's desk lamp. Peter had a new hobby, putting together model ships from model ship kits. He said he found it relaxing. She herself had helped with that one, reading the directions out loud and handing him the pieces.

She turned her head on the pillow and smiled at Peter. He smiled back at her, his eyes shining in the semi-darkness.

'Peter,' she said, 'am I normal?'

He laughed and patted her on the rump. 'I'd say from my limited experience that you're marvellously normal, darling.' She sighed; she didn't mean it that way.

'I could use another drink,' Peter said; it was his way of asking her to get one. The ashtray was removed from her back. She turned over and sat up, pulling the top sheet off the bed and wrapping it around her. 'And while you're up, flip over the record, that's a good girl.'

Marian turned the record, feeling naked in the open expanse of the living room in spite of the sheet and the venetian blinds; then she went into the kitchen and measured out Peter's drink. She was hungry – she hadn't had much for dinner – so she unboxed the cake she had bought that afternoon on the way back from Clara's. The day before had been Valentine's Day and Peter had sent her a dozen roses. She had felt guilty, thinking she ought to have given him something but not knowing what. The cake wasn't a real gift, only a token. It was a heart with pink icing and probably stale, but it was the shape that mattered.

She got out two of Peter's plates and two forks and two paper napkins; then she cut the cake. She was surprised to find that it was pink in the inside too. She put a forkful into her mouth and chewed it slowly; it felt spongy and cellular against her tongue, like the bursting of thousands of tiny lungs. She shuddered and spat the cake out into her napkin and scraped her plate into the garbage; after that she wiped her mouth off with the edge of the sheet.

She walked in to the bedroom, carrying Peter's drink and the plate. 'I've brought you some cake,' she said. It would be a test, not of Peter but of herself. If he couldn't eat his either then she was normal.

'Aren't you nice.' He took the plate and the glass from her and set them on the floor.

'Aren't you going to eat it?' For a moment she was hopeful.

'Later,' he said, 'later.' He was unwinding her from the sheet. 'You're a bit chilly, darling; come here and be warmed up.' His mouth tasted of scotch and cigarettes. He pulled her down on top of him, the sheet rustling whitely around them, his clean familiar soap-smell enfolding her; in her ears the light cocktail music went on and on.

Later, Marian was resting on her stomach with an ashtray balanced in the hollow of her back; this time her eyes were open. She was watching Peter eat. 'I really worked up an appetite,' he had said, grinning at her. He didn't seem to notice anything odd about the cake: he hadn't even winced.

Chapter Twenty-four

All at once it was the day of Peter's final party. Marian had spent the afternoon at the hairdresser's: Peter had suggested that she might have something done with her hair. He had also hinted that perhaps she should buy a dress that was, as he put it, 'not quite so mousy' as any she already owned, and she had duly bought one. It was short, red, and sequinned. She didn't think it was really her, but the saleslady did. 'It's you, dear,' she had said, her voice positive.

It had needed an alteration so she had picked it up when she came from the hairdresser's and was carrying it now in its pink and silver cardboard box as she walked towards the house across the slippery road, balancing her head on her neck as though she was a juggler with a fragile golden bubble. Even outside in the cold late-afternoon air she could smell the sweetly-artificial perfume of the hairspray he had used to glue each strand in place. Though she'd asked him not to put on too much; but they never did what you wanted them to. They treated your head like a cake: something to be carefully iced and ornamented.

She usually did her hair herself, so she had got the name of the establishment from Lucy, thinking she would know about such places; but perhaps that had been a mistake. Lucy had a face and shape that almost demanded the artificial: nailpolish and makeup and elaborate arrangements of hair blended into her, became part of her. Surely she would look peeled or amputated without them; whereas Marian had always thought that on her own body these things looked extra, stuck to her surface like patches or posters.

As soon as she had walked into the large pink room – everything had been pink and mauve, it was amazing how such frivolously feminine decorations could look at the same time so functional – she had felt as passive as though she was being admitted to a hospital to have an operation. She had checked her appointment with a mauve-haired young woman who despite her false eyelashes and iridescent talons was disturbingly nurse-like and efficient; then she had been delivered over to the waiting staff.

The shampoo girl wore a pink smock and had sweaty armpits and strong professional hands. Marian had closed her eyes, leaning back against the operating-table, while her scalp was soaped and scraped and rinsed. She thought it would be a good idea if they would give anaesthetics to the patients, just put them to sleep while all these necessary physical details were taken care of; she didn't enjoy feeling like a slab of flesh, an object.

Then they had strapped her into the chair – not really strapped in, but she couldn't get up and go running out into the winter street with wet hair and a surgical cloth around her neck – and the doctor had set to work. A young man in a white smock who smelled of cologne and had deft spindly fingers and shoes with painted toes. She had sat motionless, handing him the clamps, fascinated by the draped figure prisoned in the filigreed gold oval of the mirror and by the rack of gleaming instruments and bottled medicines on the counter in front of her. She couldn't see what he was doing behind her back. Her whole body felt curiously paralysed.

When at last all the clamps and rollers and clips and pins were in place, and her head resembled a mutant hedgehog with a covering of rounded hairy appendages instead of spikes, she was led away and installed under a dryer and switched on. She looked sideways down the assembly-line of women seated in identical mauve chairs under identical whirring mushroom-shaped machines. All that was visible was a row of strange creatures with legs of various shapes and hands that held magazines and heads that were metal domes. Inert; totally inert. Was this what she was being pushed towards, this compound of the simply vegetable and the simply mechanical? An electric mushroom.

She resigned herself to the necessity of endurance, and picked up a movie star magazine from the stack at her elbow. A blonde woman with enormous breasts spoke to her from the back cover: 'Girls! Be Successful! If you want to really Go Places, Develop Your Bust. . . .'

After one of the nurses had pronounced her dry she was returned to the doctor's chair to have the stitches taken out; she found it rather incongruous that they weren't wheeling her back on a table. She passed along the gently-frying line of those who were not yet done, and soon her head was being unwound and brushed and combed; then the doctor was smiling and holding a hand mirror at an angle so that she could see the back of her head. She looked. He had built her usually straight hair up into a peculiar shape embellished with many intricate stiff curved wisps, and had manufactured two tusk-like spitcurls which projected forward, one on each cheekbone.

'Well,' she said dubiously, frowning at the mirror, 'it's a little – um – extreme for me.' She thought it made her look like a callgirl.

'Ah, but you should wear it this way more often,' he said with Italianate enthusiasm, his rapturous expression nevertheless fading a shade. 'You should try new things. You should be *daring*, eh?' He laughed roguishly at her, displaying an unnatural number of white even teeth and two gold ones; his breath was flavoured with peppermint mouthwash.

She considered asking him to comb out some of his special effects, but decided not to, partly because she was intimidated by his official surroundings and specialist implements and dentist-like certainty – he must know what was right, it was his business – but partly because she found herself shrugging mentally. After all, she had taken the leap, she had walked through that gilded chocolate-box of her own free will and this was the consequence and she had better accept it. 'Peter will probably like it. Anyway,' she reflected, 'it will go with the dress.'

Still half etherized, she had plunged into one of the large department stores nearby, intending to take a short-cut through the basement to the subway station. She had gone quickly through the Household Wares section, past the counters that held frying-pans and casserole dishes, and the display models of vacuum-cleaners and automatic washers. They reminded her, uneasily, both of the surprise shower the girls at the office had given her the day before, her last day of work, which had involved the bestowing of tea-towels and ladles and beribboned aprons and advice, and of the several anxious letters she had got recently from her mother, urging her to choose her patterns – china and crystal and silverware – because people were wanting to know what to get for wedding presents. She had taken trips to various stores for the purpose of making the selection, but had been so far quite unable to make up her mind. And she was leaving on the bus for home the next day. Well, she would do it later.

She rounded a counter lush with artificial plastic flowers and walked along what seemed to be a main aisle that led somewhere. In front of her a small frantic man was standing on a pedestal, demonstrating a new kind of grater with an apple-coring attachment. He was pattering and grating simultaneously, non-stop, holding up a handful of shredded carrot, then an apple with a neat round hole in its centre. A cluster of women with shopping-bags watched silently, their heavy coats and overshoes drab in the basement light, their eyes shrewd and sceptical.

Marian stopped for a minute on the outer fringe of the group. The little man made a radish-rose with yet another attachment. Several of the women turned and glanced at her in an appraising way, summing her up. Anyone with a hair-style like that, they must have been thinking, would be far too trivial to be seriously interested in graters. How long did it take to acquire that patina of lower-middle income domesticity, that weathered surface of slightly mangy fur, cloth worn thin at cuff-edges and around buttons, scuffed leather of handbags; the tight slant of the mouth, the gauging eyes; and above all that invisible colour that was like a smell, the underpainting of musty upholstery and worn linoleum that made them in this bargain basement authentic in a way that she was not? Somehow Peter's future income cancelled the possibility of graters. They made her feel like a dilettante.

The little man started briskly to reduce a potato to a pulp. Marian lost her interest and continued her search for the yellow subway sign.

When she opened the front door she was met by a gabble of female voices. She took off her boots in the vestibule and put them on the newspapers that were there for that purpose. A number of other pairs had been deposited, many with thick soles and some with black fur tops. As she went past the parlour doorway she caught a glimpse of dresses and hats and necklaces. The lady down below was having a tea party; they must be the Imperial Daughters, or perhaps they were the Women Christian Temperates. The child, in maroon velvet with a lace collar, was passing cakes.

Marian climbed the stairs as noiselessly as she could. For some reason she had not yet spoken to the lady down below about giving up the apartment. She should have done it weeks ago. The delay might mean having to pay another month's rent for insufficient notice. Maybe Ainsley would want to keep it on with another room-mate; but she doubted it. In another few months that would be impossible.

When she had climbed the second flight of stairs she could hear Ainsley talking in the living room. The voice was harder, more insistent, angrier than she had ever heard it before: Ainsley did not usually lose her temper. Another voice was interrupting, answering. It was Leonard Slank's.

'Oh no,' Marian thought. They seemed to be having an argument. She definitely did not want to get involved. She intended to slip quietly into her room and close the door, but Ainsley must have heard her coming up the stairs: her head appeared abruptly from the living room, followed by quantities of loose red hair and then by the rest of her body. She was dishevelled and had been crying.

'Marian!' she half-wailed, half-commanded. 'You've got to come in here and talk to Len. You've got to make him listen to *reason*! I like your hair,' she added perfunctorily.

Marian trailed after her into the living room, feeling like a child's wheeled wooden toy being pulled along by a string, but she didn't know on what grounds, moral or otherwise, she could base a refusal. Len was standing in the middle of the room, looking even more disturbed than Ainsley.

Marian sat down on a chair, keeping her coat on as a shock-absorber. The other two both stared angrily and beseechingly at her in silence.

Then, 'My God!' Len almost shouted. 'After all that, now she wants me to *marry* her!'

'Well, what's the matter with you anyway! You don't want a homosexual son, do you?' Ainsley demanded.

'Goddamn it, I don't want any son at all! I didn't want it, you did it yourself, you should have it removed, there must be some kind of pill. . . .'

'That's not the *point*, don't be ridiculous, the point is of course I'm going to have the baby; but it should have the best circumstances, and it's your responsibility to provide it with a father. A father-image.' Ainsley was now trying a slightly more patient and cool-headed approach.

Len paced across the floor. 'How much do they cost? I'll buy you one. Anything. But I'm *not* going to marry you, dammit. Don't give me that responsibility stuff either, I'm not responsible anyway. It was all your doing, you deliberately allowed me to get myself drunk, you seduced me, you practically *dragged* me into. . . .'

'That isn't quite how I remember it,' Ainsley said, 'and I was in a condition to remember it a lot more clearly than you can. Anyway,' she continued with relentless logic, 'you thought you were seducing me. And after all, that's important too, isn't it: your motives. Suppose you really *had* been seducing me and I'd got pregnant accidentally. What would you do then? You'd certainly be responsible then, wouldn't you? So it *is* your responsibility.'

Len contorted his face, his smile an anaemic parody of cynical sarcasm. 'You're like all the rest of them, you're a sophist,' he said in a quaveringly-savage voice. 'You're twisting the truth. Let's stick to the facts, shall we dear? I *didn't* seduce you really, it was. . . .'

'That doesn't *matter*,' Ainsley said, her voice rising. 'You *thought* you. . . .'

'For God's sake can't you be *realistic*!' Leonard shrieked.

Marian had been sitting quietly, looking from one to the other, thinking how peculiarly they were acting; so out-of-control. Now she said, 'Could we please be a little less noisy? The lady down below might hear.'

'Oh, SCREW the lady down below!' Len roared.

This novel idea was so blasphemous and at the same time so ludicrous that both Ainsley and Marian broke into horrified and delighted giggles. Len glared at them. This was the final outrage, the final feminine insolence – after putting him through all that, she was laughing at him! He snatched up his coat from the back of the chesterfield and strode towards the stairs.

'You and your goddamn fertility-worship can go straight to hell!' he shouted, plunging downwards.

Ainsley, seeing the father-image escaping, remoulded her features into an imploring expression and ran after him. 'Oh Len, come back and let's talk it over seriously,' she pleaded. Marian followed them down the stairs, impelled less by a sense of being able to do anything concrete or helpful than by some obscure herd- or lemming-instinct. Everyone else was leaping over the cliff, she might as well go too.

Len's descent was halted by the spinning-wheel on the landing. He was temporarily snarled in it, and tugged and swore loudly. By the time he was able to start down the next flight of stairs Ainsley had caught up to him and was pulling at his sleeve, and all the ladies, as alert to the symptoms of wickedness as a spider to the vibrations of its web, had come fluttering out of the parlour and were gathered at the foot of the stairs, gazing up with a certain gloating alarm. The child was among them, still holding a plate of cakes, her mouth slackly open, her eyes wide. The lady down below in black silk and pearls was being dignified in the background.

Len looked over his shoulder, then down the stairs. Retreat was impossible. He was surrounded by the enemy; there was no choice but to go bravely forward.

Not only that, he had an audience. His eyes rolled in his head like those of a frenzied spaniel. 'All you clawed scaly bloody predatory whoring fucking bitches can go straight to hell! All of you! Underneath you're all the same!' he shouted, with, Marian thought, rather good enunciation.

He wrenched his sleeve out of Ainsley's clutch. 'You'll never get me!' he screamed, charging down the stairs, his coat streaming behind him like a cape, scattering the assembled ladies before him in a blither of afternoon prints and velvet flowers, and gained the front door, which closed behind him with a thunderous crash. On the wall the yellowed ancestors rattled in their frames.

Ainsley and Marian retreated up the stairs, to the sound of excited bleating and twittering from the ladies in the parlour. The voice of the lady down below was rising above the others, calm and soothing: 'The young man was obviously inebriated.'

'Well,' Ainsley said in a clipped practical voice when they were in the living room once more, 'I guess that's that.'

Marian didn't know whether she was referring to Leonard or to the lady down below. 'What's what?' she asked.

Ainsley pushed her hair back over her shoulders and straightened her blouse. 'I don't think he's going to come round. It's just as well: I doubt if he'd make a very good one anyway. I'll simply have to get another one, that's all.'

'Yes; I guess so,' Marian said vaguely. Ainsley went into the bedroom, her firm stride expressing determination, and shut the door. The matter sounded ominously settled. She seemed to have decided on another plan already, but Marian didn't even want to think about what it might be. Thinking would be of no use anyway. Whatever course it took, there would be nothing she herself could do to prevent it.

Chapter Twenty-five

She went into the kitchen and took off her coat. Then she ate a vitamin-pill, remembering as she did so that she had not had any lunch that day. She ought to put something in her stomach.

She opened the refrigerator to see what was in there that might be edible. The freezing-compartment was so thickly encrusted with ice that its door wouldn't stay shut. It contained two icecube trays and three suspicious-looking cardboard packages. The other shelves were crowded with various objects, in jars, on plates with bowls inverted over them, in waxed-paper packets and brown-paper bags. The ones toward the back had been there longer than she cared to remember. Some of them were definitely beginning to smell. The only thing she could see that interested her at all was a hunk of yellow cheese. She took it off the rack: it had a thin layer of green mould on the underside. She put it back and closed the door. She decided she wasn't hungry anyway.

'Maybe I'll have a cup of tea,' she said to herself. She looked into the cupboard where they kept the dishes: it was empty. That meant she would have to wash a cup, they had all been used. She went to the sink and peered in.

It was full of unwashed dishes: stacks of plates, glasses half-filled with organic-looking water, bowls with vestiges of things that had ceased to be recognizable. There was a saucepan that had once held macaroni and cheese; its inner surface was spotted with bluish mould. A glass dessert dish sitting in the puddle of water at the bottom of the pot was filmed over with a grey slippery-looking growth reminiscent of algae in ponds. The cups were in there too, all of them, standing one inside another, ringed with dregs of tea and coffee and scums of cream. Even the white porcelain surface of the sink had developed a skin of brown. She did not want to disturb anything for fear of discovering what was going on out of sight:

heaven only knew what further botulisms might be festering underneath. 'Disgraceful,' she said. She had a sudden urge to make a clean sweep, to turn the taps full on and squirt everything with liquid detergent; her hand even moved forward; but then she paused. Perhaps the mould had as much right to life as she had. The thought was not reassuring.

She wandered into the bedroom. It was too early to start dressing for the party, but she couldn't think of anything else she could do to fill up the time. She took her dress out of its cardboard box and hung it up; then she put on her dressing-gown and gathered together her bath equipment. She would be descending into the lady down below's territory and might have to brave an encounter; but, she thought, I'll just deny any connection with the whole mess and let her battle it out with Ainsley.

When the bathtub was filling she brushed her teeth, examining them in the mirror over the basin to make sure she hadn't missed anything, an established habit, she did it even when she hadn't been eating; it was remarkable, she thought, how much time you spend with a scouring brush in your hand and your mouth full of foam, peering down your own throat. She noticed that a tiny pimple had appeared to the right of one of her eyebrows. That's because I'm not eating properly, she decided: my metabolism or chemical balance or something has got upset. As she gazed at the small red spot it seemed to shift position a fraction of an inch. She ought to have her eyes examined, things were beginning to blur; it must be an astigmatism, she thought as she spat into the sink.

She took off her engagement ring and deposited it in the soap dish. It was a little too large for her – Peter had said they should get it cut down to size, though Clara said No, it would be best to leave it, since your fingers swelled up as you got older, especially when you were pregnant – and she had developed a fear of seeing it disappear down the drain. Peter would be furious: he was very fond of it. Then she clambered into the bathtub over the high old-fashioned side and lowered herself into the warm water.

She occupied herself with the soap. The water was lulling, relaxing. She had lots of time; she could indulge her desire to lie back with her enamelled hair placed for security against the slope of the tub, to float with the water washing gently over her nearly-submerged body. From their elevated position her eyes had a long vista of white concave enclosing walls and semi-transparent water, her body islanded, extending in a series of curves and hollows down towards the terminal peninsula of legs and the reefs of toes; and beyond that a wire rack with the soap dish, and then the taps.

There were two taps, one for the hot and one for the cold. Each had a round bulb-shaped silver base and there was a third bulb in the middle with the spout where the water came out. She looked more closely: in each of the three silver globes she could see now that there was a curiously-sprawling pink thing. She sat up, stirring the water into minor tidal waves, to see what they were. It was a moment before she recognized, in the bulging and distorted forms, her own waterlogged body.

She moved, and all three of the images moved also. They were not quite identical: the two on the outside were slanted inwards towards the third. How peculiar it was to see three reflections of yourself at the same time, she thought; she swayed herself back and forth, watching the way in which the different bright silver parts of her body suddenly bloated or diminished. She had almost forgotten that she was supposed to be taking a bath. She stretched one hand towards the taps, wanting to see it grow.

There were footsteps outside the door. She had better get out: it must be the lady down below trying to get in. She began to splash off the remaining traces of soap. Looking down, she became aware of the water, which was covered with a film of calcinous hard-water particles of dirt and soap, and of the body that was sitting in it, somehow no longer quite her own. All at once she was afraid that she was dissolving, coming apart layer by layer like a piece of cardboard in a gutter puddle.

She pulled the plug hastily and scrambled out of the tub. It was safer on the dry beach of the cold tiled floor. She slid her engagement ring back onto her finger, seeing the hard circle for a moment as a protective talisman that would help keep her together.

But the panic was still with her as she climbed the stairs. She could not face the party, all those people, Peter's friends were nice enough but they didn't really know her, fixing their uncomprehending eyes on her, she was afraid of losing her shape, spreading out, not being able to contain herself any longer, beginning (that would be worst of all) to talk a lot, to tell everybody, to cry. She contemplated bleakly the festive red dress hanging in her closet. What can I do? her mind kept thinking. She sat down on her bed.

She remained sitting on the bed, gnawing idly on the end of one of her fringed dressing-gown ties, closed in a sodden formless unhappiness that seemed now to have been clogging her mind for a long time, how long she could not remember. With its weight pressing around her it was most improbable that she would ever manage to get up off the bed. I wonder what time it is? she said to herself. I've got to get ready.

The two dolls which she had never thrown out after all were staring blankly back at her from the top of the dresser. As she looked at them their faces blurred, then re-formed, faintly malevolent. She was irritated with them for sitting there inertly on either side of the mirror, just watching her, not offering any practical suggestions. But now that she examined their faces more closely she could see that it was only the dark one, the one with the peeling paint, that was definitely watching her. Perhaps the blonde one didn't even see her, the round blue eyes in its rubbery face were gazing straight through her.

She substituted one of her fingers for the dressing-gown tie, biting at the side of her nail. Or perhaps it was a game, an agreement they had made. She saw herself in the mirror between them for an instant as though she was inside them, inside both of them at once, looking out: herself, a vague damp form in a rumpled dressing-gown, not quite focussed, the blonde eyes noting the arrangement of her hair, her bitten fingernails, the dark one looking deeper, at something she could not quite see, the two overlapping images drawing further and further away from each other; the centre, whatever it was in the glass, the thing that held them together, would soon be quite empty. By the strength of their separate visions they were trying to pull her apart.

She couldn't stay there any longer. She pushed herself off the bed and into the hallway, where she found herself crouching over the telephone and dialing a number. There was ringing, then a click. She held her breath.

'Hullo?' said a sullen voice.

'Duncan?' she said tentatively. 'It's me.'

'Oh.' There was a pause.

'Duncan, could you come to a party tonight? At Peter's place? I know it's late to ask you, but. . . .'

'Well, we're supposed to be going to a brain-picking graduate English party,' he said. 'The whole family.'

'Well, maybe you could come on later. And you could even bring them with you.'

'Well, I don't know. . . .'

'*Please*, Duncan, I don't really know anybody there, I *need* you to come,' she said with an intensity which was unfamiliar to her.

'No you don't,' he said. 'But maybe we'll come though. This other thing sounds pretty dull, all they ever do is talk about their Orals, and it would be sort of a kick to see what you're getting married to.'

'Oh thank you,' she said gratefully, and gave him directions.

When she had put down the phone she felt a lot better. So that was the answer, then: to make sure there were people at the party who really knew her. That would keep everything in the right perspective, she would be able to cope. . . . She dialled another number.

She spent half an hour on the phone; by that time she had rounded up a sufficient number of people. Clara and Joe were coming if they could get a baby-sitter, that made five counting the other three; and the three office virgins. After their initial hesitations, caused she supposed by the lateness of the invitation, she had hooked the three firmly by saying that she hadn't asked them before because she thought it was going to be mostly married people, but that several unescorted bachelors were coming, and could they do her the favour of coming along too? Things got so dull for single men at couple-parties, she had added. That made eight altogether. As an afterthought she had asked Ainsley – it would be good for her to get out – and she accepted, surprisingly: it wasn't her kind of party.

Although she considered it in passing, Marian did not think it would be a wise move to ask Leonard Slank.

Now she was all right she could begin to dress. She oozed herself into the new girdle she had got to go with the dress, noting that she hadn't really lost much weight: she had been eating a lot of noodles. She hadn't intended to buy one at all, but the saleslady who was selling her the dress and who was thoroughly corseted herself said that she ought to, and produced an appropriate model with satin panelling and a bow of ribbon at the front. 'Of course you're very *thin* dear, you don't really need one, but still that *is* a close-fitting dress and you wouldn't want it to be obvious that you haven't got one on, would you?' She had lifted her pencilled brows. At that time it had seemed like a moral issue. 'No, of course not,' Marian had said hastily, 'I'll take it.'

When she had slithered into her red dress, she found she couldn't reach behind far enough to do up the zipper. She knocked on Ainsley's door. 'Do up my zipper, please?' she asked.

Ainsley was in her slip. She had begun to put on her makeup, but thus far only one of her eyes had acquired its outline of black and her eyebrows hadn't appeared at all, which made her face look unbalanced. After she had done up Marian's zipper and the little hook at the top, she stood back and examined her critically. 'That's a good dress,' she said, 'but what are you going to wear with it?'

'With it?'

'Yes, it's very dramatic; you need some good heavy earrings or something to set it off. Have you got any?'

'I don't know,' said Marian. She went into her own room and brought back the drawer that held the trinkets accumulated from her relatives. They were all variations of clustered imitation pearls and pastel arrangements of seashells and metal-and-glass flowers and cute animals.

Ainsley pawed through them. 'No,' she said, with the decisiveness of someone who really knew. 'These won't do. I've got a pair that'll work, though.' After a search which involved much rustling in drawers and overturning of things on the bureau, she produced a couple of chunky dangly gold objects, which she screwed to Marians ears. 'That's better,' she said. 'Now smile.'

Marian smiled, weakly.

Ainsley shook her head. 'Your hair's okay,' she said, 'but really you'd better let me do your face for you. You'll never manage it by yourself. You'd just do it in your usual skimpy way and come out looking like a kid playing dress-up in her mother's clothes.'

She wadded Marian into her chair, which was lumpy with garments in progressive stages of dirtiness, and tucked a towel around her neck. 'I'll do your nails first so they can be drying,' she said, adding while she began to file them, 'looks like you've been biting them.' When the nails had been painted a shimmering off-white and Marian was holding her hands carefully in the air, she went to work on Marian's face, using mixtures and instruments from a jumble of beauty-aids that covered her dressing-table.

During the rest of the procedure, while strange things were being done to her skin, then to each eye and each eyebrow, Marian sat passively, marvelling at the professional efficiency with which Ainsley was manipulating her features. It reminded her of the mothers backstage at public-school plays, making up their precocious daughters. She had only a fleeting thought about germs.

Finally Ainsley took a lipstick-brush and painted the mouth with several coats of glossy finish. 'There,' she said, holding a hand-mirror so that Marian could see herself. 'That's better. But be careful till the eyelash-glue is dry.'

Marian stared into the egyptian-lidded and outlined and thickly-fringed eyes of a person she had never seen before. She was afraid even to blink, for fear that this applied face would crack and flake with the strain. 'Thank you,' she said doubtfully.

'Now smile,' said Ainsley.

Marian smiled.

Ainsley frowned. 'Not like *that*,' she said. 'You've got to throw yourself *into* it more. Sort of droop your eyelids.'

Marian was embarrassed: she didn't know how. She was experimenting, looking in the mirror, trying to find out which particular set of muscles would produce the desired effect, and had just succeeded in getting an approximate droop that still however had a suggestion of a squint in it, when they heard footsteps ascending the stairs; and a moment later the lady down below stood in the doorway, breathing heavily.

Marian removed the towel from her neck and stood up. Now that she had got her eyelids drooped she could not immediately get them undrooped again, back to their usual capable and level width. It was going to be impossible in this red dress and this face to behave with the ordinary matter-of-fact politeness that the situation was going to require.

The lady down below gasped a little when she saw Marian's new ensemble – bare arms and barish dress and well-covered face – but her real target was Ainsley, who stood bare-footed in her slip with one eye black-ringed and her auburn hair tendrilling over her shoulders.

'Miss Tewce,' the lady down below began. She was still wearing her tea-dress and pearls: she was going to attempt dignity. 'I have waited until I am perfectly calm to speak to you. I don't want any unpleasantness, I've always tried to avoid scenes and unpleasantness, but now I'm afraid you'll have to go.' She was not at all calm: her voice was trembling. Marian noticed that she was clenching a lace handkerchief in one hand. 'The drinking was bad enough, I know all those bottles were yours, I'm sure Miss McAlpin never drank, not more than one should' – her eyes flicked again over Marian's dress; her faith somewhat shaken, but she let the comment pass – 'though at least you were fairly discreet about all the liquor you were carrying into this house; and I couldn't say anything about the untidyness and disorder, I'm a tolerant person and what a person does in their own living-quarters has always been entirely their own business as far as I'm concerned. And I turned the other way when that young man as I'm perfectly aware, don't try to *lie* to me, was here overnight, I even went out the next morning to avoid unpleasantness. At least the child didn't know. But to make it so public' – she was shrilling now, in a vibrant accusing voice – 'dragging your disreputable, drunken friends out into the open, where people can *see* them ... and it's such a bad example for the child....'

Ainsley glared at her; the black-rimmed eye flashed. 'So,' she said in an equally accusing voice, tossing back her hair and planting her bare feet further apart on the floor, 'I've always suspected you of being a hypocrite and now I know. You're a bourgeois fraud, you have no real convictions at all, you're just worried about what the neighbours will say. Your precious reputation. Well, I consider that kind of thing immoral. I'd like you to know that *I'm* going to have a child too, and I certainly wouldn't choose to bring him up in *this* house – you'd teach him dishonesty. You'd be a bad example, and let me tell you that you're by far the most anti-Creative-Life-Force person I've ever met. I will be most pleased to move and the sooner the better; I don't want you exerting any negative pre-natal influences.'

The lady down below had turned quite pale. 'Oh,' she said faintly, clutching at her pearls. 'A baby! Oh, oh, oh!' She turned, emitting small cries of outrage and dismay, and tottered away down the stairs.

'I guess you'll have to move,' said Marian. She felt safely remote from this fresh complication. She was leaving for home the next day anyway; and now that the lady down below had finally forced a confrontation she couldn't imagine why she had ever been even slightly afraid of her. She had been so easily deflated.

'Yes, of course,' Ainsley said calmly, and sat down and began to outline her other eye.

Downstairs the doorbell rang.

'That must be Peter,' Marian said, 'already.' She had no idea it was so late. 'I'm supposed to go over with him and help get things ready – I wish we could give you a ride, but I don't think we'll be able to wait.'

'That's okay,' said Ainsley, drawing a long gracefully-curved artistic eyebrow on her forehead in the place where hers ought to have been. 'I'll come on later. I've got some things to do anyway. If it's too cold for the baby I can always take a taxi, it isn't that far.'

Marian went into the kitchen, where she had left her coat. I really should have eaten something, she said to herself, it's bad to drink on an empty stomach. She could hear Peter coming up the stairs. She took another vitamin pill. They were brown, oval-shaped, with pointed ends: like hard-cased brown seeds. I wonder what they grind up to put into these things, she thought as she swallowed.

Chapter Twenty-six

Peter unlocked the glass door with his key and fixed the latch so that the door would remain open for the guests. Then they stepped into the lobby and walked together across the wide tiled floor towards the staircase. The elevator was not yet in working order, though Peter said it would be by the end of next week. The service elevator was running but the workmen kept it locked.

The apartment building was almost finished. Each time Marian had come there she had been able to notice a minor alteration. Gradually the clutter of raw materials, pipes and rough boards and cement blocks, had disappeared, transmuted by an invisible process of digestion and assimilation into the shining skins that enclosed the space through which they were moving. The walls and the line of square supporting pillars had been painted a deep orange-pink; the lighting had been installed, and was blazing now at its full cold strength, since Peter had turned all the lobby switches on for his party. The floor-length mirrors on the pillars were new since the last time she had been there; they made the lobby seem larger, much longer than it really was. But the carpets, the furniture (imitation-leather sofas, she predicted) and the inevitable broad-leaved philodendrons twining around pieces of driftwood had not yet arrived. They would be the final rich layer, and would add a touch of softness, however synthetic, to this corridor of hard light and brittle surfaces.

They ascended the staircase together, Marian leaning on Peter's arm. In the hallways of each floor they passed as they went up Marian could see gigantic wooden crates and oblong canvas-covered shapes standing outside the apartment doors: they must be installing the kitchen equipment, the stoves and refrigerators. Soon Peter would no longer be the only person living in the building. Then they would turn the heat up to its full capacity; as it was, the building, all except Peter's place, was kept almost as cold as the outside air.

'Darling,' she said in a casual tone when they had reached the fifth floor and were pausing for a moment on the landing to catch their breath, 'something came up and I've invited a few more people. I hope you don't mind.'

All the way there in the car she had been pondering how she would tell him. It would not be a good thing for those people to arrive with Peter not knowing anything about it, though it had been a great temptation to say nothing, to rely on her ability to cope with the situation when the moment came. In the confusion she would not have to explain how she had come to invite them, she didn't want to explain, she couldn't explain, and she dreaded questions from Peter about it. Suddenly she felt totally without her usual skill at calculating his reactions in advance. He had become an unknown quantity; just after she had spoken, blind rage and blind ecstasy on his part seemed equally possible. She took a step away from him and gripped the railing with her free hand: there was no telling what he might do.

But he only smiled down at her, a slight crease of concealed irritation appearing between his eyebrows. 'Did you, darling? Well the more the merrier. But I hope you didn't ask too many: we won't have enough liquor to go around, and if there's anything I hate it's a party that goes dry.'

Marian was relieved. Now he had spoken she saw that it was exactly what he would have said. She was so pleased with him for answering predictably that she pressed his arm. He slid it around her waist, and they began to climb again. 'No,' she said, 'only about six.' Actually there were nine, but since he had been so polite about it she made the courteous gesture of minimizing.

'Anyone I know?' he asked pleasantly.

'Well ... Clara and Joe,' she said, her momentary elation beginning to vanish. 'And Ainsley. But not the others: not really....'

'My, my,' he said, teasing, 'I wasn't aware you had that many friends I've never met. Been keeping little secrets, eh? I'll have to make a special point of getting to know them so I can find out all about your private life.' He kissed her ear genially.

'Yes,' Marian said, with feeble cheerfulness. 'I'm sure you'll like them.' Idiot, she raged at herself. Idiot, idiot. How could she have been so stupid? She foresaw how it was going to be. The office virgins would be all right – Peter would just look somewhat askance at them, particularly Emmy; and Clara and Joe would be tolerated. But the others. Duncan would not give her away – or would he? He might think it was funny to drop an insinuating remark; or he might do it out of curiosity. She could take him aside when he arrived though and ask him not to. But the room-mates were an insoluble problem. She did not think either of them knew yet that she was engaged, and she could picture Trevor's shriek of surprise when he found out, the way he would glance at Duncan and say, 'But my dear, *we* thought ...' and trail off into a silence weighted with innuendos that would be even more dangerous than the truth. Peter would be furious, he would think someone had been infringing on his private property rights, he wouldn't understand at all, and what would happen then? Why in heaven's name had she invited them? What a colossal mistake; how could she stop them from coming?

They reached the seventh floor and walked along the corridor towards the door of Peter's apartment. He had spread several newspapers outside his door for people to put their overshoes and boots on. Marian took off her own boots and stood them neatly beside Peter's overshoes. 'I hope they'll follow our example,' Peter said. 'I just had the floors done, I don't want them getting all tracked up.' With no others beside them yet, the two pairs looked like black leathery bait in a large empty newspaper trap.

Inside, Peter took off her coat for her. He put his hands on her bare shoulders and kissed her lightly on the back of the neck. 'Yum

yum' he said, 'new perfume.' Actually it was Ainsley's, an exotic mixture she had selected to go with the ear-rings.

He took off his own coat and hung it up in the closet just inside the door. 'Take your coat into the bedroom, darling' he said, 'and then come on out to the kitchen and help me get things ready. Women are so much better at arranging things on plates.'

She walked across the living room floor. The only addition Peter had made to its furniture recently was another matching Danish-modern chair; most of the space was still unoccupied. At least it meant that the guests would have to circulate: there wasn't room for all of them to sit down. Peter's friends did not, as a rule, sit on floors until rather late in the evening. Duncan might though. She imagined him crosslegged in the centre of the bare room, a cigarette stuck in his mouth, staring with gloomy incredulity perhaps at one of the soap-men or at one of the Danish-modern sofa legs while the other guests circled around him, not noticing him much but being careful not to step on him, as though he were a coffee table or a conversation-piece of some kind: a driftwood-and-parchment mobile. Maybe it wasn't too late to phone them and ask them not to come. But the phone was in the kitchen and so was Peter.

The bedroom was meticulously neat as always. The books and the guns were in their usual places; four of Peter's model ships now served as book-ends. Two of the cameras had been taken out of their cases and were standing on the desk. One of them had a flash-attachment on it with a blue flashbulb already clipped inside the silver saucer-shaped reflector. More of the blue bulbs were lying near an opened magazine. Marian placed her coat on the bed; Peter had told her that the coat closet by the door wouldn't be large enough for all the coats and that the women were to put their coats in his bedroom. Her coat then, lying with its arms at its sides, was really more functional than it looked: it was acting as a sort of decoy for the other coats. By it they would see where they were supposed to go.

She turned, and saw herself reflected in the full-length mirror on the back of the cupboard door. Peter had been so surprised and pleased. 'Darling, you look absolutely marvellous,' he had said as soon as he had come up through the stairwell. The implication had been that it would be most pleasant if she could arrange to look like that all the time. He had made her turn around so he could see the back, and he had liked that too. Now she was wondering whether or not she did look absolutely marvellous. She turned the phrase over in her mind: it had no specific shape or flavour. What should it feel like? She smiled at herself. No, that wouldn't do. She smiled a different smile, drooping her eyelids; that didn't quite work either. She turned her head and examined her profile out of the corner of her eye. The difficulty was that she couldn't grasp the total effect: her attention caught on the various details, the things she wasn't used to – the fingernails, the heavy ear-rings, the hair, the various parts of her face that Ainsley had added or altered. She was only able to see one thing at a time. What was it that lay beneath the surface these pieces were floating on, holding them together? She held both of her naked arms out towards the mirror. They were the only portion of her flesh that was without a cloth or nylon or leather or varnish covering, but in the glass even they looked fake, like soft pinkish-white rubber or plastic, boneless, flexible. . . .

Annoyed with herself for slipping back towards her earlier panic, she opened the cupboard door to turn the mirror to the wall and found herself staring at Peter's clothes. She had seen them often enough before, so there was no particular reason why she should stand, one hand on the edge of the door, gazing into the dark cupboard. ... The clothes were hanging neatly in a row. She recognized all the costumes she had ever seen Peter wearing, except of course the dark winter suit he had on at the moment: there was his midsummer aspect, beside it his tweedy casual jacket that went with his grey flannels, and then the series of his other phases from late summer through fall. The matching shoes were lined up on the floor, each with its own personal shoe-tree inside. She realized that she was regarding the clothes with an emotion close to something like resentment. How could they hang there smugly asserting so much invisible silent authority? But on second thought it was more like fear. She reached out a hand to touch them, and drew it back: she was almost afraid they would be warm.

'Darling, where are you?' Peter called from the kitchen.

'Coming, darling,' she called back. She shut the cupboard door hastily, glanced into the mirror and patted one of her fronds back into place, and went to join him, walking carefully inside her finely-adjusted veneers.

The kitchen table was covered with glassware. Some of it was new: he must have bought it especially for the party. Well, they would always be able to use it after they were married. The counters held rows of bottles in different colours and sizes: scotch, rye, gin. Peter seemed to have everything well under control. He was giving some of the glasses a final polish with a clean teatowel.

'Anything I can do to help?' she asked.

'Yes darling, why don't you fix up some of these things on some dishes? Here, I've poured you a drink, scotch and water, we might as well get a head start.' He himself had wasted no time; his own glass was standing half-empty on the counter.

She sipped at her drink, smiling at him over the rim. It was far too strong for her; it burnt as it went down her throat. 'I think you're trying to get me drunk,' she said. 'Could I have another icecube?' She noticed with distaste that her mouth had left a greasy print on the rim of the glass.

'There's lots of ice in the fridge,' he said, sounding pleased that she felt in need of dilution.

The ice was in a large bowl. There was more in reserve, two polyethylene bags. The rest of the space was taken up by bottles, bottles of beer stacked on the bottom shelf, tall green bottles of gingerale and short colourless bottles of tonic water and soda on the shelves beside the freezing compartment. His refrigerator was so white and spotless and arranged; she thought with guilt of her own.

She busied herself with the potato chips and peanuts and olives and cocktail mushrooms, filling the bowls and platters that Peter had indicated, handling the foods with the very ends of her fingers so as not to get her nail-polish dirty. When she had almost finished Peter came up behind her. He put one arm around her waist. With the other hand he half-undid the zipper of her dress; then he did it back up again. She could feel him breathing down the back of her neck.

'Too bad we don't have time to hop into bed,' he said, 'but I wouldn't want to get you all mussed up. Oh well, plenty of time for that later.' He put his other arm around her waist.

'Peter,' she said, 'do you love me?' She had asked him that before as a kind of joke, not doubting the answer. But this time she waited, not moving, to hear what he would say.

He kissed her lightly on the ear-ring. 'Of course I love you, don't be silly,' he said in a fond tone that indicated he thought he was humouring her. 'I'm going to marry you, aren't I? And I love you especially in that red dress. You should wear red more often.' He let go of her, and she transferred the last of the pickled mushrooms from the bottle to the plate.

'Come in here a minute, darling,' his voice called. He was in the bedroom. She rinsed off her hands, dried them, and went to join him. He had switched on his desk lamp and was sitting at the desk adjusting one of his cameras. He looked up at her, smiling. 'Thought I'd get some pictures of the party, just for the record,' he said. 'They'll be fun to have later, to look back on. This is our first real party together, you know; quite an occasion. By the way, have you got a photographer for the wedding yet?'

'I don't know,' she said, 'I think they have.'

'I'd like to do it myself, but of course that's impossible,' he said with a laugh. He began doing things to his light-meter.

She leaned affectionately against his shoulder, glancing over it at the objects on the desk, the blue flashbulbs, the concave silver circle of the flashgun. He was consulting the open magazine; he had marked the article entitled, 'Indoors Flash Lighting'. Beside the column of print there was an advertisement: a little girl with pigtails on a beach, clutching a spaniel. 'Treasure It Forever,' the caption read.

She walked over to the window and looked down. Below was the white city, its narrow streets and its cold winter lights. She was holding her drink in one of her hands; she sipped at it. The ice tinkled against the glass.

'Darling,' Peter said, 'it's almost zero-hour, but before they come I'd like to get a couple of shots of you alone, if you don't mind. There are only a few exposures left on this roll and I want to put a new one in for the party. That red ought to show up well on a slide, and I'll get some black-and-whites too while I'm at it.'

'Peter,' she said hesitantly, 'I don't think. . . .' The suggestion had made her unreasonably anxious.

'Now don't be modest,' he said. 'Could you just stand over there by the guns and lean back a little against the wall?' He turned the desk-lamp around so that the light was on her face and held the small black light-meter out towards her. She backed against the wall.

He raised the camera and squinted through the tiny glass window at the top; he was adjusting the lens, getting her in focus. 'Now,' he said. 'Could you stand a little less stiffly? Relax. And don't hunch your shoulders together like that, come on, stick out your chest, and don't look so worried darling, look natural, come on, *smile*. . . .'

Her body had frozen, gone rigid. She couldn't move, she couldn't even move the muscles of her face as she stood and stared into the round glass lens pointing towards her, she wanted to tell him not to touch the shutter-release but she couldn't move. . . .

There was a knock at the door.

'Oh damn,' Peter said. He set the camera on the desk. 'Here they come. Well, later then, darling.' He went out of the room.

Marian came slowly from the corner. She was breathing quickly. She reached out one hand, forcing herself to touch it.

'What's the matter with me?' she said to herself. 'It's only a camera.'

Chapter Twenty-seven

The first to arrive were the three office virgins, Lucy alone, Emmy and Millie almost simultaneously five minutes later. They were evidently not expecting to see each other there: each seemed annoyed that the others had been invited. Marian performed the introductions and led them to the bedroom, where their coats joined hers on the bed. Each of them said in a peculiar tone of voice that Marian should wear red more often. Each glanced at herself in the mirror, preening and straightening, before going out to the living room. Lucy frosted her mouth and Emmy scratched hurriedly at her scalp.

They lowered themselves carefully onto the Danish-modern furniture and Peter got them drinks. Lucy was in purple velvet, with silver eyelids and false lashes; Emmy was in pink chiffon, faintly suggestive of high-school formals. Her hair had been sprayed into stiff wisps and her slip was showing. Millie was encased in pale blue satin which bulged in odd places; she had a tiny sequin-covered evening-bag, and sounded the most nervous of the three.

'I'm so glad you could all come,' Marian said. At that moment she was not at all glad. They were so excited. They were each expecting a version of Peter to walk miraculously through the door, drop to one knee and propose. What would they do when confronted with Fish and Trevor, not to mention Duncan? Moreover, what would Fish and Trevor, not to mention Duncan, do when confronted with *them*? She pictured two trios of screams and a mass exodus, one set through the door and one through the window. What have I done now? she thought. But she had almost ceased to believe in the existence of the three graduate students; they were becoming more and more improbable as the evening and the scotch wore on. Maybe they would just never show up.

The soap-men and their wives were filtering in. Peter had put a record on the hi-fi and the room was noisier and more crowded. Every time there was a knock on the door the three office virgins swivelled their heads towards the entrance; and every time they saw another successful and glittering wife step into the room with her sleek husband, they turned back, a little more frantic, to their drinks and their interchange of strained comments. Emmy was fiddling with one of the rhinestone ear-rings. Millie picked at a loose sequin on her evening-bag.

Marian, smiling and efficient, led each wife to the bedroom. The pile of coats grew higher. Peter got everybody drinks and had a number of them himself. The peanuts and potato chips and other things were circulating from hand to hand, from hand to mouth. Already the group in the living room was beginning to divide itself into the standard territories, wives on the sofa-side of the room, men on the hi-fi side, an invisible no-man's-land between. The office virgins had got stuck on the wrong side: they listened unhappily to the wives. Marian felt another pang of remorse. But she couldn't attend to them right now, she thought: she was passing the pickled mushrooms. She wondered what was keeping Ainsley.

The door opened again, and Clara and Joe walked into the room. Behind them was Leonard Slank. Marian's nerves twitched, and one of the cocktail mushrooms fell from the plate she was carrying, bounced along the floor, and disappeared under the hi-fi set. She set down the plate. Peter was already greeting them, shaking Len's hand effusively. His voice was getting louder with every drink. 'How the hell are you, good to see you here, god I've been meaning to call you up,' he was saying. Len responded with a lurch and a glazed stare.

Marian clamped her hand firmly on Clara's coatsleeve and hustled her into the bedroom. 'What's *he* doing here?' she asked, rather ungraciously.

Clara took off her coat. 'I hope you don't mind us bringing him, I didn't think you would because after all you're old friends, but really I thought we'd better, we didn't want him going off somewhere alone. As you can see, he's in piss-poor shape. He turned up just after the baby-sitter got there and he looked really awful, he'd obviously had a lot. He told us an incoherent story about some woman he's been having trouble with, it sounded quite serious, and he said he was afraid to go back to the apartment, I didn't know why, what could anybody do to him? So, poor thing, we're going to keep him up in that back room on the second floor. It's Arthur's room really, but I'm sure Len won't mind sharing. We both feel so sorry for him, what he needs is some nice home-loving type who'll take care of him, he doesn't seem to be able to cope at all. . . .'

'Did he say who she was?' Marian asked quickly.

'Why no,' Clara said, raising her eyebrows, 'he doesn't usually tell the names.'

'Let me get you a drink,' Marian said. She was feeling like another one herself. Of course Clara and Joe couldn't have known who the woman was or they never would have brought Len with them. She was surprised he had even come; he must have known there was a good chance Ainsley would be at the party, but probably by this time he was too far gone to care. What worried her most was the effect his presence might have on Ainsley. It might upset her enough to make her do something unstable.

When they reached the living room, Marian saw that Leonard had been spotted at once by the office virgins as single and available. They had him backed against the wall in the neuter area now, two of them on the sides cutting off flank escape and the third, in front. He had one of his hands pressed against the wall for balance; the other held a glass stein full of beer. While they talked he shifted his gaze continually from face to face as though he didn't want to remain looking for too long at any one of them. His own face, which was the flat whitish-grey colour of uncooked piecrust and oddly bloated, expressed a combination of sodden incredulity, boredom, and alarm. But they seemed to have pried a few words out of him, because Marian heard Lucy exclaim, 'Television! How exciting!' while the others giggled tensely. Leonard swallowed a desperate mouthful of beer.

Marian was passing the ripe olives when she saw Joe coming towards her from the men's territory. 'Hi,' he said to her. 'I'm very glad you asked us here tonight. Clara has so few chances to get out of the house.'

Both of them turned their eyes towards Clara, who was over at the sofa-side of the room, talking with one of the soapwives.

'I worry about her a lot, you know,' Joe continued. 'I think it's a lot harder for her than for most other women; I think it's harder for any woman who's been to university. She gets the idea she has a mind, her professors pay attention to what she has to say, they treat her like a thinking human being; when she gets married, her core gets invaded. . . .'

'Her what?' Marian asked.

'Her core. The centre of her personality, the thing she's built up; her image of herself, if you like.'

'Oh. Yes,' said Marian.

'Her feminine role and her core are really in opposition, her feminine role demands passivity from her. . . .'

Marian had a fleeting vision of a large globular pastry, decorated with whipped cream and maraschino cherries, floating suspended in the air above Joe's head.

'So she allows her core to get taken over by the husband. And when the kids come, she wakes up one morning and discovers she doesn't have anything left inside, she's hollow, she doesn't know who she is any more; her core has been destroyed.' He shook his head gently and sipped at his drink. 'I can see it happening with my own female students. But it would be futile to warn them.'

Marian turned to look at Clara where she stood talking, dressed in simple beige, her long hair a delicate pear-pale yellow. She wondered whether Joe had ever told Clara her core had been destroyed; she thought of apples and worms. As she watched, Clara made an emphatic gesture with one of her hands and a soap-wife stepped back looking shocked.

'Of course it doesn't help to realize all that,' Joe was saying. 'It happens, whether you realize it or not. Maybe women shouldn't be allowed to go to university at all; then they wouldn't always be feeling later on that they've missed out on the life of the mind. For instance when I suggest to Clara that she should go out and do something about it, like taking a night course, she just gives me a funny look.'

Marian looked up at Joe with an affection the precise flavour of which was blurred by the drinks she had had. She thought of him shuffling about the house in his undershirt, meditating on the life of the mind and doing the dishes and tearing the stamps raggedly off the envelopes; she wondered what he did with the stamps after that. She wanted to reach out and touch him, reassure him, tell him Clara's core hadn't really been destroyed and everything would be all right; she wanted to give him something. She thrust forward the plate she was holding. 'Have an olive,' she said.

Behind Joe's back the door opened and Ainsley came through it. 'Excuse me,' Marian said to Joe. She set the olives on the hi-fi set and went over to intercept Ainsley; she had to warn her.

'Hi,' Ainsley said breathlessly. 'Sorry I'm later than I thought but I got this urge to start packing. . . .'

Marian hurried her into the bedroom, hoping that Len hadn't seen her. She noted in passing that he was still fully enclosed.

'Ainsley,' she said when they were alone with the coats, 'Len's here and I'm afraid he's drunk.'

Ainsley unswathed herself. She looked magnificent. She was dressed in a shade of green that bordered on turquoise, with eyelids and shoes to match; her hair coiled and shone, swirled around her head. Her skin glowed, irradiated with many hormones; her stomach was not yet noticeably bulbous.

She studied herself in the mirror before answering. 'Well?' she said calmly, widening her eyes. 'Really Marian, it doesn't matter to me in the least. After the talk this afternoon I'm sure we know where we stand and we can both behave like mature adults. There's nothing he could say now that could disturb me.'

'But,' said Marian, 'he seems quite upset; that's what Clara says. Apparently he's gone to stay at their place. I saw him when he came in, he looks terrible; so I hope you won't say anything that could disturb *him*.'

'There's no reason at all,' Ainsley said lightly, 'why I should even talk to him.'

In the living room the soapmen on their side of the invisible fence were becoming quite boisterous. They gave forth bursts of laughter: one of them was telling dirty jokes. The women's voices too were rising in pitch and volume, soaring in strident competitive descants over the baritone and bass. When Ainsley appeared, there was a general surge towards her: some of the soapmen predictably deserted their side and came to be introduced, and the corresponding wives, ever alert, rose from the sofa and took rapid steps to head them off at the pass. Ainsley smiled vacantly.

Marian went into the kitchen to get a drink for Ainsley and another one for herself. The previous order of the kitchen, the neat rows of glasses and bottles, had disintegrated in the process of the evening. The sink was full of melting icecubes and shreds of food, people never seemed to know what to do with their olive-pits, and the pieces of broken glass; bottles were standing, empty and partially-empty, on the counters and the table and the top of the refrigerator; and something unidentifiable had been spilled on the floor. But there were still some clean glasses. Marian filled one for Ainsley.

As she was going out of the kitchen she heard voices in the bedroom.

'You're even handsomer than you sound on the phone.' It was Lucy's voice.

Marian glanced into the bedroom. Lucy was in there, gazing up at Peter from under her silver lids. He was standing with a camera in his hand grinning boyishly, though somewhat foolishly, down at her. So Lucy had abandoned the siege of Leonard. She must have realized it was futile, she had always been more astute about those things than the other two. But how touching of her to try instead for Peter; pathetic, actually. After all Peter was off the market almost as definitely as if he was already married.

Marian smiled to herself and retreated, but not before Peter had spotted her and called, waving the camera, his face guiltily over-cheerful. 'Hi honey, the party's really going! Almost picture-time!' Lucy turned her head towards the doorway, smiling, her eyelids raising themselves like window shades.

'Here's your drink, Ainsley,' Marian said, breaking through the circle of soapmen to hand it.

'Thanks,' said Ainsley. She took it with a certain abstraction that Marian sensed as a danger-signal. She followed the direction of Ainsley's gaze. Len was staring across the room towards them, his mouth slightly open. Millie and Emmy were still tenaciously holding him at bay. Millie had moved round to the front, blocking as much space with her wide skirt as possible and Emmy was side-stepping back and forth like a basketball guard; but one of the flanks was unprotected. Marian looked back in time to see Ainsley smile: an inviting smile.

There was a knock on the door. I'd better get it, Marian thought, Peter's busy in the bedroom.

She opened the door and found herself confronting Trevor's puzzled face. The other two were behind him, and an unfamiliar figure, probably female, in a baggy Harris-tweed coat, sunglasses and long black stockings. 'Is this the right number?' Trevor asked. 'A Mr Peter Wollander?' He evidently did not recognize her.

Marian blenched inwardly; she had forgotten all about them. Oh well, there was so much noise and chaos in there anyway that Peter might not even notice them.

'Oh, I'm so glad you could come,' she said. 'Do come in. By the way, I'm Marian.'

'Oh, hahaha, of *course*,' shrilled Trevor. 'How stupid of me! I didn't recognize you, my dear you look elegant, you should really wear red more often.'

Trevor and Fish and the other one passed by her into the room, but Duncan remained outside. He took hold of her arm, tugged her into the hall, and closed the door behind her.

He stood for a moment peering silently at her from under his hair, examining every new detail. 'You didn't tell me it was a masquerade,' he said at last. 'Who the hell are you supposed to be?'

Marian let her shoulders sag with despair. So she didn't look absolutely marvellous after all. 'You've just never seen me dressed up before,' she said weakly.

Duncan began to snicker. 'I like the ear-rings best,' he said, 'where did you dredge them up?'

'Oh stop that,' she said with a trace of petulance, 'and come inside and have a drink.' He was very irritating. What did he expect her to wear, sackcloth and ashes? She opened the door.

The sound of the talking and music and laughter swelled into the corridor. Then there was a bright flash of light, and a loud voice cried triumphantly 'Aha! Caught you in the act!'

'That's Peter,' Marian said, 'he must be taking pictures.'

Duncan stepped back. 'I don't think I want to go in there,' he said.

'But you *have* to. You have to meet Peter, I'd like you to really.' It was suddenly very important that he come with her.

'No no,' he said, 'I can't. It would be a bad thing, I can tell. One of us would be sure to evaporate, it would probably be me; anyway it's too loud in there, I couldn't take it.'

'*Please*,' she said. She was reaching for his arm, but already he was turning, almost running back down the corridor.

'Where are you going?' she called after him plaintively.

'To the laundromat!' he called back. 'Good-bye, have a nice marriage,' he added. She caught a last glimpse of his twisted smile as he rounded the corner. She could hear his footsteps retreating down the stairs.

For an instant she wanted to run after him, to go with him: surely she could not face the crowded room again. But, 'I have to,' she said to herself. She walked back through the doorway.

The first thing she encountered was Fischer Smythe's broad woolly back. He was wearing an aggressively-casual striped turtle-neck sweater. Trevor, standing beside him, was immaculately suited, shirted and tied. They were both talking to the creature in the black stockings: something about death-symbols. She side-stepped the group deftly, not wanting to be forced to account for Duncan's disappearance.

She discovered that she was standing behind Ainsley, and realized after a minute that Leonard Slank was on the other side of that rounded bluegreen form. She couldn't see his face, Ainsley's hair was in the way, but she recognized his arm and the hand holding the beer stein: freshly filled, she noted. Ainsley was saying something to him in a low urgent voice.

She heard his slurred answer: 'NO, dammit! You'll never get me. . . .'

'Alright then.' Before Marian realized what Ainsley was doing she had raised her hand and brought it down, hard, smashing her glass against the floor. Marian jumped back.

At the sound of shattering glass the conversation stopped as though its plug had been pulled out, and Ainsley said into the silence that was filled, incongruously, only by the soft sighing of violins, 'Len and I have a marvellous announcement to make.' She hesitated for effect, her eyes glittering. 'We're going to have a baby.' Her voice was bland. Oh dear, Marian thought, she's trying to force the issue.

There were a few audible gasps from the sofa-side of the room. Somebody sniggered, and one of the soapmen said, 'Atta boy Len, whoever you are.' Marian could see Len's face now. The white surface had developed a random scattering of red blotches; the underlip was quivering.

'You rotten bitch!' he said thickly.

There was a pause. One of the soap-wives began a rapid conversation about something else, but trailed off quickly. Marian watched Len: she thought he was going to hit Ainsley, but instead he smiled, showing his teeth. He turned to the listening multitudes.

'That's right folks,' he said, 'and we're going to have the christening right now, in the midst of this friendly little gathering. Baptism in utero. I hereby name it after me.' He shot out one hand and grasped Ainsley's shoulder, lifted his beer stein, and poured its contents slowly and thoroughly over her head.

The soap-wives all gave delighted screams; the soapmen bellowed 'Hey!' As the last of the suds were descending, Peter came charging in from the bedroom, jamming a flashbulb into his camera. 'Hold it!' he shouted, and shot. 'Great! That'll be a great one! Hey, this party's really getting off the ground!'

Several people gave him annoyed glances, but most paid no attention. Everyone was moving and talking at once; in the background the violins still played, saccharine-sweet. Ainsley was standing there, drenched, a puddle of foam and beer forming at her feet on the hardwood floor. Her face contorted: in a minute she would have decided whether it would be worth the effort to cry. Len had let go of her. His head dropped; he mumbled something inaudible. He looked as though he had only an imperfect idea of what he had just done and no idea at all of what he was going to do next.

Ainsley turned and started to walk towards the bathroom. Several of the soap-wives trotted forward, uttering throaty cooing noises, eager to share the spotlight by helping; but someone was there before them. It was Fischer Smythe. He was pulling his woolly turtleneck sweater over his head, exposing a muscular torso covered with quantities of tufted black fur.

'Allow me,' he said to her, 'we wouldn't want you to catch a chill, would we? Not in your condition.' He began to dry her off with his sweater. His eyes were damp with solicitude.

Ainsley's hair had come down and was lying in dripping strands over her shoulders. She smiled up at him through the beer or tears beading her eyelashes. 'I don't believe we've met,' she said.

'I think I already know who you are,' he said, patting her belly tenderly with one of his striped sleeves, his voice heavy with symbolic meaning.

It was later. The party, miraculously, was still going on, having somehow closed itself smoothly together over the rent made in it earlier by Ainsley and Len. Someone had cleaned the broken glass and beer off the floor, and in the living room now the currents of talk and music and drink were flowing again as though nothing had happened.

The kitchen however was a scene of devastation. It looked as though it had been hit by a flash-flood. Marian was scrabbling through the debris, trying to locate a clean glass; she had set her own down out there somewhere, she couldn't remember where, and she wanted another drink.

There weren't any more clean glasses. She picked up a used one, swished it under the tap, slowly and carefully poured herself another shot of scotch. She felt serene, a floating sensation, like lying on one's back in a pond. She went to the doorway and leaned in it, gazing out over the room.

'I'm coping! I'm coping!' she said to herself. The fact amazed her somewhat, but it pleased her immensely. They were all there, all of them (except, she noted as she scanned, Ainsley and Fischer, and oh yes Len – she wondered where they had gone), doing whatever people did at parties, and she was doing it, too. They were sustaining her, she could float quite watertight, buoyed up by the feeling that she was one of them. She had a warm affection for them all, for their distinct shapes and faces that she could see now so much more clearly than usual, as though they were being illuminated by a hidden floodlight. She even liked the soapwives and Trevor gesturing with one of his hands; and those people from the office, Millie, laughing over there in her shining light-blue dress, even Emmy, moving unconscious of her frazzled slip-edge. ... Peter was among them too; he was still carrying his camera and every now and then he would raise it to take a picture. He reminded her of the home-movie ads, the father of the family using up rolls and rolls of film on just such everyday ordinary things, what subjects could be better: people laughing, lifting glasses, children at birthday-parties. . . .

So that's what was in there all the time, she thought happily: this is what he's turning into. The real Peter, the one underneath, was nothing surprising or frightening, only this bungalow-and-double-bed man, this charcoal-cooking-in-the-backyard man. This home-movie man. And I called him out, she thought, I evoked him. She swallowed some of her scotch.

It had been a long search. She retraced through time the corridors and rooms, long corridors, large rooms. Everything seemed to be slowing down.

If that's who Peter really is, she thought, walking along one of the corridors, will he have a pot-belly at forty-five? Will he dress sloppily on Saturdays, in wrinkled blue jeans for his workshop in the cellar? The image was reassuring: he would have hobbies, he would be comfortable, he would be normal.

She opened a door to the right and went in. There was Peter, forty-five and balding but still recognizable as Peter, standing in bright sunlight beside a barbecue with a long fork in his hand. He was wearing a white chef's apron. She looked carefully for herself in the garden, but she wasn't there and the discovery chilled her.

No, she thought, this has to be the wrong room. It can't be the last one. And now she could see there was another door, in the hedge at the other side of the garden. She walked across the lawn, passing behind the unmoving figure, which she could see now held a large cleaver in the other hand, pushed open the door and went through.

She was back in Peter's living room with the people and the noise, leaning against the doorframe holding her drink. Except that the people seemed even clearer now, more sharply focussed, further away, and they were moving faster and faster, they were all going home, a file of soapwomen emerged from the bedroom, coats on, they teetered jerkily out the door trailing husbands, chirping goodnights, and who was that tiny two-dimensional small figure in a red dress, posed like a paper woman in a mail-order catalogue, turning and smiling, fluttering in the white empty space. . . . This couldn't be it; there had to be something more. She ran for the next door, yanked it open.

Peter was there, dressed in his dark opulent winter suit. He had a camera in his hand; but now she saw what it really was. There were no more doors and when she felt behind her for the doorknob, afraid to take her eyes off him, he raised the camera and aimed it at her; his mouth opened in a snarl of teeth. There was a blinding flash of light.

'No!' she screamed. She covered her face with her arm.

'What's the matter, darling?' She looked up. Peter was standing beside her. He was real. She put up her hand and touched his face.

'It startled me,' she said.

'You really can't hold your liquor, can you darling,' he said, fondness and irritation blending in his voice. 'You should be used to it, I've been taking pictures all evening.'

'Was that one of me?' she asked. She smiled at him in conciliation. She sensed her face as vastly spreading and papery and slightly dilapidated: a huge billboard smile, peeling away in flaps and patches, the metal surface beneath showing through. . . .

'No, actually it was of Trigger over at the other side of the room. Never mind, I'll get you later. But you'd better not have another drink darling, you're swaying.' He patted her on the shoulder and walked away.

She was still safe then. She had to get out before it was too late. She turned and set her drink down on the kitchen table, her mind suddenly rendered cunning by desperation. It all depended on getting as far as Duncan: he would know what to do.

She glanced around the kitchen, then picked up her glass and poured its contents down the sink. She would be careful, she would leave no clues. Then she picked up the telephone and dialled Duncan's number. The phone rang and rang: no answer. She put it down. From the living room there was another flash of light, and the sound of Peter laughing. She should never have worn red. It made her a perfect target.

She edged into the bedroom. I must be sure not to forget anything, she told herself. I can't come back. Before, she had wondered what their bedroom would look like after they were married, trying out various arrangements and colour-schemes. Now she knew. It would always look exactly like this. She dug among the coats, looking for her own, and could not for a moment remember what it looked like, but at last she recognized it and slipped it on; she avoided the mirror. She had no idea what time it was. She glanced at her wrist: it was blank. Of course; she had taken her watch off and left it at home because Ainsley said it didn't go with the total effect.

In the living room Peter was calling above the noise 'Come on now, let's get a group portrait. Everybody all together.'

She had to hurry. Now there was the living room to negotiate. She would have to become less visible. She took her coat back off and bundled it under her left arm, counting on her dress to act as a protective camouflage that would blend her with the scenery. Staying close to the wall, she made her way towards the door through the thicket of people, keeping behind the concealing trunks and bushes of backs and skirts. Peter was over at the other side of the room, trying to get them organized.

She opened the door and slid out; then, pausing only long enough to get her coat on again and to pick her overboots out from the tangle of trapped feet on the newspaper, she ran as fast as she could down the hallway towards the stairs. She could not let him catch her this time. Once he pulled the trigger she would be stopped, fixed indissolubly in that gesture, that single stance, unable to move or change.

She stopped on the sixth-floor landing to put on her boots, then continued down, holding on to the bannister for balance. Under the cloth and the metal bones and elastic her flesh felt numbed and compressed; it was difficult to walk, it took concentration. ... I'm probably drunk, she thought. Funny I don't feel drunk; idiot, you know perfectly well what happens to drunk people's capillaries when they go out into the cold. But it was even more important to get away.

She reached the empty lobby. Although there was no one following her, she thought she could hear a sound; it was the thin sound glass would make, icy as the tinkle of a chandelier, it was the high electric vibration of this glittering space. ...

She was outside in the snow. Running along the street, the snow squeaking under her feet, as quickly as her hampered legs would move, balancing with her eyes on the sidewalk, in winter even level surfaces were precarious, she couldn't afford to fall down. Behind her even now Peter might be tracing, following, stalking her through the crisp empty streets as he had stalked his guests in the living room, waiting for the exact moment. That dark intent marksman with his aiming eye had been there all the time, hidden by the other layers, waiting for her at the dead centre: a homicidal maniac with a lethal weapon in his hands.

She slipped on a patch of ice and almost fell. When she had recovered her balance she looked behind. Nothing.

'Take it easy,' she said, 'keep calm.' Her breath was coming in sharp gasps, crystallizing in the freezing air almost before it had left her throat. She continued on, more slowly. At first she had been running blindly; now however she knew exactly where she was going. 'You'll be all right,' she said to herself 'if only you can make it as far as the laundromat.'

Chapter Twenty-eight

It had not occurred to her that Duncan might not be in the laundromat. When she finally reached it and pulled open the glass door, breathless but relieved at having got that far at all, it was a shock to find it empty. She couldn't believe it. She stood, confronted only by the long white row of machines, not knowing where to move. She hadn't considered the time beyond that imagined encounter.

Then she saw a wisp of smoke ascending from one of the chairs at the far end. It would have to be him. She walked forward.

He was sitting slouched so far down that only the top of his head was showing over the back of the chair, his eyes fixed on the round window of the machine directly in front of him. There was nothing inside it. He didn't look up as she sat down in the chair beside his.

'Duncan,' she said. He didn't answer.

She took off her gloves and stretched out one of her hands, touching his wrist. He jumped.

'I'm here,' she said.

He looked at her. His eyes were even more shadowed than usual, more deeply-sunk in the sockets, the skin of his face bloodless in the fluorescent light. 'Oh. So you are. The Scarlet Woman herself. What time is it?'

'I don't know,' she said, 'I haven't got my watch on.'

'What're you doing here? You're supposed to be at the party.'

'I couldn't stay there any longer,' she said. 'I had to come and find you.'

'Why?'

She couldn't think of a reason that wouldn't sound absurd. 'Because I just wanted to be with you.'

He looked at her suspiciously and took another drag on his cigarette. 'Now listen, you should be back there. It's your duty, what's-his-name needs you.'

'No, you need me more than he does.'

As soon as she had said it, it sounded true. Immediately she felt noble.

He grinned. 'No I don't. You think I need to be rescued but I don't. Anyway I don't like being a test-case for amateur social-workers.' He shifted his eyes back to the washing-machine.

Marian fidgeted with the leather fingers of one of her gloves. 'But I'm not trying to rescue you,' she said. She realized he had tricked her into contradicting herself.

'Then maybe you want me to rescue you? What from? I thought you had it all worked out. And you know I'm totally inept anyway.' He sounded faintly smug about his own helplessness.

'Oh, let's not talk about rescuing,' Marian said desperately. 'Can't we just go some place?' She wanted to get out. Even talking was impossible in this white room with its rows of glass windows and its all-pervading smell of soap and bleach.

'What's wrong with here?' he said. 'I sort of like it here.'

Marian wanted to shake him. 'That isn't what I mean,' she said.

'Oh,' he said. 'Oh, that. You mean tonight's the night, it's now or never.' He dug out another cigarette and lit it. 'Well, we can't go to my place, you know.'

'We can't go to mine either.' For a moment she wondered why not, she was moving out anyway. But Ainsley might turn up, or Peter. . . .

'We could stay here, it suggests interesting possibilities. Maybe inside one of the machines, we could hang your red dress over the window to keep out the dirty old men. . . .'

'Oh come on,' she said, standing up.

He stood up too. 'Okay, I'm flexible. I guess it's about time I found out the real truth. Where are we going?'

'I suppose,' she said, 'we will have to find some sort of hotel.' She was vague about how they were going to get the thing accomplished, but tenaciously certain that it had to be done. It was the only way.

Duncan smiled wickedly. 'You mean I'll have to pretend you're my wife?' he said. 'In those ear-rings? They'll never believe it. They'll accuse you of corrupting a minor.'

'I don't care,' she said. She reached up and began to unscrew one of the ear-rings.

'Oh, leave them on for now,' Duncan said. 'You don't want to spoil the effect.'

When they were outside on the street she had a sudden horrible thought. 'Oh no,' she said, standing still.

'What's the matter?'

'I don't have any money!' Of course she hadn't thought she would need any for the party. She had only her evening-bag with her, stuffed in a coat pocket. She felt the energy that had been propelling her through the streets, through this conversation, draining away. She was powerless, paralysed. She wanted to cry.

'I think I may have some,' Duncan said. 'I usually carry some. For emergencies.' He began to search through his pockets. 'Hold this.' Into her hands he piled a chocolate-bar, then several neatly folded silver chocolate-bar wrappers, a few white pumpkin-seed shells, an empty cigarette package, a piece of grubby string tied in knots, a key-chain with two keys, a wad of chewing-gum wrapped in paper, and a shoelace. 'Wrong pocket,' he said. From his other pocket he pulled, in a cascade of small change that scattered over the sidewalk, a few crumpled bills. He picked up the change and counted all the money. 'Well, it won't be the King Eddie,' he said, 'but it'll get us something. Not around here though, this is expense-account territory; it'll have to be further downtown. Looks like this is going to be an underground movie rather than a technicolour extravaganza spectacular.' He put the money and the handfuls of junk back into his pocket.

The subway was closed down, its iron latticed gate pulled across the entrance.

'I guess we could take a bus,' Marian said.

'No; it's too cold to stand and wait.'

They turned at the next corner and walked south down the wide empty street, past the lighted storefronts. There were few cars and fewer people. It must be really late, she thought. She tried to imagine what was going on at the party – was it over? Had Peter realized yet that she was no longer there? – but all she could picture was a confusion of noises and voices and fragments of faces and flashes of bright light.

She took Duncan's hand. He wasn't wearing gloves, so she put both his hand and her own into her pocket. He looked down at her then with an almost hostile expression, but he did not remove his hand. Neither of them spoke. It was getting colder and colder: her toes were beginning to ache.

They walked for what seemed hours, gently downwards toward the frozen lake although they were nowhere near it, past blocks and blocks that contained nothing but tall brick office buildings and the vacant horizontal spaces of car-dealers, with their strings of coloured lights and little flags; not what they were looking for at all. 'I think we're on the wrong street,' Duncan said after a time. 'We should be further over.'

They went along a dark narrow cross-street whose sidewalks were treacherous with packed snow and emerged finally on a larger street gaudy with neon signs. 'This looks more like it,' said Duncan.

'What are we going to do now?' she asked, conscious of the plaintive tone in her own voice. She felt helpless to decide. He was more or less in charge. After all, he was the one with the money.

'Hell, *I* don't know how one goes about these things,' he said. 'I've never done this before.'

'Neither have I,' she said defensively, 'I mean, not like this.'

'There must be an accepted formula,' he said, 'but I guess we'll just have to make it up as we go along. We'll take them in order, from north to south.' He scanned the street. 'It looks as though they get crummier as you go down.'

'Oh, I hope it's not a real dump,' she wailed, 'with bugs!'

'Oh, I don't know, bugs might make it sort of more interesting. Anyway we'll have to take what we can get.'

He stopped in front of a narrow red brick building sandwiched between a formal-rental store with a gritty bride in the window and a dusty-looking florist's. 'Royal Massey Hotel,' its dangling neon sign said; underneath the writing there was a coat-of-arms. 'You wait here,' Duncan said. He went up the steps.

He came back down the steps. 'Door's locked,' he said.

They walked on. The next one had a more promising aspect. It was dingier, and the stone grecian-scrolled cornices over the windows were dark-grey with soot. 'The Ontario Towers,' it said, in a red sign whose preliminary 'O' had gone out. 'Cheap Rates.' It was open.

'I'll come in and stand in the lobby,' she said. Her feet were freezing. Besides, she felt a need to be courageous: Duncan was coping so well, she ought to provide at least moral support.

She stood on the dilapidated matting, trying to look respectable, and conscious of her ear-rings and of the improbability of the attempt. Duncan walked over to the night clerk, a wizened shred of a man who was staring at her suspiciously through his puckers. He and Duncan had a low-voiced conversation; then Duncan came back and took her arm and they walked out.

'What did he say?' she asked when they were outside.

'He said it wasn't that sort of place.'

'That's rather presumptuous,' she said. She was offended, and felt quite self-righteous.

Duncan snickered. 'Come now,' he said, 'no outraged virtue. All it means is that we've got to find one that *is* that sort of place.'

They turned a corner and went east along a likely-looking street. They passed a few more shabby-genteel establishments before they came to one that was even shabbier, but definitely not genteel. In place of the crumbled brick facade characteristic of the others, it had pink stucco with large signs painted on it: 'BEDS 4$ A NITE.' 'TV IN EVERY ROOM.' 'VICTORIA AND ALBERT HOTEL.' 'BEST BARGAIN IN TOWN.' It was a long building. Further down they could see the 'MEN' and 'LADIES AND ESCORTS' sign that signalled a beer-parlour, and it seemed to have a tavern too; though both would be closed at this hour.

'I think this is it,' said Duncan.

They went in. The night clerk yawned as he took down the key. 'Sort of late buddy, isn't it?' he said. 'That'll be four.'

'Better late,' Duncan said, 'than never.' He took a handful of bills out of his pocket, scattering assorted change over the carpet. As he stooped to pick it up, the night clerk looked over at Marian with an undisguised though slightly jaded leer. She drooped her eyelids at him. After all, she thought grimly, if I'm dressed like one and acting like one, why on earth shouldn't he think I really am one?

They ascended the sparsely-carpeted stairs in silence.

The room when they finally located it was the size of a large cupboard, furnished with an iron bedstead, a straight-backed chair, and a dresser whose varnish was peeling off. There was a miniature quarter-in-the-slot TV set bolted to the wall in one corner. On the dresser were a couple of folded threadbare towels in baby-blue and pink. The narrow window opposite the bed had a blue neon sign hanging outside it; the sign flashed on and off, making an ominous buzzing noise. Behind the room-door was another door that led to a cubbyhole of a bathroom.

Duncan bolted the door behind them. 'Well, what do we do now?' he said. 'You must know.'

Marian removed her boots, then her shoes. Her toes tingled with the pain of thawing. She looked at the gaunt face peering at her from between an upturned coat collar and a mass of windy hair; the face was dead white, all but the nose, which was red from the cold. As she watched he produced a tattered grey piece of kleenex from some recess in his clothing and wiped it.

God, she thought, what am I doing here? How did I get here anyway? What would Peter say? She walked across the room and stood in front of the window, looking out at nothing in particular.

'Oh boy,' said Duncan behind her, enthusiastically. She turned. He had discovered something new, a large ashtray that had been sitting on the dresser behind the towels. 'It's genuine.' The ashtray was in the form of a seashell, pink china with scalloped edges. 'It says A Gift From Burk's Falls on it,' he told her with glee. He turned it over to look on the bottom and some ashes fell out of it onto the floor. 'Made In Japan,' he announced.

Marian felt a surge of desperation. Something had to be done. 'Look,' she said, 'for heaven's sake put down that damned ashtray and take off your clothes and get into that bed!'

Duncan hung his head like a rebuked child. 'Oh, all right,' he said.

He shed his clothes with such velocity that it looked as though he had concealed zippers somewhere, or one long zipper so his clothes came off together like a single skin. He tossed them in a heap onto the chair and scuttled with alacrity into the bed and lay with the sheets pulled up around his chin, watching her with barely disguised and only slightly friendly curiosity.

With tight-lipped determination she began to undress. It was somewhat difficult to wisp off her stockings in reckless abandon or even a reasonable facsimile of it with those two eyes goggling at her in such a frog-like manner from over the top of the sheet. She scrabbled with her fingers for the zipper at the back of her dress. She could not quite reach it.

'Unzip me,' she said tersely. He complied.

She threw the dress over the back of the chair and struggled out of her girdle.

'Hey!' he said. 'A real one! I've seen them in the ads but I never got that far in real life, I've always wondered how they worked. Can I look at it?'

She handed it over to him. He sat up in bed to examine it, stretching it all of its three ways and flexing the bones. 'God, how medieval,' he said. 'How can you stand it? Do you have to wear one all the time?' He spoke of it as though it was some kind of unpleasant but necessary surgical appliance; a brace or a truss.

'No,' she said. She was standing in her slip, wondering what to do next. She refused, somewhat prudishly she supposed, to undress the rest of the way with the lights on; but he seemed to be having such a good time at the moment that she didn't want to interrupt. On the other hand the room was cold and she was beginning to shiver.

She walked doggedly towards the bed, gritting her teeth. It was an assignment that was going to take a lot of perseverance. If she had had any sleeves on she would have rolled them up. 'Move over,' she said.

Duncan flung away the girdle and pulled himself back into the bedclothes like a turtle into its shell. 'Oh no,' he said, 'I'm not letting you into this bed until you go in there and peel that junk off your face. Fornication may be all very well in its way, but if I'm going to come out looking like a piece of flowered wallpaper I reject it.'

She saw his point.

When she returned, scraped more or less clean, she snapped off the light and slithered into bed beside him. There was a pause.

'I guess now I'm supposed to crush you in my manly arms,' Duncan said out of the darkness.

She slid her hand beneath his cool back.

He groped for her head, snuffling against her neck. 'You smell funny,' he said.

Half an hour later Duncan said, 'It's no use. I must be incorruptible. I'm going to have a cigarette.' He got up, stumbled the few steps across the room in the dark, located his clothes and rummaged around in them till he had found the pack, and returned.

She could see parts of his face now and the china seashell gleaming in the light of the burning cigarette. He was sitting propped against the iron scrollwork at the head of the bed.

'I don't exactly know what's wrong,' he said. 'Partly I don't like not being able to see your face; but it would probably be worse if I could. But it's not just that, I feel like some kind of little stunted creature crawling over the surface of a huge mass of flesh. Not that you're fat,' he added, 'you aren't. There's just altogether too much flesh around here. It's suffocating.' He threw back the covers on his side of the bed. 'That's better,' he said. He rested the arm with the cigarette across his face.

Marian knelt beside him in the bed, holding the sheet around her like a shawl. She could barely trace the outlines of his long white body, flesh-white against bed-white, faintly luminous in the blue light from the street. Somebody in the next room flushed a toilet; the gurgling of the water in the pipes swirled through the air of the room and died away with a sound between a sigh and a hiss.

She clenched her hands on the sheet. She was tense with impatience and with another emotion that she recognized as the cold energy of terror. At this moment to evoke something, some response, even though she could not predict the thing that might emerge from beneath that seemingly-passive surface, the blank white formless thing lying insubstantial in the darkness before her, shifting as her eyes shifted trying to see, that appeared to have no temperature, no odour, no thickness and no sound, was the most important thing she could ever have done, could ever do, and she couldn't do it. The knowledge was an icy desolation worse than fear. No effort of will could be worth anything here. She could not will herself to reach out and touch him again. She could not will herself to move away.

The glow of the cigarette vanished; there was the hard china click of the ashtray being set down on the floor. She could sense that he was smiling in the darkness, but with what expression, sarcasm, malevolence, or even kindness, she could not guess.

'Lie down,' he said.

She sank back, still with the sheet clutched around her and her knees drawn up.

He put his arm around her. 'No,' he said, 'you have to unbend. Assuming the foetal position won't be any help at all, god knows I've tried it long enough.' He stroked her with his hand, gently, straightening her out, almost as though he was ironing her.

'It isn't something you can dispense, you know,' he said. 'You have to let me take my own time.'

He edged over, closer to her now. She could feel his breath against the side of her neck, sharp and cool, and then his face pressing against her, nudging into her flesh, cool; like the muzzle of an animal, curious, and only slightly friendly.

Chapter Twenty-nine

They were sitting in a grimy coffee-shop around the corner from the hotel. Duncan was counting the rest of his money to see what they could afford to have for breakfast. Marian had undone the buttons of her coat, but was holding it together at the neck. She didn't want any of the other people to see her red dress: it belonged too obviously to the evening before. She had put Ainsley's earrings in her pocket.

Between them on the green arborite-surfaced table was an assortment of dirty plates and cups and crumbs and splashes and smears of grease, remnants of the courageous breakfasters who had pioneered earlier into the morning when the arborite surface was innocent as a wilderness, untouched by the knife and fork of man, and had left behind them the random clutter of rejected or abandoned articles typical of such light travellers. They knew they would never pass that way again. Marian looked at their waste-strewn trail with distaste, but she was trying to be casual about breakfast. She didn't want her stomach to make a scene. I'll just have coffee and toast, maybe with jelly; surely there will be no objections to that, she thought.

A waitress with harassed hair appeared and began to clear the table. She flapped a dog-eared menu down in front of each of them. Marian opened hers and looked at the column headed 'Breakfast Suggestions'.

Last night everything had seemed resolved, even the imagined face of Peter with its hunting eyes absorbed into some white revelation. It had been simple clarity rather than joy, but it had been submerged in sleep; and waking to the sound of water sighing in the pipes and loud corridor voices, she could not remember what it was. She had lain quietly, trying to concentrate on it, on what it might possibly have been, gazing at the ceiling, which was blotched with distracting watermarks; but it was no use. Then Duncan's head had emerged from beneath the pillow where he had placed it during the night for safe-keeping. He stared at her for a moment as though he didn't have the least idea who she was or what he was doing in that room. Then 'Let's get out of here,' he said. She had leaned over and kissed him on the mouth, but after she had drawn back he had merely licked his lips, and as though reminded by the action said 'I'm hungry. Let's go for breakfast. You look awful,' he had added.

'You're not exactly the picture of health yourself,' she replied. His eyes were heavily circled and his hair looked like a raven's nest. They got out of bed and she examined her own face briefly in the yellowed wavery glass of the bathroom mirror. Her skin was drawn and white and strangely dry. It was the truth: she did look awful.

She had not wanted to put those particular clothes back on but she had no choice. They dressed in silence, awkward in the narrow space of the room whose shabbiness was even more evident in the grey daylight, and furtively descended the stairs.

She looked at him now as he sat hunched over across the table from her, muffled again in his clothes. He had lit a cigarette and his eyes were watching the smoke. The eyes were closed to her, remote. The imprint left on her mind by the long famished body that had seemed in the darkness to consist of nothing but sharp crags and angles, the memory of its painfully-defined almost skeletal ribcage, a pattern of ridges like a washboard, was fading as rapidly as any other transient impression on a soft surface. Whatever decision she had made had been forgotten, if indeed she had ever decided anything. It could have been an illusion, like the blue light on their skins. Something had been accomplished in his life though, she thought with a sense of weary competence; that was a small comfort; but for her nothing was permanent or finished. Peter was there, he hadn't vanished; he was as real as the crumbs on the table, and she would have to act accordingly. She would have to go back. She had missed the morning bus but she could get the afternoon one, after talking to Peter, explaining. Or rather avoiding explanation. There was no real reason to explain because explanations involved causes and effects and this event had been neither. It had come from nowhere and it led nowhere, it was outside the chain. Suddenly it occurred to her that she hadn't begun to pack.

She looked down at the menu. 'Bacon and Eggs, Any Style,' she read. 'Our Plump Tender Sausages.' She thought of pigs and chickens. She shifted hastily to 'Toast.' Something moved in her throat. She closed the menu.

'What do you want?' Duncan asked.

'Nothing, I can't eat anything,' she said, 'I can't eat anything at all. Not even a glass of orange juice.' It had finally happened at last then. Her body had cut itself off. The food circle had dwindled to a point, a black dot, closing everything outside. . . . She looked at the grease-spot on the cover of the menu, almost whimpering with self-pity.

'You sure? Oh well then,' said Duncan with a trace of alacrity, 'that means I can spend it all on me.'

When the waitress came back he ordered ham and eggs, which he proceeded to consume voraciously, and without apology or comment, before her very eyes. She watched him in misery. When he broke the eggs with his fork and their yellow centres ran viscously over the plate she turned her head away. She thought she was going to be sick.

'Well,' he said when he had paid the cheque and they were standing outside on the street, 'thanks for everything. I've got to go home and get to work on my term paper.'

Marian thought of the cold fuel-oil and stale cigar smell there would be inside the bus. Then she thought of the dishes in the kitchen sink. The bus would get warm and stuffy as she travelled inside it along the highway, the tires making their high grinding whine. What was living, hidden and repulsive, down there among the plates and dirty glasses? She couldn't go back.

'Duncan,' she said, 'please don't go.'

'Why? Is there more?'

'I can't go back.'

He frowned down at her. 'What do you expect me to do?' he asked. 'You shouldn't expect me to do anything. I want to go back to my shell. I've had enough so-called reality for now.'

'You don't have to do anything, couldn't you just. . . .'

'No,' he said, 'I don't want to. You aren't an escape any more, you're too real. Something's bothering you and you'd want to talk about it; I'd have to start worrying about you and all that, I haven't time for it.'

She looked down at their four feet, standing in the trodden slush of the sidewalk. 'I really can't go back.'

He peered at her more closely. 'Are you going to be sick?' he asked. 'Don't do that.'

She stood mutely before him. She could offer him no good reason for staying with her. There was no reason: what would it accomplish?

'Well,' he said, hesitating, 'all right. But not for very long, okay?'

She nodded gratefully.

They walked north. 'We can't go to my place, you know,' he said. 'They'd make a fuss.'

'I know.'

'Where do you want to go then?' he asked.

She hadn't thought about that. Everything was impossible. She put her hands over her ears. 'I don't know,' she said, her voice rising towards hysteria, 'I don't know, I might as well go back. . . .'

'Oh come now,' he said genially, 'no histrionics. We'll go for a walk.' He pulled her hands away from her ears. 'All right,' she said, letting herself be humoured.

As they walked Duncan swung their linked hands back and forth. His mood seemed to have changed from its breakfast sullenness to a certain vacant contentment. They were going uphill, away from the lake; the sidewalks were crowded with furred Saturday ladies trudging inexorably as icebreakers through the slush, brows furrowed with purpose, eyes glinting, shopping bags hung at either side to give them ballast. Marian and Duncan dodged past and around them, breaking hands when an especially threatening one bore down upon them. In the streets the cars fumed and splattered by. Pieces of soot fell from the grey air, heavy and moist as snowflakes.

'I need some clean air,' Duncan said when they had walked wordlessly for twenty minutes or so. 'This is like being in a fishbowl full of dying pollywogs. Can you face a short subway ride?'

Marian nodded. The further away, she thought, the better.

They went down the nearest pastel-tiled chute, and after an

interval smelling of damp wool and mothballs let themselves be carried up by the escalator and out again into daylight.

'Now we take the streetcar,' Duncan said. He seemed to know where he was going, for which Marian could only be thankful. He was leading her. He was in control.

On the streetcar they had to stand. Marian held on to one of the metal poles and stooped so she could see out the window. Over the top of a tea-cosy-shaped green and orange wool hat with large gold sequins sewed to it an unfamiliar landscape jolted past: stores first, then houses, then a bridge, then more houses. She had no idea what part of the city they were in.

Duncan reached over her head and pulled the cord. The streetcar ground to a halt and they squeezed their way towards the back and jumped down.

'Now we walk,' said Duncan. He turned down a side street. The houses were smaller and a little newer than the ones in Marian's district, but they were still dark and tall, many with square pillared wooden porches, the paint grey or dingy white. The snow on the lawns was fresher here. They passed an old man shovelling a walk, the scrape of the shovel sounding strangely loud in the silent air. There was an abnormal number of cats. Marian thought of how the street would smell in the spring when the snow melted: earth, bulbs coming up, damp wood, last year's leaves rotting, the winter's accumulations of the cats who had thought they were being so clean and furtive as they scratched holes for themselves in the snow. Old people coming out of the grey doors with shovels, creaking over the lawns, burying things. Spring cleaning: a sense of purpose.

They crossed a street and began to go down a steep hill. All at once Duncan started to run, dragging Marian behind him as if she was a toboggan.

'Stop!' she called, alarmed at the loudness of her own voice, 'I can't run!' She felt the curtains in all the windows swaying perilously as they went past, as though each house contained a dour watcher.

'No!' Duncan shouted back at her. 'We're escaping! Come on!'

Under her arm a seam split. She had a vision of the red dress disintegrating in mid-air, falling in little scraps behind her in the snow, like feathers. They were off the sidewalk now, slithering down the road towards a fence; there was a yellow and black chequered sign that said 'Danger.' She was afraid they would go splintering through the wooden fence and hurtle over an unseen edge, in slow motion almost, like movies of automobiles falling off cliffs, but at the last minute Duncan swerved around the end of the fence and they were on a narrow cinder path between high banks. The footbridge at the bottom of the hill came rapidly towards them; he stopped suddenly and she skidded, colliding.

Her lungs hurt: she was dizzy from too much air. They were leaning against a cement wall, one of the sides of the bridge. Marian put her arms on the top and rested. Level with her eyes there were tree-tops, a maze of branches, the ends already pale yellow, pale red, knotted with buds.

'We aren't there yet,' Duncan said. He tugged at her arm. 'We go down.' He led her to the end of the bridge. At one side was an unofficial path: the imprints of feet, a muddy track. They climbed down gingerly, their feet sideways like children learning to go down stairs, step by step. Water was dripping on them from the icicles on the underside of the bridge.

When they had reached the bottom and were standing on level ground Marian asked, 'Are we here yet?'

'Not yet,' said Duncan. He began to walk away from the bridge. Marian hoped they were going to a place where they could sit down.

They were in one of the ravines that fissured the city, but which one she didn't know. She had gone for walks close to the one that was visible from their living room window, but nothing she saw around her was familiar. The ravine was narrow here and deep, closed in by trees which looked as though they were pinning the covering of snow to the steep sides. Far above, towards the rim, some children were playing. Marian could see their bright jackets, red and blue, and hear their faint laughter.

They were going single file along a track in the crusted snow. Some other people had walked there, but not many. At intervals she noticed what she thought were the marks of horses' hooves. All she could see of Duncan was his slouched back and his feet lifting and setting down.

She wished he would turn around so she could see his face; his expressionless coat made her uneasy.

'We'll sit down in a minute,' he said as if in answer.

She didn't see any place they might possibly sit. They were

walking now through a field of tall weedstalks whose stiff dried branches scraped against them as they passed: goldenrod, teasles, burdocks, the skeletons of anonymous grey plants. The burdocks had clusters of brown burrs and the teazles their weathered-silver spiked heads but otherwise nothing interrupted the thin branching and re-branching monotony of the field. Beyond it on either side rose the walls of the ravine. Along the top now were houses, a line of them perched on the edge, careless of the erosion-gullies that scarred the ravine-face at irregular intervals. The creek had disappeared into an underground culvert.

Marian looked behind her. The ravine had made a curve; she had walked around it without noticing; ahead of them was another bridge, a larger one. They kept walking.

'I like it down here in winter,' Duncan's voice said after a while. 'Before I've only been down here in summer. Everything grows, it's so thick with green leaves and stuff you can't see three feet in front of you, some of it's poison-ivy. And it's populated. The old drunks come down here and sleep under the bridges and the kids play here too. There's a riding-stable down here somewhere, I think what we're on is one of the bridle-paths. I used to come down because it was cooler. But it's better covered with snow. It hides the junk. They're beginning to fill this place up with junk too, you know, beginning with the creek, I wonder why they like throwing things around all over the landscape ... old tires, tin cans. ...' The voice came from a mouth she couldn't see, as though from nowhere; it was foreshortened, blunted, as if it was being blotted up, absorbed by the snow.

The ravine had widened out around them and in this place there were fewer weeds. Duncan turned off the path, breaking the crusted snow; she followed him. They plodded up the side of a small hill.

'Here we are,' Duncan said. He stopped and turned, and reached a hand to draw her up beside him.

Marian gasped and took an involuntary step back: they were standing on the very edge of a cliff. The ground ended abruptly beyond their feet. Below them was a huge roughly circular pit, with a spiral path or roadway cut round and around the sides, leading to the level snowcovered space at the bottom. Directly across from where they were standing, separated from them by perhaps a quarter of a mile of empty space, was a long shed-like black building. Everything seemed closed, deserted.

'What is it?' she asked.

'It's only the brickworks,' Duncan said. 'That's pure clay down there. They go down that road with steamshovels and dig it out.'

'I didn't know there was anything like that in the ravines,' she said. It seemed wrong to have this cavity in the city: the ravine itself was supposed to be as far down as you could go. It made her suspect the white pit-bottom also; it didn't look solid, it looked possibly hollow, dangerous, a thin layer of ice, as though if you walked on it you might fall through.

'Oh, they have lots of good things. There's a prison down here somewhere, too.'

Duncan sat down on the edge, dangling his legs nonchalantly, and took out a cigarette. After a moment she sat down beside him, although she didn't trust the earth. It was the kind of thing that caved in. They both gazed down into the gigantic hole scooped into the ground.

'I wonder what time it is,' Marian said. She listened as she spoke: the open space had swallowed up her voice.

Duncan didn't answer. He finished his cigarette in silence; then he stood up, walked a short way along the brink till he came to a flat area where there were no weeds, and lay down in the snow. He was so peaceful, stretched out there looking up at the sky, that Marian walked over to join him where he was lying.

'You'll get cold,' he said, 'but go ahead if you want to.'

She lay down at arm's length from him. It did not seem right, here, to be too close. Above, the sky was a uniform light grey, made diffusely bright by a sun concealed somewhere behind it.

Duncan spoke into the silence. 'So why can't you go back? I mean, you are getting married and so on. I thought you were the capable type.'

'I am,' she said unhappily. 'I was. I don't know.' She didn't want to discuss it.

'Some would say of course that it's all in your mind.'

'I know that,' she said, impatient: she wasn't a total idiot yet. 'But how do I get it out?'

'It ought to be obvious,' Duncan's voice said, 'that I'm the last person to ask. They tell me I live in a world of fantasies. But at least mine are more or less my own, I choose them and I sort of like them, some of the time. But you don't seem too happy with yours.'

'Maybe I should see a psychiatrist,' she said gloomily.

'Oh no, don't do that. They'd only want to adjust you.'

'But I want to be adjusted, that's just it. I don't see any point in being unstable.' It occurred to her also that she didn't see any point in starving to death. What she really wanted, she realized, had been reduced to simple safety. She thought she had been heading towards it all these months but actually she hadn't been getting anywhere. And she hadn't accomplished anything. At the moment her only solid achievement seemed to be Duncan. That was something she could hang on to.

Suddenly she needed to make sure he was still there, hadn't vanished or sunk down beneath the white surface. She wanted verification.

'How was it for you last night?' she asked. He had not yet said anything about it.

'How was what? Oh. That.' He was silent for several minutes. She listened intently, waiting for his voice as though for an oracle. But when he spoke at last he said, 'I like this place. Especially now in winter, it's so close to absolute zero. It makes me feel human. By comparison. I wouldn't like tropical islands at all, they would be too fleshy, I'd always be wondering whether I was a walking vegetable or a giant amphibian. But in the snow you're as near as possible to nothing.'

Marian was puzzled. What did this have to do with it?

'You want me to say it was stupendous, don't you?' he asked. 'That it got me out of my shell. Hatched me into manhood. Solved all my problems.'

'Well. . . .'

'Sure you do, and I could always tell you would. I like people participating in my fantasy life and I'm usually willing to participate in theirs, up to a point. It was fine; just as good as usual.'

The implication sank in smoothly as a knife through butter. She wasn't the first then. The starched nurse-like image of herself she had tried to preserve as a last resort crumpled like wet newsprint; the rest of her couldn't even work up the energy to be angry. She had been so thoroughly taken in. She should have known. But after she had thought about it for a few minutes, gazing up at the blank sky, it didn't make that much difference. There was the possibility also that this revelation was just as fraudulent as so much else had been.

She sat up, brushing the snow from her sleeves. It was time for action. 'All right, that was your joke,' she said. She would let him wonder whether or not she believed him. 'Now I've got to decide what I'm going to do.'

He grinned at her. 'Don't ask me, that's your problem. It does look as though you ought to do something: self-laceration in a vacuum eventually gets rather boring. But it's your own personal cul-de-sac, you invented it, you'll have to think of your own way out.' He stood up.

Marian stood up too. She had been calm but now she could feel desperation returning in her, seeping through her flesh like the effects of a drug. 'Duncan,' she said, 'could you maybe come back with me and talk to Peter? I don't think I can do it, I don't know what to say, he's not going to understand. . . .'

'Oh no,' he said, 'you can't do that. I'm not part of that. It would be disastrous, don't you see? I mean for me.' He wrapped his arms around his torso and held on to his own elbows.

'Please,' she said. She knew he would refuse.

'No,' he said, 'it wouldn't be right.' He turned and looked down at the two imprints their bodies had made in the snow. Then he stepped on them, first on his own and then on hers, smearing the snow with his foot. 'Come here,' he said, 'I'll show you how to get back.' He led her further along. They came to a road which rose and then dipped. Below was a giant expressway, sloping up, and in the distance another bridge, a familiar bridge with subway cars moving on it. Now she knew where she was.

'Aren't you coming with me even that far?' she asked.

'No. I'm going to stay here for a while. But you have to go now.' The tone of his voice closed her out. He turned and started to walk away.

The cars rocketed past. She looked back once when she had trudged halfway up the hillside towards the bridge. She almost expected him to have evaporated into the white expanse of the ravine, but he was still there, a dark shape against the snow, crouched on the edge and gazing into the empty pit.

Chapter Thirty

Marian had just got home and was struggling with her wrinkled dress, trying to get the zipper undone, when the phone rang. She knew who it would be.

'Hello?' she said.

Peter's voice was icy with anger. 'Marian, where the hell have you been? I've been phoning everywhere.' He sounded hung-over.

'Oh,' she said with airy casualness, 'I've been somewhere else. Sort of out.'

He lost control. 'Why the hell did you leave the party? You really disrupted the evening for me. I was looking for you to get you in a group picture and you were gone, of course I couldn't make a big production of it with all those people there but after they'd gone home I looked all over for you, your friend Lucy and I got in the car and drove up and down the streets and we called your place half a dozen times, we were both so worried. Damn nice of her to take the trouble, it's nice to know there are *some* considerate women left around. . . .'

I'll bet it is, Marian thought with a momentary twinge of jealousy, remembering Lucy's silver eyelids; but out loud she said, 'Peter, please don't get upset. I just stepped outside for a breath of fresh air and something else came up, that's all. There is absolutely nothing to get upset about. There have been no catastrophes.'

'What do you mean, upset!' he said. 'You shouldn't go wandering around the streets at night, you might get *raped*, if you're going to do these things and god knows it isn't the first time why the hell can't you think of other people once in a while? You could at least have told me where you were, your parents called me long-distance, they're frantic because you weren't on the bus and what was I supposed to tell them?'

Oh yes, she thought; she had forgotten about that. 'Well, I'm perfectly all right,' she said.

'But where were you? When we'd discovered you'd left and I started quietly asking people if they'd seen you I must say I got a pretty funny story from that prince-charming friend of yours, Trevor or whatever the hell his name is. Who's this guy he was telling me about anyway?'

'Please, Peter,' she said, 'I just hate talking about things like this over the phone.' She had a sudden desire to tell him the whole story, but what good would that do since nothing had been proved or accomplished? Instead she said, 'What time is it?'

'Two-thirty,' he said, his voice surprised into neutrality by this appeal to simple fact.

'Well, why don't you come over a bit later? Maybe about five-thirty. For tea. And then we can talk it all over.' She made her voice sweet, conciliatory. She was conscious of her own craftiness. Though she hadn't made any decisions she could feel she was about to make one and she needed time.

'Well, all right,' he said peevishly, 'but it better be good.' They hung up together.

Marian went into the bedroom and took off her clothes; then she went downstairs and took a quick bath. The lower regions were silent; the lady down below was probably brooding in her dark den or praying for the swift destruction of Ainsley by heavenly thunderbolts. In a spirit approaching gay rebellion Marian neglected to erase her bath-tub ring.

What she needed was something that avoided words, she didn't want to get tangled up in a discussion. Some way she could know what was real: a test, simple and direct as litmus-paper. She finished dressing – a plain grey wool would be appropriate – and put on her coat, then located her everyday purse and counted the money. She went out to the kitchen and sat down at the table to make herself a list, but threw down the pencil after she had written several words. She knew what she needed to get.

In the supermarket she went methodically up and down the aisles, relentlessly out-manoeuvring the muskrat-furred ladies, edging the Saturday children to the curb, picking the things off the shelves. Her image was taking shape. Eggs. Flour. Lemons for the flavour. Sugar, icing-sugar, vanilla, salt, food-colouring. She wanted everything new, she didn't want to use anything that was already in the house. Chocolate – no, cocoa, that would be better. A glass tube full of round silver decorations. Three nesting plastic bowls, teaspoons, aluminium cake-decorator and a cake tin. Lucky, she thought, they sell almost everything in supermarkets these days. She started back towards the apartment, carrying her paper bag.

Sponge or angel-food? she wondered. She decided on sponge. It was more fitting.

She turned on the oven. That was one part of the kitchen that had not been over-run by the creeping skin-disease-covering of dirt, mostly because they hadn't been using it much recently. She tied on an apron and rinsed the new bowls and the other new utensils under the tap, but did not disturb any of the dirty dishes. Later for them. Right now she didn't have time. She dried the things and began to crack and separate the eggs, hardly thinking, concentrating all her attention on the movements of her hands, and then when she was beating and sifting and folding, on the relative times and textures. Spongecake needed a light hand. She poured the batter into the tin and drew a fork sideways through it to break the large air-bubbles. As she slid the tin into the oven she almost hummed with pleasure. It was a long time since she had made a cake.

While the cake was in the oven baking she re-washed the bowls and mixed the icing. An ordinary butter icing, that would be the best. Then she divided the icing into three parts in the three bowls. The largest portion she left white, the next one she tinted a bright pink, almost red, with the red food-colouring she had bought, and the last one she made dark brown by stirring cocoa into it.

What am I going to put her on? she thought when she had finished. I'll have to wash a dish. She unearthed a long platter from the very bottom of the stack of plates in the sink and scoured it thoroughly under the tap. It took quite a lot of detergent to get the scum off.

She tested the cake; it was done. She took it out of the oven and turned it upside-down to cool.

She was glad Ainsley wasn't home: she didn't want any interference with what she was going to do. In fact it didn't look as though Ainsley had been home at all. There was no sign of her green dress. In her room a suitcase was lying open on the bed where she must have left it the night before. Some of the surface flotsam was eddying into it, as though drawn by a vortex. Marian wondered how Ainsley was ever going to cram the random contents of the room into anything as limited and rectilineal as a set of suitcases.

While the cake was cooling she went into the bedroom and tidied her hair, pulling it back and pinning it to get rid of the remains of the hairdresser's convolutions. She felt lightheaded, almost dizzy: it must be the lack of sleep and the lack of food. She grinned into the mirror, showing her teeth.

The cake wasn't cooling quickly enough. She refused to put it into the refrigerator though. It would pick up the smells. She took it out of the tin and set it on the clean platter, opened the kitchen window, and stuck it out on the snowy sill. She knew what happened to cakes that were iced warm – everything melted.

She wondered what time it was. Her watch was still on the top of the dresser where she had left it the day before but it had run down. She didn't want to turn on Ainsley's transistor, that would be too distracting. She was getting jittery already. There used to be a number you could phone ... but anyway she would have to hurry.

She took the cake off the sill, felt it to see if it was cool enough, and put it on the kitchen table. Then she began to operate. With the two forks she pulled it in half through the middle. One half she placed flat side down on the platter. She scooped out part of it and made a head with the section she had taken out. Then she nipped in a waist at the sides. The other half she pulled into strips for the arms and legs. The spongy cake was pliable, easy to mould. She stuck all the separate members together with white icing, and used the rest of the icing to cover the shape she had constructed. It was bumpy in places and too many crumbs in the skin, but it would do. She reinforced the feet and ankles with tooth-picks.

Now she had a blank white body. It looked slighty obscene, lying there soft and sugary and featureless on the platter. She set about clothing it, filling the cake-decorator with bright pink icing. First she gave it a bikini, but that was too sparse. She filled in the midriff. Now it had an ordinary bathing-suit, but that still wasn't exactly what she wanted. She kept extending, adding to top and bottom, until she had a dress of sorts. In a burst of exuberance she added a row of ruffles around the neckline, and more ruffles at the hem of the dress. She made a smiling lush-lipped pink mouth and pink shoes to match. Finally she put five pink fingernails on each of the amorphous hands.

The cake looked peculiar with only a mouth and no hair or eyes. She rinsed out the cake-decorator and filled it with chocolate icing. She drew a nose, and two large eyes, to which she appended many eyelashes and two eyebrows, one above each eye. For emphasis she made a line demarcating one leg from the other, and similar lines to separate the arms from the body. The hair took longer. It involved masses of intricate baroque scrolls and swirls, piled high on the head and spilling down over the shoulders.

The eyes were still blank. She decided on green – the only other possibilities were red and yellow, since they were the only other colours she had – and with a toothpick applied two irises of green food-colouring.

Now there were only the globular silver decorations to add. One went in each eye, for a pupil. With the others she made a floral design on the pink dress, and stuck a few in the hair. Now the woman looked like an elegant antique china figurine. For an instant she wished she had bought some birthday candles; but where could they be put? There was really no room for them. The image was complete.

Her creation gazed up at her, its face doll-like and vacant except for the small silver glitter of intelligence in each green eye. While making it she had been almost gleeful, but now, contemplating it, she was pensive. All that work had gone into the lady and now what would happen to her?

'You look delicious,' she told her. 'Very appetizing. And that's what will happen to you; that's what you get for being food.' At the thought of food her stomach contracted. She felt a certain pity for her creature but she was powerless now to do anything about it. Her fate had been decided. Already Peter's footsteps were coming up the stairs.

Marian had a swift vision of her own monumental silliness, of how infantile and undignified she would seem in the eyes of any rational observer. What kind of game did she think she was playing? But that wasn't the point, she told herself nervously, pushing back a strand of hair. Though if Peter found her silly she would believe it, she would accept his version of herself, he would laugh and they would sit down and have a quiet cup of tea.

She smiled gravely at Peter as he came up out of the stairwell. The expression on his face, a scowl combined with a jutting chin, meant he was still angry. He was wearing a costume suitable for being angry in: the suit stern, tailored, remote, but the tie a paisley with touches of sullen maroon.

'Now what's all this . . .' he began.

'Peter, why don't you go into the living room and sit down? I have a surprise for you. Then we can have a talk if you like.' She smiled at him again.

He was puzzled, and forgot to sustain his frown; he must have been expecting an awkward apology. But he did as she suggested. She remained in the doorway for a moment, looking almost tenderly at the back of his head resting against the chesterfield. Now that she had seen him again, the actual Peter, solid as ever, the fears of the evening before had dwindled to foolish hysteria and the flight to Duncan had become a stupidity, an evasion; she could hardly remember what he looked like. Peter was not the enemy after all, he was just a normal human being like most other people. She wanted to touch his neck, tell him that he shouldn't get upset, that everything was going to be all right. It was Duncan that was the mutation.

But there was something about his shoulders. He must have been sitting with his arms folded. The face on the other side of that head could have belonged to anyone. And they all wore clothes of real cloth and had real bodies: those in the newspapers, those still unknown, waiting for their chance to aim from the upstairs window; you passed them on the streets every day. It was easy to see him as normal and safe in the afternoon, but that didn't alter things. The price of this version of reality was testing the other one.

She went into the kitchen and returned, bearing the platter in front of her, carefully and with reverence, as though she was carrying something sacred in a procession, an icon or the crown on a cushion in a play. She knelt, setting the platter on the coffee-table in front of Peter.

'You've been trying to destroy me, haven't you,' she said. 'You've been trying to assimilate me. But I've made you a substitute, something you'll like much better. This is what you really wanted all along, isn't it? I'll get you a fork,' she added somewhat prosaically.

Peter stared from the cake to her face and back again. She wasn't smiling.

His eyes widened in alarm. Apparently he didn't find her silly.

When he had gone – and he went quite rapidly, they didn't have much of a conversation after all, he seemed embarrassed and eager to leave and even refused a cup of tea – she stood looking down at the figure. So Peter hadn't devoured it after all. As a symbol it had definitely failed. It looked up at her with its silvery eyes, enigmatic, mocking, succulent.

Suddenly she was hungry. Extremely hungry. The cake after all was only a cake. She picked up the platter, carried it to the kitchen table and located a fork. 'I'll start with the feet,' she decided.

She considered the first mouthful. It seemed odd but most pleasant to be actually tasting and chewing and swallowing again. Not bad, she thought critically; needs a touch more lemon though.

Already the part of her not occupied with eating was having a wave of nostalgia for Peter, as though for a style that had gone out of fashion and was beginning to turn up on the sad Salvation Army clothes racks. She could see him in her mind, posed jauntily in the foreground of an elegant salon with chandeliers and draperies, impeccably dressed, a glass of scotch in one hand; his foot was on the head of a stuffed lion and he had an eyepatch over one eye. Beneath one arm was strapped a revolver. Around the margin was an edging of gold scrollwork and slightly above Peter's left ear was a thumbtack. She licked her fork meditatively. He would definitely succeed.

She was halfway up the legs when she heard footsteps, two sets of them, coming up the stairs. Then Ainsley appeared in the kitchen doorway with Fischer Smythe's furry head behind her. She still had on her bluegreen dress, much the worse for wear. So was she: her face was haggard and in only the past twenty-four hours her belly seemed to have grown noticeably rounder.

'Hi,' said Marian, waving her fork at them. She speared a chunk of pink thigh and carried it to her mouth.

Fischer had leaned against the wall and closed his eyes as soon as he reached the top of the stairs, but Ainsley focussed on her. 'Marian, what have you got there?' She walked over to see. 'It's a woman – a woman made of cake!' She gave Marian a strange look.

Marian chewed and swallowed. 'Have some,' she said, 'it's really good. I made it this afternoon.'

Ainsley's mouth opened and closed, fishlike, as though she was trying to gulp down the full implication of what she saw. 'Marian!' she exclaimed at last, with horror. 'You're rejecting your femininity!'

Marian stopped chewing and stared at Ainsley, who was regarding her through the hair that festooned itself over her eyes with wounded concern, almost with sternness. How did she manage it, that stricken attitude, that high seriousness? She was almost as morally earnest as the lady down below.

Marian looked back at her platter. The woman lay there, still smiling glassily, her legs gone. 'Nonsense,' she said. 'It's only a cake.' She plunged her fork into the carcass, neatly severing the body from the head.

PART THREE

Chapter Thirty-one

I was cleaning up the apartment. It had taken me two days to gather the strength to face it, but I had finally started. I had to go about it layer by layer. First there was the surface debris. I began with Ainsley's room, stuffing everything she had left behind into cardboard cartons: the half-empty cosmetic jars and used lipsticks, the strata of old newspapers and magazines on the floor, the desiccated banana-peel I found under the bed, the clothes she had rejected. All the things of mine I wanted to throw out went into the same boxes.

When the floors and furniture had been cleared I dusted everything in sight, including the mouldings and the tops of the doors and the window sills. Then I did the floors, sweeping and then scrubbing and waxing. The amount of dirt that came off was astounding: it was like uncovering an extra floor. Then I washed the dishes and after that the kitchen window-curtains. Then I stopped for lunch. After lunch I tackled the refrigerator. I did not examine closely the horrors that had accumulated inside it. I could see well enough from holding the little jars up to the light that they had better not be opened. The various objects within had been industriously sprouting hair, fur or feathers, each as its nature dictated, and I could guess what they would smell like. I lowered them carefully into the garbage bag. The freezing compartment I attacked with an icepick, but I discovered that the thick covering of ice, though mossy and spongelike on the outside, was hard as a rock underneath, and I left it to melt a little before attempting to chip or pry it loose.

I had just begun on the windows when the phone rang. It was Duncan. I was surprised; I had more or less forgotten about him.

'Well?' he asked. 'What happened?'

'It's all off,' I said. 'I realized Peter was trying to destroy me. So now I'm looking for another job.'

'Oh,' said Duncan. 'Actually I didn't mean that. I was wondering more about Fischer.'

'Oh,' I said. I might have known.

'I mean, I think I know what happened but I'm not sure why. He's abandoned his responsibilities, you know.'

'His responsibilities? You mean graduate school?'

'No,' said Duncan. 'I mean me. What am I going to do?'

'I haven't the faintest idea,' I said. I was irritated with him for not wanting to discuss what I was going to do myself. Now that I was thinking of myself in the first person singular again I found my own situation much more interesting than his.

'Now, now,' Duncan said, 'we can't both be like that. One of us has to be the sympathetic listener and the other one gets to be tortured and confused. You were tortured and confused last time.'

Face it, I thought, you can't win. 'Oh all right. Why don't you come over for some tea a bit later then? The apartment's a mess,' I added apologetically.

When he arrived I was finishing the windows, standing on a chair and wiping off the white glass-cleaner I had spread on them. We hadn't cleaned them for a long time and they had got quite silted over with dust, and I was thinking it was going to be curious to be able to see out of them again. It bothered me that there was still some dirt on the outside I couldn't reach: soot and rainstreaks. I didn't hear Duncan come in. He had probably been standing in the room for several minutes watching me before he announced his presence by saying 'Here I am.'

I jumped. 'Oh hi,' I said, 'I'll be right with you as soon as I finish this window.' He wandered off in the direction of the kitchen.

After giving the window one last polish with a sleeve torn from one of Ainsley's abandoned blouses I got down from the chair, somewhat reluctantly – I like to finish things once I've begun them and there were still several windows left uncleaned; besides, the prospect of discussing the love life of Fischer Smythe wasn't all that compelling – and went out to the kitchen. I found Duncan sitting in one of the chairs, regarding the open refrigerator door with a mixture of distaste and anxiety.

'What smells in here?' he asked, sniffing the air.

'Oh, various things,' I answered lightly. 'Floor polish and window cleaner and some other things.' I went over and opened the kitchen window. 'Tea or coffee?'

'Doesn't matter,' he said. 'Well, what's the real truth?'

'You must know they're married.' Tea would be easier, but a quick root through the cupboards didn't uncover any. I measured the coffee into the percolator.

'Well, yes, sort of. Fish left us a rather ambiguous note. But how did it happen?'

'How do these things ever happen? They met at the party,' I said. I turned on the coffee and sat down. I had thoughts of holding out on him but he was beginning to look hurt. 'Of course there are a few complications, but I think it will work out.' Ainsley had come in the day before after another prolonged absence and had packed her suitcases while Fischer waited in the living room, head thrown back against the cushions of the chesterfield, beard bristling with the consciousness of its own vitality, eyes closed. She had given me to understand in the few sentences she had time for that they were going to Niagara Falls for their honeymoon and that she thought Fischer would make, as she put it, 'a very good one'.

I explained all this to Duncan as well as I could. He did not seem either dismayed or delighted, or even surprised, by any of it.

'Well,' he said, 'I guess it's a good thing for Fischer, mankind cannot bear too much unreality. Trevor was quite disturbed though. He's gone to bed with a nervous headache and refuses to get up even to cook. What it all means is that I'm going to have to move out. You've heard how destructive a broken home can be and I wouldn't want my personality to get warped.'

'I hope it will be all right for Ainsley.' I really did hope so. I was pleased with her for justifying my superstitious belief in her ability to take care of herself: for a while there I had begun to lose faith. 'At least,' I said, 'she's got what she thinks she wants, and I suppose that's something.'

'Cast out into the world again,' Duncan said reflectively. He was gnawing on his thumb. 'I wonder what will become of me.' He did not seem overly interested in the question.

Talking about Ainsley made me think of Leonard. I had called Clara shortly after I had heard the news about Ainsley's marriage, so she could tell Len it was safe to come out of hiding. Later she had called back. 'I'm quite worried,' she said, 'he didn't seem nearly as relieved as he ought to have been. I thought he would go back to his apartment right away but he said he didn't want to. He's afraid to go outside the house, though he seems perfectly happy as long as he stays in Arthur's room. The children adore him most of the time and I must say it's rather nice having someone who takes them off my hands a bit, but the trouble is he plays with all of Arthur's toys and sometimes they get into fights. And he hasn't been going to work at all, he hasn't even phoned them to tell them where he is. If he just lets himself go like this much longer I'm not sure how I'm going to cope.' Nevertheless she had sounded more competent than usual.

There was a loud metallic clunk from inside the refrigerator. Duncan jerked, and took his thumb out of his mouth. 'What was that?'

'Oh, just falling ice, I expect,' I said. 'I'm defrosting the refrigerator.' The coffee smelled done. I set two cups on the table and poured.

'Well, are you eating again?' Duncan asked after a moment of silence.

'As a matter of fact I am,' I said. 'I had steak for lunch.' This last remark had been motivated by pride. It still was miraculous to me that I had attempted anything so daring and had succeeded.

'Well, it's healthier that way,' Duncan said. He looked at me directly for the first time since he had come in. 'You look better too. You look jaunty and full of good things. How did you do it?'

'I told you,' I said. 'Over the phone.'

'You mean that stuff about Peter trying to destroy you?'

I nodded.

'That's ridiculous,' he said gravely. 'Peter wasn't trying to destroy you. That's just something you made up. Actually you were trying to destroy him.'

I had a sinking feeling. 'Is that true?' I asked.

'Search your soul,' he said, gazing hypnotically at me from behind his hair. He drank some coffee and paused to give me time, then added, 'But the real truth is that it wasn't Peter at all. It was me. I was trying to destroy you.'

I gave a nervous laugh. 'Don't say that.'

'Okay,' he said, 'ever eager to please. Maybe Peter was trying to destroy me, or maybe I was trying to destroy him, or we were both trying to destroy each other, how's that? What does it matter, you're back to so-called reality, you're a consumer.'

'Incidentally,' I said, remembering, 'would you like some cake?' I had half the torso and the head left over.

He nodded. I got him a fork and took the remains of the cadaver down from the shelf where I had put it. I unwrapped its cellophane shroud. 'It's mostly the head,' I said.

'I didn't know you could bake cakes,' he said after the first forkful. 'It's almost as good as Trevor's.'

'Thank you,' I said modestly. 'I like to cook when I have the time.' I sat watching the cake disappear, the smiling pink mouth first, then the nose and then one eye. For a moment there was nothing left of the face but the last green eye; then it too vanished, like a wink. He started devouring the hair.

It gave me a peculiar sense of satisfaction to see him eat as if the work hadn't been wasted after all – although the cake was absorbed without exclamations of pleasure, even without noticeable expression. I smiled comfortably at him.

He did not smile back; he was concentrating on the business at hand.

He scraped the last chocolate curl up with his fork and pushed away the plate. 'Thank you,' he said, licking his lips. 'It was delicious.'

SURFACING

ONE

Chapter One

I can't believe I'm on this road again, twisting along past the lake where the white birches are dying, the disease is spreading up from the south, and I notice they now have sea-planes for hire. But this is still near the city limits; we didn't go through, it's swelled enough to have a bypass, that's success.

I never thought of it as a city but as the last or first outpost depending on which way we were going, an accumulation of sheds and boxes and one main street with a movie theatre, the itz, the oyal, red R burnt out, and two restaurants which served identical grey hamburger steaks plastered with mud gravy and canned peas, watery and pallid as fisheyes, and french fries bleary with lard. Order a poached egg, my mother said, you can tell if it's fresh by the edges.

In one of those restaurants before I was born my brother got under the table and slid his hands up and down the waitress's legs while she was bringing the food; it was during the war and she had on shiny orange rayon stockings, he'd never seen them before, my mother didn't wear them. A different year there we ran through the snow across the sidewalk in our bare feet because we had no shoes, they'd worn out during the summer. In the car that time we sat with our feet wrapped in blankets, pretending we were wounded. My brother said the Germans shot our feet off.

Now though I'm in another car, David's and Anna's; it's sharp-finned and striped with chrome, a lumbering monster left over from ten years ago, he has to reach under the instrument panel to turn on the lights. David says they can't afford a newer one, which probably isn't true. He's a good driver, I realize that, I keep my outside hand on the door in spite of it. To brace myself and so I can get out quickly if I have to. I've driven in the same car with them before but on this road it doesn't seem right, either the three of them are in the wrong place or I am.

I'm in the back seat with the packsacks; this one, Joe, is sitting beside me chewing gum and holding my hand, they both pass the time. I examine the hand: the palm is broad, the short fingers tighten and relax, fiddling with my gold ring, turning it, it's a reflex of his. He has peasant hands, I have peasant feet, Anna told us that. Everyone now can do a little magic, she reads hands at parties, she says it's a substitute for conversation. When she did mine she said 'Do you have a twin?' I said No. 'Are you positive,' she said, 'because some of your lines are double.' Her index finger traced me: 'You had a good childhood but then there's this funny break.' She puckered her forehead and I said I just wanted to know how long I was going to live, she could skip the rest. After that she told us Joe's hands were dependable but not sensitive and I laughed, which was a mistake.

From the side he's like the buffalo on the US nickel, shaggy and blunt-snouted, with small clenched eyes and the defiant but insane look of a species once dominant, now threatened with extinction. That's how he thinks of himself too: deposed, unjustly. Secretly he would like them to set up a kind of park for him, like a bird sanctuary. Beautiful Joe.

He feels me watching him and lets go of my hand. Then he takes his gum out, bundling it in the silver wrapper, and sticks it in the ashtray and crosses his arms. That means I'm not supposed to observe him; I face front.

In the first few hours of driving we moved through flattened cow-sprinkled hills and leaf trees and dead elm skeletons, then into the needle trees and the cuttings dynamited in pink and grey granite and the flimsy tourist cabins, and the signs saying GATEWAY TO THE NORTH, at least four towns claim to be that. The future is in the North, that was a political slogan once; when my father heard it he said there was nothing in the North but the past and not much of that either. Wherever he is now, dead or alive and nobody knows which, he's no longer making epigrams. They have no right to get old. I envy people whose parents died when they were young, that's easier to remember, they stay unchanged. I was sure mine would anyway, I could leave and return much later and everything would be the same. I thought of them as living in some other time, going about their own concerns closed safe behind a wall as translucent as jello, mammoths frozen in a glacier. All I would have to do was come back when I was ready but I kept putting it off, there would be too many explanations.

Now we're passing the turnoff to the pit the Americans hollowed out. From here it looks like an innocent hill, spruce-covered, but the thick power lines running into the forest give it away. I heard they'd left, maybe that was a ruse, they could easily still be living in there, the generals in concrete bunkers and the ordinary soldiers in underground apartment buildings where the lights burn all the time. There's no way of checking because we aren't allowed in. The city invited them to stay, they were good for business, they drank a lot.

'That's where the rockets are,' I say. *Were*. I don't correct it.

David says 'Bloody fascist pig Yanks,' as though he's commenting on the weather.

Anna says nothing. Her head rests on the back of the seat, the ends of her light hair whipping in the draft from the side window that won't close properly. Earlier she was singing, House of the Rising Sun and Lili Marlene, both of them several times, trying to make her voice go throaty and deep; but it came out like a hoarse child's. David turned on the radio, he couldn't get anything, we were between stations. When she was in the middle of St. Louis Blues he began to whistle and she stopped. She's my best friend, my best woman friend; I've known her two months.

I lean forward and say to David, 'The bottle house is around this next curve and to the left,' and he nods and slows the car. I told them about it earlier, I guessed it was the kind of object that would interest them. They're making a movie, Joe is doing the camera work, he's never done it before but David says they're the new Renaissance Men, you teach yourself what you need to learn. It was mostly David's idea, he calls himself the director: they already have the credits worked out. He wants to get shots of things they come across, random samples he calls them, and that will be the name of the movie too: *Random Samples*. When they've used up their supply of film (which was all they could afford; and the camera is rented) they're going to look at what they've collected and rearrange it.

'How can you tell what to put in if you don't already know what it's about?' I asked David when he was describing it. He gave me one of his initiate-to-novice stares. 'If you close your mind in advance like that you wreck it. What you need is flow.' Anna, over by the stove measuring out the coffee, said everyone she knew was making a movie, and David said that was no fucking reason why he shouldn't. She said 'You're right, sorry'; but she laughs about it behind his back, she calls it Random Pimples.

The bottle house is built of pop bottles cemented together with the bottoms facing out, green ones and brown ones in zig-zag patterns like the ones they taught us in school to draw on teepees; there's a wall around it made of bottles too, arranged in letters so the brown ones spell BOTTLE VILLA.

'Neat,' David says, and they get out of the car with the camera. Anna and I climb out after them; we stretch our arms, and Anna has a cigarette. She's wearing a purple tunic and white bellbottoms, they have a smear on them already, grease from the car. I told her she should wear jeans or something but she said she looks fat in them.

'Who made it, Christ, think of the work,' she says, but I don't know anything about it except that it's been there forever, the tangled black spruce swamp around it making it even more unlikely, a preposterous monument to some quirkish person exiled or perhaps a voluntary recluse like my father, choosing this swamp because it was the only place where he could fulfill his lifelong dream of living in a house of bottles. Inside the wall is an attempted lawn and a border with orange mattress-tuft marigolds.

'Great,' says David, 'really neat,' and he puts his arm around Anna and hugs her briefly to show he's pleased, as though she is somehow responsible for the Bottle Villa herself. We get back in the car.

I watch the side windows as though it's a TV screen. There's nothing I can remember till we reach the border, marked by the sign that says BIENVENUE on one side and WELCOME on the other. The sign has bullet holes in it, rusting red around the edges. It always did, in the fall the hunters use it for target practice; no matter how many times they replace it or paint it the bullet holes reappear, as though they aren't put there but grow by a kind of inner logic or infection, like mould or boils. Joe wants to film the sign but David says 'Naaa, what for?'

Now we're on my home ground, foreign territory. My throat constricts, as it learned to do when I discovered people could say words that would go into my ears meaning nothing. To be deaf and dumb would be easier. The cards they poke at you when they want a quarter, with the hand alphabet on them. Even so, you would need to learn spelling.

The first smell is the mill, sawdust, there are mounds of it in the yard with the stacked timber slabs. The pulpwood goes elsewhere to the paper mill, but the bigger logs are corralled in a boom on the river, a ring of logs chained together with the free ones nudging each other inside it; they travel to the saws in a clanking overhead chute, that hasn't been changed. The car goes under it and we're curving up into the tiny company town, neatly planned with public flowerbeds and an eighteenth century fountain in the middle, stone dolphins and a cherub with part of the face missing. It looks like an imitation but it may be real.

Anna says 'Oh wow, what a great fountain.'

'The company built the whole thing,' I say, and David says 'Rotten capitalist bastards' and begins to whistle again.

I tell him to turn right and he does. The road ought to be here, but instead there's a battered chequerboard, the way is blocked.

'Now what,' says David.

We didn't bring a map because I knew we wouldn't need one. 'I'll have to ask,' I say, so he backs the car out and we drive along the main street till we come to a corner store, magazines and candy.

'You must mean the old road,' the woman says with only a trace of an accent. 'It's been closed for years, what you need is the new one.' I buy four vanilla cones because you aren't supposed to ask without buying anything. She gouges down into the cardboard barrel with a metal scoop. Before, the ice cream came rolled in pieces of paper which they would peel off like bark, pressing the short logs of ice cream into the cones with their thumbs. Those must be obsolete.

I go back to the car and tell David the directions. Joe says he likes chocolate better.

Nothing is the same, I don't know the way any more. I slide my tongue around the ice cream, trying to concentrate on it, they put seaweed in it now, but I'm starting to shake, why is the road different, he shouldn't have allowed them to do it, I want to turn around and go back to the city and never find out what happened to him. I'll start crying, that would be horrible, none of them would know what to do and neither would I. I bite down into the cone and I can't feel anything for a minute but the knife-hard pain up the side of my face. Anaesthesia, that's one technique: if it hurts invent a different pain. I'm all right.

David finishes his cone, tossing the carton-flavoured tip out the window, and starts the car. We go through a part that's spread out from the town since I was here, freshly built square bungalows like city ones except for the pink and baby blue trim, and a few oblong shacks further along, tar-paper and bare boards. A clutch of children playing in the wet mud that substitutes for lawns; most of them are dressed in clothes too big for them, which makes them seem stunted.

'They must fuck a lot here,' Anna says, 'I guess it's the Church.' Then she says 'Aren't I awful.'

Beyond the houses, two older children, darkfaced, hold out tin cans toward the car. Raspberries perhaps.

We come to the gas station where the woman said to turn left and David groans with joy, 'Oh god look at that,' and they pile out as though it will escape if they aren't quick enough. What they're after is the three stuffed moose on a platform near the pumps: they're dressed in human clothes and wired standing up on their hind legs, a father moose with a trench-coat and a pipe in his mouth, a mother moose in a print dress and flowered hat and a little boy moose in short pants, a striped jersey and a baseball cap, waving an American flag.

Anna and I follow. I go up behind David and say 'Don't you need some gas,' he shouldn't use the moose without paying, like the washrooms they're here to attract customers.

'Oh look,' Anna says, hand going to her mouth, 'there's another one on the roof,' and there is, a little girl moose in a frilly skirt and a pigtailed blonde wig, holding a red parasol in one hoof. They get her too. The owner of the gas station is standing behind his plateglass show-window in his undershirt, scowling at us through the film of dust.

When we're back in the car I say as though defending myself, 'Those weren't here before.' Anna's head swivels round, my voice must sound odd.

'Before what?' she says.

The new road is paved and straight, two lanes with a line down the middle. Already it's beginning to gather landmarks, a few advertisement signs, a roadside crucifix with a wooden Christ, ribs sticking out, the alien god, mysterious to me as ever. Underneath it are a couple of jam jars with flowers, daisies and red devil's paintbrush and the white ones you can dry, Indian Posies, Everlasting, there must have been a car accident.

At intervals the old road crosses us; it was dirt, full of bumps and potholes, it followed the way the land went, up and down the hills and around the cliffs and boulders. They used to go over it as fast as possible, their father knew every inch of it and could take it (he said) blindfolded, which was what they often seemed to be doing, grinding up past the signs that said PETITE VITESSE and plunging down over the elevator edges and scraping around the rockfaces, GARDEZ LE DROIT, horn hooting; the rest of them clamped onto the inside of the car, getting sicker and sicker despite the Lifesavers their mother would hand out, and finally throwing up groggily by the side of the road, blue asters and pink fireweed, if he could stop in time or out the car window if he couldn't or into paper bags, he anticipated emergencies, if he was in a hurry and didn't want to stop at all.

That won't work, I can't tell them 'they' as if they were somebody else's family: I have to keep myself from telling that story. Still though, seeing the old road billowing along at a distance through the trees (ruts and traces already blurring with grass and saplings, soon it will be gone) makes me reach into my bag for the Lifesavers I brought. But they aren't needed any more, even though the new road turns from pavement into gravel ('Must've elected the wrong guy last time around,' David says jokingly) and the familiar smell of road dust fuming behind and around us mixes with the gas-and-upholstery smell of the car.

'Thought you said this would be bad,' David says over his shoulder, 'it's not bad at all.' We're nearly to the village already, the two roads joining here but widened – rock blasted, trees bulldozed over, roots in the air, needles reddening – past the flat cliff where the election slogans are painted and painted over, some faded and defaced, others fresh yellow and white, VOTEZ GODET, VOTEZ OBRIEN, along with hearts and initials and words and advertisements, THÉ SALADA, BLUE MOON COTTAGES ½ MILE, QUÉBEC LIBRE, FUCK YOU, BUVEZ COCA COLA GLACÉ, JESUS SAVES, mélange of demands and languages, an x-ray of it would be the district's entire history.

But they've cheated, we're here too soon and I feel deprived of something, as though I can't really get here unless I've suffered; as though the first view of the lake, which we can see now, blue and cool as redemption, should be through tears and a haze of vomit.

Chapter Two

We slur down the last hill, gravel pinging off the underside of the car, and suddenly there's a thing that isn't supposed to be here. MOTEL, BAR BIÈRE BEER the sign reads, neon even, someone is trying; but to no avail, there aren't any cars parked outside and the VACANCY notice is up. The building is like any other cheap motel, long grey stucco with aluminum doors; the earth around it is still chunky and raw, not yet overgrown with the road weeds.

'Let's pick up a few,' David says, to Joe; he's already swerved the car.

We head towards the door but then I stop, it's the best place to leave them, and say 'You go in and have a beer or something, I'll be back in about half an hour.'

'Right,' David says. He knows what to avoid.

'Want me to come?' Joe offers, but when I say No relief gleams through his beard. The three of them disappear through the screen door of the bar and I walk the rest of the way down the hill.

I like them, I trust them, I can't think of anyone else I like better, but right now I wish they weren't here. Though they're necessary: David's and Anna's car was the only way I could make it, there's no bus and no train and I never hitch. They're doing me a favour, which they disguised by saying it would be fun, they like to travel. But my reason for being here embarrasses them, they don't understand it. They all disowned their parents long ago, the way you are supposed to: Joe never mentions his mother and father, Anna says hers were nothing people and David calls his The Pigs.

There was a covered bridge here once, but it was too far north to be quaint. They tore it down three years before I left, to improve the dam, and replaced it with the concrete bridge which is here now, enormous, monumental, dwarfing the village. It's the dam that controls the lake: sixty years ago they raised the lake level so that whenever they wanted to flush the logs down the narrow outflow river to the mill they would have enough water power. But they don't do much logging here any more. A few men work on railway maintenance, one freight train a day; a couple of families run the stores, the small one where they used to speak English, the other where they wouldn't. The rest process the tourists, business-men in plaid shirts still creased from the cellophane packages, and wives, if they come, who sit in twos on the screened blackflyproof porches of the single-room cabins and complain to each other while the men play at fishing.

I pause to lean over the railing on the river side. The floodgates are open, the froth-coloured and brown rapids topple over the rocks, the sound rushes. The sound is one of the first things I remember, that was what warned them. It was night, I was lying in the bottom of the canoe; they had started out from the village but a heavy fog had risen, so thick they could hardly see the water. They found the shoreline and followed it along; it was dead silent, they could hear what they thought was the howling of wolves, muffled by forest and mist, it meant they had taken the right direction. Then there was the pouring noise of the rapids and they saw where they were, just as the current caught them. They were going backwards, the howling was the village dogs. If the canoe had tipped over we would have been killed, but they were calm, they didn't act like danger; what stayed in my head was only the mist whiteness, the hush of moving water and the rocking motion, total safety.

Anna was right, I had a good childhood; it was in the middle of the war, flecked grey newsreels I never saw, bombs and concentration camps, the leaders roaring at the crowds from inside their uniforms, pain and useless death, flags rippling in time to the anthems. But I didn't know about that till later, when my brother found out and told me. At the time it felt like peace.

Now I'm in the village, walking through it, waiting for the nostalgia to hit, for the cluster of nondescript buildings to be irradiated with inner light like a plug-in crêche, as it has been so often in memory; but nothing happens. It hasn't gotten any bigger, these days the children probably move to the city. The same two-storey frame houses with nasturtiums on the windowsills and squared roof-corners, motley lines of washing trailing from them like the tails of kites; though some of the houses are slicker and have changed colour. The white doll-house-sized church above on the rock hillside is neglected, peeling paint and a broken window, the old priest must be gone. What I mean is dead.

Down by the shore, a lot of boats are tied up at the government dock but not many cars parked: more boats than cars, a bad season. I try to decide which of the cars is my father's but as I scan them I realize I no longer know what kind of car he would be driving.

I reach the turnoff to Paul's, a rough dirt path rutted by tires, crossing the railroad tracks and continuing through a swamp field, logs laid side by side over the soggy parts. A few black flies catch up with me, it's July, past the breeding time, but as usual there are some left.

The road goes up and I climb it, along the backs of the houses Paul built for his son and his son-in-law and his other son, his clan. Paul's is the original, yellow with maroon trim, squat farmhouse pattern; though this isn't farming country, it's mostly rock and where there's any soil it's thin and sandy. The closest Paul ever got to farming was to have a cow, killed by the milkbottle. The shed where it and the horses used to live is now a garage.

In the clearing behind the house two 1950s cars are resting, a pink one and a red one, raised on wooden blocks, no wheels; scattered around them are the rusting remains of older cars: like my father, Paul saves everything useful. The house has added a pointed structure like a church spire, made of former car parts welded together; on top of it is a TV antenna and on top of that a lightning rod.

Paul is at home, he's in the vegetable garden at the side of the house. He straightens up to watch me, his face leathery and retained as ever, like a closed suitcase; I don't think he knows who I am.

'Bonjour monsieur,' I say when I'm at the fence. He takes a step towards me, still guarding, and I say 'Don't you remember me,' and smile. Again the strangling feeling, paralysis of the throat; but

Paul speaks English, he's been outside. 'It was very kind of you to write.'

'Ah,' he says, not recognizing me but deducing who I must be, 'Bonjour,' and then he smiles too. He clasps his hands in front of him like a priest or a porcelain mandarin; he doesn't say anything else. We stand there on either side of the fence, our faces petrified in well-intentioned curves, mouths wreathed in parentheses, until I say 'Has he come back yet?'

At this his chin plummets, his head teeters on his neck. 'Ah. No.' He gazes sideways, accusingly, down at a potato plant near his left foot. Then his head jerks up again and he says gaily, 'Not yet, ay? But maybe soon. Your fadder, he knows the bush.'

Madame has appeared in the kitchen doorway and Paul speaks with her in the nasal slanted French I can't interpret because I learned all but a few early words of mine in school. Folk songs and Christmas carols and, from the later grades, memorized passages of Racine and Baudelaire are no help to me here.

'You must come in,' he says to me, 'and take a tea,' and he bends and undoes the hook of the wooden gate. I go forward to the door where Madame is waiting for me, hands outstretched in welcome, smiling and shaking her head mournfully as though through no fault of my own I'm doomed.

Madame makes the tea on new electric stove, a blue ceramic Madonna with pink child hanging above it; when I glimpsed the stove on my way through the kitchen I felt betrayed, she should have remained loyal to her wood range. We sit on the screened porch overlooking the lake, balancing our teacups and rocking side by side in three rocking chairs; I've been given the store cushion, which has an embroidered view of Niagara Falls. The black and white collie, either the identical one I used to be afraid of or its offshoot, lies on the braided rug by our feet.

Madame, who is the same thickness all the way down, is in a long-skirted dress and black stockings and a print apron with a bib, Paul in high-waisted trousers with braces, flannel shirtsleeves rolled. I'm annoyed with them for looking so much like carvings, the habitant kind they sell in tourist handicraft shops; but of course it's the other way around, it's the carvings that look like them. I wonder what they think I look like, they may find my jeans and sweatshirt and fringed over-the-shoulder bag strange, perhaps immoral, though such things may be more common in the village since the tourists and the TV; besides, I can be forgiven because my family was, by reputation, peculiar as well as *anglais*.

I lift my cup, they are watching me anxiously: it's imperative that I mention the tea. 'Très bon,' I manage to get out in the direction of Madame. 'Délicieux.' Doubt seizes me, *thé* may be feminine.

What I'm remembering are the visits our mother was obliged to pay Madame while our father was visiting Paul. My father and Paul would be outside, talking about boats or motors or forest fires or one of their expeditions, and my mother and Madame would be inside in the rocking chairs (my mother with the Niagara Falls cushion), trying with great goodwill to make conversation. Neither knew more than five words of the other's language and after the opening Bonjours both would unconsciously raise their voices as though talking to a deaf person.

'Il fait beau,' my mother would shout, no matter what the weather was like, and Madame would grin with strain and say 'Pardon? Ah, il fait *beau*, oui, il fait beau, ban oui.' When she had ground to a stop both would think desperately, chairs rocking.

''Ow are *you*?' Madame would scream, and my mother, after deciphering this, would say '*Fine*, I am fine.' Then she would repeat the question: 'How are *you*, Madame?' But Madame would not have the answer and both, still smiling, would glance furtively out through the screen to see if the men were yet coming to rescue them.

Meanwhile my father would be giving Paul the cabbages or the string beans he had brought from his garden and Paul would be replying with tomatoes or lettuces from his. Since their gardens had the same things in them this exchange of vegetables was purely ritual: after it had taken place we would know the visit would be officially over.

Madame is stirring her tea now and sighing. She says something to Paul and Paul says, 'Your mother, she was a good woman, Madame says it is very sad; so young too.'

'Yes,' I say. Mother and Madame were about the same age and no-one would call Madame young; but then my mother never got fat like Madame.

I went to see her in the hospital, where she allowed herself to be taken only when she could no longer walk; one of the doctors told me that. She must have concealed the pain for weeks, tricked my father into believing it was only one of her usual headaches, that would be her kind of lie. She hated hospitals and doctors; she must have been afraid they would experiment on her, keep her alive as long as they could with tubes and needles even though it was what they call terminal, in the head it always is; and in fact that's what they did.

They had her on morphine, she said there were webs floating in the air in front of her. She was very thin, much older than I'd ever thought possible, skin tight over her curved beak nose, hands on the sheet curled like bird claws clinging to a perch. She peered at me with bright blank eyes. She may not have known who I was: she didn't ask me why I left or where I'd been, though she might not have asked anyway, feeling as she always had that personal questions were rude.

'I'm not going to your funeral,' I said. I had to lean close to her, the hearing in one of her ears was gone. I wanted her to understand in advance, and approve.

'I never enjoyed them,' she said to me, one word at a time. 'You have to wear a hat. I don't like liquor.' She must have been talking about Church or cocktail parties. She lifted her hand, slowly as if through water, and felt the top of her head; there was a tuft of white hair standing straight up. 'I didn't get the bulbs in. Is there snow outside?'

On the bedside table with the flowers, chrysanthemums, I saw her diary; she kept one every year. All she put in it was a record of the weather and the work done on that day: no reflections, no emotions. She would refer to it when she wanted to compare the years, decide whether the spring had been late or early, whether it had been a wet summer. It made me angry to see it in that windowless room where it was no use; I waited till her eyes were closed and slipped it into my shoulder bag. When I got outside I leafed through it, I thought there might be something about me, but except for the dates the pages were blank, she had given up months ago.

'Do what you think best,' she said from behind her closed eyes. 'Is there snow?'

We rock some more. I want to ask Paul about my father but he ought to begin, he must have news to tell me. Maybe he's avoiding it; or maybe he's being tactful, waiting until I'm ready. Finally I say 'What happened to him?'

Paul shrugs. 'He is just gone,' he says. 'I go there one day to see him, the door is open, the boats is there, I think maybe he is off somewheres near and I wait awhile. Next day I go back, everything the same, I begin to worry, where he is, I don't know. So I write to you, he has leaved your *caisse postale* and the keys, I lock up the place. His car she is here, with me.' He gestures towards the back, the garage. My father trusted Paul, he said Paul could build anything and fix anything. They were once caught in a three-week rainstorm, my father said if you could spend three weeks in a wet tent with a man without killing him or having him kill you then he was a good man. Paul justified for him his own ideal of the simpler life; but for Paul the anacronism was imposed, he'd never chosen it.

'Did you look on the island?' I say. 'If the boats are there he can't have gone off the island.'

'I look, sure,' Paul says, 'I tell the police from down-the-road, they look around, nobody find nothing. Your husband here too?' he asks irrelevantly.

'Yes, he's here,' I say, skipping over the lie even in my own mind. What he means is that a man should be handling this; Joe will do as a stand-in. My status is a problem, they obviously think I'm married. But I'm safe, I'm wearing my ring, I never threw it out, it's useful for landladies. I sent my parents a postcard after the wedding, they must have mentioned it to Paul; that, but not the divorce. It isn't part of the vocabulary here, there's no reason to upset them.

I'm waiting for Madame to ask about the baby, I'm prepared, alerted, I'll tell her I left him in the city; that would be perfectly true, only it was a different city, he's better off with my husband, former husband.

But Madame doesn't mention it, she lifts another cube of sugar from the tray by her side and he intrudes, across from me, a coffee shop, not city but roadside, on the way to or from somewhere, some goal or encounter. He peels the advertizement paper from the sugar and lets one square fall into the cup, I'm talking and his mouth turns indulgent, it must have been before the child. He smiles and I smile too, thinking of the slice of cucumber pickle that was stuck to the top of his club sandwich. A round historical plaque, on a supermarket wall or in a parking lot, marking the site where a building once stood in which an event of little importance once took place, ridiculous. He puts his hand on mine, he tries that a lot but he's easy to get rid of, easier and easier. I don't have time for him, I switch problems.

I sip at my tea and rock, by my feet the dog stirs, the lake below flutters in the wind which is beginning. My father has simply disappeared then, vanished into nothing. When I got Paul's letter ' 'Your father is gone, nobody cant find him' – it seemed incredible, but it appears to be true.

There used to be a barometer on the porch wall, a wooden house with two doors and a man and a woman who lived inside. When it was going to be fair the woman in her long skirt and apron would emerge from her door, when it was going to rain she would go in and the man would come out, carrying an axe. When it was first explained to me I thought they controlled the weather instead of merely responding to it. My eyes seek the house now, I need a prediction, but it's not there.

'I think I'll go down the lake,' I say.

Paul raises his hands, palms outward. 'We look two, three times already.'

But they must have missed something, I feel it will be different if I look myself. Probably when we get there my father will have returned from wherever he has been, he will be sitting in the cabin waiting for us.

Chapter Three

On my way back to the motel I detour to the store, the one where they're supposed to speak English: we will need some food. I go up the wooden steps, past a drowsing mop-furred mongrel roped to the porch with a length of clothesline. The screen door has a BLACK CAT CIGARETTES handle; I open it and step into the store smell, the elusive sweetish odour given off by the packaged cookies and the soft drink cooler. For a brief time the post office was here, a DEFENSE DE CRACHER SUR LE PLANCHER sign stamped with a government coat of arms.

Behind the counter there's a woman about my age, but with brassiere-shaped breasts and a light auburn moustache; her hair is in rollers covered by a pink net and she has on slacks and a sleeveless jersey top. The old priest is definitely gone, he disapproved of slacks, the women had to wear long concealing skirts and dark stockings and keep their arms covered in church. Shorts were against the law, and many of them lived all their lives beside the lake without learning to swim because they were ashamed to put on bathing suits.

The woman looks at me, inquisitive but not smiling, and the two men still in Elvis Presley haircuts, duck's ass at the back and greased pompadours curving out over their foreheads, stop talking a look at me too; they keep their elbows on the counter. I hesitate: maybe the tradition has changed, maybe they no longer speak English.

'Avez-vous du viande hâché?' I ask her, blushing because of my accent.

She grins then the two men grin also, not at me but at each other. I see I've made a mistake, I should have pretended to be an American.

'Amburger, oh yes we have lots. *H*ow much?' she asks adding the final H carelessy to show she can if she feels like it. This is border country.

'A pound, no two pounds,' I say, blushing even more because I've been so easily discovered, they're making fun of me and I have no way of letting them know I share the joke. Also I agree with them, if you live in a place you should speak the language. But this isn't where I lived.

She hacks with a cleaver at a cube of frozen meat, weighs it. 'Doo leevers,' she says, mimicking my school accent. The two men snigger. I solace myself by replaying the man from the government, he was at a gallery opening, a handicraft exhibit, string wall hangings, woven place mats, stoneware breakfast sets; Joe wanted to go so he could resent not being in it. The man seemed to be a cultural attaché of some sort, an ambassador; I asked him if he knew this part of the country, my part, and he shook his head and said 'Des barbares, they are not civilized.' At the time that annoyed me.

I pick up some fly dope in a spray can for the others, also some eggs and bacon, bread and butter, miscellaneous tins. Everything is more expensive here than in the city; no one keeps hens or cows or pigs any more, it's all imported from more fertile districts. The bread is in wax paper wrappers, tranché.

I would like to back out the door, I don't want them staring at me from behind; but I force myself to walk slowly, frontwards.

There used to be only one store. I was in front part of a house, run by an old woman who was also called Madame: none of the women had names then. Madame sold khaki-coloured penny candies which we were forbidden to eat, but her main source of power was that she had only one hand. Her other arm ended in a soft pint snout like an elephant's trunk and she broke the parcel string by wrapping it around her stump and pulling. This arm devoid of a hand was for me a great mystery, almost as puzzling as Jesus. I wanted to know how the hand had come off (perhaps she had taken it off herself) and where it was now, and especially whether my own hand could ever come off like that; but I never asked, I must have been afraid of the answers. Going down the steps, I try to remember what the rest of her was like, her face, but I can see only the potent candies, inaccessible in their glass reliquary, and the arm, miraculous in an unspecified way like the toes of saints or the cut-off pieces of early martyrs, the eyes on the plate, the severed breasts, the heart with letters on it shining like a light bulb through the trim hole painted in the chest, art history.

I find the others in the small chilly room labelled BAR; they're the only customers. They have six beer bottles and four glasses on their orange formica-topped table. A mottled boy with a haircut like the ones of the men in the store, only blonde, is sitting with them.

David waves at me as I come in: he's happy about something. 'Have a beer,' he says. 'This is Claude, his father owns this joint.'

Claude shambles off morosely to get me a beer. Underneath the bar itself is a crudely carved wooden fish with red and blue dots on it, intended possibly for a speckled trout; on its leaping back it supports the fake marble surface. Above the bar is a TV, turned off or broken, and the regulation picture, scrolled gilt frame, blown-up photograph of a stream with trees and rapids and a man fishing. It's an imitation of other places, more southern ones, which are themselves imitations, the original someone's distorted memory of a nineteenth century English gentleman's shooting lodge, the kind with trophy heads and furniture made from deer antlers, Queen Victoria had a set like that. But if this is what succeeds why shouldn't they do it?

'Claude told us business is bad this year,' David says, 'on accounta word is around the lake's fished out. They're going to other lakes, Claude's dad flies them in his seaplane, neat eh? But he says some of the men went out in the spring with a dragnet and there's all kinds of them down there, real big ones, they're just gettin' too smart.' David is slipping into his yokel dialect; he does it for fun, it's a parody of himself, the way he says he talked back in the fifties when he wanted to be a minister and was selling Bibles door-to-door to put himself through theological seminary: 'Hey lady, wanna buy a dirty book?' Now though it seems to be unconscious, maybe he's doing it for Claude, to make it clear he too is a man of the people. Or maybe it's an experiment in Communications, that's what he teaches, at night, the same place Joe works; it's an Adult Education programme. David calls it Adult Vegetation; he got the job because he was once a radio announcer.

'Any news?' Joe asks, in a neutral mumble that signals he'd prefer it if I kept from showing any reaction, no matter what has happened.

'No,' I say, 'Nothing different.' Voice level, calm. Perhaps that was what he liked about me, there must have been something, though I can't reconstruct our first meeting, now I can: it was in a store, I was buying some new brushes and a spray tin of fixative. He said Do you live around here and we went to the corner for a coffee, except I had a 7-up instead. What impressed him that time, he even mentioned it later, cool he called it, was the way I took off my clothes and put them on again later very smoothly as if I were feeling no emotion. But I really wasn't.

Claude comes back with the beer and I say 'Thank you' and glance up at him and his face dissolves and re-forms, he was about eight the last time I was here; he used to peddle worms in rusted tin cans to the fishermen down by the government dock. He's uneasy now, he can tell I recognize him.

'I'd like to go down the lake for a couple of days,' I say, to David because it's his car. 'I'd like to look around, if that's okay.'

'Great,' says David, 'I'm gonna get me one of them smart fish.'

He brought along a borrowed fishing rod, though I warned him he might not have a chance to use it: if my father had turned up after all we would have gone away without letting him find out we were here. If he's safe I don't want to see him. There's no point, they never forgave me, they didn't understand the divorce; I don't think they even understood the marriage, which wasn't surprising since I didn't understand it myself. What upset them was the way I did it, so suddenly, and then running off and leaving my husband and child, my attractive full-colour magazine illustrations, suitable for framing. Leaving my child, that was the unpardonable sin; it was no use trying to explain to them why it wasn't really mine. But I admit I was stupid, stupidity is the same as evil if you judge by the results, and I didn't have any excuses, I was never good at them. My brother was, he used to make them up in advance of the transgressions; that's the logical way.

'Oh god,' Anna says, 'David thinks he's a great white hunter.' She's teasing him, she does that a lot; but he doesn't hear, he's getting up, Claude is hustling him off to make him out a licence, it seems Claude is in charge of the licences. When David comes back I want to ask how much he paid, but he's too pleased, I don't want to spoil it. Claude is pleased also.

We find out from Claude we can hire Evans, who owns the Blue Moon Cabins, to run us down the lake. Paul would take us for nothing, he offered, but I wouldn't feel right about it; also I'm sure he would misinterpret Joe's amorphous beard and David's moustache and Three Musketeers hair. They're just a style now, like crew cuts, but Paul might feel they are dangerous, they mean riots.

David eases the car down the turnoff, two ruts and a rock hump in the centre that scrapes the car's belly. We brake in front of the cabin marked OFFICE; Evans is there, a bulky laconic American in checked shirt and peaked cap and a thick knitted jacket with an eagle on the back. He knows where my father's place is, all the older guides know every house on the lake. He moves his cigarette butt to the corner of his mouth and says he'll take us there, ten miles, for five dollars; for another five he'll pick us up two days from now, in the morning. That will give us the rest of the day to drive back to the city. He's heard of the disappearance, of course, but he doesn't mention it.

'A groovy old guy, eh?' David says when we're outside. He's

enjoying himself, he thinks this is reality: a marginal economy and grizzled elderly men, it's straight out of Depression photo essays. He spent four years in New York and became political, he was studying something; it was during the sixties, I'm not sure when. My friends' pasts are vague to me and to each other also, any one of us could have amnesia for years and the others wouldn't notice.

When David has backed the car down to the Blue Moon dock we unload our stuff, the packsacks of clothes, the camera equipment, the samsonite case with my career in it, the half dozen Red Caps they got at the motel and the paper bag of food. We scramble into the boat, a battered wood-hulled launch; Evans starts the motor and we churn out slowly. Summer cottages beginning to sprout here, they spread like measles, it must be the paved road.

David sits in front beside Evans. 'Gettin' many fish?' he asks, folksy, chummy, crafty. 'Here and there, here and there,' Evans says, giving no free handouts; then he switches the motor into high gear and I can't hear any more.

I wait until we're into the middle of the lake. At the right moment I look over my shoulder as I always did and there is the village, suddenly distanced and clear, the houses receding and grouping, the white church startling against the dark of the trees. The feeling I expected before but failed to have comes now, homesickness, for a place where I never lived, I'm far enough away; then the village shrinks, optical illusion, and we're around a point of land, it's behind us.

The three of us are together on the back seat, Anna beside me. 'This is good,' she says to me, voice shrilling over the engine roar, 'it's good for us to get away from the city'; but when I turn to answer there are tears on her cheek and I wonder why, she's always so cheerful. Then I realize they aren't tears, it's started to drizzle. The raincoats are in our packsacks; I didn't notice it had clouded over. We won't be very wet though, with his boat it will only take half an hour; before, with the heavier boats and primitive motors, it took two to three hours depending on the wind. In the city people would say to my mother, 'Aren't you afraid? What if something happened?' They were thinking of the time it would take to get to a doctor.

I'm cold, I huddle my shoulders up; drops ping onto my skin. The shoreline unrolls and folds together again as we go past; forty miles from here there's another village, in between there's nothing but a tangled maze, low hills curving out of the water, bays branching in, peninsulas which turn into islands, islands, necks of land leading to other lakes. On a map or in an aerial photograph the water pattern radiates like a spider, but in a boat you can see only a small part of it, the part you're in.

The lake is tricky, the weather shifts, the wind swells up quickly; people drown every year, boats loaded topheavy or drunken fishermen running at high speed into deadheads, old pieces of tree waterlogged and partly decayed, floating under the surface, there are a lot of them left over from the logging and the time they raised the lake level. Because of the convolutions it's easy to lose the way if you haven't memorized the landmarks and I watch for them now, dome-shaped hill, point with dead pine, stubble of cut trunks poking up from a shallows, I don't trust Evans.

But he's taken the right turns so far, we're coming into my territory, two short bends and through a passage between granite shores and out into a wider bay. The peninsula is where I left it, pushing out from the island shore with the house not even showing through the trees, though I know where it is; camouflage was one of my father's policies.

Evans arches the boat around the point and slows for the dock. The dock slants, the ice takes something away from it every winter and the water warps and rots it; it's been repaired so much all the materials are different, but it's the same dock my brother fell off the time he drowned.

He used to be kept in a chicken-wire enclosure my father built for him, large cage or small playground, with trees, a swing, rocks, a sandpile. The fence was too high for him to climb over but there was a gate and one day he learned how to open it. My mother was alone in the house; she glanced out the window, checking, and he was no longer in the cage. It was a still day, no wind noise, and she heard something down by the water. She ran to the dock, he wasn't there, she went out to the end of it and looked down. My brother was under the water, face upturned, eyes open and unconscious, sinking gently; air was coming out of his mouth.

It was before I was born but I can remember it as clearly as if I saw it, and perhaps I did see it: I believe that an unborn baby has its eyes open and can look out through the walls of the mother's stomach, like a frog in a jar.

Chapter Four

We unload our baggage while Evans idles the motor. When David has paid him he gives us an uninterested nod and backs the boat out, then turns it and swings around the point, the sound dwindling to a whine and fading as land and distance move between us. The lake jiggles against the shore, the waves subside, nothing remains but a faint iridescent film of gasoline, purple and pink and green. The space is quiet, the wind has gone down and the lake is flat, silver-white, it's the first time all day (and for a long time, for years) we have been out of the reach of motors. My ears and body tingle, aftermath of the vibration, like feet taken out of roller-skates.

The others are standing aimlessly; they seem to be waiting for me to tell them what comes next. 'We'll take the things up,' I say. I warn them about the dock: it's slippery with the drizzle, which is lighter now, almost a mist; also some of the boards may be soft and treacherous.

What I want to do is shout 'Hello!' or 'We're here!' but I don't, I don't want to hear the absence.

I hoist a packsack and walk along the dock and onto the land and towards the cabin, following the path and climbing the steps set into the hillside, lengths of split cedar held in place by a stake pounded at each end. The house is built on a sand hill, part of a ridge left by the retreating glaciers; only a few inches of soil and a thin coating of trees hold it down. On the lake side the sand is exposed, raw, it's been crumbling away: the stones and charcoal from the fireplace they used when they first lived here in tents have long since vanished, and the edge trees fall gradually, several I remember upright are leaning now. Red pines, bark scaling, needles bunched on the top branches. A kingfisher is perched on one of them, making its staccato alarm-clock cry;

they nest in the cliff, burrowing into the sand, it speeds up the erosion.

In front of the house the chicken-wire fence is still here, though one end is almost over the brink. They never dismantled it; even the dwarf swing is there, ropes frayed, sagging and blotched with weather. It wasn't like them to keep something when it was no longer needed; perhaps they expected grandchildren, visiting here. He would have wanted a dynasty, like Paul's, houses and descendants proliferating around him. The fence is a reproach, it points to my failure.

But I couldn't have brought the child here, I never identified it as mine; I didn't name it before it was born even, the way you're supposed to. It was my husband's, he imposed it on me, all the time it was growing in me I felt like an incubator. He measured everything he would let me eat, he was feeding it on me, he wanted a replica of himself; after it was born I was no more use. I couldn't prove it though, he was clever; he kept saying he loved me.

The house is smaller, because (I realize) the trees around it have grown. It's turned greyer in nine years too, like hair. The cedar logs are upright instead of horizontal, upright logs are shorter and easier for one man to handle. Cedar isn't the best wood, it decays quickly. Once my father said 'I didn't build it to last forever' and I thought then, Why not? Why didn't you?

I hope the door will be open but it's padlocked, as Paul said he left it. I dig the keys he gave me out of my bag and approach warily: whatever I find inside will be a clue. What if he returned after Paul locked it and couldn't get in? But there are other ways of getting in, he could have broken a window.

Joe and David are here now with the other packsacks and the beer. Anne is behind them with my case and the paper bag; she's singing again, Mockingbird Hill.

I open the wooden door and the screen door inside it and scan the room cautiously, then step inside. Table covered with blue oilcloth, bench, another bench which is a wooden box built against the wall, sofa with metal frame and thin mattress, it folds out into a bed. That was where our mother used to be: all day she would lie unmoving, covered with a brown plaid blanket, her face bloodless and shrunken. We would talk in whispers, she looked so different and she didn't hear if we spoke to her; but the next day she would be the same as she had always been. We came to have faith in her ability to recover, from anything; we ceased to take her illnesses seriously, they were only natural phases, like cocoons. When she died I was disappointed in her.

Nothing is out of place. Water drops fall on the roof, down from the trees.

They follow me inside. 'Is this where you lived?' Joe asks. It's unusual for him to ask me anything about myself: I can't tell whether he's pleased or discouraged. He goes over to the snow-shoes on the wall and lifts one down, taking refuge in his hands.

Anna puts the groceries on the counter and wraps her arms around herself. 'It must have been weird,' she says. 'Cut off from everything like that.'

'No,' I say. To me it felt normal.

'Depends what you're used to,' David says. 'I think it's neat.' But he's not certain.

There are two other rooms and I open the doors quickly. A bed in each, shelves, clothes hanging on nails: jackets, raincoats, they were always left here. A grey hat, he had several of those. In the right-hand room is a map of the district, tacked to the wall. In the other are some pictures, watercolours, I recall now having painted them when I was twelve or thirteen; the fact that I'd forgotten about them is the only thing that makes me uneasy.

I go back to the livingroom. David has dropped his packsack on the floor and unfolded himself along the sofa. 'Christ, am I wiped,' he says. 'Somebody break me out a beer.' Anna brings him one and he pats her on the rear and says 'That's what I like, service.' She takes out cans for herself and us and we sit on the benches and drink it. Now that we're no longer moving the cabin is chilly.

The right smell, cedar and wood stove and tar from the oakum stuffed between the logs to keep out the mice. I look up at the ceiling, the shelves: there's a stack of papers beside the lamp, perhaps he was working on them just before whatever it was happened, before he left. There might be something for me, a note, a message, a will. I kept expecting that after my mother died, word of some kind, not money but an object, a token. For a while I went twice a day to the post office box which was the only one of my addresses I'd given them; but nothing arrived, maybe she didn't have time.

No dirty dishes, no clothing strewn around, no evidence. It doesn't feel like a house that's been lived in all winter.

'What time is it?' I ask David. He holds up his watch: it's almost five. It will be up to me to organize dinner, since in a way this is my place, they are my guests.

There's kindling in the box behind the stove and a few pieces of white birch; the disease hasn't yet hit this part of the country. I find the matches and kneel in front of the stove, I've almost forgotten how to do this but after three or four matches I get it lit.

I take the round enamelled bowl from its hook and the big knife. They watch me: none of them asks me where I'm going, though Joe seems worried. Perhaps he's been expecting me to have hysterics and he's anxious because I'm not having any. 'I'm going to the garden,' I say to reassure them. They know where that is, they could see it from the lake coming in.

Grass is growing up in the path and in front of the gate; the weeds are a month tall. Ordinarily I would spend a few hours pulling them out, but it isn't worth it, we'll be here only two days.

Frogs hop everywhere out of my way, they like it here; it's close to the lake, damp, my canvas shoes are soaked through. I pick some of the leaf lettuce that hasn't flowered and turned bitter, then I pull up an onion, sliding the loose brown outer skin off from the bulb, white and eye-like.

The garden's been rearranged: before there were scarlet runners up one side of the fence. The blossoms were redder than anything else in the garden, the hummingbirds went into them, hovering, their wings a blur. The beans that were left too long would yellow after the first frost and split open. Inside were pebbles, purple-black and frightening. I knew that if I could get some of them and keep them for myself I would be all-powerful; but later when I was tall enough and could finally reach to pick them it didn't work. Just as well, I think, as I had no idea what I would do with the power once I got it; if I'd turned out like the others with power I would have been evil.

I go to the carrot row and pull up a carrot but they haven't been thinned properly, it's forked and stubby. I cut off the onion leaves and the carrot top and throw them on the compost heap, then put the things in the bowl and start back towards the gate, adding up the time, growing time, in my head. In the middle of June he was here surely; it can't be longer than that.

Anna is outside the fence, she's come to look for me. 'Where's the can?' she says. 'I'm about to burst.'

I take her to the beginning of the trail and point her along it.

'Are you okay?' she says.

'Sure,' I say; the question surprises me.

'I'm sorry he wasn't here,' she says mournfully, gazing at me out of her round green eyes as though it's her grief, her catastrophe.

'It's all right,' I tell her, comforting her, 'just keep going along the path and you'll find it, though it's quite a distance,' I laugh, 'don't get lost.'

I carry the bowl down to the dock and wash the vegetables in the lake. Below me in the water there's a leech, the good kind with red dots on the back, undulating along like a streamer held at one end and shaken. The bad kind is mottled grey and yellow. It was my brother who made up these moral distinctions, at some point he became obsessed with them, he must have picked them up from the war. There had to be a good kind and a bad kind of everything.

I cook the hamburgers and we eat and I wash the dishes in the chipped dishpan, Anna drying; then it's almost dark. I lift the bedding out from the wall bench and make up our bed, Anna can do theirs. He must have been sleeping in the main room, on the sofa.

They aren't used to going to bed as soon as it's dark though, and neither am I any more. I'm afraid they'll be bored because there's no TV or anything, I search for entertainments. A box of dominoes, a deck of cards, those were under the folded blankets. There are a lot of paperbacks on the shelves in the bedrooms, detective novels mostly, recreational reading. Beside them are the technical books on trees and the other reference books, *Edible Plants and Shoots, Tying the Dry Fly, The Common Mushrooms, Log Cabin Construction, A Field Guide to the Birds, Exploring Your Camera*, he believed that with the proper guide books you could do everything yourself; and his cache of serious books: the King James Bible which he said he enjoyed for its literary qualities, a complete Robert Burns, Boswell's *Life*, Thompson's *Seasons*, selections from Goldsmith and Cowper. He admired what he called the eighteenth century rationalists: he thought of them as men who had avoided the corruptions of the Industrial Revolution and learned the secret of the golden mean, the balanced life, he was sure they all practised organic farming. It astounded me to discover much later, in fact my husband told me, that Burns was an alcoholic, Cowper a madman, Doctor Johnson a manic-depressive and Goldsmith a pauper. There was something wrong with Thompson also; 'escapist' was the term he used. After that I liked them better, they weren't paragons any more.

'I'll light the lamp,' I say, 'and we can read.'

But David says 'Naaa, why read when you can do that in the city?' He's twiddling the dial on his transistor radio; he can't pick up anything but static and a wail that might be music, wavering in and out, and a tiny insect voice whispering in French. 'Shit,' he says, 'I wish I could get the scores.' He means baseball, he's a fan.

'We could play bridge,' I say, but no one wants to.

After a while David says 'Well children, time to break out the grass.' He opens his packsack and gropes around inside, and Anna says 'What a dumb place to put them, it's the first place they'd look.'

'Up your ass,' David says, smiling at her, 'that's where they'd look first, they grab a good thing when they see one. Don't worry, baby. I know what I'm doing.'

'Sometimes I wonder,' Anna says.

We go outside and down to the dock and sit on the damp wood, watching the sunset, smoking a little. The clouds to the west are yellow and grey, fading, and in the clear sky southeast of us the moon is rising.

'This is great,' David says, 'it's better than in the city. If we could only kick out the fascist pig Yanks and the capitalists this would be a neat country. But then, who would be left?'

'Oh Christ,' Anna says, 'don't get going on that.'

'How?' I say. 'How would you kick them out?'

'Organize the beavers,' David says, 'chew them to pieces, it's the only way. This Yank stockbroker is going along Bay Street and the beavers ambush him, drop on him from a telephone pole, chomp chomp and it's all over. You heard about the latest national flag? Nine beavers pissing on a frog.'

It's old and shoddy but I laugh anyway. A little beer, a little pot, some jokes, a little political chitchat, the golden mean; we're the new bourgeoisie, this might as well be a Rec Room. Still I'm glad they're with me, I wouldn't want to be here alone; at any moment the loss, vacancy, will overtake me, they ward it off.

'Do you realize,' David says, 'that this country is founded on the bodies of dead animals? Dead fish, dead seals, and historically dead beavers, the beaver is to this country what the black man is to the United States. Not only that, in New York it's now a dirty word, beaver. I think that's very significant.' He sits up and glares at me through the semi-darkness.

'We aren't your students,' Anna says, 'lie down.' His head rests in her lap, she's stroking his forehead, I can see her hand moving back and forth. They've been married nine years, Anna told me, they must have got married about the same time I did; but she's older than I am. They must have some special method, formula, some knowledge I missed out on; or maybe he was the wrong person. I thought it would happen without my doing anything about it, I'd turn into part of a couple, two people linked together and balancing each other, like the wooden man and woman in the barometer house at Paul's. It was good at first but he changed after I married him, he married me, we committed that paper act. I still don't see why signing a name should make any difference but he began to expect things, he wanted to be pleased. We should have kept sleeping together and left it at that.

Joe puts his arms around me, I take hold of his fingers. What I'm seeing is the black and white tugboat that used to be on the lake, or was it flat like a barge, it towed the log booms slowly down towards the dam, I waved at it whenever we went past in our boat and the men would wave back. It had a little house on it for them to live in, with windows and a stovepipe coming out through the roof. I felt that would be the best way to live, in a floating house carrying everything you needed with you and some other people you liked; when you wanted to move somewhere else it would be easy.

Joe is swaying back and forth, rocking, which may mean he's happy. The wind starts again, brushing over us, the air warm-cool and fluid, the trees behind us moving their leaves, the sound ripples; the water gives off icy light, zinc moon breaking on small waves. Loon voice, each hair on my body lifting with the shiver; the echoes deflect from all sides, surrounding us, here everything echoes.

Chapter Five

Birdsong wakes me. It's pre-dawn, earlier than the traffic starts in the city, but I've learned to sleep through that. I used to know the species; I listen, my ears are rusty, there's nothing but a jumble of sound. They sing for the same reason trucks honk, to proclaim their territories: a rudimentary language. Linguistics, I should have studied that instead of art.

Joe is half-awake too and groaning to himself, the sheet pulled around his head like a cowl. He's torn the blankets up from the bottom of the bed and his lean feet stick out, toes with the deprived look of potatoes sprouted in the bag. I wonder if he'll remember he woke me when it was still dark, sitting up and saying 'Where is this?' Every time we're in a new place he does that. 'It's all right,' I said, 'I'm here,' and though he said 'Who? Who?', repeating it like an owl, he allowed me to ease him back down into bed. I'm afraid to touch him at these times, he might mistake me for one of the enemies in his nightmare; but he's beginning to trust my voice.

I examine the part of his face that shows, an eyelid and the side of his nose, the skin pallid as though he's been living in a cellar, which we have been; his beard is dark brown, almost black, it continues around his neck and merges under the sheet with the hair on his back. His back is hairier than most men's, a warm texture, it's like teddy-bear fur, though when I told him that he seemed to take it as an insult to his dignity.

I'm trying to decide whether or not I love him. It shouldn't matter, but there's always a moment when curiosity becomes more important to them than peace and they need to ask; though he hasn't yet. It's best to have the answer worked out in advance: whether you evade or do it the hard way and tell the truth, at least you aren't caught off guard. I sum him up, dividing him into categories: he's good in bed, better than the one before; he's moody but he's not much bother, we split the rent and he doesn't talk much, that's an advantage. When he suggested we should live together I didn't hesitate. It wasn't even a real decision, it was more like buying a goldfish or a potted cactus plant, not because you want one in advance but because you happen to be in the store and you see them lined up on the counter. I'm fond of him, I'd rather have him around than not; though it would be nice if he meant something more to me. The fact that he doesn't makes me sad: no one has since my husband. A divorce is like an amputation, you survive but there's less of you.

I lie for a while with my eyes open. This used to be my room; Anna and David are in the one with the map, this one has the pictures. Ladies in exotic costumes, sausage rolls of hair across their foreheads, with puffed red mouths and eyelashes like toothbrush bristles: when I was ten I believed in glamour, it was a kind of religion and these were my icons. Their arms and legs are constrained in fashion-model poses, one gloved hand on the hip, one foot stuck out in front. They're wearing shoes with Petunia Pig toes and perpendicular heels, and their dresses have cantaloupe strapless tops like Rita Hayworth's and ballerina skirts with blotches meant for spangles. I didn't draw very well then, there's something wrong with the proportions, the necks are too short and the shoulders are enormous. I must have been imitating the paper dolls they had in the city, cardboard movie stars, Jane Powell, Esther Williams, with two-piece bathing suits printed on their bodies and cutout wardrobes of formal gowns and lacy negligées. Little girls in grey jumpers and white blouses, braids clipped to their heads with pink plastic barrettes, owned and directed them; they would bring them to school and parade them at recess, propping them up against the worn brick wall, feet in the snow, paper dresses no protection against the icy wind, inventing for them dances and parties, celebrations, interminable changing of costumes, a slavery of pleasure.

Below the pictures at the foot of the bed there's a grey leather jacket hanging on a nail. It's dirty and the leather is cracked and peeling. I see it for a while before I recognize it: it belonged to my mother a long time ago, she kept sunflower seeds in the pockets. I thought she'd thrown it out; it shouldn't still be here, he should have got rid of it after the funeral. Dead people's clothes ought to be buried with them.

another trail that went back almost as far as the swamp but it was my brother's and secret, by now it must be illegible.

He can't have left the island, both canoes are in the toolshed and the aluminum motorboat is padlocked to a tree near the dock; the gas tanks for the motor are empty.

'Anyway,' I say, 'there's only two places he can be, on the island or in the lake.' My head contradicts me: someone could have picked him up here and taken him to the village at the other end of the lake, it would be the perfect way to vanish; maybe he wasn't here during the winter at all.

But that's avoiding, it's not unusual for a man to disappear in the bush, it happens dozens of times each year. All it takes is a small mistake, going too far from the house in winter, blizzards are sudden, or twisting your leg so you can't walk out, in spring the blackflies would finish you, they crawl inside your clothes, you'd be covered with blood and delirious in a day. I can't accept it though, he knew too much, he was too careful.

I gave David the machete, I don't know what shape the trail will be in, we may have to brush it out: Joe carries the hatchet. Before we start I coat their wrists and ankles with bug spray, and my own also. I used to be immune to mosquitoes, I'd been bitten so much, but I've lost it: on my legs and body are several itchy pink bumps from last night. The sound of love in the north, a kiss, a slap.

It's overcast, lowhanging cloud, there's a slight wind from the southeast, it may rain later or it may miss us, the weather here comes in pockets, like oil. We go in through the neckhigh grass mixed with wild raspberry canes between the garden and the lake, past the burn heap and the compost heap. I should have unearthed the garbage, to see how recent it is; there's a pit also, where the burned tin cans are smashed flat and buried, that could be excavated. My father viewed as an archeological problem.

We're on the trail inside the forest; the first part is fairly open, though now and then we pass gigantic stumps, level and saw-cut, remnants of the trees that were here before the district was logged out. The trees will never be allowed to grow that tall again, they're killed as soon as they're valuable, big trees are scarce as whales.

The forest thickens and I watch for the blazes, still visible after fourteen years; the trees they're cut on have grown swollen edges around the wounds, scar tissue.

We begin to climb and my husband catches up with me again,

making one of the brief appearances, framed memories he specializes in: crystal clear image enclosed by a blank wall. He's writing his own initials on a fence, graceful scrolls to show me how, lettering was one of the things he taught. There are other initials on the fence but he's making his bigger, leaving his mark. I can't identify the date or place, it was a city, before we were married; I lean beside him, admiring the fall of winter sunlight over his cheekbone and the engraved nose, noble and sloped like a Roman coin profile; that was when everything he did was perfect. On his hand is a leather glove. He said he loved me, the magic word, it was supposed to make everything light up, I'll never trust that word again.

My bitterness about him surprises me: I was what's known as the offending party, the one who left, he didn't do anything to me. He wanted a child, that's normal, he wanted us to be married.

In the morning while we were doing the dishes I decided to ask Anna. She was wiping a plate, humming snatches of The Big Rock Candy Mountain under her breath. 'How do you manage it?' I said.

She stopped humming. 'Manage what?'

'Being married. How do you keep it together?'

She glanced at me quickly as though she was suspicious. 'We tell a lot of jokes.'

'No but really,' I said. If there was a secret trick I wanted to learn it.

She talked to me then, or not to me exactly but to an invisible microphone suspended above her head: people's voices go radio when they give advice. She said you just had to make an emotional committment, it was like skiing, you couldn't see in advance what would happen but you had to let go. Let go of what, I wanted to ask her; I was measuring myself against what she was saying. Maybe that was why I failed, because I didn't know what I had to let go of. For me it hadn't been like skiing, it was more like jumping off a cliff. That was the feeling I had all the time I was married; in the air, going down, waiting for the smash at the bottom.

'How come it didn't work out, with you?' Anna said.

'I don't know,' I said, 'I guess I was too young.'

She nodded sympathetically. 'You're lucky you didn't have kids though.'

'Yes,' I said. She doesn't have any herself; if she did she couldn't have said that to me. I've never told her about the baby; I haven't told Joe either, there's no reason to. He won't find out the usual way, there aren't any pictures of it peering out from a crib or a window or through the bars of a playpen in my bureau drawer or my billfold where he could stumble across them and act astonished or outraged or sad. I have to behave as though it doesn't exist, because for me it can't, it was taken away from me, exported, deported. A section of my own life, sliced off from me like a Siamese twin, my own flesh cancelled. Lapse, relapse, I have to forget.

The trail's winding now through high ground where there are boulders coming up out of the earth, carried and dropped by glaciers, moss on them and ferns, it's a damp climate. I keep my eyes on the ground, names reappearing, wintergreen, wild mint, Indian cucumber; at one time I could list every plant here that could be used or eaten. I memorized survival manuals, *How to Stay Alive in the Bush, Animal Tracks and Signs, The Woods in Winter*, at the age when the ones in the city were reading True Romance magazines: it wasn't till then I realized it was in fact possible to lose your way. Maxims float up: always carry matches and you will not starve, in a snow-storm dig a hole, avoid unclassified mushrooms, your hands and feet are the most important, if they freeze you're finished. Worthless knowledge; the pulp magazines with their cautionary tales, maidens who give in and get punished with mongoloid infants, fractured spines, dead mothers or men stolen by their best friends would have been more practical.

The trail dips down and across a swamp inlet at the tip of a bay, cedars here and bullrushes, blueflags, ooze. I go slowly, looking for footprints. There's nothing but a deer track, no sign of anyone: apparently Paul and the searchers didn't make it this far. The mosquitoes have scented us and swarm around our heads; Joe swears gently, David loudly, at the end of the line I hear Anna slapping.

We swing away from the shore and here it's a jungle, branches growing in across the path, hazel and moose maple, pithy junk trees. Sight is blocked two feet in, trunks and leaves a solid interlocking fence, green, green-grey, greybrown. None of the branches is chopped or broken back, if he's been here he's gone miraculously around and between them rather than through. I stand aside and

David hacks at the wall with his machete, not very well; he tatters and bends rather than slicing.

We come up against a tree fallen across the trail. It's brought several young balsams down with it: they lie tangled together, logjam. 'I don't think anyone's been through here,' I say, and Joe says 'Right on,' he's annoyed: it's obvious. I peer into the forest to see if another trail has been cut around the windfall but there's no sign; or there are too many signs, since I'm anxious every opening between two trees looks like a path.

David prods at the dead trunk with the machete, poking holes in the bark. Joe sits down on the ground: he's breathing hard, too much city, and the flies are getting to him, he scratches his neck and the backs of his hands. 'I guess that's it,' I say because I have to be the one to confess defeat, and Anna says 'Thank god, they're eating me alive.'

We start back. He could still be in there somewhere but I see now the impossibility of searching the island for him, it's two miles long. It would take twenty or thirty men at least, strung out at intervals and walking straight through the forest, and even then they could miss him, dead or alive, accident or suicide or murder. Or if for some unfathomable reason he's chosen this absence and is hiding, they'd never find him: there would be nothing easier in this country than to let the searchers get ahead of you and then follow at a distance, stopping when they stop, keeping them in sight so that no matter which way they turned you would always be behind them. That's what I would do.

We walk through the green light, feet muffled on wet decaying leaves. The trail is altered going back: I'm at the end now. Every few steps I glance to each side, eyes straining, scanning the ground for evidence, for anything human: a button, a cartridge, a discarded bit of paper.

It's like the times he used to play hide and seek with us in the semi-dark after supper, it was different from playing in a house, the space to hide in was endless; even when we knew which tree he had gone behind there was the fear that what would come out when you called would be someone else.

Chapter Six

No one can expect anything else from me. I checked everything, I tried; now I'm absolved from knowing. I should be telling someone official, filling in forms, getting help as you're supposed to in an emergency. But it's like searching for a ring lost on a beach or in the snow: futile. There's no act I can perform except waiting; tomorrow Evans will ship us to the village, and after that we'll travel to the city and the present tense. I've finished what I came for and I don't want to stay here, I want to go back to where there is electricity and distraction. I'm used to it now, filling the time without it is an effort.

The others are trying to amuse themselves. Joe and David are out in one of the canoes; I should have made them take life-jackets, neither of them can steer, they're shifting their paddles from side to side. I can see them from the front window and from the side window I can see Anna, partly hidden by trees. She's lying on her belly in bikini and sunglasses, reading a murder mystery, though she must be cold: the sky has cleared a little, but when the clouds move in front of the sun the heat shuts off.

Except for the bikini and the colour of her hair she could be me at sixteen, sulking on the dock, resentful at being away from the city and the boyfriend I'd proved my normality by obtaining; I wore his ring, too big for any of my fingers, around my neck on a chain, like a crucifix or a military decoration. Joe and David, when distance has disguised their faces and their awkwardness, might be my brother and my father. The only place left for me is that of my mother; a problem, what she did in the afternoons between the routines of lunch and supper. Sometimes she would take bread-crumbs or seeds out to the bird feeder tray and wait for the jays, standing quiet as a tree, or she would pull weeds in the garden; but on some days she would simply vanish, walk off by herself into the forest. Impossible to be like my mother, it would need a time warp; she was either ten thousand years behind the rest or fifty years ahead of them.

I brush my hair in front of the mirror, delaying; then I turn back to my work, my deadline, the career I suddenly found myself having, I didn't intend to but I had to find something I could sell. I'm still awkward with it, I don't know what clothes to wear to interviews: it feels strapped to me, like an aqualung or an extra, artificial limb. I have a title though, a classification, and that helps: I'm what they call a commercial artist, or, when the job is more pretentious, an illustrator. I do posters, covers, a little advertising and magazine work and the occasional commissioned book like this one. For a while I was going to be a real artist; he thought that was cute but misguided, he said I should study something I'd be able to use because there have never been any important woman artists. That was before we were married and I still listened to what he said, so I went into Design and did fabric patterns. But he was right, there never have been any.

This is the fifth book I've done; the first was a Department of Manpower employment manual, young people with lobotomized grins, rapturous in their padded slots: Computer Programmer, Welder, Executive Secretary, Lab Technician. Line drawings and a few graphs. The others were children's books and so is this one, *Quebec Folk Tales*, it's a translation. It isn't my territory but I need the money. I've had the typescript three weeks, I haven't come up with any final illustrations yet. As a rule I work faster than that.

The stories aren't what I expected; they're like German fairy tales, except for the absence of red-hot iron slippers and nail-studded casks. I wonder if this mercy descends from the original tellers, from the translator or from the publisher; probably it's Mr Percival the publisher, he's a cautious man, he shies away from anything he calls 'disturbing.' We had an argument about that: he said one of my drawings was too frightening and I said children liked being frightened. 'It isn't the children who buy the books,' he said, 'it's their parents.' So I compromised; now I compromise before I take the work in, it saves time. I've learned the sort of thing he wants: elegant and stylized, decoratively coloured, like patisserie cakes. I can do that, I can imitate anything: fake Walt Disney, Victorian etchings in sepia, Bavarian cookies, ersatz Eskimo for the home market. Though what they like best is something they hope will interest the English and American publishers too.

Clean water in a glass, brushes in another glass, watercolours and acrylics in their metal toothpaste tubes. Bluebottle fly near my elbow, metallic abdomen gleaming, sucker tongue walking on the oilcloth like a seventh foot. When it was raining we would sit at this table and draw in our scrapbooks with crayons or coloured pencils, anything we liked. In school you had to do what the rest were doing.

On the crest of the hill for all to see
God planted a Scarlet Maple Tree

printed thirty-five times, strung out along the top of the blackboard, each page with a preserved maple leaf glued to it, ironed between sheets of wax paper.

I outline a princess, an ordinary one, emaciated fashion-model torso and infantile face, like those I did for *Favourite Fairy Tales*. Earlier they annoyed me, the stories never revealed the essential things about them, such as what they ate or whether their towers and dungeons had bathrooms, it was as though their bodies were pure air. It wasn't Peter Pan's ability to fly that made him incredible for me, it was the lack of an outhouse near his underground burrow.

My princess tilts her head: she's gazing up at a bird rising from a nest of flames, wings outspread like a heraldic emblem or a fire insurance trademark: The Tale of the Golden Phoenix. The bird has to be yellow and the fire can only be yellow too, they have to keep the cost down so I can't use red; that way I lose orange and purple also. I asked for red instead of yellow but Mr Percival wanted 'a cool tone.'

I pause to judge: the princess looks stupified rather than filled with wonder. I discard her and try again, but this time she's crosseyed and has one breast bigger than the other. My fingers are stiff, maybe I'm getting arthritis.

I skim the story again for a different episode, but no pictures form. It's hard to believe that anyone here, even the grandmothers, ever knew these stories: this isn't a country of princesses, The Fountain of Youth and The Castle of the Seven Splendours don't belong here. They must have told stories about something as they sat around the kitchen range at night: bewitched dogs and malevolent trees perhaps, and the magic powers of rival political candidates, whose effigies in straw they burned during elections.

But the truth is that I don't know what the villagers thought or talked about, I was so shut off from them. The older ones occasionally crossed themselves when we passed, possibly because my mother was wearing slacks, but even that was never explained. Although we played during visits with the solemn, slightly hostile children of Paul and Madame, the games were brief and wordless. We never could find out what went on inside the tiny hillside church they filed into on Sundays: our parents wouldn't let us sneak up and peer through the windows, which made it illicit and attractive. After my brother began going to school in the winters he told me it was called the Mass and what they did inside was eat; I imagined it as a sort of birthday party, with ice cream – birthday parties were my only experience then of people eating in groups – but according to my brother all they had was soda crackers.

When I started school myself I begged to be allowed to go to Sunday School, like everyone else; I wanted to find out, also I wanted to be less conspicuous. My father didn't approve, he reacted as though I'd asked to go to a pool hall: Christianity was something he'd escaped from, he wished to protect us from its distortions. But after a couple of years he decided I was old enough, I could see for myself, reason would defend me.

I knew what you wore, itchy white stockings and a hat and gloves; I went with one of the girls from school whose family took a pursed-mouth missionary interest in me. It was a United Church, it stood on a long grey street of block-shaped buildings. On the steeple instead of a cross there was a thing like an onion going around which they said was a ventilator, and inside it smelled of face powder and damp wool trousers. The Sunday School part was in the cellar; it had blackboards like a regular school, with KICKAPOO JOY JUICE printed on one of them in orange chalk and underneath, in green chalk, the mysterious initials CGIT. This was a possible clue, until they translated it for me, Canadian Girls In Training. The teacher wore maroon nail-polish and a blue pancake-sized hat clipped to her head by two prongs; she told us a lot about her admirers and their cars. At the end she handed out pictures of Jesus, who didn't have thorns and ribs but was alive and draped in a bed sheet, tired-looking, surely incapable of miracles.

After church every time, the family I went with drove to a hill above the railway terminal to watch the trains shunting back and forth; it was their Sunday treat. Then they would have me to lunch, which was always the same thing, pork and beans and canned pineapple for dessert. At the beginning the father would say Grace, 'For what we are about to receive may the Lord make us truly thankful, Amen,' while the four children pinched and kicked each other under the table; and at the end he would say,

Pork and beans the musical fruit,
The more you eat the more you toot.

The mother, who had a bun of greying hair and prickles around her mouth like a schmoo, would frown and ask me what I'd learned about Jesus that morning, and the father would grin feebly, ignored by all; he was a clerk in a bank, the Sunday trains his only diversion, the little rhyme his only impropriety. For some time I had a confused notion that canned pineapple really was musical and would make you sing better, until my brother set me straight.

'Maybe I'll be a Catholic,' I said to my brother; I was afraid to say it to my parents.

'Catholics are crazy,' he said. The Catholics went to a school down the street from ours and the boys threw snowballs at them in winter and rocks in spring and fall. 'They believe in the BVM.'

I didn't know what that was and neither did he, so he said 'They believe if you don't go to Mass you'll turn into a wolf.'

'Will you?' I said.

'We don't go,' he said, 'and we haven't.'

Maybe that's why they didn't waste any sweat searching for my father, they were afraid to, they thought he'd turned into a wolf; he'd be a prime candidate since he never went to Mass at all. *Les maudits anglais*, the damned English, they mean it; they're sure we're all damned literally. There should be a *loup-garou* story in *Quebec Folk Tales*, perhaps there was and Mr Percival took it out, it was too rough for him. But in some of the stories they do it the other way round, the animals are human inside and they take their fur skins off as easily as getting undressed.

I remember the hair on Joe's back, vestigial, like appendices and little toes: soon we'll evolve into total baldness. I like the hair though, and the heavy teeth, thick shoulders, unexpectedly slight hips, hands whose texture I can still feel on my skin, roughened and leathery from the clay. Everything I value about him seems to be physical: the rest is either unknown, disagreeable or ridiculous. I don't care much for his temperament, which alternates between surliness and gloom, or for the overgrown pots he throws so skilfully on the wheel and then mutilates, cutting holes in them, strangling them, slashing them open. That's unfair, he never uses a knife, only his fingers, and a lot of the time he only bends them, doubles them over; even so they have a disagreeable mutant quality. Nobody else admires them either: the aspiring housewives he teaches two evenings a week, Pottery and Ceramics 432–A, want to make ashtrays and plates with cheerful daisies on them instead, and the things don't sell at all in the few handicraft shops that will even stock them. So they accumulate in our already cluttered basement apartment like fragmentary memories or murder victims. I can't even put flowers in them, the water would run out through the rips. Their only function is to uphold Joe's unvoiced claim to superior artistic seriousness: every time I sell a poster design or get a new commission he mangles another pot.

I wanted my third princess to be running lightly through a meadow but the paper's too wet, she gets out of control, sprouting an enormous rear; I try to salvage it by turning it into a bustle, but it's not convincing. I give up and doodle, adding fangs and a moustache, surrounding her with moons and fish and a wolf with bristling hackles and a snarl; but that doesn't work either, it's more like an overweight collie. What's the alternative to princesses, what else will parents buy for their children? Humanoid bears and talking pigs, Protestant choo-choo trains who make the grade and become successful.

Perhaps it's not only his body I like, perhaps it's his failure; that also has a kind of purity.

I crumple up my third princess, dump the paint water into the slop pail and clean the brushes. I survey from the windows: David and Joe are still out on the lake but they seem to be heading back now. Anna is halfway up the hillside stairs, towel over her arm. I see her for a moment faceted by the screen door and then she's inside.

'Hi,' she says, 'get anything done?'

'Not much,' I say.

She comes over to the table and smooths out my botched princesses. 'That's good,' she says without conviction.

'Those are mistakes,' I say.

'Oh.' She turns the sheets over, face down. 'Did you believe that stuff when you were little?' she says. 'I did, I thought I was really a princess and I'd end up living in a castle. They shouldn't let kids have stuff like that.' She goes to the mirror, blots and smooths her face, then stands on tiptoe, checking her back to see if it's pink. 'What was he *doing* up here?' she asks suddenly.

It takes me a moment to understand what she means. My father, his work. 'I don't know,' I say. 'Just, you know.'

She gives me an odd glance, as though I've violated a propriety, and I'm puzzled, she told me once you shouldn't define yourself by your job but by who you are. When they ask her what she does she talks about fluidity and Being rather than Doing; though if she doesn't like the person she just says 'I'm David's wife.'

'He was living,' I say. This is almost right, it satisfies her, she goes into the bedroom to change her clothes.

All at once I'm furious with him for vanishing like this, unresolved, leaving me with no answers to give them when they ask. If he was going to die he should have done it visibly, out in the open, so they could mark him with a stone and get it over with.

They must find it strange, a man his age staying alone the whole winter in a cabin ten miles from nowhere; I never questioned it, to me it was logical. They always intended to move here permanently as soon as they could, when he retired: isolation was to him desirable. He didn't dislike people, he merely found them irrational; animals, he said, were more consistent, their behaviour at least was predictable. To him that's what Hitler exemplified: not the triumph of evil but the failure of reason. He found war irrational too, both of my parents were pacifists, but he would have fought anyway, in defence of science perhaps, if he'd been permitted; this must be the only country where a botanist can be classified as crucial to the national defense.

As it was he withdrew; we could have lived all year in the company town but he split us between two anonymities, the city and the bush. In the city we lived in a succession of apartments and in the bush he picked the most remote lake he could find, when my brother was born there wasn't yet a road to it. Even the village had too many people for him, he needed an island, a place where he could recreate not the settled farm life of his own father but that of the earliest ones who arrived when there was nothing but forest and no ideologies but the ones they brought with them. When they say Freedom they never quite mean it, what they mean is freedom from interference.

The stack of papers is still up on the shelf by the lamp. I've been avoiding it, looking through it would be an intrusion if he were still alive. But now I've admitted he's dead I might as well find out what he left for me. Executor.

I was expecting a report of some kind, tree growth or diseases, unfinished business; but on the top page there's only a crude drawing of a hand, done with a felt pen or a brush, and some notations: numbers, a name. I flip through the next few pages. More hands, then a stiff childish figure, faceless and minus the hands and feet, and on the next page a similar creature with two things like tree branches or antlers protruding from its head. On each of the pages are the numbers, and on some a few scrawled words: LICHENS RED CLOTHING LEFT. I can't make sense out of them. The handwriting is my father's, but changed, more hasty or careless.

Outside I hear the crunch of wood on wood as the canoe hits the dock, they've brought it in too fast; then their laughter. I reach the stack of papers back to the shelf, I don't want them to see.

That's what he was doing here all winter, he was shut up in this cabin making these unintelligible drawings. I sit at the table, my heart speeded up as if I've opened what I thought was an empty closet and found myself face to face with a thing that isn't supposed to be there, like a claw or a bone. This is the forgotten possibility: he might have gone insane. Crazy, loony. Bushed, the trappers call it when you stay in the forest by yourself too long. And if insane, perhaps not dead: none of the rules would be the same.

Anna walks out of the bedroom, dressed in jeans and shirt again. She combs her hair in front of the mirror, light ends, dark roots, humming to herself, You Are My Sunshine; smoke twines up from her cigarette. *Help*, I think at her silently, *talk*. And she does.

'What's for dinner?' she says; then, waving. 'Here they come.'

Chapter Seven

At supper we finish off the beer. David wants to go fishing, it's the last night, so I leave the dishes for Anna and go down to the garden with the shovel and the tin can saved from the peas.

I dig in the weediest part near the compost heap, lifting the earth and letting it crumble, sieving the worms out with my fingers. The soil is rich, the worms scramble, red ones and pink ones.

Nobody loves me
Everybody hates me
I'm going to the garden to eat worms.

They sang that back and forth at recess: it was an insult, but perhaps they are edible. They're sold like apples in season, VERS 5¢ on the roadside signs, sometimes VERS 5¢, later VERS 10¢, inflation. French class, *vers libre*, I translated it the first time as Free Worms and she thought I was being smart.

I put the worms in the can and some dirt for them. As I walk back to the cabin I hold my palm over the top; already they're nudging with their head ends, trying to get out. I make them a cover from a piece of paper torn off the grocery bag, keeping it on with a rubber band. My mother was a saver: rubber bands, string, safety pins, jam jars, for her the Depression never ended.

David is fitting the sections of his borrowed fishing rod together; it's fibreglass, I have no faith in it. I take the steel trolling rod from its hooks on the wall. 'Come on,' I tell David, 'you can use that one for still-fishing.'

'Show me how to light the lamp,' Anna says, 'I'll stay here and read.'

I don't want to leave her alone. What I'm afraid of is my father, hidden on the island somewhere and attracted by the light perhaps, looming up at the window like a huge ragged moth; or, if he's still at all lucid, asking her who she is and ordering her out of his house. As long as there are four of us he'll keep away, he never liked groups.

'Poor sport,' David says.

I tell her I need her in the canoe for extra weight, which is a lie as we'll be too heavy already, but she takes my expert word.

While they're getting into the canoe I return to the garden and catch a small leopard frog as an emergency weapon. I put it in a jam jar and punch a few airholes in the lid.

Tackle box, smelling of stale fish, old captures; worm can and frog bottle, knife and heap of bracken fronds for the fish to bleed on. Joe in the bow, Anna behind him on a life-jacket facing me, David on another life-jacket with his back to me and his legs tangled amongst Anna's. Before I push off I clip a silver and gold spinner with glass ruby eyes to David's line and hook a worm on, looping its body seductively. Both ends twirl.

'Ech,' says Anna, who can see what I'm doing.

'It doesn't hurt them,' my brother said, 'they don't feel it.' 'Then why do they squirm?' I said. He said it was nervous tension.

'Whatever happens,' I tell them, 'stay in the middle.' We move ponderously out of the bay. I've taken on too much: I haven't been in a canoe for years, my muscles are shot, Joe paddles as though he's stirring the lake with a ladle and we're down by the bow. But none of them will know the difference. I think it's a good thing our lives don't depend on catching a fish. Starvation, bite your arm and suck the blood, that's what they do on lifeboats; or the Indian way, if there's no bait try a chunk of your flesh.

The island shoreline recedes behind us, he can't follow us here. Above the trees streaky mackerel clouds are spreading in over the sky, paint on a wet page; no wind at lake level, soft feel of the air before rain. The fish like this, the mosquitoes too, but I can't use any bug spray because it would get on the bait and the fish would smell it.

I steer us along the mainland shore. A blue heron lifts from a bay where it's been fishing and flaps overhead, neck and beak craning forward and long legs stretched back, winged snake. It notes us with a rasping pterodactyl croak and rises higher, heading south-east, there was a colony of them, it must be there. But now I have to pay more attention to David. The copper line slants down, cutting the water, vibrating slightly.

'Any action?' I ask.

'It's just sort of jigging.'

'That's the spoon turning,' I say. 'Keep the tip down; if you feel a nibble wait a second and then give it a sharp tug, okay?'

'Right,' he says.

My arms are tired. Behind me I can hear the tick tock of the frog hopping up and hitting its muzzle against the jar lid.

When we're getting near the sheer cliff I tell him to reel in, we'll still-fish and he can use his own rod.

'Lie down, Anna,' he says, 'I'm gonna use my own rod.'

Anna says 'Oh Christ, you have to do that about everything, don't you?'

He chuckles at her and reels and the line comes in, the water slipping off it; the pale gleam of the spoon wavers up out of the lake. When it skips over the surface towards us I can see the worm is gone. On one hook is a shred of worm skin; I used to wonder how the lures with their crude African-idol eyes could deceive the fish, but perhaps they've learned.

We're opposite the cliff, grey slab of rock straight as a monument, overhanging slightly, ledge like a step halfway up, brown rock-lichen growing in the fissures. I put a lead sinker and a different spoon and a fresh worm on David's line and toss it over; the worm drops, pink, pink-brown, till it disappears in the shadow of the cliff. The dark torpedo shapes of the fish are seeing it, sniffing at it, prodding it with their noses. I believe in them the way other people believe in God: I can't see them but I know they are there.

'Keep right still,' I say to Anna, who's beginning to shift uncomfortably. They can hear.

Light fading, silence; back in the forest, liquid spiral thrush voice, they call at sunset. David's arm moves up and down.

When nothing happens I tell him to reel in; the worm is gone again. I take out the little frog, the ultimate solution, and hook it on securely while it squeaks. Other people always did that for me.

'God you're cold-blooded,' Anna says. The frog goes down through the water, kicking like a man swimming.

Everyone concentrates, even Anna: they sense this is my last trick. I stare into the water, it was always a kind of meditation. My brother fished by technique, he outguessed them, but I fished by prayer, listening.

Our father who art in heaven
Please let the fish be caught.

Later when I knew that wouldn't work, just *Please be caught*, invocation or hypnosis. He got more fish but I could pretend mine were willing, they had chosen to die and forgiven me in advance.

I begin to think the frog has failed. But it's still magic, the rod bends like a diviner's and Anna shrieks with surprise.

I say 'Keep the line tight,' but David is oblivious, he's reeling like a mixmaster and saying 'Wow, wow' to himself and it's up to the surface, it jumps clear and hangs in the air like a framed photo over a bar only moving. It dives and pulls, the line slackens, it's doubling back trying to shake loose; but when it jumps again David jerks the rod with his whole body and it sails across and flops into the canoe, a dumb move, he could've lost it, on top of Anna and she lurches, screaming 'Get it off me! Get it off me!' and we almost tip. Joe says 'Holy shit' and grabs at the side, I bend the other way, counterbalancing, David is snatching at it. It slithers over the canoe ribs, flippering and snapping.

'Here,' I say, 'hit it back of the eyes.' I reach him the sheathed knife, I'd rather not kill it myself.

David swipes at it, misses; Anna cover her eyes and says 'Ugh. Ugh.' It flops towards me and I step down on it with my foot and grab the knife and whack it quickly with the knife handle, crushing the skull, and it trembles stiffly all over, that's done it.

'What is it?' David asks, amazed by what he's caught but proud too. They are all laughing, joyful with victory and relief, like the newsreels of parades at the end of the war, and that makes me glad. Their voices bounce off the cliff.

'Walleye,' I say, 'Pickerel. We'll have it for breakfast.'

It's a good size. I pick it up, fingers hooked under the gills and holding firmly, they can bite and jerk loose even when they're dead. I put it on the bracken fronds and rinse my hand and the knife. One of its eyes is bulging out and I feel a little sick, it's because I've killed something, made it dead; but I know that's irrational, killing certain things is all right, food and enemies, fish and mosquitoes; and wasps, when there are too many of them you pour boiling water down their tunnels. 'Don't bother them and they won't bother you,' our mother would say when they lit on our plates. That was before the house was built, we were living outside in tents. Our father said they went in cycles.

'Neat eh?' David says to the others; he's excited, he wants praise. 'Ugh,' says Anna, 'it's slimy, I'm not going to eat any of it.' Joe grunts, I wonder if he's jealous.

David wants to try for another; it's like gambling, you only stop if you lose. I don't remind him I have no more magic frogs; I get out a worm for him and let him hook it on himself.

He fishes for a while but he's having no luck. Just as Anna's beginning to fidget again I hear a whine, motorboat. I listen, it may be going somewhere else, but it rounds a point and becomes a roar, homing in on us, big powerboat, the white water veeing from the bow. The engine cuts and it skids in beside us, its wash rocking us sharply. American flag on the front and another at the back, two irritated-looking businessmen with pug-dog faces and nifty outfits and a thin shabby man from the village, guiding. I see it's Claude from the motel, he scowls at us, he feel we're poaching on his preserve.

'Getting any?' one of the Americans yells, teeth bared, friendly as a shark.

I say 'No' and nudge David with my foot. He'd want to tell, if only to spite them.

The other American throws his cigar butt over the side. 'This don't look like much of a place,' he says to Claude.

'Used to be,' Claude says.

'Next year I'm goin' to Florida,' the first American says.

'Reel in,' I say to David. There's no sense in staying here now. If they catch one they'll be here all night, and if they don't get anything in fifteen minutes they'll blast off and scream around the lake in their souped-up-boat, deafening the fish. They're the kind who catch more than they can eat and they'd do it with dynamite if they could get away with it.

We used to think they were harmless and funny and inept and faintly lovable, like President Eisenhower. We met two of them once on the way to the bass lake, they were carrying their tin motorboat and the motor over the portage so they wouldn't have to paddle once they were on the inner lake; when we first heard them thrashing along through the underbrush we thought they were bears. Another one turned up with a spinning reel and stepped in our campfire, scorching his new boots; when he tried to cast he sent his plug, a real minnow sealed in transparent plastic, into the bushes on the other side of the bay. We laughed at him behind his back and asked if he was catching squirrels but he didn't mind, he showed his automatic firelighter and his cook set with detachable handles and his collapsible armchair. They liked everything collapsible.

On the way back we hug the shore, avoiding the open lake in case the Americans take it into their heads to zoom past us as close as possible, they sometimes do that for fun, their wake could tip us. But before we're half the distance they whoosh away into nowhere like Martians in a late movie, and I relax.

When we get back I'll hang up the fish and wash the scales and the salty armpit odour off my hands with soap. After that I'll light the lamp and the fire and make some cocoa. Being here feels right to me for the first time, and I know it's because we're leaving tomorrow. My father will have the island to himself; madness is private, I respect that, however he may be living it's better than an instituton. Before we go I'll burn his drawings, they're evidence of the wrong sort.

The sun has set, we slide back through the gradual dusk. Loon voices in the distance; bats flitter past us, dipping over the water-surface, flat calm now, the shore things, white-grey rocks and dead trees, doubling themselves in the dark mirror. Around us the illusion of infinite space or of no space, ourselves and the obscure shore which it seems we could touch, the water between an absence. The canoe's reflection floats with us, the paddles twin in the lake. It's like moving on air, nothing beneath us holding us up; suspended, we drift home.

Chapter Eight

In the early morning Joe wakes me; his hands at any rate are intelligent, they move over me delicately as a blind man's reading braille, skilled, moulding me like a vase, they're learning me; they repeat patterns he's tried before, they've found out what works, and my body responds that way too, anticipates him, educated, crisp as a typewriter. It's best when you don't know them. A phrase comes to me, a joke then but mournful now, someone in a parked car after a highschool dance who said *With a paper bag over their head they're all the same*. At the time I didn't understand what he meant, but since then I've pondered it. It's almost like a coat of arms: two people making love with paper bags over their heads, not even any eyeholes. Would that be good or bad?

When we're finished and after we rest I get up and dress and go out to prepare the fish. It's been hanging all night, the string through its gills looped to a tree branch out of the reach of scavengers, racoons, otters, mink, skunks. A squeezing of fish shit, like a bird's only browner, drools from the anus. I untie the string and carry the fish down to the lake to clean and fillet it.

I kneel on the flat rock beside the lake, the knife and the plate for the fillets beside me. This was never my job; someone else did it, my brother or my father. I cut off the head and tail and slit the belly and open the fish into its two halves. Inside the stomach is a partly digested leech and some shreds of crayfish. I divide along the backbone, then along the two lateral lines: four pieces, blueish white, translucent. The entrails will be buried in the garden, they're fertilizer.

As I'm washing the fillets David saunters down to the dock with his toothbrush. 'Hey,' he says, 'is that my fish?' He regards the guts on the plate with interest. 'Hold it,' he says, 'that's a Random Sample.' He goes for Joe and the camera and the two of them solemnly film the fish innards, collapsed bladders and tubes and soft ropes, rearranging them between takes for better angles. It would never occur to David to have someone snap him with a Brownie camera holding his fish up by the tail and grinning, nor would he ever have it stuffed and mounted; still, he wants to immortalize it, in his own way. Photo album, I'm in it somewhere, successive incarnations of me preserved and flattened like flowers pressed in dictionaries, that was the other book she kept, the leather album, a logbook like the diaries. I used to hate standing still, waiting for the click.

I dip the fillets in flour and fry them and we eat them with strips of bacon. 'Good food, good meat, Good God, let's eat,' David says; and later, smacking his lips, 'Couldn't get this in the city.'

Anna says 'Sure you could, frozen. You can get anything there now.'

After breakfast I go into my room and begin to pack. Through the plywood wall I hear Anna walking, pouring more coffee, the creak as David stretches out on the couch.

Perhaps I should fold up all the bedding and towels and the abandoned clothes, tie them into bundles and take them back with me. No one will be living here now and the moths and the mice will get in eventually. If he doesn't ever decide to return I suppose it belongs to me, or half to me and half to my brother; but my brother won't do anything about it, after he left he's evaded them as much as I have. He set it up better though, he simply went as far away as he could: if I stuck a knitting needle straight through the earth the point would emerge where he is now, camped in the outback, inaccessible; he probably hadn't even got my letter yet. Mineral rights, that's what he explores, for one of the big international companies, a prospector; but I can't believe in that, nothing he's done since we grew up is real to me.

'I like it here,' David says. No sound from the others. 'Let's stay for a while, a week, it'd be great.'

'Don't you have that seminar?' Anna says dubiously. 'Man and his Electricity Environment, or something?'

'Electrifying. That's not till August.

'I don't think we should,' Anna says.

'How come you never want us to do anything I want to do?' David says, and there's a pause. Then he says 'What d'you think?' and Joe says 'Okay by me.'

'Great,' says David, 'we'll do some more fishing.'

I sit down on the bed. They might have asked me first, it's my house. though maybe they're waiting till I come out, they'll ask then. If I say I don't want to they can't very well stay; but what reason can I give? I can't tell them about my father, betray him; anyway they might think I was making it up. There's my work, but they know I have it with me. I could leave by myself with Evans but I'd only get as far as the village: it's David's car, I'd have to steal the keys, and also, I remind myself, I never learned to drive.

Anna makes a last feeble attempt. 'I'll run out of cigarettes.'

'Do you good,' David says cheerfully, 'filthy habit. Get you back into shape.' He's older than we are, he's over thirty, he's beginning to worry about that; every now and then he hits himself in the stomach and says 'Flab.'

'I'll get crabby,' Anna says, but David only laughs and says 'Try it.'

I could tell them there isn't enough food. But they'd spot that as a lie, there's the garden and the rows of cans on the shelves, corned beef, Spam, baked beans, chicken, powered milk, everything.

I go to the room door, open it. 'You'll have to pay Evans the five anyway,' I say.

For a moment they're startled, they realize I've overheard. Then David says 'No sweat.' He gives me a quick look, triumphant and appraising, as though he's just won something: not a war but a lottery.

When Evans turns up at the appointed time David and Joe go down to the dock to arrange things with him. I warned them not to say anything about the fish: if they do, this part of the lake will be swarming with Americans, they have an uncanny way of passing the word, like ants about sugar, or lobsters. After a few minutes I hear the boat starting again and accelerating and diminishing, he's gone.

I've avoided Evans and the explanation and negotiations by going up to the outhouse and latching myself in. That was where I went when there was something I didn't want to do, like weeding the garden. It's the new outhouse, the old one got used up. This one is built of logs; my brother and I made the hole for it, he dug with the shovel and I hauled the sand up in a pail. Once a porcupine fell in, they like to chew axe handles and toilet seats.

In the city I never hid in bathrooms; I didn't like them, they were too hard and white. The only city place I can remember hiding is behind opened doors at birthday parties. I despised them, the pew-purple velvet dresses with antimacassar lace collars and the presents, voices going Oooo with envy when they were opened, and the pointless games, finding a thimble or memorizing clutter on a tray. There were only two things you could be, a winner or a loser; the mothers tried to rig it so everyone got a prize, but they couldn't figure out what to do about me since I wouldn't play. At first I ran away, but after that my mother said I had to go, I had to learn to be polite, 'civilized,' she called it. So I watched from behind the door. When I finally joined in a game of Musical Chairs I was welcomed with triumph, like a religious convert or a political defector.

Some were disappointed, they found my hermit-crab habits amusing, they found me amusing in general. Each year it was a different school, in October or November when the first snow hit the lake, and I was the one who didn't know the local customs, like a person from another culture: on me they could try out the tricks and minor tortures they'd already used up on each other. When they boys chased and captured the girls after school and tied them up with their own skipping ropes, I was the one they would forget on purpose to untie. I spent many afternoons looped to fences and gates and convenient trees, waiting for a benevolent adult to pass and free me; later I became an escape artist of sorts, expert at undoing knots. On better days they would gather around, competing for me.

'Adam and Eve and Pinch Me,' they shouted,

> Went to the river to bathe;
> Adam and Eve fell in,
> So who do you think was saved?

'I don't know,' I said.

'You have to answer,' they said, 'that's the rules.'

'Adam and Eve,' I said craftily. '*They* were saved.'

'If you don't do it right we won't play with you,' they said. Being socially retarded is like being mentally retarded, it arouses in others disgust and pity and the desire to torment and reform.

It was harder for my brother; our mother had taught him that fighting was wrong so he came home every day beaten to a pulp. Finally she had to back down: he could fight, but only if they hit first.

I didn't last long at Sunday School. One girl told me she had prayed for a Barbara Ann Scott doll with figure skates and swansdown trim on the costume and she got it for her birthday; so I decided to pray too, not like the Lord's Prayer or the fish prayer but for something real. I prayed to be made invisible, and when in the morning everyone could still see me I knew they had the wrong God.

A mosquito lights on my arm and I let it bite me, waiting till its abdomen globes with blood before I pop it with my thumb like a grape. They need the blood before they can lay their eggs. There's a breeze, filtering through the screened window; it's better here than in the city, with the exhaust-pipe fumes and the damp heat, the burnt rubber smell of the subway, the brown grease that congeals on your skin if you walk around outside. How have I been able to live so long in the city, it isn't safe. I always felt safe here, even at night.

That's a lie, my own voice says out loud. I think hard about it, considering it, and it is a lie: sometimes I was terrified, I would shine the flashlight ahead of me on the path, I would hear a rustling in the forest and know it was hunting me, a bear, a wolf or some indefinite thing with no name, that was worse.

I look around at the walls, the window; it's the same, it hasn't changed, but the shapes are inaccurate as though everything has warped slightly. I have to be more careful about my memories, I have to be sure they're my own and not the memories of other people telling me what I felt, how I acted, what I said: if the events are wrong the feelings I remember about them will be wrong too, I'll start inventing them and there will be no way of correcting it, the ones who could help are gone. I run quickly over my version of it, my life, checking it like an alibi; it fits, it's all there till the time I left. Then static, like a jumped track, for a moment I've lost it, wiped clean; my exact age even, I shut my eyes, what is it? To have the past but not the present, that means you're going senile.

I refuse to panic, I force my eyes open, my hand, life etched on it, reference: I flatten the palm and the lines fragment, spread like ripples. I concentrate on the spiderweb near the window, flyhusks caught in it catching in turn the sun, in my mouth tongue forming my name, repeating it like a chant. . . .

Then someone knocks on the door. 'Ready or not, you must be caught,' says a voice, it's David, I can identify him, relief, I slip back into place.

'Just a minute,' I say, and he knocks again and says 'Snappy with the crap in there,' giving a Woody Woodpecker laugh.

Before lunch I tell them I'm going for a swim. The others don't want to, they say it will be too cold, and it is cold, like icewater. I shouldn't be going by myself, we were taught that, I might get cramps.

What I used to do was run to the end of the dock and jump, it was like a heart attack or lightning, but as I walk towards the lake I find I no longer have the nerve for that.

This was where he drowned, he got saved only by accident; if there had been a wind she wouldn't have heard him. She leaned over and reached down and grabbed him by the hair, hauled him up and poured the water out of him. His drowning never seemed to have affected him as much as I thought it should, he couldn't even remember it. If it had happened to me I would have felt there was something special about me, to be raised from the dead like that; I would have returned with secrets, I would have known things most people didn't.

After she'd told the story I asked our mother where he would have gone if she hadn't saved him. She said she didn't know. My father explained everything but my mother never did, which only convinced me that she had the answers but wouldn't tell. 'Would he be in the graveyard?' I said. They had a verse about the graveyard at school too:

Stick him in the bread pan,
Sock him in the jaw;
Now he's in the graveyard,
Haw, haw haw.

'Nobody knows,' she said. She was making a pie crust and she gave me a piece of the dough to distract me. My father would have said Yes; he said you died when your brain died. I wonder if he still believes that.

I go off the dock and wade in from the shore, slowly, splashing water over my shoulders and neck, the cold climbing my thighs; my footsoles feel the sand and the twigs and sunk leaves. At that time I would dive and coast along the lakefloor with my eyes open, distance and my own body blurred and eroding; or out further, diving from the canoe or the raft and turning on my back under the water to look up, the bubbles fleeing from my mouth. We would stay in until our skins became numbed and turned a strange colour, bluish-purple. I must have been superhuman, I couldn't do it now. Perhaps I'm growing old, at last, can that be possible?

I stand there shivering, seeing my reflection and my feet down through it, white as fishflesh on the sand, till finally being in the air is more painful than being in the water and I bend and push myself reluctantly into the lake.

TWO

Chapter Nine

The trouble is all in the knob at the top of our bodies. I'm not against the body or the head either: only the neck, which creates the illusion that they are separate. The language is wrong, it shouldn't have different words for them. If the head extended directly into the shoulders like a worm's or a frog's without that constriction, that lie, they wouldn't be able to look down on their bodies and move them around as if they were robots or puppets; they would have to realize that if the head is detached from the body both of them will die.

I'm not sure when I began to suspect the truth, about myself and about them, what I was and what they were turning into. Part of it arrived swift as flags, as mushrooms, unfurling and sudden growth, but it was there in me, the evidence, only needing to be deciphered. From where I am now it seems as if I've always known, everything, time is compressed like the fist I close on my knee in the darkening bedroom, I hold inside it the clues and solutions and the power for what I must do now.

I was seeing poorly, translating badly, a dialect problem, I should have used my own. In the experiments they did with children, shutting them up with deaf and dumb nurses, locking them in closets, depriving them of words, they found that after a certain age the mind is incapable of absorbing any language; but how could they tell the child hadn't invented one, unrecognizable to everyone but itself? That was in the green book at high school, *Your Health*, along with the photographs of cretins and people with thyroid deficiencies, the crippled and deformed, the examples, with back oblongs across their eyes like condemned criminals: the only pictures of naked bodies it was judged proper for us to see. The rest were diagrams, transparencies with labels and arrows, the ovaries purple sea creatures, the womb a pear.

The voices of the others and the riffle and slap of cards reach me through the closed door. Canned laughter, they carry it with them, the midget reels of tape and the On switch concealed somewhere in their chests, instant playback.

After Evans left that day I was uneasy: the island wasn't safe, we were trapped on it. They didn't realize it but I did, I was responsible for them. The sense of watching eyes, his presence lurking just behind the green leafscreen, ready to pounce or take flight, he wasn't predictable, I was trying to think of ways to keep them out of danger; they would be all right as long as they didn't go anywhere alone. He might be harmless but I couldn't be sure.

We finished lunch and I took the breadcrumbs out to the tray for the birds. The jays had discovered there were people living in the cabin; they're intelligent, they knew a figure near the tray signalled food; or perhaps a few of them were old enough to remember the image of my mother, hand outstretched. Two or three of them stood sentinel now, out of reach, wary.

Joe followed me out and watched as I spread the crumbs. He put his fingers on my arm, frowning at me, which may have meant he wanted to talk to me: speech to him was a task, a battle, words mustered behind his beard and issued one at a time, heavy and square like tanks. His hand gripped me in a preliminary spasm, but David was there with the axe.

'Hey lady,' he said, 'I see your woodpile's gettin' low. You could used a handy man.'

He wanted to do something useful; and he was right, if we were staying a week we would need a fresh supply. I asked him to find standing trees, dead but not too old or rotten, 'Yes'm,' he said, giving me a burlesque salute.

Joe took the small hatchet and went with him. They were from the city, I was afraid they might chop their feet; though that would be a way out, I thought, we'd have to go back. But I didn't need to warn them, about him, they had weapons. He would see that and run away.

When they'd disappeared along the trail into the forest I said I was going down to the weed garden, another job that had to be done. I wanted to keep busy, preserve at least the signs of order, conceal my fear, both from others and from him. Fear has a smell, as love does.

Anna could tell she was expected to help; she abandoned her

murder mystery and stubbed out her cigarette, only half-smoked, she was rationing them. We tied scarves around our heads and I went to the toolshed for the rake.

The garden was full in sunlight and steaming hot, moist as a greenhouse. We knelt down and began to pull at the weeds; they resisted, holding on or taking clumps of soil out with them or breaking their stems, leaving their roots in the earth to regenerate; I dug for the feet in the warm dirt, my hands green with weed blood. Gradually the vegetables emerged, pallid and stunted most of them, all but strangled. We raked the weeds into piles between the rows where they wilted, dying slowly; later they would be burned, like witches, to keep them from reappearing. There were a few mosquitoes and the deer flies with their iridescent rainbow eyes and stings like heated needles.

From time to time I paused, checking the fence, the border, but no one was there. Perhaps he would be unrecognizable, his former shape transfigured by age and madness and the forest, rag bundle of decaying clothes, the skin of his face woolly with dead leaves. History, I thought, quick.

It took them years to make the garden, the real soil was too sandy and anaemic. This oblong was artificial, the product of skill and of compost spaded in, black muck dredged from the swamps, horse dung ferried by boat from the winter logging camps when they still kept horses to drag the logs to the frozen lake. My father and mother would carry it in bushel baskets on the handbarrow, two poles with boards nailed across, each of them lifting an end.

I could remember before that, when we lived in tents. It was about here we found the lard pail, ripped open like a paper bag, claw scratches and toothmarks scarring the paint. Our father had gone on a long trip as he often did to investigate trees for the paper company or the government, I was never certain which he worked for. Our mother was given a three-week supply of food. The bear walked through the back of the food tent, we heard it in the night. It stepped on the eggs and tomatoes and pried open all the storage tins and scattered the wax-paper bread and smashed the jam jars, we salvaged what we could in the morning. The only thing it didn't bother with was the potatoes, and we were eating them for breakfast around the campfire when it materialized on the path, snuffling along bulky and flat-footed, an enormous fanged rug, returning for more. My mother stood up and walked towards it; it hesitated and grunted. She yelled a word at it that sounded like 'Scat!' and waved her arms, and it turned around and thudded off into the forest.

That was the picture I kept, my mother seen from the back, arms upraised as though she was flying, and the bear terrified. When she told the story later she said she'd been scared to death but I couldn't believe that, she had been so positive, assured, as if she knew a foolproof magic formula: gesture and word. She was wearing her leather jacket.

'You on the pill?' Anna asked suddenly.

I looked at her, startled. It took me a minute, why did she want to know? That was what they used to call a personal question.

'Not any more,' I said.

'Me neither,' she said glumly. 'I don't know anyone who still is any more. I got a blood clot in my leg, what did you get?' She had a smear of mud across her cheek, her pink face layer was softening in the heat, like tar.

'I couldn't see,' I said. 'Things were blurry. They said it would clear up after a couple of months but it didn't.' It was like having vaseline on my eyes but I didn't say that.

Anna nodded; she was tugging at the weeds as though she was pulling hair. 'Bastards,' she said, 'they're so smart, you think they'd be able to come up with something that'd work without killing you. David wants me to go back on, he says it's no worse for you than aspirin, but next time it could be the heart or something. I mean, I'm not taking those kinds of chances.'

Love without fear, sex without risk, that's what they wanted to be true; and they almost did it, I thought, they almost pulled it off, but as in magicians' tricks or burglaries half-success is failure and we're back to the other things. Love is taking precautions. Did you take any precautions, they say, not before but after. Sex used to smell like rubber gloves and now it does again, no more handy green plastic packages, moon-shaped so that the woman can pretend she's still natural, cyclical, instead of a chemical slot machine. But soon they'll have the artificial womb, I wonder how I feel about that. After the first I didn't ever want to have another child, it was too much to go through for nothing, they shut you into a hospital, they shave the hair off you and tie your hands down and they don't let you see, they don't want you to understand, they want you to believe it's their power, not yours. They stick needles into you so you won't hear anything, you might as well be a dead pig, your legs are up in a metal frame, they bend over you, technicians, mechanics, butchers, students clumsy or sniggering practising on your body, they take the baby out with a fork like a pickle out of a pickle jar. After that they fill your veins up with red plastic, I saw it running down through the tube. I won't let them do that to me ever again.

He wasn't there with me, I couldn't remember why; he should have been, since it was his idea, his fault. But he brought his car to collect me afterwards, I didn't have to take a taxi.

From the forest behind us came the sound of sporadic chopping: a few blows, the echoes, a pause, a few more blows, one of them laughing, echo of the laughter. It was my brother who cut the trail, the year before he left, the axe hacking and the machete slashing through the undergrowth marking his progress as he worked his way around the shore.

'Haven't we done enough?' Anna asked. 'I bet I'm getting sunstroke.' She sat back on her heels and took out the unsmoked half of her cigarette. I think she wanted us to exchange more confidences, she wanted to talk about her other diseases, but I kept on weeding. Potatoes, onions; the strawberry patch was a hopeless jungle, we wouldn't do that; in any case the season was over.

David and Joe appeared in the long grass outside the fence, one at either end of a thinnish log. They were proud, they'd caught something. The log was notched in many places as though they'd attacked it.

'Hi,' David called. 'How's the ol' plantation workers?'

Anna stood up. 'Fuck off,' she said, squinting at them against the sun.

'You've hardly done anything,' David said, unquenchable, 'you call that a garden?'

I measured their axework with my father's summarizing eye. In the city he would shake hands with them, estimating them shrewdly: could they handle an axe, what did they know about manure? They would stand there embarrassed in their washed suburban skins and highschool clothes, uncertain what was expected of them.

'That's great,' I said.

David wanted us to get the movie camera and take some footage of both of them carrying the log, for *Random Samples*; he said it would be his cameo appearance. Joe said we couldn't work the camera. David said all you did was press a button, an idiot could do it, anyway it might be even better it it was out of focus or overexposed, it would introduce the element of chance, like a painter throwing paint at a canvas, it would be organic. But Joe said what if we wrecked the camera, who would pay for it. In the end they stuck the axe in the log, after several tries, and took turns shooting each other standing beside it, arms folded and one foot on it as if it was a lion or a rhinoceros.

In the evening we played bridge, with a set of slightly greasy cards that had always been there, blue seahorses on one deck, red seahorses on the other. David and Anna played against us. They won easily: Joe didn't know how, exactly, and I hadn't played for years. I was never any good; the only part I liked was picking up the cards and arranging them.

Afterwards I waited for Anna to walk up to the outhouse with me; usually I went first, alone. We took both flashlights; they made protective circles of weak yellow light, moving with our feet as they walked. Rustlings, toads in the dry leaves; once the quick warning thump of a rabbit. The sounds would be safe as long as I knew what they were.

'I wish I had a warmer sweater,' Anna said, 'I didn't know it got so cold.'

'There's some raincoats,' I said, 'you could try those.'

When we got back to the cabin the other two were in bed; they didn't bother going as far as the outhouse after dark, they peed on the ground. I brushed my teeth; Anna started taking off her makeup by the light of a candle and her flashlight propped on end, they'd blown out the lamp.

I went into my room and got undressed. Joe mumbled, he was half asleep; I curled my arm over him.

Outside was the wind, trees moving in it, nothing else. The yellow target from Anna's flashlight was on the ceiling; it shifted, she was going into their room and I could hear them, Anna breathing, a fast panic sound as though she was running; then her voice began, not like her real voice but twisted as her face must have been, a desperate beggar's whine, *please please.* I put the pillow over my head, I didn't want to listen, I wanted it to be through but it kept on, *Shut up* I whispered but she wouldn't. She was praying to herself, it was as if David wasn't there at all. *Jesus jesus oh yes please jesus*. Then something different, not a word but pure pain, clear as water, an animal's at the moment the trap closes.

It's like death, I thought, the bad part isn't the thing itself but being a witness. I suppose they could hear us too, the times before. But I never say anything.

Chapter Ten

The sunset had been red, reddish purple, and the next day the sun held as I guessed it would; without a radio or a barometer you have to make your own prophecies. It was the second day of the week, I was ticking them off in my head, prisoner's scratches on the wall; I felt stretched, pulled tight like a drying rope, the fact that he had not yet appeared only increased the possibility that he would. The seventh day seemed a great distance away.

I wanted to get them off the island, to protect them from him, to protect him from them, save all of them from knowledge. They might start to explore, cut other trails; already they were beginning to be restless; fire and food, the only two necessities, were taken care of and there was nothing left to be done. Sun rising, drifting across the sky, shadows changing without help, uninterrupted air, absence of defining borders, the only break an occasional distant plane, vapour streak, for them it must have been like living in a hammock.

In the morning David fished from the dock, catching nothing; Anna read, she was on her fourth or fifth paperback. I swept the floor, the broom webbing itself with long threads, dark and light, from where Anna and I brushed our hair in front of the mirror; then I tried to work. Joe stayed on the wall bench, arms wrapped around his knees in lawn-dwarf position, watching me. Every time I glanced up his eyes would be there, blue as ball point pens or Superman; even with my head turned away I could feel his x-ray vision prying under my skin, a slight prickling sensation as though he was tracing me. It was hard to concentrate; I re-read two of the folk tales, about the king who learned to speak with animals and the fountain of life, but I got no further than a rough sketch of a thing that looked like a football player. It was supposed to be a giant.

'What's wrong?' I said to him finally, putting down my brush, giving up.

'Nothing.' he said. He took the cover off the butter dish and started carving holes in the butter with his forefinger.

I should have realized much earlier what was happening, I should have got out of it when we were still in the city. It was unfair of me to stay with him, he'd become used to it, hooked on it, but I didn't realize that and neither did he. When you can't tell the difference between your own pleasure and your pain then you're an addict. I did that, I fed him unlimited supplies of nothing, he wasn't ready for it, it was too strong for him, he had to fill it up, like people isolated in a blank room who see patterns.

After lunch they all sat around expectantly, as though waiting for me to dole out the crayons and plasticine or regiment the sing-song, tell them what to play. I searched through the past: what did we do when it was sunny and there was no work?

'How would you like,' I said, 'to pick some blueberries?' Offering it as a surprise; work disguised in some other form, it had to be a game.

They seized on it, glad of the novelty. 'A groove,' David said. Anna and I made peanut butter sandwiches for a mid-afternoon snack; then we basted our noses and the lobes of our ears with Anna's suntan lotion and started out.

David and Anna went in the green canoe, we took the heavier one. They still couldn't paddle very well but there wasn't much wind. I had to use a lot of energy just to keep us pointed straight, because Joe didn't know how to steer; also he wouldn't admit it, which made it harder.

We wavered aroung the stone point where the trail goes; then we were in the archipelago of islands, tips of sunken hills, once possibly a single ridge before the lake was flooded. None of them is big enough to have a name; some are no more than rocks, with a few trees clutched and knotted to them by the roots. On one of them, further along, was the heron colony. I had to strain my eyes to spot it: the young in the nests were keeping their serpent necks and blade heads immobile, imitating dead branches. The nests were all in a single tree, white pine, grouped for mutual protection like bungalows on the outskirts. If the herons get within pecking range they fight.

'See them?' I said to Joe, pointing.

'See what?' he said. He was sweating, overworked, the wind was against us. He scowled up at the sky but he couldn't make them out until one of them lifted and settled, wings balancing.

Beyond the herons' island was a larger one, flattish, with several red pines rising straight as masts from a ground harsh with blueberry bushes. We landed and tied the canoes and I gave each of them a tin cup. The blueberries were only beginning to ripen, the dots of them showing against the green like first rain pocking the lake. I took my own cup and started to work along the shore, they ripen earlier there.

During the war or was it after they would pay us a cent a cup; there was nowhere to spend it, I didn't understand at first what the metal discs were for: leaves on one side and a man's head chopped of at the neck on the reverse.

I was remembering the others who used to come. There weren't many of them on the lake even then, the government had put them somewhere else, corralled them, but there was one family left. Every year they would appear on the lake in blueberry season and visit the good places the same way we did, condensing as though from the air, five or six of them in a weatherbeaten canoe: father in the stern, head wizened and corded like a dried root, mother with her gourd body and hair pared back to her nape, the rest children or grandchildren. They would check to see how many blueberries there were, faces neutral and distanced, but when they saw that we were picking they would move on, gliding unhurried along near the shore and then disappearing around a point or into a bay as though they had never been there. No one knew where they lived during the winter; once though we passed two of the children standing by the side of the road with tin cans of blueberries for sale. It never occurred to me till now that they must have hated us.

The shore bushes rustled: it was Joe, coming down behind me. He squatted on the stone beside me; his cup was only a third full, sprinkled with leaves and green-white berries.

'Take a rest,' he said.

'In a minute.' I was almost finished. It was hot, light glared from the lake; in the sun the berries were so blue they seemed lit up from within. Falling into the cup they made a plink like water.

'We should get married,' Joe said.

I set the cup down carefully on the rock and turned to look at him, shielding my eyes. I wanted to laugh, it was incongruous, it wasn't what he would call his trip, the legal phrases and the paperwork and the vows, especially the finality; and he'd got the order wrong, he'd never asked whether I loved him, that was supposed to come first, I would have been prepared for that. 'Why?' I said. 'We're living together anyway. We don't need a certificate for that.'

'I think we should,' he said, 'we might as well.'

'But it wouldn't make any difference,' I said. 'Everything would be the same.'

'Then why not do it?' He had moved closer, he was being logical, he was threatening me with something. I swivelled, scouting for help, but they were at the far end of the island, Anna's pink shirt tiny and blazing like a gas station banner.

'No,' I said, the only answer to logic. It was because I didn't want to, that's why it would gratify him, it would be a sacrifice, of my reluctance, my distaste.

'Sometimes,' he said, placing the words evenly and deliberately, pegs in a peg-board. 'I get the feeling you don't give a shit about me.'

'I do,' I said. 'I do give a shit about you,' repeating it like a skipping rhyme. I wondered if that was the equivalent of saying I loved him. I was calculating how much getaway money I had in the bank, how long it would take me to pack and move out, away from the clay dust and the cellar mould smell and the monstrous humanoid pots, how soon I could find a new place. Prove your love, they say. You really want to marry me, let me fuck you instead. You really want to fuck, let me marry you instead. As long as there's a victory, some flag I can wave, parade I can have in my head.

'No, you don't, I can tell,' he said, unhappy rather than angry; that was worse. I could cope with his anger. He was growing larger, becoming alien, three-dimensional; panic began.

'Look,' I said, 'I've been married before and it didn't work out. I had a baby too.' My ace, voice patient. 'I don't want to go through that again.' It was true, but the words were coming out of me like the mechanical words from a talking doll, the kind with the pull tape at the back; the whole speech was unwinding, everything in order, a spool. I would always be able to say what I'd just finished saying: I've tried and failed, I'm inoculated, exempt, classified as wounded. It wasn't that I didn't suffer, I was conscientious about that, that's what qualified me. But marriage was like playing Monopoly or doing crossword puzzles, either your mind worked that way, like Anna's, or it didn't; and I'd proved mine didn't. A small neutral country.

'It would be different with us,' he said, disregarding what I said about the baby.

At my wedding we filled out forms, name, age, birthplace, blood type. We had it in a post office, a JP did it, oil portraits of former postmasters presided from the beige walls. I could recall the exact smells, glue and humid socks and the odour of second-day blouse and crystallized deodorant from the irritated secretary, and, from another doorway, the chill of antiseptic. It was a hot day, when we stepped out into the sun we couldn't see for an instant; then there was a flock of draggled pigeons pecking at the scuffed post office lawn beside the fountain. The fountain had dolphins and a cherub with part of the face missing.

'It's over,' he said, 'feel better?'

He coiled his arms around me, protecting me from something, the future, and kissed me on the forehead. 'You're cold,' he said. My legs were shaking so much I could hardly stand up and there was an ache, slow like a groan. 'Come on,' he said, 'we'd better get you home.' He lifted my face, scrutinizing it in the light. 'Maybe I should carry you to the car.'

He was talking to me as though I was an invalid, not a bride. In one hand I carried a purse or a suitcase; the other was closed. We walked through the pigeons and they blew up around us, confetti. In the car I didn't cry, I didn't want to look at him. 'I know it's tough,' he said, 'but it's better this way.' Quote, unquote. His flexible hands on the wheel. It turned, perfect circle, and the gears interlocked and spun, the engine ticked like a clock, the voice of reason.

'Why are you doing this to me?' I said, losing control. 'You'll ruin it.' Then I was sorry, as though I'd stepped on a small animal by accident, he was so miserable: he'd abdicated, betrayed what

I'd assumed were his principles, in order to be saved, by me, from me, and he'd got nothing by it.

I took his hand; he let me hold it, frowning at me, sullen as a doormat. 'I'm not good enough for you,' I said, motto, the words printed on a scroll like a fortune cookie. I kissed him on the side of the face. I was stalling for time, also I was afraid of him; the look he gave me as I drew away was one of baffled rage.

We were sitting outside in the chicken wire enclosure; Joe was in the sandbox with his back half-turned to us, scraping together a large mound of sand. He'd finished his pie, the rest of us were still eating. It was too hot to eat in the house, we had to keep the stove going for two hours. They had purple mouths and blue teeth which showed when they talked or laughed.

'That's the best pie I ever ate,' David said. 'Just like mother used to make.' He smacked his lips and posed, pretending to be a TV ad.

'Stuff it,' Anna said, 'you can't afford just one measly compliment, can you?'

David's purple mouth grinned. 'Aw,' he said, 'that *was* a compliment.'

'The hell,' Anna said. 'I've met your mother.'

David sighed and leaned back against his tree, rolling his eyes to Joe for sympathy. But he got none and so he gazed up at the sky instead. 'This is the life,' he said after a while. 'We ought to start a colony, I mean a community up here, get it together with some other people, break away from the urban nuclear family. It wouldn't be a bad country if only we could kick out the fucking pig Americans, eh? Then we could have some peace.'

Nobody answered him: he took off one of his shoes and began scratching the sole of his foot thoughtfully.

'I think it would be a copout,' Anna said abruptly.

'What would?' David said, overly tolerant, as though she'd interrupted him in mid-sentence. 'Kicking out the pigs?'

'Oh shit,' Anna said, 'you just won't.'

'What the hell are you talking about?' he said, feigning hurt. But she sat hugging her knees, smoke breathing through her nostrils. I got up and started to collect the plates.

'It turns me on when she bends over,' David said. 'She's got a neat ass. I'm really into the whole ass thing. Joe, don't you think she's got a neat ass?'

'You can have it,' Joe said. He was levelling the sand mound he had built, he was still angry.

I scraped the ends of crust into the stove and washed the plates, the water turning reddish blue, vein colour. The others ambled in; they didn't feel like playing bridge, they sat around the table reading detective novels and back issues of magazines, *Maclean's* and *The National Geographic*, some of them were ten years old. I'd read them all so I went into David's and Anna's room with a candle to look for more.

I had to climb up on the bed to reach the shelf. There was a high pile of books; I lifted it down to where the candle was. On top was a layer of paperbacks, the average kind, but underneath them were some things that were out of place: the brown leather photo album that ought to have been in a trunk in the city, along with my mother's unused wedding presents, tarnished silver bowls and lace tablecloths, and the scrapbooks we used to draw in when it rained. I thought she'd thrown them out; I wondered who had brought them here, which one of them.

There were several scrapbooks; I sat down on the bed and opened one at random, feeling as though I was opening someone else's private diary. It was my brother's: explosions in red and orange, soldiers dismembering in the air, planes and tanks; he must have been going to school by then, he knew enough to draw little swastikas on the sides. Further on there were flying men with comic-book capes and explorers on another planet, he spent hours explaining these pictures to me. The purple jungles I'd forgotten, the green sun with seven red moons, the animals with scales and spines and tentacles; and a man-eating plant, engulfing a careless victim, a balloon with HELP in it squeezing out of his mouth like bubble gum. The other explorers were rescuing him with their weapons: flame-throwers, trumpet-shaped pistols, ray-guns. In the background was their spaceship, bristling with gadgets.

The next scrapbook was mine. I searched through it carefully, looking for something I could recognize as myself, where I had come from or gone wrong; but there were no drawings at all, just illustrations cut from magazines and pasted in. They were ladies, all kinds: holding up cans of cleanser, knitting, smiling, modelling toeless high heels and nylons with dark seams and pillbox hats and veils. A lady was what you dressed up as on Hallowe'en when you couldn't think of anything else and didn't want to be a ghost; or it was what you said at school when they asked you what you were going to be when you grew up, you said 'A lady' or 'A mother,' either one was safe; and it wasn't a lie. I did want to be those things. On some of the pages were women's dresses clipped from mail order catalogues, no bodies in them.

I tried another one: mine also, earlier. The drawings were of ornately-decorated Easter eggs, singly and in groups. Some of them had people-shaped rabbits climbing up them on rope ladders; apparently the rabbits lived inside the eggs, there were doors at the tops, they could pull the ladders up after them. Beside the larger eggs were smaller ones connected to them by bridges, the outhouses. Page after page of eggs and rabbits, grass and trees, normal and green, surrounding them, flowers blooming, sun in the upper right-hand corner of each picture, moon symmetrically in the left. All the rabbits were smiling and some were laughing hilariously; several were shown eating ice-cream cones from the safety of their egg-tops. No monsters, no wars, no explosions, no heroism. I couldn't remember ever having drawn these pictures. I was disappointed in myself: I must have been a hedonistic child. I thought, and quite stodgy also, interested in nothing but social welfare. Or perhaps it was a vision of Heaven.

Behind me someone came into the room, it was David. 'Hey lady,' he said, 'what're you doing in my bed? You a customer or something?'

'Sorry,' I said. I put the album back on the shelf but I took the scrapbooks into my room and hid them under the mattress. I didn't want them spying.

Chapter Eleven

At night Joe kept turned away from me, he wasn't going to compromise. I ran my fingers over his furry back to show I wanted a truce, the borders restored to where they'd been, but after he twitched me off and grunted irritably I withdrew. I curled up, concentrating on excluding him: he was merely an object in the bed, like a sack or a large turnip. There's more than one way to skin a cat, my father used to say; it bothered me, I didn't see why they would want to skin a cat even one way. I stared at the wall and thought of maxims: two can play that game, marry in haste, repent at leisure, least said soonest mended, traditional wisdom which was never any help.

At breakfast he ignored me and the others too, hunching over his plate, mumbling replies.

'What's with him?' David said. His new beard was sprouting, a brown smudge on his chin.

'Shut up,' Anna said; but she glanced at me, inquisitive, holding me responsible for it whatever it was.

Joe wiped his sweat shirt sleeve across his mouth and went out of the house, letting the screen door slam behind him.

'Maybe he's constipated,' David said, 'it makes them grouchy. You sure he's been getting enough exercise?' Then he went 'Arf, arf' like Popeye, wiggling his ears.

'Stupid,' Anna said fondly; she rumpled his hair.

'Hey, don't do that,' he said, 'it'll all fall out.' He jumped up and went to the mirror and rearranged the hair down over his forehead; I hadn't noticed before that he combed it that way to cover the patches where it had once grown.

I gathered up the bacon rinds and the crusts from the toast and took them out to the bird tray. The jays were there, they saw I had food and told each other about it with hoarse cries. I stood quietly with my hand outstretched but they wouldn't fly down; they winged overhead, reconnoitring. Perhaps I was moving without knowing it, you had to convince them you were a thing, not an enemy. Our mother made us watch from inside the house, she said we frightened them. Once people believed the flight of birds was a portent: augury.

I heard the mosquito whine of a motor approaching; I left my handful of crumbs on the tray and went out on the point to watch. It was Paul's boat, white-painted and squarish, handmade; he waved to me from the stern. There was another man with him, sitting in the bow, backwards.

They pulled in to the dock and I ran down the steps to greet them; I caught the rope and tied it. 'Careful,' I said as they stepped out, 'it's rotten in places.'

Paul had brought me a huge wad of vegetables from his garden: he handed me a bouquet of swiss chard, a quart basket of green beans, a bundle of carrots, a brain-sized cauliflower, bashfully, as though the gift might not be acceptable. The proper reply would have been an equally large or perhaps larger assortment. I thought with dismay of the spindly broccoli and the radishes already gone to seed.

'Here is a man,' he said. 'They send him to me because I know your father.' He stepped backwards, effacing himself, and almost slipped off the dock.

'Malmstrom,' the man said as though it was a secret code; his hand shot towards me. I transferred the swiss chard to the crook of my arm and took the hand, which squeezed mine confidentially. 'Bill Malmstrom, please call me Bill.' He had trimmed grey hair and an executive moustache like the shirt ads, the vodka ads; his clothes were woodsy, semi-worn, verging on the authentic. Slung around his neck was a pair of binoculars in a suede case.

We walked to the land; he had taken out a pipe and was lighting it. I wondered if he was from the government. 'Paul, here, was telling me,' he said, looking around for Paul, 'what a nice place you have.'

'It's my father's,' I said.

His face drooped into the appropriate downward curve; if he'd been wearing a hat he would have taken it off. 'Ah yes,' he said, 'a tragedy.' I distrusted him: I couldn't place the accent, the name sounded German.

'Where are you from?' I asked, trying to be polite.

'Michigan,' he said as though it was something to be proud of. 'I'm a member of the Detroit branch of the Wildlife Protection Association of America; we have a branch in this country, quite a flourishing little branch.' He beamed at me, condescending. 'As a matter of fact that's what I wanted to discuss with you. Our place on Lake Erie is, ah, giving out so to say. I believe I can speak for the rest of the Michigan members in saying we'd be prepared to make you an offer.'

'What for?' I said. He sounded as though he wanted me to buy something, a magazine or a membership.

He swept his pipe in a semi-circle. 'This lovely piece of property,' he said. 'What we'd use it for would be a kind of retreat lodge, where the members could meditate and observe,' he puffed, 'the beauties of Nature. And maybe do a little hunting and fishing.'

'Don't you want to see it?' I asked. 'I mean, the house and all.'

'I must admit that I've already seen it; we've had our eye on this piece for quite some time. I've been coming up here to fish for years, and I've taken the liberty, when no one seemed to be here, of having a stroll around.' He gave a small harumph, a voyeur of good social standing caught in the act; then he named a price that meant I could forget about *Quebec Folk Tales* and children's books and everything else, at least for a while.

'Would you change it?' I asked. I foresaw motels, highrises.

'Well, we'd have to install a power generator, of course, and a septic tank; but apart from that, no, I expect we'd like to leave it the way it is, it has a definite,' he stroked hs moustache, 'rural charm.'

'I'm sorry but it's not for sale,' I said, 'not right now; maybe later.' If my father had been dead he might have liked the proposal but as it was he would be furious if he returned and found I'd sold his house. I wasn't sure I'd be the owner in any case. There must be deeds hidden, property titles, legal papers, I'd never had any dealings with lawyers; I would have to sign forms or charters, I might have to pay death duties.

'Well,' he said with the heartiness of a loser. 'I'm sure the offer will still be open. Indefinitely, you might say.' He drew out his wallet and gave me a card: *Bill Malmstrom, Teenie Town*, it said. *Togs for Toddlers 'n Tots.*

'Thank you,' I said, 'I'll keep it in mind.'

I took Paul by the arm and led him to the garden, as though to reciprocate for the vegetables: I felt I had to explain, at least to him, he had gone to a lot of trouble for me.

'Your garden, she is not doing so good, ay?' he said, inspecting.

'No,' I said, 'we just got it weeded; but I want you to have ...' I gazed desperately around, seized on a withered lettuce and presented it to him, roots and all, as gracefully as I could.

He held it, blinking, discouraged. 'Madame will like that,' he said.

'Paul,' I said, lowering my voice, 'the reason I can't sell is that my father's still alive.'

'Yes?' he said, perking up. 'He came back, he is here?'

'Not exactly,' I said. 'He's away right now, on a sort of trip; but perhaps he will be here soon.' For all I could tell he might have been listening to us at that moment, from behind the raspberry canes or the burn heap.

'He went for the trees?' Paul said, hurt that he hadn't been consulted: he used to go too. 'You saw him first, before?'

'No,' I said, 'he was gone when I got here; but he left me a note, more or less.'

'Ah,' he said, glancing nervously over my shoulder into the forest. It was clear he didn't believe me.

For lunch we had Paul's cauliflower and some tins, corn and fried ham. During the canned pears David said 'Who were those two old guys?' He must have seen them from the window.

'It was a man who wanted to buy the place,' I said.

'I bet he was a Yank,' David said, 'I can spot them in a crowded room.'

'Yes,' I said, 'but he was from a wildlife association, that's who he was buying it for.'

'Bullshit,' David said, 'he was a front man for the CIA.'

I laughed. 'No,' I said; I showed him the *Teenie Town* card.

But David was serious. 'You haven't seen them in operation the way I have,' he said darkly, invoking his New York past.

'What would they want up here?' I said.

'A snooping base,' he said, 'bird-watchers, binoculars, it all fits. They know this is the kind of place that will be strategically important during the war.'

'What war?' I asked, and Anna said 'Here we go.'

'It's obvious. They're running out of water, clean water, they're dirtying up all of theirs, right? Which is what we have a lot of, this country is almost all water if you look at a map. So in a while, I give it ten years, they'll be up against the wall. They'll try to swing a deal with the government, get us to give them the water cheap or for nothing in exchange for more soapflakes or something, and the government will give in, they'll be a bunch of puppets as usual. But by that time the Nationalist Movement will be strong enough so they'll force the government to back down; riots or kidnappings or something. Then the Yank pigs will send in the Marines, they'll have to; people in New York and Chicago will be dropping like flies, industry will be stalled, there'll be a black market in water, they'll be shipping it in tankers from Alaska. They'll come in through Quebec, it will have separated by then; the Pepsis will even help them, they'll be having a good old laugh. They'll hit the big cities and knock out communications and take over, maybe shoot a few kids, and the Movement guerrillas will go into the bush and start blowing up the water pipelines the Yanks will be building in places like this, to get the water down there.'

He seemed very positive about it, as if it had happened already. I thought about the survival manuals; if the Movement guerillas were anything like David and Joe they would never make it through the winters. They couldn't get help from the cities, they would be too far, and the people there would be apathetic, they wouldn't mind another change of flag. If they tried at the outlying farms the farmers would take after them with shotguns. The Americans wouldn't even have to defoliate the trees, the guerillas would die of starvation and exposure anyway.

'Where will you get food?' I said.

'What do you mean "you"?' he said. 'I'm just speculating.'

I thought of how it would appear in the history books when it was over: a paragraph with dates and a short summary of what happened. That's how it was in high school, they taught it neutrally, a long list of wars and treaties and alliances, people taking and losing power over other people; but nobody would ever go into the motives, why they wanted it, whether it was good or bad. They used long words like 'demarcation' and 'sovereignty', they wouldn't say what they meant and you couldn't ask: in high school the right thing was to stare fixedly at the teacher as though at a movie screen, and it was worse for a girl to ask questions than for a boy. If a boy asked a question the other boys would make derisive sucking noises with their mouths, but if a girl asked one the other girls would say 'Think you're so great' in the washroom afterwards. In the margins around The Treaty of Versailles I drew ornaments, plants with scrolled branches, hearts and stars instead of flowers. I got so I could draw invisibly, my fingers scarcely moving.

The generals and the historic moments looked better framed. If you put your eye down close to the photograph they disintegrated into grey dots.

Anna was squeezed in beside David on the bench, playing with one of his hands while he talked. 'Did I ever tell you that you have Murderer's Thumb?' she said.

'Don't interrupt,' he said, but when she made a whimpering face he said 'Yep, you did, almost every day,' and patted her arm.

'It's spread flat at the end,' she said, explaining to us.

'I hope you didn't sell out,' David said to me. I shook my head. 'Good girl,' he said, 'your heart's in the right place. And the rest of her too,' he said to Joe, 'I like it round and firm and fully packed. Anna, you're eating too much.'

I washed and Anna dried, as usual. Suddenly Anna said 'David is a schmuck. He's one of the schmuckiest people I know.'

I looked around at her: her voice was like fingernails, I'd never heard her talk that way about David.

'Why?' I said. 'What's wrong?' He hadn't said anything at lunch that could have upset her.

'I guess you think he's hot for you.' Her mouth stretched down tight with the lips inside, a toad's.

'No,' I said, bewildered, 'why would I think that?'

'Those things he says, you know, like about your ass and being fully packed,' she said impatiently.

'I thought he was teasing.' I had thought that too, it was just a habit like picking your nose, only verbal.

'Teasing, shit. He was doing it to me. He always does stuff like that to other women in front of me, he'd screw them with me in the room if he could. Instead he screws them somewhere else and tells me about it afterwards.'

'Oh,' I said. I hadn't deduced that. 'Why? I mean, why does he tell you?'

Anna brooded, her dishtowel slack. 'He says it's being honest. What a turd. When I get mad he says I'm jealous and possessive and I shouldn't get uptight, he says jealousy is bourgeois, it's a leftover from the property ethic, he thinks we should all be swingers and share it around. But I say there are these basic emotions, if you feel something you should let it out, right?' It was an article of faith, she glared at me, challenging me to affirm or deny; I wasn't certain so I didn't say anything. 'He pretends he doesn't feel those things, he's so cool,' she said, 'but really it's just to show me he can do it and get away with it, I can't stop him; all that theorizing about it is coverup bullshit garbage.' She raised her head, smiling, friendly again. 'I thought I should warn you so you'd know if he grabs you or anything it won't have much to do with you, it's all about me really.'

'Thank you,' I said. I was sorry she'd told me; I still wanted to believe that what they called a good marriage had remained possible, for someone. But it was kind of her, thoughtful; I knew in her place I wouldn't have done it, I would have let her take care of herself, My Brother's Keeper always reminded me of zoos and insane asylums.

Chapter Twelve

The slop pail was full; I carried it to the garden to pour the dirty water into the trench. Joe was lying by himself on the dock, face down; when I came to rinse the pail he didn't move. Anna passed me on the steps, wearing her orange bikini, oiled for her sun ritual.

In the cabin I set the pail under the counter. David was pondering his chin bristles in the mirror; he slid his arm half around me and said in a guttural voice, 'Come wiz me to zee outhouse.'

'Not right now,' I said, 'I have to do some work.'

He mimed regret. 'Ah well,' he said, 'some other time.'

I took out my samsonite case and sat down at the table. He leaned over my shoulder. 'Where's old Joe?'

'Down on the dock,' I said.

'He seems out of sorts,' David said, 'maybe he has worms; when you get back to the city you should take him to the vet.' And a moment later, 'How come you never laugh at my jokes?'

He hung around while I set out the brushes and paper. Finally he said, 'Well, Nature calls,' and soft-shoed out the door like the end of a vaudeville act.

I swivelled the caps back onto the paint tubes, I had no intention of working: now they were all out of the way I would search for the will, the deed, the property title. Paul had been certain he was dead, that made me doubt my theory. Perhaps the CIA had done away with him to get the land, Mr Malmstrom was not quite plausible; but that was preposterous, I couldn't start suspecting people for no reason.

I rummaged in the cavity under the wall bench, went through the shelves, groped under the beds where the tents were stored. He might have filed the papers in a safety-deposit box, earlier, in a city bank, I'd never find them. Or he might have burned them. At any rate they weren't here.

Unless they were in among the pages of a book: I checked Goldsmith and Burns, holding them by the spines and shaking, then I thought of his lunatic drawings, the only clue I had that he might not be dead. I'd never gone through all of them. In a way that would be the logical hiding place; he'd always been logical, and madness is only an amplification of what you already are.

I lifted down the stack of drawings and began to look. The paper was thin and soft, like rice paper. First the hands and antlered figures, always with numbers scrawled in the corner, then a larger sheet, a half-moon with four sticks coming out of it, bulbed at the ends. I righted the page, judging by the numbers, and it became a boat with people, the knobs were their heads. It was reassuring to find I could interpret it, it made sense.

But the next one was nothing I could recognize. The body was long, a snake or a fish; it had four limbs or arms and a tail and on the head were two branched horns. Lengthwise it was like an animal, an alligator; upright it was more human, but only in the positions of the arms and the front-facing eyes.

Total derangement. I wondered when it had started; it must have been the snow and the loneliness, he'd pushed himself too far, it gets in through your eyes, the thin black cold of mid-winter night, the white days dense with sunlight, outer space melting and freezing again into different shapes, your mind starts doing the same thing. The drawing was something he saw, a hallucination; or it might have been himself, what he thought he was turning into.

I uncovered the next page. But it wasn't a drawing, it was a typed letter, I skimmed it quickly. Addressed to my father.

Dear Sir:

Many thanks for forwarding the photographs and tracings and the corresponding map. The material is most valuable and I shall include some of it in my forthcoming work on the subject, with your permission and giving due credit. Details of any subsequent discoveries you may make would be most welcome.

I include a copy of one of my recent studies which you may find of interest.

Yours sincerely.

The letter had an illegible signature and a university crest. Paper-clipped to it were half a dozen xeroxed sheets: *Rock Paintings of the Central Shield, by Dr Robin M. Grove*. The first few pages were maps and graphs and statistics; I skimmed them quickly. At the end of the article there were three short paragraphs, subtitled *Aesthetic Qualities and Possible Significance*.

The subject matter falls into the following categories: Hands, Abstract Symbols, Humans, Animals and Mythological Creatures. In treatment they are reminiscent, with their elongated limbs and extreme distortion, of the drawings of children. The static rigidity is in marked contrast to the rock paintings of other cultures, most notably the European cave paintings.

From the above features we may deduce that the creators of the paintings were interested exclusively in symbolic content, at the expense of expressiveness and form. However we can only indulge in conjecture as to the nature of this content, since no historical records exist. Informants, questioned have supplied conflicting traditions. Some state that the sites of the paintings are the abodes of powerful or protective spirits, which may explain the custom, persisting in remote areas, of leaving offerings of clothing and small bundles of 'prayer' sticks. One gives more credence to the theory that the paintings are associated with the practice of fasting to produce significant or predictive dreams.

Doubtful also is the technique employed. The paintings seem to have been executed either with the fingers or with a crude brush of some sort. The predominant colour is red, with minor occurrences of white and yellow; this may be due either to the fact that red among the Indians is a sacred colour or to the relative availability of iron oxides. The bonding agent is being investigated; it may prove to be bears' fat or birds' eggs, or perhaps blood or spittle.

The academic prose breathed reason; my hypotheses crumbled like sand. This was the solution, the explanation: he never failed to explain.

His drawings were not originals then, only copies. He must have been doing them as a sort of retirement hobby, he was an incurable amateur and enthusiast: if he'd become hooked on these rock paintings he would have combed the area for them, collecting them with his camera, pestering the experts by letter whenever he found one; an old man's delusion of usefulness.

I pressed my fingers into my eyes, hard, to make the pool of blackness ringed with violent colour. Release, red spreading back in, abrupt as pain. The secret had come clear, it had never been a secret, I'd made it one, that was easier. My eyes came open, I began to arrange.

I thought, I suppose I knew it from the beginning, I shouldn't have tried to find out, it's killed him. I had the proof now, indisputable, of sanity and therefore of death. Relief, grief, I must have felt one or the other. A blank, a disappointment: crazy people can come back, from wherever they go to take refuge, but dead people can't, they are prohibited. I tried to recall him, picture his face, the way he'd been when he was alive. I found I couldn't; all I could see was the cards he used to hold up, testing us: 3X9=? He was as absent now as a number, a zero, the question mark in place of the missing answer. Unknown quantity. His way. Everything had to be measured.

I was staring down at the drawings, they were framed by my two arms lain parallel on the table. I began to notice them again. There was a gap, something not accounted for, something left over.

I spread the first six pages out on the table and studied them, using what they called my intelligence, it shortcircuits those other things. The notes and numbers were apparently a location code, it was like a puzzle he'd left for me to solve, an arithmetic problem; he taught us arithmetic, our mother taught us to read and write. Geometry, the first thing I learned was how to draw flowers with compasses, they were like acid patterns. Once they thought you could see God that way but all I saw was landscapes and geometrical shapes; which would be the same thing if you believed God was a mountain or a circle. He said Jesus was a historical figure and God was a supersitition, and a superstition was a thing that didn't exist. If you tell your children God doesn't exist they will be forced to believe you are the god, but what happens when they find out you are human after all, you have to grow old and die? Resurrection is like plants, Jesus Christ is risen today they sang at Sunday School, celebrating the daffodils; but people are not onions, as he so reasonably pointed out, they stay under.

The numbers were a system, a game; I would play it with him, it would make him seem less dead. I lined up the pages and compared the notes, carefully as a jeweller.

On one of the drawings, another antlered figure, I finally spotted the key: a name I recognized, White Birch Lake where we went bass fishing, it was connected to the main lake by a portage. I went into David's and Anna's room where the map of the district was tacked to the wall. Marked on a point of land was a tiny red X and a number, identical with the number on the drawing. The printed name was different, *Lac des Verges Blanches*, the government had been translating all the English names into French ones, though the Indian names remained the same. Scattered here and there were other Xs, like a treasure map.

I wanted to go there and verify, match the drawing with reality; that way I'd be sure I'd followed the rules and done it right. I could disguise it as a fishing trip, David hadn't caught anything since his first attempt, though he'd been trying. We'd have time to go there and get back with two days to spare.

I heard Anna's voice approaching, singing, the words trailing off as her breath gave out climbing the steps. I went back to the main room.

'Hi,' she said, 'do I look burnt?'

She was pink now, parboiled, white showing around the orange edges of her suit, neck dividing body colour from applied face colour. 'A little,' I said

'Listen,' she said, her voice shifting into concern, 'what's wrong with Joe? I was down on the dock with him and he didn't say one word.'

'He doesn't talk much,' I said.

'I know, but this was different. He was just lying there.' She was pushing, demanding answers.

'He thinks we should get married,' I said.

Her eyebrows lifted like antennae. 'Really? Joe? That's not. . . .'

'I don't want to.'

'Oh,' she said. 'then that's awful. You must feel awful.' She'd found out; now she was rubbing after-sun lotion on her shoulders. 'Mind?' she said, handing me the plastic tube.

I didn't feel awful; I realized I didn't feel much of anything, I hadn't for a long time. Perhaps I'd been like that all my life, just as some babies are born deaf or without a sense of touch; but if that was true I wouldn't have noticed the absence. At some point my neck must have closed over, pond freezing or a wound, shutting me into my head; since then everything had been glancing off me, it was like being in a vase, or the village where I could see them but not hear them because I couldn't understand what was being said. Bottles distort for the observer too: frogs in the jam jar stretched wide, to them watching I must have appeared grotesque.

'Thanks,' Anna said, 'I hope I won't peel. I think you should go talk to him or something.'

'I have,' I said; but her eyes were accusing, I hadn't done enough, conciliation, expiation. I went obediently towards the door.

'Maybe you can work it out,' she called after me.

Joe was still on the dock but he was sitting on the edge now with his feet in the water, I crouched down beside him. His toes had dark hairs on the tops, spaced like the needles on a balsam twig.

'What is it?' I said. 'Are you sick?'

'You know fucking well,' he said after a minute.

'Let's go back to the city,' I said, 'the way it was before.' I took hold of his hand so I could feel the calloused palm, thickened by the wheel, concrete.

'You're screwing around with me,' he said, still not looking at me. 'All I want is a straight answer.'

'About what?' I said. Near the dock there were some water skippers, surface tension holding them up; the fragile shadows of the dents where their feet touched fell on the sand underwater, moving when they moved. His vulnerability embarrassed me, he could still feel, I should have been more careful with him.

'Do you love me, that's all,' he said. 'That's the only thing that matters.'

It was the language again. I couldn't use it because it wasn't mine. He must have known what he meant but it was an imprecise word; the Eskimoes had fifty-two names for snow because it was important to them, there ought to be as many for love.

'I want to,' I said. 'I do in a way.' I hunted through my brain for any emotion that would coincide with what I'd said. I did want to, but it was like thinking God should exist and not being able to believe.

'Fucking jesus,' he said, pulling his hand away, 'just yes or no, don't mess around.'

'I'm trying to tell the truth,' I said. The voice wasn't mine, it came from someone dressed as me, imitating me.

'The truth is,' he said bitterly, 'you think my work is crap, you think I'm a loser and I'm not worth it.' His face contorted, it was pain: I envied him.

'No,' I said, but I couldn't say it right and he needed more than that.

'Come up to the cabin,' I said; Anna was there, she would help. 'I'll make some tea.' I got up but he wouldn't follow.

While the stove was heating I took the leather album from the shelf in their room and opened it on the table, where Anna was reading. It was no longer his death but my own that concerned me; perhaps I would be able to tell when the change occurred by the diferences in my former faces, alive up to a year, a day, then frozen. The duchess at the French court before the Revolution, who stopped laughing or crying so her skin would never change or wrinkle, it worked, she died immortal.

Grandmothers and grandfathers first, distant ancestors, strangers, in face-front firing-squad poses: cameras weren't ordinary then, maybe they thought their souls were being stolen, as the Indians did. Underneath them were labels in white, my mother's cautious printing. My mother before she was married, another stranger, with bobbed hair and a knitted hat. Wedding pictures, corseted smiles. My brother before I was born, then pictures of me beginning to appear. Paul taking us down the lake with his sleigh and horses before the ice went out. My mother, in her leather jacket and odd long 1940s hair, standing beside the tray for the birds, her hand stretched out; the jays were there too, she's training them, one is on her shoulder, peering at her with clever thumbtack eyes, another is landing on her wrist, wings caught as a blur. Sun sifting around her through the pines, her eyes looking straight at the camera, frightened, receding into the shadows of her head like a skull's, a trick of the light.

I watched myself grow larger. Mother and father in alternate shots, building the house, walls and then the roof, planting the garden. Around them were borders of blank paper, at each corner a hinge, they were like small grey and white windows opening into a place I could no longer reach. I was in most of the pictures, shut in behind the paper; or not me but the missing part of me.

School pictures, my face lined up with forty others, colossal teachers towering above us. I could find myself always, I was the one smudged with movement or turning the other way. Further on, glossy colour prints, forgotten boys with pimples and carnations, myself in the stiff dresses, crinolines and tulle, layered like store birthday cakes; I was civilized at last, the finished product. She would say 'You look very nice, dear,' as though she believed it; but I wasn't convinced, I knew by then she was no judge of the normal.

'Is that you?' Anna said, putting down *The Mystery At Sturbridge*. 'Christ, how could we ever wear that stuff?'

The last pages of the album were blank, with some loose prints stuck in between the black leaves as though my mother hadn't wanted to finish. After the formal dresses I disappeared; no wedding pictures, but of course we hadn't taken any. I closed the cover, straightening the edges.

No hints or facts, I didn't know when it had happened. I must have been all right then; but after that I'd allowed myself to be cut in two. Woman sawn apart in a wooden crate, wearing a bathing suit, smiling, a trick done with mirrors, I read it in a comic book; only with me there had been an accident and I came apart. The other half, the one locked away, was the only one that could live; I was the wrong half, detached, terminal. I was nothing but a head, or no, something minor like a severed thumb; numb. At school they used to play a joke, they would bring little boxes with cotton wool in them and a hole cut in the bottom; they would poke their finger through the hole and pretend it was a dead finger.

Chapter Thirteen

We pushed off from the dock at ten by David's watch. The sky was watercolour blue, the cloud bunches white on the backs and grey on the bellies. Wind from the stern, waves overtaking, my arms lifting and swinging, light and automatic as though they knew what to do. I was at the front, figurehead; behind me Joe shoved at the water, the canoe surged forward.

The landmarks passed, unscrolling, one-dimensional map thickening into stone and wood around us: point, cliff, leaning dead tree, heron island with the intricate bird silhouettes, blueberry island sailed by its mast pines, foregrounds. On the next island there was once a trapper's cabin, logs chinked with grass and a straw mound where the bed had been; I could see nothing left but a muddle of rotting timber.

In the morning we talked, uselessly but in calm rational voices as though discussing the phone bill; which meant it was final. We were still in bed, his feet stuck out at the bottom. I could hardly wait till I was old so I wouldn't have to do this any more.

'When we get back to the city,' I said, 'I'll move out.'

'I will if you like,' he said generously.

'No, you've got all your pots and things there.'

'Have it your way,' he said, 'you always do.'

He thought of it as a contest, like the children at school who would twist your arm and say Give in? Give in? until you did; then they would let go. He didn't love me, it was an idea of himself he loved and he wanted someone to join him, anyone would do, I didn't matter so I didn't have to care.

The sun was at twelve. We had lunch on a jagged island almost out in the wide part of the lake. After we landed we found that someone had built a fireplace already, on the shore ledge of bare granite; trash was strewn around it, orange peelings and tin cans and a rancid bulge of greasy paper, the tracks of humans. It was like dogs pissing on a fence, as if the endless, anonymous water and unclaimed land, compelled them to leave their signature, stake their territory, and garbage was the only thing they had to do it with. I picked up the pieces of clutter and piled them to one side, I would burn them afterwards.

'That's disgusting,' Anna said. 'How can you touch it?'

'It's the sign of a free country,' David said. 'Germany under Hitler was very tidy.'

'We didn't need to use the axe, the island was covered with dry sticks, branches discarded from trees. I boiled the water and made tea and we had chicken noodle soup, out of a package, and sardines and tinned applesauce.

We sat in the shade, white smoke and the smell of scorching orange peels wrapping over us when the wind swerved. I hooked the billy tin off the fire and poured the tea; ashes and bits of twig were floating in it.

'Gentlemen,' David said, raising his tin cup, 'Up the Queen. Did that once in a bar in New York and these three Limeys came over and wanted to start a fight, they thought we were Yanks insulting their Queen. But I said she was our Queen too so we had the right, and they ended up buying us a drink.'

'I think it would be more fair,' Anna said, 'if you did it, "Ladies and Gentleman, Up the Queen and Duke."'

'None of that Women's Lib,' David said, his eyes lidding, 'or you'll be out on the street. I won't have one in the house, they're preaching random castration, they get off on that, they're roving the streets in savage bands armed with garden shears.'

'I'll join if you will,' Anna said to me, joking.

I said 'I think men ought to be superior.' But neither of them heard the actual words; Anna looked at me as though I'd betrayed her and said 'Wow, are you ever brainwashed,' and David said 'Want a job?' and to Joe, 'Hear that, you're superior.' But when Joe only grunted he said 'You should wire him for sound. Or fix him up with a plug and a shade, he'd make a great end-table lamp. I'm having him give a guest lecture in Adult Vegetation next year, 'How Pots Communicate', he'll walk in and say nothing for two hours, that'll freak them.' Joe smiled at last, wanly.

In the night I had wanted rescue, if my body could be made to sense, respond, move stongly enough, some of the red lightbulb synapses, blue neurons, incandescent molecules might seep into my head through the closed throat, neck membrane. Pleasure and pain are side by side they said but most of the brain is neutral; nerveless, like fat. I rehearsed emotions, naming them: joy, peace, guilt, release, love and hate, react, relate; what to feel was like what to wear, you watched others and memorized it. But the only thing there was the fear that I wasn't alive: a negative, the difference between the shadow of a pin and what it's like when you stick it in your arm, in school caged in the desk I used to do that, with pen-nibs and compass points too, instruments of knowledge, English and Geometry; they've discovered rats prefer any sensation to none. The insides of my arms were stippled with tiny wounds, like an addict's. They slipped the needle into the vein and I was falling down, it was like diving, sinking from one layer of darkness to a deeper, deepest; when I rose up through the anaesthetic, pale green and then daylight, I could remember nothing.

'Don't bother him,' Anna said.

'Or maybe I'll make it a short course this time,' David said. 'For the businessmen how to open the Playboy centrefold with the left hand only, keeping the right free for action, for the housewives how to switch on TV and switch off their heads, that's all they need to know, then we can go home.'

But he wouldn't, he needed to be rescued himself and neither of us would put on the cape and boots and the thunderbolt sweat-shirt, we were both afraid of failure; we lay with our backs to each other, pretending to sleep, while Anna prayed to nobody through the plywood wall. Romance comic books, on the cover always a pink face oozing tears like a melting popsicle; men's magazines were about pleasure, cars and women, the skins bald as inner tubes. In a way it was a relief, to be exempt from feeling.

'The trouble with you is you hate women,' Anna said savagely; she threw the rest of her tea and the tealeaves out of her tin cup into the lake, they hit with a splat.

David grinned. 'That's what they call a delayed reaction,' he said. 'Goose Anna in the bum and three days later she squeals. Cheer up, you're so cute when you're mad.' He crawled over to her on all fours and rubbed his bristly burdock chin against her face and asked her how she would like to be raped by a porcupine. 'You know that one?' he said. 'How do porcupines do it? Carefully!' Anna smiled at him as though he was a brain-damaged child.

The next minute he had scrambled up and was capering on the point, shaking his clenched fist and yelling 'Pigs! Pigs!' as loud as he could. It was some Americans, going past on their way to the village, their boats sloshing up and down in the waves, spray pluming, flags cocked fore and aft. They couldn't hear him because of the wind and the motor, they thought he was greeting, they waved and smiled.

I washed the dishes and soaked the fireplace, the hot stones sizzling, and we packed and started again. It was rougher, there were whitecaps on the open lake, the canoe rolled under us, we had to fight to keep it from turning broadside on; foam trailed on the dark water, spent waves. Paddle digging the lake, ears filled with moving air; breath and sweat, muscle hurt, my body at any rate was alive.

The wind was too strong, we had to change course; we headed across to the lee shore and followed it, as close to the land as possible, threading the maze of rocks and shallows. It was the long way around but the trees sheltered us.

Finally we reached the narrow bay where the portage was; the sun was at four, we'd been delayed by the wind. I hoped I would be able to find the place, the beginning of the path; I knew it was on the opposite side. As we rounded the point I heard a sound, human sound. At first it was like an outboard starting; then it was a snarl. Chainsaw, I could see them now, two men in yellow helmets. They'd left a trail, trees felled at intervals into the bay, trunks cut cleanly as though by a knife.

Surveyors, the paper company or the government, the power company. If it was the power company I knew what it meant: they were going to raise the lake level as they had sixty years ago, they were plotting a new shoreline. Twenty feet up again and this time they wouldn't cut off the trees as they had before, it would cost too much, they would be left to rot. The garden would go but the cabin would survive; the hill would become an eroding sand island surrounded by dead trees.

As we went by they glanced at us, then turned back to their work, indifferent. Advance men, agents. Swish and crackle as the tree tottered, whump and splash as it hit. Near them was a post driven into the ground, numbers on it in fresh red paint. The lake didn't matter to them, only the system: it would be a reservoir. During the war. I would be able to do nothing, I didn't live there.

The landing place at the portage was clogged with driftwood, sodden and moss-grown. We pushed in among the slippery logs as far as we could, then clambered out and waded, dragging the canoes up over, soaking our shoes. It was bad for the canoes, it scraped the keels. There were other paint marks, recent.

We unloaded the canoes and I knotted the paddles into position across the thwarts. They said they would take the tents and canoes and Anna and I could take the packs and the leftovers, the fishing rods and the tackle box with the jar of frogs I'd caught that morning, the movie equipment. David had insisted on it, though I warned him we might tip.

'We have to use up the film,' he said, 'we've only got it rented for another week.'

Anna said 'But there won't be anything you want,' and David said 'How do you know what I want?'

'There's an Indian rock painting,' I said, 'prehistoric. You might take that.' A point of interest, it would go with the Bottle Villa and the stuffed moose family, a new anomaly for their collection.

'Wow,' David said,'Is there? Neat,' and Anna said 'For god's sake don't encourage him.'

Neither of them had portaged before; we had to help them lift and balance the canoes. I said maybe they should double up, both of them under one canoe, but David insisted they could do it the real way. I said they should be careful; if the canoe slipped sideways and you didn't get out in time it would break your neck. 'What's the matter,' he said, 'don't you trust us?'

The trail hadn't been brushed out recently but there were deep footprints, bootprints, in the muddy places. Two sets, they pointed in but not out: whoever they were, Americans maybe, spies, they were still in there.

The packs were heavy, food for three days in case the weather turned bad and marooned us; the straps cut into my shoulders, I leaned forward against the weight, feet squishing in the wet shoes as I walked.

The portage was up over a steep ridge of rock, watershed, then down through ferns and saplings to an oblong pond, a shallow mudhole we'd have to paddle across to reach the second portage. Anna and I got there first and set down the packs; Anna had time to smoke half a cigarette before David and Joe came staggering down the trail, bumping into the sides like blinkered horses. We held the canoes and they crouched out from under, they were pink and breathless.

'Better be fish in there,' David said, sleeving off his forehead.

'The next one's shorter,' I told them.

The water was covered with lily pads, the globular yellow lilies with their thick centre snouts pushing up from among them. It swarmed with leeches, I could see them undulating sluggishly under the brown surface. When the paddles hit bottom on the way across, gas bubbles from decomposing vegetation rose and burst with a stench of rotten eggs or farts. The air fogged with mosquitoes.

We reached the second portage, marked by a trapper's blaze weathered to the colour of the tree. I got out and stood holding the canoe steady while Joe climbed forward.

It was behind me, I smelled it before I saw it; then I heard the flies. The smell was like decaying fish. I turned around and it was hanging upside down by a thin blue nylon rope tied round its feet and looped over a tree branch, its wings fallen open. It looked at me with its mashed eye.

Chapter Fourteen

'Heavy,' David said. 'What is it?'

'A dead bird,' Anna said. She held her nose with two fingers.

I said 'It's a heron. You can't eat them.' I couldn't tell how it had been done, bullet, smashed with a stone, hit with a stick. This would be a good place for herons, they would come to fish in the shallow water, standing on one leg and striking with the long spear bill. They must have got it before it had time to rise.

'We need that,' David said, 'we can put it next to the fish guts.'

'Shit,' Joe said, 'it really stinks.'

'That won't show in the movie,' David said, 'you can stand it for five minutes, it looks so great, you have to admit.' They began to set up the camera; Anna and I waited, sitting on the packs.

I saw a beetle on it, blueblack and oval; when the camera whirred it burrowed in under the feathers. Carrion beetle, death beetle. Why had they strung it up like a lynch victim, why didn't they just throw it away like the trash? To prove they could do it, they had the power to kill. Otherwise it was valueless: beautiful from a distance but it couldn't be tamed or cooked or trained to talk, the only relation they could have to a thing like that was to destroy it. Food, slave or corpse, limited choices; horned and fanged heads sawed off and mounted on the billiard room wall, stuffed fish, trophies. It must have been the Americans; they were in there now, we would meet them.

The second portage was shorter but more thickly overgrown: leaves brushed, branches pushed into the corridor of air over the trail as though preventing. Newly broken stubs, wood and pith exposed like splintered bones, ferns trampled, they'd been here, their tractor-tread footsteps dinting the mud path in from of me like excavations, craters. The slope descended, slits of the lake gleamed through the trees. I wondered what I would say to them, what could be said, if I asked them why it would mean nothing. But when we reached the end of the portage they were nowhere in sight.

The lake was a narrow crescent, the far end was hidden. Lac des verges blanches, the white birch grew in clumps by the shore edge, doomed eventually by the disease, tree cancer, but not yet. The wind swayed the tops of them; it was blowing crossways over the lake. The surface corrugated, water flapping against the shore.

We got into the canoes again and paddled towards the bend; I remembered there was an open space where we could camp. On the way there were several abandoned beaver lodges shaped like dilapidated beehives or wooden haystacks; I memorized them, the bass like underwater tangle.

We were later than I had planned, the sun was red and weakening. David wanted to fish right away but I said we had to pitch the tents and collect wood first. There was garbage at this site too but it was ancient garbage, the labels on the beer bottles illegible, the cans corroded. I gathered it up and took it with me when I went back among the trees to dig the toilet hole.

Layer of leaves and needles, layer of roots, damp sand. That was what used to bother me most about the cities, the white zero-mouthed toilets in their clean tiled cubicles. Flush toilets and vacuum cleaners, they roared and made things vanish, at that time I was afraid there was a machine that could make people vanish like that too, go nowhere, like a camera that could steal not only your soul but your body also. Levers and buttons, triggers, the machines sent them up as roots sent up flowers; tiny circles and oblongs, logic become visible, you couldn't tell in advance what would happen if you pressed them.

I showed the three of them where I had dug the hole. 'Where do you sit?' Anna asked, squeamish.

'On the ground,' David said, 'good for you, toughen you up. You could use an ass job.' Anna poked him on the belt buckle and said 'Flab,' imitating him.

I opened more tins and heated them, baked beans and peas, and we ate them with smokey tea. From the rock where I washed the dishes I could see part of a tent, in among the cedars at the distand end of the lake: their bunker. Binoculars trained on me, I could feel the eye rays, cross of the rifle sight on my forehead, in case I made a false move.

David was impatient, he wanted his money's worth, what he'd come for. Anna said she'd stay at the campsite: fishing didn't interest her. We left her the insect spray and the three of got into the green canoe with the fishing rods. I put the frog jar in the stern where I could reach it. David was facing me this time; Joe sat in the bow, he was going to fish too, though he didn't have a licence.

The wind had dwindled, the lake was pink and orange. We went along the shore, birches cool, overhanging us, ice pillars. I was dizzy, too much water and sun glare, the skin of my face was shimmering as though burned, afterglow. In my head when I closed my eyes the shape of the heron dangled, upside down. I should have buried it.

The canoe steered over to the nearest beaver lodge and they tied up to it. I opened the tackle box and clipped a lure onto David's line. He was happy, whistling under his breath.

'Hey, maybe I'll hook a beaver,' he said. 'The national emblem. That's what they should've put on the flag instead of a maple leaf, a split beaver; I'd salute that.'

'Why should it be split?' I said. It was like skinning the cat, I didn't get it.

He looked exasperated. 'It's a joke,' he said; and when I still didn't laugh, 'Where've you been living? It's slang for cunt. The Maple Beaver for Ever, that would be neat.' He lowered his line into the water and began to sing, off-key:

> In days of yore, from Britains shore
> Wolfe, the gallant hero, came:
> It spread all o'er the hooerhouse floor
> On Canada's fair domain. . . .

They sing that at your school?'

'The fish will hear you,' I said, and he stopped.

A part of the body, a dead animal. I wondered what part of them the heron was, that they needed so much to kill it.

Into my head the tugboat floated, the one that was on the lake before, logboom trailing it, men waving from the cabin, sunlight and blue sky, the perfect way. But it didn't last. One spring when we got to the village it was beached near the government dock, abandoned. I wanted to see what the little house was like, how they had lived; I was sure there would be a miniature table and chairs, beds that folded down out of the walls, flowered window curtains. We climbed up; the door was open but inside it was bare wood, not even painted; there was no furniture at all and the stove was gone. The only things we could find were two rusted razor blades on the windowsill and some pictures drawn on the walls in pencil.

I thought they were plants or fish, some of them were shaped like clams but my brother laughed, which meant he knew something I didn't; I nagged at him until he explained. I was shocked, not by those parts of the body, we'd been told about those, but that they should be cut off like that from the bodies that ought to have gone with them, as though they could detach themselves and crawl around on their own like snails.

I'd forgotten about that; but of course they were magic drawings like the ones in caves. You draw on the wall what's important to you, what you're hunting. They had enough food, no need to draw tinned peas and Argentine corned beef, and that's what they wanted instead during those monotonous and not at all idyllic trips up down the lake, nothing to do but play cards, they must have detested it, back and forth chained to the logs. All of them now or old, they probably hated each other.

The bass struck on both lines at once. They fought hard, the rods doubled over. David landed one but Joe let his escape into the labyrinth of sticks, where it wound the line around a branch and snapped it.

'Hey,' David was saying, 'kill it for me.' The bass was fierce, it was flipping around the inside of the canoe. It spat water from its undershot jaw with a hissing sound; it was either terrified or enraged, I couldn't tell which.

'You do it,' I said, handing him the knife. 'I showed you how, remember?'

Thud of metal on fishbone, skull, neckless headbody, the fish is whole, I couldn't any more, I had no right to. We didn't need it, our proper food was tin cans. We were committing this act, violation, for sport or amusement or pleasure, recreation they call it, these were no longer the right reasons. That's an explanation but no excuse my father used to say, a favourite maxim.

While they admired David's murder, cadaver, I took the bottle with the frogs in it out of the tackle box and unscrewed the top; they slipped into the water, green with black leopard spots and gold eyes, rescued. Highschool, each desk with a tray on it and a frog, exhaling ether, spread and pinned flat as a doily and slit open, the organs explored and clipped out, the detached heart still gulping slowly like an adam's apple, no martyr's letters on it, the intestines messy string. Pickled cat pumped full of plastic, red for the arteries, blue for the veins, at the hospital, the undertaker's. Find the brain of the worm, donate your body to science. Anything we could do to the animals we could do to each other: we practised on them first.

Joe flipped his broken line back to me and I rummaged among the lures and found another leader, a lead sinker, another hook: accessory, accomplice.

The Americans had rounded the point, two of them in a silver canoe; they were barging towards us. I assessed them, their disguises: they weren't the bloated middle-aged kind, those would stick to powerboats and guides; they were younger, trimmer, with the candid, tanned astronaut finish valued by the magazines. When they were even with us their mouths curved open, showing duplicate sets of teeth, white and even as false ones.

'Gettin' any?' the front man said with a midwestern accent; traditional greeting.

'Lots,' David said, smiling back. I was expecting him to say something to them, insult them, but he didn't. They were quite large.

'Us too,' the front one said. 'We been in here three-four days, they been biting the whole time, caught our limit every day.' They had a starry flag like all of them, a miniature decal sticker on the canoe bow. To show us we were in occupied territory.

'Well, see ya,' the back one said. Their canoe moved past us towards the next beaver house.

Raygun fishing rods, faces impermeable as space-suit helmets, sniper eyes, they did it; guilt glittered on them like tinfoil. My brain recited the stories I'd been told about them: the ones who stuffed the pontoons of their seaplane with illegal fish, the ones who had a false bottom to their car, two hundred lake trout on dry ice, the game warden caught them by accident. 'This is a lousy country,' they said when he wouldn't take the bribe, 'we ain't never coming back here.' They got drunk and chased loons in their powerboats for fun, backtracking on the loon as it dived, not giving it a chance to fly, until it drowned or got chopped up in the propeller blades. Senseless killing, it was a game; after the war they'd been bored.

The sunset was fading, at the other side of the sky the black was coming up. We took the fish back, four of them by now, and I cut a Y-shaped sapling stringer to go through the gills.

'Poo,' Anna said to us, 'you smell like a fish market.'

David said 'Wish we had some beer. Maybe we could get some off the Yanks, they're the type.'

I went down to the lake with the bar of soap to wash the fish blood off my hands. Anna followed me.

'God,' she said, 'what'm I going to do? I forgot my makeup, he'll kill me.'

I studied her: in the twilight her face was grey. 'Maybe he won't notice,' I said.

'He'll notice, don't you worry. Not now maybe, it hasn't all rubbed off, but in the morning. He wants me to look like a young chick all the time, if I don't he gets mad.'

'You could let you face get really dirty,' I said.

She didn't answer that. She sat down on the rock and rested her forehead on her knees. 'He'll get me for it,' she said fatalistically. 'He's got this little set of rules. If I break one of them I get punished, except he keeps changing them so I'm never sure. He's crazy, there's something missing in him, you know what I mean? He likes to make me cry because he can't do it himself.'

'But that can't be serious,' I said, 'the makeup thing.'

A sound came out of her throat, a cough or a laugh. 'It's not just that; it's something for him to use. He watches me all the time, he waits for excuses. Then either he won't screw at all or he slams it in so hard it hurts. I guess it's awful of me to say that.' Her eggwhite eyes turned towards me in the half-darkness. 'But if you said any of this to him he'd just make funny cracks about it, he says I have a mind like a soap opera, he says I invent it. But I really don't, you know.' She was appealing to me for judgment but she didn't trust me, she was afraid I would talk to him about it behind her back.

'Maybe you should leave,' I said, offering my solution, 'or get a divorce.'

'Sometimes I think he wants me to, I can't tell any more. It used to be good, then I started to really love him and he can't stand that, he can't stand having me love him. Isn't that funny?' She had my mother's leather jacket over her shoulders, she'd brought it because she didn't have a heavy sweater. With Anna's head attached to it it was incongruous, diminished. I tried to think about my mother but she was blanked out; the only thing that remained was a story she once told about how, when she was little, she and her sister had made wings for themselves out of an old umbrella; they'd jumped off the barn roof, attempting to fly, and she broke both her ankles. She would laugh about it but the story seemed to me then chilly and sad, the failure unbearable.

'Sometimes I think he'd like me to die,' Anna said, 'I have dreams about it.'

We walked back and I built up the fire and mixed some cocoa, using powdered milk. Everything was dark now except for the flames, sparks going up in spirals, coals underneath pulsing red when the night breeze hit them. We sat on the groundsheets, David with his arm around Anna, Joe and I a foot apart.

'This reminds me of Girl Guides,' Anna said in the cheerful voice I once thought was hers. She began to sing, the notes hesitant, quavering:

There'll be bluebirds over
The white cliffs of Dover
Tomorrow, when the world is free...

The words went out towards the shadows, smoke-thin, evaporating. Across the lake a barred owl was calling, quick and soft like a wing beating against the eardrum, cutting across the pattern of her voice, negating her. She glanced behind her: she felt it.

'Now everybody sing,' she said, clapping her hands.

David said 'Well, goodnight children,' and he and Anna went into their tent. The tent lit up from inside for a moment, flashlight, then went out.

'Coming?' Joe said.

'In a minute.' I wanted to give him time to go to sleep.

I sat in the dark, the stroking sound of the night lake surrounding me. In the distance the Americans' campfire glowed, a dull red cyclops eye: the enemy lines. I wished evil towards them: Let them suffer, I prayed, tip their canoe, burn them, rip them open. Owl: answer, no answer.

I crawled into the tent through the mosquito-netting; I groped for the flashlight but didn't switch it on, I didn't want to disturb him. I undressed by touch; he was obscure beside me, inert, comforting as a log. Perhaps that was the only time there could be anything like love, when he was asleep, demanding nothing. I passed my hand lightly over his shoulder as I would touch a tree or a stone.

But he wasn't sleeping; he moved, reached over for me.

'I'm sorry,' I said, 'I thought you were asleep.'

'Okay,' he said, 'I give up, you win. We'll forget everything I said and do it like you want, back to the way it was before, right?'

It was too late, I couldn't. 'No,' I said. I had already moved out.

His hand tightened in anger on my arm; then he let go. 'Sweet flaming balls of Christ,' he said. His outline lifted in the darkness, I crouched down, he was going to hit me; but he turned over away from me, muffling himself in the sleeping bag.

My heart bumped, I held still, translating the noises on the other side of the canvas wall. Squeaks, shuffling in the dry leaves, grunting, nocturnal animals; no danger.

Chapter Fifteen

The tent roof was translucent, wet parchment, spotted on the outside with early dew. Bird voices twirled over my ears, intricate as skaters or running water, the air filling with liquid syllables.

In the middle of the night there was a roar, Joe having a nightmare. I touched him, it was safe, he was trapped in the straitjacket sleeping bag. He sat up, not yet awake.

'This is the wrong room,' he said.

'What was it?' I asked. 'What were you dreaming?' I wanted to know, perhaps I could remember how. But he folded over and went back.

My hand was beside me; it had the cured hide smell of wood-smoke mingled with sweat and earth, fish lingering, smell of the past. At the cabin we would soak the clothes we'd been wearing, scrub the forest out of them, renew our coating of soap and lotion.

I dressed and went down to the lake and dipped my face into it. This water was not clear like the water in the main lake: it was brownish, complicated by more kinds of life crowded more closely together, and it was colder. The rock ledge dropped straight down, lake of the edge. I woke the others.

After I'd cleaned the fish I dipped them in flour and fried them and boiled coffee. The fish flesh was white, blue-veined; it tasted like underwater and reeds. They ate, not talking much; they hadn't slept well.

Anna's face in the daylight was dried and slightly shrivelled without its cream underfilm and pink highlights; her nose was sunburned and she had prune crinkles under her eyes. She kept turned away from David, but he didn't seem to notice, he didn't say anything, except when she knocked her foot against his cup and tipped some of his coffee out onto the ground. Then all he said was 'Watch it Anna, you're getting sloppy.'

'Do you want to fish any more this morning?' I said to David, but he shook his head: 'Let's go take that rock painting.'

I burned the fish bones, the spines fragile as petals; the innards I planted in the forest. They were not seeds, in the spring no minnows would sprout up. Deer skeleton we found on the island, shreds of flesh on it still, he said the wolves had killed it in the winter because it was old, that was natural. If we dived for them and used our teeth to catch them, fighting on their own grounds, that would be fair, but hooks were substitutes and air wasn't their place.

The two of them fiddled with the movie camera, adjusting and discussing it; then we could start.

According to the map the rock painting was in a bay near the Americans' camp. They didn't seem to be up yet, there was no smoke coming from their fireplace. I thought, maybe it worked and they're dead.

I looked for a dip in the shore, a line that would fit the mapline. It was there, site of the X, unmistakable: cliff with sheer face, the kind they would have chosen to paint on, no other flat rock in sight. He had been here and long before him the original ones, the first explorers, leaving behind them their sign, word, but not its meaning. I leaned forward, scanning the cliff surface; we let the canoes drift in sideways till they scraped the stone.

'Where is it?' David said; and to Joe, 'You'll have to steady the canoe, there's no way we can shoot from land.'

'It might be hard to see at first,' I said, 'Faded. It ought to be right here somewhere.' But it wasn't: no man with antlers, nothing like red paint or even a stain, the rock surface extended under my hand, coarse-grained, lunar, broken only by a pink-white vein of quartz that ran across it, a diagonal marking the slow tilt of the land; nothing human.

Either I hadn't remembered the map properly or what he'd written on the map was wrong. I'd reasoned it out, unravelled the clues in his puzzle the way he taught us and they'd led nowhere. I felt as though he'd lied to me.

'Who told you about it?' David said, cross-examining.

'I just thought it was here,' I said. 'Someone mentioned it. Maybe it was another lake.' For a moment I knew: of course, the lake had been flooded, it would be twenty feet under water. But that was the other lake, this one was part of a separate system, the watershed divided them. The map said he'd found them on the main lake too; according to the letter he'd been taking pictures of them. But when I'd searched the cabin there had been no camera. No drawings, no camera, I'd done it wrong, I would have to look again.

They were disappointed, they'd expected something picturesque or bizarre, something they could utilize. He hadn't followed the rules, he'd cheated, I wanted to confront him, demand an explanation: You said it would be here.

We turned back. The Americans were up, they were still alive; they were setting out in their canoe, the front one had his fishing rod trailing over the bow. Joe and I were ahead, we approached them at right angles.

'Hi,' the front one said, to me, bleached grin. 'Any luck?' That was their armour, bland ignorance, heads empty as weather balloons: with that they could defend themselves against anything. Straight power, they mainlined it; I imagined the surge of electricity, nerve juice, as they hit it, brought it down, flapping like a crippled plane. The innocents get slaughtered because they exist, I thought, there is nothing inside the happy killers to restrain them, no conscience or piety; for them the only things worthy of life were human, their own kind of human, framed in the proper clothes and gimmicks, laminated. It would have been different in those countries where an animal is the soul of an ancestor or the child of a god, at least they would have felt guilt.

'We aren't fishing,' I said, my lips clipping the words. My arm wanted to swing the paddle sideways, blade into his head: his eyes would blossom outwards, his skull shatter like an egg.

The corners of his mouth wilted. 'Oh,' he said. 'Say, what part of the States are you all from? It's hard to tell, from your accent. Fred and me guessed Ohio.'

'We're not from the States,' I said, annoyed that he'd mistaken me for one of them.

'No kidding?' his face lit up, he'd seen a real native. 'You from here?'

'Yes,' I said. 'We all are.'

'So are we,' said the back one unexpectedly.

The front one held out his hand, though five feet of water separated us. 'I'm from Sarnia and Fred here, my brother-in-law, is from Toronto. We thought you were Yanks, with the hair and all.'

I was furious with them, they'd disguised themselves. 'What're you doing with that flag on your boat then?' I said, my voice loud, it surprised them. The front one withdrew his hand.

'Oh that,' he said with a shrug. 'I'm a Mets fan, have been for years, I always root for the underdog. Bought that when I was down there for the game, the year they won the pennant.' I looked more closely at the sticker: it wasn't a flag at all, it was a blue and white oblong with red printing, GO METS.

David and Anna had caught up with us. 'You a Mets fan?' David said. 'Out of sight.' He slid his canoe in beside theirs and they shook hands. But they'd killed the heron anyway. It doesn't matter what country they're from, my head said, they're still Americans, they're what's in store for us, what we are turning into. They spread themselves like a virus, they get into the brain and take over the cells and the cells change from inside and the ones that have the disease can't tell the difference. Like the late show sci-fi movies, creatures from outer space, body snatchers injecting themselves into you dispossessing your brain, their eyes blank eggshells behind the dark glasses. If you look like them and talk like them and think like them then you are them, I was saying, you speak their language, a language is everything you do.

But how did they evolve, where did the first one come from, they weren't an invasion from another planet, they were terrestrial. How did we get bad. For us when we were small the origin was Hitler, he was the great evil, many-tentacled, ancient and indestructible as the Devil. It didn't matter that he had shrunk to a few cinders and teeth by the time I heard about him; I was certain he was alive, he was in the comic books my brother brought home in the winters and he was in my brother's scrapbook too, he was the swastikas on the tanks, if only he could be destroyed everyone would be saved, safe. When our father made bonfires to burn the weeds we would throw sticks into the flames and chant 'Hitler's house is burning down, My Fair Lady-O'; we knew it helped. All possible horrors were measured against him. But Hitler was gone and the thing remained; whatever it was, even then, moving away from them as they smirked and waved goodbye, I was asking Are the Americans worse than Hitler. It was like cutting up a tapeworm, the pieces grew.

We landed at the campsite and rolled up the sleeping bags and struck the tents and packed them. I covered the toilet hole and smoothed it, camouflaging it with sticks and needles. Leave no traces.

David wanted to stay and have lunch with the Americans and talk about baseball scores, but I said the wind was against us, we would need the time. I hurried them, I wanted to get away, from my own anger as well as from the friendly metal killers.

We reached the first portage at eleven. My feet moved over the rocks and mud, stepping in my own day-old footprints, backtracking; in my brain the filaments, trails reconnected and branched, we killed other people besides Hitler, before my brother went to school and learned about him and the games became war games. Earlier we would play we were animals; our parents were the humans, the enemies who might shoot us or catch us, we would hide from them. But sometimes the animals had power too: one time we were a swarm of bees, we gnawed the fingers, feet and nose off our least favourite doll, ripped her cloth body open and pulled out the stuffing, it was grey and fluffy like the insides of mattresses; then we threw her into the lake. She floated and they found the body and asked us how she got lost, and we lied and said we didn't know. Killing was wrong, we had been told that: only enemies and food could be killed. Of course the doll wasn't hurt, it wasn't alive; though children think everything is alive.

At the midway pond the heron was still there, hanging in the hot sunlight like something in a butcher's window, desecrated, unredeemed. It smelled worse. Around its head the flies vibrated, laying their eggs. The king who learned to speak with animals, in the story he ate a magic leaf and they revealed a treasure, a conspiracy, they saved his life; what would they really say? Accusation, lament, an outcry of rage; but they had no spokesman.

I felt a sickening complicity, sticky as glue, blood on my hands, as though I had been there and watched without saying No or doing anything to stop it: one of the silent guarded faces in the crowd. The trouble some people have being German, I thought, I have being human. In a way it was stupid to be more disturbed by a dead bird than by those other things, the wars and riots and the massacres in the newspapers. But for the wars and riots there was always an explanation, people wrote books about them saying why they happened: the death of the heron was causeless, undiluted.

The laboratory, he was older then. He never caught birds, they were too quick for him, what he caught was the slower things. He kept them in jars and tin cans on a board shelf back in the forest, near the swamp; to reach them he made a secret path, marked only by small notches on the trees, a code. Sometimes he forgot to feed them or perhaps it was too cold at night, because when I went there by myself that day one of the snakes was dead and several of the frogs, their skin dry and their yellow stomachs puffed up, and the crayfish was floating in the clouded water with its legs uppermost like a spider's. I emptied those bottles into the swamp. The other things, the ones still alive, I let out. I rinsed the jars and tins and left them in a row on the board.

After lunch I hid but I had to come out finally for dinner. He couldn't say anything in front of them but he knew it was me, there was no one else. He was so angry he was pale, his eyes twisted as though they couldn't see me. 'They were mine,' he said. Afterwards he trapped other things and changed the place; this time he wouldn't tell me. I found it anyway but I was afraid to let them out again. Because of my fear they were killed.

I didn't want there to be wars and death, I wanted them not to exist; only rabbits with their coloured egg houses, sun and moon orderly above the flat earth, summer always, I wanted everyone to be happy. But his pictures were more accurate, the weapons, the disintegrating soldiers: he was a realist, that protected him. He almost drowned once but he would never allow that to happen again, by the time he left he was ready.

The leeches were there again in the tepid pond water, clumps of young ones hanging from the lily pad stems like fingers, larger ones swimming, flat and soft as noodles. I didn't like them but distaste excused nothing. In the other lake they never bothered us when we were swimming but we would catch the mottled kind, bad kind he called them, and throw them on the campfire when our mother wasn't watching, she prohibited cruelty. I didn't mind that so much, if only they would die; but they would writhe out and crawl painfully, coated with ashes and pine needles, back towards the lake, seeming to be able to smell where the water was. The he would pick them up with two sticks and put them back in the flames again.

It wasn't the city that was wrong, the inquisitors in the school-yard, we weren't better than they were; we just had different victims. To become like a little child again, a barbarian, a vandal: it was in us too, it was innate. A thing closed in my head, hand, synapse, cutting off my escape: that was the wrong way, the entrance, redemption was elsewhere, I must have overlooked it.

We reached the main lake and re-loaded the canoes and shoved them out over the snarl of logs. In the bay the felled trees and numbered posts showed where the surveyors had been, power company. My country, sold or drowned, a reservoir; the people were sold along with the land and the animals, a bargain, sale, *solde*. Les soldes they called them, sellouts, the flood would depend on who got elected, not here but somewhere else.

Chapter Sixteen

It was the sixth day, I had to find out; it would be my last chance, tomorrow Evans was coming to take us back. My brain was rushing, covering over the bad things and filling the empty spaces with an embroidery of calculations and numbers, I needed to finish, I had never finished anything. To be exact, to condense myself to a pinpoint, impaling a fact, a certainty.

As soon as I could I re-checked the map. The X was where is should have been, I hadn't made a mistake. There was only one theory I could retreat to: some of the crosses might be places he thought suitable for paintings but hadn't examined yet. I ran my finger around the shore, looking for the nearest marked site; it was the cliff where we had been fishing the first evening, it would be underwater, I would have to dive. If I found something it would vindicate him, I would know he'd been right; if not I could try the next X, near the heron island, and then the next one.

I had my bathing suit on already; we'd been washing the clothes down on the dock, rubbing them on the ribbed washboard with the worn-down bar of yellow soap, standing in the lake to rinse them. They were pegged out to dry now on the line behind the cabin, shirts, jeans, socks, Anna's coloured lingerie, our cast skins. Anna had seemed more relaxed, she hummed from behind her fresh facade of makeup. She had stayed down by the lake to shampoo the smoke out of her hair. I pulled on a sweat shirt in case there were Americans. Before leaving I searched once more for his camera, the one he must have used to take the photographs, but it wasn't there; he must have had it with him. At the time, the last time.

I had started down the steps before I saw them. The three of them were on the dock, split into parts by the treetrunk bars. Anna was kneeling in her orange bikini, with a towel draped over her head like a nun; David was standing over her, hands on hips. Joe was further back with the movie camera, sitting on the dock with his legs dangling, head averted as if waiting politely for them to be through. When I heard what they were saying I stood still. The canoes were there and I needed one of them but it was too dangerous. It was a calm day, the sound carried.

'Come on, take it off,' David said; his light-humour voice.

'I wasn't bothering you.' Anna was muted, avoiding.

'It won't hurt you, we need a naked lady.'

'What the hell for?' Anna was peevish now, her veiled head upturned; her eyes would be squinting.

'*Random Samples*,' David said patiently, and I thought, They've used up everything, there's nothing left here now for them to take pictures of except each other, next it will be me. 'You'll go in beside the dead bird, it's your chance for stardom, you've always wanted fame. You'll get to be on Educational TV' he added as though it was a special bribe.

'Oh for Christ's sake,' Anna said. She picked up her murder mystery again and pretended to read.

'Come on, we need a naked lady with big tits and a big ass,' David said in the same tender voice; I recognized that menacing gentleness, at school it always went before the trick, the punchline.

'Look, will you leave me alone?' Anna said. 'I'm minding my own business, mind yours why don't you.' She stood up, her towel sliding off, and tried to get past him to the land, but he sidestepped in front of her.

'I won't take her if she doesn't want to,' Joe said.

'It's token resistance,' David said, 'she wants to, she's an exhibitionist at heart. She likes her lush bod, don't you? Even if she is getting too fat.'

'Don't think I don't know what you're trying to do,' Anna said, as though she'd guessed a riddle. 'You're trying to humiliate me.'

'What's humiliating about your body, darling?' David said caressingly. 'We all love it, you ashamed of it? That's pretty stingy of you, you should share the wealth; not that you don't.'

Anna was furious now, goaded, her voice rose. 'Fuck off, you want bloody everything don't you, you can't use that stuff on me.'

'Why not,' David said evenly, 'it works. Now just take it off like a good girl or I'll have to take it off for you.'

'Leave her alone,' Joe said, swinging his legs, bored or excited, it was impossible to tell.

I wanted to run down to the dock and stop them, fighting was wrong, we weren't allowed to, if we did both sides got punished as in a real war. So we battled in secret, undeclared, and after a while I no longer fought back because I never won. The only defence was flight, invisibility. I sat down on the top step.

'Shut up, she's my wife,' David said. His hand clamped down above her elbow. She jerked away, then I saw his arms go around her as if to kiss her and she was in the air, upside down over his shoulder, hair hanging in damp ropes. 'Okay twatface,' he said, 'is it off or into the lake?'

Anna's fists grabbed bunches of his shirt. 'If I go in, you go in too.' The words spurted from behind her fallen hair, she was kicking, I couldn't see whether she was laughing or crying.

'Shoot,' David said to Joe, and to Anna, 'I'll count to ten,'

Joe swivelled the camera and trained it on them like a bazooka or a strange instrument of torture and pressed the button, lever, sinister whirr.

'All right,' Anna said under its coercion, 'you shmuck bastard, God damn you.' He set her down and stepped aside. Her arms, elbows out, struggled with the fastener like a beetle's on its back and the top dropped away: I saw her cut in half, one breast on either side of a thin tree.

'Bottoms too,' David said as though to a recalcitrant child. Anna glanced at him, contemptuous, and bent. 'Look sexy now, move it; give us a little dance.'

Anna stood for a moment, brown-red with yellow fur and white markings like underwear, glaring at them. Then she stuck her middle finger in the air at them and ran to the end of the dock and jumped into the lake. It was a bellyflop, the water splattered out like a dropped egg. She came up with her hair in streaks over her forehead and started to swim around towards the sand point, clumsy, arms flailing.

'Get that?' David said mildly over his shoulder.

'Some of it,' Joe said. 'Maybe you could order her to do it again.' I thought he was being sarcastic but I wasn't sure. He began to unscrew the camera from the tripod.

I could hear Anna splashing and then stumbling below on the sand point; she was really crying now, her indrawn breaths rasping. The bushes rustled, she swore; then she appeared over the top of the hill, she must have climbed up by holding onto the leaning trees. Her pink face was dissolving, her skin was covered with sand and pine needles like a burned leech. She went into the cabin without looking at me or saying anything.

I stood up. Joe was gone but David was still on the dock, sitting now crosslegged. One at a time they were safer; I went down for the canoe.

'Hi' he said, 'how goes it?' He didn't know I'd been watching. He had his shoes off and was picking at a toenail as though nothing had happened.

David is like me, I thought, we are the ones that don't know how to love, there is something essential missing in us, we were born that way, Madame at the store with one hand, atrophy of the heart. Joe and Anna are lucky, they do it badly and suffer because of it: but it's better to see than to be blind, even though that way you had to let in the crimes, and atrocities too. Or perhaps we are normal and the ones who can love are freaks, they have an extra organ, like the vestigial eye in the foreheads of amphibians they've never found the use for.

Anna's bikini lay on the dock, crumpled, a shed chrysalis. He picked up the top and began pleating and unpleating the strap. I hadn't meant to say anything aout it, it wasn't my concern, but I found myself asking him anyway. 'Why did you do that?' My voice was neutral and I realized it wasn't for Anna I was aksing, I wasn't defending her; it was for myself, I needed to understand.

For a moment he acted. 'What?' he said, grinning and innocent.

'What you just did to her,'

He looked hard at me to see if I was accusing him but I was untying the canoe, I was impersonal as a wall, a confessional, and that reassured him. 'You don't know what she does to me,' he said with a slight whine. 'She asks for it, she makes me do it.' His voice turned crafty. 'She goes with other men, she thinks she can get away with it, but she's too dumb, every time I find out; I can smell it on her. Not that I'd mind if she'd do it openly and be honest about it, God knows, it's not that I'm jealous.' He smiled broad-mindedly. 'But she's devious, I can't stand that.'

Anna hadn't told me, she had left something out; or else he was lying. 'But she loves you,' I said.

'Bullshit,' he said 'she's trying to cut my balls off.' His eyes were sad rather than hostile, as though he had once believed better of her.

'She loves you,' I repeated, petals off a daisy; it was the magic word but it couldn't work because I had no faith. My husband, saying it over and over like a Dial the Weather recording, trying to engrave it on me; and with the same bewilderment, as though I was the one who'd been hurting him and not the other way round. An accident, that's what he called it.

'She never tells *me* that,' he said. 'I get the impression she wants out, she's waiting for the chance to leave. But I haven't asked, we don't talk much any more except with other people around.'

'Maybe you should,' I said; unconvinced, unconvincing.

He shrugged. 'What would we talk about? She's too dumb, she can't figure out what I'm saying to her, Jesus, she moves her lips when she watches the TV even. She doesn't know anything, every time she opens her mouth she makes an ass of herself. I know what you're thinking,' he said, almost pleading, 'but I'm all for the equality of women; she just doesn't happen to be equal and that's not my fault, is it? What I married was a pair of boobs, she manipulated me into it, it was when I was studying for the ministry, nobody knew any better then. But that's life.' He wiggled his moustache and gave a Woody Woodpecker laugh, his eyes baffled.

'I think you could work it out,' I said. I braced the paddle across the gunwhales and clambered into the canoe. I remembered what Anna had said about emotional commitments: they've made one, I thought, they hate each other; that must be almost as absorbing as love. The barometer couple in their wooden house, enshrined in their niche on Paul's front porch, my ideal; except they were glued there, condemned to oscillate back and forth, sun and rain, without escape. When he saw her next there would be no recantations, no elaborate reconciliation or forgiveness, they were beyond that.

Neither of them would mention it, they had reached a balance almost like peace. Our mother and father at the sawhorse behind the cabin, mother holding the tree, white birch, father sawing, sun through the branches lighting their hair, grace.

The canoe pivoted. 'Hey,' he said, 'where you off to?'

'Oh. . . .' I gestured towards the lake.

'Want a stern paddler?' he said. I'm great, I've had lots of practice by now.'

He sounded wistful, as though he needed company, but I didn't want him with me, I'd have to explain what I was doing and he wouldn't be able to help. 'No,' I said, 'Thanks just the same.' I knelt, slanting the canoe to one side.

'Okay,' he said, 'see you later, alligator,' He unwound his legs and stood up and strolled off the dock towards the cabin, his striped T-shirt flashing between slats of the trees, receding behind me as I glided from the bay into the open water.

Chapter Seventeen

I moved towards the cliff. The sun sloped, it was morning still, the light not yellow but clear white. Overhead a plane, so far up I could hardly hear it, threading the cities together with its trail of smoke; an X in the sky, unsacred crucifix. The shape of the heron flying above us the first evening we fished, legs and neck stretched, wings outspread, a bluegrey cross, and the other heron or was it the same one, hanging wrecked from the tree. Whether it died willingly, consented, whether Christ died willingly, anything that suffers and dies instead of us is Christ; if they didn't kill birds and fish they would have killed us. The animals die that we may live, they are substitute people, hunters in the fall killing the deer, that is Christ also. And we eat them, out of cans or otherwise; we are eaters of death, dead Christ-flesh resurrecting inside us, granting us life. Canned Spam, canned Jesus, even the plants must be

Christ. But we refuse to worship; the body worships with blood and muscle but the thing in the knob head will not, wills, not to, the head is greedy, it consumes but does not give thanks.

I reached the cliff, there were no Americans. I edged along it, estimating the best place to dive: it faced east, the sun was on it, it was the right time of day; I would start at the left-hand side. Diving by myself was hazardous, there ought to be another person. But I thought I remembered how: we took the canoes or we built rafts from strayed logs and board ends, they would often snap their ropes and escape in the spring when the ice went out; sometimes we would come across them again later, drifting loose like pieces broken from a glacier.

I shipped the paddle and took off my sweatshirt. I would dive several feet out from the rockface and then swim down and in: otherwise I'd risk hitting my head, the drop looked sheer but there might be a ledge underwater. I knelt, facing backwards with both knees on the stern seat, then put a foot on each gunwale and stood up slowly. I bent my knees and straightened, the canoe teetered like a springboard. My other shape was in the water, not my reflection but my shadow, foreshortened, outline blurred, rays streaming out from around the head.

My spine whipped, I hit the water and kicked myself down, sliding through the lake strata, grey to darker grey, cool to cold. I arched sideways and the rockface loomed up, grey pink brown; I worked along it, touching it with my fingers, snail touch on slime-surface, the water unfocusing my eyes. Then my lungs began to clutch and I curled and rose, letting out air like a frog, my hair swirling over my face,towards the canoe, where it hung split between water and air, mediator and liferaft. I canted it with my weight and rolled into it over the side and rested; I hadn't seen anything. My arms ached from the day before and the new effort, my body stumbled, it remembered the motions only imperfectly, like learning to walk after illness.

I waited a few minutes, then moved the canoe further along and dived again, my eyes straining, not knowing what shape to expect, handprint or animal, the lizard body with horns and tail and front-facing head, bird or canoe with stick paddlers; or a small thing, an abstraction, a circle, a moon; or a long distorted figure, stiff and childish, a human, Air gave out, I broke surface. Not here, it must be further along or deeper down; I was convinced it was there, he would not have marked and numbered the map so methodically for nothing, that would not be consistent, he always observed his own rules, axioms.

On the next try I thought I saw it, a blotch, a shadow, Just as I turned to go up. I was dizzy, my vision was beginning to cloud, while I rested my ribs panted, I ought to pause, half an hour at least; but I was elated, it was down there, I would find it. Reckless I balanced and plunged.

Pale green, then darkness, layer after layer, deeper than before, seabottom; the water seemed to have thickened, in it pinprick lights flicked and darted, red and blue, yellow and white, and I saw they were fish, the chasm-dwellers, fins lined with phosphorescent sparks, teeth neon. It was wonderful that I was down so far, I watched the fish, they swam like patterns on closed eyes, my legs and arms were weightless, free-floating; I almost forgot to look for the cliff and the shape.

It was there but it wasn't a painting, it wasn't on the rock. It was below me, drifting towards me from the furthest level where there was no life, a dark oval trailing limbs. It was blurred but it had eyes, they were open, it was something I knew about, a dead thing, it was dead.

I turned, fear gushing out of my mouth in silver, panic closing my throat, the scream kept in and choking me. The green canoe was far above me, sunlight radiating around it a beacon, safety.

But there was not one canoe, there were two, the canoe had twinned or I was seeing double. My hand came out of the water and I gripped the gunwale, then my head; water ran from my nose, I gulped breath, stomach and lungs contracting, my hair sticky like weeds, the lake was horrible, it was filled with death, it was touching me.

Joe was in the other canoe. 'He told me you went over this way,' he said. He must have been almost there before I dived but I hadn't seen him. I couldn't say anything, my lungs were urgent, my arms would hardly pull me into the canoe.

'What the hell are you doing?' he said.

I lay on the bottom of the canoe and closed my eyes; I wanted him not to be there. It formed again in my head: at first I thought it was my drowned brother, hair floating around the face, image I'd kept from before I was born; but it couldn't be him, he had not drowned after all, he was elsewhere. Then I recognized it: it wasn't ever my brother I'd been remembering that had been a disguise.

I knew when it was, it was in a bottle curled up, staring out at me like a cat pickled; it had huge jelly eyes and fins instead of hands, fish gills, I couldn't let it out, it was dead already it had drowned in air. It was there when I woke up, suspended in the air above me like a chalice, an evil grail and I thought. Whatever it is, part of myself or a separate creature, I killed it. It wasn't a child but it could have been one, I didn't allow it.

Water was dripping from me into the canoe, I lay in a puddle. I had been furious with them, I knocked it off the table, my life on the floor, glass egg and shattered blood, nothing could be done.

That was wrong, I never saw it. They scraped it into a bucket and threw it wherever they throw them, it was travelling through the sewers by the time I woke, back to the sea, I stretched my hand up to it and it vanished. The bottle had been logical, pure logic, remnant of the trapped and decaying animals, secreted by my head, enclosure, something to keep the death away from me. Not even a hospital, not even that sanction of legality, official procedures. A house it was, shabby front room with magazines, purple runner on the hall floor, vines and blossoms, the smell of lemon polish, furtive doors and whispers, they wanted you out fast. Pretense of the non-nurse, her armpits acid, face powdered with solicitude. Stumble along the hall, from flower to flower, her criminal hand on my elbow, other arm against the wall. Ring on my finger. It was all real enough, it was enough reality for ever, I couldn't accept it, that mutilation, ruin I'd made, I needed a different version. I pieced it together the best way I could, flattening it, scrapbook, collage, pasting over the wrong parts. A faked album, the memories fraudulent as passports; but a paper house was better than none and I could almost live in it, I'd lived in it until now.

He hadn't gone with me to the place where they did it; his own children, the real ones, were having a birthday party. But he came afterwards to collect me. It was a hot day, when we stepped out into the sun we couldn't see for an instant. It wasn't a wedding, there were no pigeons; the post office and the lawn were in another part of the city where I went for stamps; the fountain with the dolphins and the cherub with half a face was from the company town, I'd put it in so there would be something of mine.

'It's over,' he said, 'feel better?'

I was emptied, amputated; I stank of salt and antiseptic, they had planted death in me like a seed.

'You're cold,' he said, 'come on, we'd better get you home.' Scrutinizing my face in the light, hands on the wheel, tough, better this way. In my deflated lap there was a purse, suitcase. I couldn't go there, home, I never went there again, I sent them a postcard.

They never knew, about that or why I left. Their own innocence, the reason I couldn't tell them; perilous innocence, closing them in glass, their artificial garden, greenhouse. They didn't teach us about evil, they didn't understand about it, how could I describe it to them? They were from another age, prehistoric, when everyone got married and had a family, children growing in the yard like sunflowers; remote as Eskimoes or mastodons.

I opened my eyes and sat up. Joe was still there beside me; he was holding on to the edge of my canoe.

'You all right?' he said. His voice came to me faintly, as though muffled.

He said I should do it, he made me do it; he talked about it as though it was legal, simple, like getting a wart removed. He said it wasn't a person, only an animal; I should have seen that was no different, it was hiding in me as if in a burrow and instead of granting it sanctuary I let them catch it. I could have said no but I didn't; that made me one of them too, a killer. After the slaughter, the murder, he couldn't believe I didn't want to see him any more; it bewildered him, he resented me for it, he expected gratitude because he arranged it for me, fixed me so I was as good as new; others, he said, wouldn't have bothered. Since then I'd carried that death around inside me, layering it over, a cyst, a tumour, black pearl; the gratitude I felt now was not for him.

I had to go onto the shore and leave something: that was what you were supposed to do, leave a piece of your clothing as an offering. I regretted the nickels I'd taken dutifully for the collection plate, I got so little in return: no power remained in their bland oleotinted Jesus prints or in the statues of the other ones, rigid and stylized, holy triple name shrunken to swearwords. These gods, here on the shore or in the water, unacknowledged or forgotten, were the only ones who had ever given me anything I needed; and freely.

The map crosses and the drawings made sense now: at the

beginning he must have been only locating the rock paintings, deducing them, tracing and photographing them, a retirement hobby; but then he found out about them. The Indians did not own salvation but they had once known where it lived and their signs marked the sacred places, the places where you could learn the truth. There was no painting at White Birch Lake and none here, because his later drawings weren't copied from things on the rocks. He had discovered new places, new oracles, they were things he was seeing the way I had seen, true vision; at the end, after the failure of logic. When it happened the first time he must have been terrified, it would be like stepping through a usual door and finding yourself in a different galaxy; purple trees and red moons and a green sun.

I swung the paddle and Joe's hand came unstuck and the canoe went towards the shore. I slipped on my canvas shoes and bundled up the sweatshirt and stepped out, looping the rope to a tree, then I climbed the slope towards the cliff, trees on one side, rockface on the other, balsam smell, underbrush scratching my bare legs. There was a ledge, I'd noticed it from the lake, I could throw my sweatshirt onto it. I didn't know the names of the ones I was making the offering to; but they were there, they had power. Candles in front of statues, crutches on the steps, flowers in jam jars by the roadside crosses, gratitude for cures, however wished-for and partial. Clothing was better, it was closer and more essential; and the gift had been greater, more than a hand or any eye, feeling was beginning to seep back into me, I tingled like a foot that's been asleep.

I was opposite the ledge; reindeer moss feathered it, clumps intricate with branches, the tips red, glowing in the sun. It was only an arm's length away on the sheer cliff; I folded my sweatshirt neatly and reached it across.

Behind me something lumbered, crashing. It was Joe, I'd forgotten about him. When he caught up with me he took me by the shoulders.

'You all right?' he said again.

I didn't love him, I was far away from him, it was as though I was seeing him through a smeared window or glossy paper; he didn't belong here. But he existed, he deserved to be alive. I was wishing I could tell him how to change so he could get there, the place where I was.

'Yes,' I said. I touched him on the arm with my hand. My hand touched his arm. Hand touched arm. Language divides us into fragments, I wanted to be whole.

He kissed me; I stood on my side of the window. When his head drew away I said 'I don't love you,' I was going to explain but he didn't seem to hear me, mouth on my shoulder, fingers at the clasp behind my back, then sliding down my flanks, he was pushing on me as though trying to fold up a lawn chair, he wanted me to lie down on the ground.

I stretched out inside my body, twigs and pine needles under me. At that moment I thought; perhaps for him I am the entrance, as the lake was the entrance for me. The forest condensed in him, it was noon, the sun was behind his head; his face was invisible, the sun's rays coming out from a centre of darkness, my shadow.

His hands descended, zipper sound, metal teeth on metal teeth, he was rising out of the fur husk, solid and heavy; but the cloth separated from him and I saw he was human, I didn't want him in me, sacrilege, he was one of the killers, the clay victims damaged and strewn behind him, and he hadn't seen, he didn't know about himself, his own capacity for death.

'Don't,' I said, he was lowering himself down on me, 'I don't want you to.'

'What's wrong with you?' he said, angry; then he was pinning me, hands manacles, teeth against my lips, censoring me, he was shoving against me, his body insistent as one side of an argument.

I slid my arm between us, against his throat, windpipe, and pried his head away. 'I'll get pregnant,' I said, 'it's the right time.' It was the truth, it stopped him: flesh making more flesh, miracle, that frightens all of them.

He reached the dock first, outdistancing me, his fury propelling the canoe like a motor. By the time I got there he had vanished.

Chapter Eighteen

There was no one in the cabin. It was different, larger, as though I hadn't been there for a long time: the half of me that had begun to return was not yet used to it. I went back outside and unhooked the gate of the fenced oblong and sat down on the swing, carefully, the ropes still held my weight; I swayed myself gently back and forth, keeping my feet on the ground. Rocks, trees, sandbox where I made houses with stones for windows. The birds were there, chickadees and jays; but they were wary of me, they weren't trained.

I turned the ring on my left-hand finger, souvenir: he gave it to me, plain gold, he said he didn't like ostentation, it got us into the motels easier, opener of doors; in the intervening time I wore it on a chain around my neck. The cold bathrooms, interchangeable, feel of tile on footsoles, walking into them wrapped in someone else's towel in the days of rubber sex, precautions. He would prop his watch on the night-tables to be sure he wasn't late.

For him I could have been anyone but for me he was unique, the first, that's where I learned. I worshipped him, non-child-bride, idolater, I kept the scraps of his handwriting like saints' relics, he never wrote letters, all I had was the criticism in red pencil he paperclipped to my drawings. CS and DS, he was an idealist, he said he didn't want our relationship as he called it to influence his aesthetic judgment. He didn't want our relationship to influence anything; it was to be kept separate from life. A certificate framed on the wall, his proof that he was still young.

He did say he loved me though, that part was true; I didn't make it up. It was the night I locked myself in and turned on the water in the bathtub and he cried on the other side of the door. When I gave up and came out he showed me snapshots of his wife and children, his reasons, his stuffed and mounted family, they had names, he said I should be mature.

I heard the thin dentist's-drill sound of a powerboat approaching, more Americans; I got off the swing and went halfway down the steps where I would be shielded by the trees. They slowed their motor and curved into the bay. I crouched and watched, at first I thought they were going to land: but they were only gazing, surveying, planning the attack and the takeover. They pointed up at the cabin and talked, flash of binoculars. Then they accelerated and headed off towards the cliff where the gods lived. But they wouldn't catch anything, they wouldn't be allowed. It was dangerous for them to go there without knowing about the power; they might hurt themselves, a false move, metal hooks lowered into the sacred water, that could touch it off like electricity or a grenade. I had endured it only because I had a talisman, my father had left me the guides, the man-animals and the maze of numbers.

It would be right for my mother to have left something for me also, a legacy. His was complicated, tangles, but hers would be simple as a hand, it would be final. I was not completed yet; there had to be a gift from each of them.

I wanted to search for it but David was jogging down the path from the outhouse. 'Hi,' he called, 'you seen Anna?'

'No,' I said. If I went back to the house or into the garden he would follow me and talk. I stood up and walked down the rest of the steps and ducked into the trail entrance through the long grass.

In the cool green among the trees, new trees and stumps, the stumps with charcoal crusts on them, scabby and crippled, survivors of an old disaster. Sight flowing ahead of me over the ground, eyes filtering the shapes, the names of things fading but their forms and uses remaining, the animals learned what to eat without nouns. Six leaves, three leaves, the root of this is crisp. White stems curved like question marks, fish-coloured in the dim light, corpse plants, inedible. Finger-shaped yellow fungi, unclassified, I never memorized all of them; and further along a mushroom with cup and ring and chalk gills and a name: Death Angel, deadly poison. Beneath it the invisible part, threadlike underground network of which this was the solid flower, temporary as an icicle, growth frozen; tomorrow it would be melted but the roots would stay. If our bodies lived in the earth with only the hair sprouting up through the leafmould it would seem as if that was all we were, filament plants.

The reason they invented coffins, to lock the dead in, preserve them, they put makeup on them; they didn't want them spreading or changing into anything else. The stone with the name and the date was on them to weight them down. She would have hated it, that box, she would have tried to get out; I ought to have stolen her out of that room and brought her here and let her go away by herself into the forest, she would have died anyway but quicker, lucidly, not in that glass case.

It sprang up from the earth, pure joy, pure death, burning white like snow.

The dry leaves shuffled behind me: he had shadowed me along the trail. 'Hi, whatcha doin'?' he said.

I didn't turn or speak but he didn't wait for an answer, he sat down beside me and said 'What's that?'

I had to concentrate in order to talk to him, the English words seemed imported, foreign; it was like trying to listen to two separate conversations, each interrupting the other. 'A mushroom,' I said. That wouldn't be enough, he would want a specific term. My mouth jumped like a stutterer's and the Latin appeared. 'Amanita.'

'Neat,' he said, but he wasn't interested. I willed him to go away but he didn't; after a while he put his hand on my knee.

'Well?' he said.

I looked at him. His smile was like a benevolent uncle's; under his forehead there was a plan, it corrugated the skin. I pushed his hand off and he put it back again.

'How about it?' he said. 'You wanted me to follow you.'

His fingers were squeezing, he was drawing away some of the power, I would lose it and come apart again, the lies would recapture. 'Please don't,' I said.

'Come on now, don't give me hassle,' he said. 'You're a groovy chick, you know the score, you aren't married.' He reached his arm around me, invading, and pulled me over towards him; his neck was creased and freckled, soon he would have jowls, he smelled like scalp. His moustache whisked my face.

I twisted away and stood up. 'Why are you doing this?' I said. 'You're interfering.' I wiped at my arm where he had touched it.

He didn't understand what I meant, he smiled even harder. 'Don't get uptight,' he said, 'I won't tell Joe. It'll be great, it's good for you, keeps you healthy,' Then he went 'Yuk, yuk' like Goofy.

He was speaking about it as though it was an exercising programme, athletic demonstration, ornamental swimming in a chlorine swimming pool noplace in California. 'It wouldn't keep me healthy,' I said, 'I'd get pregnant.'

He lifted his eyebrows, incredulous. 'You're putting me on,' he said, 'this is the twentieth century.'

'No it isn't,' I said. 'Not here,'

He stood up also and took a step towards me. I backed away. He was turning mottled pink, turkey neck, but his voice was still rational. 'Listen,' he said, 'I realize you walk around in never-never land but don't tell me you don't know where Joe is; he's not so noble, he's off in the bushes somewhere with cunt on four legs, right about now he's shoving it into her.' He glanced quickly at his wristwatch as though timing them; he seemed elated by what he'd said, his eyes gleamed like test-tubes.

'Oh,' I said; I thought about it for a minute. 'Maybe they love each other.' It would be logical, they were the ones who could. 'Do you love me,' I asked in case I hadn't understood him, 'is that why you want me to?'

He thought I was being either smart or stupid and said 'Christ.' Then he paused, aiming. 'You aren't going to let him get away with it, are you?' he said. 'Tit for tat as they say.' He folded his arms, resting his case, retaliation was his ultimate argument: he must have felt it was a duty, an obligation on my part, it would be justice. Geometrical sex, he needed me for an abstract principle; it would be enough for him if our genitals could be detached like two kitchen appliances and copulate in mid-air, that would complete his equation.

His wristwatch glittered, glass and silver: perhaps it was his dial, the key that wound him, the switch. There must be a phrase, a vocabulary that would work. 'I'm sorry,' I said, 'but you don't turn me on.'

'You,' he said, searching for words, not controlled any more, 'tight-ass bitch.'

The power flowed into my eyes, I could see into him, he was an imposter, a pastiche, layers of political handbills, pages from magazines, *affiches*, verbs and nouns glued on to him and shredding away, the original surface littered with fragments and tatters. In a black suit knocking on doors, young once, even that had been a costume, a uniform; now his hair was falling off and he didn't know what language to use, he'd forgotten his own, he had to copy. Second-hand American was spreading over him in patches, like mange or lichen. He was infested, garbled, and I couldn't help him: it would take such time to heal, unearth him, scrape down to were he was true.

'Keep it to yourself then,' he said, 'I'm not going to sit up and beg for a little third-rate cold tail.'

I detoured around past him, back towards the cabin. More than ever I needed to find it, the thing she had hidden; the power from my father's intercession wasn't enough to protect me, it gave only knowledge and there were more gods than his, his were the gods of the head, antlers rooted in the brain. Not only how to see but how to act.

I thought he would stay there, at least till I was out of range, but he followed along behind me. 'Sorry I blew my cool,' he said. His voice had changed again, now it was deferential. 'It's between us, okay? No need to mention it to Anna, right?' If he'd succeeded he would have told her as soon as he could. 'I respect you for it, I really do.'

'That's all right,' I said; I knew he was lying.

They sat around the table in the regular places and I served dinner. There hadn't been any lunch but no one mentioned that.

'What time is Evans coming tomorrow?' I said.

'Ten, ten-thirty,' David said. 'Have a nice afternoon?' he said to Anna. Joe stuck a new potato with his fork and put it into his mouth.

'Fantastic,' Anna said. 'I got some sun and finished my book, then I had a long talk with Joe and went for a stroll.' Joe chewed, his closed mouth moving, silent refutation. 'And you?'

'Great,' David said, his voice buoyant, inflated. He bent his arm onto the table, his hand brushing mine casually, as though by accident, for her to see. I flinched away, he was lying about me, the animals don't lie.

Anna smiled mournfully at him. I watched him, he wasn't laughing, he was staring at her, the lines in his face deepening and sagging. They know everything about each other, I thought, that's why they're so sad; but Anna was more than sad, she was desperate, her body her only weapon and she was fighting for her life, he was her life, her life was the fight: she was fighting him because if she ever surrendered the balance of power would be broken and he would go elsewhere. To continue the war.

I didn't want to join. 'It's not what you think,' I said to Anna. 'He asked me to but I wouldn't.' I wanted to tell her I hadn't acted against her.

Her eyes flicked from him to me. 'That was pure of you,' she said. I'd made a mistake, she resented me because I hadn't given in, it commented on her.

'She's pure all right,' David said, 'she's a little purist.'

'Joe told me she won't put out for him any more,' Anna said, still looking at me. Joe didn't say anything; he was eating another potato.

'She hates men,' David said lightly. 'Either that or she wants to be one. Right?'

A ring of eyes, tribunal; in a minute they would join hands and dance around me, and after that the rope and the pyre, cure for heresy.

Maybe it was true, I leafed through all the men I had known to see whether or not I hated them. But then I realized it wasn't the men I hated, it was the Americans, the human beings, men and women both. They'd had their chance but they had turned against the gods, and it was time for me to choose sides. I wanted there to be a machine that could make them vanish, a button I could press that would evaporate them without disturbing anything else, that way there would be more room for the animals, they would be rescued.

'Aren't you going to answer?' Anna said, taunting.

'No,' I said.

Anna said, 'God, she really is inhuman,' and they both laughed a little, sorrowfully.

Chapter Nineteen

I cleared the table and scraped the canned ham fat scraps from the plates into the fire, food for the dead. If you fed them enough they would come back; or was it the reverse, if you fed them enough they would stay away, it was in one of the books but I'd forgotten.

Anna said she would wash the dishes. It was an apology perhaps, reparation for the fact that she'd found it easier to fight on his side than against him. For once. She rattled the cutlery in the pan, singing to avoid discussion, we were beyond the time for confidences; her voice occupied the room, territorial.

It had to be inside the house. Before supper I searched the toolshed, while I was getting the shovel, and the garden when I dug up the potatoes; but it wasn't there, I would have recognized it. It had to be something out of place, something that wasn't here when I left, apple in the row of oranges like the old arithmetic workbooks. She would have brought it here especially for me and hidden it where I would discover it when I was ready; like my father's puzzle it would mediate, we cannot approach them directly. I dried the dishes as Anna washed, inspecting each one to make sure it was familiar. But nothing had been added since I'd been here, the gift was not a dish.

It wasn't anywhere in the main room. When we'd finished I went into David's and Anna's room: her leather jacket was there, hanging up, it hadn't been put back since the trip. I examined the pockets; there was nothing in them but an empty metal aspirin container and an ancient kleenex, and the husks from sunflower seeds; and a charred filter from one of Anna's cigarettes, which I dropped on the floor and crushed with my foot.

My room was the only one remaining. As soon as I stepped inside it I sensed the power, in my hands and running along my arms, I was close to it. I scanned the walls and shelves, it wasn't there; my painted ladies watched me with their bristling eyes. Then I was certain: it was in the scrapbooks, I'd shoved them under the mattress without reading through all of them. They were the last possibility and they weren't supposed to be here, they belonged in the city, in the trunk.

I heard a motor droning from down the lake, a different pitch, deeper than a powerboat.

'Hey look,' Anna called from the main room, 'A big boat!' We went out on the point: it was a police launch like the ones driven by the game wardens, they were checking us they way they used to, to see if we had any dead fish and a licence to go with them; it was routine.

The launch slowed and drew into the dock. David was down there anyway, I would let him meet it, he was the one with the papers. I re-entered the house and stood by the window. Anna, inquisitive, sauntered down to join them.

There were two men, police or probably game wardens, they were wearing ordinary clothes; and a third man, blond, Claude from the village probably, and a fourth one, older, the size of Paul. It was odd that Paul was on the launch: if he were coming for a visit he would bring his own boat. David shook hands with them and they clustered on the dock, talking in low voices. David dug into his pocket, for the licence; then he scratched his neck as if worried. Joe appeared from the outhouse path and the talking started over again; Anna's head turned up towards me.

Then I saw David hurrying, taking the hill steps two at a time. The screen door banged shut behind him. 'They found your father,' he said, breathing hard from the climb. He squinted his face, as if to show sympathy.

The door slammed again, it was Anna; he put his arm around her and they both studied me with the intent pouncing look they'd had at supper.

'Oh,' I said. 'Where?'

'Some American guys found him in the lake. They were fishing, they hooked him by mistake; the body was unrecognizable but an old guy named Paul something-or-other down there, says he knows you, he identified the clothes. They figured he'd fallen off a cliff or something, he had a skull fracture.' Seedy department-store magician, producing my father out of nowhere like a stuffed rabbit out of a hat.

'Where?' I said again.

'It's awful,' Anna said, 'I'm really sorry.'

'They don't know where it happened,' David said, 'he must've drifted; he had a camera around his neck, big one, they think the weight kept him down or he would've been found sooner.' His eyes gloating.

It was clever of him to have guessed the missing camera, since I'd told them nothing. He must have thought quickly in order to make it all up in such a short time: I knew it was a lie, he was doing it to get back at me. 'Did they ask to see your fishing licence?' I said.

'No,' he said, faking surprise. 'You want to talk to them?'

That was a risk, he should have calculated better, it would expose his whole construction. Maybe that's what he wanted, maybe it was intended as a practical joke. I decided to act as though I believed him, see how he'd get out of it. 'No,' I said, 'tell them I'm too upset. I'll speak to Paul tomorrow when we get to the village, about the arrangements.' That was what they were called, the arrangements. 'He'd want to be buried around here.' Convincing details, if he could invent I could invent also, I'd read enough murder mysteries. The detectives, eccentric hermits, orchid-raisers, sharp bluehaired old ladies, girls with jackknives and flashlights, for them everything fitted. But not in real life, I wanted to tell him, you've outsmarted yourself.

He and Anna glanced at each other: they'd planned on hurting me. 'Okay,' he said.

Anna said, 'Wouldn't you rather ...' and then stopped. They walked back down the steps, disappointed both of them, their trap had failed.

I went into the other room and took the scrapbooks out from under the mattress. There was still enough light to see by but I closed my eyes, touching the covers with my hands, fingertips. One of them was heavier and warmer; I lifted it, let it fall open. My mother's gift was there for me, I could look.

The rest of the scrapbook had early people, hairs blazing out of their heads like rays or spikes, and suns with faces, but the gift itself was a loose page, the edge torn, the figures drawn in crayon. On the left was a woman with a round moon stomach: the baby was sitting up inside her gazing out. Opposite her was a man with horns on his head like cow horns and a barbed tail.

The picture was mine, I had made it. The baby was myself before I was born, the man was God, I'd drawn him when my brother learned in the winter about the Devil and God: if the Devil was allowed a tail and horns, God needed them also, they were advantages.

That was what the pictures had meant then but their first meaning was lost now like the meanings of the rock paintings. They were my guides, she had saved them for me, pictographs, I had to read their new meaning with the help of the power. The gods, their likenesses: to see them in their true shape is fatal. While you are human; but after the transformation they could be reached. First I had to immerse myself in the other language.

Launch vibration, going away. I slid the page back into the scrapbook and replaced it under the mattress. Trample of the others on the hill, I stayed inside the room.

They lit the lamp. Noise of David fumbling and then the cards, he was laying out a game of solitaire; then Anna's voice, she wanted to set up the other deck. They were playing doubles, slapping the cards down expertly as gamblers, monosyllables as they gained or lost. Joe sat in the corner on the bench, I could hear him scuffling against the wall.

For him truth might still be possible, what will preserve him is the absence of words; but the others are already turning to metal, skins galvanizing, heads congealing to brass knobs, components and intricate wires ripening inside. The cards tick on the table.

I unclose my fist, releasing, it becomes a hand again, palm a network of trails, lifeline, past present and future, the break in it closing together as I purse my fingers. When the heartline and the headline are one, Anna told us, you are either a criminal, an idiot or a saint. How to act.

Their voices murmur, they can't discuss me, they know I'm listening. They're avoiding me, they find me inappropriate; they think I should be filled with death, I should be in mourning. But nothing has died, everything is alive, everything is waiting to become alive.

THREE

Chapter Twenty

The sunset was red, a clear tulip colour paling to flesh webs, membrane, Now there are only streaks of it, mauve and purple, sky visible through the window, divided by the window squares and then by the interlacing branches, leaves overlapping leaves. I'm in the bed, covered up, clothes in a pile on the floor, he will be here soon, they can't postpone it forever.

Mumbles, cards gathered, swish and spit of teeth being brushed. Blown breath and guttering, the lamp goes out, the flashlight beams wash over the ceiling. He opens the door and stands hesitating, darkening the light he holds, after the morning and the afternoon he isn't sure how to approach me. I feign sleep and he feels his way into the room, stealthy as moss, and unzips his human skin.

He thinks I'm in pain, he wants to evade it, he bends himself away from me; but I stroke him, move my hand over his body, he's startled because I'm awake. After a minute he turns to me stiffening, arms going around me and over me and I smell Anna on him, suntan lotion and pink face grease and smoke, but that doesn't matter; what matters is the other smell, smells, the sheets, wool and soap, chemically treated hides, I can't here. I sit up, swing my legs out of the bed.

'Now what?' he says, whispers.

I tug at his hands. 'Not here.'

'Christ!' He tries to pull me back down but I brace my legs, hooking them onto the side.

'Don't talk,' I say.

He stumbles out of the bed then and follows me, from this room to the other and across the outer floor. When I've unlatched the screen door and the wooden door I take his hand: there is something outside which I have protection against but he doesn't, I have to keep him close to me, inside the radius.

We go over the ground, feet and skin bare; the moon is rising, in the greygreen light his body gleams and the trunks of trees, the white ovals of his eyes. He walks as though blind, blundering into the shadow clumps, toes stubbing, he had not yet learned to see in the dark. My tentacled feet and free hand scent out the way, shoes are a barrier between touch and the earth. Double thump, clutched heartbeat: rabbits, warning us and each other. On the far shore an owl, its voice feathered and clawed, black on black, blood in the heart.

I lie down, keeping the moon on my left hand and the absent sun on my right. He kneels, he is shivering, the leaves under and around us are damp from the dew, or is it the lake, soaking up through the rock and sand, we are near the shore, the small waves riffle. He needs to grow more fur.

'What is it?' he says. 'What's wrong?' My hands are on his shoulders, he is thick, undefined, outline but no features, hair and beard a mane, moon behind him. He turns to curve over me; his eyes glint, he is shaking, fear or tensed flesh or the cold. I pull him down, his beard and hair fall over me like ferns, mouth as soft as water. Heavy on me, warm stone, almost alive.

'I love you,' he says into the side of my neck, catechism. Teeth grinding, he's holding back, he wants it to be like the city, baroque scrollwork, intricate as a computer, but I'm impatient, pleasure is redundant, the animals don't have pleasure. I guide him into me, it's the right season, I hurry.

He trembles and then I can feel my lost child surfacing within me, forgiving me, rising from the lake where it has been prisoned for so long, its eyes and teeth phosphorescent; the two halves clasp, interlocking like fingers, it buds, it sends out fronds. This time I will do it by myself, squatting, on old newspapers in a corner alone; or on leaves, dry leaves a heap of them, that's cleaner. The baby will slip out easily as an egg, a kitten, and I'll lick it off and bite the cord, the blood returning to the ground where it belongs; the moon will be full, pulling. In the morning I will be able to see it: it will be covered with shining fur, a god, I will never teach it any words.

I press my arms around him, smoothing his back; I'm grateful to him, he's given me the part of himself I needed. I'll take him back to the cabin, through the force that presses in on us now like deepsea on a diver, then I can let him go.

'Is it all right?' he says. He's lying on top of me, breathing, molten. 'Was it all right?'

He means two different things; but 'Yes' I say, answer to a third question, unasked. Nobody must find out or they will do that to me again, strap me to the death machine, emptiness machine, legs in the metal framework, secret knives. This time I won't let them.

'Then it's okay,' he says; he's leaning on his elbows, with his fingers and lips he soothes me, my cheek, hair. 'It wasn't anything this afternoon, it didn't mean anything; it was her that wanted it.' He rolls off me, lies beside me, nuzzling against my shoulder for warmth; he's shivering again. 'Shit,' he says, 'it's bloody freezing.' Then, cautiously, 'Now do you?'

It's love, the ritual word, he wants to know again; but I can't give redemption, even as a lie. We both wait for my answer. The winds moves, rustling of tree lungs, water lapping all around us.

Chapter Twenty-one

When I wake up it's morning, we're in the bed again. He is awake already, head hovering above me, he was surveying me while I slept. He smiles, a plump smile, contented, his beard puffed up like a singing toad throat, and lowers his face to kiss me. He still doesn't understand, he thinks he has won, act of his flesh a rope noosed around my neck, leash, he will lead me back to the city and tie me to fences, doorknobs.

'You slept in,' he says. He begins to shift himself over onto me but I look at the sun, it's late, eight-thirty almost. In the main room I can hear metal on metal, they're up.

'There's no hurry,' he says, but I push him away and get dressed.

Anna is making food, scraping a spoon in the frying pan. She has her purple tunic on and her white bellbottoms, urban costume, and her makeup is slabbed down over her face like a visor.

'I thought I'd do it,' she says, 'so you two could sleep in.' She must have heard the door opening and closing in the night; she produces a smile, warm, conspiratorial, and I know what circuits are closing in her head: by screwing Joe she's brought us back together. Saving the world, everyone wants to; men think they can do it with guns, women with their bodies, love conquers all, conquerors love all, mirages raised by words.

She dishes out breakfast. It's baked beans from a can, the usual morning food is gone.

'Pork and beans and musical fruit, the more you eat the more you toot,' David says and quacks like Daffy Duck, jaunty, mimicking satisfaction.

Anna helps him, co-operative community life; she taps him on the knuckles with her fork and says 'Oh you.' Then she remembers and adjusts to her Tragedy mask: 'How long will it take you, in the village I mean?'

'I don't know,' I say. 'Not very long.'

We pack and I help them carry the baggage down, my own also, caseful of alien words and failed pictures, canvas bundle of clothes, nothing I need. They sit on the dock talking; Anna is smoking, she's reduced to the last one.

'Christ,' she says, 'I'll be glad to hit the city. Stock up again.'

I go up the steps once more to make sure they haven't left anything. The jays are there, flowing from tree to tree, voices semaphoring, tribal; they retreat to the upper branches, they still haven't decided whether I can be trusted. The cabin is the way we found it; when Evans arrives I'll snap the lock.

'You should take the canoes up before he comes,' I say when I'm back down. 'They go in the toolshed.'

'Right,' David says. He consults his watch, but they don't get up. They have the camera out, they're discussing the movie; the zipper bag of equipment is beside them, the tripod, the reels of film in their cannisters.

'I figure we can start cutting it in two or three weeks,' David says, his version of a pro. 'We'll take it into the lab first thing.'

'There's part of a reel left,' Anna says. 'You should get her, you got me but never got her.' She looks at me, fumes ascending from her nose and mouth.

'Now that's an idea,' David says. 'The rest of us are in it, she's the only one who isn't.' He assesses me. 'Where would we fit her in though? We don't have anyone fucking yet; but I'd have to do it,' he says to Joe, 'we need you running the camera.'

'I could run the camera,' Anna says, 'you could both do it,' and everyone laughs.

They get up after a while and hoist the red canoe, one at each end, and carry it up the hill. I stay with Anna on the dock.

'Is my nose peeling?' she says, rubbing it. From her handbag she takes a round gilt compact with violets on the cover. She opens it, unclosing her other self, and runs her fingertip around the corners of her mouth, left one, right one; then she unswivels a pink stick and dots her cheeks and blends them, changing her shape, performing the only magic left to her.

Rump on a packsack, harem cushion, pink on the cheeks and black discreetly around the eyes, as red as blood as black as ebony, a seamed and folded imitation of a magazine picture that is itself an imitation of a woman who is also an imitation, the original nowhere, hairless lobed angel in the same heaven where God is a circle, captive princess in someone's head. She is locked in, she isn't allowed to eat or shit or cry or give birth, nothing goes in, nothing comes out. She takes her clothes off or puts them on, paper doll wardrobe, she copulates under strobe lights with the man's torso while his brain watches from its glassed-in control cubicle at the other end of the room, her face twists into poses of exultation and total abandonment, that is all. She is not bored, she has no other interests.

Anna sits, darkness in her eye sockets, skull with a candle. She clicks the compact shut and stubs out her cigarette against the dock; I remember the way she was crying, climbing up the sand hill, it was yesterday, since then she has crystallized. The machine is gradual, it takes a little of you at a time, it leaves the shell. It was all right as long as they stuck to dead things, the dead can defend themselves, to be half dead is worse. They did it to each other also, without knowing.

I unzip the bag with the camera equipment and lift out the cannisters of film.

'What're you doing?' Anna says, listlessly however.

I unwind the film, standing full in the sun, and let it spiral into the lake. 'You better not do that,' Anna says, 'they'll kill you.' But she doesn't interfere, she doesn't call them.

When I've unravelled the reels I open the back of the camera.

The film coils onto the sand under the water, weighted down by its containers; the invisible captured images are swimming away into the lake like tadpoles, Joe and David beside their defeated log, axemen, arms folded, Anna with no clothes on jumping off the end of the dock, finger up, hundreds of tiny naked Annas no longer bottled and shelved.

I study her to see if her release has made any difference, but the green eyes regard me unaltered from the enamel face. 'They'll get you,' she says, doleful as a prophet. 'You shouldn't have done it.'

They're at the top of the hill now, coming back for the other canoe. I run quickly towards it, flip it over right side up, throw a paddle inside and drag it along the dock.

'Hey!' David calls. 'What're you doing?' They're almost here, Anna watches me, biting a knuckle, she can't decide whether or not to tell: if she keeps quiet they'll treat her as an accomplice.

I slide the canoe stern first into the water, squat, step in, shove.

'She dumped out your film,' Anna says behind me.

I push the blade into the water, I don't turn, I can hear them peering down into the lake.

'Shit,' David says, 'shit, shit, oh shit, why the shit didn't you stop her?'

When I'm as far as the sand point I look back. Anna stands, arms slack at her sides, uninvolved; David is kneeling, his hands fishing in the water, pulling up the film in spaghetti handfuls though he must know it's futile, everything has escaped.

Joe is not there. He appears then at the top of the sand cliff, running, halting. He yells my name, furiously: if he had a rock he would throw it.

The canoe glides, carrying the two of us, around past the leaning trees and out of range. It's too late for them to get the other canoe and follow; probably they haven't thought of it, surprise attacks work by confusing. The direction is clear. I see I've been planning this, for how long I can't tell.

I go along near the trees, boat and arms one movement, amphibian; the water closes behind me no track. The land bends and we bend with it, a narrowing and then a space and I'm safe, hidden in the shore maze.

Here there are boulders; they loom under the water, brown shadows like clouds or threats, barricade. Slope of ground on either side, rock hung with creepers. The lake floor, once land floor, slants upwards, so shallow now a motor could not pass. Another turning and I'm in the bay, landlocked swamp, layer of tepid water with reeds and cat-tails nosing up through the black vegetable ooze, around the sawed stumps of the once tower-high trees. This is where I threw the dead things and rinsed the tins and jars.

I float, no need to paddle. Further in, the trees they didn't cut before the flood are marooned, broken and grey-white, tipped on their sides, their giant contorted roots bleached and skinless; on the sodden trunks are colonies of plants, feeding on disintegration, laurel, sundew the insect-eater, its toenail-sized leaves sticky with red hairs. Out of the leaf nests the flowers rise, pure white, flesh of gnats and midges, petals now, metamorphosis.

I lie down on the bottom of the canoe and wait. The still water gathers the heat; birds, off in the forest a woodpecker, somewhere a thrush. Through the trees the sun glances; the swamp around me smoulders, energy of decay turning to growth, green fire. I remember the heron; by now it will be insects, frogs, fish, other herons. My body also changes, the creature in me, plant-animal, sends out filaments in me; I ferry it secure between death and life, I multiply.

The motor approaching wakes me: it's out on the lake, it will be Evans. I beach the canoe, knot the rope to a tree. They won't be expecting me, not from this direction; I have to make sure they leave with him as they should, it would be their way to pretend but stay behind to catch me when I come back.

It's less than a quarter of a mile through the trees, swerving to avoid branches, careful where I step, along the vestiges of the coded trail to where the laboratory shelves were, if I didn't know the trail was there I could never find it. As Evans' boat pulls into the dock I am behind them, near the piled wood, head down and lying flat, I can see them through the screen of plant stems.

They stoop, they're loading the things into the boat. I wonder if they're taking mine as well, my clothes, fragments of pictures.

They stand talking with Evans, their voices low, inaudible; but they'll be explaining, they'll have to invent some reason, accident, say why I'm not with them. They will be plotting, a strategy for recapture; or will they really go off and discard me, vanish into the catacombs of the city, giving me up for lost, stashing me away in their heads with all the obsolete costumes and phrases? For them I'll soon be ancient as crew cuts and world war songs, a half-remembered face in a highschool year-book, a captured enemy medal: memorabilia, or possibly not even that.

Joe comes up the steps, shouting; Anna shouts too, shrill, like a train whistle before departure, my name. It's too late, I no longer have a name. I tried for all those years to be civilized but I'm not and I'm through pretending.

Joe goes around to the front of the cabin, concealed from me. After a minute he reappears, stumping back down the hill to them, shoulders sloped in defeat. Perhaps by now he understands.

They clamber into the boat. Anna pauses for a moment, turned directly towards me, face in the sunlight puzzled, oddly forlorn: does she see me, is she going to wave goodbye? Then the others reach out hands to her and lift her in, a gesture that looks from a distance almost like love.

The boat chugs backwards into the bay, then swings into forward and roars. Bullhead Evans at the wheel, checkshirted and stolid, American, they are all Americans now. But they are really going, really gone, a ringing in my ears and then a silence. I get to my feet slowly, my body is cramped from not moving; on the bare flesh of my legs are the imprints of leaves and twigs.

I walk to the hill and scan the shoreline, finding the place, opening, where they disappeared: checking, reassuring. It's true, I am by myself; this is what I wanted, to stay here alone. From any rational point of view I am absurd; there are no longer any rational points of view.

Chapter Twenty-two

They've locked the doors, on the toolshed, on the cabin; it was Joe, he may have assumed I'd take the canoe to the village. No, it was ill will. I shouldn't have left the keys hanging on the nail, I should have put them in my pocket. But it was stupid of them to think they could keep me out. Soon they will reach the village, the car, the city; what are they saying about me now? That I was running away; but to go with them would have been running away, the truth is here.

I stand on the front step and lean sideways, clutching the windowledge, looking in. The canvas packsack with my clothes had been moved, it's back inside now, on the table with my case; beside it is Anna's detective novel, her last one, cold comfort but comfort, death is logical, there's always a motive. Perhaps that's why she read them, for the theology.

Sun gone, sky darkening, it may rain later. Clouds building over the hills, anvils, ominous hammerheads, it will be a storm; it might miss though, sometimes they eddy for days, approaching but never striking. I'll have to get inside. Breaking into my own house, go in and out the window they used to sing, holding their arms up like bridges; as we have done before.

The handbarrow is underneath the cabin, beside the stacked wood where it was always kept, two poles with boards nailed across like rungs. I haul it out and prop it against the wall under the window, the one with no screen. The window is hooked on the inside at the corners, I'll have to break four of the little squares of glass. I do it with a rock, my head turned away, eyes closed because of the splinters. I reach carefully in through the jagged holes and undo the hooks and lift the window inwards onto the couch. If I could open the toolshed I could use the screw-driver to take the padlock hasp off the door, but the toolshed has no windows. Axe and machete inside it, saw, metal utensils.

I step on the couch and then on the floor, I'm in. I sweep up the broken glass; after that I hook the window back in place. It will be a nuisance, climbing in and out, removing the window each time, but the other windows have screens and I've nothing to cut them with. I could try the knife: if I had to leave in a hurry it would be better to use one of the back windows, they're nearer the ground.

I've succeeded; I don't know what to do now. I pause in the middle of the room, listening: no wind, stillness, held breath of the lake, the trees.

To be busy I unpack my clothes again and hang them on the nails in my room. My mother's jacket is back, I last saw it in Anna's room, it's been shifted. My footsteps are the only sounds, reverberation of shoes on wood.

There must be something that comes next but the power has drained away, my fingers are empty as gloves, eyes ordinary, nothing guides me.

I sit down at the table and leaf through an old magazine, shepherds knitting their own socks, weather gnarling their faces, women in laced bodices and red lipstick balancing washing baskets on their heads, smiling to show their teeth and happiness; rubber plantations and deserted temples, jungle crawling over the serene carved gods. Ring from a wet cup on the cover, printed there yesterday or ten years ago.

I open a can of peaches and eat two of the yellow fibrous halves, sugary juice dribbling from the spoon. Then I lie down on the couch and sleep descends over my face, black oblong, dreamless.

When I wake up the diffused light outside is further west, it feels late, it must be almost six, dinner hour; David had the only watch. Hunger is there in me, a contained whimper. I unhook the window and climb out, one foot on the wobbling handbarrow, scraping my knee as I let myself drop to the ground. I should build a ladder; but there are no implements, no boards.

I go down to the garden. I've forgotten the knife and the bowl but they aren't needed, fingers wll do. I unlatch the gate, the chicken wire walls are around me; outside the fence the trees droop as though wilting, the plants inside are pale in the greyish light; the air is heavy, oppressive. I start to pull up the onions and the carrots.

I'm crying finally, it's the first time, I watch myself doing it: I'm crouching down beside the lettuces, flowers finished now, gone to seed, my breath knots, my body tightens against it; the water fills my mouth, fish taste. But I'm not mourning, I'm accusing them, *Why did you*? They chose it, they had control over their death, they decided it was time to leave and they left, they set up this barrier. They didn't consider how I would feel, who would take care of me. I'm furious because they let it happen.

'Here I am,' I call. 'I'm here!' Voice rising and rising with the frustration and then the terror of hearing no answer, the time we were playing after supper and I hid too well, too far away and they couldn't find me. The treetrunks are so much alike, the same size, the same colour, impossible to retrace the path, instead locate the sun, the direction, whichever way you go you're bound to hit water. The dangerous thing is to panic, to walk in circles.

'I'm here!' But nothing happens. I wipe the salt off my face, my fingers earth-smeared.

If I will it, if I pray, I can bring them back. They're here now, I can sense them waiting, beyond sight on the path or in the long grass outside the fence, they are pulling against me but I can make them come out, from wherever it is they are hiding.

I start a fire in the stove and cook the food in the darkening room. There's no reason to set out plates; I eat from the pot and the frying pan with a spoon. I'll save the dirty dishes till there are enough; when the dishwasher pail is full I will have to lower it through the window with a rope.

I climb out again and set the scraps from the tinned meat on the tray for the birds. Deep grey, the clouds descending, closing in; the puffs of wind have begun, they advance across the lake like shudders; to the south there's a column of rain. Flickers of light but no thunder, gust of leaves.

I walk up the hill to the outhouse, forcing myself to go slowly, holding the panic at a distance, looking at it. Inside I hook the door shut, it's doors I'm afraid of because I can't see through them, it's the door opening by itself in the wind I'm afraid of. I run back down the path, telling myself to stop it, I'm old enough, I'm old.

The power would have protected me but it's gone, exhausted, no more use now than silver bullets or the sign of the cross. But the house will defend me, it's the right shape. Back inside I put the window up again, hooking it to the frame, barricading myself in, wood bars. The four broken panes, how can I close them. I try stuffing them with pages torn from the magazines and crumpled, *National Geographic, Macleans*, but it doesn't work, the holes are too big, the wads of paper fall to the floor. If only I had nails, a hammer.

I light the lamp but the air drafting in through the broken window makes it flutter and turn blue, and with the lamp on I can't see what's happening outside. I blow it out and sit in darkness, listening to the gush of the wind, but it doesn't rain.

After a while I decide to go to bed. I'm not tired, I slept in the afternoon, but there's nothing else to do. In my room I stand for a long time wondering why I'm afraid to take off my clothes: and I worried that they'll come back for me, if they do I'll have to get out quickly: but they wouldn't try it in a storm, Evens knows better than that, the open lake is the worst place because of the electricity, flesh and water both conduct.

I tie back the curtain so there will be more light. My mother's jacket is hanging on a nail beside the window, there's nobody in it; I press my forehead against it. Leather smell, the smell of loss; irrecoverable. But I can't think about that. I lie down on the bed in my clothes and in a moment the first rain hits the roof. It patters, changes to a steady drumming, sound of an avalanche, surrounding. I feel the lake rising, up over the shore and the hill, the trees toppling into it like sand collapsing, roots overturned, the house unmoored and floating like a boat, rocking and rocking.

In the middle of the night silence wakes me, the rain has stopped. Blank dark, I can see nothing, I try to move my hands but I can't. The fear arrives like waves, like footfalls, it has no center; it encloses me like armour, it's my skin that is afraid, rigid. They want to get in, they want me to open the windows, the door, they can't do it by themselves. I'm the only one, they are depending on me but I don't know any longer who they are; however they come back they won't be the same, they will have changed. I willed it, I called to them, that they should arrive is logical; but logic is a wall, I built it, on the other side is terror.

Above on the roof is the finger-tapping of water dripping from the trees. I hear breathing, withheld, observant, not in the house but all around it.

Chapter Twenty-three

In the morning I remember the window outline, beginning to emerge; I must have been watching till nearly dawn. Then I think it might have been a dream, the kind that creates the illusion of being awake.

For breakfast I eat canned stew, heating it first in a pot, and instant coffee. There are too many windows, I move so I'm sitting on the wall bench, from there I can see all of them.

I stack the dishes in the pan with the ones from last night and pour the rest of the hot water over them. Then I turn to the mirror to brush my hair.

But when I pick up the brush there is a surge of fear in my hand, the power is there again in a different form, it must have seeped up through the ground during the lightning. I know that the brush is forbidden, I must stop being in the mirror. I look for the last time at my distorted glass face: eyes lightblue in dark red skin, hair standing tangled out from my head, reflection intruding between my eyes and vision. Not to see myself but to see. I reverse the mirror so it's toward the wall, it no longer traps me, Anna's soul closed in the gold compact, that and not the camera is what I should have broken.

I unfasten the window and go out; at once the fear leaves me like a hand lifting from my throat. There must be rules: places I'm permitted to be, other places I'm not. I'll have to listen carefully, if I trust them they will tell me what is allowed. I ought to have let them in, it may have been the only chance they will give me.

The enclosure with the swing and the sandpile is forbidden, I know that without touching it. I walk down to the lake. It is flat calm, the water is pollen-streaked, mist is drifting up off the bays and from behind the islands, the sun burning it away as it rises, the sun itself hot and bright as light through a lens. Something glimmers out on the surface, a swimming animal or a dead log; when there is no wind things venture out from the shore. The air smells of earth, midsummer.

I step on the dock: the fear says No, I can be near the lake but not on the dock. I wash my hands from the flat stone. If I do everything in the right order, if I think of nothing else. What sacrifice, what do they want?

When I'm certain I've guessed what is required I go back to the cabin, enter it. The fire I made for breakfast is still smouldering: I add another stick of wood and open the draft.

I snap the catches on my case and take out the drawings and the typescript, *Quebec Folk Tales*, it's easily replaceable for them in the city, and my bungled princesses, the Golden Phoenix awkward and dead as a mummified parrot. The pages bunch in my hands; I add them one by one so the fire will not be smothered, then the paint tubes and brushes, this is no longer my future. There must be some way of cancelling the samsonite case, it can't be burned. I draw the big knife across it, x-ing it out.

I slip the ring from my left hand, non-husband, he is the next thing I must discard finally, and drop it into the fire, altar, it may not melt but it will at least be purified, the blood will burn off. Everything from history must be eliminated, the circles and the arrogant square pages. I rummage under the mattress and bring out the scrapbooks, ripping them up, the ladies, dress forms with decorated china heads, the suns and the moons, the rabbits and their archaic eggs, my false peace, his wars, aeroplanes and tanks and the helmeted explorers; perhaps at the other side of the world my brother feels the weight lifting, freedom feathering his arms. Even the guides, the miraculous double woman and the god with horns, they must be translated. The ladies on the wall too with their watermelon breasts and lampshade skirts, all my artifacts.

Theirs too, the map torn from the wall, the rock paintings, left to me by my father's will; and the album, the sequence of my mother's life, the confining photographs. My own faces curl, blacken, the imitation mother and father change to flat ashes. It is time that separates us, I was a coward, I would not let them into my age, my place. Now I must enter theirs.

When the paper things are burned I smash the glasses and plates and the chimney of the lamp. I rip one page from each of the books, Boswell and *The Mystery at Sturbridge*, the Bible and the common mushrooms and *Log Cabin Construction*, to burn through all the words would take too long. Everything I can't break, frying pan, enamel bowl, spoons and forks, I throw on the floor. After that I use the big knife to slash once through the blankets, the sheets and the beds and the tents and at the end my own clothes and my mother's grey leather jacket, my father's grey felt hat, the raincoats: these husks are not needed any longer, I abolish them, I have to clear a space.

When nothing is left intact and the fire is only smouldering I leave, carrying one of the wounded blankets with me, I will need it until the fur grows. The house shuts with a click behind me.

I untie my feet from the shoes and walk down to the shore; the earth is damp, cold, pockmarked with raindrops. I pile the blanket on the rock and step into the water and lie down. When every part of me is wet I take off my clothes, peeling them away from my flesh like wallpaper. They sway beside me, inflated, the sleeves bladders of air.

My back is on the sand, my head rests against the rock, innocent as plankton; my hair spreads out, moving and fluid in the water. The earth rotates, holding my body down to it as it holds the moon; the sun pounds in the sky, red flames and rays pulsing from it, searing away the wrong form that encases me, dry rain soaking through me, warming the blood egg I carry. I dip my head beneath the water, washing my eyes.

Inshore a loon; it lowers its head, then lifts it again and calls. It sees me but it ignores me, accepts me as part of the land.

When I am clean I come up out of the lake, leaving my false body floated on the surface, a cloth decoy; it jiggles in the waves I make, nudges gently against the dock.

They offered clothing as a token, formerly; that was partial but the gods are demanding, absolute, they want all.

The sun is three-quarters, I have become hungry. The food in the cabin is forbidden, I'm not allowed to go back into that cage, wooden rectangle. Also tin cans and jars are forbidden; they are glass and metal. I head for the garden and prowl through it, then squat, wrapped in my blanket. I eat the green peas out of their shells and the raw yellow beans, I scrape the carrots from the earth with my fingers, I will wash them in the lake first. There is one late strawberry, I find it among the matted weeds and suckers. Red foods, heart colour, they are the best kind, they are sacred; then yellow, then blue; green foods are mixed from blue and yellow. I pull up one of the beets and scratch the dirt from it and gnaw at it but the rind is tough, I'm not strong enough yet.

At sunset I devour the washed carrots, taking them from the grass where I've concealed them, and part of a cabbage. The outhouse is forbidden so I leave my dung, droppings, on the ground and kick earth over. All animals with dens do that.

I hollow a lair near the woodpile, dry leaves underneath and dead branches leaned over, with fresh needle branches woven to cover. Inside it I curl with the blanket over my head. There are mosquitoes, they bite through; it's best not to slap them, the blood smell brings others. I sleep in relays like a cat, my stomach hurts. Around me the space rustles; owl sound, across the lake or inside me, distance contracts. A light wind, the small waves talking against the shore, multilingual water.

Chapter Twenty-four

The light wakes me, speckled through the roof branches. My bones ache, hunger is loose in me, belly a balloon, floating shark stomach. It's hot, the sun is almost at noon, I've slept most of the morning. I crawl outside and run towards the garden where the food is.

The gate stops me. Yesterday I could go in but not today: they are doing it gradually. I lean against the fence, my feet pawprinting the mud damp from the rain, the dew, the lake oozing up through the ground. Then my belly cramps and I step to one side and lie down in the long grass. A frog is there, leopard frog with green spots and gold-rimmed eyes, ancestor. It includes me, it shines, nothing moves but its throat breathing.

I rest on the ground, head propped on hands, trying to forget the hunger, looking through the wire hexagons at the garden: rows, squares, stakes, markers. The plants are flourishing, they grow almost visibly, sucking moisture up through the roots and succulent stems, their leaves sweating, flushed in the sunrays to a violent green, weeds and legitimate plants alike, there is no difference. Under the ground the worms twine, pink veins.

The fence is impregnable; it can keep out everything but weed seeds, birds, insects and the weather. Beneath it is a two-foot-deep moat, paved with broken glass, smashed jars and bottles, and covered with gravel and earth, the woodchucks and skunks can't burrow under. Frogs and snakes get through but they are permitted.

The garden is a stunt, a trick. It could not exist without the fence.

Now I understand the rule. They can't be anywhere that's marked out, enclosed: even if I opened the doors and fences they could not pass in, to houses and cages, they can move only in the spaces between them, they are against borders. To talk with them I must approach the condition they themselves have entered; in spite of my hunger I must resist the fence, I'm too close now to turn back.

But there must be something else I can eat, something that is not forbidden. I think of what I might catch, crayfish, leeches, no not yet. Along the trail the edible plants, the mushrooms, I know the poisonous kinds and the ones we used to collect, some of them can be eaten raw.

There are raspberries on the canes, shrivelled and not many but they are red. I suck those, their sweetness, sourness, piercing in my mouth, teeth crackling on the seeds. Into the trail, tunnel, cool of the trees, as I walk I search the ground for shapes I can eat, anything. Provisions, they will provide, they have always favoured survival.

I find the six-leaved plants again, two of them, and dig up the crisp white roots and chew them, not waiting to take them back to the lake to wash them. Earth caked beneath my jagged nails.

The mushrooms are still there, the deadly white one, I'll save that till I'm immune, ready, and the yellow food, yellow fingers. By now many of them are too old, wrinkled, but I break off the softer ones. I hold them in my mouth a long time before swallowing, they taste musty, mildewed canvas, I'm not sure of them.

What else, what else? Enough for a while. I sit down, wrapping myself in the blanket which is damp from the grass, my feet have gone cold. I will need other things, perhaps I can catch a bird or a fish, with my hands, that will be fair. Inside me it is growing, they take what they require, if I don't feed it it will absorb my teeth, bones, my hair will thin, come out in handfuls. But I put it there, I invoked it, the fur god with tail and horns, already forming. The mothers of gods, how do they feel, voices and light glaring from the belly, do they feel sick, dizzy? Pain squeezes my stomach, I bend, head pressed against knees.

Slowly I retrace the trail. Something has happened to my eyes, my feet are released, they alternate, several inches from the ground. I'm ice-clear, transparent, my bones and the child inside me showing through the green webs of my flesh, the ribs are shadows, the muscles jelly, the trees are like this too, they shimmer, their cores glow through the wood and bark.

The forest leaps upwards, enormous, the way it was before they cut it, columns of sunlight frozen; the boulders float, melt, everything is made of water, even the rocks. In one of the languages there are no nouns, only verbs held for a longer moment.

The animals have no need for speech, why talk when you are a word

I lean against a tree, I am a tree leaning

I break out again into the bright sun and crumple, head against the ground

I am not an animal or a tree, I am the thing in which the trees and animals move and grow, I am a place

I have to get up, I get up. Through the ground, break surface, I'm standing now; separate again. I pull the blanket over my shoulders, head forward.

I can hear the jays, crying and crying as if they've found an enemy or food. They are near the cabin, I walk towards them up the hill. I see them in the trees and swooping between the trees, the air forming itself into birds, they continue to call.

Then I see her. She is standing in front of the cabin, her hand stretched out, she is wearing her grey leather jacket; her hair is long, down to her shoulders in the style of thirty years ago, before I was born; she is turned half away from me, I can see only the side of her face. She doesn't move, she is feeding them: one perches on her wrist, another on her shoulder.

I've stopped walking. At first I feel nothing except a lack of surprise: that is where she would be, she has been standing there all along. Then as I watch and it doesn't change I'm afraid, I'm cold with fear, I'm afraid it isn't real, paper doll cut by my eyes, burnt picture, if I blink she will vanish.

She must have sensed it, my fear. She turns her head quietly and looks at me, past me, as though she knows something is there but she can't quite see it. The jays cry again, they fly up from her, the shadows of their wings ripple over the ground and she's gone.

I go up to where she was. The jays are there in the trees, cawing at me; there are a few scraps on the feeding tray still, they've knocked some to the ground. I squint up at them, trying to see her, trying to see which one she is; they hop, twitch their feathers, turn their heads, fixing me first with one eye, then the other.

Chapter Twenty-five

It's day again, my body jumps out of sleep. What I heard was a powerboat, attacking. It's almost too late, they were pulling around into the bay and slowing and nearly to the dock when I woke up. I scramble on hands and knees out of my den, blanket over me, brown plaid camouflage, and run stooping further back among the trees and flatten, worming into a thicket, hazel bushes, where I can see.

They may have been sent to hunt for me, perhaps the others asked them to, they may be the police; or they may be sightseers, curious tourists. Evans will have told at the store, the whole village will know. Or the war may have started, the invasion, they are Americans.

They can't be trusted. They'll mistake me for a human being, a naked woman wrapped in a blanket: possibly that's what they've come here for, if it's running around loose, ownerless, why not take it. They won't be able to tell what I really am. But if they guess my true form, identity, they will shoot me or bludgeon in my skull and hang me up by the feet from a tree.

They're hulking out of the boat now, four or five of them. I can't see them clearly, their faces, the stems and leaves are in the way; but I can smell them and the scent bring nausea, it's stale air, bus stations and nicotine smoke, mouths lined with soiled plush, acid taste of copper wiring or money. Their skins are red, green in squares, blue in lines, and it's a minute before I remember that these are fake skins, flags. Their real skins above the collars are white and plucked, with tufts of hair on top, piebald blend of fur and no fur like mouldy sausages or the rumps of baboons. They are evolving, they are halfway to machine, the leftover flesh atrophied and diseased, porous like an appendix.

Two of them climb the hill to the cabin. They are talking, their voices are distinct but they penetrate my ears as sounds only, foreign radio. It must be either English or French but I can't recognize it as any language I've ever heard or known. Scrapes and grunts, they're getting in, through the door or the open window, crunch of their boots inside on the broken glass. One of them laughs, spike scratched on slate.

The other three are still on the dock. Then they shout: they must have found my clothes, one is kneeling down. Is it Joe, I try to picture what Joe looks like. But it makes no difference, he wouldn't help me, he would be on their side; he may have given them the keys.

The two come out of the cabin and thud down to the dock again, their false skins flapping. They cluster, they chitter and sizzle like a speeded-up tape, the forks and spoons on the ends of their arms waving excitedly. Perhaps they think I drowned myself, that would be the kind of blunder they would make.

Keep quiet I say, I bite into my arm but I can't hold it back, the laughter extrudes. It startles me, I stop at once but it's too late, they've heard me. Rubber feet stomping off the dock and bulletproof heads moving towards me, who could they be, David and Joe, Claude from the village, Evans, Malmstrom the spy, the Americans, the humans, they're here because I wouldn't sell. I don't own it, nobody owns it I tell them, you don't have to kill me. Rabbit's choices: freeze, take the chance they won't see you; then bolt.

I have a good start on them and no shoes. I run silently, dodging branches, heading for the path to the swamp, the canoe is there, I can easily reach it first. On the open lake they could cut me off with the motorboat but if I go into the swamp, among the dead tree roots. I'll be safe, they'd have to wade for me, the mud is soft, they'll sink like bulldozers. Behind me they crash, their boots crash, language ululating, electronic signals thrown back and forth between them, hooo, hooo, they talk in numbers, the voice of reason. They clank, heavy with weapons and iron plating.

But they've half-circled and are closng, five metal fingers converging to a fist. I double back. Other tricks: up a tree, but no time and no tree is big enough. Crouch behind boulders, at night yes but not now and there are no boulders, they've pulled themselves back into the earth just when I need them. Flight, there's no alternative, though I'm praying the power has deserted me, nothing is on my side, not even the sun.

I swerve toward the lake, there's a high bank here, steep slope, sand mostly. I go over the edge and slide down it, on a knee and elbow it seems, gouging furrows, I hope they won't see the tracks. I keep the blanket over me so the white won't show and crouch with my face against the treeroots that dangle over the eroded side. Twisted: cedars. One of my feet is gashed and the arm, I can feel the blood swelling out like sap.

The clangs and shouts thrash past me and continue, further away, then nearer. I stay unmoving, don't give yourself away. Back in the woods they group: talking, laughter. Maybe they've brought food, in hampers and thermos bottles, maybe they thought of it as a picnic. My heart clenches, unclenches, I listen to it.

The sound of the starting motor prods me. I pull myself up onto the bank and squat behind the hedge of trunks, if I stay by the shore they might see me. The noise surges out from behind the point and they rocket past, so near I could hit them with a stone. I count them, making sure, five.

That is the way they are, they will not let you have peace, they don't want you to have anything they don't have themselves. I stay on the bank, resting, licking the scratches; no fur yet on my skin, it's too early.

I make my way back towards the cabin, resenting the gods although perhaps they saved me, limping, blood is still coming out of my foot but not as much. I wonder if they have set traps; I will have to avoid my shelter. Caught animals gnaw off their arms and legs to get free, could I do that.

I haven't had time to be hungry and even now the hunger is detached from me, it does not insist; I must be getting used to it, soon I will be able to go without food altogether. Later I will search along the other trail; at the end of it is the stone point, it has blueberry bushes.

As I approach the toolshed the fear, the power is there, in the soles of my feet, coming out of the ground, a soundless humming. I am forbidden to walk on the paths. Anything that metal has touched, scarred; axe and machete cleared the trails, order is made with knives. His job was wrong, he was really a surveyor, he learned the trees, naming and counting them so the others could level and excavate. He must know that by now. I step to one side, skirting the worn places where shoes have been, descending towards the lake.

He is standing near the fence with his back to me, looking in at the garden. The late afternoon sunlight falls obliquely between the treetrunks on the hill, down on him, clouding him in an orange haze, he waves as if through water.

He has realized he was an intruder; the cabin, the fences, the fires and paths were violations; now his own fence excludes him, as logic excludes love. He wants it ended, the borders abolished, he wants the forest to flow back into the places his mind cleared: reparation.

I say Father.

He turns towards me and it's not my father. It is what my father saw, the thing you meet when you've stayed here too long alone.

I'm not frightened, it's too dangerous for me to be frightened of it; it gazes at me for a time with its yellow eyes, wolf's eyes, depthless but lambent as the eyes of animals seen at night in the car headlights. Reflectors. It does not approve of me or disapprove of me, it tells me it has nothing to tell me, only the fact of itself.

Then its head swings away with an awkward, almost crippled motion: I do not interest it, I am part of the landscape, I could be anything, a tree, a deer skeleton, a rock.

I see now that although it isn't my father it is what my father has become. I knew he wasn't dead.

From the lake a fish jumps
An idea of a fish jumps
A fish jumps, carved wooden fish with dots painted on the sides, no, antlered fish thing drawn in red on cliffstone, protecting spirit. It hangs in the air suspended, flsh turned to icon, he has changed again, returned to the water. How many shapes can he take.

I watch it for an hour or so; then it drops and softens, the circles widen, it becomes and ordinary fish again.

When I go to the fence the footprints are there, side by side in the mud. My breath quickens, it was true, I saw it. But the prints are too small, they have toes; I place my feet in them and find that they are my own.

Chapter Twenty-six

In the evening I make a different lair, further back and better hidden. I eat nothing but I lie down on the rocks and drink from the lake. During the night I have a dream about them, the way they were when they were alive and becoming older; they are in a boat, the green canoe, heading out of the bay.

When I wake in the morning I know they have gone finally, back into the earth, the air, the water, wherever they were when I summoned them. The rules are over. I can go anywhere now, into the cabin, into the garden, I can walk on the paths. I am the only one left alive on the island.

They were here though, I trust that. I saw them and they spoke to me, in the other language.

I'm not hungry any more but I trudge back to the cabin and climb through the window again and open a tin of yellow beans. To prefer life, I owe them that. I sit crosslegged on the wall bench and eat the beans out of the can with my fingers, a few at a time, too much at first is bad. Junk on the floor, things broken, did I do that?

David and Anna were here, they slept in the far bedroom; I remember them, but indistinctly and with nostalgia, as I remember people I once knew. They live in the city now, in a different time. I can remember him, fake husband, more clearly though, and now I feel nothing for him but sorrow. He was neither of the things I believed, he was only a normal man, middle-aged, second-rate, selfish and kind in the average proportions; but I was not prepared for the average, its needless cruelties and lies. My brother saw the danger early. To immerse oneself, join in the war, or to be destroyed. Though there ought to be other choices.

Soon it will be autumn, then winter; the leaves will turn by late August, as early as October it will begin to snow and it will keep on until the snow is level with the tops of the windows or the bottom of the roof, the lake will freeze solid. Or before that they'll close the floodgates on the dam and the water will rise, I'll watch it day by day, perhaps that's why they came in the motorboat, not to hunt but to warn me. In any case I can't stay here forever, there isn't enough food. The garden won't last and the tins and bottles will give out; the link between me and the factories is broken, I have no money.

If they were searches they will go back and say maybe that they saw me, maybe that they only thought they did. If they weren't searchers they'll say nothing.

I could take the canoe that's roped up in the swamp and paddle the ten miles to the village, now, tomorrow, when I've eaten and I'm strong enough. Then back to the city and the pervasive menace, the Americans. They exist, they're advancing, they must be dealt with, but possibly they can be watched and predicted and stopped witout being copied.

No gods to help me now, they're questionable once more, theoretical as Jesus. They've receded, back to the past, inside the skull, is it the same place. They'll never appear to me again, I can't afford it; from now on I'll have to live in the usual way, defining them by their absence; and love by its failures, power by its loss, its renunciation. I regret them; but they give only one kind of truth, one hand.

No total salvation, resurrection, Our father, Our mother, I pray, Reach down for me, but it won't work: they dwindle, grow, become what they were, human. Something I never gave them credit for; but their totalitarian innocence was my own.

I try to think for the first time what it was like to be them: our father, islanding his life, protecting both us and himself, in the midst of war and in a poor country, the effort it must have taken to sustain his illusions of reason and benevolent order, and perhaps he didn't. Our mother, collecting the seasons and the weather and her children's faces, the meticulous records that allowed her to omit the other things, the pain and isolation and whatever it was she was fighting against, something in a vanished history, I can never know. They are out of reach now, they belong to themselves, more than ever.

I set the half-empty tin down on the table and walk carefully across the floor, my bare feet avoiding the broken glass. I turn the mirror around: in it there's a creature neither animal nor human, furless, only a dirty blanket, shoulders huddled over into a crouch, eyes staring blue as ice from the deep sockets; the lips move by themselves. This was the stereotype, straws in the hair, talking nonsense or not talking at all. To have someone to speak to and words that can be understood: their definition of sanity.

That is the real danger now, the hospital or the zoo, where we are put, species and individual, when we can no longer cope. They would never believe it's only a natural woman, state of nature, they think of that as a tanned body on a beach with washed hair waving like scarves; not this, face dirt-caked and streaked, skin grimed and scabby, hair like a frayed bathmat stuck with leaves and twigs. A new kind of centrefold.

I laugh, and a noise comes out like something being killed: a mouse, a bird?

Chapter Twenty-seven

This above all, to refuse to be a victim. Unless I can do that I can do nothing. I have to recant, give up the old belief that I am powerless and because of it nothing I can do will ever hurt anyone. A lie which was always more disastrous than the truth would have been. The word games, the winning and losing games are finished; at the moment there are no others but they will have to be invented, withdrawing is no longer possible and the alternative is death.

I drop the blanket on the floor and go into my dismantled room. My spare clothes are here, knife slashes in them but I can still wear them. I dress, clumsily, unfamiliar with buttons; I re-enter my own time.

But I bring with me from the distant past five nights ago the time-traveller, the primaeval one who will have to learn, shape of a goldfish now in my belly, undergoing its watery changes. Word furrows potential already in its proto-brain, untravelled paths. No god and perhaps not real, even that is uncertain; I can't know yet, it's too early. But I assume it: if I die it dies, if I starve it starves with me. It might be the first one, the first true human; it must be born, allowed.

I'm outside in the garden when the boat comes. It isn't Evans; it's Paul's boat, thick and slow and painted white, he built it himself. Paul is at the back, beside the antique motor; in the front is Joe.

I go out through the gate and retreat behind the trees, white birches clumped beside the path, not hurrying, not running away but cautious.

The motor cuts, the nose of the boat bumps the dock. Paul stands up with an oar, pulling in; Joe gets out and ropes the boat and takes several steps towards the land.

He calls my name, then pauses, 'Are you here?' Echo: here, here?

He must have been waiting in the village, the searchers must have told him they'd seen me, perhaps he was with them. He stayed behind when David and Anna went away in their car, or he drove to the city with them and then hitched back, walked back, what's important is that he's here, a mediator, an ambassador, offering me something: captivity in any of its forms, a new freedom?

I watch him, my love for him useless as a third eye or a possibility. If I go with him we will have to talk, wooden houses are obsolete, we can no longer live in spurious peace by avoiding each other, the way it was before, we will have to begin. For us it's necessary, the intercession of words; and we will probably fail, sooner or later, more or less painfully. That's normal, it's the way it happens now and I don't know whether it's worth it or even if I can depend on him, he may have been sent as a trick. But he isn't an American, I can see that now; he isn't anything, he is only half-formed, and for that reason I can trust him.

To trust is to let go. I tense forward, towards the demands and questions, though my feet do not move yet.

He calls for me again, balancing on the dock which is neither land nor water, hands on hips, head thrown back and eyes scanning. His voice is annoyed: he won't wait much longer. But right now he waits.

The lake is quiet, the trees surround me, asking and giving nothing.

LADY ORACLE

PART ONE
Chapter One

I planned my death carefully; unlike my life, which meandered along from one thing to another, despite my feeble attempts to control it. My life had a tendency to spread, to get flabby, to scroll and festoon like the frame of a baroque mirror, which came from following the line of least resistance. I wanted my death, by contrast, to be neat and simple, understated, even a little severe, like a Quaker church or the basic black dress with a single strand of pearls much praised by fashion magazines when I was fifteen. No trumpets, no megaphones, no spangles, no loose ends, this time. The trick was to disappear without a trace, leaving behind me the shadow of a corpse, a shadow everyone would mistake for solid reality. At first I thought I'd managed it.

The day after I arrived in Terremoto I was sitting outside on the balcony. I'd been intending to sunbathe, I had visions of myself as a Mediterranean splendor, golden-brown, striding with laughing teeth into an aqua sea, carefree at last, the past discarded; but then I remembered I had no suntan lotion (Maximum Protection: without it I'd burn and freckle), so I'd covered my shoulders and thighs with several of the landlord's skimpy bath towels. I hadn't brought a bathing suit; bra and underpants would do, I thought, since the balcony was invisible from the road.

I'd always been fond of balconies. I felt that if I could only manage to stand on one long enough, the right one, wearing a long white trailing gown, preferably during the first quarter of the moon, something would happen: music would sound, a shape would appear below, sinuous and dark, and climb towards me, while I leaned fearfully, hopefully, gracefully, against the wrought-iron railing and quivered. But this wasn't a very romantic balcony. It had a geometric railing like those on middle-income apartment buildings of the fifties, and the floor was poured concrete, already beginning to erode. It wasn't the kind of balcony a man would stand under playing a lute and yearning or clamber up bearing a rose in his teeth or a stiletto in his sleeve. Besides, it was only five feet off the ground. Any mysterious visitor I might have would be more likely to approach by the rough path leading down to the house from the street above, feet crunching on the cinders, roses or knives in his head only.

That at any rate would be Arthur's style, I thought; he'd rather crunch than climb. If only we could go back to the way it had once been, before he had changed. . . . I pictured him coming to retrieve me, winding up the hill in a rented Fiat which would have something wrong with it; he would tell me about this defect later, after we'd thrown ourselves into each other's arms. He would park as close to the wall as possible. Before getting out he would check his face in the rearview mirror, adjusting the expression: he never liked to make a fool of himself, and he wouldn't be sure whether or not he was about to. He would unfold himself from the car, lock it so his scanty luggage could not be stolen, place the keys in an inside jacket pocket, peer left and right, and then with that curious ducking motion of the head, as if he were dodging a thrown stone or a low doorway, he'd sneak past the rusty gate and start cautiously down the path. He was usually stopped at international borders. It was because he looked so furtive; furtive but correct, like a spy.

At the sight of lanky Arthur descending towards me, uncertain, stony-faced, rescue-minded, in his uncomfortable shoes and well-aged cotton underwear, not knowing whether I would really be there or not, I began to cry. I closed my eyes: there in front of me, across an immense stretch of blue which I recognized as the Atlantic Ocean, was everyone I had left on the other side. On a beach, of course; I'd seen a lot of Fellini movies. The wind rippled their hair, they smiled and waved and called to me, though of course I couldn't hear the words. Arthur was the nearest; behind him was the Royal Porcupine, otherwise known as Chuck Brewer, in his long pretentious cape; then Sam and Marlene and the others. Leda Sprott fluttered like a bedsheet off to one side, and I could see Fraser Buchanan's leather-patched elbow sticking out from where he lurked behind a seaside bush. Further back, my mother, wearing a navy-blue suit and a white hat, my father indistinct by her side; and my Aunt Lou. Aunt Lou was the only one who wasn't looking at me. She was marching along the beach, taking deep breaths and admiring the waves and stopping every now and then to empty the sand out of her shoes. Finally she took them off, and continued, in fox fur, feathered hat and stocking feet, towards a distant hot-dog and orangeade stand that beckoned to her from the horizon like a tacky mirage.

But I was wrong about the rest of them. They were smiling and waving at each other, not at me. Could it be that the Spiritualists were wrong and the dead weren't interested in the living after all? Though some of them were still alive, and I was the one who was supposed to be dead; they should have been mourning but instead they seemed quite cheerful. It wasn't fair. I tried to will something ominous onto their beach – a colossal stone head, a collapsing horse – but with no result. In fact it was less like a Fellini movie than that Walt Disney film I saw when I was eight, about a whale who wanted to sing at the Metropolitan Opera. He approached a ship and sang arias, but the sailors harpooned him, and each of his voices left his body in a different-coloured soul and floated up towards the sun, still singing. *The Whale Who Wanted to Sing at the Met*, I think it was called. At the time I cried ferociously.

It was this memory that really set me off. I never learned to cry with style, silently, the pearl-shaped tears rolling down my cheeks from wide luminous eyes, as on the covers of *True Love* comics, leaving no smears or streaks. I wished I had; then I could have done it in front of people, instead of in bathrooms, darkened movie theaters, shrubberies and empty bedrooms, among the party coats on the bed. If you could cry silently people felt sorry for you. As it was I snorted, my eyes turned the color and shape of cooked tomatoes, my nose ran, I clenched my fists, I moaned, I was embarrassing, finally I was amusing, a figure of fun. The grief was always real but it came out as a burlesque of grief, an overblown imitation like the neon rose on White Rose Gasoline stations, gone forever now. ... Decorous weeping was another of those arts I never mastered, like putting on false eyelashes. I should've had a governess, I should have gone to finishing school and had a board strapped to my back and learned water-color painting and self-control.

You can't change the past, Aunt Lou used to say. Oh, but I wanted to; that was the one thing I really wanted to do. Nostalgia convulsed me. The sky was blue, the sun was shining, to the left a puddle of glass fragments shimmered like water; a small green lizard with iridescent blue eyes warmed its cool blood on the railing; from the valley came a tinkling sound, a soothing moo, the lull of alien voices. I was safe, I could begin again, but instead I sat on my balcony, beside the remains of a kitchen window broken before my time, in a chair made of aluminum tubes and yellow plastic strips, and made choking noises.

The chair belonged to Mr Vitroni, the landlord, who was fond of felt-tipped pens with different colors of ink, red, pink, purple, orange, a taste I shared. He used his to show the other people in the town that he could write. I used mine for lists and love letters, sometimes both at once: *Have gone to pick up some coffee, XXX*. The thought of these abandoned shopping trips intensified my sorrow . . . no more grapefruits, cut in half for two, with a red maraschino cherry like a navel boss, which Arthur habitually rolled to the side of the plate; no more oatmeal porridge, loathed by me, extolled by Arthur, lumping and burning because I hadn't taken his advice and done it in a double boiler. . . . Years of breakfasts, inept, forsaken, never to be recovered. . . . Years of murdered breakfasts, why had I done it?

I realized I'd come to the worst place in the entire world. I should have gone somewhere fresh and clean, somewhere I'd never been before. Instead I'd returned to the same town, the same house even, where we'd spent the summer the year before. And nothing had changed: I'd have to cook on the same two-burner stove with the gas cylinder, *bombola*, that ran out always in the middle of a half-done meal; eat at the same table, which still had the white rings on the varnish from my former carelessness with hot cups; sleep in the same bed, its mattress furrowed with age and the anxieties of many tenants. The wraith of Arthur would pursue me; already I could hear faint gargling noises from the bathroom, the crunch of glass as he scraped back his chair on the balcony, waiting for me to pass his cup of coffee out to him through the kitchen window. If I opened my eyes and turned my head, surely he would be there, newspaper held six inches from his face, pocket dictionary on one knee, left index finger inserted (perhaps) in his ear, an unconscious gesture he denied performing.

It was my own stupidity, my own fault. I should have gone to Tunisia or the Canary Islands or even Miami Beach, on the

Greyhound Bus, hotel included, but I didn't have the willpower; I needed something more familiar. A place with no handholds, no landmarks, no past at all: that would have been too much like dying.

By this time I was weeping spasmodically into one of the landlord's bath towels and I'd thrown another one over my head, an old habit: I used to cry under pillows so as not to be found out. But through the towel I could now hear an odd clicking sound. It must've been going on for a while. I listened, and it stopped. I raised the towel. There, at the level of my ankles and only three feet away, floated a head, an old man's head, topped by a ravelling straw hat. The whitish eyes stared at me with either alarm or disapproval; the mouth, caved in over the gums, was open at one side. He must've heard me. Perhaps he thought I was having an attack of some kind, in my underwear, towel-covered on a balcony. Perhaps he thought I was drunk.

I smiled damply, to reassure him, clutched my towels around me and tried to get out of the aluminum chair, remembering too late its trick of folding up if you struggled. I lost several of the towels before I was able to back in through the door.

I'd recognized the old man. It was the same old man who used to come one or two afternoons a week to tend the artichokes on the arid terrace below the house, cutting the larger weeds with a pair of rusty shears and snipping off the leathery artichoke heads when they were ready. Unlike the other people in the town, he never said anything to me or returned a word of greeting. He gave me the creeps. I put on my dress (out of sight of the picture window, behind the door) and went into the bathroom to swab my face with a dampened washcloth and blow my nose on some of Mr Vitroni's scratchy toilet paper; then to the kitchen to make a cup of tea.

For the first time since arriving, I began to feel afraid. It was more than depressing to have returned to this town, it was dangerous. It's no good thinking you're invisible if you aren't and the problem was: if I had recognized the old man, perhaps he had recognized me.

Chapter Two

I sat down at the table to drink my tea. Tea was consoling and it would help me think; though this tea wasn't very good, it came in bags and smelled of Band-aids. I'd bought it at the main grocery store, along with a package of Peek Frean biscuits, imported from England. The store had laid in a large supply of these, anticipating a wave of English tourists which so far hadn't arrived. *By Appointment to Her Majesty the Queen, Biscuit Manufacturers*, it said on the box, which I found morale-building. The Queen would not snivel: regret is gauche. *Pull yourself together*, said a stern royal voice. I sat straighter in my chair and considered what I should do.

I'd taken precautions, of course. I was using my other name, and when I'd gone to see if Mr Vitroni's flat was available I'd worn my sunglasses and covered my head with the scarf I'd bought at the Toronto airport, printed with pink Mounted Policeman performing a musical ride against a background of purple Rocky Mountains, made in Japan. I shrouded my body in one of the sacklike print dresses, also pink, with baby-blue flowers, that I'd bought off a street rack in Rome. I would've preferred the big red roses or the orange dahlias: this dress made me look like an expanse of wallpaper. But I wanted something inconspicuous. Mr Vitroni hadn't remembered me, I was sure of that. However, the old man had caught me without my disguise, and, worse still, with my hair showing. Waist-length red hair was very noticeable in that part of the country.

The biscuits were hard as plaster and tasted of shelf. I ate the last one, dipping it into the tea and chewing it up mechanically before I realized I'd finished the package. That was a bad sign, I'd have to watch that.

I decided I'd have to do something about my hair. It was evidence, its length and color had been a sort of trademark. Every newspaper clipping, friendly or hostile, had mentioned it, in fact a lot of space had been devoted to it: hair in the female was regarded as more important than either talent or the lack of it. *Joan Foster, celebrated author of* Lady Oracle, *looking like a lush Rossetti portrait, radiating intensity, hypnotized the audience with her unearthly ...* (The Toronto Star). *Prose-poetess Joan Foster looked impressively Junoesque in her flowing red hair and green robe; unfortunately she was largely inaudible ...* (The Globe and Mail). They could trace my hair much more easily than they could ever trace me. I would have to cut it off and dye the rest, though I wasn't sure where I'd be able to get the hair dye. Certainly not in this town. I might have to go back to Rome for it. I should've bought a wig, I thought; that was an oversight.

I went into the bathroom and dug the nail scissors out of my zippered makeup bag. They were too small, but it was a choice between that and one of Mr Vitroni's dull paring knives. It took me quite a while to saw the hair off, strand by strand. I tried shaping what remained, but it got shorter and shorter, though no less uneven, until I saw that I'd cropped my head like a concentration camp inmate's. My face looked quite different, though: I could pass for a secretary on vacation.

The hair lay in mounds and coils in the bathroom sink. I wanted to save it; I thought briefly of stowing it in a bureau drawer. But how could I explain if it were found? They'd start looking for the arms and legs and the rest of the body. I'd have to get rid of it. I considered flushing it down the toilet, but there was too much of it, and the septic tank had already begun to act up, burping swamp gas and shreds of decomposing toilet paper.

I took it into the kitchen and lit one of the gas burners. Then, strand by strand, I began to sacrifice my hair. It shrivelled, blackened, writhed like a handful of pinworms, melted and finally burned, sputtering like a fuse. The smell of singed turkey was overpowering.

Tears ran down my cheeks; I was a sentimentalist without doubt, of the sloppiest kind. The thing was: Arthur used to like brushing my hair for me, and that small image dissolved me; though he never learned not to pull at the tangles and it hurt like hell. Too late, too late. ... I could never manage the right emotions at the right times, anger when I should have been angry, tears when I should have cried; everything was mismatched.

When I was halfway through the pile of hair I heard footsteps coming down the gravel path. My heart clumped together, I stood frozen: the path led to nowhere but the house, there was no one in the house but me, the other two flats were empty. How could Arthur have found me so soon? Perhaps I had been right about him after all. Or it wasn't Arthur, it was one of the others. . . . The panic I hadn't allowed myself to feel for the past week rolled in an ice-gray wave back over my head, carrying with it the shapes of my fear, a dead animal, the telephone breathing menace, killer's notes cut from the Yellow Pages, a revolver, anger. . . . Faces formed and disintegrated in my head, I didn't know who to expect, what did they want? The question I could never answer. I felt like screaming, rushing into the bathroom, there was a high square window I might be able to squeeze through; then I could run up the hill and drive away in my car. Another fast getaway. I tried to remember where I'd put the keys.

There was a knock at the door, a stolid confident knock. A voice called, 'Hello? You are within?'

I could breathe again. It was only Mr Vitroni, Signor Vitroni, Reno Vitroni of the broad smile, inspecting his property. It was his sole piece of property, as far as I knew; nevertheless he was supposed to be one of the richest men in the town. What if he wanted to check the kitchen, what would he think of the sacrifical hair? I turned off the burner and stuffed the hair into the paper bag I used for garbage.

'Coming,' I called, 'just a minute.' I didn't want him walking in: my bed was unmade, my clothes and underwear were draped over chairbacks and strewn on the floor, there were dirty dishes on the table and in the sink. I hooded myself with one of the towels and snatched my dark glasses from the table as I went past.

'I was just washing my hair,' I said to him when I'd opened the door.

He was puzzled by the dark glasses: a little, but not much. Foreign ladies, for all he knew, had strange beauty rituals. He beamed and held out his hand. I held out my own hand, he lifted it as though to kiss it, then shook it instead.

'I am most pleasant to see you,' he said, bringing his heels together in a curiously military bow. The colored felt pens were lined up across his chest like medals. He'd made his fortune in the war, somehow; no one questioned these things now that they were all over. At the same time he'd learned a bit of English, and scraps of several other languages as well. Why had he come to my flat in the early evening, surely not the right time for him to visit a young foreign woman, this respectable middle-aged man with the right kind of barrel-shaped wife and numerous grandchildren? He was carrying something under his arm. He looked past my shoulder as if he wanted to go in.

'You are possibly cooking your meal?' he said. He'd picked up the smell of burning hair. God knew what these people ate, I could hear him thinking. 'I wish I do not disturb?'

'No, not at all,' I said heartily. I stood squarely in the doorway.

'Everything with you is fine? The light is going on again?'

'Yes, yes,' I said, nodding more than was necessary. There was no electricity when I moved in, as the last tenant hadn't paid the bill. But Mr Vitroni had pulled strings.

'There is much of the sunshine, no?'

'Very much,' I said, trying not to show impatience. He was standing too close.

'This is good.' Now he got to the point. 'I have something here for you. So you will find yourself more' – he lifted his free arm, palm up, expansive, welcoming, ushering me in – 'so you will be at home with us.'

How embarrassing, I thought, he was giving me a housewarming present. Was this customary, what should I say? 'That's terribly kind of you,' I said, 'but. . . .'

Mr Vitroni dismissed my gratitude with a wave of the hand. From under his arm he produced his square bundle, set it on the plastic chair, and began to untie the strings. He paused at the last knot, for suspense, like a magician. Then the brown wrapping paper fell open, revealing five or six pictures, paintings, done – O lord! – on black velvet, with gilded plaster frames. He lifted them out and displayed them to me one by one. They were all of historical sites in Rome, each done in an overall color tone. The Colosseum was a feverish red, the Pantheon mauve, the Arch of Constantine a vaporous yellow, St Peter's pink as a cake. I frowned at them like an adjudicator.

'You like?' he asked commandingly. I was a foreigner, this was the sort of thing I was supposed to like and he'd brought them as a gift, to please me. Dutifully I was pleased; I couldn't bear to hurt his feelings.

'Very nice,' I said. I didn't mean the paintings but the gesture.

'My, how you say,' he said. 'The son of my brother, he has a genius.'

We both looked silently at the pictures, lined up now on the window ledge and glowing like highway signs in the light of the low golden sun. As I stared at them they began to take on, or give off, a certain horrible energy, like the closed doors of furnaces or tombs.

It wasn't going fast enough for him. 'Who you like?' he said. 'This one?'

How could I choose without knowing what the choice would mean? The language was only one problem; there was also that other language, what is done and what isn't done. If I accepted a picture, would I have to become his mistress? Was the choice of picture significant, was it a test?

'Well,' I said tentatively, pointing to the neon Colosseum. . . .

'Two hundred fifty thousand lire,' he said promptly. I was immediately relieved: simple cash transactions weren't mysterious, they were easy to handle. Of course the paintings hadn't been done by his nephew at all, I thought; he must've bought them in Rome, from a street vendor, and was reselling them at a profit.

'Fine,' I said. I couldn't afford it at all, but I'd never learned to haggle, and anyway I was afraid of insulting him. I didn't want my electricity to go off. I went to get my purse.

When he'd folded and pocketed the money he began to gather up the paintings. 'You have two maybe? To send your family?'

'No thank you,' I said. 'This one is just lovely.'

'Your husband will come soon also?'

I smiled and nodded vaguely. This was the impression I'd given him when I rented the flat. I wanted it known in the town that I had a husband, I didn't want any trouble.

'He will like these picture,' he said, as if he knew.

I began to wonder. Did he recognize me after all, despite the dark glasses, the towel and the different name? He was fairly rich; surely he didn't need to go around peddling cheap tourist pictures. The whole thing might have been an exuse, but for what? I had the feeling that much more had happened in the conversation than I'd been able to understand, which wouldn't have been unusual. Arthur used to tell me I was obtuse.

When Mr Vitroni was safely off the balcony I took the picture inside and looked around for a place to hang it up. It had to be the right place: for years I'd needed to have the main objects in my room arranged in the proper relationship to each other, because of my mother, and whether I liked it or not this was going to be a main object. It was very red. I hung it finally on a nail to the left of the door; that way I could sit with my back to it. My habit of rearranging the furniture, suddenly and without warning, used to annoy Arthur. He never understood why I did it; he said you shouldn't care about your surroundings.

But Mr Vitroni was wrong: Arthur wouldn't have liked the picture. It wasn't the sort of thing he liked, though it was the sort of thing he believed I liked. Appropriate, he'd say, the Colosseum in blood-red on vulgar black velvet, with a gilt frame, noise and tumult, cheering crowds, death on the sands, wild animals growling, snarling, screams, and martyrs weeping in the wings, getting ready to be sacrificed; above all, emotion, fear, anger, laughter and tears, a performance on which the crowd feeds. This, I suspected, was his view of my inner life, though he never quite said so. And where was he in the midst of all the uproar? Sitting in the front row center, not moving, barely smiling, it took a lot to satisfy him; and, from time to time, making a slight gesture that would preserve or destroy: thumbs up or thumbs down. You'll have to run your own show now, I thought, have your own emotions. I'm through acting it out, the blood got too real.

By now I was furious with him and there was nothing to throw except the plates, which were Mr Vitroni's, and no one to throw them at except Mr Vitroni himself, now plodding doubtlessly up the hill, puffing a little because of his short legs and pillowy belly. What would he think if I came raging up behind him, hurling plates? He'd call a policeman, they'd arrest me, they'd search the flat, they'd find a paper bag full of red hair, my suitcase. . . .

I was quickly practical again. The suitcase was under a big fake-baroque chest of drawers with peeling veneer and an inlaid seashell design. I pulled it out and opened it; inside were my wet clothes, in a green plastic Glad Bag. They smelled of my death, of Lake Ontario, spilled oil, dead gulls, tiny silver fish cast up on the beach and rotting. Jeans and a navy-blue T-shirt, my funerary costume, my former self, damp and collapsed, from which the many-colored souls had flown. I could never wear such clothes in Terremoto, even if they weren't evidence. I thought of putting them in the garbage, but I knew from before that the children went through the garbage cans, especially those of foreigners. There had been no place to discard them on the well-traveled road to Terremoto. I should have thrown them away at the Toronto airport or the one in Rome; however, clothes discarded in airports were suspicious.

Though it was dusk, there was still enough light to see by. I decided to bury them. I scrunched the Glad Bag up and shoved it under my arm. The clothes were my own, I hadn't done anything wrong, but I still felt as though I was getting rid of a body, the corpse of someone I'd killed. I scrambled down the path beside the house, my leather-soled sandals skidding on the stones, till I was among the artichokes at the bottom. The ground was like flint and I had no shovel; there was no hope of digging a hole. Also the old man would notice if I disturbed his garden.

I examined the foundation of the house. Luckily it was shoddily built and the cement was cracking in several places. I found a loose chunk and pried it out, using a flat rock. Behind the cement there was plain dirt: the house was built right into the hillside. I scraped out a cavity, wadded the Glad Bag up as small as I could, and shoved it in, wedging the piece of cement back on top of it. Perhaps, hundreds of years from now, someone would dig up my jeans and T-shirt and deduce a forgotten rite, a child murder or a protective burial. The idea pleased me. I scuffed the fallen earth around with my foot so it wouldn't be noticeable.

I climbed back up to the balcony, feeling relieved. Once I'd dyed my hair, all the obvious evidence would be taken care of and I could start being another person, a different person entirely.

I went into the kitchen and finished burning the hair. Then I got out the bottle of Cinzano which I'd hidden in the cupboard, behind the plates. I didn't want it known here that I was a secret drinker, and I wasn't really, there just wasn't any place where I could do it in public. Here, women were not supposed to drink alone in bars. I poured myself a small glassful and toasted myself. 'To life,' I said. After that it began to bother me that I'd spoken out loud. I didn't want to begin talking to myself.

The ants were into the spinach I'd bought the day before. They lived in the outside wall, spinach and meat were the only things they'd actively hunt, everything else they'd ignore as long as you put out a saucer of sugar and water for them. I'd already done this and they'd found it, they were marching back and forth between the saucer and their nest, thin on the way there, fat on the way back, filling themselves like miniature tankers. There was a circle of them around the edge of the water and a few had gone in too far and drowned.

I poured myself another drink, then dipped my finger into the saucer and wrote my initials in sugar-water on the windowsill. I waited to see my name spelled out for me in ants: a living legend.

Chapter Three

When I woke up the next morning my euphoria was gone. I didn't exactly have a hangover, but I didn't feel like getting up too suddenly. The Cinzano bottle was standing on the table, empty; what I found ominious about this was that I couldn't remember finishing it. Arthur used to tell me not to drink so much. He wasn't a great drinker himself, but he had a habit of bringing a bottle home from time to time and leaving it out where I would see it. I suppose I was like a kid's chemistry set for him: secretly he liked mixing me up, he knew something exciting would happen. Though he was never sure what, or what he wanted; if I'd known that it would've been easier.

Outside it was drizzling, and I had no raincoat. I could've bought one in Rome, but I'd remembered the climate as unbroken sunshine and warm nights. I hadn't brought my own raincoat or umbrella or many of my own things at all, since I hadn't wanted to leave any obvious signs of packing. Now I began to regret my closet, my red-and-gold sari, my embroidered caftan, my apricot velvet gown with the ripped hem. Though where could I have worn them, here? Nevertheless I lay in bed, longing for my fan made out of peacock feathers, only one feather missing, my evening bag with gas-blue beads, a real antique.

Arthur had a strange relationship with my clothes. He didn't like me spending money on them because he thought we couldn't afford it, so at first he said they clashed with my hair or they made me look too fat. Later, when he took up Women's Liberation for flagellation purposes, he tried to tell me I shouldn't want to have clothes like that, I was playing into the hands of the exploiters. But it went beyond that; he found these clothes an affront of some kind, a personal insult. At the same time he was fascinated by them, as he was by all the things about me he disapproved of. I suspect he found them arousing and was irritated with himself because of it.

At last he made me so self-conscious that I found it hard to wear my long dresses in public. Instead I would close the bedroom door, drape myself in silk or velvet, and get out all the dangly gold earrings and chains and bracelets I could find. I would dab myself with perfume, take off my shoes, and dance in front of the mirror, twirling slowly around, waltzing with an invisible partner. A tall man in evening dress, with an opera cloak and smoldering eyes. As he swept me in circles (bumping occasionally into the dressing table or the end of the bed) he would whisper, 'Let me take you away. We will dance together, always.' It was a great temptation, despite the fact that he wasn't real. . . .

Arthur would never dance with me, even in private. He said he had never learned.

I lay in bed, watching it rain. From somewhere in the town I could hear a plaintive mooing sound, hoarse and metallic, like an iron cow. I felt sad, and there was nothing in the flat to cheer me up. *Flat* was a good word for it. An advertisement in the back of a British newspaper would have called it a *villa*, but it was only two rooms and a cramped kitchen. The walls were covered with unpainted plaster, splotched and mottled from water seepage. Across the ceiling ran beams of naked wood – Mr Vitroni must have thought they'd be rustic and picturesque – and these harbored centipedes, which dropped from them sometimes, usually at night. In the cracks between the walls and the floor and occasionally in the tiny bathtub there were medium-sized brown scorpions, which were not supposed to be deadly. Because of the rain outside it was dark and cold, it was dripping somewhere, and it seemed to echo like a cave, perhaps because the two flats above were still empty. Before, there had been a family of South Americans above us who played their guitars late into the evening, wailing and stamping their feet so that chips of plaster fell like hail. I wanted to go up and wail and stamp my feet too, but Arthur thought it would be pushy to introduce ourselves. He grew up in Fredericton, New Brunswick.

I rolled over, and the mattress got me in the spine. There was one prong that stuck up, right in the middle; but I knew that if I turned the mattress over there would be four prongs. It was the same mattress, with its chasms and pinnacles and treachery, unchanged by a year of others. We'd made love on it with an urgency reminiscent of motel rooms. Arthur was stimulated by the centipedes, which lent an aura of danger (a well-known aphrodisiac, witness the Black Death). Also he liked living out of suitcases. It must've made him feel like a political refugee, which was probably one of his fantasies, though he never said so.

In addition he could think we were going somewhere, somewhere better; and in fact whenever we moved he did perceive the new place as better, for a while. After that he would perceive it as merely different, and after that as merely the same. But he valued the illusion of transience more highly than the illusion of permanence, and our entire marriage took place in a kind of spiritual train station. Perhaps it had to do with the way we met. Because we started out by saying goodbye, we became accustomed to it. Even when he was just going to the corner for a package of cigarettes, I would gaze at him as if I would never see him again. And now I would never see him again.

I burst into tears and shoved my head under the pillow. Then I decided this would have to stop. I couldn't let Arthur go on controlling my life, especially at such a distance. I was someone else now, I was almost someone else. People used to say to me, 'You don't look at all like your photographs,' and it was true; so with a few adjustments I'd be able to pass him on the street one day and he wouldn't even recognize me. I untangled myself from the sheets – Mr Vitroni's sheets, thin and carefully mended – went into the bathroom, and ran cold water over a washcloth to deflate my face, noticing just in time the small brown scorpion concealed in the folds. It was hard to get used to these ambushes. If Arthur had been there I would have screamed. As it was I dropped the washcloth on the floor and crushed the scorpion with the tin bottom of a can of cleansing powder, also supplied by Mr Vitroni. He'd stocked the flat well with products for keeping it clean – soap, toilet disinfectant, scrub brushes – but for cooking there was only a single frying pan and two pots, one minus the handle.

I shambled out to the kitchen and turned on the burner. I was never any good in the mornings before coffee. I needed something warm in my mouth to make me feel safe; here it was filter coffee and milk from the triangular cupboard container on the windowsill. There was no refrigerator, but the milk wasn't sour yet. I had to boil it anyway, everything had to be boiled.

I sat at the table with my hot cup, adding another white ring to the varnish, eating a package of rusks and trying to organize my life. One step at a time, I told myself. Luckily I'd brought some felt pens; I would make a list. *Hair dye*, I wrote at the top in apple green. I would go to Tivoli or perhaps Rome for it, the sooner the better. With my hair dyed there would be nothing linking me to the other side, except my fingerprints. And no one would bother about the fingerprints of a woman pronounced officially dead.

I wrote *Money*, and underlined it twice. Money was important. I had enough for about a month, if I was frugal. Realistically I had enough for about two weeks. The black velvet Colosseum had set me back. I hadn't been able to take much out of my bank account, since a large withdrawal the day before my death would've looked funny. If I'd had more time I could have arranged it through my other bank account, the professional one. If there had been anything in the other bank account. Unfortunately I usually transferred most of it to my own as soon as it came in. I wondered who would get the money; Arthur, probably.

Postcard to Sam, I wrote. I'd bought the postcard already, at the Rome airport. It had a picture of the Leaning Tower of Pisa. I printed the agreed-upon message in green block letters:

> HAVING A SUPER TIME. ST PETER'S IS WONDERFUL. SEE YOU SOON, LOVE, MITZI AND FRED.

That would tell him I'd arrived safely. If there had been complications, I would have written: WEATHER COOL AND FRED HAS DYSENTERY. THANK GOD FOR ENTEROVIOFORM! LOVE, MITZI AND FRED.

I decided to mail the postcard first and worry about the money and the hair dye later. I finished my coffee, ate the last rusk, and changed into the second of my new baggy dresses, a white one with gray and mauve lozenges on it. I noticed that my nightgown had a rip halfway down the seam, at thigh level. With no one looking at me, watching for these transgressions, would I become sluttish? Why don't you take better care of yourself, a voice said, don't you want to make something of yourself? *Needles and thread*, I wrote on my list.

I wrapped my head up in the scarf with the pink Mounties and put on my dark glasses. It was no longer raining but it was still gray; the glasses would look odd, but I couldn't help it. I walked up the winding cobbled street towards the market square, running the gauntlet of old women who sat every day on the doorsteps of their agressively historical stone houses, their huge obsolete torsos crammed into black dresses as if in mourning, their legs like bloated sausages encased in wool. They were the same old women that had looked me over on the previous afternoon, the same ones that had been there a year ago and two thousand years ago. They did not vary.

Buongiorno, each one said as I went past, and I nodded at them, smiling and repeating the word. They didn't seem very curious about me. They already knew where I lived, what my car looked like, that I was foreign, and every time I bought something in the square they would know about that also. What else was there to know about a foreigner? The only thing that might bother them was that I lived alone: it wouldn't seem natural to them. But it didn't seem natural to me, either.

The post office was in the front part of one of the damp historical houses. It contained only a bench, a counter and a bulletin board, with some pictures tacked to it that looked like WANTED posters: surly men, front and side. A couple of policemen, or were they soldiers, were lounging on the bench in their leftover Mussolini uniforms: high stiff boots, leg stripes, sheaves of wheat on the pocket flaps. The back of my neck prickled as I stood at the counter, trying to make the woman understand that I wanted an airmail stamp. All I could think of was *Par Avion*, wrong language. I flapped my arms like wings, feeling idiotic, but she caught on. Behind me the policemen laughed. Surely they would sniff out my passport, which was glowing through the leather sides of my bag like molten iron, like a siren, surely they would ask to see it, question me, notify the authorities. ... And what would the authorities do?

The woman behind the counter took the card in through her slotted window. As soon as Sam got it he could let me know how well we'd succeeded. I went out, followed by the shiny beetle eyes of the policemen.

It was a good plan, I thought; I was pleased with myself for having arranged it. And suddenly I wanted Arthur to know how clever I'd been. He always thought I was too disorganized to plot my way across the floor and out the door, much less out of the country. I was the one who would charge off to do the shopping with a carefully drawn-up list, many of the items suggested by him, and forget my handbag, come back for it, forget the car keys, drive away, forget the list; or return with two tins of caviar and a box of fancy crackers and a half bottle of champagne, then try to justify these treasures by telling him they were on sale, a lie every time but the first. I would love him to know I'd done something complicated and dangerous without making a single mistake. I'd always wanted to do something he would admire.

Remembering the caviar made me hungry. I crossed the market square to the main grocery store, where you could get tins and packages, and bought another box of Peek Freans and some cheese and pasta. Outside, near the café, there was an ancient vegetable truck; that must have been the horn I'd heard earlier. It was surrounded by plump housewives, in their morning cotton dresses and bare legs, calling their orders and waving their bundles of paper money. The vegetable man was young, with an oiled mane of hair; he stood in the back of the truck, filling baskets and joking with the women. When I walked over he grinned at me and shouted something that made the women laugh and shriek. He offered me a bunch of grapes, wiggling it suggestively, but I wasn't up to it, my vocabulary was too limited; so I went instead to the regular vegetable stand. The produce wasn't fresh but the man was old and kindly and I could get away with pointing.

At the butcher's I bought two expensive, paper-thin slices of beef, which I knew would have a pallid taste. It was from yearlings, because no one could afford to pasture a cow for longer than that, and I never did learn to cook it properly, it always came out like vinyl.

I walked back down the hill, carrying my packages. My red Hertz Rent-A-Car was parked opposite the wrought-iron gate that led to the path. I'd got it at the airport and there was already a scratch on it, from a street in Rome that turned out to be one-way, *senso unico*. Some of the town's children were clustered around it, drawing pictures in the film of dust that covered it, peeping through the windows almost fearfully, running their hands along the fenders. When they saw me they drew back from the car and huddled whispering.

I smiled at them, thinking how charming they looked, with their round brown eyes, alert as a squirrel's; several had blond hair, startling against their olive skin, and I remembered having been told that the barbarians used to come this way, ten or fifteen centuries ago. That was why all the towns were built on hills.

'*Bongiorno,*' I said to them. They giggled shyly. I turned in at the gate and crunched down the path. Two dwarfish hens, the color of shredded cardboard, scuttled out of my way. Halfway down I stopped: I was trying to remember whether or not I'd locked the door. Despite my apparent safety, I couldn't afford to get careless or lazy. It was irrational, but I had the feeling that there was someone inside the flat, sitting in the chair by the window, waiting for me.

Chapter Four

But there was nobody in the flat. If anything, it was emptier than ever. I cooked lunch without mishap, nothing exploded or boiled over, and ate it at the table. Soon, I thought, I'd be eating in the kitchen, standing up, out of the pots and pans. That was how people got when they lived alone. I felt I should try to establish some sort of routine.

After lunch I counted my money, some in cash, some in traveler's checks. There was less than I'd thought, as always; I'd have to get down to business and earn some more. I went over to the bureau, pulled open the underwear drawer, and dug among the contents, wondering what had inspired me to buy a pair of red bikini briefs with *Sunday* embroidered on them in black. It was the Royal Porcupine, of course; among other things, he was an underwear freak. It had been part of a Weekend Set; I had *Friday* and *Saturday* too, all bilingual. I took them out of the cellophane package and the Royal Porcupine said, 'Put on *Sunday/Dimanche*'; he liked creating images of virtue violated. I did. 'Dynamite,' said the Royal

Porcupine. 'Now turn round.' He prowled towards me and we ended up in a lustful tangle on his mattress. There was a flesh-coloured brassiere too, with front closing. *For lovers only*, the ad said, so I bought it to go with my lover. I was a sucker for ads, especially those that promised happiness.

I'd brought this incriminating underwear with me because I was afraid Arthur would discover it after my death and realize he'd never seen it before. During my life he would never have looked into that particular drawer; he shied away from underwear, he liked to think his mind was on higher things, which, to give him credit, it was, most of the time. So I used my underwear drawer as a hiding place, and from force of habit I was still doing this.

I took out Fraser Buchanan's black notebook. Under it, at the bottom, wrapped in a slip, was the manuscript I'd been working on at the time of my death.

Charlotte stood in the room where he had left her, her hands still unconsciously clasping the casket of jewels. A fire was crackling in the spacious fireplace, its reflections gleaming warmly on the marble family crests that adorned the richly carved mantel, yet she felt quite cold. At the same time, her cheeks were burning. She could still see the curl of his lip, the tilt of the cynical eyebrows in the dark but compelling face, his hard mouth, thin-lipped and rapacious. . . . She remembered the way his eyes had moved over her, appraising the curves of her firm young body, which were only partially concealed by her cheap, badly fitting black crepe dress. She had sufficient experience with the nobility to know how they looked upon women like herself, who through no fault of their own were forced to earn their own livings. He would be no different from the rest. Her breasts moved tumultuously beneath the black crepe as she thought of the humiliations she had suffered. Liars and hypocrites, all of them! Already she had begun to hate him.

She would finish resetting the emeralds and leave Redmond Grange as quickly as possible. There was menace lurking somewhere in the vast house, she could almost smell it. She remembered the puzzling words of the coachman, Tom, as he handed her none too graciously out of the coach. 'Don't go near the maze, Miss, is my advice to you,' he had said. He was a sinister, ratlike man with bad teeth and a furtive manner.

'What maze?' Charlotte had asked.

'You'll find out soon enough,' he had replied with a snigger. 'Many a young girl afore you has come to grief in the maze.' But he had refused to explain further.

From outside the French windows came a trail of silvery laughter, a woman's voice. . . . At this hour, and in November, who could be walking on the terrace? Charlotte shivered, remembering those other footsteps she had heard in the same place the night before; but when she had looked down onto the terrace from her bedroom window, she could see nothing but moonlight and the shadows of the shrubberies moving in the wind.

She went towards the door, intending to mount the stairs to her own small room, which was on the same floor as the maid's quarters. That was how highly Redmond valued her, she thought with scorn. She might as well have been a governess, one step above a parlor maid or a cook but definitely not a lady. Yet she was as wellbred as he was, if the truth were known.

Outside the drawing-room door Charlotte paused in amazement. At the foot of the stairs, blocking her way, stood a tall woman in a sable traveling cloak. The hood was thrown back, revealing flame-red hair; the bodice of her scarlet dress was cut low, displaying the swell of her white breasts. It was evident that the skill of Bond Street's most fashionable and expensive dressmakers had been lavished on her costume; yet beneath this veneer of civilized sophistication, her body moved with the sensuousness of a predatory animal. She was ravishingly beautiful.

She glared at Charlotte, her green eyes gleaming in the light from the silver candelabrum, decorated with cupids and festoons of grapes, which she was holding in her left hand. 'Who are you and what are you doing in this house?' she demanded in an imperious voice. Before Charlotte could answer, the woman's glance fell upon the casket she was carrying. 'My jewels!' she cried. She struck Charlotte across the face with her gloved hand.

'Softly, Felicia,' said Redmond's voice. He emerged from the shadows. 'I had intended the restoration of your jewels as a surprise to welcome you home. But it is I who am surprised, as you have come before expected.' He laughed, a dry, mocking laugh.

The woman called Felicia turned to him, her smoldering eyes possessive, her provocative smile revealing small white teeth of a perfect uniformity. Redmond lifted her gloved hand gallantly to his lips.

Eight pages were missing, the first eight pages. For a moment I thought I'd left them behind, in the apartment, where Arthur would be sure to find them. But I couldn't have done that, I couldn't have been that sloppy. Fraser Buchanan must've taken them, slipped them up his jacket sleeve, folded them and stuffed them into a pocket when he was in the bedroom, before I could get to him. I had his black notebook though, and my hostage was better.

It wouldn't be too difficult to reconstruct the opening pages. Charlotte would round the curve of the spacious lime-tree-bordered driveway in the Redmond carriage, the second-best one, which had been sent to the station to fetch her. She'd be clutching her inadequate shawl around her, worrying about the shabbiness of her clothes and her battered trunk in the boot: would the servants sneer? Then she would glimpse the Grange itself, with its feminine bulk and its masculine turrets and its air of pervasive evil. She'd be ushered by a contemptuous butler into the Library, where, after keeping her waiting in an inconsiderate manner, the master of the house would interview her. He would express surprise that the jewel restorers had sent a woman, and would imply that she wasn't up to the job. She would answer him firmly, even a little defiantly. He would notice the challenge in her lustrous blue eyes, and remark that she was perhaps a little too independent for her own good.

'In my position, Sir,' she would reply with a tinge of bitterness, 'one is forced to be independent.' Charlotte of course was an orphan. Her father had been the younger son of a noble house, disowned by his family for marrying her mother, a sweet-natured woman who danced in an Opera-house. Charlotte's parents had died in a smallpox epidemic. She herself had escaped with only a few pockmarks, which lent piquancy to her expression. She was brought up by her uncle, her mother's brother, who was rich but a miser, and who'd forced her to learn her present trade before he'd perished of yellow fever. He'd left her nothing, he'd always hated her, and her father's noble family would have nothing to do with her. She wished Redmond to know that she was not in his house, in his power, by choice but from necessity. Everyone had to eat.

I'd need a working title. *The Lord of Redmond Grange*, I thought, or, better still, *Terror at Redmond Grange*. Terror was one of my specialties; that and historical detail. Or perhaps something with the word *Love* in it: love was a big seller. For years I'd been trying to get love and terror into the same title, but it was difficult. *Love and Terror at Redmond Grange* would be far too long, and it sounded too much like *The Bobbsey Twins at Sunset Beach. My Love Was Terror* ... too Mickey Spillane. *Stalked by love*, that would do in a pinch.

I'd also need a typewriter. I touch-typed everything; it was faster, and in my business speed was important. I was a good typist; at my high school typing was regarded as a female secondary sex characteristic, like breasts. Perhaps I could buy a second-hand typewriter in Rome. Then I could fill in the opening pages, write another eight or nine chapters, and send them to Hermes Books with a covering letter explaining that I'd moved to Italy on account of my health. They'd never seen me, they knew me only by my other name. They thought I was a middle-aged ex-librarian, overweight and shy. Practically a recluse, in fact, and allergic to dust, wool, fish, cigarette smoke and alcohol, as I'd explained to them when declining lunches. I'd always tried to keep my two names and identities as separate as possible.

Arthur never found out that I wrote Costume Gothics. At first I worked on them only when he was out. Later I would go into the bedroom, close the door, and tell him I was studying for some university extension course or other: Chinese Pottery, Comparative Religion, courses I never managed to complete for the simple reason that I never really took them.

Why did I never tell him? It was fear, mostly. When I first met him he talked a lot about wanting a woman whose mind he could respect, and I knew that if he found out I'd written *The Secret of Morgrave Manor* he wouldn't respect mine. I wanted very much to have a respectable mind. Arthur's friends and the books he read, which always had footnotes, and the causes he took up made me feel deficient and somehow absurd, a sort of intellectual village idiot, and revealing my profession would certainly have made it worse. These books, with their covers featuring gloomy, foreboding castles and apprehensive maidens in modified nightgowns, hair streaming in the wind, eyes bulging like those of a goiter victim, toes poised for flight, would be considered trash of the lowest order. Worse than trash, for didn't they exploit the masses, corrupt by distracting, and perpetuate degrading stereotypes of women as helpless and persecuted? They did and I knew it, but I couldn't stop.

'You're an intelligent woman,' Arthur would have said. He always said this before an exposition of some failing of mine, but also he really believed it. His exasperation with me was like that of a father with smart kids who got bad report cards.

He wouldn't have understood. He wouldn't have been able to understand in the least the desire, the pure quintessential need of my readers for escape, a thing I myself understood only too well. Life had been hard on them and they had not fought back, they'd collapsed like soufflés in a high wind. Escape wasn't a luxury for them, it was a necessity. They had to get it somehow. And when they were too tired to invent escapes of their own, mine were available for them at the corner drugstore, neatly packaged like the other painkillers. They could be taken in capsule form, quickly and discreetly, during those moments when the hair-dryer was stiffening the curls around their plastic rollers or the bath oil in the bath was turning their skins to pink velvet, leaving a ring in the tub to be removed later with Ajax Cleanser, which would make their hands smell like a hospital and cause their husbands to remark that they were about as sexy as a dishcloth. Then they would mourn their lack of beauty, their departing youth. . . . I knew all about escape, I was brought up on it.

The heroines of my books were mere stand-ins: their features were never clearly defined, their faces were putty which each reader could reshape into her own, adding a little beauty. In hundreds of thousands of houses these hidden selves rose at night from the mundane beds of their owners to go forth on adventures so complicated and enticing that they couldn't be confessed to anyone, least of all to the husbands who lay snoring their enchanted snores and dabbling with nothing more recondite than a Playboy Bunny. I knew my readers well, I went to school with them, I was the good sport, I volunteered for committees, I decorated the high-school gym with signs that read HOWDY HOP and SNOWBALL STOMP and then went home and ate peanut butter sandwiches and read paperback novels while everyone else was dancing. I was Miss Personality, confidante and true friend. They told me all.

Now I could play fairy godmother to them, despite their obvious defects, their calves which were too skinny, those disfiguring hairs on their upper lips, much deplored in cramped ads at the backs of movie magazines, their elbows knobby as chickens' knees. I had the power to turn them from pumpkins to pure gold. War, politics and explorations up the Amazon, those other great escapes, were by and large denied them, and they weren't much interested in hockey or football, games they couldn't play. Why refuse them their castles, their persecutors and their princes, and come to think of it, who the hell was Arthur to talk about social relevance? Sometimes his goddamned theories and ideologies made me puke. The truth was that I dealt in hope, I offered a vision of a better world, however preposterous. Was that so terrible? I couldn't see that it was much different from the visions Arthur and his friends offered, and it was just as realistic. So you're interested in the people, the workers, I would say to him during my solitary midnight justifications. Well, that's what the people and the workers read, the female ones anyway, when they have the time to read at all and they can't face the social realism of *True Confessions*. They read my books. Figure that out.

But that would have been going too far, that would have been treading on Arthur's most sensitive and sacred toe. It would be better to approach it from a materialist-determinist angle: 'Arthur, this happens to be something I'm good at and suited for. I discovered it by accident but then I became hooked, I turned professional and now it's the only way I know of earning a living. As the whores say, why the hell should I be a waitress? You're always telling me women should become whole people through meaningful work and you've been nagging at me to get some. Well, this is my work and I find it meaningful. And I'm hardly an idle drone, I've written fifteen of these things.'

Arthur wouldn't have bought this, however. Marlene the paragon had worked as a typesetter for three months ('You can't really understand the workers until you've been on the inside with them'), and for Arthur, the snob, nothing less would do.

Poor Arthur. I thought about him, all alone in our apartment, surrounded by the rubble of our marriage. What was he doing at that instant? Was he stuffing my red and orange gowns into a Crippled Civilians bag, emptying my makeup drawer into the garbage? Was he leafing through the scrapbook I'd started to keep in those first weeks of childish excitement after *Lady Oracle* had appeared? How naive to have thought they would all finally respect me. ... The scrapbook would go into the trash, along with all those other scraps of me that were left on the other side. What would he keep, a glove, a shoe?

Perhaps he was regretting. This was a new thought: he was feeling melancholy, bereaved even, as I was. It struck me that I might have misjudged him. Suppose he no longer hated me, suppose he had given up revenge. Perhaps I'd done something terrible to him, something final. Should I send him an anonymous postcard from Rome – *Joan is not dead, signed, A Friend* – to cheer him up?

I should have trusted him more. I should have been honest from the beginning, expressed my feelings, told him everything. (But if he'd known what I was really like, would he still have loved me?) The trouble was that I wanted to maintain his illusions for him intact, and it was easy to do, all it needed was a little restraint: I simply never told him anything important.

But it wasn't more honesty that would have saved me, I thought; it was more dishonesty. In my experience, honesty and expressing your feelings could lead to only one thing. Disaster.

PART TWO
Chapter Five

If you let one worm out of a can of worms, all the other worms will follow. Aunt Lou used to say that; she had many useful maxims, some traditional, some invented by her. For instance, I've heard 'The tongue is the enemy of the neck' elsewhere, but never 'There's more than one cat in any bag' or 'Don't count on your rabbits before they're out of the hat.' Aunt Lou believed in discretion, though only in important matters.

That was one reason I never told Arthur much about my mother. If I'd started on her, he would've found out about me soon enough. I invented a mother for his benefit, a kind, placid woman who died of a rare disease – lupus, I think it was – shortly after I met him.

Luckily he was never curious about my past: he was too busy telling me about his. I heard all about his own mother: how she'd claimed to have known the very instant Arthur was conceived and dedicated him to the ministry (Anglican) right then and there in her womb, how she'd threatened to cut his thumbs off when she caught him playing with himself at the age of four. I knew about his contempt for her and for her belief in hard work and achievement, so curiously like his own, and about his fear of her orderliness, symbolized by her flower borders which he was forced to weed. I heard about her dislike of drinking and also about his father's bar in the recreation room in that Fredericton judge's mansion he claimed to have left so far behind, with the miniature gold Scotsmen's heads on the bottletops, perversely like nipples, or so I imagined them. I knew about the various hysterical letters his mother had written, disowning him for this or that, politics, religion, sex. One came when she learned we were living together, and she never did forgive me.

To all these monstrosities and injustices I listened faithfully, partly out of a hope that I would gradually come to understand him, but mostly from habit. At one stage of my life I was a good listener, I cultivated listening, I figured I'd better be good at it because I wasn't very good at anything else. I would listen to anyone about anything, murmuring at appropriate moments, reassuring, noncommittal, sympathetic as a pillow. I even took up eavesdropping behind doors and in buses and restaurants, but this was hardly the same, since it was unilateral. So it was easy to listen to Arthur, and I ended up knowing a lot more about his mother than he did about mine, not that it did me much good. Knowledge isn't necessarily power.

I did tell him one thing though, which should've made more of an impression on him than it did: my mother named me after Joan Crawford. This is one of the things that always puzzled me about her. Did she name me after Joan Crawford because she wanted me to be like the screen characters she played – beautiful, ambitious, ruthless, destructive to men – or because she wanted me to be successful? Joan Crawford worked hard, she had willpower, she built herself up from nothing, according to my mother. Did she give me someone else's name because she wanted me never to have a name of my own? Come to think of it, Joan Crawford didn't have a name of her own either. Her real name was Lucille LeSueur, which would have suited me much better. Lucy the Sweat. When I was eight or nine and my mother would look at me and say musingly, 'To think that I named you after Joan Crawford,' my stomach would contract and plummet and I would be overcome with shame; I knew I was being reproached, but I'm still not sure what for. There's more than one side to Joan Crawford, though. In fact there was something tragic about Joan Crawford, she had big serious eyes, an unhappy mouth and high cheekbones, unfortunate things happened to her. Perhaps that was it. Or, and this is important: Joan Crawford was thin.

I was not, and this is one of the many things for which my mother never quite forgave me. At first I was merely plump; in the earliest snapshots in my mother's album I was a healthy baby, not much heftier than most, and the only peculiar thing is that I was never looking at the camera; instead I was trying to get something into my mouth: a toy, a hand, a bottle. The photos went on in an orderly series, though I didn't exactly become rounder, I failed to lose what is usually referred to as baby fat. When I reached the age of six the pictures stopped abruptly. This must have been when my mother gave up on me, for it was she who used to take them; perhaps she no longer wanted my growth recorded. She had decided I would not do.

I became aware of this fairly soon. My mother enrolled me in a dancing school, where a woman called Miss Flegg, who was almost as slender and disapproving as my mother, taught tap dancing and ballet. The classes were held in a long room over a butcher shop, and I could always remember the way the smell of sawdust and raw meat gave way to the muggy scent of exhausted feet, mingled with Miss Flegg's Yardley cologne, as I trudged up the dusty stairs. My mother took this step partly because it was fashionable to enroll seven-year-old girls in dancing schools – Hollywood musicals were still popular – and partly because she hoped it would make me less chubby. She didn't say this to me, she said it to Miss Flegg; she was not yet calling me fat.

I loved dancing school. I was even quite good at the actual dancing, although Miss Flegg sometimes rapped her classroom pointer sharply on the floor and said, 'Joan dear, I wish you would stop thumping.' Like most little girls of that time I idealized ballet dancers, it was something girls could do, and I used to press my short piggy nose up against jewelry store windows and goggle at the china music-box figurines of shiny ladies in brittle pink skirts, with roses on their hard ceramic heads, and imagine myself leaping through the air, lifted by a thin man in black tights, light as a kite and wearing a modified doily, my hair full of rhinestones and glittering like hope. I worked hard at the classes, I concentrated, and I even used to practice at home, wrapping myself in a discarded lace bathroom curtain I had begged from my mother as she was about to stuff it into the garbage can. She washed it first though; she didn't like dirt. I longed for a pair of satin toe shoes, but we were too young, Miss Flegg explained, the bones in our feet had not hardened. So I had to settle for black slippers with an unromantic elastic over the instep.

Miss Flegg was an inventive woman; I suppose these days she would be called creative. She didn't have much scope for her inventiveness in the teaching of elementary steps to young children, which was largely a matter of drill, but she let herself go on the annual spring recital. The recital was mostly to impress the parents, but it was also to impress the little girls themselves so they would ask to be allowed to take lessons the next year.

Miss Flegg choreographed the entire program. She also constructed the sets and props, and she designed the costumes and handed out patterns and instructions to the mothers, who were supposed to sew them. My mother disliked sewing but for this event she buckled down and cut and pinned just like all the other mothers. Maybe she hadn't given up on me after all, maybe she was still making an effort.

Miss Flegg organized the recital into age groups, which corresponded to her dancing classes. There were five of them: Teenies, Tallers, Tensies, Tweeners and Teeners. Underneath her spiny exterior, the long bony hands, the hair wrenched into a bun, and the spidery eyebrows, done, I realized later, with a pencil, she had a layer of sentimentality, which set the tone for her inventions.

I was a Teenie, which was in itself a contradiction in terms, for as well as being heavier than everyone else in the class I had begun to be taller. But I didn't mind, I didn't even notice, for I was becoming more wildly excited about the recital every day. I practiced for hours in the basement, the only place I was allowed to do it after I had accidentally knocked over and broken my mother's white-and-gold living-room lamp in the shape of a pineapple, one of a set. I twirled beside the washing machine, humming the dance music in my head, I curtseyed to the furnace (which in those days still burned coal), I swayed in and out between the sheets drying double-folded on the line, and when I was exhausted I climbed the cellar stairs, out of breath and covered with coal dust, to be confronted by my mother with her mouth full of pins. After I'd been scrubbed I would be stood on a chair and told to turn around slowly. I could barely hold still even to have my costumes tried on.

My mother's impatience was almost equal to my own, though it was of another sort. She may have started to regret sending me to dancing school. For one thing, I wasn't getting any slimmer; for another, I now made twice as much noise as I had at first, especially when I rehearsed my tap number in my patent leather shoes with metal tips toe and heel, on the hardwood of the hall floor, which I had been ordered not to do; and for another, she was having trouble with the costumes. She'd follow the instructions, but she couldn't get them to look right.

There were three of them, for the Teenies were doing three numbers: 'Tulip Time,' a Dutch ballet routine for which we had to line up with partners and move our arms up and down to simulate windmills; 'Anchors Aweigh,' a tap dance with quick turns and salutes (this was soon after the end of the war and military motifs were still in vogue); and 'The Butterfly Frolic,' a graceful number whose delicate flittings were more like my idea of what dancing should be. It was my favorite, and it had my favorite costume too. This featured a gauzy skirt, short, like a real ballerina's, a tight bodice with shoulder straps, a headpiece with spangled insect antennae, and a pair of colored cellophane wings with coathanger frames, supplied by Miss Flegg. The wings were what I really longed for but we weren't allowed to put them on until the day itself, for fear of breakage.

But it was this costume that was bothering my mother. The others were easier: the Dutch outfit was a long full skirt with a black bodice and white sleeves, and I was the rear partner anyway. The 'Anchors Aweigh' number had middy dresses with naval braid trim, and this was all right too since they were high-necked, long-sleeved and loose around the waist. I was in the back row because of my height; I hadn't been picked as one of the three stars, all with Shirley Temple curls, who were doing solos on drums made out of cheese crates. But I didn't mind that much: I had my eye on the chief butterfly spot. There was a duet with the only boy in the class; his name was Roger. I was slightly in love with him. I hoped the girl who was supposed to do it would get sick and they would have to call me in. I'd memorized her part as well as my own, more or less.

I stood on the chair and my mother stuck pins into me and sighed; then she told me to turn slowly, and she frowned and stuck in some more pins. The problem was fairly simple: in the short pink skirt, with my waist, arms and legs exposed, I was grotesque. I am reconstructing this from the point of view of an adult, an anxious, prudish adult like my mother or Miss Flegg; but with my jiggly thighs and the bulges of fat where breasts would later be and my plump upper arms and floppy waist, I must have looked obscene, senile almost, indecent; it must have been like watching a decaying stripper. I was the kind of child, they would have thought back then in the early months of 1949, who should not be seen in public with so little clothing on. No wonder I fell in love with the nineteenth century: back then, according to the dirty postcards of the time, flesh was a virtue.

My mother struggled with the costume, lengthening it, adding another layer of gauze to conceal the outlines, padding the bodice; but it was no use. Even I was a little taken aback when she finally allowed me to inspect myself in the three-sided mirror over her vanity table. Although I was too young to be much bothered by my size, it wasn't quite the effect I wanted. I did not look like a butterfly. But I knew the addition of the wings would make all the difference. I was hoping for magic transformations, even then.

The dress rehearsal was in the afternoon, the recital the same evening. They were so close together because the recital was to be held, not in the room over the butcher shop, which would have been too cramped, but in the public school auditorium, rented for a single Saturday. My mother went with me, carrying my costumes in a cardboard dress box. The stage was cramped and hollow-sounding but was redeemed by velvet curtains, soft purple ones; I felt them at the first opportunity. The space behind it was vibrating with excitement. A lot of the mothers were there. Some of them had volunteered to do makeup and were painting the faces of theirs and other people's daughters, the mouths with dark-red lipstick, the eyelashes with black mascara which stiffened them into spikes. The finished and costumed girls were standing against the wall so as not to damage themselves, inert as temple sacrifices. The bigger pupils were strolling about and chatting; it wasn't as important to them, they had done it before, and their numbers were to be rehearsed later.

'Tulip Time' and 'Anchors Aweigh' went off without a hitch. We changed costumes backstage, in a tangle of arms and legs, giggling nervously and doing up each other's hooks and zippers. There was a crowd around the single mirror. The Tallers, who were alternating with us, did their number, 'Kitty Kat Kapers,' while Miss Flegg stood in the wings, evaluating, waving time with her pointer, and occasionally shouting. She was wrought up. As I was putting on my butterfly costume, I saw my mother standing beside her.

She was supposed to be out in the front row where I'd left her, sitting on a folding chair, her gloves in her lap, smoking and jiggling one of her feet in its high-heeled open-toed shoe, but now she was talking with Miss Flegg. Miss Flegg looked over at me; then she walked over, followed by my mother. She stood gazing down at me, her lips pressed together.

'I see what you mean,' she said to my mother. When resenting this scene later on, I always felt that if my mother hadn't interfered Miss Flegg would have noticed nothing, but this is probably not true. What she was seeing, what they were both seeing, was her gay, her artistic, her *spiritual* 'Butterfly Frolic' being reduced to something laughable and unseemly by the presence of a fat little girl who was more like a giant caterpillar than a butterfly, more like a white grub if you were really going to be accurate.

Miss Flegg could not have stood this. For her, the final effect was everything. She wished to be complimented on it, and whole-heartedly, not with pity or suppressed smiles. I sympathize with her now, although I couldn't then. Anyway, her inventiveness didn't desert her. She leaned down, placed her hand on my round bare shoulder, and drew me over to a corner. There she knelt down and gazed with her forceful black eyes into mine. Her blurred eyebrows rose and fell.

'Joan, dear,' she said, 'how would you like to be something special?'

I smiled at her uncertainly.

'Would you do something for me, dear?' she said, warmly.

I nodded. I liked to help.

'I've decided to change the dance a little,' she said. 'I've decided to add a new part to it; and because you're the brightest girl in the class, I've chosen you to be the special, new person. Do you think you can do that, dear?'

I had seen enough of her to know that this kindness was suspect, but I fell for it anyway. I nodded emphatically, thrilled to have been selected. Maybe I'd been picked to do the butterfly duet with Roger, maybe I would get bigger, more important wings. I was eager.

'Good,' said Miss Flegg, clamping her hand on my arm. 'Now come and hop into your new costume.'

'What am I going to be?' I asked as she led me away.

'A mothball, dear,' she answered serenely, as if this were the most natural thing in the world.

Her inventive mind, and possibly earlier experiences, had given her a fundamental rule for dealing with situations like this: if you're going to be made to look ridiculous and there's no way out of it, you may as well pretend you meant to. I didn't learn this rule till much later, not consciously. I was wounded, desolated in fact, when it turned out that Miss Flegg wanted me to remove my cloudy skirt and spangles and put on one of the white teddy-bear costumes the Tensies were using for their number, 'Teddy Bears' Picnic.' She also wanted me to hang around my neck a large sign that said MOTHBALL, 'So they'll all understand, dear, what you're supposed to be.' She herself would make the sign for me, in the interval between the rehearsal and the performance.

'Can I wear my wings?' I asked. It was beginning to seep through to me, the monstrousness of the renunciation she was asking me to make.

'Now, who ever heard of a mothball with wings?' she said in what was supposed to be a jocular but practical manner.

Her idea was that once the butterflies had finished their cavorting, I would lumber among them in the white suit and the sign, and the butterflies would be coached to scatter. It would be cute, she told me.

'I liked the dance the way it was,' I said tentatively. 'I want it to be the way it was.' I was on the verge of crying; probably I had already begun.

Miss Flegg's manner changed. She put her face down close to mine so I could see the wrinkles around her eyes up close and smell the sour toothpaste smell of her mouth, and said, slowly and distinctly, 'You'll do as I say or you won't be in the dance at all. Do you understand?'

Being left out altogether was too much for me. I capitulated, but I paid for it. I had to stand in the mothball suit with Miss Flegg's hand on my shoulder while she explained to the other Teenies, sylphlike in their wispy skirts and shining wings, about the change in plans and my new, starring role. They looked at me, scorn on their painted lips; they were not taken in.

I went home with my mother, refusing to speak to her because she had betrayed me. It was snowing lightly, though it was April, and I was glad because she had on her white open-toed shoes and her feet would get wet. I went into the bathroom and locked the door so she couldn't get at me; then I wept uncontrollably, lying on the floor with my face against the fluffy pink bath mat. Afterwards I pulled the laundry hamper over so I could stand on it and look into the bathroom mirror. My made-up face had run, there were black streaks down my cheeks like sooty tears and my purple mouth was smudged and swollen. What was the matter with me? It wasn't that I couldn't dance.

My mother pleaded briefly with me through the locked bathroom door, then she threatened. I came out, but I wouldn't eat any dinner: someone besides me would have to suffer. My mother wiped the makeup off my face with Pond's Cold Cream, scolding me because it would have to be done over, and we set out again for the auditorium. (Where was my father? He wasn't there.)

I had to stand enviously in the wings, red-faced and steaming in the hated suit, listening to the preliminary coughs and the scraping of folding chairs, then watching while the butterflies tinkled through the movements I myself had memorized, I was sure, better than any of them. The worst thing was that I still didn't understand quite why this was being done to me, this humiliation disguised as a privilege.

At the right moment Miss Flegg gave me a shove and I lurched onto the stage, trying to look, as she had instructed me, as much like a mothball as possible. Then I danced. There were no steps to my dance, as I hadn't been taught any, so I made it up as I went along. I swung my arms, I bumped into the butterflies, I spun in circles and stamped my feet as hard as I could on the boards of the flimsy stage, until it shook. I threw myself into the part, it was a dance of rage and destruction, tears rolled down my cheeks behind the fur, the butterflies would die; my feet hurt for days afterwards. 'This isn't me,' I kept saying to myself, 'they're making me do it'; yet even though I was concealed in the teddy-bear suit, which flopped about me and make me sweat, I felt naked and exposed, as if this ridiculous dance was the truth about me and everyone could see it.

The butterflies scampered away on cue and much to my surprise I was left in the center of the stage, facing an audience that was not only laughing but applauding vigorously. Even when the beauties, the tiny thin ones, trooped back for their curtsey, the laughter and clapping went on, and several people, who must have been fathers rather than mothers, shouted 'Bravo mothball!' It puzzled me that some of them seemed to like my ugly, bulky suit better than the pretty ones of the others.

After the recital Miss Flegg was congratulated on her priceless touch with the mothball. Even my mother appeared pleased. 'You did fine,' she said, but I still cried that night over my thwarted wings. I would never get a chance to use them now, since I had decided already that much as I loved dancing school I was not going back to it in the fall. It's true I had received more individual attention that the others, but I wasn't sure it was a kind I liked. Besides, who would think of marrying a mothball? A question my mother put to me often, later, in other forms.

Chapter Six

At first, every time I repeated this story to myself, underneath my pillow or inside the refuge of the locked bathroom, it filled me with the same rage, helplessness and a sense of betrayal I'd felt at the time. But gradually I came to see it as preposterous, especially when I thought about telling it to anyone else. Instead of denouncing my mother's injustice, they would probably laugh at me. It's hard to feel undiluted sympathy for an overweight seven-year-old stuffed into a mothball suit and forced to dance; the image is simply too ludicrous. But if I described myself as charming and skinny, they would find the whole thing pathetic and grossly unfair. I knew this even when I was ten. If Desdemona was fat who would care whether or not Othello strangled her? Why is it that the girls Nazis torture on the covers of the sleazier men's magazines are always good-looking? The effect would be quite different if they were overweight. The men would find it hilarious instead of immoral or sexually titillating. However, plump unattractive women are just as likely to be tortured as thin ones. More so, in fact.

The year after the dancing school fiasco, when I was eight, we moved from the cramped duplex where we had been living to a slightly bigger house, a bungaloid box near a Loblaws supermarket. It wasn't at all the sort of house my mother pictured as the proper dwelling place for her, but it was better than the fugitive quarters, the rundown apartments and the top floors of old houses she'd had to put up with earlier. This meant a new school and a new neighborhood, and my mother felt the best way to get me adjusted, as she put it, was to enroll me in Brownies. It was characteristic of her that she didn't choose the nearest Brownies, the one most of the girls in my class actually went to. Instead she picked one farther away, in a better neighborhood, attended by children from different schools entirely. Thus her ploy served none of her purposes. It didn't help to acquaint me with the girls in my own school, the reverse in fact as I had to leave school early on Brownie Tuesdays in order to get there in time; and at the Brownies itself I was an alien from beyond the borders.

To get to this Brownies I had to take the streetcar, and to reach the streetcar stop I had to cross one of the many ravines that wound through the city. My mother was terrified of this ravine: it crawled with vines and weedy undergrowth, it was dense with willow trees and bushes, behind every one of which she pictured a lurking pervert, an old derelict rendered insane by rubbing alcohol, a child molester or worse. (Sometimes she called them 'exhibitionists,' which always caused me to have second thoughts about the Canadian National Exhibition.) Every Tuesday she would give me a lecture about them before I set out for school, wearing, even that early in the morning, my brown uniform and the shoes which I had laboriously polished the evening before. 'Don't talk to any bad men,' she would say. 'If one comes up to you in that ravine, run away as fast as you can.' She would deliver this warning during breakfast, in a voice that suggested that no matter how fast I ran I would never be able to get away, I was doomed, and my oatmeal porridge would twist itself into a lump and sink to the bottom of my stomach. She never suggested what these men would look like or what they would do if they caught me, which left the field wide open to my imagination. And the way she put it made me somehow responsible, as if I myself had planted the bushes in the ravine and concealed the bad men behind them, as if, should I be caught, it would be my own doing.

To cross the ravine you had to walk down a long gravelled hill, then across a wooden bridge, which was quite old. It slanted, and some of the planks had rotted away completely so you could see the ground a long way beneath. Then you had to go up a path on the other side, with the leaves and branches almost touching you, like evil vegetable fingers. I would run down the hill and across the bridge, heavily as a trundled barrel, but by the time I got to the upward climb I would be so out of breath I would have to walk. This was the worst part.

After I had gone a number of times by myself, my mother hit on a solution. Like most of her solutions, it was worse than the problem. She discovered that several other mothers on our side of the bridge had aspirations like her own; or at any rate they'd enrolled their own daughters in the same Brownies. I'd known this for some time but hadn't told her, because these girls were older than I was, they were in higher grades, and they seemed formidable to me. Though we followed the same route to Brownies, I made sure that I walked either a safe distance ahead of them or a safe distance behind, and on the streetcar I kept at least four seats between us. But my mother was a great arranger at that period of her life, and she phoned up the other mothers, who knew about the bad men too, and simply arranged that I was to walk to Brownies with these girls. They made me nervous, but I did feel a little safer crossing the ravine with them.

The trouble was that despite the terrors involved in getting there, I worshiped Brownies, even more than I had worshiped dancing classes. At Miss Flegg's you were supposed to try to be better than everyone else, but at Brownies you were supposed to try to be the same, and I was beginning to find this idea quite attractive. So I liked wearing the same baggy uniform with its odd military beret and tie, learning the same ritual rhymes, handshakes and salutes, and chanting in unison with the others,

> A Brownie gives in to the *older* folk;
> A Brownie does NOT give in to her*self!*

There was even some dancing involved. At the beginning of every session, when the slightly dilapidated papier-mâché toadstool which was the group fetish had been set in place on its grassy-green felt mat, and the gray-haired woman in the blue Guide uniform had said, with a twinkle in her eye, 'Hoot! Hoot!' the Brownies would hurtle from the four corners of the room, six at a time, and perform a whirling, frenzied dance, screeching out the words to their group songs as loud as they could. Mine was:

> Here you see the laughing Gnomes,
> Helping mothers in our homes.

This was not strictly true: I didn't help my mother. I wasn't allowed to. On the few occasions I'd attempted it, the results had not pleased her. The only way I could have helped her to her satisfaction would have been to change into someone else, but I didn't know this yet. My mother didn't approve of my free-form style of making beds, nor of the crashes and fragments when I dried the dishes. She didn't like scraping the charcoal off the bottoms of the pots when I tried to cook ('a cooked dessert' was one Brownies test requirement), or having to reset the table after I'd done it backwards. At first I tried to surprise her with sudden Good Turns, as suggested in the Brownie handbook. One Sunday I brought her breakfast in bed on a tray, tripped, and covered her with wet cornflakes. I polished her good navy-blue suede shoes with black boot polish. And once I carried out the garbage can, which was too heavy for me, and tipped it down the back steps. She wasn't a very patient woman; she told me quite soon that she would rather do things right herself the first time than have to do them over again for me. She used the word 'clumsy,' which made me cry; but I was excused from household chores, which I saw as an advantage only much later. I sang out the words unflinchingly though, as I stomped around the toadstool in clouds of church-basement dust, with a damp Gnome hand clutched in each of mine.

The lady who ran the pack was known as Brown Owl; owls, we were told, meant wisdom. I always remembered what she looked like: the dried-apple face, the silvery gray hair, the snapping blue eyes, quick to spot a patch of tarnish on the brass fairy pin or a dirty fingernail or a poorly tied shoelace. Unlike my mother, she was impartial and kind, and she gave points for good intentions. I was entranced by her. It was hard to believe that an adult, older than my mother even, would actually squat on the floor and say things like 'Tu-whit, Tu-whoo' and 'When Brownies make their fairy ring. They can magic everything!' Brown Owl acted as though she believed all this, and thought that we did too. This was the novelty: someone even more gullible than I was. Occasionally I felt sorry for her, because I knew how much pinching, shoving and nudging went on during Thinking Time and who made faces behind Brown Owl's back when we were saying, 'I promise to do my duty to God and the King and to help others every day, especially those at home.' Brown Owl had a younger sidekick known as Tawny Owl. Like vice-principals everywhere, she was less deceivable and less beloved.

The three girls with whom I crossed the ravine each Brownie

day were called Elizabeth, Marlene and Lynne. They were ten, and almost ready to join the Girl Guides; 'flying up,' it was called if you had obtained your Golden Wings. Otherwise you had to walk up. Elizabeth was going to fly, no doubt about it: she was plastered with badges like a diplomat's suitcase. Marlene probably would, and Lynne probably wouldn't. Elizabeth was a Sixer and had two stripes on her arm to prove it. Marlene was a Pixie and I can't remember what Lynne was. I admired Elizabeth and feared the other two, who competed for her attention in more or less sinister ways.

At first they tolerated me, on those long perilous walks to the streetcar stop. I had to walk a little behind, but that was a small enough price to pay for protection from the invisible bad men. That went on through September and October, while the leaves turned yellow and fell and were burned in the sidewalk fires that were not yet illegal, during roller skating and skipping, past knee socks and into long stockings and winter coats. The days became shorter, we walked home in the dark across the bridge, which was lit only by one feeble bulb at either end. When it began to snow we had to go into leggings, heavy lined pants that were pulled on over our skirts, causing them to bunch into the crotch, and held up by elastic shoulder straps. In those days girls were not allowed to wear slacks to school.

The memory of this darkness, this winter, the leggings, and the soft snow weighing down the branches of the willow trees in the ravine so that they made a bluish arch over the bridge, the white vista from its edge that should have been so beautiful, I associate with misery. Because by that time Elizabeth and her troop had discovered my secret: they had discovered how easy it was to make me cry. At our school young girls weren't supposed to hit each other or fight or rub snow in each other's faces, and they didn't. During recess they stayed in the Girls' Yard, where everything was whispering and conspiracy. Words were not a prelude to war but the war itself, a devious, subterranean war that was unending because there were no decisive acts, no knockdown blows that could be delivered, no point at which you could say *I give in*. She who cried first was lost.

Elizabeth, Marlene and Lynne were in other grades or they would have found out about me sooner. I was a public sniveller still, at the age of eight; my feelings were easily hurt, despite my mother, who by this time was telling me sharply to act my age. She herself was flint-eyed, distinct, never wavery or moist; it was not until later that I was able to reduce her to tears, a triumph when I finally managed it.

Elizabeth was the leader of the Gnomes, and I was one of her five followers during those dusty Tuesdays of rituals and badges and the sewing on of buttons. It was over knots that I came to grief. We had mastered the reef, and Tawny Owl, who was the knot specialist, had decided we were ready for the clove hitch; so with her lanyard – from the end of which hung a splendid and enviable silver whistle – looped over a chairback, she was demonstrating. I was cross-eyed with concentration, I was watching so hard I didn't see a thing, and when it came to my turn to duplicate the magic feat the rope slipped through my fingers like spaghetti and I was left with nothing but a snarl. Tawny Owl did it again, for my benefit, but with no better results.

'Joan, you weren't paying attention,' Tawny Owl said.

'But I *was*,' I said earnestly.

Tawny Owl huffed up. Unlike Brown Owl, she knew about the things that went on behind her back, which made her suspicious. She took my protest for lippiness. 'If you won't cooperate, Gnomes, I'll just have to go over and work with the Pixies. I'm sure they are more interested in learning.' And she marched off, taking her whistle with her. Of course I started oozing right away. I hated being falsely accused. I hated being accurately accused too, but injustice was worse.

Elizabeth narrowed her eyes. She was about to say something, but Brown Owl, ever alert, came trotting over and said brightly, 'Now, now, Joan, we don't like to see unhappy faces at Brownies; we like to see cheerfulness. Remember, "Frowns and scowls make ugly things, Smiling gives them fairy wings."' This only made me cry harder, and I had to be secluded in the cloakroom so as not to embarrass everyone until I had, as Brown Owl put it, got my Brownie smile back again. 'You must learn to control yourself,' she said kindly, patting me on the beret as I heaved and choked. She didn't know what a lot of territory this covered.

That blue-black evening, as we crunched our way home over the snow, Elizabeth paused under the last streetlight before the bridge and looked at the others. Then, without warning, they all took off down the hill in a flurry of hilarious giggles and disappeared into the darkness of the ravine before I knew what was happening, shouting back, 'The bad man's gonna getcha!' – abandoning me at the top of the hill to make the crossing by myself. First I called, then I ran after them, but they were too far ahead. I sniffled over the bridge, wiping my mucous nose on the backs of my mittens and glancing fearfully behind me, though of course no child molester or exposure artist in his right mind would have been abroad in near-zero weather. They would all have been lurking in railroad stations or the backs of churches, but I didn't know this. I heaved my way up the final hill; they were waiting in ambush at the top.

'Are you ever a crybaby,' Elizabeth said with scorn and delight, and that set the pattern for the rest of the year.

The game for the three of them was to think up ingenious variations. Sometimes they would just run off; other times they would threaten to run off. Sometimes they would claim that their running off was a punishment, deserved by me, for something I had done or hadn't done that day: I had skipped too heavily in the fairy ring, I hadn't stood straight enough, my tie was rumpled, I had dirty fingernails, I was fat. Sometimes they would say they wouldn't run off, or would swear to come back and get me, if I would only perform certain acts: I had to crawl around in the snow, barking like a dog, or throw a snowball at a passing old lady, whereupon they would point at me and jeer, '*She* did it! *She* did it!' Sometimes they would ask me, 'What would the bad man do to you if he caught you?' It wasn't enough for me to say I didn't know; they would merely take flight, giggling behind their hands: 'She doesn't know, she doesn't know!' I spent half an hour one night standing at the top of the hill, singing over and over in a quavering voice, a hundred times exactly, 'We're the Brownies, here's our aim, Lend a hand and play the game,' before I realized they weren't going to keep their promise and retrieve me. Once they told me to stick my tongue onto an iron fence on the way down the ravine, but it wasn't cold enough and my tongue didn't freeze to the fence as they'd hoped.

The funny thing was that though the conditions, directions and demands, were issued by Elizabeth, I knew it was the other two who thought them up. Lynne was especially inventive: her position was precarious, she didn't have the strength of character, she could so easily turn into me. I couldn't tell my mother about any of this because I felt that whatever she would say, underneath it her sympathies would lie with them. 'Stand up for yourself,' she would exhort. How could a daughter of hers have turned out to be such a limp balloon?

Sometimes, when they'd left me alone in the darkness and cold, I would stand there almost hoping that the bad man would really come up out of the ravine and do whatever he was fated to do. That way, after I'd been stolen or killed, they would be punished, and they would be forced to repent at last for what they'd done. I imagined him as a tall man, very tall, in a black suit, heaving up out of the snow like an avalanche in reverse, blue-faced and covered with ice, red-eyed, hairy-headed, with long sharp teeth like icicles. He would be frightening but at least he would be an end to this misery that went on and seemed as if it would go on forever. I would be taken away by him, no trace of me would ever be found. Even my mother would be sorry. Once I actually waited for him, counting under my breath – he would come after a hundred, he would come after two hundred – for so long that I was half an hour late for dinner and my mother was furious.

'What have you been doing?' she said.

'Playing,' I said, and she told me I was selfish and inconsiderate.

The snow finally changed to slush and then to water, which trickled down the hill of the bridge into rivulets, one on either side of the path; the path itself turned into mud. The bridge was damp, it smelled rotten, the willow branches turned yellow, the skipping ropes came out. It was light again in the afternoons, and on one of them, when for a change Elizabeth hadn't run off but was merely discussing the possibilities with the others, a real man actually appeared.

He was standing at the far side of the bridge, a little off the path, holding a bunch of daffodils in front of him. He was a nice-looking man, neither old nor young, wearing a good tweed coat, not at all shabby or disreputable. He didn't have a hat on, his taffy-colored hair was receding and the sunlight gleamed on his high forehead. I was walking ahead, as ordered (they liked to keep an eye on me from behind), and the others were deep in their plans, so I saw him first. He smiled at me, I smiled back, and he lifted his daffodils up to reveal his open fly and the strange, ordinary piece of flesh that was nudging flaccidly out of it.

'Look,' I said to the others, as if I had just discovered something of interest. They did look, and immediately began to scream and run up the hill. I was so startled – by them, not by him – that I didn't move.

The man looked slightly dismayed. His pleasant smile faded and he turned away, pulling his coat together, and began to walk in the other direction, across the bridge. Then he turned back, made a little bow to me, and handed me the daffodils.

The others were waiting above, clustered a safe way along the street. 'What did he say? What did he do?' they asked. 'Don't you know that was a bad man? You sure had the nerve,' Elizabeth said grudgingly. For once I had impressed them, though I wasn't sure why; there hadn't been anything frightening about the man, he had smiled. I liked the daffodils too, though I threw them into a ditch before I reached our house. I was astute enough to know that I wouldn't be able to explain where I'd got them in a way my mother would approve of.

On the walk home from the next Brownie meeting the girls were especially nice to me, and I thought that now, after my long probation, I was going to become their friend. That seemed to be true, because Elizabeth said, 'Would you like to be in our club? We have a club, you know.' This was the first I'd heard of it, though clubs were popular at school, but yes, of course I wanted to be in it. 'You have to go through the ceremony first,' Marlene said. 'It isn't hard.'

We all knew about ceremonies, Brownies was full of them, and I think they got some of the details of what followed from the joining-up ritual, in which you were led across cardboard stepping stones that read CHEERFULNESS, OBEDIENCE, GOOD TURNS and SMILES. You then had to close your eyes and be turned around three times, while the pack chanted,

> Twist me and turn me and show me the elf,
> I looked in the water and there saw . . .

Here you were supposed to open your eyes, look into the enchanted pool, which was a hand-mirror surrounded by plastic flowers and ceramic bunnies, and say, 'Myself.' The magic word.

So when Elizabeth said, 'Close your eyes,' I closed them. Marlene and Lynne each took one of my hands, and I felt something soft being tied across my eyes. Then they took me downhill, warning me when there was a hole or a rock. I felt the bridge under my feet and they turned me around several times, then back, so I no longer knew which way I was facing. I started to be frightened.

'I don't want to join the club,' I said, but Elizabeth said reassuringly, 'Sure you do, you'll like it,' and they led me farther on. 'Stand over here,' Elizabeth said, and a hard surface came up against my back 'Now put your hands at your sides.' I felt something being passed around each of my arms, then around my body, and pulled tight.

'Now,' said Elizabeth, still in the same soothing voice, 'we're going to leave you here for the bad man.' The other two started to giggle uncontrollably, and I could hear them running off. Now I knew where I was: they had tied me with Elizabeth's skipping rope to the post at the end of the bridge, right where we had seen the man the week before. I started to whimper.

Then I stopped. I knew they were probably watching to see what I would do, so I decided for a change to do nothing. Surreptitiously I wriggled my arms to find out if I could get free. They had pulled the rope quite tight enough, so I would simply wait until they got bored with it and came to untie me. I knew they couldn't just leave me there: that would be going too far. When I didn't show up my mother would phone their mothers and they would get hell.

At first I could hear them faintly, tittering among themselves at the top of the hill, and once they called down, 'How do ya like the club?' I didn't answer; at last I was tired of them. But after a while I could hear nothing but the repetitive singing of the birds from the ravine below, and then it started to get colder. They must have gone away, intending to come back later, and forgotten about me.

I was snivelling to myself and struggling in the ropes with rising desperation, trying to get one hand across to the other so I could slip the loop down and off, when I heard the footsteps coming towards me across the bridge. I froze: maybe it was one of the bad kind, maybe something horrible would finally happen, though I can't have been a very exciting sexual object, a fat, snotty-nosed eight-year-old in a Brownie outfit. But a voice said, 'What's this?' and the blindfold was lifted off my eyes. (It was Marlene's Brownie tie.)

The man was neither old nor young; he was wearing a tweed coat and carrying a newspaper under his arm. He smiled at me, and I couldn't tell at all whether or not it was the man from the week before, because he had a hat on. I had looked most at the balding head and the daffodils. This man, unlike the other, was smoking a pipe. 'Got all tied up, did you?' he asked as I looked up at him with dubious, swollen eyes. He knelt and undid the knots.

'Those are good knots,' he said. He asked me where I lived and I told him. 'I'll take you home,' he said. I said it was all right, I knew where I lived, but he said it was getting dark and little girls should not be running around by themselves after dark. He took my hand and we started to walk up the hill together.

But suddenly my mother was hurrying down towards us. Her hair was flying, she did not have gloves on, and when she came closer I could see that she was enraged. I dodged behind the man's tweed coat but she wrenched me out and slapped me across the face. She had never done this before.

'What have you been up to?' she said. I said nothing; I stood and glared at her, I didn't cry, and this impressed her as even more unnatural. I'd decided I was through crying in public, though of course I wasn't.

At this point the man interceded. He explained how he had found me tied up and how he had untied me and offered to see me home. My mother then became overly gracious, as she usually was with adults. They shook hands and she led me off. She phoned up the other mothers, full of moral indignation, and that was it for Brownies. It was too bad, because I really did like it. Brown Owl was one of the most pleasant women I had encountered so far, besides Aunt Lou, and I missed her.

My mother used this incident as an example of my own feckless-ness and general lack of wisdom. 'You were stupid to let the other girls fool you like that,' she said.

'I thought they were my friends,' I said.

'Friends wouldn't tie you up like that, would they? And in that ravine. Who knows what might have happened to you. You could've been killed. You were just lucky that nice man came along and untied you when he did, that's all.'

'Mother,' I said solemnly, eager to redeem myself in some way but unsure how to do it – perhaps by demonstrating that she was wrong? – 'I think that was a bad man.'

'Don't be an idiot,' she said. 'That nice man?'

'I think he was the same one. The daffodil man.'

'What daffodil man?' she asked. 'What have you been doing?'

'Nothing,' I said, backpedaling frantically; but it was too late, the first worm was out of the can and the rest had to follow. My mother was not pleased. In addition to everything else, I was now accused of sneaking around behind her back: I should have told her immediately.

I still wasn't sure, though: was it the daffodil man or not? Was the man who untied me a rescuer or a villian? Or, an even more baffling thought: was it possible for a man to be both at once?

I turned this puzzle over in my mind time after time, trying to remember and piece together the exact features of the daffodil man. But he was elusive, he melted and changed shape like butterscotch or warm gum, dissolving into a tweedy mist, sending out menacing tentacles of flesh and knotted rope, forming again as a joyful sunburst of yellow flowers.

Chapter Seven

One of the bad dreams I used to have about my mother was this. I would be walking across the bridge and she would be standing in the sunlight on the other side of it, talking to someone else, a man whose face I couldn't see. When I was halfway across, the bridge would start to collapse, as I'd always feared it would. Its rotten planks buckled and split, it tilted over sideways and began to topple slowly into the ravine. I would try to run but it would be too late, I would throw myself down and grab onto the far edge as it rose up, trying to slide me off. I called out to my mother, who could still have saved me, she could have run across quickly and reached out her hand, she could have pulled me back with her to firm ground – but she didn't do this, she went on with her conversation, she didn't notice that anything unusual was happening. She didn't even hear me.

In the other dream I would be sitting in a corner of my mother's bedroom, watching her put on her makeup. I did this often as a small child: it was considered a treat, a privilege, by both my mother and myself, and refusing to let me watch was one of my mother's ways of punishing me. She knew I was fascinated by her collection of cosmetics and implements: lipsticks, rouges, perfume in dainty bottles which I longed to have, bright red nail polish (sometimes, as an exceptional bribe, I was allowed to have some brushed on my toes, but never on my fingers: 'You're not old enough,' she'd say), little tweezers, nail files and emery boards. I was forbidden to touch any of these things. Of course I did, when she was out, but they were arranged in such rigid rows both on the dressertop and in the drawers that I had to be very careful to put them back exactly where I'd found them. My mother had a hawk's eye for anything out of place. I later extended this habit of snooping through her drawers and cupboards until I knew everything that each of them contained; finally I would do it not to satisfy my curiosity – I already knew everything – but for the sense of danger. I only got caught twice, early on: once when I ate a lipstick (even then, at the age of four, I was wise enough to replace the cover on the tube and the tube in the drawer, and to wash my mouth carefully; how did she know it was me?), and once when I couldn't resist covering my entire face with blue eye shadow, to see how I would look blue. That got me exiled for weeks. I almost gave the whole game away the day I found a curious object, like a rubber clamshell, packed away neatly in a box. I was dying to ask her what it was, but I didn't dare.

'Sit there quietly, Joan, and watch Mother put on her face.' she'd say on the good days. Then she would tuck a towel around her neck and go to work. Some of the things she did seemed to be painful; for instance, she would cover the space between her eyebrows with what looked like brown glue, which she heated in a little pot, then tear it off, leaving a red patch; and sometimes she'd smear herself with pink mud which would harden and crack. She often frowned at herself, shaking her head as if she was dissatisfied; and occasionally she'd talk to herself as if she'd forgotten I was there. Instead of making her happier, these sessions appeared to make her sadder, as if she saw behind or within the mirror some fleeting image she was unable to capture or duplicate; and when she was finished she was always a little cross.

I would stare at the proceedings, fascinated and mute. I thought my mother was very beautiful, even more beautiful when she was colored in. And this was what I did in the dream: I sat and stared. Although her vanity tables became more grandiose as my father got richer, my mother always had a triple mirror, so she could see both sides as well as the front of her head. In the dream, as I watched, I suddenly realized that instead of three reflections she had three actual heads, which rose from her toweled shoulders on three separate necks. This didn't frighten me, as it seemed merely a confirmation of something I'd always known; but outside the door there was a man, a man who was about to open the door and come in. If he saw, if he found out the truth about my mother, something terrible would happen, not only to my mother but to me. I wanted to jump up, run to the door, and stop him, but I couldn't move and the door would swing slowly inward. . . .

As I grew older, this dream changed. Instead of wanting to stop the mysterious man, I would sit there wishing for him to enter. I wanted him to find out her secret, the secret that I alone knew: my mother was a monster.

I can never remember calling her anything but Mother, never one of those childish diminutives; I must have, but she must have discouraged it. Our relationship was professionalized early. She was to be the manager, the creator, the agent; I was to be the product. I suppose one of the most important things she wanted from me was gratitude. She wanted me to do well, but she wanted to be responsible for it.

Her plans for me weren't specific. They were vague but large, so that whatever I did accomplish was never the right thing. But she didn't push all the time; for days and even weeks she would seem to forget me altogether. She would become involved in some other project of hers, like redecorating her bedroom or throwing a party. She even took a couple of jobs: she was a travel agent, for instance, and she once worked for an interior decorator, searching out lamps and carpets that would match living-room color designs. But none of these jobs lasted long, she would get discouraged, they weren't enough for her and she would quit.

It wasn't that she was aggressive and ambitious, although she was both these things. Perhaps she wasn't aggressive or ambitious enough. If she'd ever decided what she really wanted to do and had gone out and done it, she wouldn't have seen me as a reproach to her, the embodiment of her own failure and depression, a huge edgeless cloud of inchoate matter which refused to be shaped into anything for which she could get a prize.

In the image of her that I carried for years, hanging from my neck like an iron locket, she was sitting in front of her vanity table, painting her fingernails a murderous red and sighing. Her lips were thin but she made a larger mouth with lipstick over and around them, like Bette Davis, which gave her a curious double mouth, the real one showing through the false one like a shadow. She was an attractive woman, even into her late thirties, she had kept her figure, she had been popular in her youth. In her photograph album there were snapshots of her in party dresses and bathing suits, with various young men, her looking at the camera, the young men looking at her. One young man recurred often, in white flannels, with a big motor car. She said she'd been engaged to him, more or less.

There were no pictures of her as a girl though, none of her parents, none of the two brothers and the sister I later found out she had. She almost never talked about her family or her early life, though I was able to piece a little of it together. Her parents had both been very strict, very religious. They hadn't been rich; her father had been a stationmaster for the CPR. She'd done something that offended them – what it was I never learned – and she'd run away from home at the age of sixteen and never gone back. She'd worked at various jobs, clerking in Kresge's, waitressing. When she was eighteen she'd been a waitress at a resort in Muskoka, which was where she later met my father. The young men in the pictures were guests at the resort. She could only wear the party dresses and the bathing suits on her day off.

My father hadn't been staying at the resort; it wasn't the kind of thing he would do. He met my mother by accident, when he'd dropped by to visit a friend. There were a couple of pictures of them before the wedding, in which my father looked embarrassed. My mother held his arm as if it were a leash. Then the wedding portrait. After that some photos of my mother alone, which my father must have taken. Then nothing but me, drooling on rugs, eating stuffed animals or fists; my father had gone off to the war, leaving her pregnant, with nobody to take pictures of her.

My father didn't come back until I was five, and before that he was only a name, a story which my mother would tell me and which varied considerably. Sometimes he was a nice man who was coming home soon, bringing with him all kinds of improvements and delightful surprises: we would live in a bigger house, eat better, have more clothes, and the landlord would be put in his place once and for all. At other times, when I was getting out of hand, he was retribution personified, the judgment day that would catch up with me at last; or (and I think this was closest to her true feelings) he was a heartless wretch who had abandoned her, leaving her to cope with everything all by herself. The day he finally returned I was almost beside myself, torn between hope and fear: what would he bring me, what would he do to me? Was he a bad man or a nice man? (My mother's two categories: nice men did things for you, bad men did things to you.) But when the time came, a stranger walked through the door, kissed my mother and then me, and sat down at the table. He seemed very tired and said little. He brought nothing and did nothing, and that remained his pattern.

Most of the time he was simply an absence. Occasionally, though, he would stroll back into reality from wherever he had been, and he even had his moments of modest drama. I was thirteen, it must have been 1955, it was a Sunday. I was sitting in the kitchenette, eating half of an orange layer cake, for which I would later be scolded. But I'd already eaten one piece and I knew the number of words for that one piece would be as great as for half a cake, so I ate on, speedily, trying to get it all down before being discovered.

By this time I was eating steadily, doggedly, stubbornly, anything I could get. The war between myself and my mother was on in earnest; the disputed territory was my body. I didn't quite know this though I sensed it in a hazy way; but I reacted to the diet booklets she left on my pillow, to the bribes of dresses she would give me if I would reduce to fit them – formal gowns with layers of tulle and wired busts, perky little frocks, skirts with slim waists and frothy crinolines – to her cutting remarks about my size, to her pleas about my health (I would die of a heart attack, I would get high blood pressure), to the specialists she sent me to and the pills they prescribed, to all of these things, with another Mars Bar or a double helping of french fries. I swelled visibly, relentlessly, before her very eyes, I rose like dough, my body advanced inch by inch towards her across the dining-room table, in this at least I was undefeated. I was five feet four and still growing, and I weighed a hundred and eighty-two pounds.

Anyway: I was sitting in the kitchenette, eating half of an orange layer cake. It was a Sunday in 1955. My father was in the living room, sitting in an easy chair reading a murder mystery, his favorite way of relaxing. My mother was on the chesterfield, pretending to read a book on child psychology – she put a certain amount of time demonstrating that, God knew, she was doing her best – but actually reading *The Fox*, an historical novel about the Borgias. I had already finished it, in secret. The chesterfield had a diminutive purple satin cushion at either end, and these two cushions were sacrosanct, ritual objects which were not to be moved. The chesterfield itself was a dull pink, a nubby material shot through with silver threads. It had a covering of transparent plastic, which was removed for entertaining. The rug, which picked up the purple of the cushions, was also covered with a sheet of plastic, heavier in texture. The lampshades were protected with cellophane. On each of my father's feet was a slipper of maroon leather. My mother's feet and my own were similarly encased, as by this time my mother had made it a rule that no shoes were to be allowed inside the house. It was a new house and she had just finished getting it into shape; now that it was finally right she didn't want anything touched, she wanted it static and dustless and final, until that moment when she would see what a mistake she had made and the painters or movers would arrive once more, tailing disruption.

(My mother didn't want her living rooms to be different from everyone else's, or even very much better. She wanted them to be acceptable, the same as everybody else's, although her idea of everybody else changed as my father's salary increased. Perhaps this was why they looked like museum displays or, more accurately, like the show windows of Eaton's and Simpsons, those magic downtown palaces I would approach, with Aunt Lou, every December along a vista of streetcar tracks. We didn't go to see the furniture though, we were heading for the other windows, where animals, fairies and red-cheeked dwarfs twirled mechanically to the sound of tinkle bells. When I was old enough to go Christmas shopping it was Aunt Lou who took me. One year I announced I wasn't going to get my mother a Christmas present. 'But, dear,' Aunt Lou said, 'you'll hurt her feelings.' I didn't think she had any, but I gave in and bought her some bubble bath, enclosed in a lovely pink squeezable swan. She never used it, but I knew in advance she wouldn't. I ended up using it myself.)

I finished the slab of leftover cake and rose to my feet, my stomach bumping the table. My slippers were large and furry; they made my feet look twice as big. I clomped in them sullenly through the dining room, into the living room and past my parents and their books, without saying anything. I had developed the habit of clomping silently but very visibly through rooms in which my mother was sitting; it was a sort of fashion show in reverse, it was a display, I wanted her to see and recognise what little effect her nagging and pleas were having.

I intended to go into the hall, then up the stairs with a sasquatch-like, banister-shaking tread, and along the hall to my room, where I was going to put on an Elvis Presley record and turn the volume up just loud enough so she would repress the desire to complain. She was beginning to worry about her ability to communicate with me. I didn't have any intentional plans, I was merely acting according to a dimly felt, sluggish instinct. I was aware only of a wish to hear 'Heartbreak Hotel' at the maximum volume possible without reprisals.

But when I was halfway across the room there was a sudden pounding at the front door. Someone was hammering on it with balled fists; then there was the thud of a hurled body and a hoarse voice, a man's voice, screaming, 'I'll kill you! You bastard, I'll kill you!'

I froze. My father leapt from his chair and doubled over in a kind of wrestler's crouch. My mother put a bookmark between the pages of her book and closed it; then she removed her reading glasses, which she wore on a silver chain around her neck, and looked at my father with irritation. It was obviously his fault: who would call her a bastard? My father straightened up and went to the door.

'Oh, it's you, Mr Currie,' he said. 'I'm glad to see you're up and about again.'

'I'll sue you,' the voice shouted. 'I'll sue you within an inch of your life! Why couldn't you just leave me alone? You've ruined everything!' The voice broke into long, raucous sobs.

'You're a little upset right now,' my father's voice said.

The other voice wept, 'You messed it up! I did it right this time and you messed it up! I don't want to live. . . .'

'Life is a gift,' my father said with quiet dignity but a slight edge of reprimand, like the kindly dentist who demonstrated about cavities on the television set we'd acquired two years before. 'You should be grateful for it. You should respect it.'

'What do you know?' the voice roared. Then there was a scuffling sound and the voice receded into the distance, trailing muffled words behind it like a string of bubbles underwater. My father shut the door quietly and came back to the living room.

'I don't know why you do it,' my mother said. 'They're never grateful.'

'Do what?' I said, bulgy-eyed, breaking my vow of silence in my eagerness to know. I had never heard a man cry before and the knowledge that they sometimes did was electrifying.

'When people try to kill themselves,' my mother said, 'your father brings them to life again.'

'Not always, Frances,' my father said sadly.

'Often enough,' my mother said, opening her book. 'I'm tired of getting abusive phone calls in the middle of the night. I really wish you would stop.'

My father was an anesthetist at the Toronto General Hospital. He had studied to be one at my mother's urging, as she felt specialization was the coming thing, everyone said that specialists did better than family doctors. She had even been willing to make the necessary financial sacrifices while he was training. But I thought all my father did was put people to sleep before operations. I didn't know about this resurrectionist side of his personality.

'Why do people try to kill themselves?' I asked. 'How do you bring them to life again?'

My father ignored the first part of this question, it was far too complicated for him. 'I'm testing experimental methods,' he said. 'They don't always work. But they only give me the hopeless cases, when they've tried everything else.' Then he said, to my mother rather than to me, 'You'd be surprised how many of them are glad. That they've been able to . . . come back, have another chance.'

'Well,' said my mother. 'I only wish the ones who aren't so glad would keep it to themselves. It's a waste of time, if you ask me. They'll simply try all over again. If they were serious they'd just stick a gun in their mouth and pull the trigger. That takes the chance out of it.'

'Not everyone,' said my father, 'has your determination.'

Two years later, I learned something else about my father. We were in another house, with a bigger dining room, wood-paneled and impressive. My mother was having a dinner party, entertaining two couples whom she claimed privately to dislike. According to her, it was necessary to have them to dinner because they were my father's colleagues, important men at the hospital, and she was trying to help him with his career. She paid no attention when he said that it didn't matter one iota to his career whether she had these people to dinner or not; she went ahead and did it anyway. When she finally realized he'd been telling the truth, she stopped giving dinner parties and began drinking a little more heavily. But she must have already started by this evening, for which I can remember the menu: chicken breasts in cream sauce with wild rice and mushrooms, individual jellied salads with cranberries and celery, topped with mayonnaise, Duchess potatoes, and a complex dessert with mandarin oranges, ginger sauce and some kind of sherbet.

I was in the kitchen. I was fifteen, and I'd reached my maximum growth: I was five feet eight and I weighed two hundred and forty-five, give or take a few pounds. I no longer attended my mother's dinner parties; she was tired of having a teenaged daughter who looked like a beluga whale and never opened her mouth except to put something into it. I cluttered up her gracious-hostess act. On my side, much as I would have welcomed the chance to embarrass her, strangers were different, they saw my obesity as an unfortunate handicap, like a hump or a club foot, rather than the refutation, the victory it was, and watching myself reflected in their eyes shook my confidence. It was only in relation to my mother that I derived a morose pleasure from my weight; in relation to everyone else, including my father, it made me miserable. But I couldn't stop.

I was in the kitchen then, eavesdropping through the passageway and devouring spare parts and leftovers. They had reached the dessert, so I was making away with the extra chicken and cranberry salads and Duchess potatoes, and listening to the conversation in the other room halfheartedly, as if to a tepid radio drama. One of the visiting doctors had been in the war, mostly in Italy as it turned out; the other one had enlisted but had never made it farther than England. Then of course there was my father, who apart from acknowledging that he had been over there too, never said much about it. I'd listened in on conversations like this before and they didn't interest me. From the war movies I'd seen, there was nothing much for women to do in wars except the things they did anyway.

The man who had served in Italy finished recounting one of his exploits, and after a chorus of ruminative murmurs, asked, 'Where were you stationed, Phil?'

'Oh, um,' said my father.

'In France,' my mother said.

'Oh, you mean after the invasion,' said the other man.

'No,' said my mother, and giggled; a danger sign. She had taken to giggling during dinner parties lately. The giggle, which had a bleary, uncontrolled quality, had replaced the high, gay company laugh she used to wield as purposefully as a baseball bat.

'Oh,' said the Italy man politely, 'what were you doing?'

'Killing people,' said my mother promptly and with relish, as if she were enjoying a private joke.

'Fran,' said my father. It was a warning, but the tone was also imploring; something new and rare. I was gnawing the last shreds of the carcass of a breast, but I stopped in order to listen more closely.

'Well, everyone kills a few people in a war, I guess,' said the second man.

'Up close?' said my mother. 'I bet you didn't kill them up close.'

There was a silence, of the kind that comes into a room when everyone knows that something exciting and probably unpleasant is going to happen. I could picture my mother looking around at the attentive faces, avoiding my father's eyes.

'He was in Intelligence,' she said importantly. 'You wouldn't think it to look at him, would you? They dropped him in behind the lines and he worked with the French underground. You wouldn't ever hear it from him, but he can speak French like a native; he gets it from his last name.'

'My,' said one of the women, 'I've always wanted to go to Paris. Is it as beautiful as they say?'

'His job was to kill the people they thought were fakes,' my mother continued. 'He had to just take them out and shoot them. In cold blood. Sometimes he wouldn't even know if he'd shot the right one. Isn't that something?' Her voice was thrilled and admiring. 'The funny thing is, he doesn't like me to mention it ... the funny thing is, he told me once that the frightening thing about it was, he started to *enjoy* it.'

One of the men laughed nervously. I got up and retreated on my furry slippered feet to the stairs (I could walk quietly enough when

I wanted to) and lowered myself down halfway up. Sure enough, a moment later my father marched through the swinging door into the kitchen, followed by my mother. She must have realized she had pushed it too far.

'There's nothing *wrong* with it,' she said. 'It was in a good cause. You never make the most of yourself.'

'I asked you not to talk about it,' my father said. He sounded very angry, enraged. It was the first time I realized he could feel rage; he was usually very calm. 'You have no idea what it was like.'

'I think it's great,' said my mother, earnestly. 'It took real courage, I don't see what's wrong with. . . .'

'Shut up,' said my father.

Those are stories from later; earlier he wasn't there, which is probably why I remember him as nicer than my mother. And after that he was busy studying, he was someone who was not to be disturbed, and then he was at the hospital a lot. He didn't know quite what to make of me, ever; though I never felt he was hostile, only bemused.

The few things we did together were wordless things. Such as: he took to growing house plants – vines and spider plants and ferns and begonias. He liked to tinker with them, snipping off cuttings and repotting and planting, on Saturday afternoons if he had the free time, listening to the Texaco Company Metropolitan Opera broadcasts on the radio, and he would let me help him with the plants. As he never said much of anything, I would pretend his voice was the voice of Milton Cross, kindly and informed, describing the singers' costumes and the passionate, tragic and preposterous events in which they were involved. There he would be, puffing away on the pipe he took up after he quit cigarettes, poking at his house plants and conversing to me about lovers being stabbed or abandoned or betrayed, about jealousy and madness, about unending love triumphing over the grave; and then those chilling voices would drift into the room, raising the hair on the back of my neck, as if he had evoked them. He was a conjuror of spirits, a shaman with the voice of a dry, detached old opera commentator in a tuxedo. Or that's how I imagined him sounding, when I thought up the conversations I would have liked to have had with him but never did. I wanted him to tell me the truth about life, which my mother would not tell me and which he must have known something about, as he was a doctor and had been in the war, he'd killed people and raised the dead. I kept waiting for him to give me some advice, warn me, instruct me, but he never did any of these things. Perhaps he felt as if I weren't really his daughter; he'd seen me for the first time five years after I was born, and he treated me more like a colleague than a daughter, more like an accomplice. But what was our conspiracy? Why hadn't he come back on leave during those five years? A question my mother asked also. Why did they both act as though he owed my mother something?

Then there were those other conversations I overheard. I used to go into the upstairs bathroom, lock the door, and turn on the tap so they would think I was brushing my teeth. Then I would arrange the bath mat on the floor so my knees wouldn't get cold, put my head into the toilet, and listen to them through the pipes. It was almost a direct line to the kitchen, where they had most of their fights, or rather my mother had them. She was a lot easier to hear than my father.

'Why don't you try doing something with her for a change, she's your daughter, too. I'm really at the end of my rope.'

My father: silence.

'You don't know what it was like, all alone with her to bring up while you were there over there enjoying yourself.'

My father: 'I didn't enjoy myself.'

And once: 'It's not as though I wanted to have her. It's not as though I wanted to marry you. I had to make the best of a bad job if you ask me.'

My father: 'I'm sorry it hasn't worked out for you.'

And once, when she was very angry: 'You're a doctor, don't tell me you couldn't have done something.'

My father: (inaudible).

'Don't give me that crap, you killed a lot of people. Sacred my foot.'

At first I was shocked, mainly by my mother's use of the word *crap*. She tried so hard to be a lady in front of other people, even me. Later I tried to figure out what she'd meant, and when she'd say, 'If it wasn't for me you wouldn't be here,' I didn't believe her.

I ate to defy her, but I also ate from panic. Sometimes I was afraid I wasn't really there, I was an accident; I'd heard her call me an accident. Did I want to become solid, solid as a stone so she wouldn't be able to get rid of me? What had I done? Had I trapped my father, if he really was my father, had I ruined my mother's life? I didn't dare to ask.

For a while I wanted to be an opera singer. Even though they were fat they could wear extravagant costumes, nobody laughed at them, they were loved and praised. Unfortunately I couldn't sing. But it always appealed to me: to be able to stand up there in front of everyone and shriek as loud as you could, about hatred and love and rage and despair, scream at the top of your lungs and have it come out music. That would be something.

Chapter Eight

'Sometimes I think you haven't got a brain in your head,' my mother used to say. When I was crying, for some invalid reason or other. To her mind, tears were an evidence of stupidity. I'll give you something to cry about. That's nothing to cry about. Don't cry over spilled milk.

'I'm lonely,' I told her. 'I don't have anyone to play with.'

'Play with your dolls,' she said, outlining her mouth.

I did play with them, those crotchless frizzy-haired plastic goddesses, with their infantile eyes and their breasts that emerged and receded gently as knees, unalarming, devoid of nipples. I dressed them up for social events they never attended, undressed them again and stared at them, wishing they would come alive. They were chaste, unloved, widowed: in those days there were no male dolls. They danced by themselves or stood against the wall, catatonic.

When I was nine I tried for a dog. I knew I wouldn't get one but I was softening her up for a kitten; I'd been offered one by a girl at school whose cat had six, one with seven toes on each foot. This was the one I wanted. What I really wanted was a baby sister but this was out of the question, and even I knew it. I'd heard her say over the phone that one was more than enough. (Why wasn't she happier? Why could I never make her laugh?)

'Who would feed it?' my mother asked. 'Three times a day.'

'I would,' I said.

'You wouldn't,' my mother said, 'you don't come home for lunch.' Which was true, I took my lunch to school in a lunch box.

With the kitten it was house-training and scratching the furniture. Next I tried a turtle; there didn't seem much that could go wrong with a turtle, but my mother said it would be smelly.

'No it wouldn't,' I said, 'they've got one at school and it doesn't smell.'

'It would get lost behind the furniture,' my mother said, 'and starve to death.'

She wouldn't hear of a guinea pig or a hamster or even a bird. Finally after nearly a year of failures I backed her into a corner. I asked for a fish. It would be noiseless, odorless, germ-free and clean; after all, it lived in water. I wanted it to have a bowl with colored pebbles and a miniature castle.

She couldn't think of any good reason why not, so she gave in and I bought a goldfish at Kresge's. 'It will only die,' my mother said. 'Those cheap goldfish all have diseases.' But when I'd had it a week she did give in enough to ask me its name. I was sitting with my eye against the glass, watching it as it swam up to the top and back down again, burping out pieces of its food.

'Susan Hayward,' I said. I had just seen *With a Song in My Heart*, in which Susan Hayward made a comeback from a wheelchair. The odds were stacked against this goldfish and I wanted it to have a courageous name. It died anyway; my mother said it was my fault, I overfed it. Then she flushed it down the toilet before I had a chance to weep over it and bury it properly. I wanted to replace it but my mother said that surely I had learned my lesson. I was always supposed to be learning some lesson or other.

My mother said movies were vulgar, though I suspected she'd once gone to a lot of them; otherwise how would she know about Joan Crawford? So it was my Aunt Lou who took me to see Susan Hayward. 'There, you see?' she said to me afterwards. 'Red hair can be very glamorous.'

Aunt Lou was tall and heavy and built like an Eaton's Catalog corset ad for the mature figure, but she didn't seem to mind. She piled her graying yellowish hair onto the top of her head and stuck extravagant hats with feathers and bows onto the mound with pearl hatpins and wore bulky fur coats and heavy tweeds, which made her look even taller and fatter. In one of my earliest memories of her I'm sitting on her wide, woolly lap – hers was the only lap I remember sitting on, and my mother would say, 'Get down, Joan, don't bother your Aunt Louisa' – and stroking the fur of the fox she wore around her neck. This was a real fox, it was brown, it wasn't as mangy as it later became; it had a tail and four paws, black beady eyes and a cool plastic nose, though underneath its nose, instead of a lower jaw, it had a clamp by which it held its tail in place. Aunt Lou would open and shut the clamp and pretend that the fox was talking. It often revealed secrets, such as where Aunt Lou had hidden the gumdrops she had bought me, and it asked important questions also, like what I wanted for Christmas. When I grew older this game was dropped, but Aunt Lou still kept the fox in her closet, although it had gone out of style.

Aunt Lou took me to the movies a lot. She loved them, especially the ones that made you cry; she didn't think a movie was much good unless it made you cry. She rated pictures as two-Kleenex, three-Kleenex or four-Kleenex ones, like the stars in restaurant guides. I wept also, and these binges of approved sniveling were amongst the happiest moments of my childhood.

First there was the delightful feeling of sneaking out on my mother; for although she claimed to give her consent when I asked permission, I knew she didn't really. Then we would take the streetcar or a bus to the theater. In the lobby we would stock up on pocket-packs of Kleenex, popcorn and candy bars; then we would settle down in the furry, soothing darkness for several hours of guzzling and sniffling, as the inflated heroines floating before us on the screen were put through the wringer.

I suffered along with sweet, patient June Allyson as she lived through the death of Glenn Miller; I ate three boxes of popcorn while Judy Garland tried to cope with an alcoholic husband, and five Mars Bars while Eleanor Parker, playing a crippled opera singer, groped her mournful way through *Interrupted Melody*. But the one I like best was *The Red Shoes*, with Moira Shearer as a ballet dancer torn between her career and her husband. I adored her: not only did she have red hair and an entrancing pair of red satin slippers to match, she also had beautiful costumes, and she suffered more than anyone. I munched faster and faster as she became more and more entangled in her dilemma – I wanted those things too, I wanted to dance and be married to a handsome orchestra conductor, both at once – and when she finally threw herself in front of a train I let out a bellowing snort that made people three rows ahead turn around indignantly. Aunt Lou took me to see it four times.

I saw a number of *Adult* pictures long before I was an adult, but no one ever questioned my age. I was quite fat by this time and all fat women look the same, they all look forty-two. Also, fat women are not more noticeable than thin women; they're less noticeable, because people find them distressing and look away. To the ushers and the ticket sellers I must've appeared as a huge featureless blur. If I'd ever robbed a bank no witness would have been able to describe me accurately.

We would come out of the movie red-eyed, our shoulders still heaving, but with a warm feeling of accomplishment. Then we would go for a soda or two or for a snack at Aunt Lou's apartment – grilled crab-meat sandwiches with mayonnaise, cold chicken salad. She kept a number of these things in her refrigerator or in cans on her cupboard shelves. Her apartment building was an older one, with dark wood trim and large rooms. The furniture was dark and large, too, frequently dusty and always cluttered: newspapers on the chesterfield, afghan shawls on the floor, odd shoes or stockings under the chairs, dishes in the sink. To me this disorder meant you could do what you liked. I imitated it in my own bedroom, scattering clothes and books and chocolate-bar wrappers over the surfaces so carefully planned by my mother, the dressing table with the sprigged muslin flounce, bedspread to match, rug in harmony. This was the only form of interior decoration I ever did, and the drawback was that sooner or later it had to be cleaned up.

When we'd had our snack Aunt Lou would pour herself a drink, slip off her shoes, settle into one of her podgy chairs, and ask me questions in her rasping voice. She actually seemed interested in what I had to say, and she didn't laugh when I told her I wanted to be an opera singer.

One of my mother's ways of dismissing Aunt Lou was to say that she was bitter and frustrated because she didn't have a husband, but if this was true Aunt Lou kept it well hidden. To me she seemed a lot less bitter and frustrated than my mother, who, now that she'd achieved and furnished her ultimate house, was concentrating more and more of her energy on forcing me to reduce. She really did try everything. When I refused to take the pills or stick to the diets – neatly drawn up by her, with menus for every day of the week listing the number of calories – she sent me to a psychiatrist.

'I like being fat,' I told him, and burst into tears. He sat looking at me with the tips of his fingers together, smiling benevolently but with a trace of disgust as I gasped and puffed.

'Don't you want to get married?' he asked when I had subsided. This started me off afresh, but the next time I saw Aunt Lou I asked her, 'Didn't you want to get married?'

She gave one of her raucous laughs. She was sitting in her overstuffed easy chair, drinking a martini. 'Oh, I was married, dear,' she said. 'Didn't I ever tell you?'

I'd always assumed Aunt Lou was an old maid because her last name was the same as my father's, Delacourt, pronounced *Delacore*. 'French nobility, no doubt,' said Aunt Lou. Her great-grandfather had been a farmer, before he decided to improve himself. He got into the railroad, she said, on the ground floor, sold the farm to do it; that was how the family made its money. 'They were all crooks, of course,' Aunt Lou said, sipping at her drink, 'but nobody called it that.'

It turned out Aunt Lou had been married at nineteen, to a man eight years her senior, of good social standing and approved by the family. Unfortunately he was a compulsive gambler. 'In one pocket and out the other,' she wheezed, 'but what did I know? I was madly in love with him, dear, he was tall, dark and handsome.' I began to see why she liked the kind of movies she did: they were a lot like her own life. 'I tried, dear, I really did, but it was no use. He would be gone for days on end, and it wasn't as though I knew anything about running a house or managing money. I'd never shopped for food in my life; all I knew was you picked up the phone and someone brought it to your house in a box. The first week I was married I ordered a pound of everything: one pound of flour, one pound of salt, one pound of pepper, one pound of sugar. I thought that was what you were supposed to do. The pepper lasted years.' Aunt Lou's laugh sounded like an enraged walrus. She liked telling jokes on herself, but sometimes it made her choke. 'Then he'd come back and if he'd lost he'd tell me how much he loved me, if he'd won he'd complain about being tied down. It was very sad, really. One day he just never came back. Maybe they shot him for not paying. I wonder if he's still alive; if he is, I suppose I'm still married to him.'

I found out even later that Aunt Lou had a boyfriend of sorts. His name was Robert, he was an accountant, he had a wife and children, and he came to her apartment on Sunday evenings for dinner. 'Don't tell your mother, dear,' Aunt Lou said. 'I'm not sure she'd understand.'

'Wouldn't you like to marry him?' I asked her when she told me about him.

'Once bitten, twice shy,' said Aunt Lou. 'Besides, I never got a divorce, what was the point? I just took back my own name, that way I don't have to answer so many questions. Take my advice and don't get married until you're at least twenty-five.'

She assumed there would be suitors clamoring at my heels; she didn't even acknowledge the possibility that no one would ask me. My mother's version was that nobody who looked like me could ever accomplish anything, but Aunt Lou was all for dismissing handicaps or treating them as obstacles to be overcome. Crippled opera singers could do it if they would only try. Gross as I was, something might be expected of me after all. I wasn't sure I was up to it.

After her bad experience with the gambler Aunt Lou had gone out and gotten herself a job. 'I couldn't type, dear,' she said, 'I couldn't do anything, the way I was brought up; but it was the Depression, you know. The family didn't have money any more. So I had to, didn't I? I worked my way up.'

When I was younger my father and mother were vague about Aunt Lou's job, and so was she. All they would say was that she worked in an office for a company and she was head of a department. I found out what she actually did when I was thirteen.

'Here,' said my mother, 'I suppose it's time you read this,' and she put into my hands a pink booklet with a wreath of flowers festooning the front. *You're Growing Up*, the cover said. On the inside page was a letter, which began, 'Growing up can be fun. But there are also some things about it which can be puzzling. One of them is menstruation. . . .' At the bottom of this page was a picture of Aunt Lou, smiling maternally but professionally, taken before her jowls were quite so large. Around her neck was a single strand of pearls. Although she did wear pearls in real life, it was never just one strand. Underneath the letter was her signature: 'Sincerely yours, Louisa K. Delacourt.' I studied the diagrams in the pink booklet with interest; I read the etiquette hints for tennis games and high-school proms, the wardrobe suggestions, the advice on washing your hair; but I was even more impressed by Aunt Lou's picture and signature – like a movie star, sort of. My Aunt Lou was famous, in a way.

I asked her about it the next time I saw her. 'I'm head of Public Relations, dear,' she said. 'Just for Canada. But I didn't really write that booklet, you know. That was written by Advertising.'

'Then what do you do?' I asked.

'Well,' she said. 'I go to a lot of meetings, and I advise on the ads. And I answer the letters. My secretary helps me, of course.'

'What kind of letters?' I asked.

'Oh, you know,' she said. 'Complaints about the product, requests for advice, that sort of thing. You'd think they'd all be from young girls, and a lot of them are. Girls wanting to know where their vagina is and things like that. We have a form letter for those. But some of them are from people who really need help, and those are the ones I answer personally. When they're afraid to go to the doctor or something, they write me. Half the time I don't know what to say.' Aunt Lou finished her martini and went to pour herself another one. 'I got one just the other day from a woman who thought she'd been impregnated by an incubus.'

'An incubus?' I asked. It sounded like some sort of medical appliance. 'What's that?'

'I looked it up in the dictionary,' said Aunt Lou. 'It's a sort of demon.'

'What did you tell her?' I asked, horrified. What if the woman was right?

'I told her,' said Aunt Lou reflectively, 'to get a pregnancy test, and if it came out positive it wouldn't be an incubus. If it's negative, then she won't have to worry, will she?'

'Louisa is beyond the pale,' my mother said when she was explaining to my father why she didn't have Aunt Lou to dinner more often. 'People are sure to ask her what she does, and she always tells them. I can't have her using those words at the dinner table. I know she's good-hearted but she just doesn't care what kind of an impression she makes.'

'Count your blessings,' Aunt Lou said to me with a chuckle. 'They pay well and it's a friendly office. I've got nothing to complain about.'

The psychiatrist gave up on me after three sessions of tears and silence. I resented the implication that there were yet more things wrong with me in addition to being fat, and he resented my resentment. He told my mother it was a family problem which couldn't be resolved by treating me alone, and she was indignant. 'He has his nerve,' she said to my father. 'He just wants to get more money out of me. They're all quacks, if you ask me.'

After that she entered her laxative phase. I think by this time she was frantic; certainly she was obsessed with my bulk. Like most people she probably thought in images, and her image of me then must have been a one-holed object, like an inner tube, that took things in at one end but didn't let them out at the other: if she could somehow uncork me I would deflate, all at once, like a dirigible. She started to buy patent medicines, disguising her attempts to get me to take them – 'It'll be good for your complexion' – and occasionally slipping them into the food. Once she even iced a chocolate cake with melted Ex-Lax, leaving it on the kitchen counter where I found and devoured it. It made me wretched but it didn't make me thin.

By this time I was in high school. I resisted my mother's plan to send me to a private girls' school, where the pupils wore kilts and little plaid ties. Ever since Brownies I'd been wary of any group composed entirely of women, especially women in uniforms. So instead I went to the nearest high school, which was second-best in my mother's opinion but not as bad as it might have been, since by now we were living in a respectable neighborhood. The catch was that the children of the families my mother viewed as her peers and models were sent to the kind of private school she wanted to send me to, so the high school got mostly the leftovers, from the smaller houses around the fringes of the area, the brash new apartment building which had been opposed by the established residents, and even worse, the flats above the stores on the commercial streets. Some of my classmates were not at all what she had in mind, though I didn't tell her this as I didn't want to be forced into uniform.

At this time my mother gave me a clothing allowance, as an incentive to reduce. She thought I should buy clothes that would make me less conspicuous, the dark dresses with tiny polka-dots and vertival stripes favored by designers for the fat. Instead I sought out clothes of a peculiar and offensive hideousness, violently colored, horizontally striped. Some of them I got in maternity shops, others at cut-rate discount stores; I was especially pleased with a red felt skirt, cut in a circle, with a black telephone appliquéd onto it. The brighter the colors, the more rotund the effect, the more certain I was to buy. I wasn't going to let myself be diminished, neutralized, by a navy-blue polka-dot sack.

Once, when I arrived home in a new lime-green car coat with toggles down the front, flashing like a neon melon, my mother started to cry. She cried hopelessly, passively; she was leaning against the banister, her whole body slack as if she had no bones. My mother had never cried where I could see her and I was dismayed, but elated too at this evidence of my power, my only power. I had defeated her: I wouldn't ever let her make me over in her image, thin and beautiful.

'Where do you find them?' she sobbed. 'You're doing it on purpose. If I looked like you I'd hide in the cellar.'

I'd waited a long time for that. She who cries first is lost. 'You've been drinking,' I said, which was true. For the first time in my life I experienced, consciously, the joy of self-righteous recrimination.

'What have I done to make you behave like this?' my mother said. She was wearing a housecoat and slippers, even though it was four-thirty in the afternoon, and her hair could have been cleaner. I stomped past her, up to my room, feeling quite satisfied with myself. But when I thought about it, I had doubts. She was taking all the credit for herself, I was not her puppet; surely I was behaving like this not because of anything she had done but because I wanted to. And what was so bad, anyway, about the way I was behaving?

'That's just the way I am,' Aunt Lou said once. 'If other people can't handle it, that's their problem. Remember that, dear. You can't always choose your life, but you can learn to accept it.' I was accustomed to thinking of Aunt Lou as wise; she was certainly generous. The only trouble was that the bits of wisdom she dispensed could have several meanings, when you thought hard about them. For instance, was I supposed to accept my mother, or was she supposed to accept me?

In one of my daydreams I used to pretend Aunt Lou was my real mother, who for some dark but forgivable reason had handed me over to my parents to be brought up. Maybe I was the child of the handsome gambler, who would one day reappear, or Aunt Lou had had me out of wedlock when she was very young. In this case my father was not my real father, and my mother ... but here it broke down, for what could have persuaded my mother to take me in if she hadn't been obliged to? When my father would comment on how fond Aunt Lou was of me, my mother would reply acidly that it was only because she didn't have me on her hands all the time. On her hands, in her hair, these were the metaphors my mother used about me, despite the fact that she seldom touched me. Her hands were delicate and long-fingered, with red nails, her hair carefully arranged; no nests for me among those stiff immaculate curls. I could always recall what my mother looked like but not what she felt like.

Aunt Lou however was soft, billowy, woolly, befurred; even her face, powdered and rouged, was covered with tiny hairs, like a bee. Wisps escaped from her head, threads from her hems, sweetish odors from the space between her collar and her neck, where I would rest my forehead, listening to the stories of her talking fox. In the summers, when I was small and we wandered the grounds of the Canadian National Exhibition, she would hold me by the hand. My mother didn't hold me by the hand, there were her gloves to think of. She held me by the arm or the back of the collar. And she would never take me to the Ex, which she said was not worthwhile. Aunt Lou and I thought it was worthwhile, we loved it, the shouting barkers and the pipe bands and the wads of pink cotton candy and greasy popcorn we would stuff into ourselves while rambling from one pavilion to another. We would head for the Pure Foods first every year to see the cow made of real butter; one year they made the Queen instead.

But there was something I could never quite remember. We went to the midway, of course, and on rides, the slower ones – Aunt Lou liked the Ferris wheel – but there were two tents Aunt Lou wouldn't let me visit. One had women in harem costumes and enormous jutting breasts painted on it, and two or three of these women would pose on a little stage outside the door in their gauzy pants with their midriffs showing, while a man with a megaphone tried to get people to buy tickets. The other was the Freak Show, and this tent had the fire-eater and the sword-swallower in it, as well as the Rubber Man and the Siamese Twins, JOINED HEAD TO HEAD AND STILL ALIVE, the man said, and the fattest woman in the world. Aunt Lou didn't want to go into this tent either. 'It's wrong to laugh at other people's misfortunes,' she said, sterner than usual. I found this unfair: other people laughed at mine, I should get a chance too. But then, nobody regarded being fat as a misfortune; it was viewed simply as a disgusting failure of will. It wasn't fated and therefore glamorous, like being a Siamese twin or living in an iron lung. Nevertheless, the Fat Lady was in that tent and I wanted to see her; but I never did.

What I couldn't remember was this: were there two tents, or was there only one? The man with the megaphone sounded the same for freaks and dancing girls alike. They were both spectacular, something that had to be seen to be believed.

Aunt Lou's favorite midway place was the one with the giant mouth on the outside, from which canned laughter issued in a never-ending stream. 'Laugh in the Dark,' it was called. It had phosphorescent skeletons, and distorting mirrors that stretched you and shrank you. I found those mirrors disturbing. I didn't want to be fatter than I already was, and being thinner was impossible.

I used to imagine the Fat Lady sitting on a chair, knitting, while lines and lines of thin grey faces filed past her, looking, looking. I saw her in gauze pants and a maroon satin brassiere, like the dancing girls, and red slippers. I thought about what she would feel. One day she would rebel, she would do something; meanwhile she made her living from their curiosity. She was knitting a scarf, for one of her relatives who had known her from a child and didn't find her strange at all.

Chapter Nine

I had one picture of Aunt Lou. I used to cart it around with me and stand it on whatever bureau happened to be there, but when I escaped to Terremoto I left it behind: Arthur might have noticed it was missing. It was taken on a hot August day on the grounds of the Canadian National Exhibition, outside the Colosseum

Building, by one of those roving photographers who snap your picture and hand you a slip of paper with a number on it.

'Is that your mother?' Arthur asked once when I was unpacking it.

'No,' I said, 'that's my Aunt Lou.'

'Who's the other one? The fat one.'

For a moment I hesitated, on the verge of telling him the truth. 'That's my other aunt,' I said. 'My Aunt Deirdre. Aunt Lou was wonderful, but Aunt Deirdre was a bitch.'

'Looks like she had thyroid problems,' Arthur said.

'She didn't, she just ate too much. She worked as a telephone operator,' I said. 'She liked that because she could sit down all day and she had a loud voice. She got promoted to one of those people who phone you up to find out why you haven't paid the bill.' What lies I told him, and it wasn't just in self-defense: already I'd devised an entire spurious past for this shadow on a piece of paper, this woman of no discernible age who stood squinting at the camera, holding a cone of pink spun sugar, her face puffed and empty as a mongoloid idiot's: my own shucked-off body.

'She looks a bit like you,' he said.

'A bit,' I admitted. 'I didn't like her. She was always trying to tell me how to run my life.'

It hurt me a little to betray myself like that. The picture was an opening and I should have taken it, it was still early enough for such risks. Instead I retreated behind the camouflage of myself as Arthur perceived me. I suppose I couldn't trust him with all that discarded misery, I didn't think he would be able to handle it. He wanted me to be inept and vulnerable, it's true, but only superficially. Underneath this was another myth: that I could permit myself to be inept and vulnerable only because I had a core of strength, a reservoir of support and warmth that could be drawn on when needed.

Every myth is a version of the truth, and the warmth and support were there all right. I learned commiseration early, I gave dollar bills to the Salvation Army at Christmas and to legless men selling pencils on streetcorners, I was the sort children approach with lies about having lost their bus fare and I forked over every time. When I walked down Yonge Street I got hit by the Hare Krishna at each red light, it was like a parade, I don't know how they spotted me. I empathized with anything in pain: cats hit by cars, old women who fell on icy sidewalks and were mortified by their own weakness and displayed underpants, aldermen who wept on television when they lost an election. For this reason, as Arthur pointed out more that once, my politics were sloppy. I didn't like firing squads; I never felt that those toppled from power deserved what got done to them, no matter what they'd done in their turn. 'Naive humanism,' Arthur called it. He liked it fine when it was applied to him, though.

What he didn't know was that behind my compassionate smile was a set of tightly clenched teeth, and behind that a legion of voices, crying, *What about me? What about my own pain? When is it my turn?* But I'd learned to stifle these voices, to be calm and receptive.

I made it through high school on warmth and supportiveness. In the *Braeside Banner*, under the group pictures in which girls with dark mouths and penciled brows and pageboys or ponytails were arranged in front of boys with crew cuts or oily duck's asses, eyes front, feet crossed at the ankles, the epigram for me always said, 'Our happy-go-lucky gal with the terrific personality!!!' or 'A great pal!!!!' or 'Joanie's a laugh a minute!!' or 'A swell kid who never seems to get excited.' For other girls they said things like, 'She likes them tall!!' or 'Oh, those Don Mills parties!!' or 'Her main attraction is a certain Simpson's Rep!' or even, 'Good things come in small packages.' At home I was sullen or comatose, at the movies I wept with Aunt Lou, but at school I was doggedly friendly and outgoing, I chewed gum, smoked in the washroom, and painted my lips Precious Pink or Sultry Red, my tiny cupid's mouth lost in a sea of face. I was good at volleyball, though not at basketball, in which you had to run around a lot. I was elected to committees, usually as the secretary, and I joined the United Nations Club and was part of a delegation to the Model U.N., representing the Arabs. I made quite a good speech on the plight of the Palestinian refugees, as I recall. I helped with the decorations for the dances, stringing endless limp wreaths of Kleenex flowers along the walls of the sweaty gymnasium, though of course, I never attended. My marks were reasonable but not so high as to be offensive. More importantly, I played kindly aunt and wisewoman to a number of the pancake-madeup, cashmere-sweatered, pointy-breasted girls in the class. It was for this reason that the yearbook said such cozy things about me.

There were two other fat girls in the school. One of these,

Monica, was a year ahead of me. She had greasy hair, cut short and combed back, like a boy's, and she wore a black leather jacket with silver studs. At noon hour she hung out with some of the tougher, stupider boys in the parking lot, where they drank from mickeys hidden in glove compartments and exchanged dirty jokes. She was accepted by them, more or less, but as another boy. They didn't seem to think of her as a woman at all. Theresa, the other one, was in the same year as I was but a different class. She was pallid and reticent; she never said much and had few friends. She waddled along the halls by herself, shoulders stooped and books clasped to her chest to hide some of her frontal bulk, peering shyly and myopically at her own feet. She wore cream-colored rayon blouses with discreet embroidery on them, like the forty-five-year-old office secretary's. Yet it was she rather than brazen Monica who had the traditional fat-girl reputation, it was Theresa at whom boys would shout from the other side of the street, 'Hey Theresa, hey fatty! Wanta go out behind the field house with me?' for the benefit of other, less forthright boys. Theresa would turn her head away, blushing; no one knew whether or not the rumors were true, that she would 'do it' under the right circumstances, but everyone believed them.

As for me, I had a terrific personality and my friends were nice girls, the kind boys wanted to take out to dances and movies, where they would be seen in public and admired. No one shouted things at me on the street; no one who went to our school, at any rate. These girls liked to walk home with me, asking my advice and confiding in me, for two reasons: if a boy who was not wanted approached them, there I was, a fat duenna, the perfect excuse, it was like having your own private tank; and if a more desirable boy turned up, how could my friends help but look good beside me? In additon, I was very understanding, I always knew the right moment to say, 'See you tomorrow,' and vanish into the distance like a blimp in a steady wind, leaving the couple gazing at each other on the sidewalk in front of those trim Braeside houses, those clipped lawns. The girls would phone me up later, breathlessly, and say 'Guess what happened,' and I would say 'Oh, what?' as though I were thrilled and delighted and could hardly wait to find out. I could be depended upon not to show envy, not to flirt competitively, and not to wonder why I wasn't invited to the mixed-couples parties of these, my dearest friends. Though immersed in flesh, I was regarded as being above its desires, which of course was not true.

Everyone trusted me, no one was afraid of me, though they should have been. I knew everything about my friends, their hopes, their preferences, the brand of china and the style of wedding dress they had lined up for themselves already at the age of fifteen, the names of the unsuspecting boys on whom they wished to bestow these treasures, how they really felt about the boys they went out with, those drips and creeps, and about the other ones they would rather have gone out with, those living dolls. I knew what they thought about each other and what they said behind each other's backs. But they guessed nothing about me; I was a sponge, I drank it all in but gave nothing out, despite the temptation to tell everything, all my hatred and jealousy, to reveal myself as the duplicitous monster I knew myself to be. I could just barely stand it.

About the only advantage to this life of strain was that I gained a thorough knowledge of a portion of my future audience: those who got married too young, who had babies too early, who wanted princes and castles and ended up with cramped apartments and grudging husbands. But I couldn't forsee that at the time.

Monica dropped out of school as soon as she could. So did Theresa, in order to get married to a garage mechanic, an older man who didn't go to my school or any other. It was said she was pregnant, though as one of my friends remarked, how could you tell? I hung on, grimly; I wanted to graduate in order to be finished with it, but I had no idea what I was going to do next. My mother wished me to go to Trinity College at the University of Toronto, which was prestigious, and I almost wanted to myself, I wanted to study archaeology or perhaps history; but I couldn't bear the thought of four or more years of acute concealed misery, with the horrors of sororities, engagements, football games and spring weddings thrown in. I started taking part-time jobs; I opened a bank account. I told Aunt Lou, but no one else, that as soon as I had enough money I was going to leave home.

'Do you think that's wise, dear?' she said.

'Do you think staying there would be wise?' I asked. She knew my mother, she should have sympathized with me. Perhaps she was worried about what would happen to me, out there in the world. I was worried about that too. I wanted to leave, but I was also afraid to.

I'd been feeling guilty about Aunt Lou: I hadn't been going to the movies with her as much as I used to. The truth was that I was afraid one of my friends, Barbara or Carole-Ann (who was a cheerleader) or Valerie, done up in a cashmere sweater, with little trussed breasts sticking out jaunty as cocked thumbs, a wreath of artificial flowers twined around the elastic band which held the ponytail, towing a boy wearing a jacket with the letter B on it, would turn up at the same movie and see me snivelling beside my fur-draped, hefty aunt.

'Don't go before you're ready,' said Aunt Lou sagely, and as usual it could have meant anything.

The kinds of jobs I was able to get were unskilled and not very pleasant. Employers as a rule didn't want to hire anyone so fat, but some were too embarrassed to turn me away completely, especially when they'd advertised. I would look at them accusingly from between my bloated eyelids and say, 'Here's the advertisement, right here,' and they would take me on for a couple of weeks, making up a lie about one of their regular staff being away on holiday. Thus I worked in the five-and-dime for three weeks, as a theater usher for two, a cashier in a restaurant for three, and so on. Some employers welcomed me: I was as cheap as a woman but didn't cause the disruption among male employees and customers other women did. However, these were often hard, disagreeable jobs, like washing dishes, and I didn't stay at them long.

My mother was baffled by these jobs. 'What do you have to work for?' she asked, many times. 'We give you all the money you need.' She found the jobs I took degrading to her personally, which was a bonus. They must have reminded her, also, of her own early life.

When sexual frankness became fashionable, I read a lot of accounts of other people's first sexual experiences: masturbatation with doorknobs, water faucets and the handles of electric shavers, gropings in the back seats of cars at drive-in movies, scramblings among bushes and so forth. None of these were like mine. I myself did have two early sexual experiences, though for the most part I suppressed my interest in sex as completely as I suppressed my interest in war films. There was no available role for me, so I ignored the whole thing as much as possible. Although I pretended to, I didn't really join in my friends' collective passion for male singers. The most I would permit myself was an idealized lust for the figure of Mercury, with winged hat and sandals, impressive muscles and a telephone cable wrapped discreetly around his loins, that used to appear on the front of the Toronto telephone directory. It disappeared years ago. Perhaps the phone company discovered that he was the god of thieves and trickery as well as speed.

But I had vicarious access to the sexual mysteries through the Barbaras and Valeries with whom I ate lunch and walked home, though they tended to discuss such things more with each other than they did with me. They excluded me out of respect, as one would exclude a nun or a saint. Sexually they were prudish, doling themselves out in approved amounts, a kiss after the third date, more serious kissing only if you were going steady, protection below the neck. It was before the pill, and there were enough dismal examples held in front of their eyes, by mothers and by gossip about girls who had to get married, or even worse, who had to get married but couldn't, to keep them rigid. If they went further than you were supposed to, they didn't tell.

My first sexual experience went like this. I was walking home with Valerie, who has since made several guest appearances in the pages of my Costume Gothics, once dressed in a farthingale, once in an ersatz-Grecian dress of the Regency, cut low on the bosom. This day, however, she was wearing a red sweater with a poodle pin on it, a matching red plaid skirt and penny loafers, with a navy-blue trench coat over all. She was telling me about an important phone call she'd had the evening before, when she was in the middle of washing her hair. Several blocks before the street where I usually turned off, we were intercepted by a boy who had been trying to get Valerie to go out with him for weeks. She wasn't interested – in her opinion, as I knew, he was a pill – but etiquette dictated that she not be too openly rude to him, as that might get her the reputation of being stuck-up. So he strolled along beside us, making nervous conversation to Valerie and ignoring me as much as he could.

Valerie gave me a significant look so I didn't turn off down my street. Instead I walked with her all the way to her house, knowing she would call later and thank me for having caught on. At her driveway she said goodbye, then turned and lilted up the walk, her ponytail swinging. The back door closed behind her. I stood there on the sidewalk, my feet bulging over the sides of my penny loafers. My ankles hurt, I'd gone three blocks out of my way and would now have to retrace them, it was time for me to go home and make myself a triple-decker Kraft Cheese and peanut butter sandwich and get ready for my usherette job at the Starlite Theater, where Natalie Wood was playing in *Splendor in the Grass*. The boy, whom even I judged unacceptable, was now supposed to say, 'See ya,' and stride away from me as fast as he could go. But instead he did a curious thing. He knelt down in front of me, right in a mud puddle – it was April and had been raining – and buried his face against my enormous stomach.

What did I do? I was stupefied; I was compassionate; I stroked his hair. My hand smelled of Brylcreem for days.

After a few minutes of this he got up, the knees of his pants dripping wet, and walked away. That was my first sexual experience. I went home and ate my sandwich.

As to why this particular boy, whose name I could never remember, though I could picture quite clearly the strained, even agonized expression on his face, performed this grotesque though almost ritual act on a muddy sidewalk in the suburb of Braeside Park in front of an ordinary house of red brick with white trim and two clipped cedars, one on either side of the front door, I had no clue. Perhaps it was sorrow over thwarted love and he was looking for consolation. Then again, it might have been an instinctive act of belly worship; or perhaps, judging from the way he threw his arms around me as far as they could go, his chemistry textbook lying forgotten on the sod, and dug in his fingers, he might have perceived me as a single enormous breast. But this is a later speculation. At the time I was so shocked by the novelty of being touched by a boy that I forgot about the incident as soon as possible. It hadn't been very pleasant. I didn't even use it to make fun of him, as I might have if I had been thinner. On his part, he avoided me and didn't try to get Valerie to go out with him again.

My second sexual experience took place during one of my part-time jobs. It was when I was working as a cashier in a restaurant, a small, mediocre one called the Bite-A-Bit. It served hot dogs, hamburgers, milk shakes, coffee, pieces of pie; and if you wanted a full-course dinner, fried chicken and shrimp, minute steaks, grilled pork chops and roast beef. I worked from four-thirty to nine-thirty, when it closed, and part of my pay was a free meal, from the lower price ranges. I perched on a high stool behind the cash register and took in the money. I also looked after the customers who sat at the counter beside my stool, and for this purpose I had a telephone connected with the cooking area, over which I gave the orders.

The cooking area was at the back, with a pass-through hatchway decorated in fake-brick wallpaper and several copper pans which were never used. There were two cooks, a lethargic, resentful Canadian and a sprightly, bright-eyed foreigner, either Italian or Greek, I wasn't sure which. This was always the way, in my experience with jobs. The Canadians who had the jobs like that didn't expect to rise any higher: despite the advantage of knowing the language and the terrain, this was the best they could do. The foreigners, on the other hand, were on the way up, they were saving money and learning, they didn't intend to stay on the menial level. The foreign cook took half the time of the other and was twice as polite. He beamed as he handed the waitresses their plates of food, he scampered around in his ovenlike enclosure like a baking chipmunk, humming snatches of exotic song, and you could see the other man would have liked to kill him.

My relationship with him began when he started to reach for the phone every time I called in an order. He had a clear view of me through the hatchway.

'Alloo,' he would sing sweetly.

'A cheeseburger and a side of french fries, ' I would say.

'For you, I make it extra special.'

I thought he was teasing me and ignored him, but one day he asked over the intercom, 'You have coffee with me, eh? After work?'

I was too startled to say no. No one had ever asked me for coffee before.

He helped me on with my coat and opened the door for me, darting around me like a tugboat around the Queen Elizabeth; he was five inches shorter than I was and probably eighty pounds lighter. Once we were sitting across from each other in a nearby coffee shop, he got straight to the point.

'I require for you to marry me.'

'What?' I said.

He leaned across the table, gazing at me with his sparkling black eyes. 'I am serious. I want to meet with your father, and look, I show you my bank account.' To my consernation he pushed a little blue bankbook towards me.

'My father?' I stammered. 'Your bank account ...'

'See,' he said, 'I have right intentions. I wish to open restaurant of my own now soon, I have saved enough. You are a serious girl, you are not like many in this country, you are a good girl, I have watched you, and I do not know how to speak. You would work the cash register for me, and welcome the people. I would cook, much better things than in there.' He gestured across the street towards the Bite-A-Bit. 'I will serve the wine, who but a pig can eat without wine?'

'But,' I said. Just for a moment I could not think of any reason why not. Then I imagined the expression on my mother's face as I loomed down the aisle in white satin with this tiny foreign man slung over my arm like a purse.

'I will give you babies,' he said, 'lots of babies, I see you like the babies. You are a good girl. Then, when we have enough money, we go and visit my country. You will like.'

'But,' I said, 'I'm not the same religion as you.'

He waved his hand. 'You will change.'

When I first visited Terremoto it was more obvious what he saw in me: I was the shape of a wife already, I was the shape it took most women several years to become. I had just started a little early, that was all. But at the time I couldn't overcome the suspicion that he was making fun of me; either that, or it was simply a commercial propositon. How easy it would be, though; for despite his size he was obviously used to making decisions, I myself would not have to make any ever again. However, I did not want to be a cashier for much more of my life. I wasn't good at adding.

'Thank you very much,' I said, 'but I'm afraid it's impossible.'

He was not discouraged. Over the next few weeks he behaved as if he'd been expecting a rejection, as a matter of form. It was proper and modest of me to have refused him and now all I needed was persuasion; after the correct amount I would give in. He flirted with me through the hatchway when I went to pick up my orders, making cat's eyes and wiggling his small brown moustache at me, he called me over the intercom to sigh and plead, watching me all the while from his post at the griddle. When it was time for me to take my break and eat dinner he cooked expensive, forbidden things for me, piling my plate high with shrimps, which he knew I liked, and topping the mound with a sprig of parsley. My appetite, usually gargantuan, began to fall off, partly from the effects of being in contact with other people's food for hours at a time, but partly because at every meal I felt I was being bribed.

The whole thing had the air of a ceremony, a performance that it was necessary to go through before I gave in and did what he wanted; yet like all ceremonies that are believed in, it was sincere and oddly touching. I liked him, but he was disturbing me. I knew I didn't merit such attentions, and besides, there was something absurd about them; it was like being pursued by Charlie Chaplin. I was relieved when the permanent cashier returned and I could quit.

For a while I daydreamed about this man in school (I never did learn his real name; in his determination to become Canadian, he insisted that it was John). For the most part I saw him merely as a landscape, a region of blue skies and balmy climate, with white sand beaches and a stately classical ruin on a cliff, with pillars; a place that would be in marked contrast to dour Toronto and its gritty winter winds, its salt slush that decayed your boots, or its humid, oppressive summers; a place where I would fit in at last, where I would be the right shape. Sometimes I thought it would be pleasant to have married him, it would be as good as having a pet, for with his black eyes and his soft moustache he would be like a friendly animal, a squirrel or an otter, scurrying over my body, enormous to him as a peninsula. But gradually these images faded and as I tuned out the drone of the history teacher, talking monotonously about natural resources and other things that didn't interest me, I returned to an earlier fantasy.

In this one I was sitting in a circus tent. It was dark, something was about to happen, the audience was tense with expectation. I was eating popcorn. Suddenly a spotlight cut through the blackness and focused on a tiny platform at the top of the tent. Upon it stood the Fat Lady from the freak show at the Canadian National Exhibition. She was even fatter that I had imagined her, fatter than the crude picture of her painted on the hoarding, much fatter than me. She was wearing pink tights with spangles, a short fluffy pink skirt, satin ballet slippers and, on her head, a sparkling tiara. She carried a diminutive pink umbrella; this was a substitute for the wings which I longed to pin on her. Even in my fantasies I remained faithful to a few ground rules of reality.

The crowd burst out laughing. They howled, pointed and jeered; they chanted insulting songs. But the Fat Lady, oblivious, began to walk carefully out onto the high wire, while the band played a slow, stately melody. At this the crowd stilled, and a murmur of dismay arose. It was obvious this was a dangerous thing for her to be doing, she was so enormously fat, how could she keep her balance, she would topple and fall. 'She'll be killed,' they whispered, for there was no safety net.

Gradually, inch by inch, the Fat Lady proceeded along the wire, pausing to make sure of her balance, her pink umbrella raised defiantly above her head. Step by step I took her across, past the lumbering enterprises of the West Coast, over the wheatlands of the prairies, walking high above the mines and smokestacks of Ontario, appearing in the clouds like a pink vision to the poor farmers of the St Lawrence Valley and the mackerel fishermen of the Maritimes. 'Good Christ, what is it?' they muttered, pausing in the endless hauling-in of their nets. Several times she faltered and the crowd drew in its breath; the wire oscillated, she concentrated all her forces on this perilous crossing, for a fall meant death. Then, just before the bell went and the period was over – this was the trick – she would step to safety on the other side and the people would rise to their feet, the roar of their voices her tribute. A large crane would appear and lower her to the ground.

You'd think I would have given this Fat Lady my own face, but it wasn't so simple. Instead she had the face of Theresa, my despised fellow-sufferer. At school I avoided her, but I wasn't altogether a heartless monster, I wished to make reparation, I had good intentions.

I knew how Arthur would analyze this fantasy. What a shame, he'd say, how destructive to me were the attitudes of society, forcing me into a mold of femininity that I could never fit, stuffing me into those ridiculous pink tights, those spangles, those outmoded, cramping ballet slippers. How much better for me if I'd been accepted for what I was and had learned to accept myself, too. Very true, very right, very pious. But it's still not so simple. I wanted those things, that fluffy skirt, that glittering tiara. I liked them.

As for the Fat Lady, I knew perfectly well that after her death-defying feat she had to return to the freak show, to sit in her oversized chair with her knitting and be gaped at by the ticket-buyers. That was her real life.

Chapter Ten

When I was in my third year at Braeside High, Aunt Lou invited me to dinner one Sunday. I was surprised, as I knew she reserved Sunday evenings for Robert, the accountant from her company. But when she said, 'Wear something nice, dear,' I realized she was going to let me meet him. I didn't have anything nice to wear, but it was like Aunt Lou not to acknowledge this. I wore my felt skirt with the telephone on it.

I was prepared to be jealous of Robert. I'd pictured him as tall, overpowering and a little sinister, taking advantage of my Aunt Lou's affections. But instead he was small and dapper, the most trimly dressed man I'd ever seen. Aunt Lou had even cleaned up the apartment for him, more or less; though I could see the toe of a nylon stocking nosing out from under the best chair, where he sat sipping at the edge of his martini.

Aunt Lou was ornamented from head to toe. Things dangled from her, her wrists jingled, South Sea odors wafted from her. As she bustled about, putting the final touches to the feast she'd prepared, she seemed to warm and expand, filling the room. Robert watched her as if she were a gorgeous sunset. I wondered if any man would ever look at me like that.

'I don't know what your aunt sees in a dry old stick like me,' he said, ostensibly to me but really to Aunt Lou.

Aunt Lou bellowed. 'Don't let him fool you,' she said. 'Underneath it he's a devil.'

After we'd finished the chocolate mousse, Aunt Lou said, 'Joan, dear, we were wondering if you'd like to go to church with us.'

This was even more of a surprise. My mother went to church for social reasons; she'd subjected me to several years of Sunday school, with white gloves and round navy-blue felt hats held on by elastic bands and patent-leather Mary Janes. Aunt Lou had sympathized when I said it was boring. She herself had occasionally taken me to a small Anglican church, though only on Easter Sundays, for the hymns, she said, but that was as far as it went. Now, however, she applied one of her astonishing hats to the top of her head, powdered her nose, and took her white gloves matter-of-factly in hand.

'It's not exactly a church,' she said to me, 'but Robert goes every Sunday.'

We went in Robert's car, which he parked on a pokey side street north of Queen. The semi-detached houses were old two-story red brick with front porches; the neighborhood looked squalid and sagging. Dirty snow fringed the lawns. One of the houses stood out from the others because it had bright red window curtains, illuminated from behind so that they glowed, and it was this house we entered.

In the front hall there was a table with a large brass tray, a pile of paper slips and several pencils; beneath it, overshoes, rubbers and galoshes drained onto spread newspapers. Aunt Lou and Robert each wrote a number on one of the slips of paper, then placed the folded paper on the tray. 'You write a number too, dear,' Aunt Lou said. 'Maybe you'll get a message.'

'A message?' I said. 'Who from?'

'Well, you never know,' said Aunt Lou. 'But you might as well try.'

I thought I would wait and see what happened. When we'd gone through a pair of purple velvet curtains, we were in the Chapel, as I later learned to call it. It had once been the living room of the house, but now it contained five or six rows of folding bridge-table chairs, each with a hymnbook on it. In what had once been the dining room there was a raised stage with a pulpit covered in red velvet, and a small electric organ. Only a third of the chairs were occupied; the room filled up a little more before the service began, but on my subsequent visits I never saw it completely full. Most of the regular members of the congregation were quite old, and many had chronic coughs. Aunt Lou and Robert were among the youngest.

We settled into our front-row seats, Aunt Lou ruffling herself like a chicken, Robert sitting primly upright. Nothing happened for a while; from behind us came throat-clearings and shufflings. I opened the hymnbook, which was quite thin, not at all like the

Anglican one. *The Spiritualist Hymnbook*, it was called; and, rubber-stamped below the title, *Property of Jordan Chapel*. I read two of the hymns, at random. One was about a joyous boat ride across a river to the Other Side, where loved ones were awaiting. The other was about the blessed spirits of those who've gone before, watching o'er us for our safety till we reach the other shore. This thought made me uncomfortable. Being told in Sunday school that God was watching you every minute of every hour had been bad enough, but now I had to think about all these other people I didn't even know who were spying on me. 'What kind of a church is this?' I whispered to Aunt Lou.

'Shh, dear, they're starting,' Aunt Lou said placidly, and sure enough the lights dimmed and a short woman in a brown rayon dress, with gold button earrings and a matching pin, crossed the stage and began to play the electric organ. A chorus of quavery voices rose around me, tiny and shrill as crickets.

Halfway through the hymn, two people entered from the door that led to the kitchen, and stood behind the pulpit. One, as I came to know, was the Reverend Leda Sprott, the leader. She was a stately older woman with blue eyes, blue hair and a Roman nose, dressed in a long white satin gown, with an embroidered purple band, like a bookmark, around her neck. The other was a skinny gray man who was referred to as 'Mr Stewart, our visiting medium.' I later wondered in what sense he was visiting, since he was always there.

When the hymn had wavered to its close, Leda Sprott raised her hands above her head. 'Let us meditate,' she said, in a deep, resonant voice, and there was silence, broken only by the sound of uncertain footsteps, which went out through the purple curtains and then, very slowly, up the stairs. Leda Sprott began a short prayer, asking for the help of our loved ones who had gained the greater light for those of us still wandering in the mists on this side. Distantly, we heard a toilet flush, and the footsteps came back down.

'We will now have an inspiring message from our visiting medium, Mr Stewart' said the Reverend Leda, stepping aside.

By the end of my time with the Spiritualists I'd practically memorized Mr Stewart's message, since it was the same every week. He told us not to be downhearted, that there was hope; that when things seemed darkest, it was almost dawn. He quoted a few lines from 'Say Not the Struggle Naught Availeth,' by Arthur Hugh Clough:

> And not by eastern windows only,
>   When daylight comes, comes in the light;
> In front, the sun climbs slow, how slowly,
>   But westward, look, the land is bright.

And another line, from the same poem: 'If hopes were dupes, fears may be liars.' 'Fears may indeed be liars, my friends; which reminds me of a little story I heard the other day, and which can be of help to us all at those moments when we are feeling down, when we're feeling nothing matters and what's the use of struggling on. There were once two caterpillars, walking side by side down a road. The pessimistic caterpillar said he'd heard that soon they would have to go into a dark narrow place, that they would stop moving and be silent. 'That will be the end of us,' he said. But the optimisitic caterpillar said, 'That dark place is only a cocoon; we will rest there for a time, and after that we will emerge with beautiful wings; we will be butterflies, and fly up toward the sun.' Now, my friends, that road was the Road of Life, and it's up to each of us which we will choose to be, the pessimistic caterpillar, filled with gloom and looking forward only to death, or the optimistic caterpillar, who was filled with trust and hope and looked forward to the higher life.'

The congregation never seemed to mind that the message was always the same. In fact, they'd probably have felt cheated if it had varied.

After the message the collection was taken up by the brown rayon woman, and after that came the serious business. This was what everyone had come for, really: their own personal messages. The brown rayon woman brought in the brass tray, and Leda Sprott took up the pieces of paper one by one. She would hold each piece unopened in her hand, close her eyes, and give the message. Then she would open the paper and read the number. The messages were largely about health: 'There's an old white-haired lady with light coming out from around her head, and she is saying, 'Be careful going down stairs, especially on Thursday'; and she's saying the word *sulphur*. She's warning you; she sends you love and greetings.' 'There's a man wearing a kilt, and he has a set of bagpipes; he must be Scottish; he has red hair. He's giving you a lot of love, and he's saying, 'Cut down on the sweet foods, they're not good for you.' He's telling you – I can't quite catch the word. It's a mat of some kind. 'Be careful of mats,' that's what he's saying.'

After the pieces of paper were finished, Mr Stewart took over and did free-form messages, pointing to members of the congregation and describing spirits which were standing behind their chairs. I found this much more disturbing than the numbers: Leda Sprott's messages seemed to come from inside her head, but Mr Stewart did it with his eyes open, he could actually *see* dead people right there in the room. I slouched down in my chair, hoping he wouldn't point at me.

After this there were more hymns; then Leda Sprott reminded us about the Healing Hands session on Tuesday, the Automatic Writing on Wednesday, and the private sittings on Thursday, and that was all. There was some scuffling and crowding in the hall as several elderly men struggled with their galoshes. At the door people thanked her warmly; she knew most of them, and would ask, 'Did you get what you wanted, Mrs Hearst?' 'How was that, Mrs Dean?'

'I'll throw that medicine away right now,' they'd say, or, 'It was my Uncle Herbert, that was just the kind of coat he used to wear.'

'Well, Robert,' said Aunt Lou in the car. 'I'm sorry she didn't come tonight.'

Robert was visibly disappointed. 'Maybe she was busy,' he said. 'I don't know who that other woman was, the one in the evening dress.'

'A large woman,' Aunt Lou said. 'Hah. It sounded like me.' She asked Robert up for a drink, but he said he was discouraged and should probably go home, so I went up instead and had a hot chocolate and some petit fours and a shrimp sandwich. Aunt Lou had a double Scotch.

'It's his mother,' she said. 'That's the third week in a row she hasn't turned up. She was always a little thoughtless. Robert's wife couldn't stand her, she refuses to go to church with him at all. 'If you ever do get to talk to that old horror,' she told him, 'I don't want to be there.' I think that's a bit cruel, don't you?'

'Aunt Lou,' I said, 'do you really *believe* all that stuff?'

'Well, you never can tell, can you?' she said. 'I've seen them give a lot of accurate messages. Some of them don't mean all that much, but some of them are quite helpful.'

'But it could just be mind reading,' I said.

'I don't know how it's done,' said Aunt Lou, 'but they all find it very comforting. I know Robert does, and he likes me to take an interest. I feel you have to keep an open mind.'

'It gives me the willies,' I said.

'I keep getting messages from that Scotsman,' Aunt Lou said musingly. 'The one with the red hair and bagpipes. I wonder what he meant about the mats. Maybe he meant mutts, and I'm going to be bitten by a dog.'

'Who is he?' I said.

'I haven't the faintest idea,' Aunt Lou said. 'Nobody I know of ever played the bagpipes. He's certainly not a relation.'

'Oh,' I said, relieved. 'Have you told them that?'

'I wouldn't dream of it,' said Aunt Lou. 'I wouldn't want to hurt their feelings.'

I fell into the habit of going regularly to the Jordan Chapel on Sunday nights. It was a way of seeing Aunt Lou which, by now, I preferred to the movies, as I was absolutely certain that nobody from Braeside High would ever see me there. I even spent a certain amount of time worrying about the Spiritualist doctrines: if The Other Side was so wonderful, why did the spirits devote most of their messages to warnings? Instead of telling their loved ones to avoid slippery stairs and unsafe cars and starchy foods, they should have been luring them over cliffs and bridges and into lakes, spurring them on to greater feats of intemperance and gluttony, in order to hasten their passage to the brighter shore. Some of the Spiritualists also believed in multiple incarnations, and some in Atlantis. Others were standard Christians. Leda Sprott didn't mind what you believed as long you also believed in her powers.

I was willing to watch it all, with the same suspension of disbelief I granted to the movies, but I drew the line at putting a number on the tray. I didn't know any dead people and I had no wish to know any. One night, however, I did get a message, which was much more peculiar than anything I'd feared. It was during Leda Sprott's number session, and she was just about to process the last folded paper on the brass tray. As usual she'd closed her eyes, but then she opened them suddenly.

'I have an urgent message,' she said, 'for someone without a number.' She was looking straight at me. 'There's a woman standing behind your chair. She's about thirty, with dark hair, wearing a navy-blue suit with a white collar and a pair of white gloves. She's telling you . . . what? She's very unhappy about something. . . . I get the name *Joan*. I'm sorry, I can't hear. . . .' Leda Sprott listened for a minute, then said, 'She couldn't get through, there was too much static.'

'That's my mother!' I said to Aunt Lou in a piercing whisper. 'She's not even dead yet!' I was frightened, but I was also outraged: my mother had broken the rules of the game. Either that, or Leda Sprott was a fraud. But how could she know what my mother looked like? And if she'd snooped around, she wouldn't have made the mistake of using a living person.

'Later, dear,' Aunt Lou said.

After the service was over I confronted Leda Sprott. 'That was my mother,' I said.

'I'm happy for you,' said Leda. 'I had the feeling she's been trying to contact you for some time. She must be very concerned about you.'

'But she's still alive!' I said. 'She isn't dead at all!'

The blue eyes wavered, but only for a moment. 'Then it must've been her astral body,' she said placidly. 'That happens sometimes, but we don't encourage it; it confuses things, and the reception isn't always good.'

'Her *astral body*?' I'd never heard of such a thing. Leda Sprott explained that everyone had an astral body as well as a material one, and that your astral body could float around by itself, attached to you by something like a long rubber band. 'She must've come in through the bathroom window,' she said. 'We always leave it open a little; the radiator overheats.' You had to be very careful about your rubber band, she said; if it got broken, your astral body could get separated from the rest of you and then where would you be? 'A vegetable, that's what,' said Leda Sprott. 'Like those cases you read about, in the hospital. We keep telling the doctors that in some cases brain operations do more harm than good. They should be leaving the window open a bit, so the astral body can get back in.'

I did not like this theory at all. I particularly didn't like the thought of my mother, in the form of some kind of spiritual jello, drifting around after me from place to place, wearing (apparently) her navy-blue suit from 1949. Nor did I want to hear that she was concerned about me: her concern always meant pain, and I refused to believe in it. 'That's crazy,' I said, in as rude a voice as possible.

To my surprise, Leda Sprott laughed. 'Oh, we're used to being told *that*,' she said. 'We can certainly live with that.' Then, to my embarrassment, she took hold of my hand. 'You have great gifts,' she said, looking into my eyes. 'Great powers. You should develop them. You should try the Automatic Writing, on Wednesday. I can't tell whether you're a sender or a receiver ... a receiver, I think. I'd be glad to help you train; you could be better than any of us, but it would take hard work, and I must warn you, without supervision there's some danger. Not all the spirits are friendly, you know. Some of them are very unhappy. If they bother me too much, I rearrange the furniture. That confuses them, all right.' She patted my hand, then let go of it. 'Come back next week and we'll talk about it.'

I never went back. I'd been shaken by the apparition of my mother (who, when I returned that Sunday night, didn't look at all as if she'd been astral-traveling; she was the same as ever, and a little tight). Leda Sprott's opinion of my great powers was even more terrifying, especially since I had to admit I found the thought appealing. Nobody had ever told me I had great powers before. I had a brief, enticing vision of myself, clad in a white flowing robe with purple trim, looking stately and radiating spiritual energy. Leda Sprott was quite fat ... perhaps this was to be my future. But I wasn't sure I really wanted great powers. What if something went wrong? What if I failed, enormously and publicly? What if no messages would come? It was easier not to try. It would be horrible to disappoint any congregation, but especially the one at the Jordan Chapel. They were so trusting and gentle, with their coughs and reedy voices. I couldn't stand the responsibility.

Several months later I confided in Aunt Lou. At the time, she'd seen I was upset and hadn't pressed for details. 'Leda Sprott told me I had great powers,' I said.

'Did she, dear?' Aunt Lou said. 'She told me the same thing. Maybe we both have them.'

'She said I should try the Automatic Writing.'

'Do you know,' Aunt Lou said thoughtfully, 'I *did* try it. You'll probably think I'm silly.'

'No,' I said.

'You see, I've always wanted to know whether my husband is

still alive or not. I felt that if he wasn't, he might have the, well, the politeness to let me know.'

'What happened?' I asked.

'Well,' Aunt Lou said slowly, 'it was quite strange. She gave me a ballpoint pen, just an ordinary ballpoint pen. I don't know what I was expecting, a goose quill or something. Then she lit a candle and put it in front of a mirror, and I was supposed to stare at the candle – not the real one, the reflection. I did this for a while and nothing happened, except that I could hear a sort of humming noise. I think I fell asleep or sort of dozed off or something, just for a minute. After that it was time to go.'

'Did you write anything?' I asked eagerly.

'Not exactly,' said Aunt Lou. 'Just a sort of scribble, and a few letters.'

'Maybe he's still alive then,' I said.

'You never can tell,' said Aunt Lou. 'If he is dead, it would be just like him not to say anything. He always wanted to keep me in suspense. But Leda Sprott said it was a good beginning and I should go back. She says it takes them a while to get through.'

'So did you?'

Aunt Lou frowned. 'Robert wanted me to. But you know, I'm not sure it's a good idea. I looked at the paper afterwards, and it wasn't at all like my handwriting. Not at all. I didn't like that feeling of being, well, taken over. I felt I should leave it alone, and I would too if I were you, dear. You can't fly on one wing. That's what I think.'

Despite Aunt Lou's advice, I was strongly tempted to try some Automatic Writing myself, at home in my bedroom; and one evening when my parents were out, I did. I got one of the candles from the dining room downstairs, a red ballpoint pen, and my mother's Jot-a-Note from the telephone table. I lit the candle, turned out my bedroom light, and sat in front of the vanity-table mirror, staring at the small flame in the glass and waiting for something to happen. I was trying very hard to keep from moving my hand consciously: that would be cheating, and I wanted it to be real. Nothing happened, except that the candle flame seemed to get bigger.

The next thing I knew my hair was on fire: I'd leaned imperceptibly towards the candle. At that time I had bangs, and they'd started to sputter and frizzle. I slapped my hand over my forehead and ran to the bathroom; my front hair was badly singed, and I had to cut it off, which caused a scene with my mother the next day, as she'd just contributed five dollars towards a hairdo. I decided I'd better leave the Automatic Writing alone.

There was something on the notepad, though: a single long red line that twisted and turned back on itself, like a worm or a snarl of wool. I couldn't remember drawing it; but if that was all the Other Side had to tell me, why should I go to the trouble?

For a while I embroidered Leda Sprott's advice into a classroom daydream (I could do it if I wanted to; humble beginnings in unknown chapel; miraculous revelations; fame spreads; auditoriums packed; thousands helped; whispered comments, awe and admiration – 'She may be a *large* woman, but what powers!'). After several months, however, it gradually faded away, leaving nothing but Mr Stewart's sermon, indelibly engraved on my brain, to surface at inopportune moments: the pessimistic caterpillar and the optimistic caterpillar, inching their way along the Road of Life, involved in their endless dialogue. Most of the time I was on the side of the optimistic caterpillar; but in my gloomiest moments I would think. So what if you turn into a butterfly? Butterflies die too.

Chapter Eleven

The next job I got, after the Bite-A-Bit Restaurant, was at the Sportsmen's Show. This took place in March every year, down on the grounds of the Exhibition, in the Colosseum Building. It was like an auto show or a fall fair; speedboat, fiberglass canoe, and kayak peddlers all had booths, and fishing-rod and rifle companies did too. The Boy Scouts put on demonstrations of tent-pitching and fire-lighting, teams of them in their green uniforms grinding away at fire drills, with their pink bare knees sticking out of their short pants. Beside their platform the Ministry of Lands and

Forests had a poster on forest-fire prevention. At stated times there were Indian dances, given by a group of bitter Indians in costumes that were too new to look real. I knew they were bitter because they ate hot dogs at the same hot-dog stand I did, and I overheard some of the things they said. One of them called me 'Fatso.'

There was a grandstand show too, with log-rolling contests and fly-casting competitions, and a Miss Outdoors pageant, and a seal named Sharky who could play 'God Save the Queen' by tooting on a set of blowpipes.

I liked it better than any job I'd ever had. It was untidy and a little tawdry, and I could walk through the crowd without feeling too out of place. For all they knew I was an expert fly-caster or a female logroller. I worked after school and all day Saturday and Sunday. On my dinner break I would eat five or six hot dogs and drink a few Honey Dews, then wander around, stopping to watch the ladies' outdoor fashion show, the latest in parkas and kapok life jackets, which Miss Outdoors would head off with a demonstration of her plug-casting technique; or perhaps I would go to one of the grandstand archways and look in while someone shot a balloon with an arrow, balancing on the gunwale of a canoe, or a man pushed another man off a spinning log into a plastic swimming pool.

My own job was fairly simple. I stood at the back of the archery range, wearing a red leather change apron, and rented out the arrows. When the barrels of arrows were almost used up, I'd go down to the straw targets, leaving the customers standing back of the rope barrier: a few children, some sports-minded younger men and their wives or girl friends, quite a few boys in black leather jackets who otherwise hung out around the shooting gallery. I'd pull the arrows out, drop them into the barrels, and start over again.

There were two other employees. Rob gave the spiel; he had experience as a huckster and carneyman, he worked the Ex in the summers – rides, cotton-candy stands, win-a-Kewpie-doll games. He stood with a foot on either edge of a barrel and called, 'THREE for a dime, nine for a quarter, step right up and show your skill, break the balloon and you get one free, would the little lady like to try?' Bert, a shy first-year university student with glasses and crew-neck sweaters, helped me pass out the arrows and rake in the quarters.

The difficulty was that we couldn't make sure all the arrows had actually been shot before we went to clear the targets. Rob would shout, 'Bows DOWN please, arrows OFF the string,' but occasionally someone would let an arrow go, on purpose or by accident. This was how I got shot. We'd pulled the arrows and the men were carrying the barrels back to the line; I was replacing a target face, and I'd just bent over to stick in the last target pin when I felt something hit me in the left buttock. There was a sound from behind, a sort of screaming laugh, and Rob yelled 'Who did that?' before I had time to feel any pain. The fellow said he didn't mean to, which I didn't believe. The sight of my moonlike rump had probably been too much for him.

I had to go to the first-aid station to have the arrow taken out, and hitch up my skirt while the wound was plugged up and dressed. Luckily it was only a target arrow and it hadn't gone in very far. 'Just a flesh wound,' the nurse said. Rob wanted me to go home but I insisted on staying till closing time. Afterward he drove me back himself, in his ancient Volkswagen. He was very sweet. Although he was cynical about almost everything else, he was sympathetic to anyone who had been injured due to this kind of occupational hazard. He himself had nearly been killed once by a Mighty Mouse car that went off the track. When we stopped at a red light, he took his right hand off the wheel and patted me on the knee with it. 'Too bad you can't piss standing up,' he joked. That was my third sexual experience.

When I came in through the front door, my father's voice called to me from the living room, which was unusual. By that time my parents were letting me come and go as I pleased. They were sitting in their usual places. My father looked careworn and drained, my mother furious.

'We have some bad news for you, Joan,' my father said gently.

'Your Aunt Lou died,' said my mother. 'Of a heart attack. I always knew she would.' When it came to disasters, my mother's prophecies were discouragingly accurate.

At first I didn't believe it. My impulse was to sit down, which I did, heavily. I yelped with pain.

'What on earth,' said my mother.

'Someone shot me with an arrow,' I said. 'In the behind.'

My mother looked at me as if I was out of my mind. 'Isn't that just like you,' she said, as if it was my fault. 'She left you some money,' she continued belligerently. 'It's the most idiotic thing I ever heard of. It's a total and complete waste of time, if you ask me.'

My mother, never one to beat around the bush, had gone over to Aunt Lou's apartment as soon as she'd heard the news from the apartment building superintendent, who had found poor Aunt Lou on the bathroom floor in her kimono. She'd slipped on the bath mat, either before or after the attack. The real will was with Aunt Lou's lawyer, but my mother had found a copy among Aunt Lou's papers. 'A mess,' she said. 'The whole apartment's a mess. You'll have to come over and help me with it.' For we were Aunt Lou's only relatives.

Aunt Lou had indeed left me some money. Two thousand dollars, in fact, which was a lot at that time, for someone of my age. But there was a condition: I could have it only if I reduced, and Aunt Lou had even picked the proper weight. I had to lose a hundred pounds.

This was what had made my mother so angry. She didn't think me capable of it. In her eyes, the money might as well have been thrown away. The only other person who got any was Aunt Lou's husband, the gambler, provided he could be found.

I spent the night mourning Aunt Lou, fitfully and noisily, though my tears were not yet completely felt, as I didn't yet believe she was dead. The finality of her disappearance didn't get through to me till the following morning, when, light-headed from lack of sleep, I limped after my mother into the now-empty apartment. It was much as I had last seen it, but without Aunt Lou's assurance and vitality it looked unkempt, grubby, shabby even. Aunt Lou always made you feel as though she had intended, even planned the disorder. Now it seemed like mere carelessness; or worse, as though someone had gone through it, searching for something that could not be found and throwing clothes and objects about with no regard for their owner. It was clear Aunt Lou hadn't expected to die or she would have been tidier. And yet she had expected it, or she wouldn't have left her curious will.

Now in her apartment I felt like an intruder, as though we'd broken into her privacy without asking or were observing an intimate scene through a knothole in the wall. But it got worse. My mother started rifling her closets, pulling the clothes off the hangers, folding them and ramming them into a large brown

Crippled Civilians donation bag she had brought, making remarks about them as she did so. 'Look at that, will you,' she said of Aunt Lou's best gold-sequinned evening dress. 'Cheap.' I saw Aunt Lou disappearing, piece by piece, into the brown paper bag which was swallowing her endlessly, her breezy clothes, her gay scarves and follies, her jokes about herself which my mother took seriously (that magenta blouse, for instance), and I couldn't stand it. I managed to save the fox, stuffing it surreptitiously into my purse while my mother's back was turned. Then I went into the kitchen, to commune with Aunt Lou one last time, via her refrigerator. My mother didn't comment, or complain that I wasn't helping her; I knew in some obscure way that I hadn't been brought along to help in any case, I'd been brought as a devious form of punishment for having loved Aunt Lou while she was alive.

I found a can of lobster in the cupboard and made myself a sandwich. Aunt Lou's purse was there, and I opened it. I felt like a spy, but I knew my mother would open it later and junk the contents. I took out Aunt Lou's wallet, her compact and one of her handkerchiefs with lace edging, which still had her characteristic smell, and put them in my own purse. It was not stealing, it was rescuing. I wanted to keep as much of her in existence as I could, for my mother was determined on obliteration.

My mother had been in a slump lately, but Aunt Lou's death perked her up again; it gave her something to supervise. She made all the funeral arrangements, efficiently and with a certain grim relish. She sent out notices and replied to cards and telephone calls (from Aunt Lou's office, all of them) and placed an announcement in the paper. My father wasn't up to it. He took several days off from the hospital and wandered about the house in his maroon leather slippers, getting in my mother's way as she bustled about and saying, 'Poor Lou,' over and over, like some melancholy bird. The only other things he said to me were, 'She practically brought me up,' and, 'She knit me a pair of socks during the war. They didn't fit.' He had been fonder of her and closer to her than I had guessed, yet I couldn't help wondering how someone brought up by Aunt Lou could have turned out to be as inexpressive as my father. She used to say, 'Still waters run deep,' and, 'If you can't say anything nice, don't say anything at all.' Perhaps that explained it. She didn't leave him any money, though; he didn't need it and the gambler did, that would have been her reason.

Aunt Lou was put on display at O'Dacre's Funeral Home, surrounded by baskets of white chrysanthemums (ordered by my mother) and visited by equally middle-aged girls from the sanitary napkin company, who sniffed audibly, squeezed my mother's hand, and said what a wonderful personality she had. I disgraced myself at the funeral by crying too much and too loudly.

Robert the accountant was there, his eyes red and shrunken. After the service he pressed my hand. 'She'll be in touch,' he said. 'We can count on her.' But I couldn't believe it.

When we got back to the house my mother said, 'Well, that's over with.' The next thing I remembered was looking up at the ceiling of the living room. I'd fainted, knocking over an end table (scratched), a Swedish Modern lamp (broken), and a copper-enameled ashtray (undamaged).

It turned out that I had blood poisoning, from the arrow wound. The nurse at the first-aid station hadn't put enough disinfectant on it. The doctor said I must have been running a fever for days. It's true I'd been dizzy, my ears had been singing and objects had been shrinking and swelling around me, but I had attributed this to grief. I was put to bed and injected with penicillin. The doctor said it was a good thing I was so fat ('fleshy,' he said); he seemed to hold a kind of blotter theory about fat and germs. My mother brought me chicken bouillon cubes dissolved in hot water.

I developed a raging fever, with delirium. One of the results of this was the notion that I'd been hit with the arrow at precisely the moment Aunt Lou died and that the shot had been guided by her departing spirit. She'd been letting me know, saying goodbye, in a rather eccentric manner, true – and she wouldn't have wanted me to get blood poisoning – but this was characteristic of her. I never quite got rid of this idea, although I knew it was farfetched. At the time it bothered me a lot; indeed it filled me with remorse, for I hadn't recognized this message from the dead, a cry for help perhaps. I should have dropped everything and rushed off to her apartment, not stopping even to remove the arrow. I might have been in time. I seemed to hear her voice, from a great distance, saying, 'Most said soonest mended,' and, 'For want of a nail the man was lost,' though I knew that both of these were wrong.

In my lucid moments, and when I was convalescing, I thought about her other message to me, the one in her will. How was I to interpret it? Did it mean she hadn't really accepted me for what I was, as I thought she had – that she too found me grotesque, that for her also I would not do? Or was it just pragmatism on her part, her realization that I would have an easier life if I were thinner? She'd offered me the money to get away, to escape from my mother, as she knew I wished to do; but on terms that would force me to capitulate, or so it seemed.

One day, while I was sitting up in bed, leafing through one of my father's detective novels, I happened to glance down at my body. I'd thrown the bedcovers off, as it was warm, and my nightgown had ridden up. I didn't usually look at my body, in a mirror or in any other way; I snuck glances at parts of it now and then, but the whole thing was too overwhelming. There, staring me in the face, was my thigh. It was enormous, it was gross, it was like a diseased limb, the kind you see in pictures of jungle natives; it spread on forever, like a prairie photographed from a plane, the flesh not green but bluish-white, with veins meandering across it like rivers. It was the size of three ordinary thighs. I thought, That is really my thigh. It really is, and then I thought, This can't possibly go on.

When I was up and around again I told my mother I was going to reduce. She didn't believe me, but I went downtown to Richmond Street and weighed in, as the will stipulated, with Aunt Lou's lawyer, a Mr Morrisey, who kept saying, 'She was a character, your aunt.' I'd already lost some weight during my illness, and I had only seventy pounds to go.

I had somehow expected that once I'd made my decision I would simply deflate, like an air mattress. I wanted it to happen suddenly and with little effort on my part, and I was annoyed when it didn't. I started taking my mother's miraculous remedies, all at once: a couple of fat pills in the morning, a dose of laxatives, half a box of Ayds, a little RyKrisp and black coffee, a waddle around the block for exercise. Of course I developed some spectacular side effects: blinding headaches, stomach cramps, accelerated heartbeat from the fat pills, and an alarming clarity of vision. The world, which I'd seen for so long as a blur, with the huge but ill-defined figure of my mother blocking the foreground, came sharply into focus. Sunshine and brilliant colors hurt my eyes. I suffered from fits of weakness and from alarming, compulsive relapses during which I would eat steadily, in a kind of trance, anything and everything in sight – I recall with horror consuming nine orders of fried chicken in a row – until my shrunken and abused stomach would protest and I would throw up.

I'd lost some time at school through sickness, and I couldn't catch up; it was too difficult to concentrate. I spent the mornings resisting the thought of lunch hour and the afternoons regretting it. I became listless and crabby; I snapped at my friends, I told them I didn't want to hear any more about their stupid boyfriends, I turned down requests to help with the decorations for the Senior Formal, which was to be called 'April Antics.' I was fed up with Kleenex flowers. My marks plummetted; my skin sagged into the loosefolds of the chronically ill or aged, it flopped around me like a baggy sweat suit. Around May I was put through a surreal interview with the Guidance Counselor, during which I, bug-headed on diet speed, my mind zapping around like a mechanical mouse, stared walleyed at this non-credible bright-gray man while he said, 'We know you have the ability, Joan. Is there something bothering you at home?' 'My Aunt died,' I said, and then began to giggle so hard I choked. The rest of the interview consisted of him whacking me on the back. I think he called my mother on the telephone.

At home I spent hours in front of the mirror, watching as my eyebrows, then my mouth, began to spread across my face. I was dwindling. The sight of a fat person on the street, which used to inspire fellow feeling, I now found revolting. The wide expanse of flesh that had extended like a sand dune from my chin to my ankles began to recede, my breasts and hips rising from it like islands. Strange men, whose gaze had previously slid over and around me as though I wasn't there, began to look at me from truck-cab windows and construction sites; a speculative look, like a dog eyeing a fire hydrant.

As for my mother, at first she was gratified, though she phrased it in her own way: 'Well, it's about time, but it's probably too late.' As I persevered, she said things like, 'You're ruining your health,' and, 'Why do you have to go to extremes with everything?' and even, 'You should eat something more than that, you'll starve to death.' She went on baking sprees and left pies and cookies around the kitchen where they would tempt me, and it struck me that in a lesser way she had always done this. While I grew thinner, she herself became distraught and uncertain. She was drinking quite heavily now and she began to forget where she had put things, whether or not her dresses had been sent to the cleaners, what she had said or not said. At times she would almost plead with me to stop taking the pills, to take better care of myself; then she would have spasms of rage, a dishevelled piecemeal rage unlike her former purposeful fury. 'You are the limit,' she would say with contempt. 'Get out of here, the sight of you makes me sick.'

About the only explanation I could think of for this behavior of hers was that making me thin was her last available project. She'd finished all the houses, there was nothing left for her to do, and she had counted on me to last her forever. I should have been delighted by her distress, but instead I was confused. I'd really believed that if I became thinner she would be pleased; a smug, masterful pleasure, but pleasure nonetheless: her will being done. Instead she was frantic.

One afternoon when I'd dragged myself home from school, weak with hunger, and had gone into the kitchen for the single piece of RyKrisp which was my reward, she wandered in from the living room, a glass of Scotch in one hand, still in her pink dressing gown and furred mules.

'Look at you,' she said. 'Eat, eat, that's all you ever do. You're disgusting, you really are, if I were you I'd be ashamed to show my face outside the house.' This was the sort of thing she used to say to me when I was fat and she was trying to browbeat me into reducing, but I felt this speech was not necessary any more.

'Mother,' I said, 'I'm on a diet, remember? I'm eating a piece of RyKrisp, if you don't mind, and I've lost eighty-two pounds. As soon as I lose eighteen more I'm going down to Mr Morrisey's office and pick up Aunt Lou's money, and after that I'm moving out.'

I shouldn't have given away my plans. She looked at me with an expression of rage, which changed quickly to fear, and said, 'God will not forgive you! God will never forgive you!' Then she took a paring knife from the kitchen counter – I had been using it to spread cottage cheese on my RyKrisp – and stuck it into my arm, above the elbow. It went through my sweater, pricked the flesh, then bounced out and fell to the floor. Neither of us could believe she had done this. We both stared, then I picked up the paring knife, put it down on the kitchen table, and placed my left hand casually over the wound in my sweater, as if I myself had inflicted it and was trying to conceal it. 'I think I'll make myself a cup of tea,' I said conversationally. 'Would you like one, Mother?'

'That would be nice,' she said. 'A cup of tea picks you up.' She sat down unsteadily on one of the kitchen chairs. 'I'm going shopping on Friday,' she said as I filled the kettle. 'I don't suppose you'd like to come.'

'That would be nice,' I said.

That evening, when there were no longer any sounds from my mother's room – she'd gone to bed early and my father was still at the hospital – I packed a suitcase and left. I'd been badly frightened, not so much by the knife (the scratch hadn't been deep and I'd washed it thoroughly with Dettol, to avoid blood poisoning) as by my mother's religious sentiments. After her mention of God I'd decided she was crazy. Though she'd forced me to go to Sunday school, she had never been a religious woman.

PART THREE

Chapter Twelve

The morning was bright with sunshine. It streamed through the windows of the Library, where Charlotte sat, neatly attired in her modest gray gown, its white collar fastened at the throat with her mother's cameo brooch. The brooch aroused sad reveries: her mother, whose delicate pale features Charlotte had inherited, had pressed it into her hand moments before she died. She had smiled at Charlotte, a single tear rolling down her cheek, and had made her promise to always tell the truth, to be pure, circumspect and obedient. 'When the right man appears, my darling,' she had said, 'you will know it; your heart will tell you. With my dying breath I pray for your safety.' Charlotte had always treasured the picture of her mother's face, framed in the gently curling tresses of blond hair fine as spiders' webs, and her sad but hopeful smile.

Charlotte shook off these unhappy thoughts. She bent again over her jeweler's glass; she was repairing the tiny clasp of an emerald bracelet. For a fleeting moment she pictured how the emeralds would look against Felicia's white skin, how their green would enhance her green eyes and complement her fiery hair. But she dismissed these thoughts too, they were unworthy of her, and concentrated on the work at hand.

There was a light laugh, like the drowsy twitter of some tropical bird. Charlott glanced up. Through the gauzy white curtains she could see a couple strolling arm in arm at a short distance from the window, deep in what looked like a confidential conversation. By her red hair she recognized Felicia, who was wearing a very costly morning costume of blue velvet, trimmed with white ostrich feathers at the throat and cuffs, with a dashing hat to match. Her hands were concealed in an ermine muff, and as she threw back her head to laugh once more, the sunlight glimmered on her milky throat and on her small teeth.

The man by her side, bending closer now to whisper something into her ear, was wearing a short cape; in his gloved left hand he carried a gold-handled riding crop, which he dangled nonchalantly. Charlotte thought it must surely be Redmond, and a pang of dismay shot through her; but as he straightened and turned his profile towards her, she realized that this man, although he certainly resembled Redmond, was not he. Redmond's nose was more aquiline.

Charlotte did not mean to eavesdrop, but she could not help overhearing part of the conversation. The man said something in a low voice, and Felicia replied, with a contemptuous toss of her head and another laugh:

'No, you are mistaken ... Redmond suspects nothing. He is occupying himself completely these days with that whey-faced chit he hired to repair my emeralds, and has eyes for nothing else.'

What could she mean? Charlotte was still gazing out the window at the departing couple when a slight sound made her turn. Redmond was standing in the doorway, regarding her with a fixed stare; his eyes burned like coals.

'How do you like my wife's new riding costume?' he asked her, with a sneer in his voice that let her know he had seen her looking through the window. A hot flush rose to Charlotte's cheek: was he accusing her of meddling, of spying and intruding?

'It becomes her very well,' she answered with reserve. 'I could not help seeing it, as she passed so very near the window.'

Redmond laughed and came towards her. She rose from her chair and shrank back against the shelves of fine leather-bound books, each with Redmond's family crest stamped in gold on the spine. Her heart was beating with alarm. His face was flushed with drink, although it was still midmorning, and she recalled the strange stories she'd been hearing about his behavior from kindly Mrs Ryerson, the housekeeper. His wife Felicia, Lady Redmond, also had a scandalous reputation. They could escape gossip because of their position, but Charlotte knew that if she herself once fell from virtue she would be doomed, fated to wander the polluted night streets of London or to find asylum only in a house of shame.

'I do not admire such fine plumage,' he said. 'That dress of yours now ... that would be more fitting ... in a wife. But you wear your hair too severely.' He approached her and disengaged a tendril of her hair; then his hand crept towards her throat, his lips sought hers, his features distorted and savage. Charlotte pulled away, seeking wildly for some object with which to defend herself. She seized a weighty copy of Boswell's Life of Johnson: *if he attempted to humiliate her in this way again, she would not scruple to strike him with it. He was not the first importunate nobleman she'd had to fend off, and it was not her fault she was young and pretty.*

'I beg you to remember, sir,' she cried, 'that I am alone and unprotected under your roof. Remember your duty!' Redmond looked at her with a new respect; but before he could reply, there was a low laugh. In the doorway stood Felicia in all her opulent splendor, dangling her plumed hat in one dainty hand. Beside her stood the cloaked stranger.

'Prettily spoken,' said the stranger, grinning at Charlotte. 'Redmond, I hope you take it to heart.'

Felicia ignored her and addressed herself to Redmond.

'It seems to me, Redmond, that your little Miss Jeweler is overly long about my emeralds. Surely it does not take such a time to repair a few broken catches and mount a few gems. When will she be done?'

Charlotte flinched at being thus spoken of in the third person, but Redmond bowed to his wife, an ironic bow. 'You must ask her yourself, my dear,' he said. 'The ways of a professional are unfathomable, like the ways of a woman.' He strode towards the doorway. 'Good of you to ride over, Otterly,' he said, shaking hands with the tall stranger. 'You know I am always glad to see you for luncheon, even when unannounced.'

'I like a little brisk exercise of a morning,' the man replied. The two strolled away. Felicia remained a moment, studying Charlotte with an appraising glance, as if she were a piece of furniture.

'I would not remain here too long, if I were you,' she said. 'The drains in this house are not good; for those with sensitive natures, such as your own, they have been known to have a bad effect on the health, and even on the mind. If you care for some outdoor exercise, however, you might enjoy a stroll in our maze. I'm told it's interesting.' She swept away in a swirl of velvet.

Charlotte sat in a whirl of confused emotions. How dare these people treat her like this! But yet with Redmond, though he could be so disagreeable, she had found herself wishing that his hand had remained on her throat just a moment longer. ... And the cloaked stranger, he must be Redmond's half brother, the Earl of Otterly. The things she had heard about him from Mrs Ryerson had not been pleasant.

She was too upset to continue working. She locked the emeralds back into their box, locked the box into the room as Redmond had instructed her, and went upstairs to her own room to compose herself.

But when she opened the door of her bedroom, it was all she could do to keep from uttering a scream. There, spread out on her bed, was her good back silk dress, viciously slashed to ribbons. Great gashes had been cut into the skirt, the bodice had been mutilated beyond repair, the sleeves were in shreds. It looked as though some sharp instrument had been employed, a knife or a pair of scissors.

Charlotte entered the room and closed the door behind her. Her knees felt weak and she was a little dizzy. Who had done this? She knew she had left the dress in the wardrobe when she had gone down to commence her work on the jewels. She opened the wardrobe door. ... All of her other clothes had been treated in similar fashion: her travelling cloak, her one other dress, her nightrail, her petticoats, her tippet. She had nothing left to wear but the clothes she had on her back.

But why? *she asked herself, as she sank, trembling, onto her small, hard bed. It occurred to her that someone wanted to frighten her away, someone wanted her to leave Redmond Grange . . . or perhaps it was a warning, a sign left by a well-wisher. She had looked for a note but there had been none. Only those ominous slashes.*

She had left her room at nine o'clock; she had breakfasted, then worked alone until eleven-thirty, when she had overheard the conversation between Felicia and Otterly. In that time, anyone in the household – or someone from beyond it! – could have entered her room, unseen by her, and committed the deed. Redmond, Felicia, Otterly, kindly Mrs Ryerson . . . the maids, the cook, William the gardener, Tom the coachman, with his ratlike smile. It could have been any of them.

Fearfully, she recalled Felicia's remark about the badness of the drains. Had it been a threat? And if she disobeyed the warning, to what lengths would her unknown enemy be prepared to go in order to rid Redmond Grange of her . . . forever?

I wrote this in Terremoto with my apple-green felt pen. It took me four days, which was far too slow. Usually I wrote my Costume Gothics on the typewriter, with my eyes closed. It was somehow inhibiting to have to see what I'd put on the page, and in apple-green it was more lurid than I'd intended.

I decided I'd have to make the trip to Rome for the typewriter and the hair dye. I'd never be finished with Charlotte at the rate I was going, and my own financial future depended on hers. The sooner she could be safely established the better.

Meanwhile she was in peril, my eternal virgin on the run, my goddess of quick money. The house was after her, the master of the house as well, and possibly the mistress. Things were closing in on her, though so far she was being sensible. She was a plucky girl who refused to be intimidated. Otherwise she'd take the next coach out. I myself didn't have the least idea who'd slashed up her clothes. Redmond, of course, would buy her a new wardrobe, which would fit perfectly, unlike the shabby discards she'd been wearing. She'd hesitate to accept, but what could she do? She didn't have a stitch to her name. Bad things always happened to the clothes of my heroines: bottles of ink got poured over them, holes were burned in them, they got thrown out of windows, shredded, ripped. In *The Turrets of Tantripp* someone stuffed them full of hay, like a scarecrow or a voodoo effigy, and floated them down a river. Once they were buried in a cellar.

Felicia wouldn't like Charlotte's new wardrobe though. 'If you're going to set this girl up as your mistress, Redmond,' she'd say, within Charlotte's hearing, 'I wish you'd do it somewhere else.' She was a cynical woman, and used to his escapades.

I replaced the manuscript in my underwear drawer, put on my disguise, and set out for Rome, locking the door carefully behind me.

Driving in Italy made me nervous. People steered cars as if they were horses. They didn't think in terms of roads but in terms of where they wanted to go: a road was where someone else wanted you to go, a road was an insult. I admired this attitude, as long as I wasn't driving. When I was it made me jumpy. The road from the town was a series of zigzags, with no fences or posts on the drop side. I beeped the horn all the way down, and chickens and children scattered.

I made it to Tivoli without accidents, then down the long hill to the plain. Rome hovered in the distance. The closer I came to it, the more raw earth there was, the more huge pipes and pieces of red, blue and orange machinery lay strewn like dinosaur bones beside the highway. Men were digging, excavating, tearing down, abandoning; it was beginning to look like North America, like any big junk city. The road was now crowded with trucks, small ones and large ones with trailer carrying more pipes, more machines, in and out, but I couldn't tell whether it was evidence of growth or of decay. For all I knew the country was teetering on the edge of chaos, it would be plunged into famine and revolt next week. But I couldn't read the newspapers, and the disasters of this landscape were invisible to me, despite the pipes and machines; I floated along serenely as through a movie travelog, the sky was blue and the light golden. Huge blockish apartment buildings lined the road to Rome, their balconies festooned with washing, but I couldn't guess what kind of life went on inside them. In my own country I would have known, but here I was deaf and dumb.

I pushed my way through the stifling traffic and found a place to park. The American Express office was crowded; long lines of women in sunglasses like mine and men in rumpled summer suits jammed the wickets. The American dollar was unstable and banks were refusing to cash traveler's checks. I should've taken Canadian, I thought. After waiting my turn I was given some fresh money and went out to search for a typewriter.

I found a secondhand portable Olivetti and bought it, using my limited vocabulary and finger signals. I came out of the store weighed down by the typewriter but nevertheless feeling light as a dancer, anonymous and unwatched in the procession of sidewalk people I would never have to know.

Then suddenly I remembered Arthur. He'd been there with me, we'd been on this very same street together, I could feel him still beside me, real as touch. We'd been holding hands. We'd stopped to consult our map, right here in front of this store, it even smelled the same. Had it happened or was I making it up? Had we really walked through the maze of Roman streets together, did we meander in a rented Fiat, did we drive along the Appian Way with its tombs and rumored ghosts, did we descend into the Catacombs, stuffed with the dried shells of Christians, were we guided by a short Bulgarian priest, did we rise again after thirty minutes? Did we go round and round the Colosseum, unable to find the right exit while thunderous trucks swayed past on either side, loaded with metal and cement, pillars, lions for the games, loot, slaves? My feet hurt a lot but I'd been happy. Arthur had been with me, he wasn't with me now, we had been walking along a street like this one and then the future swept over us and we were separated. He was in the distance now, across the ocean, on a beach, the wind ruffling his hair, I could hardly see his features. He was moving at an ever-increasing speed away from me, into the land of the dead, the dead past, irretrievable.

Chapter Thirteen

I first met Arthur in Hyde Park. It was an accident: I collided with him between an anti-vivisectionist speaker and a man who was predicting the end of the world. I was living with a Polish Count in London at the time, and I still wasn't sure how I'd gotten into it.

When I'd walked out my mother's front door two years earlier, closing it gently behind me so as not to wake her up, I had no such plans. In fact I had no plans at all. I had a suitcase in one hand and my purse in the other. The suitcase contained the few clothes that would still fit me, skirts with belts that could be pulled in, blouses that could be gathered and tucked; I'd had to discard a whole wardrobe over the year I'd been deflating. It was the end of June, almost my nineteenth birthday. I'd written the grade thirteen examinations and I knew I'd failed at least four papers, but the results wouldn't be available till August. In any case I didn't care.

Aunt Lou's fox was in my suitcase, and in my purse I had her birth certificate and the picture of us at the National Exhibition. I had about thirty dollars, seventeen of my own and thirteen from the petty cash box my mother kept in the kitchen; I would repay it later. I could not yet collect Aunt Lou's legacy as I was still overweight, but I had money in the bank from my various jobs and I could get some out in the morning.

I took a bus downtown, where I checked into the Royal York Hotel. This made me nervous: I'd never stayed in a hotel before in my life. I used Aunt Lou's name, as I didn't want my mother to trace me. That was stupid, she would have recognized Aunt Lou's name at once, but I didn't think of that. Instead I was prepared to be challenged by the desk clerk for being underage, and I would then have been able to whip out Aunt Lou's birth certificate and demonstrate that I was forty-nine.

But all he said was, 'Anyone with you?'

'No,' I said. He looked over my shoulder and around the gilded lobby to make sure I was telling the truth. It didn't strike me at the time that he might have suspected I was a prostitute. I attributed my success not to the fact that the lobby was empty, but to the white gloves I'd worn as a symbol of adulthood and social status. 'A lady never goes out of the house without putting on her gloves,' said my mother. Aunt Lou lost gloves continually.

(Perhaps it was to the Royal York Hotel, that bogus fairyland of nineteenth-century delights, red carpeting and chandeliers, moldings and cornices, floor-to-ceiling mirrors and worn plush sofas and brass-trimmed elevators, that the first stirrings of my creative impulse could be traced. To me, such a building seemed designed for quite other beings than the stodgy businessmen and their indistinct wives who were actually to be found there. It demanded ball gowns and decorum and fans, dresses with off-the-shoulder necklines, like those on the Laura Secord chocolate boxes, Summer Selection, crinolines and dapper gentlemen. I was upset when they remodeled it.)

Once the bellhop was finally gone – he hung around for a long time turning the lights on and off and opening and closing the venetian blinds until I remembered what I'd read about tipping – I opened all the bureau drawers. I longed to write an elegant note on the aristocratic stationery, but there was no one at all I could write to. I took a bath, using up all the monogrammed towels. I washed my hair and rolled it up in a set of plastic-mesh-covered rollers. All the time I was fat I'd worn my hair cropped short, which emphasized the roundness of my face. My mother kept making proposals for improvement; she'd wanted me to wear a pageboy, then a poodle cut, but I'd rejected everything. Now, however, I'd been growing my hair for a year and it was shoulder-length, dark red and straight. I didn't wear it loose but kept it back with a bobby pin behind each ear. When my hair was neatly rolled, I stood in front of the full-length mirror on the back of the bathroom door and examined myself, much as a real estate agent might examine a swamp, with an eye to future development. I was still overweight and I was still baggy. There were stretch marks on my thighs, and my face was that of a thirty-five-year-old housewife with four kids and a wandering husband: I looked worn down. But I had green eyes and small white teeth, and luckily I didn't have pimples. I had only eighteen pounds to go.

In the morning I bought a paper and went through the want ads, looking for a room. I found one on Isabella Street, called up the landlady and represented myself over the phone as a twenty-five-year-old office girl, non-drinking and non-smoking. I pinned my hair back, put on my white gloves and went off to inspect it. I gave my name as Miss L. Delacourt, and I used this name also when I opened a new bank account later in the day. I withdrew all my money from my other account and closed it; I didn't want my mother tracking me down. This was the formal beginning of my second self. I was amazed at how easily everyone believed me, but then, why should they suspect?

That afternoon I went to the hospital to see my father. I'd never been inside it before, so I had no idea how to find him. I asked receptionists and they asked each other until they discovered he was in an operating room. They wanted me to make an appointment or stay in the reception area – I hadn't told them I was his daughter – and I said I would. But I'd heard the floor number, and when none of them was watching I got up quietly and went to the elevator.

I stood outside the door, waiting, and finally he came out. I'd never seen him dressed in his official uniform: he had a white cap on and a gown, and a mask over the lower half of his face, which he was in the act of pulling down. He looked much more impressive than he ever had at home, he looked like someone with power. He was talking with two other doctors. I had to call out to him before he noticed me.

'Your mother's been worried sick,' he said without annoyance.

'She's been worried sick all my life,' I said. 'I just wanted to tell you that I'm all right. I'm not coming back, I have a room and enough money.'

He stared down at me with an expression I could not place then because I'd rarely had it directed my way. It was admiration, and perhaps even envy: I had done what he couldn't bring himself to do, I had run away. 'Are you sure you're all right?' he said. When I nodded, he said, 'I don't suppose I could persuade you to go around and see her?'

'She tried to kill me,' I said. 'Did she tell you that?' I was exaggerating, as the knife hadn't gone in very far, but I wanted to impress on him the fact that it wasn't my fault. 'She stuck a knife in my arm.' I rolled up my sleeve to show him the scratch.

'She shouldn't have done that,' he said, as if she'd made a left-hand turn where a right was required. 'I'm sure she didn't mean to.'

I agreed to keep in touch with him – I kept this promise, more or less – but I refused to have anything more to do with my mother. He understood my position. He said it in those words exactly, like a man who has spent a lot of time understanding people's positions. I've remembered that phrase, and it occurred to me along time afterwards that no one ever understood his position; not me, not my mother or Aunt Lou, not anyone. I don't think it was because he didn't have one. His position was the position of a man who has killed people and brought them back to life, though not the same ones, and these mysteries are hard to communicate. Other than that, his position was that of a man who wears maroon leather slippers and fiddles with house plants on weekends, and for this reason is thought of as an inconsequential fool by his wife. He was a man in a cage, like most men; but what made him different was his dabbling in lives and deaths.

For the next couple of months I lived in my Isabella Street room, for which I paid fourteen dollars a week. That included a change of sheets and towels and a hot plate, on which I boiled cups of tea and prepared low-calorie snacks. The house itself was a red-brick Victorian one – they've torn it down since and built a highrise – with dark, creaky wooden-floored hallways, a staircase which has been useful to me on several occasions ('She glided up the staircase, one hand on the banister . . .'), and a smell of furniture polish. Undercutting the furniture polish was another smell, probably vomit. Both the house and the neighborhood had gone downhill; but the landlady was a Scot and severe, so whatever vomiting went on was done behind closed doors.

Other people lived in the house but I seldom saw them, partly because I was out a lot. I trotted briskly down the steps every morning as if I had a job, but actually I was starving myself so I would be able to collect Aunt Lou's money. In the evenings I would return to my room and boil up a package of peas or some corned beef on the single hot plate. While I ate I mourned Aunt Lou. Now that she was dead I had no one to talk to; I'd get out her fox fur, which smelled of mothballs, and stare at it, hoping it would miraculously open it's mouth and speak, in the voice of Aunt Lou, as it had during my childhood. I tried going to the movies, by myself, but it only depressed me more, and with Aunt Lou absent I had to deal with the attentions of strange men, which interrupted the films. In August I went to the Canadian National Exhibition, a melancholy pilgrimage. I hadn't been there with Aunt Lou for three years – she must've felt I was getting too old for it – and it seemed different, shoddier somehow, the gaiety forced and raucous.

I went to the museum a lot, and the art gallery, places where I could walk around and look as if I was doing something, places where I would not be tempted by food. I took bus trips: to St Catherines, to London, Ontario, to Windsor, and to Buffalo and Syracuse and Albany. I was searching for a city I could move to, where I would be free not to be myself. I didn't want anything too different or startling, I just wanted to fit in without being known.

It was on these bus trips that I first discovered there was something missing in me. This lack came from having been fat; it was like being without a sense of pain, and pain and fear are protective, up to a point. I'd never developed the usual female fears: fear of intruders, fear of the dark, fear of gasping noises over the phone, fear of bus stops and slowing cars, fear of anyone or anything outside whatever magic circle defines safety. I wasn't whistled at or pinched on elevators, I was never followed down lonely streets. I didn't experience men as aggressive lechers but as bashful, elusive creatures who could think of nothing to say to me and who faded away at my approach. Although my mother had warned me about bad men in the ravine, by the time I reached puberty her warnings rung hollow. She clearly didn't believe I would ever be molested, and neither did I. It would have been like molesting a giant basketball, and secretly, though I treasured images of myself exuding melting femininity and soft surrender, I knew I would be able to squash any potential molester against a wall merely by breathing out. So when I shrank to normal size I had none of these fears, and I had to develop then artificially. I had to keep reminding myself; Don't go there alone. Don't go out at night. Eyes front. Don't look, even if it interests you. Don't stop. Don't get out of the car. Keep going.

I would be sitting near the center of the bus. Behind me would be a man smoking a cigar, beside me a stranger. Every couple of hours we would stop at a roadside restaurant where I would make sleepwalking trips to the Ladies', which smelled always of disinfectant and liquid soap. There I would wipe from my face with dampened paper towels the bus fumes, oily and brownish; and later, when the side of my head was bumping against the cold metal of the window frame and my body itched with the desire to sleep, a hand would appear on my thigh, stealthy, not moving, an exploratory hand, tense with the knowledge of its solitary mission.

When the hands appeared I couldn't cope with them. They took me by surprise. Men didn't make passes at fat girls, so I had no experience, and I was acutely uncomfortable. The hands didn't frighten or arouse me, they simply made me aware that I didn't know what to do. So I would pretend I didn't notice the hand; I would gaze out the window at the pitch-black landscape, while deft fingers crept up my thigh. At the next stop I would excuse myself politely and stumble off the bus, without much idea of what to do next.

Sometimes I would look for a motel; more often, though, I'd head for the bus-station restaurant and eat all the dry doughnuts and pieces of fish-glue pie I could afford. At these times I felt very lonely; I also longed to be fat again. It would be an insulation, a cocoon. Also it would be a disguise. I could be merely an onlooker again, with nothing too much expected of me. Without my magic cloak of blubber and invisibility I felt naked, pruned, as though some essential covering was missing.

Despite these relapses I dwindled. Suddenly I was down to the required weight, and I was face to face with the rest of my life. I was now a different person, and it was like being born fully grown at the age of nineteen: I was the right shape, but I had the wrong past. I'd have to get rid of it entirely and construct a different one for myself, a more agreeable one. And I decided against any of the places I'd visited. Living in a rented room in Albany would be the same, finally, as living in a rented room in Toronto, except that there would be less chance of running into my mother on the street. Or anyone else who might recognize me.

The thought of going on with the same kind of life for ever and ever depressed me. I wanted to have more than one life, and when at last I stepped triumphantly down from the scales in Mr Morrisey's office and collected the money, I went straight to a travel agency and bought a plane ticket for England.

Chapter Fourteen

'You have the body of a goddess,' the Polish Count used to say, in moments of contemplative passion. (Did he rehearse?)

'Do I have the head of one too?' I replied once, archly.

'Do not make such jokes,' he said. 'You must believe me. Why do you refuse to believe in your own beauty?'

But which goddess did he mean? There was more than one, I knew. The one on the Venus pencil package, for instance, with no arms and all covered with cracks. Some goddesses didn't have bodies at all; there was one in the museum, three heads on top of a pillar, like a fire hydrant. Many were shaped like vases, many like stones. I found his compliment ambiguous.

The Polish Count was an accident. I met him first when I fell off a double-decker bus near Trafalgar Square. Luckily I didn't fall from the upper deck; I had one foot halfway to the ground, but I wasn't used to having the bus start before people were safely off it and it leapt from under me, sending me sprawling onto the sidewalk. The Polish Count happened to be passing by, and he picked me up.

At the time I was living in a damp bed-sitter in Willesden Green. I found it through Canada House, which was the first place I went when I got to London. I was homesick already. I knew no one, I had nowhere to stay, and I was disappointed by what I'd seen of England on the bus from the airport. So far it was too much like what I had left, except that everything looked as though two giant hands had compressed each object and then shoved them all closer together. The cars were smaller, the houses were crowded, the people were shorter; only the trees were bigger. And things were not as old as I'd expected them to be. I wanted castles and princesses, the Lady of Shalott floating down a winding river in a boat, as in *Narrative Poems for Juniors*, which I studied in Grade Nine. I'd looked up *shalott*, fatally, in the dictionary: *shallot, kind of small onion.* The spelling was different but not different enough.

I am half-sick of shadows, said
The Lady of Small Onion.

Then there was that other line, which caused much tittering among the boys and embarrassment among the girls:

The curse is come upon me, cried
The Lady of Shalott.

Why did boys think blood running down a girl's leg was funny? Or was it terror that made them laugh? But none of it put me off, I was a romantic despite myself, and I really wanted, then, to have someone, anyone, say that I had a lovely face, even if I had to turn into a corpse in a barge-bottom first.

Instead of the castles and ladies, though, there was only a lot of traffic and a large number of squat people with bad teeth.

Canada House, when I got there, was a marble mausoleum, impressive but silent. A woman behind a dark wooden counter in a cavernous, dimly lit room, in which a few dour Canadians were reading week-old Toronto newspapers and collecting their mail, handed me a list of rooms to let. Since I knew nothing about the topography of London I took the first one I could get. Unfortunately it was an hour's ride from the center via the underground, which was like a traveling front parlor lined in purple plush; I kept expecting to see footstools and potted palms. Toronto's new subway, on the other hand, with its pastel tiles and smell of Dust-Bane, was more like a traveling bathroom. Already I was feeling provincial.

When I came up from the underground, I walked along a street lined with tiny shops; an unhealthy number of them were candy stores. The woman at Canada House had drawn me a rough map; she had also advised me to purchase a small Maple Leaf and wear it on my lapel, so as not to be mistaken for an American.

The house was a Tudor cottage, the same as all the others on the street, fake Tudor, fake cottage, with a walled front garden. The landlord was a surly man in shirtsleeves and braces who seemed to be afraid I would have orgiastic parties and skip without paying the rent. The room itself was on the ground floor and smelled of rotting wood; it was so damp that the furniture actually was rotting, though very slowly. As I lay in my clammy bed the first night, wondering if I had taken off so much weight and come so far for nothing, a black man climbed in through the front window. But all he said was, 'Wrong window, sorry,' and climbed out again. I could hear faint sounds of a lively party going on farther down the street. I was disgustingly lonely. I was already thinking about moving somewhere else, a flat would be better, I would have more space; but this room was inexpensive and I wanted Aunt Lou's money to last as long as possible. When it was gone I would have to make a decision, choose what I was going to do, get a job (I could touch-type) or go back to school (perhaps I could be an archeologist after all), but I wasn't ready yet, I wasn't adjusted. I'd spent all my life learning to be one person and now I was a different one. I had been an exception, with the limitations that imposed; now I was average, and I was far from used to it.

I wasn't supposed to cook in my room – the landlord felt his tenants were conspiring to set his house on fire, though this would have been difficult as it was so damp – but I was permitted to boil a kettle on the single gas ring. I took to drinking tea and eating Peek Frean biscuits, in bed, with all the covers pulled up around me. It was the end of October and piercingly chilly, and the heat in my room was controlled by shillings in the slot. So was the hot water in the shared bathroom; I took few baths. I began to understand why people on the underground smelled the way they did: not dirty exactly, but cooped-up. Aside from the tea and biscuits, I ate in cheap restaurants and soon learned to avoid the things I would ordinarily have eaten. 'Hot dog,' I found out, meant a reddish, thin object fried in lamb fat. 'Hamburger' was a square, sawdusty-beige thing between two halves of a hard bun, and 'milk shakes' tasted like chalk. I ate fish and chips, or eggs, peas and chips, or sausage and mash. I bought an undershirt.

I began to feel I should be doing something besides watching my stash of traveler's checks dwindle. Travel was supposed to be broadening; why did I feel narrower? So I bought a map of England and picked out names that sounded familiar from high school, like York, or names that intrigued me, like Ripon. I would go to these places on the British Railway, stay overnight in a second-rate inn or a bed-and-breakfast, and come back the next day. I looked at historic buildings. I inspected churches and collected the pamphlets they had on racks with a slot for a sixpence, which I didn't always contribute. I learned what a 'clerestory' was, and bought postcards, which made me feel I had been somewhere. These postcards I sent to my father, addressed to the hospital, with cryptic notes on them like, 'Big Ben's not so big,' and, 'Why do they call it the Lake District? They should call it the Puddle District, ha ha.' I began to feel that England was a message in code which I didn't know how to decipher, and that I would have to read a lot of books in order to understand it.

I'd been in England about six weeks when I fell off the bus. The Polish Count helped me up, and I thanked him. It was a simple enough beginning.

He was slightly shorter than I was, with wispy light-brown hair receding from his forehead, sloping shoulders, and rimless spectacles, which were not fashionable at the time. He was wearing a navy-blue overcoat, a little frayed and shiny, and carrying a briefcase. In order to help me up he set down the briefcase, placed a hand under each of my armpits, and gave a gallant heave. I almost toppled him over but we regained our balance, and he picked up his briefcase.

'Are you all right?' he asked, in a vaguely English accent. If I had been English I might have been able to tell he was a Polish Count; as it was, I could not.

'Thank you very much,' I said. I had ripped a stocking and scraped my knee, and my akle was badly twisted.

'You must sit down,' he said. He steered me across the road and into a restaurant called, as I remember, The Golden Egg, and brought me some tea and a blackcurrant tart, slightly squashed. His manner was warm but patronizing, as if I were an unusually inept child. 'There,' he said, beaming. I noticed that he had an aquiline nose, though it didn't achieve its potential due to his height. 'This tea is the English remedy for everything. They are a strange people.'

'Aren't you English?' I asked.

His eyes – which were greenish-gray, or perhaps grayish-green – clouded over behind his spectacles, as if I'd asked a rude personal question. 'No,' he said. 'But in these days, one must adapt. You, of course, are American.'

I explained that I wasn't, and he seemed disappointed. He asked me if I liked to ski, and I replied that I had never learned. 'I owe my life to skis,' he said enigmatically. 'All Canadians ski. How else would one get around, over the snow?'

'Some of us use toboggans,' I said. The word puzzled him, and I explained.

I finished my tea. This was the moment, I felt, when I should thank him graciously for his kindness and leave. Otherwise we would have to exchange the stories of our lives and I was too depressed about mine to want to do that. So I thanked him and stood up. Then I sat back down again. My ankle had swollen and I could barely walk.

He insisted on taking me all the way back to Willesden Green, supporting me as I hobbled to the underground station and along the street past the candy stores.

'But this is appalling,' he said when he saw my rooming house. 'You can't live here. *Nobody* lives here.' Then he volunteered to wrap my ankle in towels wrung out in cold water. He was doing this, kneeling in front of me while I sat on the bed, when the landlord appeared and gave me a week's notice. The Polish Count informed him that the lady had sprained her ankle. The landlord replied that he didn't care what I had sprained, I was out come Thursday, as he couldn't have that kind of carryings-on in his house. It was the sight of my naked, tumescent foot that had offended him.

When he had gone, the Polish Count shrugged. 'They are a small-minded people, the English,' he said. 'A nation of shop-keepers.' I didn't know this was a quotation and thought it was very clever of him. I had been shocked to find Stonehenge surrounded by a fence, with a gate in it for taking tickets. 'You have seen the Tower of London?' he asked. I hadn't. 'We will go there tomorrow.'

'But I can't walk!'

'We will go in a taxi, and by boat.' He had not asked me, he had told me, so I didn't think of saying no. Also, he seemed old to me; in fact he was forty-one, but I put him in the category of aged and therefore harmless men.

On this excursion, he told me the story of his life. He requested mine first, as politeness demands. I said I'd come to London to study art at the art school, but I'd decided I had no talent. He sighed. 'You are a wise girl,' he said, 'to have made this discovery so early in life. You will not delude yourself with false hopes. I myself once wished to be a writer, I wished to be like Tolstoy, you understand; but now I am exiled from my own language, and this one is fit for nothing but to make hoardings with. It has no music, it does not sing, it is always trying to sell you something.'

I didn't know who Tolstoy was; I nodded and smiled. He went on to relate his personal history. His family had belonged to the upper class, before the war; he wasn't a Count exactly, but he was something or other, and he showed me a signet ring he wore on his little finger. It was a mythical bird, a griffin or a phoenix, I forget which. The family had scrabbled along under the Germans, but when the Russians invaded he knew he had to get out or be shot.

'Why?' I said. 'You hadn't done anything.'

He gave me a pitying look. 'It is not what you do,' he said, 'but who you are.'

He and a party of six others had skied to the border, where a guide was to meet them and take them across. But he became ill. He insisted the others go on without him, and crawled into a cave, certain he would die. The others were caught at the border and executed. He recovered and made his own way across, travelling at night and taking the direction from the stars. When he first arrived in England, he washed dishes in Soho restaurants to make a living; but once he had learned enough English, he obtained a position as a clerk in a bank, working in the foreign exchange department. 'I am the last,' he said, 'of a dying race. The last of the Mohicans.' In fact he had a daughter back in Poland, as well as a mother; but he had no son, and this weighed on him.

My first reaction to this story was that I had met a liar as compulsive and romantic as myself. But my usual impulse was to believe everything I was told, as I myself wished to be believed, and in this case it was the right impulse, since his story was essentially true. I was very impressed. He seemed to belong to a vanished and preferable era, when courage was possible. I limped through the Tower of London on his rather stringy arm with a mixture of emotions new to me: I felt sorry for him because of the sufferings he had undergone, I admired his daring, I was flattered by the attention he was paying to me and grateful for it, and especially I was pleased to be thought wise. I later found that almost anyone would tell you you were wise if you confessed you had no talent.

That was a Sunday. On Monday he had to work at the bank in the daytime, but in the evening he took me to dinner at a club for Polish expatriates, which was full of one-eyed Generals and other Polish Counts. 'We are the few that are left,' he said. 'The Russians killed off the others.'

'But weren't you both against the Germans?' I asked. He laughed gently and explained, at some length.

My own ignorance amazed me. All sorts of things had been happening behind my back, it appeared: treacheries and famines, diplomatic coups, ideological murders and doomed heroic exploits. Why had no one told me? They had, perhaps, but I hadn't been listening. I had been worrying about my weight.

On Tuesday he took me to a chamber music concert, a benefit for some Polish political organization I had never heard of. I mentioned that I hadn't yet found another room.

'But you will live with me!' he exclaimed. 'I have a nice place, very nice, very charming, with lots of room. Of course you must do this.' He had the entire second floor of a house in Kensington, which was owned by a nonagenarian English Lord who was usually in a nursing home. The third floor was occupied by three working girls, but of good class, he assured me: they worked in offices.

I thought it was very considerate and kind of him to offer to share his apartment with me. As he had never touched me, except to help me across the street or along it, because of my ankle, and had never made any suggestive remarks, I was quite surprised when, after I had brushed my teeth and was about to climb into bed (wearing, I believe, a heavy sack-shaped flannel gown I'd bought at Marks & Spencer's the week before), there was a discreet knock at the my door and this man, whose first name I didn't even know, appeared in the doorway, dressed in a pair of blue-and-white-striped pajamas. He understood that he was getting into bed with me, and he understood that I understood this also.

The story I told Arthur later, about being seduced under a pine tree at the age of sixteen, by a summer camp sailing instructor from Montreal, was a lie. I was not seduced at all. I was a victim of the Miss Flegg syndrome: if you find yourself trapped in a situation you can't get out of gracefully, you might as well pretend you chose it. Otherwise you will look ridiculous. Innocence has its hazards, and in my case one of them was that the Polish Count couldn't conceive of anyone being as simpleminded as I was. If you ask a woman to move into your apartment and she consents, naturally she is consenting to be your mistress. It's an odd term, 'mistress,' but that was how he thought of me, these were the categories into which his sexual life was arranged: wives and mistresses. I was not the first mistress. For him there was no such thing as a female lover.

When describing the episode with the Montreal sailing instructor to Arthur, I took care to include some salacious details. I added a few convincing small touches as well, the pine needles sticking into my bum, his Jockey undershorts, the smell of Brylcreem; I was good at things like that. Of course I never went to summer camp in my life. My mother wanted me to, but it meant being shut up for two months with a pack of sadistic overgrown Brownies, with no escape. So I spent the summers lying about the house, eating and reading trashy books, some of which had salacious details. It was these I used in the story of my life; I had to borrow, because the first experience with the Polish Count was not at all erotic. My ankle hurt, the pajamas turned me off, and he looked weird without his spectacles. Also it was painful; and although he was patient and instructive later, though inclined to give performance points – it was almost like taking tap-dancing lessons – he wasn't on this occasion.

When he discovered I wasn't the easygoing art student manquée he'd thought I was – when he realized he had deprived me of my virginity – the Polish Count was filled with remorse. 'What have I done?' he said mournfully. 'My poor child. Why didn't you say something?' But anything I could have said would have been implausible. This was the reason I fabricated my life, time after time: the truth was not convincing.

So I said nothing,and he patted my shoulder anxiously. He felt he'd injured my chances for a good marriage. He wanted to make it up to me and couldn't understand why I wasn't more upset. I was sitting up in bed, pulling my flannel gown back on (for it was just as cold and damp in his flat as it had been in mine) and watching his long, melancholy face with the green-gray eyes slightly askew. I was glad it had happened. It proved to me finally that I was normal, that my halo of flesh had disappeared and I was no longer among the untouchables.

Chapter Fifteen

I often wondered what would have happened if I'd stayed with the Polish Count instead of moving in with Arthur. Maybe I would be fat and content, sitting in his apartment during the day, wearing a flowered negligee, doing a little embroidering, a little mending, reading trashy books and eating chocolates; in the evenings we would dine out at the Polish Officer's Club and I would be treated with respect, more or less; I would have an acknowledged position, I would be 'Paul's mistress.' But it wouldn't have worked, he was too methodical. His first name was Tadeo but he preferred to be called Paul, his third name, after Saint Paul, who was a systematic man, no loose ends. His idea of the good life was that it should be tidy.

Even his escape over the Polish border had been tidy. ('But it was chance that saved your life!' I exclaimed. 'No,' he said, 'I would have been dead anyway if I had not used my head.') He calculated his course precisely and emerged from the forest at the exact point he intended. To keep himself awake and to dispel the hallucinations he was having, he recited the multiplication tables as he plodded through the snow and the darkess (plodded, for he had given his skis to a member of the doomed party). He didn't panic, as I would have done; he paid no attention to the vivid geometrical shapes and, later, the menacing faces that appeared before him in the air. I too had seen the shapes and the faces, during my attack of blood poisoning, and I knew that my response, especially in the depths of that Polish forest, dense as hair, cold as despair, would have been to sit down in the snow and let disaster overtake me. Details would distract me, the candle stubs and bones of those who had gone before; in any labyrinth I would have let go of the thread in order to follow a wandering light, a fleeting voice. In a fairy tale I would be one of the two stupid sisters who open the forbidden door and are shocked by the murdered wives, not the third, clever one who keeps to the essentials: presence of mind, foresight, the telling of watertight lies. I told lies but they were not watertight. My mind was not disciplined, as Arthur sometimes pointed out.

So did Paul. He was compulsive about time, he had to leave the house at precisely eight-fifteen, and before that he spent ten minutes by the clock polishing his shoes and brushing his suit. He found my lack of order charming, but not for long; soon he was making speeches about how much easier it was to hang up one's clothes at the time, rather than leaving them in a heap on the floor till the next morning. He didn't expect much of me – after all, I was only a mistress – but those few things he expected absolutely. I think he considered training me to live with him a minor and tedious challenge, sort of like training a dog: a limited number of tricks, learned thoroughly.

With the exception of that first surprising night he confined sex to weekends. He believed in separate rooms, so I slept on a fold-out bed in the room he called the library. He was not stingy or repressive by nature, but he was a man with a mission, and because I slept in the library I soon discovered what it was.

The first day, after he left for the bank, I slept in till eleven. Then I got up and browsed around the flat, opening the kitchen cupboards, looking for something to eat but also exploring the personality of this man who the night before had, as they say, violated my honor. I was curious, and you can tell a lot about a person from their kitchen cupboards. Paul's were very well-organized; tinned goods prevailed, with some utilitarian dried soups and a package of water biscuits. The foods were of two kinds, bare necessities and exotica: squid, I recall, and some seal meat (which we had later; it was rank and oily). Next I did the refrigerator, which was spotless and almost empty. I ate several water biscuits with some tinned sardines, then made myself a cup of tea and went into Paul's room to go through his closet and bureau drawers. I was careful not to disturb anything. There were some tinted photos on the bureau, the lips purplish, the hair yellowish-gray. Boxer shorts; all his pajamas were striped except for a pair of silk ones. Under the boxer shorts there was a revolver, which I didn't touch.

I went back to the library, intending to get dressed, but I thought I'd go through the bookshelves first. The books were mostly old, cloth- and leather-bound with marbled endpapers, the kind you find on secondhand book tables. A number of them were in Polish, though there were English ones too: Sir Walter Scott, quite a lot of that, and Dickens and Harrison Ainsworth and Wilkie Collins; I remember the names because I subsequently read most of them. But there was one shelf that puzzled me. It consisted of nurse novels, the mushy kind that have a nurse on the cover and a doctor in the background gazing at her with interest and admiration, though never pop-eyed with desire. They had titles such as *Janet Holmes, Student Nurse; Helen Curtis, Senior Nurse*; and *Anne Armstrong, Junior Nurse*. Some had more daring titles, such as *Romance in Paradise* and *Lucy Gallant, Army Nurse*. They were all by a woman with the improbable name of Mavis Quilp. I skimmed through a couple, remembering them well. I'd read dozens, back in my fat days. They were standard fare, each ending with nurse and doctor wrapped in each other's arms as firmly and antiseptically as elastic bandages. There was something odd about the language, the clichés were a little off, distorted just slightly. For instance, someone said, 'They're selling like pancakes' instead of 'hotcakes,' someone else said, 'Keep a stiff upper jaw,' and Anne Armstrong 'trombled' rather than trembled when the doctor brushed past her, though that could have been a typo. Other than this, however, they weren't remarkable; but they were so out of place in Paul's library that I asked him about them that evening.

'Paul,' I said, when we were seated opposite each other at the kitchen table, eating the tinned seal meat and drinking the half-bottle of champagne he had brought back as a propitiation offering, 'why do you read those trashy books by Mavis Quilp?'

He gave me a peculiar, twisted smile. 'I never read those trashy books by Mavis Quilp.'

'Then why do you have fourteen of them in your library?' Perhaps Paul was a secret agent – which would explain the revolver – and the Quilp books were messages in code.

He was still smiling. 'I write those trashy books by Mavis Quilp.'

I dropped my fork. 'You mean, *you're* Mavis Quilp?' I started to laugh, but was stopped by the offended look on his face.

'I have a mother and a daughter on the inside,' he replied stiffly.

The story he told me was this. On first arriving in England, he had still fancied himself a writer. He had written a three-volume epic dealing with the fortunes of a petit-aristocratic family (his) before, during and after the war, laboring away at it with the help of a dictionary in the intervals between his ten-hour stints as a dishwasher. He would rather have written in Polish, but felt it was no use. His novel had thirteen major characters, all of them related, and each with an entourage of wives, mistresses, friends, children and uncles. When he'd finished his book at last and had typed it, painfully, himself, he took it to a publisher. He knew nothing of publishers; inadvertently, he had chosen one that did nothing but Westerns, nurse novels and historical romances.

They rejected his novel, of course, but they were impressed by the quality and especially the quantity of his work. 'You can turn it out, all right, mate,' the man had told him. 'Here's a story line for you, write it up and keep it simple, a hundred quid. Fair enough?' He had needed the money.

While his three-volume epic went the rounds of other, more respectable publishers – it never did get accepted – he churned out junky novels, using at first the story lines provided for him, later supplying his own. He was now receiving between two and three hundred pounds a book, no royalties. With his new job at the bank he earned exactly enough to support himself, so the nurse-novel money was extra, and he sent it to his mother and daughter in Poland. He had a wife there too, but she had divorced him.

The publisher had offered him Westerns and historical romances, but he stuck to his specialty. For Westerns you had to use words like 'pard' which he didn't feel comfortable with; and historical romances would depress him, they would remind him of his old, privileged life. (Escape literature, he told me, should be an escape for the writer as well as the reader.) With nurse novels he didn't need to learn anything extra or use any strange words except a few medical terms easily found in a first-aid handbook. He had chosen his pseudonym because he found the name Mavis to be archetypically English. As for Quilp. . . .

'Ah, Quilp,' he sighed. 'This is a character from Dickens, it is a deformed, malicious dwarf. This is what I see myself to be, in this country; I have been deprived of my stature, and I am filled with bitter thoughts.'

Status, I thought; but I did not say it. I was leaning not to correct him.

'What about something more like you,' I suggested. 'Spy stories, you know, with intrigue and international villains. . . . '

'That would be too much like life,' he sighed.

'For nurses, nurse novels may be too much like life,' I said.

'Nurses do not read the nurse novels. They are read by women who wish mistakenly to be a nurse. In any case, if the nurses wish to avoid the problems of their life, they must write spy stories, that is all. What is gravy for the goose will be misplaced on the gander, such is fate.' Paul believed in fate.

It was to Paul, then, that I owed my choice of career. Aunt Lou's money was running out, much faster than I'd anticipated, though I was trying to be economical, and I didn't like the thought of getting a job. Nobody likes that thought, really, they only do it because they have to. I could touch-type, but it seemed to me I could make money faster by typing at something of my own, and other people's business letters are very boring. Also, there was nothing much for me to do on weekday evenings while Paul sat bashing away at his current book, *Judith Morris, Arctic Expedition Nurse*, chain-smoking Gauloises stuck in a short gold cigarette holder he kept clenched between his teeth, and drinking one glass of tawny port per evening. At such times, contempt for his readers and for himself hovered in the room like a cloud of smoke, and his temper after one of these sessions was foul but cold, like smog.

I asked Paul to get me some samples of historical romances from Columbine Books, his publisher, and I set to work. I joined the local library and took out a book on costume design through the ages. I made lists of words like 'fichu' and 'paletot' and 'pelisse'; I spent whole afternoons in the costume room of the Victoria and Albert Museum, breathing in the smell of age and polished wood and the dry, sardonic odor of custodians, studying the glass cases and the collections of drawings. I thought if I could only get the clothes right, everything else would fall into line. And it did; the hero, a handsome, well-bred, slightly balding man, dressed in an immaculately tailored tweed cloak, like Sherlock Holmes's, pursued the heroine, crushing his lips to hers in a hansom cab and rumpling her *pelisse*. The villain, equally well-bred and similarly clad, did just about the same thing, except that in addition he thrust his hand inside her *fichu*. The rival female had a lithe body like that of a jungle animal beneath her exquisitely stitched corset, and like all such women, she came to a bad end. I wasn't as good at bad ends as I later became: I think she merely tripped on her *paletot*, going downstairs. But she deserved this, as she'd attempted to reduce the heroine to a life of shame by tying her up and leaving her in a brothel, under the supervision of a madam to whom I gave the features of Miss Flegg.

But I had aimed too high. My first effort came back with instructions to the effect that I could not use words like 'fichu' and 'paletot' and 'pelisse' without explaining what they meant. I made the necessary revisions and received my first hundred pounds, with a request for more material. Material, they called it, as if it came by the yard.

I was quite thrilled when two copies of *The Lord of Chesney Chase* arrived in a brown-paper parcel, with a dark-haired woman in a plum-colored traveling cloak on the cover and my pen name in white lettering: Louise K. Delacourt. For of course I used Aunt Lou's name; it was a kind of memorial to her. Several years later, when I'd switched to a North American publisher, I was asked for a photograph. It was for the files, they said, to be used for publicity; so I sent them the shot of Aunt Lou at the Ex, with me standing beside her. This picture was never used. The women who wrote my kind of book were supposed to look trim and healthy, with tastefully grayed hair. Unlike the readers, they had brisk shoulders and were successful. They weren't supposed to squint into the sun, displaying both rows of teeth and holding a cone of spun sugar. The readers preferred not to think of their fairy godmothers, the producers of their delicate nightly masquerades, as overblown and slighly frowsy, with slip straps that showed and necklines that gaped, like Aunt Lou's. Or my own.

Initially Paul encouraged me, partly because of the money. He liked the idea of having a mistress, but he couldn't really afford to keep one. After the first five or six months, when I started earning more per book than he did, he even began to charge me rent, though having me sleeping in his library didn't cost him any extra. I was grateful for his belief, not in my talent exactly, for he didn't feel that writing this kind of book required any, but in my perseverance: I could think up plots almost as fast as he could, and I was a better typist, so I could equal him page for page on a good night. At first he was paternal and indulgent.

In some ways he reminded me of the man with the bouquet of daffodils who had exposed himself in that chivalrous and touching way on the wooden bridge when I was a young Brownie. Paul too had that air of well-meaning but misplaced gallantry; they were both, I thought, gentle and harmless beneath their eccentricities, asking only simple gratifications that didn't impose too much on the partner or watcher. And both of them had rescued me, perhaps, though the identity of the daffodil man was still not clear to me.

I couldn't tell about Paul's identity either, for as time went on he began to change. Or possibly I merely learned more about him. For instance, he viewed the loss of my virginity as both totally his fault – thus making him responsible for me – and a fall from grace which disqualified me from ever being a wife, or his wife at any rate. He thought my lack of guilt was a sign of barbarism. Anyone from across the Atlantic Ocean was a kind of savage to him, and even the English were questionable, they were too far west. So he ended by being angry with me for my failure to cry, though I told him over and over that this wasn't the sort of thing I cried about.

Then there were his views on the war. He seemed to think that the Jews were in some obscure metaphysical way responsible for it, and thus for the loss of his family château.

'But that's ridiculous,' I said, outraged; he couldn't mean it. 'That's like saying a rape victim is responsible for being raped, or a murder victim. . . . '

He drew imperturbably on his Gauloise. 'This also is true,' he said. 'They have brought it upon themselves.'

I thought about the revolver. I couldn't ask him about it without revealing that I'd snooped in his room, and I knew by now he would find this unforgivable. I began to feel a little like Eva Braun in the bunker: what was I doing with this madman, how did I get into this thoroughly sealed place, and how could I get out? For Paul had an end-of-the-world fatalism: civilization for him had either already collapsed or was about to. He thought there would be another war, in fact he hoped there would; not that he thought it would solve or improve anything, but so that he himself might fight in it and distinguish himself by acts of bravery. He hadn't resisted enough in the last one, he felt; he'd been too young to know that he should've stayed and perished in the forest with the rest of the slaughtered army. To have lived, to have survived, to have escaped was a kind of disgrace. But he didn't picture war as tanks, missiles and bombs, he pictured it as himself on horseback, with a sabre, charging against impossible odds. 'Women do not understand these things,' he'd say, clenching his teeth down on the end of his cigarette holder. 'They believe that life is babies and sewing.'

'I can't sew,' I said, but he would merely say, 'Later you will sew. You are so young,' and go on to prophesy more doom.

I recited slogans of hope, in vain; he would only smile his twisted little smile and say, 'You Americans are so naive, you have no history.' I'd given up trying to tell him I was not an American. 'It is all the same thing, isn't it?' he would say. 'The lack of one kind of history is the same as the lack of another.'

Ultimately our differences were: I believed in true love, he believed in wives and mistresses; I believed in happy endings, he in cataclysmic ones; I thought I was in love with him, he was old and cynical enough to know I wasn't. I had merely been deluded into this belief by my other belief, the one in true love. How could I be sleeping with this peculiar man, who was no Bell Telephone Mercury, without being in love with him? Surely only true love could justify my lack of taste.

Because Paul knew I was not in love with him, because he thought of me as a mistress and of mistresses as unfaithful by nature, he began to have fits of jealousy. It was all right as long as I did nothing but loll around the flat, reading and typing out my Costume Gothics and going nowhere except with him. He didn't even mind my trips to the Victoria and Albert; he didn't notice them much, because I was always home before he was and I didn't go there on the weekends. It was over the Portobello Road that we came to the parting of the ways. He himself introduced me to it, and it quickly became an obsession with me. I would pore for hours over the stalls of worn necklaces, sets of gilt spoons, sugar tongs in the shape of hen's feet or midget hands, clocks that didn't work, flowered china, spotty mirrors and ponderous furniture, the flotsam left by those receding centuries in which, more and more, I was living. I had never seen things like this before; here there was age, waves of it, and I pawed through it, swam in it, memorized it – a jade snuffbox, an enameled perfume bottle, piece after piece, exact and elaborate – to fix and make plausible the nebulous emotions of my costumed heroines, like diamonds on a sea of dough.

What amazed me was the sheer volume of objects, remnants of lives, and the way they circulated. The people died but their possessions did not, they went round and round as in a slow eddy. All of the things I saw and coveted had been seen and coveted previously, they had passed through several lives and were destined to pass through several more, becoming more worn but also more valuable, harder and more brilliant, as if they had absorbed their owners' sufferings and fed on them. How difficult these objects are to dispose of, I thought; they lurk passively, like vampire sheep, waiting for someone to buy them. I myself could afford almost nothing.

After these excursions I would return to the flat exhausted, my energy drained, while back in their stalls the coral rose brooches, the cairngorm pins, the cameos with their ivory profiles would be glowing in the dusk, sated as fleas. No wonder Paul began to suspect I had a lover and was sneaking off to visit him. Once he followed me; he thought I didn't see him, dodging in and out of the racks of used evening gowns and feather boas, like a comic private eye. It was beneath his dignity, of course, to actually accuse me of anything. Instead he threw tantrums because I wanted to go to the Portobello Road on Saturday, the good day, and he felt this day should be reserved for him. He began to attack my novels too, calling them cheap and frivolous, and it infuriated him when I agreed with him pleasantly. Of course they were cheap and frivolous, I said, but I had never claimed I was a serious writer. He took this as a dig at his own previous ambitions. Probably he would rather have found out I had a lover than discovered I didn't. A lover would have been less humiliating.

Paul was beginning to frighten me. He would wait for me at the top of the stairs after my orgies in the Portobello Road, standing there like a newel post, not saying anything, and as I came up the steps he would fix me with a reproachful, vindictive stare. 'I saw a wonderful Victorian jack-in-the-box today,' I would begin, but my voice would sound false, even to myself. I'd always found other people's versions of reality very influential and I was beginning to think that maybe he was right, maybe I did have a secret lover. I certainly began to want one, for making love with Paul had begun to resemble a shark fight, he was no longer gentle, he was pinching and biting and coming into the library on weekdays. It would have been all right except for the baleful glances and the oppressive silences, and the revolver, which was making me anxious.

Also, he'd just announced that the Polish government had agreed to let his mother out of Poland. He had saved up for it and at last it would happen, it was easier to get the old ones out than the young ones, he said. But I didn't want a Polish Countess living with us – where would she sleep? – discussing me in Polish and siding with Paul against me and ironing his boxer shorts, which I refused to do. He was devoted to his mother, which was tolerable only at a distance. But when I mentioned moving out, to give them more space, I said, he wouldn't hear of it.

Chapter Sixteen

I never told Arthur about Paul, which was perhaps a mistake. Not that he would have minded the fact that I was living with another man; but he would have been horrified by Paul's title, such as it was, and by his politics. Any woman who could live with such a man would have been stamped *wrong* by Arthur right away, and this was obvious to me fifteen minutes after I met him.

I was walking in Hyde Park, in July 1963. From either side came the sound of orations, doom-laden as the Old Testament, but I only half heard them. It was almost my twenty-first birthday, but I wasn't thinking about that either. I was pacing out the route which was about to be taken by Samantha Deane, the heroine of *Escape from Love*, as she fled from the illicit attentions of Sir Edmund DeVere. He'd just tried to take advantage of her in the children's schoolroom while everyone else had gone off to the Crystal Palace for the day.

As Samantha hurried down the stairs, her cheeks burned with the memory of what had just occurred. She'd been sitting alone in the schoolroom, working on the piece of crewelwork she kept for her few leisure moments. She hadn't heard the door open, hadn't heard Sir Edmund approach until he was within two yards of her chair. With an exclamation of surprise, she had risen to her feet. Sir Edmund was flushed and dishevelled. His usual iron control had vanished. As he gazed at her, his eyes flamed like those of some wild animal that scents its quarry.

'Sir Edmund,' Samantha said, trying to keep her voice level. 'What is the meaning of this intrusion? Why are you not at the Crystal Palace with the others?' Yet despite her efforts her knees were weak, either with fright or with a response she tried in vain to deny.

'I knew you were alone,' he said, moving closer. 'I slipped away. You must take pity upon me, you must know that my life is hell.' Yet he was not pleading, he was demanding. He seized her by the wrist and drew her toward him, pressing his hard mouth against hers. In vain she struggled, fighting both him and her own unbidden desires. His avid hands were already at her throat, tearing aside her fichu. . . .

'Remember who you are!' she managed to gasp. 'You are a married man!' His only answer was a harsh laugh. Desperately she remembered the short thick needle she still grasped in her right hand. She lifted it and raked it across his cheek. More in surprise than in pain, he released her, and she made use of this moment to run for the door, to slam it behind her and twist the heavy key in the lock. She was too terrified to think of taking a cloak or even a shawl.

Now she was hurrying through the Park, without knowing how she'd gotten there. Her thin black dress was little protection against the chill air of evening. Where was she to go, what to do? What explanation would Sir Edmund give the others, especially Lady Letitia, when they returned to find him locked in the schoolroom and the governess gone? Whatever he said would be to her discredit, she was sure; she could not return; and after that he would seek her out, hunt her down. . . . She had only a few pennies in her reticule. Where was she to spend the night?

Dark shapes flitted by on either side, and from time to time she heard low, mocking laughter. . . . Daughters of sin, vile abandoned creatures such as she herself might have become had she not struggled. . . . But perhaps she was now in even more danger. Alone, weak, unprotected – to what dissolute reveler might she not fall prey? She had not forgotten the lecherous advances of the Earl of Darcy, Sir Edmund's uncle. Then she had fled from his residence to Sir Edmund's, seeking protection; but the protector had failed her. . . .

There were footsteps behind her. She shrank into the shade of a tree, hoping to escape notice, but a shadow loomed against the seting sun, there was a hand on her arm, and a voice, hoarse with passion, breathed her name. . . .

At this point in my rehearsal I felt something on my arm. I looked down at it; there *was* a hand on it. I screamed, quite loudly, and the next thing I knew I was lying on top of a skinny, confused-looking young man. Pieces of paper were scattered over us like outsized confetti. Then I was being helped to my feet by several members of the crowd that had immediately gathered.

'Tryin' to molest yer, was he, love?' said one, burly and beer-scented. 'Bleedin' agitators.'

'I was just handing her a leaflet,' said my assailant. To my horror I saw that he had a slight cut on his cheek. I felt like an idiot.

'Want to call a bobby, love? They should be put away, they should, bothering young girls.'

'No, thank you,' I said. An antivivisectionist and a prophet of doom had both come over from their soap boxes to help. They were almost identical, saintly refined old men with pale-blue Ancient Mariner eyes. When they saw I wasn't hurt, each gave me a pamphlet.

'It was entirely my fault,' I told everyone. 'It was a mistake. I thought he was someone else, I just panicked, that's all. Here, let me get you a Kleenex,' I said to the young man. 'I'm very sorry I scratched you.' I rummaged in my purse but was unable to find one.

'It's all right,' he said stoically. He was on his knees, gathering up his leaflets, and I knelt to help him. The leaflets had a black-and-white drawing of an atomic bomb explosion, and the motto,

KEEP THE WORLD FROM GOING UP IN SMOKE. 'Banning the bomb?' I asked.

'Yes,' he said gloomily. 'Not that it's doing any good. But you have to keep on.'

I looked at him more closely. He was wearing a black crew-neck sweater, which I found quite dashing. A melancholy fighter for almost-lost causes, idealistic and doomed, sort of like Lord Byron, whose biography I had just been skimming. We finished collecting the pamphlets, I fell in love, and we went for a drink at the nearest pub. That wasn't hard to maneuver: all I had to do was express interest in the cause. I would've preferred it if he'd had a British accent; unfortunately he was only a Canadian, like me, but I overlooked this defect.

While Arthur stood in line at the bar for my double Scotch and his Guinness – when he drank at all, he tended to drink things that were supposed to have health-giving minerals in them – I felt anxiously through my brain for whatever scraps of political lore might have lodged there inadvertently, like bits of spinach among front teeth. I'd presented myself as someone who was at least semi-informed; now I'd have to come across. I even took out the pamphlets I'd been handed and glanced rapidly through them, hoping for some hint or topic. Do *you know that* DOG *spelled backwards is* GOD? one of them began. DOG, apparently, was the fourth member of the Holy Trinity, and was going to be in on the Last Judgment. The other pamphlet was more orthodox: Armageddon was at hand and if you wanted to come out of it you had to lead a pure life.

When Arthur returned with the drinks I was ready for him. Whenever the conversation got too specific, I switched the subject to the plight of the Palestinian refugees. I knew quite a lot about this from my days in the U.N. Club at Braeside High. At the time, this area was obscure enough to catch Arthur's attention, and I was ashamed to see that he was moderately impressed.

I let him walk me as far as the Marble Arch tube station. I couldn't invite him home with me, I explained, because I shared a flat with a clerk-typist who was very fat and homely, and who became quite unhappy and depressed if I asked any men into the flat for whatever reason. It was best to avoid phoning, I told him, but if he could give me his number. . . . He didn't have a phone, but, even better, he invited me to a rally the next day. Faint with lust, I went to the public library – the same one where I got my costume books – and took out all of Bertrand Russell's books I could find, which caused some difficult moments with Paul when he came across them. 'Communistic trash,' he raged. 'I will not allow them within my household.'

'I was only doing research,' I said. 'I thought I might do something a little more modern this time, set in the twenties.'

'It will not sell,' said Paul. 'If you raise the skirts and cut the hair, it will not sell. They prefer it if the woman should retain her mystery. As I do,' he added, kissing me on the collarbone.

At one time I would have found remarks like this very European and charming, but they were beginning to irritate me. 'Some mystery,' I said, 'if all it takes is a few yards of cloth and a wig. Men are mysterious too, you know, and I don't notice them wearing ringlets and waltz-length ballgowns.'

'Ah, but the mystery of man is of the mind,' Paul said playfully, 'whereas that of the woman is of the body. What is a mystery but a thing which is remaining hidden? It is more easy to uncover the body than it is the mind. For this reason, a bald man is not looked upon as an unnatural horror, but a bald woman is.'

'And I suppose a moronic woman is more socially acceptable than an idiot man,' I said, intending sarcasm.

'Just so,' said Paul. 'In my country they were often used as the lowest form of prostitute, whereas a man with no mind, for him there was no use.' He smiled, feeling he'd proved his point.

'Oh, for heaven's sake,' I said. I stomped out to the kitchen to make myself a cup of tea. Paul was puzzled. He was also suspicious: he still couldn't understand my sudden interest in Bertrand Russell.

I had a lot of trouble with these books, and, I discovered, with theories and politics in general. I didn't want to be blown up by an atomic bomb, but on the other hand I couldn't believe that anything I could do would prevent it. I might as well be trying to abolish the automobile: if I got run over by one, I'd be just as dead, I reasoned. I thought Lord Russell had a very appealing face, though, and I immediately gave him a bit part in *Escape from Love* as a benevolent old eccentric who rescues Samantha Deane in Hyde Park by beating her assailant over the head with his umbrella. (*'Take that, sir! Are you all right, my dear?' 'How can I ever express my gratitude?' 'I see you are well brought up, and I believe your explanation. Allow me to offer you asylum for the night. . . . My housekeeper will lend you a nightgown. Mrs Jenkins, a cup of tea, if you please, for this young lady.*') I even supplied him with a hobby – he raised guppies – which made me feel quite friendly towards all his frontispieces and able to tolerate his policies and the awe-tinged admiration with which Arthur regarded him.

If Arthur had known about my little dramatization of Lord Russell, he would've been appalled. 'Trivializing,' he would have called it, and did call it in later years, when I was less able to conceal this particular habit of mind. Also when I was less willing to simulate adoration of Arthur's hero-of-the-day: Arthur was fickle, he changed allegiances, and after I'd been through this a few times I became wary. 'What about *Mrs* Marx?' I would say, or, 'I bet Marx's wife wanted him to be a doctor.' All I would get would be a disgusted look, so I would go into the kitchen and fantasize about the home life of Marx. 'Not tonight, dear, I have a headache, you intellectuals are all the same, mooning around, why don't you get out there and make something of yourself if you're so smart, god knows you have the talent.'

I thought of Castro as a tiger in bed though, with those cigars and that beard, which would explain his vogue in North America. But Mao was my favorite, you could tell he liked to eat. I pictured him wolfing down huge Chinese meals, with relish and no guilt, happy children climbing all over him. He was like an inflated Jolly Green Giant except yellow, he wrote poetry, he had fun. He was fat but successful and he didn't take any shit about it. The home life of Stalin was boring, too much was known about it, he was such a puritan anyway. But Mao, what a garden of delights. He encouraged jugglers and spectacles, he liked the color red and flags and parades and table tennis; he knew the people needed food and escape, not just sermons. I liked to think about him in the bathtub, all covered with soap, like an enormous cherub, beaming away and very appreciative while some adoring female – me! – scrubbed his back.

As far as I was concerned, it was impossible to love a theory. I didn't love Arthur for his theories, although they lent him a kind of impersonal grandeur, like a crimson-lined opera cloak. I loved him for the way his ears stuck out, just slightly; for the way he pronounced certain words – 'Aunt,' for instance, and 'grass.' Being from the Maritimes, he said *ahnt* and *grahss*, whereas I was from Ontario and said *ant* and *graass*. I found this exotic. I loved his deliberate threadbareness, his earnest idealism, his ridiculous (to me) economies – he used tea bags twice – the way he stuck his finger in his ear, his farsightedness and the battered reading glasses he had to wear for it. Once I said, 'I guess that's why you like me, you can't see what I look like up close.' It was a little early to make this joke; he said, 'No, that isn't the reason.' Then there was a long, awkward pause, as if he was trying to think very hard about the reason he did like me. Or perhaps, I thought with a sinking of the stomach, about whether he liked me at all.

This was a problem. I couldn't tell what Arthur felt about me, if anything. He seemed to enjoy discussing the philosophy of civil disobedience with me, or rather telling me about it, for I was wise enough not to reveal my ignorance and mostly nodded. He allowed me to go around handing out leaflets with him, and ate with relish the sandwiches I would bring on these occasions. He told me about his background, his father the judge, his mother the religious nut. He father had wanted him to be a lawyer, his mother had insisted he be a medical missionary at the very least. He'd thwarted both of them by going into Philosophy, but he hadn't been able to stick it through all the syllogisms ('A bald man is bald,' he said, 'what does that have to do with the human condition?' and for once I could agree without hypocrisy ... until I started thinking about it; what if you *were* a bald man?). He'd left after his third year, to take a break and meditate on the true path. (That was the difference between us: for Arthur there were true paths, several of them perhaps, but only one at a time. For me there were no paths at all. Thickets, ditches, ponds, labyrinths, morasses, but no paths.)

Then he'd gotten involved in the ban-the-bomb movement, which had absorbed him for two years. He'd devoted a lot of time and energy to the movement, but somehow he was still on the fringes, a leaflet man. Perhaps it was because he was a Canadian.

I radiated sympathy and understanding. We were sitting in a cheap restaurant, which smelled of lamb fat, eating plates of fried eggs, chips and peas, which was what Arthur mostly ate. He was running out of money; soon he'd have to take another occasional job, sweeping floors or folding napkins or, worst of all, washing dishes; either that or accept what he considered his parents' bribery and go back to school at the University of Toronto, which he hated with a cool, abstract passion.

His Earls Court flat had a small kitchen, but he didn't like cooking, and the kitchen itself was a shambles. He shared the flat with two other men, a New Zealander who was studying at the London School of Economics and who ate cold, ketchup-covered canned baked beans and left the unwashed plates around like the scenes of tiny slaughters, and a gazelle-eyed radical from India who cooked brown rice and curries for himself and also left the plates around. Arthur was fastidious; he didn't like messes. But he was so fastidious he wouldn't clean them up, so we ate out. Once or twice I went over and tidied the kitchen for them, but this had no good effects and a couple of bad ones. Arthur was given another false impression about me: I wasn't at heart a kitchen-tidier, and he was disappointed later when he found this out. The New Zealander, whose name was Slocum, pursued me around the kitchen with pleas ('Be a sport, I haven't had one bit since I got to this bleeding cold-hearted country, not one bit'), and the Indian radical lost the initial respect he'd had for me as a politico of sorts and began to make cow-eyes and flare his nostrils. One could not, apparently, be both a respected female savant and a scullery maid.

Meanwhile, I couldn't get any further with Arthur than holding hands; and life with Paul was becoming more and more insupportable. What if he were to follow me, find me handing out leaflets with Arthur, and challenge him to a duel, or something equally upsetting? It was Arthur I loved, not Paul, I decided. I took drastic measures.

I waited till Paul had left for the bank; then I packed everything I owned, including my typewriter and the half-finished manuscript of *Escape from Love*. I scribbled a note for Paul. I wanted to say, 'Darling, it's better this way,' but I knew this was not dramatic enough, so instead I wrote, 'I have been making you unhappy and we cannot go on like this. It was not to be.' I didn't think he would be able to trace me, and I didn't really think he would try. Still, he was a great one for points of honour. Perhaps he would materialize in the doorway one evening with some grotesque, theatrical weapon, a paper knife or a straight razor. I didn't see him using the revolver; it was too modern. Before I could lose my nerve, I bundled all my luggage into a taxi, and unbundled it onto Arthur's doorstep. He would be home, I knew, I'd checked it out the day before.

'I've been evicted,' I told him.

He blinked. 'Just like that?' he said. 'I think that's illegal.'

'Well, it's happened,' I said. 'Because of my political sympathies. The landlord found some of those leaflets . . . he's violently right-wing, you know. There was a terrible row.' (This was a version of the truth, I felt. Paul was the landlord, sort of, and he was right-wing. Nevertheless I was an imposter, and I felt like one.)

'Oh,' said Arthur. 'Well, in that case. . . .' I was a political refugee. He invited me in so we could consider what I should do, and he even helped me carry the luggage up the stairs.

'I don't have any money,' I said, over a cup of tea which I'd made myself in the filthy kitchen. Neither did Arthur. Neither did either of his roommates, he knew for a fact. 'I don't know anyone else in London.'

'I guess you can sleep on the sofa,' he said, 'until you get a job.' What else could he say? We both looked at the sofa, which was ancient and lumpy; stuffing dripped from its mangled side.

I slept on the sofa for two nights; after that I slept with Arthur. We even made love. I'd been expecting fervor of a kind, because of his politics, but the first few times it was a lot more rapid than I was used to 'Arthur,' I said tactlessly, 'have you ever slept with a woman before?' There was a pause, during which I could feel his neck muscles tense. 'Of course I have,' Arthur said coldly. It was the only direct lie he ever consciously told me.

Once I was there, installed in his own house under his very nose, Arthur began to pay more attention to me. He even became affectionate, in his own way; he would brush my hair for me, clumsily but with concentration, and he would sometimes come up behind me and hug me, apropos of nothing, as if I were a teddy bear. I myself was bliss-filled and limpid-eyed: the right man had come along, complete with a cause I could devote myself to. My life had significance.

There were difficulties, though: the Indian and the New Zealander were ubiquitous, opening our door in the mornings to borrow shillings from Arthur, the New Zealander leering, the Indian remote with the ascetic disapproval he'd assumed as soon as he found out we were sleeping together. Or the New Zealander would sit on the sofa, listening to his transistor radio and doing rapid calculations under his breath, while the Indian took baths, leaving the wet towels on the floor; he was fond of saying that no one understood the evils of the class system the way he did, since he'd been raised in it, but he couldn't get over the habit of regarding anyone who picked up a towel as a servant. Both resented my presence; or rather, they resented what they regarded as Arthur's good fortune. Arthur himself wasn't conscious of their resentment, or of his good fortune either.

The other difficulty was that I could find neither time nor space to work on *Escape from Love*. When Arthur went out, he expected me to go with him; and if by any chance I could avoid that, one of the others was sure to be there. I kept the manuscript in a locked suitcase, as I suspected the New Zealander of snooping in our room. One day I returned to find that the Indian had hocked my typewriter. He'd repay me later, he promised, but after that I resented every grain of brown rice he ate. I didn't have enough money left to get it out of the pawnshop myself, and I'd counted on at least two hundred pounds for the finished work. I grew daily and secretly more desperate. Arthur didn't know about this problem; he kept wondering why I hadn't yet got a job as a waitress. In the fictitious past I'd constructed for his benefit I'd included a few items of truth, and I'd told him I had once been a waitress. I also told him I'd once been a cheerleader, and we laughed together over my politically misguided past.

When I'd been with them three weeks I was almost broke. Nevertheless, one day I blew a few precious shillings on some remnant material for bathroom curtains, a red-and-orange floral print. They'd make the bathroom less chilly and cavernous, I thought. I was going to sew them myself, by hand. I'd never sewn anything before in my life. I came up the stairs, humming to myself, and unlocked the door of the flat.

There, standing in the middle of the parlor floor, was my mother.

Chapter Seventeen

How had she found me?

She was standing, very upright, on the clay-colored rug, dressed in her navy-blue suit with the white collar; her white gloves, hat and shoes were immaculate, and she was clutching her purse under her arm. Her face was made up, she'd drawn a bigger mouth around her mouth with lipstick, but the shape of her own mouth showed through. Then I saw that she was crying, soundlessly, horribly; mascara was running from her eyes in black tears.

Through her back I could see the dilapidated sofa; it looked as though the stuffing was coming out of her. The hair on the back of my neck bristled, and I leapt back through the front door, shut it behind me, and leaned against it. It was her astral body, I thought, remembering what Leda Sprott had told me. Why couldn't she keep the goddamned thing at home where it belonged? I pictured my mother floating over the Atlantic Ocean, her rubber band getting thinner and thinner the farther it was stretched; she'd better be careful or she'd break that thing and then she'd be with me forever, lurking around in the parlor like a diaphanous dustball or a transparent Kodak slide of herself taken in 1949. What did she want from me? Why couldn't she leave me alone?

I opened the door again, to confront her and have it out finally; but she was gone.

I immediately rearranged all the furniture, which was difficult as it was old and heavy. Then I went through the flat, checking for open windows, but there weren't any. How had she gotten in?

I didn't tell the others about this visitation. They were a little put out about the furniture; not that they cared, but they felt I should have consulted them. 'I was trying to save you the trouble,' I said. 'I just think it looks better this way.' They put it down to housewifely instincts and forgot about the incident. I didn't, though: if my mother had managed to get her astral body across the Atlantic Ocean once, she'd be able to do it again, and I didn't welcome the next visit. I wasn't sure that rearranging the furniture would keep her out. Leda Sprott had used it for unfriendly spirits, but my mother wasn't a spirit.

I got the telegram five days later. It had been sitting in Canada House for four days; I'd continued to get my mail there and I'd used it as my return address on the infrequent postcards I'd been sending my father, in case my mother should ever have taken it into her head to sleuth me out and hunt me down. I didn't pick up my mail very often, because all I ever got was the occasional postcard from my father, with a picture of the Toronto skyline as seen at night from Centre Island – he must've bought several dozen of them at once – and the message, 'Everything all right here,' as if he were sending me a report card.

The telegram said; YOUR MOTHER DIED YESTERDAY. RETURN PLEASE. FATHER.

I read it three times. At first I decided it was a trap: my mother had sent it herself, she'd got the address off one of my postcards left carelessly lying around by my father, she was trying to lure me back within striking distance. But in that case she would have said YOUR FATHER DIED YESTERDAY. However, she might have realized that I wouldn't want to return while she was still alive, and sent the telegram as a false all-clear signal.

But what if she really was dead? In that case she'd turned up in my front parlor to tell me about it. I didn't at all want this to be true, but I suspected it was. I would have to go back.

When I reached the flat, the Indian radical was sitting cross-legged on the floor, explaining to Arthur, who was on the sofa, that if he had sexual intercourse too much he would weaken his spirit and thereby his mind, and would become politically useless. The thing to do, he said, was to draw the seminal fluid up the spinal column into the pituitary gland. He used the example of Gandhi. I listened to this conversation for a couple of minutes through the half-opened door (listening outside doors was a habit I'd retained), but since I couldn't hear what Arthur was answering, if anything, I walked in.

'Arthur,' I said, 'I have to go back to Canada. My mother died.'

'If she's dead already,' he said, 'why go back? There's nothing you can do.'

He was right, but I needed to know she was really dead. Even if I phoned the house long-distance and spoke with my father, I couldn't be sure ... I would have to see her. 'I can't explain,' I said, 'it's a family thing. I just have to go back.'

Then we both remembered that I didn't have any money. Why hadn't my father sent me some? He'd assumed that I was competent and solvent; he always assumed that there was nothing the matter with me, I was a sensible girl. My mother would have known better. 'I'll think of something, ' I said. I sat on the bed and chewed my fingers. My typewriter was in hock, *Escape from Love* was locked in my suitcase, untouched since I'd moved in with Arthur; it was only half done. I had hardly enough money for the paper to complete it. I could write my father for money, but that would be a precious pound, and besides, my bank account here was in the name of Louisa K. Delacourt. That would be hard to explain to my father, especially by telegram. It might hurt his feelings.

I slipped the manuscript into my bag. 'I'm going to the library,' I told Arthur. Before I left, I pinched one of the New Zealander's cheap yellow notepads and a ballpoint pen. No use to borrow: there would have been an inquisition.

For the next two days I sat in the library reading room, laboriously block-printing and tuning out the rustlings, creakings, wheezings and catarrhal coughs of the other occupants. Samantha Deane was kidnapped precipitously from her bedroom in the house of the kindly guppy man; threatened with rape at the hands of the notorious Earl of Darcy, the hero's disreputable uncle; rescued by the hero; snatched again by the agents of the lush-bodied, evil-minded Countess of Piedmont, the jealous semi-Italian beauty who had once been the hero's mistress. Poor Samantha flew back and forth across London like a beanbag, ending up finally in the hero's arms, while his wife, the feeble-minded Lady Letitia, died of yellow fever, the Countess, now quite demented, plunged to her death off a battlement during a thunderstorm and the Earl was financially ruined by the Pacific Bubble. It was one of the shortest books I'd ever written. Fast-paced though, or, as the jacket put it, event followed event to a stunning climax. I picked up a copy in Toronto when it came out. Samantha was charming in blue, her hair rippling like seaweed against an enormous cloud; Castle DeVere turreted with menace in the background.

But I got less for it than usual, partly because of the length – Columbine paid by the word – and partly because the bastards knew I needed the money. 'The conclusion is a little *unresolved*,' said the letter. But it was enough for a one-way airplane ticket.

My mother was dead, all right. Not only that, I'd missed the funeral. I didn't think to telephone from the airport, so as I walked up the front steps of the house in Toronto I didn't know whether or not anyone would be there to welcome me.

It was evening and the lights in the house were on. I knocked; no one answered so I tried the door, found it open, and walked in. I could see she was dead right away because some of the plastic covers were on the chairs and some were off. My mother would never have done a thing like that. For her, they were either on or off: the living room had two distinct and separate personalities, depending on whether or not she was entertaining. The uncovered chairs looked faintly obscene, like undone flies.

My father was sitting in one of the chairs, wearing his shoes. This was another clue. He was reading a paperback book, though abstractedly, as if he no longer needed to absorb himself in it completely. I saw this just for an instant before he noticed me.

'Your mother's dead,' he said. 'Come in and sit down, you must have had a long trip.'

His face was more furrowed than I'd remembered it, and also more defined. Previously it had been flat, like a coin, or even like a coin run over by a train; it had looked as though the features had been erased, but not completely, they were smudged and indistinct as if viewed through layers of gauze. Now however his face had begun to emerge, his eyes were light blue and shrewd, I'd never thought of him as shrewd; and his mouth was thin, even a little reckless, the mouth of a gambler. Why had I never noticed?

He told me that he'd found my mother at the bottom of the cellar stairs when he'd returned from the hospital one evening. There was a bruise on her temple and her neck was oddly twisted, broken, as he recognized almost immediately. He had called an ambulance for form's sake although he knew she was dead. She was wearing her housecoat and pink mules, and she must have tripped, my father said, and fallen down the stairs, hitting her head several times and breaking her neck at the bottom. He hinted at the amount she had been drinking lately. The verdict at the inquest was accidental death. It could not have been anything else, as there was no signs of anyone having been in the house and nothing had been taken. This was the longest conversation I ever had with him.

I was overcome by a wave of guilt, for many reasons. I had left her, walked out on her, even though I was aware that she was unhappy. I had doubted the telegram, suspecting a plot, and I hadn't even made it back for the funeral. I had closed the door on her at the very moment of her death – which, however, couldn't be determined exactly, as she had been dead for five or six hours at least by the time my father found her. I felt as if I'd killed her myself, through this was impossible.

That night I went to the refrigerator, *her* refrigerator, and gorged myself on the contents, eating with frantic haste and no enjoyment half a chicken, a quarter of a pound of butter, a banana cream pie, store-bought, two loaves of bread and a jar of strawberry jam from the cupboard. I kept expecting her to materialize in the doorway with that disgusted, secretly pleased look I remembered so well – she liked to catch me in the act – but despite this ritual, which had often before produced her, she failed to appear. I threw up twice during the night and did not relapse again.

My suspicions began the next day, when my father said to me at breakfast, looking at me with his new, sly eyes and sounding as if he'd rehearsed it, 'You may find this difficult to believe, but I loved your mother.'

I did find it difficult to believe. I knew about the twin beds, the recriminations, I knew that in my mother's view both I and my father had totally failed to justify her life the way she felt it should have been justified. She used to say that nobody appreciated her, and this was not paranoia. Nobody did appreciate her, even though she'd done the right thing, she had devoted her life to us, she had made her family her career as she had been told to do, and look at us: a sulky fat slob of a daughter and a husband who wouldn't talk to her, wouldn't move back to Rosedale, that stomping ground of respectable Anglo-Saxon money where his family had once lived, was he ashamed of her? The answer was probably yes, although during these conversations my father would say nothing; or he would say that he hadn't liked Rosedale. My mother would say that my father didn't love her, and I believed my mother.

Stranger still was his need to say to me, 'I loved your mother.' He wanted to convince me, that was clear; but it was also clear that he hadn't really been expecting me to come back from England. He'd already given my mother's clothes to the Crippled Civilians, he'd made footmarks all over the rug, there were dirty dishes in the sink at least three days old, he was systematically violating all the rules. He said an even more suspicious thing on the second day. He said, 'It isn't the same without her,' sighing and looking at me as he did so. His eyes pleaded with me to believe him, join the conspiracy, keep my mouth shut. I had a sudden image of him sneaking out of the hospital, wearing his white mask so he would not be recognized, driving back to the house, letting himself in with his key, removing his shoes, putting on his slippers and creeping up behind her. He was a doctor, he'd been in the underground, he'd killed people before, he would know how to break her neck and make it look like an accident. Despit his furrows and sighs he was smug, like a man who'd gotten away with something.

I told myself, in vain, that this was not the sort of thing he would do. Anything is the sort of thing anyone would do, given the right circumstances. I began to hunt for motives, another woman, another man, an insurance policy, a single overwhelming grievance. I examined my father's shirt collars for lipstick, I sifted through official-looking papers in his bureau drawers, I listened in on the few phone calls he received, crouching on the stairs. But nothing turned up, and I abandoned my search a lot sooner than I would have if I'd been convinced. Besides, what would I have done if I'd found out my father was a murderer?

I switched to speculations about my mother; I could afford to speculate about her, now that she was no longer there. What had been done to her to make her treat me the way she did? More than ever, I wanted to ask my father whether she was pregnant before they got married. And what about that young man in her photograph album, with the white flannels and expensive car, the one she said she'd been more or less engaged to? More or less. Some tragedy lurked there. Had he thrown her over because her father had been a stationmaster for the CPR? Was my father second-best, even though he was a step up for her?

I got the photograph album to refresh my memory. Perhaps in the expressions of the faces there would be some clue. But in all the pictures of the white-flannelled man, the face had been cut out, neatly as with a razor blade. The faces of my father also were missing. There was only my mother, young and pretty, laughing gaily at the camera, clutching the arms of her headless men. I sat for an hour with the album open on the table before me, stunned by this evidence of her terrible anger. I could almost see her doing it, her long fingers working with precise fury, excising the past, which had turned into the present and betrayed her, stranding her in this house, this plastic-shrouded tomb from which there was no exit. That was what she must have felt. It occurred to me that she might have committed suicide, though I'd never heard of anyone committing suicide by throwing themselves down the cellar stairs. That would explain my father's furtiveness, his wish to be believed, his eagerness to get rid of her things, which would remind him perhaps that he was partly to blame. For the first time in my life I began to feel it was unfair that everyone had liked Aunt Lou but no one had liked my mother, not really. She'd been too intense to be likable.

It was partly my failure as well. Had I been wrong to take my life in my own hands and walk out the door? And before that I had been the fat mongoloid idiot, the defective who had shown her up, tipped her hand: she was not what she seemed. I was a throw-back, the walking contradiction of her pretensions to status and elegance. But after all she was my mother, she must once have treated me as a child, though I could remember only glimpses, being held up by her to look at myself in the triple mirror when she'd brushed my hair, or being hugged by her in public, in the company of other mothers.

For days I brooded about her. I wanted to know about her life, but also about her death. What had really happened? And especially, if she'd died in her pink housecoat and mules, why had she turned up in my front parlor wearing her navy-blue suit from 1949? I decided to find Leda Sprott and ask her for a private sitting.

I looked her up in the phone book, but she wasn't there. Neither was the Jordan Chapel. I took a streetcar to the district where it had stood, and walked up and down the streets, searching for it. Finally I found the house; no doubt about it, I remembered the gas station on the corner. But a Portuguese family lived there now, and they could tell me nothing. Leda Sprott and her tiny band of Spiritualists had vanished completely.

I stayed with my father for nine days, watching my mother's house disintegrate. Her closets and dresser drawers were empty, her twin bed stood made but unused. Dandelions appeared on the lawn, rings around the bathtub, crumbs on the floor. My father did not exactly resent my presence, but he didn't urge me to stay. We had been silent conspirators all our lives, and now that the need for silence was removed, we couldn't think of anything to say to each other. I used to imagine that my mother was keeping us apart and if it weren't for her we could live happily, like Nancy Drew and her understanding lawyer Dad, but I was wrong. In fact she'd held us together, like a national emergency, like the Blitz.

Finally I got a room by myself, on Charles Street. I couldn't really afford it, but my father told me he was planning to sell the house and move into a one-bedroom apartment on Avenue Road. (He eventually married again, a nice legal secretary he met after my mother's death. They moved to a bungalow in Don Mills.)

For a while after my mother's death I couldn't write. The old plots no longer interested me, and a new one wouldn't do. I did try – I started a novel called *Storm over Castleford* – but the hero played billiards all the time and the heroine sat on the edge of her bed, alone at night, doing nothing. That was probably the closest to social realism I ever came.

The thought of Arthur contributed to my depression. I should never have left, I told myself. We'd kissed goodbye at the airport – well not the airport exactly, but he'd seen me to the BOAC bus terminal – and I'd told him I'd come back as soon as I could. I'd written him faithfully every week, and I'd explained that I couldn't return just yet as I didn't have the money. For a while he'd answered; odd letters, full of news about his leaflet activities, which he signed 'Yours sincerely.' (I signed mine, 'Love and a thousand kisses, XXXX.') But then there was silence. I didn't dare to think about what had happened. Was there another woman, some pamphlet-distributing chippy? Maybe he'd simply forgotten about me. But how could he, when I'd left most of my luggage in his apartment?

I got a job as a makeup demonstrator at the cosmetics counter in Eaton's, selling mascara. But I cried a lot at night and my eyes were puffy, so they switched me to wigs. Not even the good wigs, the synthetic ones. It wasn't very interesting work, and the customers' fruitless quest for youth and beauty depressed me. Occasionally when no one was lookng I would try on the wigs myself, but it was mostly the gray ones. I wanted to see how I would look when I was older. I would soon be old, I felt, and nothing would happen to me in the meantime because I wasn't interested in anything or anyone. I'd been deserted, I was convinced of it now. I was miserable.

Chapter Eighteen

I sat in exile on the Roman curb, on top of my portable Olivetti in its case, and wept. Pedestrians paused; some said things to me. I wanted Arthur back, I wanted him right here, with me. If I explained, how could he be angry? I'd handled things very badly ...

I stood up, wiped my face with a corner of my scarf, and looked around for a newsstand. I bought the first postcard I could find and wrote on the back of it, *I'm not really dead, I had to go away. Come over quickly.* XXX. I didn't sign my name or put any address: he would know who it was and where to find me.

After I'd mailed it I felt much better. Everything would be all right; as soon as he got the postcard Arthur would fly across the ocean, we would embrace, I'd tell him everything, he would forgive me, I would forgive him, and we could start all over again. He would see that I couldn't possibly go back to the other side, so he would change his name. Together we would bury all his clothes and buy new ones, once I'd sold *Stalked by Love*. He would grow a beard or a moustache – something distinguished and pointed, not the amorphous frizz that made men look like out-of-control armpits – and he might even dye his hair.

I remembered the hair dye. I located the equivalent of a drugstore and spent some time going through the rinses, tints, washes and colorings. I finally settled for Lady Janine's 'Carissima,' a soft, glowing chestnut, autumn-kissed, laced with sunlight and sprinkled with sparkling highlights. I liked a lot of adjectives on my cosmetic boxes; I felt cheated if there were only a few.

To celebrate the birth of my new personality (a sensible girl, discreet, warm, honest and confident, with soft green eyes, regular habits and glowing chestnut hair), I bought myself a *fotoromanzo* and sat down at an outdoor café to read it and eat a *gelato*.

If Arthur were here he'd be helping me to read the *fotoromanzo*.

We practiced our Italian that way, reading the speeches from the rectangular voice balloons out loud to each other, looking up the hard words in our pocket dictionary and figuring out the meanings from the black-and-white photos. Arthur found this faintly degrading; I found it fascinating. The stories were all of torrid passion, but the women and men never had their mouths open and their limbs were arranged like those of mannequins, their heads sat on their necks precise as hats. I understood that convention, that sense of decorum. Italy was more like Canada than it seemed at first. All that screaming with your mouth closed.

In this one the mother was secretly the lover of the daughter's fiancé, *fidanzato*. 'I love you,' she said, plaster-faced; *Ti amo*. She was wearing a negligee. 'Do not despair,' he said, gripping her shoulders. They never seemed to say anything I really needed, like 'How much are the tomatoes?' In the next square the woman's negligee was slipping off her shoulder.

A shadow loomed over me. I started and looked up: it was only a stranger though, white teeth and overpressed suit, nylon tie, pink and green. I knew that single women weren't supposed to sit alone in bars, but this wasn't a bar and it was the middle of the day. Perhaps it was the *fotoromanzo* that had attracted him. I closed it, but he'd already sat down at my table.

'*Scusi, signora.*' He asked me a question; I had no idea what it meant. I smiled weakly and said, '*Inglese, no parlo Italiano*,' but he grinned even more intensely. In his eyes our clothes fell to the floor, we fell to the floor, the white glass-topped table overturned and there was broken glass everywhere. Don't move, Signora, not even your hand with the wedding ring, where is your husband? Or you will cut yourself and there will be a lot of blood. Stay here on the floor with me and let me run my tongue over your belly.

I scrambled to my feet, gathering up my purse, hoisting the typewriter. The man behind the counter grinned as I paid my bill. How could I have allowed it, a man with such pointed shoes and a pink-and-green nylon tie? He reminded me of the vegetable man in the market square, with his grape-colored eyes, caressing the furry peaches, hefting the grapefruits possessively as breasts. My hand slid through his lambswool hair, we surged together on a wave of plums and tangerines, grapevines twined around us. . . .

Arthur, I thought, you'd better get my postcard fairly soon or something regrettable is going to happen.

It was midafternoon by the time I got back to Terremoto. I went to the post office, as I'd been doing every day, hoping for news from Sam. So far there had been nothing. 'Louisa Delacourt,' I said as usual, but this time the woman behind the counter turned her whole body, like the wax fortune-teller at the Canadian National Exhibition, who would pick out a card for you if you gave her a dime. Her hand came through the slot in the window, holding a blue airmail letter.

Outside, beyond the eyes of the lounging policemen, I tore it open and read a single word: BETHUNE. That was the code word for success. If there had been a fiasco, the letter would have said TRUDEAU. Sam was convinced the Mounties examined his mail; not only the mail he received but also the mail he sent out. 'That'll fix the buggers,' he said. 'Let them try to figure that one out.'

I crumpled the thin blue letter and stuffed it into my purse. Relief flooded through me, I was really free now; the inquest had gone all right, the stories of Sam and Marlene had been believed, I'd had a boating accident. I was officially dead even though no body had been found.

Charlotte was having tea with Mrs Ryerson, the plump, friendly housekeeper. So far, she was the only person in the entire household that Charlotte could trust. A fire was blazing on the hearth, shedding warmth and rosy reflections. Nevertheless, Charlotte did not feel quite safe. She wondered whether she should tell Mrs Ryerson about her destroyed wardrobe; but she decided not to, not just yet. . . .

'Mrs Ryerson,' Charlotte said, buttering a scone, 'what is the maze?'

A shadow crossed Mrs Ryerson's face. 'What maze, miss?'

'Tom, the coachman, warned me not to go near it.'

'And I wouldn't if I was you, miss,' Mrs Ryerson said emphatically. 'It's not a good place, the maze, especially for young girls.'

'But what is it?' Charlotte asked, puzzled.

'It's one of them mazes, miss, as was planted by the Master's forebears, hundreds of years ago, in the reign of Good Queen Bess it was, or so they say. The Master won't talk of it, ever since the first Lady Redmond was lost there, and the second one too, in broad daylight it was. Some say the Little Folk dance there and they don't like intruders, but that's just superstition. The first Lady Redmond, she said so too, and she went into it just to prove it was harmless, but she never did come out. They searched it later but nothing was found, nothing but one of her gloves, white kid it was.'

Charlotte was astonished. 'You mean . . . there's been more than one Lady Redmond?' she asked.

Mrs Ryerson nodded. 'This one's the third,' she said. 'The second one, a sweet girl she was too, she got so curious about what happened to the first, she went in as well. That time they heard her screaming, but when they went in – Tom the coachman it was and two of the grooms – she was gone. Spirited right away, as you might say. It's all overgrown, you know, miss.'

In spite of herself, Charlotte shivered. 'Why. . . . That's extraordinary,' she murmured. She felt a strong desire to visit the maze, to look at it, if only from the outside. She didn't believe in supernatural agencies. 'What about the present Lady Redmond?' she asked.

'She don't go near it, as I know of,' Mrs Ryerson replied. 'Some say as how there's no center to the maze and that's how they get lost, they gets into it and can't find their way out. Some say as how the first Lady Redmond and the second one are still in there, wandering around in circles.' Mrs Ryerson glanced over her shoulder; despite the warmth of the room, she drew her shawl more closely about her.

Charlotte finished the scone and licked her fingers fastidiously. 'Why, that's ridiculous,' she said. 'Who ever heard of a maze without a center?' But she was thinking uneasily of the events of the night before. . . . She'd been in her bedroom, and she'd heard a sound . . . a sound that came from outside, below, on the terrace . . . the sound of footsteps . . . and then, surely she was not mistaken, the sound of someone calling her name. *An icy tremor of fear shot through her. She arose and went to the window. There, below her, clearly visible in the eerie light from the moon, which had just appeared from behind a wisp of gauzy cloud, stood a figure . . . a figure swathed in a dark cloak, its features concealed.*

As Charlotte gazed, the figure turned and stalked away with measured steps. Who was trying to mystify her? Anger replaced her fear, and curiosity: she would get to the bottom of this. Hastily she made her way down the back stairs, which terminated, she knew, in a side door opening onto the terrace.

She was just in time to see the figure plunge into a yawning portal at the end of the terrace walk. Charlotte followed rashly; she hurried down a flight of stone steps. Before her was the lawn, with its formal Elizabethan flower plots, and beyond that . . . the entrance to the maze. The cloaked figure plunged into the entrance-way and disappeared; from somewhere came a low laugh.

Charlotte stood still. . . . Suddenly she was terrified. She felt drawn towards the maze, irresistibly, against her will, yet she knew that if she went in, something terrible would happen to her.

A hand on her arm made her start and scream, and she was looking up into the dark, enigmatic face of Redmond.

'A little late to be out walking, is it not?' he said mockingly. 'Or perhaps you were intending to ... meet someone. You seem dressed for some such occasion.'

Charlotte blushed crimson. She realized she was wearing nothing but her nightrail; beneath its snowy covering her breasts moved with agitation.

'I ... I must have been walking in my sleep,' she said in confusion. 'I do not recall ever having done so before.'

'A dangerous custom,' Redmond remarked, tightening his grip on her arm – for she had attempted to pull away – 'and dangerous customs must be paid for.' His face bent closer to her own; his eyes were gleaming in the light from the crescent moon. 'And now ...'

I'd been typing at the table, with my eyes closed; but as I paused to consider how Charlotte was going to get away this time (there were no library books around, no candelabra, no pokers from the fireplace she could hit him with; perhaps a good swift knee in the groin? But that was out of bounds in my books; it would have to be an interruption by a third party), I heard a sound.

There was someone outside, on the path. I could hear stealthy footsteps, coming down towards me. A shoe slid on gravel. The footsteps paused.

'Arthur?' I said in a small voice. But it wasn't Arthur, it couldn't be, so soon. I wanted to scream, to rush into the bathroom and shut and bolt the door, I could squeeze through the small window and run up the hill to my car, where did I put the keys? Faces formed and disintegrated in my head ... What did they want?

I realized how visible I must be, back-lit behind the picture window. I froze, listening, then turned out the light and crouched down behind the table. Was it Mr Vitroni, come back for some dubious reason in the middle of the night? Was it a stranger, someone, some man, who'd heard I lived alone? I couldn't remember whether or not I'd locked the door.

For a long time I huddled behind the table, listening for a sound, feet coming toward me, feet retreating. I could hear insects, a distant whine, a car winding up the hill toward the square ... but nothing else.

Finally I got up and looked out the front window onto the balcony, then out the kitchen window, then out the bathroom window. Nothing and nobody.

It was nerves, I told myself. I would have to watch that. I

climbed into bed, taking my *fotoromanzo* with me to calm myself down. I could read it without a dictionary, almost, since there were a lot of words and phrases I already knew. *I am not afraid of you. I don't trust you. You know that I love you. You must tell me the truth. He looked so strange. Is something the matter? Our love is impossible. I will be yours forever. I am afraid.*

PART FOUR

Chapter Nineteen

'So!' cried Felicia, breaking in upon them. 'This is how you disport yourself when my back is turned. Really, Redmond, I wish you would have more consideration.' She was wearing a dark cloak, thrown loosely over a sumptuous costume of flaming orange silk, with blue velvet trim. In an instant Charlotte was certain that it was Felicia who had called her name, lured her out of the house in her nightrail. It was Felicia who had written BEWARE in blood across her yellowing, warped bedroom mirror . . . Perhaps it was a conspiracy between the two of them. But Felicia seemed in earnest and her surprise appeared genuine. Charlotte's conviction wavered as she watched them confront each other.

'First it was the upstairs maid,' Felicia stormed. 'Then that girl you hired to repair the leather bindings in the Library. If you must behave this way, you might have a little more taste. Next time have the goodness to select someone from your own class.'

'Of what do you accuse me, madam?' Redmond growled. Despite herself, Charlotte felt a surge of sympathy toward him. Surely he only behaved this way because of the unhappiness of his marriage; surely if he were truly loved, unselfishly and purely instead of with Felicia's jealous possessiveness, he would be a different man. But she quickly suppressed this thought.

'Of carrying on in a shameless manner with this . . . this . . .'

'May I ask what you yourself are doing out at this time of night?' Redmond asked, his voice a menacing purr.

Before Felicia could answer, Charlotte found her own anger coming to her rescue. 'I refuse to stand here any longer. You may believe me or not, both of you, as you choose.' She turned and ran back toward the house, holding back the tears that she knew would come unbidden as soon as she could reach the safety of her room. She felt humiliated and degraded. Behind her, she could hear Felicia laughing, and perhaps Redmond was laughing too. She hated both of them.

As she ran along the terrace, a heavy stone jar, one of the ornaments of the balcony above, toppled over and crashed on the balustrade beside her, breaking into pieces, missing her by inches. Charlotte stifled a scream; she glanced up into the darkness. She knew now, it was beyond a doubt, she'd seen a black-cloaked shape whisking away, someone was trying to kill her ...

I'd set up the typewriter on the tabel. It worked all right, but there was no letter *k* in the Italian alphabet: I substituted *x*. And the keyboard was different, which meant I had to look. It was distracting, like some curious Martian code. I began to write the *k*'s in by hand, wondering what 'xill' meant. I stared at the word ... A kind of Aztec lizard, a Roman numeral?

Arthur would have known. He was good at crossword puzzles. But Arthur wasn't there.

Arthur, I thought, my eyes filling with tears, where are you? Why won't you come and find me? At any moment he might appear at the door, unexpectedly. He had done it once.

He had arrived at night, in the middle of a rainstorm. The landlady knocked at the door of my room. 'Miss Delacourt,' she said, 'it's ten o'clock. You know you aren't supposed to have visitors after seven.' I was lying on the bed, staring at the ceiling.

'I don't have any visitors in here,' I said, opening the door to show her it was true. I never had any visitors.

'There's one downstairs,' she said. 'I told him he couldn't come in. Said his name was Arthur something,' she said, as she slopped off down the hall in her kimono and shower thongs.

I ran down the front stairs, clutching the banister. It couldn't be Arthur, I'd given him up for lost. His last letter was dated September 8; it was now November. But if by some miracle it was Arthur and the landlady had sent him away ... I flung open the front door, prepared to gallop down the street after him in my terrycloth bathrobe. He was just turning to go back down the steps.

'Arthur', I screamed, throwing my arms around him from behind. He was wearing a yellow plastic raincoat with the collar turned up about his ears; his head was cold and soaking wet. We teetered on the edge of the top step; then I let go and he turned around.

'Where the hell have you been?' he said.

I couldn't ask him in, since the landlady was keeping watch around the corner of the upstairs hall, so I got my umbrella and rubber boots and went off into the night with him. We had some granular coffee in a late-night hamburger-and-chile place and unravelled the past.

'Why didn't you write?' I said.

'I did but the letters got returned.' He'd sent them to my father's address; he, of course, was no longer there.

'But I sent you my new address,' I said, 'as soon as I moved. Did't you get it?'

'I've been back here since the middle of September,' he said. 'Slocum was supposed to be forwarding my mail, but I didn't get any of it till today.'

How unjust I'd been to doubt him. I was overjoyed to see him, I felt we should immediately go somewhere to celebrate and then hop into bed. 'It's great that you're back!' I said.

Arthur didn't think it was great. He was quite depressed, and looked it: all his corners were turned down, eyes, mouth, shoulders. 'What's the matter?' I asked, and he told me, at some length.

The Movement had fallen to pieces. He dropped dark hints, but I could never figure out whether it had been crushed by a show of force from without, had been infiltrated and destroyed from within, or had disintegrated through general lack of morale and squabbles among its members. Whatever the reason, something he'd believed in and worked for had failed, and this failure had plunged him into a state of existential gloom. He'd spent some time being torpid, and then in despair he'd agreed to accept money from his parents – surely I must see how bad things had been – and return to the University of Toronto. He was supposed to be writing a paper on Kant.

So it wasn't purely a longing to see me that had brought him across the ocean. It was inertia and the absence of a sense of purpose. I didn't mind that much, so long as he was there, and he had gone to a lot of trouble to find me. He'd walked at least three blocks in the rain: that meant dedication of a sort.

We spent the rest of the evening, and many evenings that followed, discussing whether or not it was ethical for him to stay in Toronto and go to the university on money that he considered tainted. 'But if it's for a good end —' I would say. I didn't care whether it was ethical or not: I wanted him to stay with me, and the alternative he was proposing was a trip to northern British Columbia to work in an asbestos mine. 'It's not for a good end,' he would reply mournfully. 'What use is Kant anyway? It's all abstract bullshit . . .' But he lacked the willpower to quit.

All that winter I devoted myself to cheering Arthur up. I took him to movies, I listened to his complaints about the university, I typed his papers for him, complete with footnotes. We ate hamburgers at Harvery's Hamburgers and went for walks in Queen's Park, and on jaunts to the Riverdale Zoo, about the only entertainments, aside from the movies, that we could afford. We slept together, when we could. Arthur was living in residence, and that sort of thing was tolerated only if you did it furtively; my landlady, on the other hand, would tolerate nothing, no matter how furtive.

Sometimes during these nights I would wake up to find Arthur clinging to me as if the bed was an ocean full of sharks and I was a big rubber raft. Asleep he was desperate, he sometimes talked to people who weren't there and ground his teeth. But awake he was apathetic and unresponsive, or coldly dialectical. Without his political enthusiasms he was quite different from the way he'd been in England. He allowed me to do things for him, but he didn't participate.

None of this bothered me very much. His aloofness was even intriguing, like a figurative cloak. Heroes were supposed to be aloof. His indifference was feigned, I told myself. Any moment now his hidden depths would heave to the surface; he would be passionate and confess his long-standing devotion. I would then confess mine, and we would be happy. (Later I decided that his indifference at that time was probably not feigned at all. I also decided that passionate revelation scenes were better avoided and that hidden depths should remain hidden; façades were at least as truthful.)

In the spring Arthur proposed. We were stting on a Queen's Park bench, eating take-out hamburgers and drinking milk shakes.

'I have a good idea,' Arthur said. 'Why don't we get married?'

I said nothing. I couldn't think of any reasons why not. Arthur could, though, and he proceeded to analyze them: neither of us had much money, we were probably too young and unsettled to make such a serious commitment, we didn't know each other very well. But to all these objections he had the answers. He'd been giving it quite a lot of thought, he said. Marriage itself would settle us down, and through it, too, we would become better acquainted. If it didn't work out, well, it would be a learning experience. Most importantly, we could live much more cheaply together than we could seperately. He'd move out of residence and we'd both move into a larger rented room than the one I had, or even a small flat. I would keep my job, of course; that way he wouldn't have to accept so much money from his parents. He'd been thinking of switching into policital science, which would mean several more years at school, and he wasn't too sure his parents would support him through that.

I chewed the rest of my hamburger and swallowed it thoughtfully; then I slurped up the rest of my milk shake. Now or never was the time for courage, I thought. I longed to marry Arthur, but I couldn't do it unless he knew the truth about me and accepted me as I was, past and present. He'd have to be told I'd lied to him, that I'd never been a cheerleader, that I myself was the fat lady in the picture. I would also have to tell him that I'd quit my job as a wig-seller several months before and was currently finishing *Love Defied*, on the proceeds of which I expected to live for at least the next six months.

'Arthur,' I said, 'marriage is serious. There are a few things I think you should know about me, in advance.' My voice was trembling: surely he would be horrified, he would find me unethical, he would be disgusted, he would leave . . .

'If you mean you were living with another man when you met me,' he said, 'I already know that. It doesn't bother me in the least.'

'How did you find out?' I asked. I thought I'd been very careful.

'You didn't expect me to believe that story about your fat roommate, did you?' he said indulgently. He smiled and put his arm around me. 'Slocum followed you home,' he said. 'I asked him to.'

'Arthur,' I said, 'you sneaky old spy.' I was delighted that he'd been jealous or curious enough to have done this; I also saw that he was pleased at having penetrated my disguise. But how annoyed he'd be if he discovered he'd only made it as far as the first layer.

. . . I decided to postpone my revelations to some later date.

The only difficulty with the actual wedding was that Arthur refused to be married in a church, since he disapproved of religion. He also refused to be married in a city hall, because he disapproved of the current government. When I protested that these were the only choices, he said there had to be some other way. I went through the Yellow Pages, under 'Bridal' and 'Weddings,' but these departments covered only gowns and cakes. Then I looked under 'Churches.' There was one division labeled 'Interdenominational.'

'Will this do?' I said. 'If they'll marry anyone to anyone else, they can't have very strict religious convictions.' I talked him into it, and he phoned the first name on the list, a Reverend E. P. Revele.

'It's all set,' he told me, coming out of the pay phone. 'He says we can have it at his house, he'll supply the witnesses, and it'll only take ten minutes. He says they like to do a little ceremony, nothing religious.'

That was fine with me. I didn't want to be done out of a ceremony, I wouldn't feel married without one. 'What did you say?'

'As long as he keeps it short.'

Arthur also told me that it would only cost fifteen dollars, which was lucky since we didn't have very much money. I was torn between asking him to postpone the wedding – I'd think of some excuse, but really so I could finish *Love Defied* and buy a good wedding dress – and rushing to the Interdenominationalists right away, before Arthur found out the truth. Fear prevailed over vanity, and I bought a white cotton dress with nylon daisies on it at Eaton's Budget Floor. It would be a little disappointing, but I could stand the disappointment of a cheap cotton wedding a lot better than I could stand the thought of no wedding at all. I was terrified that I'd be exposed at the last minute as a fraud, liar and impostor. Under the strain I started to eat extra helpings of English muffins covered with butter, loaves of bread and honey, banana splits, doughnuts, and secondhand cookies from Kresge's. Though these indulgences were not obvious to Arthur, I was gaining weight; the only thing that saved me from bloating up like a drowned corpse was the wedding date itself, and even so, I'd gained thirteen pounds by the time it arrived. I could just barely get my zipper done up.

No one we knew came to our wedding, for the simple reason that we knew no one. Arthur's parents were out of the question: Arthur had written them an aggressively frank letter saying that we'd been sleeping together for a year, so they needn't think his marriage was a capitulation to convention. They, of course, denounced both of us and cut off Arthur's funds. I thought of inviting my father, but he might reveal more of my past than I wanted Arthur to know. I sent him a postcard afterward, and he sent me a waffle iron. Arthur didn't like any of the philosophy students, and I hadn't become friends with any of my fellow wig demonstrators, so we wouldn't even get any wedding presents I went out and bought myself a soup kettle, a pair of oven mitts and, on impulse, a gadget for taking the stones out of cherries and the pits out of olives, to make myself feel more like a bride.

On the day itself, Arthur picked me up at my rooming house and we got on the northbound subway together. We sat on the black leatherette seats and watched the pastel tiles flash by; we held hands. Arthur seemed apprehensive. He'd lost weight and was skinny as a funeral brass; our reflections in the subway-car windows had deep hollows under the eyes. I didn't see how he was possibly going to be able to carry me over the threshold. We didn't even have a threshold: we hadn't rented an apartment yet, because I still had two paid-in-advance weeks left at my rented room, and Arthur said there was no point wasting money.

We got off the subway and transferred to a bus. It wasn't till after it had started that the name on the front of it registered. 'Where did you say this man lives?' I said. Arthur handed me the piece of paper on which he'd scribbled the address and told me. I was in Braeside Park.

I began to sweat. The bus went past the stop where I used to get off; up a side street I glimpsed my mother's house. My face must have been white, for when Arthur glanced at me, squeezing my hand to reassure me or for reassurance, he said, 'Are you all right?'

'Just a little nervous, I guess,' I said, with a ducklike laugh.

We got off the bus and walked along the sidewalk, into the dank interior of upper Braeside Park, past the trim, respectable, haunted fake-Tudor dwellings of my obese adolescence. My terror was growing. Surely the minister would be someone I knew, someone whose daughter I'd gone to school with, someone who would recognize me despite my change of shape. He wouldn't be able to contain himself, he would exclaim at my transformation and tell humorous stories about my former size and weight, and Arthur would know – on our very wedding day! – how deeply I'd decieved him. He'd know I hadn't gone steady with a basketball player, or been third runner-up in the Rainbow Romp queen-of-the-prom contest. The maple trees were heavy with drooping green leaves, the air was humid as soup, laden with car fumes which had drifted in from the nearest thoroughfare. Moisture beaded our upper lips; I could feel the sweat spreading under my arms, staining the purity of my white dress.

'I think I'm having a sunstroke,' I said, leaning against him.

'But you haven't been in the sun,' Arthur said reasonably. 'That's the house, right up there, we'll get inside and you can have a drink of water.' He was pleased in a way that I was reacting with such distress; it camouflaged his own.

Arthur helped me up the cement front steps of Number 52 and rang the bell. There was a small, ornately lettered sign on the door that said 'Paradise Manor'; I read it without comprehension. I was trying to decide whether or not to faint. Then, even if there was a revelation, I could exit with dignity, in an ambulance. The aluminum screen door had the silhouette of a flamingo on it.

The door was opened by a tiny old woman in pink gloves, pink high-heeled shoes, a pink silk dress and a pink hat decorated with blue cloth carnations and forget-me-nots. There was a round circle of rouge on each of her cheeks, and her eyebrows were two thinly penciled arcs of surprise.

'We're looking for the Reverend E. P. Revele,' Arthur said.

'Oh, what a lovely dress!' the old woman chirped. 'I love weddings; I'm the witness, you know, my name is Mrs Symons. They always have me for the witness. Here comes the bride,' she called to the house in general.

We went in. I was recovering; surely this was no one I knew. Thankfully I breathed in the smell of upholstery and warm furniture polish.

'The Revered does the ceremonies in the parlor,' said Mrs Symons. 'It's such a lovely ceremony, I'm sure you'll like it.' We followed her, and found ourselves in a grotto.

It was the standard Braeside living room, poorer section, with a dining room opening onto it, which in turn opened into the kitchen; however, the walls contained, not the traditional soothing landscapes (Brook in Winter, Country Lane in Fall), but several peacock fans, some framed pieces of embroidery, a picture of a ballet dancer that lit up from behind ornamented with sprays of dried leaves, a painting of a North American Indian woman smiling winsomely, a shellwork picture – flowers in a vase, the petals of each made from a different kind of shell – and a number of fading photographs, also in frames, with signatures across the bottom. The chesterfield and matching easy chairs were of plum-colored velvet and each easy chair had a matching footstool; all were smothered in many-colored doilies crocheted in wool. The mantel of the fireplace was crowded with objects: little Buddhas, Indian gods, a china dog, several brass cigarette cases and a stuffed owl under a glass bell.

'Here comes the Reverend,' said Mrs Symons in an excited whisper. There was shuffling noise behind us. I turned, then collapsed into a plum-colored armchair; for there, standing in the doorway in her long white gown with the purple bookmark, leaning now on a silver-headed cane and surrounded by a nimbus of Scotch whiskey, was Leda Sprott.

She looked me straight in the face, and I could tell she knew exactly who I was. I moaned and closed my eyes.

'Wedding nerves,' shrilled Mrs Symons. She grabbed my hand and began chafing my wrist. 'I fainted three times during my own wedding. Get the smelling salts!'

'I'm all right,' I said, opening my eyes. Leda Sprott hadn't said anything: maybe she'd keep my secret.

'Are you all right?' Arthur said to me. I nodded. 'We were looking for a minister named E. P. Revele,' he said to Leda Sprott.

'I am E. P. Revele,' she said. 'Eunice P. Revele.' She smiled, as if she was used to incredulity.

'Are you qualified?' Arthur asked.

'Of course,' said Leda. She waved at an official-looking framed certificate on the wall. 'They wouldn't let me perform weddings if I weren't. Now, what will you have? I specialize in mixed marriages. I can do Jewish, Hindu, Catholic, five kinds of Protestant, Buddhist, Christian Scientist, agnostic, Supreme Being, any combination of these, or my own speciality.'

'Maybe we should take the speciality,' I said to Arthur. I wanted it over and done with as soon as possible, so I could get away.

'That is the one I myself prefer,' said Leda. 'But first, the picture.' She went to the hall, where she called, 'Harry!' I took this chance to look at the certificate. 'Eunice P. Revele,' it said, right enough. I was confused: either she was really Leda Sprott, in which case the ceremony would be invalid, or she was really Eunice P. Revele; if so, why had she used another name at the

Jordan Chapel? But then, I thought, men who changed their names were likely to be con-men, criminals, undercover agents or magicians, whereas women who changed their names were probably just married. Beside the certificate was a photo of Leda, much younger, shaking hands with Mackenzie King. It was signed, I noticed.

Mrs Symons was trying to get Arthur to put a plastic wreath of flowers around his neck, with no success. She put one on me, though, and a man in a gray suit came in with a Polaroid camera. It was Mr Stewart, the visiting medium. 'Smile,' he said, squinting through the viewfinder. He himself smiled broadly.

'Look,' Arthur said, 'this isn't ...' But there was a flash, and Mrs Symons whipped off my wreath.

'When the gong sounds, you stand to attention,' Mrs Symons said. She was very excited. 'You look lovely, dear.'

'It sounded all right over the phone,' Arthur said to me in a low voice.

'Who were you talking to?' I asked. 'You said it was a man.'

'I thought it was,' Arthur said.

The gong sounded and Leda paced in, wearing a different robe, a purple one, trimmed in red velvet. I recognized the remains of the Jordan Chapel curtains and pulpit: times were evidently hard. With the help of Mr Stewart, she got up onto the footstool that stood in front of the fireplace.

'Arthur Edward Foster,' she intoned. 'Joan Elizabeth Delacourt. Advance.' She broke into a fit of coughing as, hand in hand, we approached her.

'Kneel,' she said, stretching out her arms in front of her as if about to dive off the stool. We did. 'No, no,' she said irritably, 'on either side. How can I join you together if you're already joined?' We got up, kneeled again, and Leda placed a slightly trembling hand on each of our heads.

'For true happiness,' she said, 'you must approach life with a feeling of reverence. Reverence for life, for those loved ones who are still with us, and also for those who have gone before. Remember that all we do and all that is in our hearts is watched and recorded, and will someday be brought to light. Avoid deception and falsehood; treat your lives as a diary you are writing and that you know your loved one will someday read, if not here on this side, then on the other side, where all the final reconciliations will take place.

Above all, you should love each other for what you are and forgive each other for what you are not. You have a beautiful aura, my children; you must work to preserve it.' Her voice dropped to a mumble; I think she was praying. She swayed dangerously and I hoped she would not fall off the stool.

'Amen,' said Mrs Symons.

'You may rise,' said Leda. She asked for our rings – I'd insisted on double rings, and we'd got them in a pawn shop – and circled them three times around the statue of the Buddha, though it might have been the stuffed owl; from where I was standing, I couldn't see. 'For wisdom, for charity, for tranquillity,' she said. She gave Arthur's ring to me and my ring to Arthur.

'Now,' she said, 'holding the rings in your *left* hands, place your *right* hands on each other's hearts. when I count to three, *press*.'

'Three is the mystical number,' Mrs Symons said. 'Four is too, but . . .' By this time I'd recognized her: she was one of the old Jordan Chapel regulars. 'My name comes out to five,' she continued. 'That's numerology, you know.'

'There's a story I heard recently that would be appropriate for this occasion,' said Mr Stewart. 'There were once two caterpillars who were walking down the Road of Life, the optimistic caterpillar and the pessimistic . . .'

'Not now, Harry,' Leda Sprott said sharply. The ceremony was getting out of hand. She told us to put the rings on each other's fingers, hastily pronounced us man and wife, and clambered down off the footstool.

'Now the presents!' cried Mrs Symons. She scurried from the room. Leda produced a certificate, which we were all supposed to sign.

'There's someone standing behind you,' Mr Stewart said. His eyes were glazed and he seemed to be talking to himself. 'She's a young woman, she's unhappy, she has on white gloves . . . she's reaching out towards you . . . '

'Harry,' Leda said, 'go and help Muriel with the presents.'

'We don't want any presents, really,' I said, and Arthur agreed, but Leda Sprott said, 'A wedding isn't a wedding without presents,' and pink Mrs Symons was already hurrying in from the hall with several packages wrapped in white tissue paper. We thanked them; we were both acutely embarrassed because these well-meaning, rather pathetic old people had gone to so much trouble and we were secretly so ungrateful. Mr Stewart gave us the Polaroid snapshot, in which our faces were a sickly blue and the sofa was brownish-red, like dried blood.

'Now I have something to say to the bride and groom ... separately,' said Leda Sprott. I followed her into the kitchen. She shut the door and we sat down at the kitchen table, which was an ordinary one covered with checked oilcloth. She poured herself a shot from a half-empty bottle, then looked at me and grinned. One of her eyes, I could see now, was not quite focused; perhaps she was going blind.

'Well,' she said. 'I'm pleased to see you again. You've changed, but I never forget a face. How is your aunt?'

'She died,' I said, 'didn't you know?'

'Yes, yes,' she said, waving one of her hands impatiently, 'of course. But she must still be with you.'

'No, I don't think so,' I said.

Leda Sprott looked disappointed. 'I can see you haven't taken my advice,' she said. 'That's unfortunate. You have great powers, I told you that before, but you've been afraid to develop them.' She took my hand and peered at it for some moments, then dropped it. 'I could tell you a lot of mumbo jumbo, which would probably mean just as little to you as the truth,' she said. 'But I liked your aunt, so I won't. You do not choose a gift, it chooses you, and if you deny it it will make use of you in any case, though perhaps in a less desirable way. I used my own gift, as long as I had it. You may think I'm a stupid old woman or a charlatan, I'm used to that. But sometimes I had the truth to tell; there's no mistaking it when you do. When I had no truth to tell, I told them what they wanted to hear. I shouldn't have done that. You may think it's harmless, but it isn't.' She paused, staring down at her fingers, which were knotted with arthritis. Suddenly I believed in her. I wanted to ask her all the questions I'd saved up for her: she could tell me about my mother .... But my belief faded: hadn't she just hinted that the Jordan Chapel was fraudulent and her revelations guesswork and playacting?

'People have faith in you,' Leda said. 'They trust you. That can be dangerous, especially if you take advantage of it. Everything catches up to you sooner or later. You should stop feeling so sorry for yourself.' She was looking at me sharply with her one good eye, her head on one side, like a bird. She seemed to expect some reply.

'Thank you,' I said awkwardly.

'Don't say what you don't mean,' she said irritably. 'You do enough of that already. That's really all I have to say to you, except . . . yes, you should try the Automatic Writing. Now, send in your new husband.'

I didn't want Arthur to be alone with her. If she'd been this blunt with me, what was she likely to say to him?

'You won't tell him, will you?' I said.

'Tell him what?' Leda asked sharply.

It was hard to put into words. 'What I was like,' I said. What I meant was: *What I looked like.*

'What do you mean?' Leda said. 'You were a perfectly nice young girl, as far as I could tell.'

'No, I mean . . . my shape. I was, you know.' I couldn't say 'fat'; I used that word about myself only in my head.

She saw what I meant, but it only amused her. 'Is that all?' she said. 'To my mind it's a perfectly proper shape. But don't worry, I won't give away your past, though I must say there are worse tragedies in life than being a little overweight. I expect you not to give mine away, either. Leda Sprott owes a little money here and there.' She laughed wheezily, then started to cough. I went to get Arthur.

Five minutes later he came out of the kitchen. As we left, Mrs Symons teetered along the hall after us, down the steps and along the walk, throwing handfuls of rice and confetti at us and chirping gaily. 'Good luck,' she called, waving her pink-gloved hand.

We walked to the bus stop, carrying the packages. Arthur didn't say anything; his jaw was grim.

'What's the matter?' I asked. Had Leda told him about me after all?

'The old fraud ripped me off for fifty bucks,' he said. 'On the phone she told me fifteen.'

When we got back to my rented room we opened the tissuepaper packages. They contained a plastic punch bowl with matching cups, a ninety-eight-cent book on health-food cookery, a framed print of Leda, shaking hands with Mackenzie King, and some government pamphlets about the health-giving properties and correct use of yeast. 'She must make quite a profit,' Arthur said.

Surely we would have to go through it all over again at the City Hall, I thought; the ceremony with the footstool and the stuffed owl couldn't possibly be legal. 'Do you think we're really married?' I asked.

'I doubt it,' Arthur said. But strangely enough we were.

Chapter Twenty

We went on our Honeymoon four years later, in 1968. It was Arthur's Quebec separatist incarnation, so he insisted on going to Quebec City, where he confused all the waiters by trying to speak *joual* to them. Most of them found it insulting; the ones who really were separatists sneered at his pronunciation, it was too Parisian for them. We spent the first night watching the funeral of Robert Kennedy on the bunny-eared television set in the cheap motel where we were staying. It wouldn't work unless you held onto the bunny ears with one hand and put your other hand on the wall. I did the wall-touching, Arthur did the watching. By that time I was feeling truly married.

It took me a while. At first our life was unsettled. We had no money except what I could earn by writing Costume Gothics and pretending to take odd jobs, and we lived in rooming houses instead of the tawdry apartments we later sought out. Sometimes there would be a kitchen alcove concealed by a bamboo curtain or a plastic accordion door, but more often there would be only a single-burner hot plate. I would cook dinners of vegetables in boilable plastic packages, or tins of ravioli, and we would eat them sitting on the edge of the bed and trying not to get any more tomato sauce on the sheets. After the meal I would scrape the plates into the rooming-house toilet and rinse them in the bathtub, as these rooms rarely had sinks. This meant that during baths, which we took together, with me soaping Arthur's back, his ribs sticking out like Death's in a medieval woodcut, we would often be surprised by the odd noodle or pea, floating in the soap scum like an escaped fragment of Sargasso Sea. I felt it added a welcome touch of the tropics to those otherwise polar bathrooms but Arthur didn't like it. Although he denied it, he had a thing about germs.

I complained a lot about the inconvenience of this improvised suitcase life, and after two years of it, when Arthur was a teaching assistant in Political Science and had a salary of sorts, he broke down and we got a real apartment. It was in a slum – which has since become fashionably white-painted and coach-lamped – but at least it had a full kitchen in addition to the cockroaches. I then discovered to my dismay that Arthur expected me to cook, actually cook, out of raw ingredients such as flour and lard. I'd never cooked in my life. My mother had cooked, I had eaten, those were our roles; she wouldn't even let me in the kitchen when she was cooking, for fear I would break something, stick my germ-laden finger in a sauce, or tread too heavily, causing her cake to fall. I hadn't taken Home Economics in high school; I took Business Practices instead. I wouldn't have minded the cooking, though from the other girls' accounts it was mostly about nutrition; but I shrank from the thought of sewing. How could I possibly sit there, sewing a huge billowing tent for myself, while the others worked away at their trim tailored skirts and ruffled blouses?

But for Arthur's sake I would try anything, though cooking wasn't as simple as I'd thought. I was always running out of staples such as butter or salt and making flying trips to the corner store, and there were never enough clean dishes, since I hated washing them; but Arthur didn't like eating in restaurants. He seemed to prefer my inedible food: the Swiss fondue which would turn to lymph and balls of chewing gum from too high a heat, the poached eggs which disintegrated like mucous membranes and the roast chickens which bled when cut; the bread that refused to rise, lying like quicksand in the bowl; the flaccid pancakes with centers of uncooked ooze; the rubbery pies. I seldom wept over these failures, as to me they were not failures but successes, they were secret triumphs over the notion of food itself. I wanted to prove that I didn't really care about it.

Occasionally I neglected to produce any food at all because I had forgotten completely about it. I would wander into the kitchen at midnight to find Arthur making himself a peanut-butter sandwich and be overwhelmed with guilt at the implication that I'd been starving him. But though he criticized my cooking, he always ate it, and he resented its absence. The unpredictability kept him diverted; it was like mutations, or gambling. It reassured him, too. His view of the world featured swift disasters set against a background of lurking doom, and my cooking did nothing to contradict it. Whereas for me these mounds of dough, these lumps burning at the edges, this untransformed blood, represented something quite different. Each meal was a crisis, but a crisis out of which a comfortable resolution could be forced to emerge, by the addition of something . . . a little pepper, some vanilla . . . At heart I was an optimist, with a lust for happy endings.

It took me a while to realize that Arthur enjoyed my defeats. They cheered him up. He loved hearing the crash as I dropped a red-hot platter on the floor, having forgotten to put on my oven mitt; he liked to hear me swearing in the kitchen; and when I would emerge sweaty-faced and disheveled after one of my battles, he would greet me with a smile and a little joke, or perhaps even a kiss, which was as much for the display, the energy I'd wasted, as for the food. My frustration and anger were real, but I wasn't that bad a cook. My failure was a performance and Arthur was the audience. His applause kept me going.

That was all right with me. Being a bad cook was much easier than learning to be a good one, and the extra noise and flourishes didn't strain my powers of invention. My mistake was in thinking that these expectations of Arthur's were confined to cooking. It only looked that way at first, because as far as he could tell I attempted nothing else.

It wasn't that Arthur was dishonest: what he thought and what he said he thought were the same. It was just that both of these things were different from what he felt. For years I wanted to turn into what Arthur thought I was, or what he thought I should be. He was full of plans for me, ambitions, ways in which I could exercise my intelligence constructively, and there I would be, lying lumpishly in bed in the mornings while he was up and making himself black coffee and pursuing one of his goals. That was what was wrong with me, he told me, I didn't have any goals. Unfortunately I was unable to think of this word except in connection with hockey, a game I didn't much enjoy.

But Arthur wasn't always an early riser. He had his down moments too. After his disillusionment with the atom-bomb people he'd stayed out of politics for a while. But soon he was on the upswing. This time it was civil rights: he went down to the States and almost got shot. But then that came apart and he was into another period of depression. In quick succession he went through Vietnam and sheltering draft dodgers, student revolt, and an infatuation with Mao. Every one of these involved extensive reading, not just for Arthur but for me. I made a real effort, but somehow I was always out of date, perhaps because I found it so hard to read theories. By the time I'd adjusted my views to Arthur's, his had already changed. Then I would have to be converted anew, improved, made to see the light once more. 'Here,' he would say, 'read this book,' and I'd know the cycle had begun again.

The trouble with Arthur was that he meant well, he meant too well, he wanted everyone to mean as well as he did. When he would find out they didn't, that not all of them burned with his own pure flame but some had pride, others were self-interested and power-hungry, he would become angry. He was a prisoner of conscience.

Once I'd thought of Arthur as single-minded, single-hearted, single-bodied; I, by contrast, was a sorry assemblage of lies and alibis, each complete in itself but rendering the others worthless. But I soon discovered there were as many of Arthur as there were of me. The difference was that I was simultaneous, whereas Arthur was a sequence. At the height of his involvment with any of these causes, Arthur would have the electricity of six, he'd scarcely sleep at all, he'd rush about stapling things and making speeches and carrying signs. But at the low points he'd barely be able to make it out of bed, he'd sit in a chair all day, chain-smoking and looking out the window, watching television, or doing crosswords or jigsaw puzzles of Jackson Pollock paintings and Oriental rugs. It was only on the way up or the way down that I existed for him as any kind of distinct shape; otherwise I was just a kind of nourishing blob. We made love only during the middle periods. When he was way up he had no time, when he was way down he had no energy.

I admired and evied his purity of conscience, despite its drawbacks: when Arthur was going down, overcome by disillusionment and clouds of doom, he'd write letters to all the people he'd worked with during the up period, denouncing them as traitors and scoundrels, and I was the one who would get the phone calls from them, outraged, puzzled or hurt. 'Well, you know how Arthur is,' I'd say to them. 'He hasn't been feeling very well, he's been discouraged.'

I wished he would do his own explaining, but he specialized in ambushes. He never had fights with people, he never talked things out with them. He would simply decide, by some dark, complicated process of evaluation, that these people were unworthy. Not that they'd done something unworthy, but that unworthiness was innate in them. Once he'd made his judgment, that was it. No trial, no redress. I once told him that I thought he was behaving a little like Calvin's God, but he was offended and I didn't press it. Secretly I was afraid of this same kind of judgment being applied to me.

I often hoped Arthur would find some group that would be able to sustain the overwhelming burden of his trust. It wasn't just that I wanted Arthur to be happy, though I did. I had two other reasons. One was that his depressions made me miserable, because they made me feel inadequate. The love of a good woman was supposed to preserve a man from this kind of thing, I knew that. But at these times I wasn't able to make him happy, no matter how badly I cooked. Therefore I was not a good woman.

The other was that I couldn't write Costume Gothics when Arthur was depressed. He hung around the house much of the time, and when he wasn't doing anything he didn't want me to do anything either. If I went into the bedroom and closed the door, he would open it, stand in the doorway looking at me reproachfully, and say he had a headache. Or he would want me to help him with his crossword puzzle. It was very hard to concentrate on my heroine's tumultuous breasts, my hero's thin rapacious mouth, with this kind of thing going on. I would have to pretend I was going out to look for a job, and from time to time I would really get one, in self-defense.

It was only after I got married that my writing became for me anything more than an easy way of earning a living. I'd always felt sly about it, as if I was getting away with something and nobody had found me out; but now it became important. The really important thing was not the books themselves, which continued to be much the same. It was the fact that I was two people at once, with two sets of identification papers, two bank accounts, two different groups of people who believed I existed. I was Joan Foster, there was no doubt about that; people called me by that name and I had authentic documents to prove it. But I was also Louisa K. Delacourt.

As long as I could spend a certain amount of time each week as Louisa, I was all right, I was patient and forbearing, warm, a sympathetic listener. But if I was cut off, if I couldn't work at my current Costume Gothic, I would become mean and irritable, drink too much and start to cry.

Thus we went on from year to year, with Arthur's frenzied cycles alternating with my own, and it was fine really, I loved him. Every once in a while I'd suggest that perhaps it was time for us to settle down somewhere, a little more permanently, and have children. But Arthur wasn't ready, he would say, he had work to do, and I had to admit that I myself had mixed feelings. I wanted children, but what if I had a child who would turn out like me? Even worse, what if I turned out to be like my mother?

All this time I carried my mother around my neck like a rotting albatross. I dreamed about her often, my three-headed mother, menacing and cold. Sometimes she would be sitting in front of her vanity table, sometimes she would be crying. She never laughed or smiled.

In the worst dream I couldn't see her at all. I would be hiding behind a door, or standing in front of one, it wasn't clear which. It was a white door, like a bathroom door or perhaps a cupboard. I'd been locked in, or out, but on the other side of the door I could hear voices. Sometimes there were a lot of voices, sometimes only two; they were talking about me, discussing me, and as I listened I would realize that something very bad was going to happen. I felt helpless, there was nothing I could do. In the dream I would back into the farthest corner of the cubicle and wedge myself in, press my arms against the walls, dig my heels against the floor. They wouldn't be able to get me out. Then I would hear the footsteps, coming up the stairs and along the hall.

Arthur would shake me awake. 'What's the matter?' I would say.

'You were grunting.'

Grunting? Humiliation. Screaming would be one thing, but grunting ... 'I was having a nightmare,' I'd say. But Arthur couldn't understand why I would have nightmares. Surely nothing that terrible had ever happened to me, I was a normal girl with all kinds of advantages, I was beautiful and intelligent, why didn't I make something of myself? I should try to be more of a leader, he would tell me.

What he failed to understand was that there were really only two kinds of people: fat ones and thin ones. When I looked at myself in the mirror, I didn't see what Arthur saw. The outline of my former body still surrounded me, like a mist, like a phantom moon, like the image of Dumbo the Flying Elephant superimposed on my own. I wanted to forget the past, but it refused to forget me; it waited for sleep, then cornered me.

Chapter Twenty-one

When I stopped to think about it, I felt our marriage was happier than most. I even became a little smug about it. In my opinion, most women made one basic mistake: they expected their husbands to understand them. They spent much precious time explaining themselves, serving up their emotions and reactions, their love and anger and sensitivities, their demands and inadequacies, as if the mere relating of these things would get results. Arthur's friends tended to be married to women like this, and these women, I knew, thought of me as placid, sloppy and rather stupid. They themselves made it from crisis to crisis, with running commentaries, on a combination of nerve ends, cigarettes, bludgeoning honesty and what used to be called nagging. Because I didn't do this, Arthur's friends envied him a bit and confided to me in the kitchen. They were beleaguered and exhausted; their wives had a touch of the shrill self-righteousness familiar to me from my mother.

But I didn't want Arthur to understand me: I went to great lengths to prevent this. Though I was tempted sometimes, I resisted the impulse to confess. Arthur's tastes were Spartan, and my early life and innermost self would have appalled him. It would be like asking for a steak and getting a slaughtered cow. I think he suspected this; he certainly headed off my few tentative attempts at self-revelation.

The other wives, too, wanted their husbands to live up to their own fantasy lives, which except for the costumes weren't that different from my own. They didn't put it in quite these terms, but I could tell from their expectations. They wanted their men to be strong, lustful, passionate and exciting, with hard rapacious mouths, but also tender and worshipful. They wanted men in mysterious cloaks who would rescue them from balconies, but they also wanted meaningful in-depth relationships and total openness. (The Scarlet Pimpernell, I would tell them silently, does not have time for meaningful in-depth relationships.) They wanted multiple orgasms, they wanted the earth to move, but they also wanted help with the dishes.

I felt my own arrangement was more satisfactory. There were two kinds of love, I told myself; Arthur was terrific for one kind, but why demand all things of one man? I'd given up expecting him to be a cloaked, sinuous and faintly menacing stranger. He couldn't be that: I lived with him, and cloaked strangers didn't leave their socks on the floor or stick their fingers in their ears or gargle in the mornings to kill germs. I kept Arthur in our apartment and the strangers in their castles and mansions, where they belonged. I felt this was quite adult of me, and it certainly allowed me to be more outwardly serene than the wives of Arthur's friends. But I had the edge on them: after all, when it came to fantasy lives I was a professional, whereas they were merely amateurs.

And yet, as time went by, I began to feel something was missing. Perhaps, I thought, I had no soul; I just drifted around, singing vaguely, like the Little Mermaid in the Andersen fairy tale. In order to get a soul you had to suffer, you had to give something up; or was that to get legs and feet? I couldn't remember. She'd become a dancer, though, with no tongue. Then there was Moira Shearer, in *The Red Shoes*. Neither of them had been able to please the handsome prince; both of them had died. I was doing fairly well by comparison. Their mistake had been to go public, whereas I did my dancing behind closed doors. It was safer, but. . . .

It was true I had two lives, but on off days I felt that neither of them was completely real. With Arthur I was merely playing house, I wasn't really working at it. And my Costume Gothics were only paper; paper castles, paper costumes, paper dolls, as inert and lifeless finally as those unsatisfactory blank-eyed dolls I'd dressed and undressed in my mother's house. I got a reputation for being absentminded, which Arthur's friends found endearing. Soon it was expected of me, and I added it to my repertoire of deficiencies.

'You apologize too much,' one of the strident wives told me, and I began to wonder about that. It was true, I did apologize. But why did I feel I had to be excused? Why did I want to be exempted, and what from? In high school you didn't have to play baseball if you had your period or a pain in your stomach, and I preferred the sidelines. Now I wanted to be acknowledged, but I feared it. If I brought the separate parts of my life together (like uranium, like plutonium, harmless to the naked eye, but charged with lethal energies) surely there would be an explosion. Instead I floated, marking time.

It was September. Arthur was in one of his slumps, having just written a batch of letters denouncing everyone connected with the Curriculum Reform movement, which had been his latest cause. I'd just started a new book; *Love, My Ransom* was the working title. With Arthur hanging around the apartment it was hard to close my eyes and drift off into the world of shadows; also, the old sequence of chase and flight, from rape or murder, no longer held my attention as it once had. I needed something new, some new twist: there was now more competition, Costume Gothics were no longer regarded as mere trash but as money-making trash, and I felt I was in danger of being crowded out. From scanning the works of my rivals, as I did every week, anxiously, in the corner drugstore, I could see that the occult was the latest thing. It was no longer enough to have a hero with a cloak; he had to have magical powers as well. I went to the Central Reference Library and read up on the seventeenth century. What I needed was a ritual, a ceremony, something sinister but decorative. . . .

When Penelope awoke, she found she was blindfolded; she could move neither hand nor foot. They had tied her to a chair. The two of them were whispering together at the opposite end of the room; she strained to catch their words, knowing that her life and that of Sir Percy might depend upon it.

'We can use her to gain access to the knowledge, I tell you,' Estelle was saying. She was a tempestuous beauty with gypsy blood.

'It would be better to put her out of the way,' muttered François. 'She has seen too much.'

'Yes, yes,' said Estelle, 'but first we can use her. It is not often that one with such great but undeveloped powers comes into my hands.'

'Have your way,' François said, between his teeth, 'so long as you will then allow me to have mine.' His flashing eyes swept over Penelope's trembling and helpless young body. 'Hush ... she is awake.'

Estelle approached, moving with savage, untamed grace. Her small white teeth flashed in the semi-darkness, and she threw back her long, dishevelled red hair. 'So, my child,' she said with false friendliness. 'You are awake. Now you will perform a small service for us, hein?'

'I will do nothing for you,' Penelope said. 'I know you for what you are.'

Estelle laughed. 'Such courage, little one,' she said. 'But you will not be able to help yourself. Drink this.' She forced some liquid from an exotic flask between Penelope's teeth. Then she removed Penelope's blindfold and placed a small table with a mirror on it before her, lit a candle, and set the candle in front of the mirror.

Penelope felt an aura of evil gather in the room; it grew thick around her. Despite herself, she felt her gaze being drawn to the flame; her mind fluttered, fascinated, helpless as a moth, her own reflction disappeared ... further into the mirror she went, and further, till she seemed to be walking on the other side of the glass, in a land of indistinct shadows. Ahead of her, voices murmured in the mist.

'Do not be frightened,' Estelle's voice said from a great distance. 'Tell us what you see. Tell us what you hear.'

I'd been typing with my eyes closed, as usual, but at this point I opened them. I'd come up against a blank wall: I hadn't the least idea what Penelope would see or hear next. I thought about it for half an hour, with no result. I'd have to act it through. This was a long-standing habit of mine: when I came to a dead end, I tried to simulate the scene as much as possible and block out the action, like a stage director.

It was risky, since Arthur was watching television in the next room. Also, I didn't think we had any candles. I went out to the kitchen, rummaged through the drawers, and came up with a short, dust-covered stub which had once gone with the chafing dish I'd bought in a moment of delusion and thrown out in a moment of rage. I stuck it to a saucer, found the matches, and went back into the bedroom, closing the door. Arthur thought I was writing an essay on the sociology of pottery for the university extension course I claimed to be taking.

I lit the candle end and set it in front of my dressing-table mirror. (I'd recently bought a three-sided one, like my mother's.) It was only when I was sitting in front of the mirror that I remembered my previous experiment with Automatic Writing, back in high school. That time I'd set fire to my bangs. I pinned my hair back from my face, just in case. I wasn't expecting to get any messages, only to set the scene for my book, but I felt I should have a pen or a pencil handy.

Penelope, of course, was a natural medium. She was easily hypnotized. She had also just had some liquid from an exotic flask, which would help. I went out to the kitchen again, poured myself a Scotch and water, and drank it. Then I sat myself in front of the mirror and tried to concentrate. Maybe Penelope should get a message from Sir Percy, telling her that he was in danger. Maybe she should transmit one. . . . Was she a sender or a receiver? Bell Telephone would go out of business if this method could be perfected. . . .

My attention was wandering. *You are Penelope*, I told myself sternly.

I stared at the candle in the mirror, the mirror candle. There was more than one candle, there were three, and I knew that if I moved the two sides of the mirror toward me there would be an infinite number of candles, extending in a line as far as I could see. . . . The room seemed very dark, darker than it had before; the candle was very bright, I was holding it in my hand and walking along a corridor, I was descending, I turned a corner. I was going to find someone. I needed to find someone.

There was movement at the edge of the mirror. I gasped and turned around. Surely there had been a figure, standing behind me. But there was no one. I was wide awake now, I could hear a faint roar from the television in the next room, and the voice of the announcer, 'He shoots, he scores! A blistering drive from the point. There may have been a rebound. . . . Here comes the replay. . . .'

I looked down at the piece of paper. There, in a scrawly handwriting that was certainly not my own, was a single word:

Bow

I blew out the candle and turned on the overhead light. *Bow.* What the hell was that supposed to mean? I got out the paperback Roget's Thesaurus I kept for synonyms of words I used often, such as 'tremble' – v. *flutter, throb* (SHAKE); *quiver, shiver, shudder* (FEAR) – and looked it up.

bow–n. curtsey, obseisance, salaam (RESPECT, GESTURE); prow, stem, nose (FRONT); longbow, crossbow (ARMS); curve, bend, arch (CURVE, BEND).

bow–v. nod, salaam, curtsey (RESPECT, GESTURE); arch, round, incline (CURVE, BEND); cringe, stoop, kneel (SLAVERY); submit, yield, defer (SUBMISSION).

What a dumb word, I thought; there was no way that was going to help out with Penelope and Estelle. But then I felt the impact of what had happened. I had actually written a word, without being conscious of doing it. Not only that, I'd seen someone in the mirror, or rather in the room, standing behind me. I was sure of it. Everything Leda Sprott had told me came back to me; it was real, I was convinced it was real and someone had a message for me. I wanted to go down that dark, shining corridor again, I wanted to see what was at the other end. . . .

On the other hand, I didn't want to. It was too frightening. It was also too ridiculous: what was I doing playing around with candles and mirrors, like one of Leda Sportt's octogenarian Spiritualists? I needed a message for Penelope, true, but I didn't have to run the risk of setting myself on fire to get one.

I went out to the kitchen and pured myself another drink.

That was how it began. The mirror won, curiosity prevailed. I set Penelope aside, I left her sitting in her chair: I would attend to her later. The word hadn't been for her, it had been for me, and I wanted to find out what it meant. The next morning I went to the nearest Loblaws and bought six pairs of dinner candles, and that evening, when Arthur was watching a football game, I went again into the mirror.

The experience was much the same as before, and it remained the same for the three months or so during which I continued with this experiment. There was the sense of going along a narrow passage that led downward, the certainty that if I could only turn the next corner or the next – for these journeys became longer – I would find the thing, the truth or word or person that was mine, that was waiting for me. Only one thing changed: the feeling that someone was standing behind me was not repeated. When I would emerge from the trance, as I suppose it could be called, there would usually be a word, sometimes several words, occasionally even a sentence, on the notepad in front of me, though twice there was nothing but a scribble. I would stare at these words, trying to make sense of them; I would look them up in Roget's Thesaurus, and most of the time, other words would fill in around them:

Who is the one standing in the prow
Who is the one voyaging
under the sky's arch, under the earth's arch
under the arch of arrows
in the death boat, why does she sing

She kneels, she is bent down
under the power
her tears are dark
her tears are jagged
her tears are the death you fear
Under the water, under the water sky
her tears fall, they are dark flowers

I wasn't at all sure what this meant, nor could I ever get to the end of the corridor.

However, the words I collected in this way became increasingly bizarre and even threatening: 'iron,' 'throat,' 'knife,' 'heart.' At first the sentences centered around the same figure, the same woman. After a while I could almost see her: she lived under the earth somewhere, or inside something, a cave or a huge building; sometimes she was on a boat. She was enormously powerful, almost like a goddess, but it was an unhappy power. This woman puzzled me. She wasn't like anyone I'd ever imagined, and certainly she had nothing to do with me. I wasn't at all like that, I was happy. Happy and inept.

Then another person, a man, began to turn up. Something was happening between the two of them; cryptic love letters formed on the pages, obscure, frightening. This man was evil, I felt, but it was hard to tell. Sometimes he seemed good. He had many disguises. Occasionally there would be passages that looked as if they came from somewhere else, and some rather boring prosy sermons about the meaning of life.

I kept all the words, and the longer sections I worked out from them, in a file folder marked *Recipes*. I'd sometimes hidden notes for Costume Gothics in the same file, though I stored the manuscripts themselves in my underwear drawer.

Between these sessions, in the daytime, when I was doing the dishes or coasting along the aisles of the supermarket, I would have moments of sudden doubt about this activity. What was I doing, why was I doing it? If I was going to hypnotize myself like this, shouldn't it be for some good end, like giving up drinking? Was I going (perhaps) just a little crazy? What would Arthur think if he found out?

I don't know what would have happened if I'd kept on, but I was forced to stop. I went into the mirror one evening and I couldn't get out again. I was going along the corridor, with the candle in my hand as usual, and the candle went out. I think the candle really did go out and that was why I was stuck there, in the midst of darkness, unable to move. I'd lost all sense of direction; I was afraid to turn around even, in case I ended up going farther in. I felt as though I was suffocating.

I don't know how long it was; it felt like centuries, but then Arthur was shaking me. He sounded angry.

'Joan, what're you doing?' he said. 'What's the matter with you?'

I was back in our bedroom. I was so thankful I threw my arms around Arthur and started to cry. 'I've had the most terrible experience,' I said to him.

'What?' he said. 'I found you in here with the lights out, staring into the mirror. What happened?'

I couldn't tell him. 'I saw someone outside the window,' I said. 'A man. He was looking in.'

Arthur rushed over to the window to look, and I quickly checked the piece of paper. There was nothing on it at all; not a mark, not a scratch. I vowed I would stop this stupidity right then and there. Leda Sprott had said you needed training, and now I was ready to believe it. The next day I threw out my remaining candles and went back to Penelope and Sir Percy Somerville. I wanted to forget all about this little adventure into the extranatural. I wasn't cut out for the occult, I told myself. I scrapped Penelope's mirror scene: she would have to make do with rape and murder like everyone else.

But I was left with the collection of papers. Several weeks later, I got them out and looked through them. They seemed to me to be as good as a few similar books I'd seen in bookstores. I thought maybe one of the small experimental publishing houses might be interested in them, so I typed them up and sent them off to Black Widow Press. I got back what I thought was a rather rude letter, almost by the next post:

Dear Ms. Foster:
Quite frankly, these reminded us of a cross between Kahlil Gibran and Rod McKuen. Though some of the pieces are not without literary merit, unfortunately the whole collection is uneven in tone and unresolved. Perhaps you should begin with submissions to the literary magazines. Or you might try Morton and Sturgess; it might be their kind of thing.

This depressed me for a while. Maybe they were right, maybe it wasn't any good. I didn't suppose it would help if I said the manucript had been dictated by powers beyond my control. Why did I want to publish it anyway? Who did I think I was? 'Who do you think you are?' my mother used to ask me, but she would never wait for an answer.

But I had as much right to try as the next person. I screwed up my nerve and bundled the pages off to Morton and Sturgess. I wasn't at all prepared for what happened.

The decisive meeting took place in the bar at the Inn on the Park. I'd never been in this place before: it wasn't the sort of place Arthur would ever go. It was too expensive, for one thing, and it was obviously for capitalists. Despite myself, I was impressed.

There were three of them at the meeting: John Morton, the original owner of the company, who was distinguished-looking; Doug Sturgess, his partner and the one in charge of promotion, who struck me as an American; and a haggard-eyed young man, introduced to me as an editor, Colin Harper. 'A poet himself,' said Sturgess heartily.

They all ordered martinis. I wanted a double Scotch, but I didn't want to be thought unladylike, not right away. They would find out soon enough, I felt. So I ordered a Grasshopper.

'Well,' said John Morton, looking at me benevolently, with the tips of his fingers pressed together.

'Yes, indeed,' said Sturgess. 'Well, Colin, you might as well begin.'

'We thought it was – ah – reminiscent – of a mixture of Kahlil Gibran and Rod McKuen,' said Colin Harper unhappily.

'Oh,' I said. 'It's that bad, is it?'

'*Bad*?' said Sturgess. 'Is she saying bad? You know how many copies those guys *sell*? It's like having the *Bible*, man.' He was wearing a suit with a safari jacket top.

'You mean you want to do it?' I said.

'It's dymamite,' said Sturgess. 'And isn't she a great little lady? We'll have a great cover. Four-color, the works. Do you play the guitar?'

'No,' I said, surprised. 'Why?'

'I thought we might do you as a sort of female Leonard Cohen,' said Sturgess.

The other two were slightly embarrassed by this. 'Of course, it will need a little editing,' said Morton.

'Yes,' said Colin. 'We might take out the more, well. . . . '

'A bit of it could come out, here and there,' said Sturgess. 'I mean, there's some of it I don't understand too much: for instance, who's the man with the daffodils and the icicle teeth?'

'I sort of like that,' Colin said. 'It's, you know, Jungian. . . . '

'But the part about the Road of Life, well. . . . '

'I like that,' Sturgess said. 'That's clear, that's something you can get your teeth into.'

'Well, gentlemen, those are details,' said Morton. 'We can clear all that up later. It's evident that this is a book that has something for everyone. My dear,' he said, turning to me, 'we would be most happy to publish your book. Now, do you have a title for it?'

'Not yet,' I said. 'I haven't thought much about it. I guess I didn't really think it would ever get published. I don't know much about these things.'

'What about this bit, right here,' Sturgess said, thumbing through the manuscrapt. 'This sort of caught my eye. Section Five:

She sits on the iron throne
She is one and three
The dark lady the redgold lady
the blank lady oracle
of blood, she who must be
obeyed forever
Her glass wings are gone

She floats down the river
singing her last song

and so forth.'

'Yes,' said Morton, 'that's resonant. That reminds me of something.'

'What I mean is, here's your title,' said Sturgess. '*Lady Oracle*. That's it, I have a nose for them. The women's movement, the occult, all of that.'

'I don't want to publish this book if it isn't really any good,' I said. I was on my third Grasshopper, and I was beginning to feel undignified. I was also beginning to wonder about Arthur. What was he going to think about it, this unhappy but torrid and, I was feeling now, slightly preposterous love affair between a woman in a boat and a man in a cloak, with icicle teeth and eyes of fire?

'Good,' said Sturgess. 'Don't you worry your pretty little head about good. We'll worry about good, that's our business, right? I know just the way to handle this. I mean, there's lots of good, but this is *terrific*.'

Chapter Twenty-two

'Arthur,' I said, 'I'm having a book published.' I said this while Arthur was watching the eleven PM *National News* on the CBC, hoping he wouldn't quite hear me. But he did.

'What?' he said. 'A book? You?'

'Yes,' I said.

Arthur looked dismayed. He turned down the volume on the news. 'What's it about?' he said.

'Well, it's sort of, you could say it's about the male-female roles in our society.' I was uneasy about this; I was thinking of Section Fourteen, which had the embrace between the Iron Maiden, smooth on the outside but filled with spikes, and the man in the inflated rubber suit. But I was trying to think of something he'd find respectable, and this seemed to be all right, as he stopped frowning.

'That's good,' he said. 'I've always told you that you had the ability. I could look it over for you, if you like. Fix it up for you.'

'Thank you, Arthur,' I said, 'but it's already been edited.' This was true: poor Colin Harper had been over the manuscript several times, scratching things out and writing *delete* in the margins. He had tried to be tactful, but the book obviously embarrassed him. He'd used the word 'melodramatic' twice, and once he'd said 'Gothic sensibility,' which gave me a fright – *he knew*. But it was only a coincidence. 'It's already at the printer's,' I told Arthur. 'They want me to be on television,' I added, I suppose to impress him.

Arthur was displeased again, as I knew he would be. 'Why didn't you tell me sooner?'

'You've been so busy,' I murmured. 'I didn't want to bother you.' This was true enough, as Arthur had met a whole new group of people and was into a fresh upward spiral of activity.

'Well, that's wonderful,' he said. 'I'll have to read it. We should go out to celebrate; there're some people I've been wanting you to meet anyway.'

Arthur's idea of going out to celebrate was the Young Lok Gardens on Spadina. 'It's the way Sai Woo's used to be,' said Arthur, 'before it got famous.' What he meant was that it was cheap. We'd eaten there once before, and the food was good; but for me a celebration should have drinks at least, and candles if possible. Young Lok Gardens didn't have a liquor license.

But Arthur was feeling touchy, so I didn't suggest anything else. We walked over to Spadina and took a bus. Arthur still refused to let us have a car; wasteful, he said. I knew he was morally right; he was always morally right. This was admirable, but it was beginning to be a strain.

The people we were going to meet, Arthur told me, were Don and Marlene Pugh. Arthur and Don taught in the same university department and shared the same views. Arthur respected Don's mind, he told me. He was very good at respecting people's minds, initially. But he would always manage to find some flaw, some little corner of dry rot. 'Nobody's perfect,' I would tell him. Not even you, I increasingly wanted to add.

We walked into the Young Lok Gardens, which was crowded, as usual. A couple sitting against the far wall waved at us, and we squeezed ourselves through the tables to reach them.

'Joan, this is Don Pugh and his wife Marlene,' Arthur said, and I suddenly felt sick to my stomach. I knew Marlene. I'd gone to Brownies with her.

She hadn't changed that much, she was still a lot thinner than I was. She was wearing a faded-denim jacket and jeans, with a flower embroidered on the jacket pocket; she had sparse blond hair, worn raggedly about her shoulders, and round silver-rimmed glasses. She was slim and muscular, with chunky silver rings on all four fingers of her left hand, like knuckle dusters. I could tell she'd flown up to Guides, covered her sleeves with badges, gone on to take modern dancing, Gestalt therapy, karate, carpentry. She smiled up at me, cool and competent. I, of course, was wearing fringes: a shawl, a dangly necklace with which I could easily be strangled, a scarf. My hair needed washing, my fingernails were dirty, my shoelaces felt untied, although I wasn't wearing any.

Wads of fat sprouted on my thighs and shoulders, my belly bulged out like a Hubbard squash, a brown wool beret popped through my scalp, bloomers coated my panic-stricken loins. Tears swelled behind my eyes. Like a virus meeting an exhausted throat, my dormant past burst into rank life.

'Great to meet you,' Marlene said.

'Excuse me,' I said. 'I have to go to the bathroom.'

I headed for the ladies', followed by their astonished eyes. Once there, I locked myself into a cubicle, where I sat, helpless with self-pity, snorting and blowing my nose. Some celebration. Marlene my tormentor, who'd roped me to a bridge and left me there, a living sacrifice, for the monster of the ravines; Marlene the ingenious inquisitor. I was trapped again in the nightmare of my childhood, where I ran eternally after the others, the oblivious or scornful ones, hands outstretched, begging for a word of praise. She hadn't recognized me, but when she did I knew what would happen: she would have a smile of indulgence for her former self, and I would be overcome with shame. Yet I hadn't done anything shameful; she was the one who'd done it. Why then should I be the one to feel guilt, why sould she go free? Hers was the freedom of the strong; my guilt was the guilt of those who lose, those who can be exposed, those who fail. I hated her.

I couldn't stay in there all night. I wiped my face with a damp paper towel and repaired my makeup. I would just have to tough it out.

When I came back to the table, they were eating a whole sweet-and-sour fish, complete with bulging, baked eyes. They hardly noticed my return: they were deep into a discussion of United States cultural imperialism. Another man had joined them, sad-eyed, sandy-haired and balding. I gathered that his name was Sam, though no one bothered to introduce me.

I sat and listened as they batted their ideas back and forth like ping-pong balls, scoring their various points. They were deciding the future of the country. Should it be nationalism with a socialist flavor, or socialism with a nationalist flavor? Don, it appeared, had all the statistics; Arthur had the fervor. Sam seemed to be the theoretician; it came out that he'd trained as a rabbinical student. Marlene pronounced the judgements. Self-righteousness was hers, I thought. She was even more self-righteous that Arthur. She had all the aces, she'd once worked in a factory, which impressed hell out of the others. No one said anything to me; Arthur might have mentioned my book, I felt, but maybe he was protecting himself. He didn't want to say anything about it before he'd read it; he didn't trust me. The only one at the table I had any hope of communicating with was the baked fish, now reduced to a spine and a head.

'Let's get some fortune cookies,' I said with forced cheerfulness. 'I love them, don't you?' Arthur ordered some, with the air of indulging a spoiled child. Marlene gave me a look of contempt.

I decided to tackle her head-on. I might as well know the worst, right now. 'I think we went to the same Brownies,' I said.

Marlene laughed. 'Oh, Brownies,' she said, 'Everyone went to Brownies.'

'I was a Gnome,' I said.

'I really can't remember what I was,' she said. 'I can't remember much about it at all. We used to hide in the cloakroom afterwards though, and phone people up on the church phone. When they answered we would say, "Is your refrigerator running?" and when they'd say yes, we'd say, "Then you better catch it." That's about all I remember.'

I could recall this game very well, since they would never let me play. I was astonished at how much I still resented this. But I resented even more the fact that she hadn't recognized me. It seemed very unjust that an experience so humiliating to me hadn't touched her at all.

The fortune cookies came. Don and Arthur ignored theirs, but the rest of us opened them. I got *A new love awaits you.* Sam got one that promised riches, and Marlene's said, *It is often best to be oneself.*

'I obviously got the wrong one,' Sam said.

'I don't know,' Marlene said. 'You've always been a closet capitalist.' They seemed to know each other better than I'd thought.

'I got the wrong one too,' I said. Marlene's, I felt, was meant for me. *It is often best to be oneself,* whispered the small, crumby voice, like a conscience. But which one, which one? And if I was ever to begin, think how appalled they would be.

'What was wrong with you?' Arthur said when we were back at the apartment.

'I don't know,' I said. 'To be perfectly honest, I didn't go for Marlene all that much.'

'Well, she liked you, a lot,' Arthur said. 'She told me when you were in the can.'

'The first time?' I said.

'No,' he said, 'I think it was the third.'

Thank God for toilet cubicles, I thought, the only places left for solitary meditation and prayer. What had I been praying for? I'd prayed, with all my heart, that Marlene would fall down a hole.

During the following week, Marlene and Don, with Sam in their wake, practically moved in with us. Marlene became Arthur's Platonic ideal. Not only did she have a mind he could respect, she was also a tip-top cook, mostly vegetarian. Don and Marlene had two young children, and despite the fact that it was Arthur who'd festooned our bedroom with every known form of birth-control device, urged me to take the Pill, grouched when it made me throw up, and turned guacamole-green every time my period was late, I was now silently reproached for not having any.

Marlene was the managing editor of *Resurgence*, a small Canadian-nationalist left-wing magazine, of which Don was the editor and Sam the assistant editor. Arthur quickly became a contributing editor, and wrote a carefully researched article on branch plants, which Marlene read, chain-smoking (her only vice), nodding thoughtfully, and sayng things like, 'Good point you've got there,' while Artur beamed. The Muse, I thought angrily; she never bothered to help me make the coffee, I did it all. It was the least I could do, as Arthur said, and I was determined to do the least.

I was jealous of Marlene, but not in the ordinary way. It didn't occur to me that Arthur would ever think of laying a hand on her skinny little rump, any more than a devout Catholic would palpate the Madonna. And it was soon obvious to me that Marlene was having an affair with Sam, although Don didn't know. I decided not to tell anyone, not yet. I was immediately more good-natured; I bought cookies, which I served with the coffee, and began to sit in on the editorial sessions. I was especially friendly to Sam; I could see that he was under a lot of pressure. Although one side of him was as dedicated and earnest as Arthur, he had a less intimidating side which he revealed only in the kitchen while he helped with the coffee. I liked the fact that he helped with the coffee, and that he was much clumsier than I was.

Meanwhile, the galley proofs of *Lady Oracle* had come from the publisher. I corrected them, with growing apprehension. On rereading, the book seemed quite peculiar. In fact, except for the diction, it seemed a lot like one of my standard Costume Gothics, but a Gothic gone wrong. It was upside-down somehow. There were the sufferings, the hero in the mask of a villain, the villain in the mask of a hero, the flights, the looming death, the sense of being imprisoned, but there was no happy ending, no true love. The recognition of this half-likeness made me uncomfortable. Perhaps I should have taken it to a psychiatrist instead of a publisher; but then, I remembered the psychiatrist my mother had sent me to. He hadn't been much help, and no one would understand about the Automatic Writing. Perhaps I shouldn't have used my own name, Arthur's name rather; then I wouldn't have had to show him the book. More and more I dreaded this. He hadn't mentioned the book since I'd first told him about it, and neither had I. Though I resented his lack of interest, I welcomed the chance to postpone the day of judgment. Arthur wouldn't like the book, I was certain of it, and neither would anyone else.

I called up Mr Sturgess, of Morton and Sturgess. 'I've changed my mind,' I said. 'I don't want the book published.'

'What?' said Sturgess. 'Why not?'

'I can't explain,' I said. 'It's personal.'

'Look,' Sturgess said, 'you've signed a contract, remember?'

But not in blood, I thought. 'Couldn't we just sort of call the whole thing off?'

'We're in production,' Sturgess said. 'Why don't you meet me for a drink and we'll discuss it.'

He patted me on the back, figuratively, and told me it would be all right. I allowed myself to believe him. After that he began making special phone calls, to keep my morale bolstered.

'We're revving up the engines,' he would say one day. Then, 'We've got you on a couple of key spots.' Or, 'We're sending you on tour, trans-Canada.' This last made me think of the Queen, standing on the back platform of a train, waving. Would I have to do that? It also made me think of Mr Peanut, who would come to the Loblaws parking lot on special Saturdays. He had ordinary legs and arms, with spats and white gloves, but his body was a huge peanut; he would dance in a blind, shambling way while girl attendants sold coloring books and packages of peanuts. As a child I'd loved him, but suddenly I saw what it was like to be the peanut: clumsy, visible and suffocating. Maybe I shouldn't have signed the contract, so carelessly, so recklessly, after my fifth Grasshopper. As the publication date approached, I would wake every morning with a sense of unspecified foreboding, before I remembered.

I was reassured by the advance copies of the book, though. It looked like a real book, and there was my picture on the back, like a real author's. Louisa K. Delacourt never got her picture on the back. I was a little alarmed by the jacket blurb: 'Modern love and the sexual battle, dissected with a cutting edge and shocking honesty.' I didn't think the book was about that, exactly; but Sturgess assured me he knew what he was doing. 'You write it, you leave it to us to sell it,' he said. He also told me jubilantly that he'd 'placed' the most important review.

'What does that mean?' I said.

'We made sure the book went to someone who'd like it.'

'But isn't that cheating?' I asked, and Sturgess laughed. 'You're incredible,' he said. 'Just stay that way.'

UNKNOWN BURSTS ON LITERARY SCENE LIKE COMET, said the first review, in the *Toronto Star*. I cut it out with the kitchen scissors and pasted it into the new scrapbook I'd bought from Kresge's. I was beginning to feel better. The *Globe* review called it 'gnomic' and 'chthonic,' right in the same paragraph. I looked these words up in the dictionary. Maybe it wasn't too bad, after all.

(But I didn't stop to reflect on the nature of comets. Lumps of cosmic debris with long red hair and spectacular tails, discovered by astronomers, who named them after themselves. Harbingers of disaster. Portents of war.)

Chapter Twenty-three

I gave Arthur a copy of *Lady Oracle*, inscribed in the front, *For Arthur, With All My Love*, XXXX, *Joan*. But he didn't say one word about it, and I was afraid to ask him what he thought. His manner became distant, and he began to spend a lot of time at the university, or so he said. I would catch him giving me hurt looks when he thought I wasn't watching. I couldn't figure it out. I'd been expecting him to tell me the book was bourgeois or tasteless or obscure or a piece of mystification, but instead he was acting as though I'd committed some unpardonablé but unmentionable sin.

I complained to Sam, who was in the habit now of dropping over for a beer or two in the afternoons. He knew I knew about Marlene, so he could complain to me.

'I'm in deep shit,' he said. 'Marlene's got me by the balls, and she's twisting. She wants to tell Don. She thinks we should be open and honest. That's okay in theory, but . . . she wants to move in with me, kids and all. It'd drive me crazy. Also,' he said, with a return to sanctimoniousness, 'think what it would do to *Resurgence*, it'd fall apart.'

'That's too bad,' I said. 'I have a problem.'

'*You* have a problem?' Sam said. 'But you never have problems.'

'This time I do,' I said. 'It's about Arthur and my book. I mean, he hasn't even told me it's bad,' I said. 'It's not like him at all. He's acting as though it just doesn't exist, but at the same time he's hurt by it. Is it really that terrible?'

'I'm not a metaphor man, myself,' Sam said, 'but I thought it was a pretty good book. I thought there was a lot of truth in it. You got the whole marriage thing, right on. It isn't how Arthur would've struck me, but another guy can never see that side, right?'

'Oh my God,' I said. 'You think that book is about Arthur?'

'So does Arthur,' Sam said. 'That's why he's hurt. Isn't it?'

'No,' I said. 'Not at all.'

'Who's the other fellow then? Sam wanted to know. 'If he finds out it's someone else, he's going to be even more pissed off, you know.'

'Sam, it isn't about anyone. I don't have any secret lover, I really don't. It's all sort of, well, imaginary.'

'You're in deep shit,' Sam said. 'He's never going to believe that.'

This was what I feared. 'Maybe you could have a talk with him.'

'I'll try,' said Sam, 'but I don't think it'll work. What am I supposed to tell him?'

'I don't know,' I said. Sam must have said something though, because Arthur's attitude modified a little. He continued to look at me as though I'd betrayed him to the Nazis, but he was going to be a good sport and not mention it. The only thing he said was, 'When you write your next book, I'd appreciate it if you'd let me see it first.'

'I'm not going to write any more books,' I said. I was hard at work on *Love, My Ransom*, but he didn't have to know about that.

I had other things to worry about. Sturgess' battle plan was now in full swing, and my first television show was coming up. After that, Morton and Sturgess were throwing a party for me. I was very nervous. I put on a lot of Arrid Extra-Dry and a long red gown, and tried to remember what Aunt Lou's etiquette booklet had said about sweaty palms. Talcum powder, I thought. I sprinkled some on my hands and set off in a taxi for the television station. Just be yourself, Sturgess had told me.

The interviewer was a man, a young man, very intense. He joked with the technicians while they put the noose around my neck; a microphone, they said. I swallowed several times. I felt like Mr Peanut, big and cumbersome. The strong lights went on and the intense young man turned towards me.

'Welcome to *Afternoon Hot Spot*. Today we have with us Joan Foster, author, I guess that's author*ess*, of the runaway bestseller *Lady Oracle*. Tell me, Mrs Foster – or do you prefer to be called M*s* Foster?'

I was taking a drink of water, and I set it down so quickly I spilled it. We both pretended the water was not running across the table and into the interviewer's shoes. 'Whichever you like,' I said.

'Oh, then you're not in Women's Lib.'

'Well, no,' I said. 'I mean, I agree with some of their ideas, but . . .'

'Mrs Foster, would you say you are a happily married woman?'

'Oh *yes*,' I said. 'I've been married for years.'

'Well, that's strange. Because I've read your book, and to me it seemed very angry. It seemed like a very angry book. If I were your husband, I'm not sure I'd like it. What do you think about that?'

'It's not about my *marriage*,' I said earnestly. The young man smirked.

'Oh, it's not,' he said. 'Then perhaps you'll tell us what inspired you to write it.'

At this point I told the truth. I shouldn't have done it, but once I'd started I couldn't stop. 'Well, I was trying some experiments with Automatic Writing,' I said. 'You know, you sit in front of a mirror, with a paper and pencil and a lighted candle, and then . . . Well, these words would sort of be given to me. I mean, I'd find them written down, without having done it myself, if you know what I mean. So after that . . . well, that's how it happened.' I felt like a total idiot. I wanted another drink of water, but there wasn't any, I'd spilled it all.

The inverviewer was at a loss. He gave me a look that clearly said, You're putting me on. 'You mean these poems were dictated to you by a spirit hand,' he said jocularly.

'Yes,' I said. 'Something like that. You might try it yourself, when you get home.'

'Well,' said the interviewer. 'Thank you very much for being with us this afternoon. That was the lovely Joan Foster, or should I say Mrs Foster – oh, she'll get me for that one! – M*s* Joan Foster, authoress of *Lady Oracle*. And this is Barry Finkle, signing off for *Afternoon Hot Spot*.'

At the party, Sturgess took my elbow and steered me around the room as if I were a supermarket pushcart.

'I'm sorry about the interview,' I told him. 'I shouldn't have said that.'

'What do you mean?' he crowed. 'It was sensational! How'd you think it up? You sure put him in his place!'

'I didn't mean to,' I said. No use to tell him that what I'd said was true.

There were a lot of people at the party, and I was bad at remembering names. I made a mental note not to drink too much. I'd made a fool of myself once that day, I felt. I had to keep calm.

When Sturgess finally let go of my elbow, I backed up against the wall. I was hiding from a newspaper columnist who'd seen the television program and wanted to have a conversation about psychic phenomena. I felt like crying. What was the use of being Princess-for-a-day if you still felt like a toad? Acted like one, too. Arthur would be humiliated. What I'd said, coast to coast, was way off the party line. Not that he had a party. This was a party, some party. I finished my double Scotch and went for another.

When I was getting my drink at the bar, a man came up beside me.

'Are you Lady Oracle?' he said.

'It's the name of my book,' I said.

'Terrific title,' he said. 'Terrible book. It's a leftover from the nineteenth century. I think it's a combination of Rod McKuen and Kahlil Gibran.'

'That's what my publisher thought, too,' I said.

'I guess you're a publishing success,' he said. 'What's it like to be a successful bad writer?'

I was beginning to feel angry. 'Why don't you publish and find out?' I said.

'Hey,' he said, grinning, 'temper. You've got fantastic hair, anyway. Don't ever cut it off.'

This time I looked at him. He too had red hair, and he had an elegant moustache and beard, the moustache waxed and curled upward at the ends, the beard pointed. He was wearing a long black cloak and spats, and carrying a gold-headed cane, a pair of white gloves, and a top hat embroidered with porcupine quills.

'I like your hat,' I said.

'Thanks,' he said. 'I got a girl to do it for me. A girl I knew. She did some gloves to match, but I kept getting stuck on things – people in breadlines, dead dogs, nylon stockings, stuff like that. This is my dress uniform. Why don't you come home with me?'

'Oh, I couldn't,' I said. 'Thank you anyway.'

He didn't seem disappointed. 'Well, at least you can come to my show,' he said. He handed me an invitation, slightly smudged. 'The opening's tonight. Its just a couple of blocks from here; that's how come I crashed this party, I got tired of my own.'

'All right,' I said There didn't seem any harm in it, I thought. Secretly I was flattered: it was a long time since anyone had propositioned me. Also I found him attractive. Him or the cape, I wasn't sure which. And I wanted to get away from the columnist.

'The opening was at a minor art gallery, The Takeoff, and the show itself was called SQUAWSHT. 'It's a pun, like,' he told me as we walked across to Yonge Street. '*Squaw* and *squashed*, get it?'

'I think so,' I said. I was studying the invitation, in the light from a store window. 'The Royal Porcupine,' it said. 'Master of the CON-CREATE POEM.' There was a picture of him in full dress, flanked by a shot of a dead porcupine, taken from underneath so its long front teeth were showing.

'What's your real name?' I said.

'That is my real name,' he said, a little offended. 'I'm having it changed legally.'

'Oh,' I said. 'What made you happen to pick that particular one?'

'Well, I'm a Royalist,' he said. 'I really dig the Queen. I felt I should have a name that would reflect that. It's like the Royal Mail or the Royal Canadian Mounted Police. Also I thought it would be memorable.'

'What about the porcupine?'

'I've always figured the beaver was wrong, as a national symbol,' he said. 'I mean, the beaver. A dull animal and too nineteenth-century; all that industry. And you know what they used to be hunted for? The skin was for hats, and then they cut the nuts off for perfume. I mean, what a fate. The porcupine though, it does what it likes, it's covered with prickles so nobody messes with it. Also it has strange tastes, I mean beavers chew trees, porcupines chew toilet seats.

'I thought they were easy to kill,' I said. 'You hit them with a stick.'

'Propaganda,' he said.

As we arrived, a number of people were leaving; outside, the

SPCA was picketing with signs that read SAVE OUR ANIMALS. The show itself consisted of several freezers with glass tops and fronts, like the display cases for ice cream and frozen juice in supermarkets. Inside these freezers there were a number of dead animals, all of which had apparently been run over by cars. They were quick-frozen in exactly the poses they'd been discovered in, and attached to the side of each one, in the position usually reserved for the name of the painting, the size and the materials – composition #72, 5' X 9', acrylic and nylon tubing – there was a little card with the species of the animal, the location where it had been found, and a description of its injuries: RACCOON AND YOUNG, DON MILLS AND 401, BROKEN SPINE, INTERNAL HEMORRHAGE, for instance; or DOMESTIC PUSSYCAT, RUSSELL HILL ROAD, CRUSHED PELVIS. There were a skunk, several dogs, a fawn and a porcupine, as well as the usual cats, groundhogs and squirrels. There was even a snake, mangled almost beyond recognition.

'What do you think of it?' asked the Royal Porcupine when we'd made the rounds.

'Well,' I said, 'I don't know . . . I guess I don't know much about art.'

'It's not art, it's poetry,' the Royal Porcupine said, slightly offended. 'Con-create poetry, I'm the man who put the creativity back in concrete.'

'I don't know much about that either.'

'That's obvious from the stuff you write,' he said. 'I could write that stuff with my toes. The only reason you're so famous is your stuff is obsolete, man, they buy it because they haven't caught up with the present yet. Rearview mirror, like McLuhan says. The new poetry is the poetry of *things*. Like, this has never been done before,' said the Royal Porcupine, looking morosely over towards the front door of the gallery, where another bunch of queasy first-nighters was making a green-faced exit. 'Do you realize that?'

'Have you sold anything?' I asked brightly.

'No,' he said, 'but I will. I should take this show to the States, people up here are so cautious, they're unwilling to take a chance. That's how come Alexander Graham Bell had to go south.'

'That's what my husband says,' I offered.

The Royal Porcupine looked at me with new interest. 'You're married,' he said. 'I didn't know that. 'You've got the sexiest elbows I've ever seen. I'm thinking of doing a show on elbows, it's a very unappreciated part of the body.'

'Where would you get them?' I asked.

'Around,' he said. He took me by the elbow. 'Let's get out of here.'

As we went past the group of SPCA picketers outside the front door, he muttered, 'They missed the *point.* I don't squash them, I just recycle them, what's wrong with that?'

'Where are we going?' I asked the Royal Porcupine, who still had hold of my elbow.

'My place,' he said.

'I'm hungry,' I said evasively.

So we went to Mr Zums on Bloor Street, where I had a Zumburger with the works and the Royal Porcupine had a chocolate milk shake. I paid – he didn't have any money – and we debated the pros and cons of going back to his place.

'I want to make love to your elbow,' he said. 'With fringe benefits.'

'But I'm married,' I said, chewing thoughtfully on my Zumburger. I was resisting temptation, and it was a temptation. Arthur had frozen me out; as far as he was concerned I might as well have been a turnip. I'd been finding myself attracted to the most inappropriate men lately: CBC news commentators, bus conductors, typewriter repairmen. In my fantasies I wasn't even bothering with the sets and custumes, I was going straight to the heavy breathing. Things must have been bad.

'That's okay,' said the Royal Porcupine, 'I prefer married women.'

'My husband might not prefer it,' I said.

'He doesn't have to know, does he?'

'He'd know. He has intuition.' This wasn't true; what was really worrying me was: even if Arthur did know, would he care? And what if he didn't care, what then? 'He'd think you're decadent, he'd think you were bad for my ideology.'

'He can have your ideology, I'll take the rest, fair enough? Come on, let me sweep you off your feet. You're the type, I can tell.'

I finished my Zumburger. 'It's impossible,' I said.

'Have it your way,' he said, 'you win one, you lose one. You're missing something though.'

'I don't have the energy,' I said.

He said he'd walk me home, and we set off along Bloor, heading west toward the street of old three-story red-brick houses, with porches and gables, where Arthur and I were living at that time, temporarily as ever. The Royal Porcupine seemed to have forgotten about his proposition already. He was worrying about the success of his show. 'The last one I did, there was only one review. The old fart said it was an unsuccessful attempt to be disgusting. You can't even shock the bourgeoisie any more; you could put on a show of amputated orphans' feet and someone would ask you to sign them.'

We passed the Museum and the Varsity Stadium and continued west, through a region of tiny, grubby old stores which were turning into boutiques, past a wholesale truss concern. On Brunswick we turned north, but after several houses the Royal Porcupine stoped and shouted. He'd found a dead dog, quite a large one; it looked like a husky.

'Help me get it into the bag,' he said, for he'd taken a green plastic garbage bag out from under his cloak. He jotted down the location in a notebook he carried for the purpose. Then he lifted the hind end and I slid the garbage bag over it. The bag wasn't big enough and the dog's head stuck out the top, its tongue lolling.

'Well, goodnight,' I said, 'it was nice meeting you.'

'Just a minute,' he said, 'I can't get this thing back by myself.'

'I'm not going to carry it,' I said. the blood was still wet.

'Then take my cane.'

He hoisted the dog and concealed it under his cloak. We smuggled it into a taxi, for which I ended up paying, and went to the Royal Porcupine's lair. It was in a downtown warehouse that had been converted into artists' studios. 'I'm the only one who lives here though,' he said. 'I can't afford not to. The others have real houses.'

We went up the heavy industrial elevator to the third floor. The Royal Porcupine didn't have very much furniture, but he did have a large freezer, and he took the dog over to it immediately and lowered it in. Then he tied the limbs so the corpse would freeze in the position in which we'd found it.

While he was doing this, I explored. Most of the space was empty. In one corner was his bed, a mattress on the floor, no sheets; on top of it were several mangy sheep-skin rugs, and over it hung a tattered red velvet canopy with tassels. He had a card table and two card chairs; on both the table and the chairs there were used plates and cups. On one wall was a blow-up of himself, in costume, holding a dead mouse by the tail. Beside it was a formal portrait of the Queen and Prince Philip, with decorations and tiaras, in a heavy gilt frame like the kind in the principal's office at high school. Aganst the other wall stood a kitchen counter, with none of the plumbing installed. It held a collection of stuffed animals. Some were toys, teddy bears and tigers and bunnies. Some were real animals, expertly finished and mounted, birds mostly: a loon, an owl, a bluejay. Then there were a few chipmunks and squirrels, not done well at all. The stitches were visible, they had no bead eyes, and they were long and fat, live liverwursts, their legs sticking straight out.

'I tried taxidermy first,' said the Royal Porcupine, 'but I wasn't any good at it. Freezing's a lot better, that way they don't get moths.'

He had taken off his cloak, and as I turned I saw that he was now taking off his shirt as well. The dog blood left red stains as he unbuttoned; his chest emerged, covered with auburn hair.

His green eyes lit up like a lynx's, and he walked towards me, growling softly. The backs of my knees were weak with lust, and I felt a curious tingling sensation in my elbows.

'Well, I guess I'd better be going now,' I said. He said nothing. 'How do you work the elevator?'

'For Christ's sake,' I said a minute later, 'wash your hands!'

'I've always wanted to know what it was like to fuck a cult figure,' the Royal Porcupine said reflectively. He was lying on his mattress, watching me as I scrubbed the dog blood off my belly with a corner of his shirt, dipped in the toilet. He didn't have a sink.

'Well,' I said a little sharply, 'what's it like?'

'You have a nice ass,' he said. 'But it's not that different from anyone else's ass.'

'What were you expecting?' I said. Three buttocks. Nine tits. I felt like a moron for wanting to get the dog blood off, I felt I was violating one of his rituals, I was letting him down. I hadn't risen to the occasion, and already I was feeling guilty about Arthur.

'It's not what there is,' he said, 'it's what you do with it.'

He didn't say whether what I did with it would pass his standards or not, and at that moment I didn't care. I just wanted to go home.

Chapter Twenty-four

This was the beginning of my double life. But hadn't my life always been double? There was always that shadowy twin, thin when I was fat, fat when I was thin, myself in silvery negative, with dark teeth and shining white pupils glowing in the black sunlight of that other world. While I watched, locked in the actual flesh, the uninteresting dust and never-emptied ashtrays of daily life. It was never-never land she wanted, that reckless twin. But not twin even, for I was more than double, I was triple, multiple, and now I could see that there was more than one life to come, there were many. The Royal Porcupine had opened a time-space door to the fifth dimension, cleverly disguised as a freight elevator, and one of my selves plunged recklessly through.

Not the others, though. 'When can I see you again?' he asked.

'Soon,' I said. 'Don't call me, though, I'll call you. Okay?'

'I'm not applying for a job, you know,' he said.

'I know. Please understand.' I kissed him goodnight. Already I was beginning to feel that I couldn't see him again. It would be too dangerous.

When I got back to the apartment Arthur wasn't there, although it was almost twelve o'clock. I threw myself on the bed, stuck my head under the pillow, and began to cry. I felt I'd ruined my life, again. I would repent, I would turn over a new leaf, I wouldn't call the Royal Porcupine, although I was longing to. What could I do to make it up to Arthur? Perhaps I could write a Costume Gothic, just for him, putting his message into a form that the people could understand. Nobody, I knew, read *Resurgence* except the editors, some university professors, and all the rival radical groups who edited magazines of their own and spent a third of each issue attacking each other. But at least a hundred thousand people read my books, and among them were the mothers of the nation. *Terror at Casa Loma*, I'd call it, I would get in the evils of the Family Compact, the martyrdom of Louis Riel, the horrors of colonialism, both English and American, the struggle of the workers, the Winnipeg General Strike ...

But it would never work. In order for Arthur to appreciate me I'd have to reveal the identity of Louisa K., and I knew I couldn't do that. No matter what I did, Aurther was bound to despise me. I could never be what he wanted. I could never be Marlene.

It was two in the morning when Arthur came back.

'Where have you been?' I asked, snuffling.

'At Marlene's place,' Arthur said, and my heart dropped. He'd gone for consolation, and ...

'Was Don there?' I asked in a small voice.

It turned out that Marlene had told Don about Sam, and Don had hit her in the eye. Marlene had called up the entire editorial staff of *Resurgence,* including Sam. They'd come over to Marlene's house, where they'd had a heated discussion about whether or not Don had been justified. Those in favor said the workers often hit their wives in the eye, it was an open and direct method of expressing your feelings. Those against it said it was degrading to women. Marlene had announced she was moving out. Sam said she couldn't move in with him, and another debate began. Some said he was a prick for not letting Marlene move in with him, others felt that if he didn't really want her to he was right to say so. In the middle of this, Don, who'd been out getting drunk at Grossman's Tavern, came back and told them all to get the hell out of his house.

I was secretly glad of this uproar. Arthur could no longer consider Marlene the paragon he once had, and it took some of the heat off me.

'What about Marlene?' I said, with false concern. 'Was she all right?'

'She's outside the door,' Arthur said heavily, 'sitting on the stairs. I thought I should check with you first. I couldn't just leave her there, not with him in that condition.'

He didn't say anything about the television interview though, and for this I was grateful. Perhaps he hadn't seen it. It would have been a terrible humiliation to him. I hoped no one would tell him about it.

Marlene slept on the chesterfield that night, and the next night, and the next. It appeared she'd moved in with us. I couldn't do anything about it, for wasn't she in trouble, wasn't she a political refugee? That was how she saw it, and Arthur did too.

During the days she negotiated over the phone with Don and, strangely enough, with Sam. Between these conversations she sat at my kitchen table, chain-smoking and drinking my coffee and asking me what she should do. She was no longer neat and tidy; her eyes were dark-circled, her hair stringy, her nails ragged from biting. Should she keep on seeing Sam, should she go back to Don? Don had the children, temporarily. As soon as she got a place of her own, she'd get them away from him if she had to go to court to do it.

I refrained from asking her when she was going to get a place of her own. 'I don't know,' I said, 'which of them do you love?' I sounded exactly like the friendly housekeepers in my own Costume Gothics, I thought, but what else could I say?

'Love,' Marlene snorted. 'Love isn't the *point*. The point is, which of them is up to having a truly equal relationship. The point is, which is the least exploitive.'

'Well,' I said, 'offhand I'd say Sam was.' He was my friend, Don wasn't, so I was putting in my plug for Sam. On the other hand, I still didn't like Marlene very much, so why was I wishing her on my friend? 'But I'm sure Don's very nice, too,' I added.

'Sam is a swine,' Marlene said. When Women's Lib had appeared, Marlene had dismissed it as bourgeois; now she was a convert. 'It takes a personal experience to really open your eyes,' she told me. She kept implying I hadn't suffered enough; in this too I was deficient. I knew I shouldn't feel defensive about it, but I did.

When Marlene was off visiting Sam, Don would drop by to consult me. 'Well, maybe you should move to another city,' I said. That was what I would have done.

'That would be running away,' Don said. 'She's my wife. I want her back.'

Then, in the evenings, when Marlene was seeing her children, Sam would come over and I'd make him a drink. 'God, it's driving me crazy,' he'd say. 'I'm in love with her, I just don't want to live with her all the time. I tell her we can spend *important* time together, significant time, much better if we live in separate houses. And I don't see why we can't have other relationships, as long as ours is the main one, but she can't see it. I mean, I'm not the jealous type.'

With all the coming and going, I began to feel I was living in a train station. Arthur was hardly ever there, since Marlene and Don had resigned from *Resurgence* and he himself was trying to keep it going. Marlene was too distraught to help much with the cooking and cleaning up, and she was no help with the rest of my life either. Increasingly, I was daydreaming aout the Royal Porcupine. I hadn't called him yet, but any moment now I knew I would give in. I searched the papers for reviews of SQUAWSHT, and found one in the Saturday entertainment supplement. 'A telling and incisive commentary on our times,' it said.

'How would you like to go to an art show?' I asked Marlene. The show was still on, it wouldn't hurt just to walk through it.

'That pretentious bourgeois shit?' she said. 'No thanks.'

'Oh, have you seen it?' I asked.

'No, but I read the review. You can tell.'

Meanwhile there was my literary career. The day after the television show, the phone calls had begun. They were mostly from people who'd believed me and who wanted to know how to get in touch with the Other Side, though some were hate calls from people who thought I'd been making fun of the interviewer, or Spiritualism, or both. Some thought I could foretell the future and wanted me to foretell theirs. None of them asked for love potions or wart remover, but I felt it would come to that.

Then there were the letters, which Morton and Sturgess forwarded to me. They were mostly from people who wanted help getting published. At first I tried answering them, but I soon discovered that these people did not want their fantasies destroyed. When I explained that I had no surefire contacts in the publishing world, they were outraged to be told I was powerless. It overwhelmed me with guilt that I couldn't live up to their expectations, so after a while I started throwing the letters out unanswered, and after that, unread. Then the people started arriving at the apartment, demanding to know why I hadn't answered their letters.

New articles were appearing every week, with titles like 'The Selling of *Lady Oracle*' and '*Lady Oracle*: Hoax or Delusion?' And because of that first, calamitous television interview, which had made the papers – AUTHOR CLAIMS SPIRIT GUIDANCE – the other interviewers Sturgess had lined up wouldn't leave the subject alone. It did no good for me to say I didn't want to talk about it; that only whetted their curiosity.

'I hear *Lady Oracle* was written by angels, sort of like the Book of Mormon,' they'd say.

'Not exactly,' I'd say. Then I'd try to change the subject, hoping that Arthur wasn't watching. Sometimes they would be seriously interested, which was even worse. 'So you think there *is* a life after death,' they'd say.

'I don't know. I guess no one really knows that, do they?'

After these shows I would phone up Sturgess, in tears, and beg to be excused from the next one. Sometimes he would bolster up my sagging self-confidence: I was great, I was doing fine, sales were terrific. Sometimes he would act hurt and say it was our understanding when we signed the contract that I'd do a certain number of shows, didn't I remember?

I felt very visible. But it was as if someone with my name were out there in the real world, impersonating me, saying things I'd never said but which appeared in the newspapers, doing things for which I had to take the consequences: my dark twin, my funhouse-mirror reflection. She was taller than I was, more beautiful, more threatening. She wanted to kill me and take my place, and by the time she did this no one would notice the difference because the media were in on the plot, they were helping her.

And that wasn't all. Now that I was a public figure I was terrified that sooner or later someone would find out about me, trace down my former self, unearth me. My old daydreams about the Fat Lady returned, only this time she'd be walking across her tightrope, in her pink tutu, and she'd fall, in slow motion, turning over and over on the way down . . . Or she'd be dancing on a stage in her harem costume and her red slippers. But it wouldn't be a dance at all, it would be a striptease, she'd start taking off her clothes, while I watched, powerless to stop her. She'd wobble her hips, removing her veils, one after another, but no one would whistle, no one would yell *Take it off baby*. I tried to turn off these out-of-control fantasies, but couldn't, I had to watch them through to the end.

After Sam left one afternoon, I sat at the kitchen table, drinking Scotch. Marlene was out seeing a lawyer; she'd left her breakfast dishes on the table, a mound of orange peels and a bowl half full of water-logged Rice Krispies. Her healthy eating habits had gone down the drain. So had mine. I was a nervous wreck, I realized, and I'd been one for some time. My home was a campground littered with other people's garbage, physical, emotional; Arthur was never there, for which I didn't blame him; I'd been unfaithful to him but I didn't have the courage either to tell him or to do it again, as I wished to. It wasn't willpower that was keeping me away from the Royal Porcupine, it was cowardice. I was inept, I was slovenly and hollow, a hoax, a delusion. Tears trickled down my face, onto the crumb-strewn table.

Pull yourself together, I told myself. You've got to get out.

Marlene came back from her lawyer, teeth clenched, eyes glinting; visits to her lawyer usually had this effect on her. She sat down and lit a cigarette.

'I've got that prick,' she said.

I wasn't sure which one she meant, but I wasn't interested.

'Marlene,' I said, 'I have a wonderful idea. This place is really too small for the three of us.'

'You're right,' she said. 'It's a little crowded. I'll be moving out as soon as I can find a place of my own.'

'No,' I said, '*we'll* move out. Term's almost over. Arthur and I will go away for the summer and you can stay here. It'll help you get things sorted out.'

Arthur wasn't enthusiastic when I told him. At first he said we couldn't afford it, but I told him my aunt had died and left me some money.

'I thought your aunt died a long time ago,' Arthur said.

'That was my other aunt, that was Aunt Lou. This was Aunt Deirdre. We never got on that well, but I guess she didn't have anyone else to leave it to.' The truth was that I'd sold *Love, My Ransom* for a reasonable sum. My own life was a mess, but Louisa K. was doing all right.

'What about the magazine?' Arthur asked. 'I can't just dump it.'

'You need a rest,' I told him. 'Marlene will take it over again. She needs something to get her mind off everything else.'

I told Sturgess my mother was dying of cancer and I had to go to Saskatchewan to look after her.

'What about all those appearances,' he said, aggrieved, 'and the trans-Canada tour?'

'Postpone them,' I said. 'I'll do it when I get back.'

'Could you at least do an interview in Regina?'

'My mother's dying, remember?' I said, and he had to make do with that.

It was Sam who suggested Italy and gave us Mr. Vitroni's address. He'd got it from a friend. Arthur wanted to go to Cuba, but we couldn't get visas in time.

We took a plane to Rome and rented a red Fiat, which we drove to Terremoto. I navigated, using Sam's friend's directions and a map. The gearshift knob came off a few times, but Arthur always had trouble with cars. We moved into the flat, and there we were, away from everyone, ready to sort out our life.

I suppose I'd been hoping for a reconciliation, or at least for a return to the way things had been before *Lady Oracle*, and in a way this did happen. My tortuous Fat-Lady fantasies disappeared. Away from the *Resurgence* group, Arthur was sweeter, more pensive. I made coffee in the mornings and passed it out to him through the kitchen window. Then we would sit among the pieces of broken glass on the balcony, drinking it and practicing our Italian from the *fotoromanzi* or just gazing out over the valley. We went for walks on the hills above the town and admired the view. Arthur wanted to do some field work, as he called it, dealing with the system of land ownership, but his Italian wasn't good enough, so he let the project drop. From time to time he scratched away at an article for *Resurgence*, on the difficulty of making feature films in Canada; but he seemed to have lost his fervor. We made love a lot and visited ruins.

One day we went Tivoli. We bought some ice-cream cones, then went to see the Cardinal's gardens, with the famous waterwork statues. We went down a staircase bordered with sphinxes, water shooting from their nipples, and wandered from grotto to grotto. At the end we came to Diana of Ephesus, the guidebook said, rising from a pool of water. She had a serene face, perched on top of a body shaped like a mound of grapes. She was draped in breasts from neck to ankle, as though afflicted with a case of yaws: little breasts at the top and bottom, big ones around the middle. The nipples were equipped with spouts, but several of the breasts were out of order.

I stood licking my ice-cream cone, watching the goddess coldly. Once I would have seen her as an image of myself, but not any more. My ability to give was limited, I was not inexhaustible. I was not serene, not really. I wanted things, for myself.

Chapter Twenty-five

Almost as soon as we got back from Italy, I called the Royal Porcupine. He didn't sound surprised. 'What took you so long?' he said.

'I was away,' I said ambiguously. 'I tried to call you before I left, but you weren't there.'

We met at the Red Hot stand in Simpson's Basement. The Royal Porcupine explained that he was even poorer than usual and this was the cheapest place in town to have lunch, as you could get two hot dogs and an orange drink for a dollar. I found his cape a little incongruous in Simpson's Basement, and the sexual fantasies I'd been having aout him drooped slightly. Still, there was something Byronic about him. Byron, I remembered, had kept a pet bear in his rooms and drunk wine from a skull.

He borrowed a subway token from me and we went back to his place. 'I have to explain something first,' I said in the freight elevator. 'We have to keep this light.' Arthur, I said, was very important to me and I didn't want to do anything that would hurt him.

The Royal Porcupine said that was fine wih him, and the lighter things were, the better.

At first they were very light. Finally I had someone who would waltz with me, and we waltzed all over the ballroom floor of his warehouse, he in his top hat and nothing else, I in a lace tablecloth, to the music of the Mantovani strings, which we got at the Crippled Civilians. We got the record player there, too, for ten dollars. When we weren't waltzing or making love, we frequented junk shops, combing them for vests, eight-button gloves, black satin Merry Widows and formal gowns of the fifties. He wanted a sword cane, but we never did find one. We did find a store in Chinatown which had button boots for sale, left over from 1905.

They hadn't sold because they were odd sizes, and I had to sit down on the curb and let the Royal Porcupine try to cram my feet into each pair, beautiful half-tones, white glacé kid, pearl gray. I felt like Cinderella's ugly sister. The only pair I could get on were black lace-ups with steel toes, washerwoman boots, but even these were desirable. We bought them, and later a pair of black net stockings to go with them.

I soon discovered that my own interest in nineteenth-century trivia was no match for the Royal Porcupine's obsession with cultural detritus. Whereas I liked antique silver and snuffboxes, he lusted after green Coca-Cola bottles, worn Captain Marvel comic books, Mickey Mouse watches, Big Little Books, and movie star paper dolls from the twenties. He didn't have very much money, so he couldn't buy everything he wanted, but he was a walking catalog of ephemera, of the irrelevant and the disposable. Everything, for him, was style; nothing was content. Beside him I felt almost profound.

Unfortunately the lace-up black ankle boots gave me severe pains in the feet if I wore them for more than half an hour; but it was enough for a couple of good waltzes. When we'd tired ourselves out we'd go to the Kentucky Fried Chicken place on the corner and order a bucket and two Cokes. These we would eat in the warehouse. The Royal Porcupine wanted to save the chicken bones, boil them, and glue and wire them into a sculpture, which he would call 'Joan Foster Kentucky Fried'; he wanted to exhibit it at his next show. It was a terrific idea, he said. The black shoes would be called 'Foster Dances #30,' and he'd cover a Mantovani record with clumps of my hair and call it 'Hairy Foster Music.' And if he could have a pair of my Weekend Set underpants, he could . . .

'That's very creative,' I said, 'but I don't think it's a good idea.'

'Why not?' he said, a litle hurt.

'Arthur would find out.'

'Arthur,' he said. 'It's always Arthur.'

He was beginning to resent Arthur. He made a point of telling me about his two other women. They were both married, one to a psychologist, the other to a chemistry professor. He said they were both very dumb and no good in bed. The chemistry professor's wife used to leave baked goods for him beside the freight elevator, without warning. We would lie on his grubby mattress, eating the damp pumpkin cakes and the flat high-protein bread (she was a health-food freak) while the Royal Porcupine talked about her deficiencies. I began to wonder whether he did the same with both of them, about me. I minded, but I couldn't afford to.

'Why do you see them, if they're so boring?' I asked.

'I have to do something when you're not here,' he said petulantly. Already he'd decided they were my fault.

Occasionally I would have an attack of guilt about Arthur and cook special meals for him, which failed even more miserably then the meals I usually cooked. I even toyed with the idea of telling him, trying openness and honesty as Marlene had; but then, it hadn't done any wonders for her, and I was fairly sure it wouldn't do much for me either. I was afraid that Arthur would laugh, denounce me as a traitor to the cause, or kick me out. I didn't want that: I still loved him, I was sure of it. 'Maybe we should have an open marriage,' I said to Arthur one night as he was hacking his way through a pork chop that I'd put under the broiler and then forgotten about. But he didn't even answer, which might've been because his mouth was full, and that was as far as I got.

When we'd returned from Italy, Marlene was no longer in our apartment. She'd gone back to Don. They'd 'worked it out,' they said; but she was still seeing Sam. Nobody was supposed to know, but of course Sam told me immediately.

'Where does that leave you?' I said.

'Back where we started,' he said, 'but with more experience.'

That was where Arthur and I seemed to be also. The trouble with me, I thought, was that I had experience all right, but I couldn't seem to learn from it.

Arthur was back at his teaching job, and the *Resurgence* group had reunited, which should have made him happy. He wasn't happy though, I could tell. Once I would have made a big effort to cheer him up, but I was beginning to resent the gray aura he gave off constantly, like a halo in reverse. Some days I felt his unhappiness was all my fault, I was neglecting him. But more often I tried to dismiss it. Perhaps he simply had a talent for unhappiness, as others had a talent for making money. Or perhaps he was trying to destory himself in order to prove to me that I was destructive. He was beginning to accuse me of not taking enough interest in his work.

From this soggy domestic atmosphere the Royal Porcupine was

a welcome escape. He didn't make many demands; with him it was easy come, easy go. I began to get careless. I started calling him from the apartment when Arthur was out, and then when Arthur was merely in the next room. My work was suffering too: I'd completely lost interest in Costume Gothics. What did I need them for now?

When I finally went on Sturgess' trans-Canada tour, the Royal Porcupine came along, and we had a lot of fun smuggling him into the motel rooms. Sometimes we dressed up in middle-aged tourist outfits, bought at the Crippled Civilians, and registered under assumed names. In Toronto I started going to parties, not exactly with him, but five minutes before or after. We'd get other people to introduce us to each other. These games were childish, but a relief.

It was at one of these parties that I met Fraser Buchanan. He came up to me, glass in hand, and stood smirking while I asked the Royal Porcupine what he did for a living.

'I'm a mortician,' he said. We both thought this was funny.

'Excuse me, Ms. Foster,' Fraser Buchanan said, extending his hand. 'My name is Fraser Buchanan. Perhaps you've heard of me.' He was a short man, tidily dressed in a tweed jacket and turtle-neck sweater, with sideburns that he obviously found daring, as he turned his head often to give you the benefit of a side view.

'I'm afraid I haven't,' I said. I smiled at him; I was feeling good. 'This is the Royal Porcupine, the con-create poet.'

'I know,' said Fraser Buchanan, giving me an oddly intimate smile. 'I'm familiar with his ... work. But really, Ms Foster, I'm more interested in you.' He sidled closer, wedging himself between me and the Royal Porcupine. I leaned backward a little. 'Tell me,' he said in a half-whisper, 'how is it that I never saw any of your work in print before *Lady Oracle?* Most poets, or should I say poetesses, go through an, ah, an apprentice period. In the little magazines and so forth. I follow them closely, but I never saw anything of yours.'

'Are you a journalist?' I asked.

'No, no,' he said. 'I used to write a little poetry myself.' His tone suggested that he had since outgrown this. 'You might call me an interested observer. A lover,' he smirked, 'of the arts.'

'Well,' I said, 'I guess I just never thought any of my stuff was good enough to be published. I never sent any of it in.' I gave what I hoped was a modest laugh and looked over his shoulder at the

Royal Porcupine, hoping for rescue. Fraser Buchanan's thigh was resting ever so lightly against my own.

'So then you sprang fully formed, like Athena from the head of Zeus,' he said. 'Or rather, from the head of John Morton. That man certainly has a nose for young talent.'

I couldn't put my finger on it, but there was some very unpleasant insinuation going on. I laughed again and told him I was going to get another drink. It occurred to me that I'd seen him before, front row center at a television talk show, taking notes in a little book. Several talk shows. Several out-of-town talk shows. A motel lobby.

'Who is that strange little man?' I asked the Royal Porcupine later, as we lay exhausted on his mattress. 'What does he do?'

'He knows everyone,' he said. 'He used to be with the CBC, I guess everyone did. Then he started a literary magazine called *Reject*; the idea was that it would print only stuff that'd been rejected by other literary magazines, the more the merrier, plus the rejection slips. He was going to give a prize for the best rejection slip, he said it was an art. But it flopped because nobody wanted to admit they'd been rejected. He printed a lot of his own stuff in the first issue, though. I think he's English. He goes to all the parties, he goes to every party he can get into. He used to go around saying, 'Hello, I'm Fraser Buchanan, the Montreal Poet.' I think he once lived in Montreal.'

'But how come you know him?'

'I submitted stuff to *Reject*,' the Royal Porcupine said. 'That was when I was still doing words. He rejected it. He hates my stuff, he thinks it's too far out.'

'I think he's been following me around,' I said. What I thought was worse: he's been following *us* around.

'He's freaky,' said the Royal Porcupine. 'He has this thing about celebrities. He says he's writing a history of our times.'

That evening I took a taxi home early. I was suffering again from self-doubt. The difficulty was that I found each of my lives perfectly normal and appropriate, but only at the time. When I was with Arthur, the Royal Porcupine seemed like a daydream from one of my less credible romances, with an absurdity about him that I tried to exclude from my fictions. But when I was with the Royal Porcupine, he seemed plausible and solid. Everything he did and said made sense in his own terms, whereas it was Arthur who became unreal; he faded to an insubstantial ghost, a washed-out photo on some mantelpiece I'd long ago abandoned. Was I hurting him, was I being unfaithful? How could you hurt a photograph?

When I walked into the apartment that evening, I was still thinking about this. The *Resurgence* crowd was there in force; something exciting was going on. Sam was the only one who said hello. They had a captive union organizer there, a real one, backed into the corner. He called them 'you kids.'

'If you kids want to get involved, okay,' he was saying, 'but if the workers want to spit on policemen, let *them* spit on policemen. It's *their* jobs. You kids can go to jail, you don't have steady jobs, you can miss some time, but for them it's different.

Don started to argue that this was precisely why they and not the workers should do it, but the union organizer waved his hand in dismissal. 'No, no,' he said. 'I know you kids mean well, but believe me. Sometimes the wrong kind of help is worse than no help at all.'

'What's going on?' I asked Sam.

'It's a strike down at a mattress factory,' Sam said. 'Trouble is, most of the workers are Portuguese, and they don't buy our line all that much. Canadian nationalism means bugger all to them, you know? Not that we can get it across to them, we're still looking for an interpreter.'

'Who spit on a policeman?'

'Arthur did,' Sam said, and I could tell from the smug yet chastised look on Arthur's face that indeed he had. For some reason this annoyed me.

If I hadn't just come from the Royal Porcupine's, I wouldn't have said anything; but he thought politics were boring, especially Canadian nationalism. 'Art is universal,' he'd say. 'They're just trying to get attention.'

When I was with Arthur, I believed in the justice of his cause, his causes, every one of them; how could I live with him otherwise? But the Royal Porcupine took the edge off causes. It was the Cavaliers and the Roundheads all over again.

'Oh, for heaven's sake,' I said to Arthur. 'I suppose you can hardly wait to be arested. But what'll that solve, not a damn thing. You don't live in the real world, you won't join any kind of a political party and go out there and really change things, instead you sit around and argue and attack each other. You're like the Plymouth Brethren, all you're interested in is defining your own purity by excluding everyone else. And then you go out and make some useless, *meaningless* gesture like spitting on a policeman.'

No one said anything; everyone was too stunned. I was the last person they'd have expected such a tirade from, and come to think of it, who was I to talk? I was hardly saving the world myself.

'Joan's right,' Marlene said, in a voice cold with tactics. 'But let's hear what kind of useful, meaningful gesture she'd like to suggest instead.'

'Oh, I don't know,' I said. I immediately started backing up and apologizing. 'I mean, it's really none of my business, I don't know all that much about politics. Maybe you could blow up the Peace Bridge or something.'

I was horrified to see that they were taking me seriously.

The next evening a small deputation arrived at the apartment. Marlene, Don, Sam and a couple of the younger Resurgenites.

'We've got it out there in the car,' Marlene said.

'Got what?' I asked. I'd just washed my hair, I hadn't been expecting them. Arthur was off teaching his night class in Canadian Literature; he'd barely spoken to me that day, and I wasn't happy about that.

'The dynamite,' she said. She was quite excited. 'My father's in construction, it was easy to pinch it, plus the detonator and a couple of blasting caps.'

'Dynamite? What're you doing with dynamite?'

'We talked over your idea,' she said. 'We decided it wasn't such a bad one. We're going to blow up the Peace Bridge, as a gesture. It's the best one to blow up, because of the name.

'Wait a minute,' I said, 'you might hurt someone.'

'Marlene says we'll do it at night,' Don said quickly. 'We won't blow it all up anyway, it's more like a symbol. A gesture, like you said.'

They wanted me to hide the dynamite for them. They'd even thought out a plan. They wanted me to buy a used car, under an assumed name, using a fake address, the apartment of a new Resurgenite who was going away for a couple of months anyway. Then I had to put the dynamite in the trunk of the car and move the car around every day, from one street to another, from one all-night parking lot to the next.

'A used car costs money,' I said slowly.

'Look, it was your idea,' Marlene said. 'The least you can do is help us out. Besides, you can get a cheap one for a couple of hundred.'

'Why me?'

'They'd never suspect you,' Marlene said. 'You don't look much like the dynamite type.'

'How long will I have to do this?' I asked.

'Only till we get the plan together. Then we'll take over the car.'

'All right, I'll do it,' I said. 'Where's the dynamite?'

'Here,' Don said, handing me a cardboard carton.

I never had any intention of carrying out their plan. The next day I took a taxi to the Royal Porcupine's and stowed the box in the cellar. There were a lot of crates and boxes there anyway. I told him it was an ugly statue I'd got for a wedding present and I couldn't bear to have it in the house any longer.

'I'd rather you didn't open it,' I said. 'For sentimental reasons.'

Chapter Twenty-six

The Royal Porcupine couldn't let well enough alone. That was one of the things I like about him: he didn't believe in well enough, he believed in cataclysmic absolutes.

'Where'd you get the dynamite?' he said. We were lying on his mattress; he always kept serious questions till afterwards.

'I asked you not to open that box,' I said.

'Come on, you knew I would. You know I love ugly statues. Where'd you get it?

'It's not my dynamite,' I said. 'It belongs to some other people.'

'I've never seen any of that stuff go off,' he said thoughtfully. 'I always liked Victoria Day though, that was my favorite holiday. That and Hallowe'en.'

'If you're thinking of blowing anything up,' I said, 'forget it. You'd get me in deep trouble if they found out it was missing.'

'We could replace it,' he said, 'with other dynamite.'

'No,' I said. I was remembering the time he'd almost electrocuted us. He'd heard from one of his friends, also a con-create artist, that if you got a string of christmas tree lights, plugged it in, unscrewed one of thelights, and stuck your finger in the socket at the moment of ejaculation, not only you but your partner would have the greatest orgasm in the world. His friend's recipe also included several joints, but the Royal Porcupine had given up dope. 'Jejune,' he called it. 'Fred Astaire didn't smoke dope, right?' He'd spent days trying to persuade me to perform this act, or 'art-if-act,' as he called it; the 'if' stood for the element of chance. He'd even bought a third-hand string of Christmas tree lights. 'I refuse to turn myself into an electric toaster to satisfy one of your demented whims,' I told him; so he'd hidden the lights under the mattress and plugged them in just before my next visit. He was planning to sneak his finger into the socket without my knowing, at the crucial moment; but we'd hardly begun before wisps of smoke began to curl our from under the mattress. I was afraid something similar would happen with the dynamite.

As usual, the more I resisted, the more excited he became. He got up off the mattress and started pacing the room. He put his fur hat on, a recent one, with Mountie earflaps. 'Come *on*,' he said, 'it would be terrific! We wouldn't blow anything up, we'd just set it off, at night somewhere, and watch it go. Wow, it'd be sensational. It would be, like, an *event*, and we'd be the only audience, it would be all for us. *Ka-boom*. It's the only chance you'll ever get, how could you pass up something like that?'

'Easily,' I said. 'I don't like loud meaningless noises.'

'Then you're with the wrong man,' he said. He started licking my ear.

'Chuck, be reasonable.'

'Reasonable,' he said sullenly. 'If I was reasonable, you wouldn't love me. Everyone else is reasonable.' He took off his fur hat and flung it across the room. 'And don't call me *Chuck*.' (I'd recently found out that his real name was Chuck Brewer, and he even had a job: he was a part-time commercial artist, specializing in layout and design. He told me this in deepest confidence, as if it were disreputable.)

Five days later we were walking across High Park, looking for a suitable place. It was eleven at night, it was the middle of March; there was still ice in the ponds and snow under the trees, it was a late spring. The Royal Porcupine had on one of his fur coats and his fur hat with the earflaps down. Under his coat he was carrying the dynamite in the cardboard box, with the fuse and detonator. He said he'd found out how to work it. I didn't believe him; also I didn't trust his motives.

'I'm not going along with this if you blow up any people,' I said.

'I told you, I won't.'

'Or any animals. Or any houses, or any trees.'

'You still don't get it,' he said impatiently . 'The point isn't to blow anything up, it's just to blow up the dynamite. It's a pure act.'

'I don't believe in pure acts,' I said.

'Then you don't have to come with me,' he said craftily, but I felt if I didn't he might break his promise and blow up something important, like a reservoir or the Gzowski Memorial down by the lakefront, which he'd mentioned in passing.

After inspecting a few likely sites, he settled on a stretch of open ground near a medium-sized pond. There didn't seem to be any structures nearby and it was quite far from the road, so I approved it. I crouched shivering in a clump of bushes while he fiddled with the dynamite, ataching the blasting cap and unraveling the wire.

'Are we far enough away?' I asked.

'Oh, sure,' he said. Though when he set off the charge, it made an impressive enough WHUMP, and we were showered with bits of earth and a few small stones.

'Hah!' cried the royal Porcupine. 'Did you see that!'

I hadn't seen anything, as I'd closed my eyes and covered them with my mittened hands. 'It was great,' I said admiringly.

'Great,' he said. 'Is that all you can say? It was fuckin' *terrific*, it's the best art-if-act I've ever done!' He pulled me into his fur coat and began undoing buttons.

'We've got to get out of here,' I protested. 'Someone must've heard it, the police will come, they patrol this park.'

'Come on,' he begged, and I couldn't refuse, it was obviously so important to him. We made seismographic love inside his coat, listening for the sound of sirens, which never arrived.

'You're one in a million,' he said. 'Nobody else would've done that. I think I'm in love with you.' I should've felt ironic about this, but I didn't. I kissed him gratefully, I must admit.

He was a little disappointed that the explosion didn't make the front page. For a whole day it didn't even make the newspapers, but on the second day he located a paragraph buried in the *Star*.

MYSTERIOUS EXPLOSION IN HIGH PARK

Police were puzzled by a small blast Wednesday, apparently caused by dynamite. No one was injured, although the sewer system of a nearby park restaurant was temporarily disrupted. There was no apparent reason for the blast; vandalism is suspected.

The Royal Porcupine was enthralled by this report, which he read out loud to me several times. 'No apparent reason,' he crowed. 'Fabulous!' He took the clipping to a photo blow-up service, had it enlarged, framed it in a carved frame from the Crippled Civvies, and mounted it beside the Queen.

For weeks after the explosion, Marlene and Don and the rest believed that I was moving the dynamite around the city, in a 1968 powder-blue Chevy. Meanwhile they were debating their contemplated act. Not how to do it, for they never got that far. They didn't even get as far as maps and strategy, they were stuck at the level of pure theory: would they be blowing up the right thing? It would be a nationalist act, true, but was it nationalist enough, and if so, would it serve the people? Some decisive act was necessary, Don argued; otherwise they would be outflanked. Already ideas they'd thought were theirs alone were beginning to appear in newspaper editorials, and the Gallup poll showed a swing in their direction. They viewed these developments with alarm: the revolution was getting into the wrong hands.

I didn't mind moving their imaginary dynamite around the city. It gave me a perfect chance to leave the apartment any time I felt like it. 'Time to move the dynamite,' I'd say cheerfully, and there wasn't much Arthur could say. In fact he was even proud of me. 'You've got to admit she's intrepid,' Sam said. They felt I was being very cool.

Most of the time I'd go over to the Royal Porcupine's. But something was changing. The lace tablecloth in which I waltzed with him was turning itself back into a lace tablecloth, with a rip in it; the black pointed boots were no longer worth the pain they inflicted. Motels became motels, and what they meant to me now was hard work and embarrassment. Sturgess was sending me on yet more trips, to Sudbury, to Windsor, and it was costing me more and more to get through the interviews.

Afterward I would go back to the motel and wash out my underwear and pantyhose in the bathroom sinks, squeezing them in towels and draping them over coat hangers. In the mornings they were never quite dry but I would put them on anyway, feeling the clammy grub-gray touch against my skin. It was like dressing in the used breath of other people. While the Royal Porcupine sat on the bed's edge, white and skinny as a root, and asked me questions.

'What's he like?'

'Who?'

'You know, Arthur. How often do you . . . '

'Chuck, it's none of your business.'

'It is my business,' he said. He didn't pick up on the name; he was becoming less and less like the Royal Porcupine and more and more like Chuck. 'I don't ask you those things about your lady friends.'

'I made those other women up,' he said sulkily. 'There's no one but you.'

'So who leaves the pumpkin cakes?'

'My mother,' he said. I knew this was a lie.

He'd always lived in his own unwritten biography, but now he started seeing the present as though it was already the past, bandaged in gauzy nostalgia. Every restaurant we ate in he left with a sigh and a backward glance; he spoke of things we'd done the week before as if they were snapshots in some long-buried photograph album. Each of my gestures was petrified as I performed it, each kiss embalmed, as if he was saving things up. I felt like a collectable. 'I'm not dead yet,' I told him more than once, 'so why are you looking at me like that?'

This was one of his moods. In another he would be openly hostile towards me. He began to take a morbid interest, not in his own newspaper clippings, which weren't numerous, but in mine. He'd cut them out and use them to belabor me.

'It says here you're a challenge to the male ego.'

'Isn't that silly,' I said.

'But you are a challenge to the male ego,' he said.

'Oh, come on,' I said. 'Who've I ever challenged?'

'It says here you're a threat.'

'What the hell do you mean?' I said. I'd been especially nice all afternoon, I felt.

'You stomp all over people's egos without even knowing your're doing it,' he said. 'You're emotionally clumsy.'

'If we're going to have this conversation, would you please put on your clothes?' I said. My lower lip was trembling; somehow I couldn't argue with a naked man.

'See what I mean?' he said. 'You're telling me what to do. You're a threat.'

'I am not a threat,' I said.

'If you aren't a threat,' he said, 'why are you screaming?'

I began to cry. He put his arms around me, I put my arms around him, oozing tears like an orphan, like an onion, like a slug sprinkled with salt. 'I'm sorry,' he said. 'I don't have a male ego anyway, I probably have the ego of a wombat.'

'I thought we were going to keep it light,' I said, between damp snorts.

'It's light, it's light,' he said. 'Wait'll it gets heavy. I'm just depressed because it's raining and I don't have any money.'

'Let's go out for some Kentucky Fried,' I said, wiping my nose. But he wasn't hungry.

One rainy afternoon when I arrived at his warehouse, he was waiting for me all dressed up in his cape and a tie I'd never seen before, a Crippled Civilians maroon one with a mermaid on it. He grabbed me by the waist and whirled me around the floor; his eyes sparkled.

What is it?' I said when I'd caught my breath. 'What's gotten into you?'

'A surprise,' he said. He led me over to the bed: lying on it was a truly grotesque white pancake hat from the fifties, with a feather and a veil.

'Where did you get *that?*' I said, wondering what new fantasy had gripped him. The fifties had never been his favorite period.

'It's your going-away hat,' he said. 'I got it at the Sally Ann, eighty-nine cents.'

'But what's it for?'

'Going away, of course,' he said, still elated. 'I thought we might, you know, go away together. Elope.'

'You must be crazy,' I said. 'Where would we go?'

'How about Buffalo?'

I started to laugh, then saw that he was serious. 'That's very sweet of you,' I said, 'but you know that I can't.'

He wanted me to leave Arthur and move in with him. That's what it amounted to, and finally he admitted it. We sat side by side on the bed, staring at the floor. 'I want to live a normal life with you,' he said.

'I don't think we could,' I said. 'I'm a terrible cook. I burn things.'

'I want to wake up in the morning and eat breakfast with you and read *The Globe and Mail*.'

'I could come over for breakfast,' I said. 'A late breakfast.'

'I want to brush your hair.'

I began to snivel. I'd once told him Arthur liked brushing my hair; or used to.

'What's he got that I haven't got?'

I didn't know. But I didn't want him to spoil things, I didn't want him to become gray and multi-dimensional and complicated like everyone else. Was every Heathcliff a Linton in disguise? What did I want, adventure or security, and which of them offered what? Perhaps neither of them offered either, they both wanted me to offer these things, and once more I was deficient. The Royal Porcupine lay with his head against my stomach, waiting for the answer.

'I don't know,' I said. 'It isn't that.'

He sat up again. 'That's the trouble with you, you have no motives. Don't you know how dangerous that is? You're like an out-of-control school bus.'

'I don't mean to be,' I said. To make up for it, I bought him a bottle of One-A-Day vitamin pills and a pair of socks and dusted off his stuffed animals. I even gave him my fox, the one that had been Aunt Lou's. This was a real gift: I valued it. Once it would have delighted him, but he barely glanced at it.

'At least you could tell him about us,' he said. 'Sometimes I think you're ashamed of me.'

But I drew the line at that. 'I can't,' I said, 'it would ruin everything. I love you.'

'You're afraid to take a chance on me,' he said mournfully. 'I can see that. I'm not much now, I admit it, but think of the potential!'

'I like you the way you are,' I said, but he couldn't believe me. It wasn't that I didn't love him. I did, in a peculiar way, but I knew I couldn't live with him. For him, reality and fantasy were the same thing, which meant that for him there was no reality. But for me it would mean there was no fantasy, and therefore no escape.

The next time I stepped out of the freight elevator, there was an ambush waiting for me. The Royal Porcupine was there, but he was no longer the Royal Procupine. He'd cut his hair short and shaved off his beard. He was standing in the middle of the floor, no cape, no cane, no gloves; just a pair of jeans and a T-shirt that said *Honda* on it. He was merely Chuck Brewer; had he always been, underneath his beard? He looked plundered.

'My God,' I said, almost screamed. 'What did you do that for?'

'I killed him,' Chuck said. 'He's over with, he's finished.'

I started to cry. 'Oh, I forgot these,' he said. He ripped down his picture of the Queen, then his dynamite poster, and threw them onto the pile he'd made of his costumes.

'What about your animals?' I said stupidly.

'I'm getting rid of them,' he said. 'They aren't any good to me now.'

I was staring at his chin; I'd never seen it before. 'Now will you move in?' he said. 'It doesn't have to be here, we could get a house.'

It was horrible. He'd thought that by transforming himself into something more like Arthur he could have Arthur's place; but by doing this he'd murdered the part of him that I loved. I scarcely knew how to console the part that remained. Without his beard, he had the chin of a junior accountant.

I hated myself for thinking this. I felt like a monster, a large, blundering monster, irredeemably shallow. How could I care about his chin at a time like this? I threw my arms about him. I couldn't do what he wanted, it was all wrong.

'I can tell you aren't going to,' he said, disengaging my arms.

'Well, I guess there's only one thing to do. How about a double suicide? Or maybe I could shoot you and then jump off the Toronto Dominion Centre with your body in my arms.' He managed a white smile, but he didn't fool me. He was completely serious.

Chapter Twenty-seven

The Freight elevator ponderously descended. I imagined the Royal Porcupine pounding down three flights of stairs, shedding his clothes, to confront me on the ground floor, stark naked; but when the door grated open he wasn't there. I ran three blocks to the Kentucky Fried Chicken, ducked inside and ordered a Family Bucket. Then I took a taxi back to the apartment. I would tell all, I would cry. I would be forgiven, I would never do it again, if only Arthur would pardon me and take me back to safety.

I climbed the stairs to the apartment and flung open the door, breathing hard. I was ready for the scene. It wouldn't be just a confession, it would be an accusation too: why had Arthur driven me to it, what did he propose to do about it, shouldn't we discuss our relationship to find out what had gone wrong? For some complicated and possibly sadistic reason of his own he'd allowed me to become involved with a homicidal maniac, and it was time he knew about it. I didn't ask much, I only wanted to be loved. I only wanted some human consideration. Was that so terrible, was that so impossible, was I some kind of mutation?

Arthur was watching television. His back was toward me, and the nape of his neck was vulnerable. I noticed that he needed a haircut, and this hurt me. He was like a child, whole in his beliefs and trusts. What was I doing?

'Arthur,' I said, 'there's something I have to discuss with you.'

He said, without turning, 'Could you wait till it's over?'

I sat down on the floor beside his chair and opened the Family Bucket. Silently I offered it to him. 'How can you eat that American crap?' he said, but he took a breast and began to chew. He was watching the Olympic doubles figure-skating championships; once he would watch only the news, but now it was anything he could get, situation comedies, hockey games, police series, talk shows.

The television set had vertical foldover on the lower third of the screen, so that the people on the talk shows had four hands, like Indian gods and goddesses, and the chase sequences on the police shows appeared upside down, with two sets of cops and two sets of robbers; but Arthur wouldn't get it fixed because of the expense. He said he knew someone who could fix it.

The Austrian skaters, in long white sleeves, the girl in a dark bodice, glided backwards around the rink at incredible speed, completely synchronized. Each of them had four legs. They turned and the girl flew up into the air and posed, upside down, two-headed, while the man held her with one arm. Down she came – 'Her right foot touched,' said the commentator – and they both fell, multiplying as they hit the ice. They got up and continued their routine, but it wasn't quite the same. Canada's pair fell down too, although they were daring at first.

The Fat Lady skated out onto the ice. I couldn't help myself. It was one of the most important moments in my life, I should have been able to keep her away, but out she came in a pink skating costume, her head ornamented with swan's-down. With her was the thinnest man in the world. She smiled at the crowd, nobody smiled back, they didn't believe what they were seeing because she was whirling around the rink with exceptional grace, spinning like a top on her tiny feet, then the thin man lifted her and threw her and she floated up, up, she hung suspended . . . her secret was that although she was so large, she was very light, she was hollow, like a helium balloon, they had to keep her tethered to her bed or she'd drift away, all night she strained at the ropes . . .

There's something I have to tell you, I thought of saying during the commercial. But Arthur was rooting through the Family Bucket for an unconsumed piece, his fingers were covered with grease, and he had a little piece of chicken on his chin. Tenderly I wiped it off. This was a defenseless moment: how could I violate it? Arthur would need dignity.

A famous figure-skater praised margarine, unconvincingly, her eyes hypnotized by the cue cards. Then the competition came back on. The Fat Lady was still there, bobbing against the ceiling. The U.S. team scooted across the bottom of the screen like a centipede, but no one paid any attention, they were all distracted by the huge pink balloon that bobbed with such poor taste above their heads. . . . The Fat Lady kicked her skates feebly; her tights and the huge moon of her rump were visible. Really it was an outrage. 'They've gone for the harpoon gun,' I heard the commentator say. They were going to shoot her down in cold blood, explode her, despite the fact that she had now burst into song . . .

Why am I doing this? I thought, *Who's doing this to me?* 'I'm going to bed,' I told Arthur. I couldn't act, I couldn't even think straight; at any moment the Royal Porcupine might come hammering at the door, or scream some terrible message over the phone, the moment before he jumped, and I was paralyzed, there was nothing I could do. I could only wait for the ax to fall and, knowing him, it wouldn't even be an ax, it would be a rubber turkey from some joke shop; that or a huge explosion. He had no sense of proportion. Russia won the title, again.

The next morning I got the first of the phone calls. No voice, nothing, though I said hello three times. Just some breathing and a click. I knew it had to be him, but I was surprised by his lack of originality. The second phone call came at six, and the third one at nine. The next day I got a letter from him, or I felt it had to be from him. It was just a blank sheet of paper with a little woodcut of Death, holding a scythe, and the caption, MAY I HAVE THIS WALTZ? The letters and words had been cut from the Yellow Pages and pasted on; Death was from a magazine. I crumpled it up and threw it into the garbage. He'd certainly gone to work fast, but I wasn't going to let him see he was getting to me.

What I really expected was an anonymous letter to Arthur. I started censoring his mail, though to do it I had to get up early and make it to the downstairs hallway in time to snatch the mail as it came through the letter slot. I'd ponder the envelopes, and if the contents weren't obvious I would save them to steam open later. I did this for five days, but nothing happened. The phone calls continued. I didn't know whether Arthur got any: if so, he didn't mention it.

Everything depended on whether the Royal Porcupine wanted me back – if so, he wouldn't tell Arthur – whether he wanted to kill me, which I doubted, or whether he just wanted revenge. I thought of phoning to ask him; he might tell me the truth if I got him at the right moment. I should never have given him this power, the power to ruin my life; for it wasn't yet completely ruined, something could still be salvaged. I hinted to Arthur that it might be a nice change for us to move to another city.

On the sixth day I got another letter. The address was typewritten; there was no stamp, it must've been delivered by hand. Inside there was another cut-out message: OPEN THE DOOR. I waited half an hour and opened it. On the doorstep there was a dead porcupine with an arrow stuck into it. A label attached to the arrow read JOAN.

'Oh, for Christ's sake,' I said. If the landlord, or Arthur had found it first there would have been an uproar or at least an inquisition. I had to get rid of it in a hurry. It was a large porcupine, with extensive wounds, and it was already beginning to rot. I pulled it to the side of the porch and dumped it among the hydrangeas, hoping that none of the neighbors was watching. Then I went upstairs, got a green plastic Glad Bag, stuffed the procupine into it, and managed to get it into the garbage can labeled 'Tenants' in the hinged bin at the back. I pictured the Royal Porcupine unfreezing all his animals, one by one, and leaving them on my doorstep. He had a lot of them, they'd last for weeks.

I felt he was going too far. In the afternoon I went out to a pay phone and called him. 'Chuck, is that you?' I said when he answered.

'Who is this,' he said, 'Myrna?'

'You know bloody well it's not Myrna, whoever she may be,' I said. 'It's Joan, and I want you to know I don't think you're funny at all.'

'What do you mean?' he said. He really did sound surprised.

'You know,' I said. 'Your little notes. I suppose you thought you were being very clever, cutting the letters out of the Yellow Pages like that so I wouldn't know it was you.'

'No, I didn't,' he said. 'I mean, what notes? I've never sent you any notes.'

'What about that *thing* you left on my doorstep this morning? I suppose that wasn't one of your precious mangled animals.'

'What are you talking about?' he said 'You must be crazy. I haven't done a thing.'

'And you can stop phoning and breathing at me over the phone, too.'

'I swear to God I haven't called you once. Has someone been calling you?'

I felt defeated. If he was lying, that meant he was going to continue. If he wasn't, then who was doing it? 'Chuck, be honest,' I said.

'I thought I asked you not to call me that,' he said coldly. 'I haven't done anything to you. Why should I? You told me it's over. Okay, I was mad at the time, but I thought about it, and if you say it's over, it's over. You know me, here today, gone tomorrow. Easy come, easy go. Why should I worry?'

I was hurt that he was taking it so calmly. 'So that's really all I meant to you,' I said.

'Look, you were the one who backed out, not me. If you don't want to live with me, what do you expect me to do? Stick my head in the oven?'

'Maybe I was wrong,' I said, 'maybe we should talk about it.'

'Why prolong the agony?' he said. 'Besides, I've got company.'

Then he hung up on me. I slammed down the phone and jiggled the coin return; I felt I should definitely get my dime back, he owed me that. But from the black machine, no satisfaction.

I ran back to the apartment, closed myself into the bedroom, got out my typewriter, and shut my eyes, A tall man in a cloak, that was what I needed. All the time I'd been with the Royal Porcupine I hadn't written a word. Was this why my creatures seemed more real than usual, nearer to me, charged with an energy greater than I gave them?

But it was no good; I couldn't stop time, I could shut nothing out.

That night there was another call, and the next day another note: COME INTO THE FUNERAL PARLOR, with a picture of a spider glued to it. The day after that, a dead bluejay on the doorstep. That night I thought I heard someone climbing the fire escape.

I began to hesitate before picking up the phone. I thought of getting a shrill whistle, the kind you were supposed to use on obscene phone callers. Once I screamed 'Stop it!' into the phone before realizing it was only Sam. I wasn't afraid, exactly; I still thought of it as a prolonged and revengeful practical joke, and the Royal Porcupine – for I was still convinced he was the one – probably thought of it as a work of art. Maybe he was taking pictures of me opening the door and finding his smelly little tokens of esteem, maybe he'd put the prints on exhibition. I thought about going over to his warehouse and trying to reason with him . . .

The phone rang. I let it ring three times, then picked it up, prepared for the breathing and maybe even a threatening laugh. 'Hello,' I said.

'This is Joan Delacourt?' A man's voice, thick and odd somehow.

'Yes,' I said automatically, before I'd had time to think about this use of my maiden name. Everyone called me Joan Foster now.

'Joan. At last I have founded you.'

'Who is this?' I said.

'You cannot guess?' the voice said coyly. Now it was sounding familiar. 'This is your friend Mavis.' A flirtatious laugh.

'Paul,' I said. 'Oh, my God.'

'I have read about you in the newspaper,' Paul said, undaunted by my dismay, 'I have recognized the picture, though it is not so beautiful as you. I have been so happy about your success, you do not need to write the Gothic Romance any more, you are a true writer. I have read your book. It is promising, I think, for a first book, by a woman.'

Behind me I could hear Arthur coming in the door. I had to get Paul off the phone, but I didn't want to hurt his feelings. 'Paul,' I said, 'I must see you. I'd like to see you.'

'This, too, is what I desire,' said Paul. 'I know of a good restaurant . . . '

I met him at it the next day, for a late lunch. Zerdo's, the restaurant was called. There never used to be restaurants in Toronto with names like Zerdo's, but now there were many. It was like Paul to pick a restaurant with a name like some sort of drain cleaner, I thought as I opened the door. It was a narrow darkened room with tables covered with checked cloths and lamps in the shape of candles. Artificial grapevines festooned the walls. At the back of the room was a pass-through hatchway covered with fake brick wallpaper and hung with copper pans . . . The maître d' bustled toward me, short and alert, gold-tasselled menus under his arm.

'John,' I said involuntarily. I'd know that soft moustache anywhere . . .

'I beg your pardon, madame,' he said. 'My name is Zerdo.'

Paul was already walking toward me. Ceremoniously he kissed my hand and led me with gentle melancholy towards a table. When we were seated he did not speak, but gazed at me with reproachful eyes from behind his glasses, which were now, I noticed, tinted: a pale mauve.

'This used to be called the Bite-A-Bit,' I said. I didn't say I'd been the cashier, but there was my double behind the cash register, a heavy woman with bunned hair, wearing a black dress which showed her rippling elbows but not her bosom. One of my once-potential futures, in the flesh; Mrs Zerdo, no doubt. At this moment I envied her.

'Joan,' said Paul. 'Why have you fleed from me?' He'd taken the plastic rose out of its vase and was twirling it between his fingers, apparently unaware that it wasn't real. What could I say that would be appropriate?

'It was all for the best,' I said.

'No, Joan,' he said sadly. 'It was not. You know I have loved you. I have wished to marry you, once you were older; I planned that, I should have told you. Yet you run away from me. You have made me very unhappy.' He said this, yet I didn't altogether believe him. I noticed his suit, which was certainly a more expensive one than he'd once been able to afford; and he had an air of confidence that was new to him. The bitter, threadbare aristocrat had been blurred a little; superimposed on that was a layer of succesful businessman.

Zerdo appeared with the wine list. He was deferential to Paul, who ordered flawlessly. Paul took out a Gauloise, offered me one, and inserted one for himself in his cigarette holder, which was new and sumptuous.

'I am pleased I have discovered you,' Paul said, as we sipped our lemon soup. 'Now we will have to think what to do, as I see you have married.'

'Paul,' I said to change the subject, 'do you live here now? Have you moved to Canada?'

'No,' he said, 'but I am here often. On business. I am no longer with the bank since six years, I have another business. I am – ' he hesitated ' – importer.'

'What do you import?' I asked.

'Many things,' he said vaguely. 'Wood carvings, the chess sets and the boxes for cigarettes, from Czechoslovakia; garments from India, they are popular now, and from Mexico. It is helpful to have a knowledge of many languages. I do not speak all myself, but one can always arrange.' He didn't really want to talk about it. I remembered the revolver. Was that a slight bulge under his arm, could he possibly be wearing a shoulder holster? I thought, in rapid succession, of heroin, opium, atomic weapons, jewels and state secrets.

'I have extracted my mother,' he said, 'from Poland, but she has died.'

We talked about that, and about his daughter, during the moussaka.

'I read in the paper that your husband is some sort of a Communist,' he said when we'd reached the baklava. 'Joan, how could you marry a man like this? I have told you what they are like.'

'He's not exactly a Communist,' I said. 'It's hard to explain, but it's different here. Besides, it doesn't mean anything here, it's respectable, sort of. They don't *do* anything; they just have meetings and talk a lot, sort of like the Theosophists.'

'Talk is dangerous,' said Paul darkly. 'All such things begin by talk. They are good at talk, they are like the Jesuits. Poor child, this is how he made you marry him. You have had your brain washed out by him.

'No,' I said, 'it wasn't like that,' but Paul was convinced.

'I can tell you are very unhappy,' he said.

This was true enough, and I didn't deny it. In fact I was enjoying the sensation of all this sympathy lapping around me, like warm washcloths. I'd thought Paul would be angry with me, but he was being so nice. I drank another glass of wine and Paul ordered brandy.

'You can trust me,' he said, patting my hand. 'You were a child, you did not know your own mind. Now you are a woman. You will leave this man, you will divorce, we will be happy.'

'Paul, I can't leave,' I said. He swam before me in a haze of nostalgia. Was this my lost love, my rescuer? My eyes filled with tears, and so did my nose. I blotted myself with the table napkin. Any minute now I was really going to cry.

Paul's jaw tightened. 'He will not let you. I see,' he said. 'They are like that. If you tell him it is I you love, he will . . . But I have friends. If necessary I shall steal you.'

'No,' I said, 'Paul, you can't do that. That would be dangerous. Besides, people don't do things like that here.'

Paul patted my hand. 'Do not worry,' he said. 'I know what I am doing. I will wait, and then, at the right moment, I will strike.' His eyes gleamed; it was a challenge, he wanted to win.

I couldn't tell him I didn't want to be stolen; that would be too rude, and painful for him as well. 'Well,' I said, 'it's important that you don't tell anyone you've seen me. And you shouldn't phone ... Paul, did you phone me before, without saying anything?'

'Maybe once,' he said. 'I thought it was wrong number.' So it wasn't him.

We got up to leave. Paul took my arm. 'Do you still write Mavis Quilps?' I said, remembering. 'I guess you don't have to any more.'

'I continue to write them, as a recreation,' Paul said. 'It is soothing to the mind, after a hard day's work.' He paused for a moment, searched an inside pocket. 'Here,' he said. 'I have brought a gift, for you. You are a specialty. I am alone in my life, no one else would care. But I know you would like it.'

He handed me the book. *Nurse of the High Arctic*, it said on the cover. By Mavis Quilp. The pink-cheeked nurse smiled winsomely from the nimbus of her parka.

'Oh, Paul,' I said, 'thank you so much.' I was touched, ludicrously; it was like the end of the whale movie, he was so sad, so trusting, so hopeless, consolation was so impossible. I threw my arms around his neck and burst into tears.

Now you've done it, I thought as I sobbed against his shoulder. I had to stoop a little to do this. He was wearing Hai Karate shaving lotion, which made me cry even harder. How could I get out of it? I had been too encouraging, again.

Chapter Twenty-eight

Paul wanted to put me into a taxi. It was part of his image that I should go off in a taxi, but I said I wanted to walk, so he got into the taxi himself. I watched as he was swept away, north on Church Street in the glinting metal traffic. Then I started to walk home.

My eyes were still swollen and I was numbed and depressed. Paul's wish to rescue me was gallant but futile, as all gallantry now seemed to me futile. Besides, I didn't want to be rescued by him, but hadn't had the courage to tell him. Sullenly I would iron his boxer shorts and eat his caviar, in some tacky hideout, pretending to be happy and grateful; sullenly I would escape again, leaving him punctured and perhaps, this time, vengeful. I'd once thought I was in love with him. Maybe I had been.

'There's magic in love and smiles. Use them every day, in all you do, and see what wonderful things happen,' Brown Owl used to say chirpily, readng it from her little book. I'd believed that slogan, I'd believed that the absence of wonderful things happening had been due to my own failure, my insufficient love. Now it seemed to me that the name of a furniture polish could be substituted for 'love' in this maxim without at all violating its meaning. Love was merely a tool, smiles were another tool, they were both just tools for accomplishing certain ends. No magic, merely chemicals. I felt I'd never really loved anyone, not Paul, not Chuck the Royal Porcupine, not even Arthur. I'd polished them with my love and expected them to shine, brightly enough to return my own reflection, enhanced and sparkling.

At that moment it seemed to me impossible that anyone could ever really love anyone, or if they could, that anything lasting or fine would come of it. Love was the pursuit of shadows, and I was a shadow for Paul, doomed to flee before him, evanescent as a cloud. Some cloud, I thought, already my feet hurt. He probably didn't want me at all, he wanted the adventure of kidnapping me from what he imagined to be a den of fanged and dangerous Communists, armed to the teeth with brain-suction devices and slaughterous rhetoric, I in their midst bound hand and foot by jargon. Once he had me he wouldn't know at all what to do with me. He hadn't been able to live with me before, he couldn't stand the mess, and the years hadn't made me any neater. I was not the same as my phantom.

When I got home there was another anonymous note, something about coffins, but I scarcely glanced at it. I climbed the stairs to the apartment, slowly; I had a blister on one foot. I hoped Arthur would be there so I'd have at least the comfort of a familiar body; but he wasn't, and I remembered he'd said he'd be at a meeting. The apartment was empty and desolate, as it would be, I thought, without him. I'd better get used to it; any day now the Royal Porcupine would get tired of his game and escalate it.

I went into the bathroom, ran the tub full of warm water, added some Vitabath and climbed in with my Mavis Quilp. The bathroom had always been my refuge, it was the only room in the house, all the houses, where I could lock the door. I'd wallow in the tub like a steamy walrus while my mother cleared her throat discreetly outside the door, torn between the grunts and shouts of the body she refused to admit she possessed and her unwillingness to be explicit.

'Joan, what are you doing in there?'

Long pause. 'Taking a bath.'

'You've been in there for an hour. Other people might want to use the bathroom too, you should be more considerate.'

I covered myself with bubbles and submerged myself in *Nurse of the High Arctic*. Why had Sharon ever left her comfortable hospital in England to come up north where there were no conveniences and where the handsome doctor sneered at her every time she dropped a scalpel? She sped over the ice floe in her runaway dogsled, pursued on foot by the grouchy doctor. *Stop, you silly little fool. I can't, I don't know how.* I knew what would happen, I was familiar with Paul's style . . . Only when the doctor saw her upside down and covered with fur would he realize how much he loved her, and after that he would have to earn her love in return. He would have an accident, or she would have an accident, one or the other. Pure ice, pure snow, chaste kiss.

I longed for the simplicity of that world, where happiness was possible and wounds were only ritual ones. Why had I been closed out from that impossible white paradise where love was as final as death, and banished to this other place where everything changed and shifted?

The phone rang, but I let it ring. I wasn't going to get out of the bathtub and leave puddles on the floor to listen to someone breathe; I would stay here with Sharon and Doctor Hunter. *He touched her cheek, brushing away a strand of hair. Brusquely he told her that she should keep her hair pinned back: didn't she remember her training?* Seductive ringlets, tendrils and strands, they always featured in Paul's books, as in Milton's. *Sharon blushed and turned away to hide it.*

Three quarters of an hour later, as the helicopter with the rescued Eskimo was touching down (any moment now, the declaration, the embrace), as the water was getting tepid for the second time, I thought I heard someone in the next room. I listened, careful not to make a ripple: there were definite footsteps, crossing the main room and heading towards my bedroom.

I froze in the bathtub; I went rigid with fear. For a moment I lay there like a giant popsicle; visions of knife-wielding rapists, their fangs dripping blood, flashed before me, visions of burglars, dope-crazed and lethal, visions of perverts who would chop me into pieces and leave choice cuts in every trash bin in the city. There was no bathroom window. Perhaps if I stayed quiet he would simply take what he could find, which wouldn't be much, and leave the way he had come. I could have sworn I'd put the catch on the window that opened onto the fire escape, and he hadn't come in the door, it squeaked so much I would have heard it.

Slowly I eased myself out of the bathtub. I didn't pull the plug, it would've gurgled. I spread out the bath mat, then knelt on it and applied my eye to the keyhole. At first I could see nothing. The mysterious visitor was out of sight in the bedroom. I waited, and he crossed the doorway. His face was turned the other way, but he was short and he looked familiar.

It was Paul, I decided. I hadn't been expecting him quite so soon. There were some rummaging sounds, a few mutterings: what was he doing? He was supposed to be looking for me, not going through my closet. I felt like calling out, 'Oh, for heaven's sake, Paul, I'm in here.' I wrapped my torso in a bath towel; I'd have to go out and have a serious talk with him, apologize to him, tell him I was sorry but he'd minunderstood me, I was happy with my husband and the past was the past. He could hardly carry me off after that. Then we would become old friends.

I unlocked the door and padded in my bare feet across to the bedroom. 'Paul,' I said, 'I want to . . .'

The man turned around, and it wasn't Paul. It was Fraser Buchanan, in his tweed jacket with the leather patches and a trendy turtle-neck sweater, plus a pair of black gloves. He'd been going through my bureau drawers, and it was obvious from his thoroughness and air of method that this wasn't the first time he'd done this sort of thing.

'What are you doing in here?' I shouted at him.

I'd startled him, but he recovered quickly. He bared his teeth like a cornered chinchilla.

'I'm doing research,' he said, very cool. Obviously it wasn't the first time he'd been caught.

'I could have you arrested,' I said. I can't have looked too dignified: I was holding the towel together at the back.

'The fact is, I know a good deal more about you than you think. I know things I'm sure you would rather keep ... private. Just between us two.'

What had he found out? Who would he tell? *Arthur*, I thought. *Arthur will know*. My hidden selves, my other lives, unworthy. I couldn't let that happen.

'What?' I managed to squeak. 'What are you talking about?'

'I think you understand me well enough, Mrs Foster. Or should I say Miss Delacourt, Miss Louisa K. Delacourt, author of *Love Defied* and others?'

He'd got as far as my underwear drawer, then.

'I've read a number of your books,' he continued, 'though I didn't know at the time they were yours. They aren't bad, for that kind of thing. But they don't exactly go with *Lady Oracle*, do they? Wrong image, I should think. I don't expect your Women's Libber fans will be too overjoyed when they hear the news, though some other people I could think of might find it amusing. Not to mention the *Braeside Banner*. Those pictures of you are really fine. Tell me, how did you manage to lose all that avoirdupois?'

'What do you want?' I said.

'Well, that depends,' he said crisply, 'on what you've got to offer. In exchange, you might say.'

'Let me put on some clothes,' I said, 'and we'll talk it over.'

'I prefer you this way,' said Fraser Buchanan.

I was furious, but I was also frightened. He'd discovered at least two of my secret identities, and I was so confused at that point I couldn't remember whether I had any more. If I hadn't become a culture heroine it wouldn't have mattered quite so much, though I couldn't stand the thought of Arthur knowing about my previous life as Pneumatic Woman. And if he told the media people the truth about Lousia K. Delacourt, my brief interlude of being taken seriously would be over. Unpleasant as it had been, I'd discovered it was much better than not being taken seriously. I would rather dance as a ballerina, though faultily, than as a flawless clown.

I put on my apricot velvet gown, piled my hair on top of my head with a few seductive tendrils twining around my neck, and attached some dangly gold earrings. I put on makeup, I even put on some perfume. Something would have to be done about Fraser

Buchanan, but I hadn't yet figured out what. I decided to admire him. As I entered the living room, I smiled at him. He was sitting on the chesterfield with his hands on his knees, as if waiting for the dentist.

I suggested we go out for a drink, as there was nothing to drink in the apartment (a lie). He agreed readily, as I thought he would. He felt he had won and there was nothing to be discussed but the terms.

The bar he chose was the Fourth Estate. He hoped a lot of journalists would see him with me. I ordered a Dubonnet on the rocks with a twist of lemon, he a double Scotch. I offered to pay, but he didn't go for that.

'I also know about your little fling with that fraudulent artist, or poet, or whatever he calls himself,' he confided, leaning across the chic round mirror-topped table. 'I've been following you around.'

My stomach went cold. This was the thing I had feared the most. I'd been so careful; had Chuck told him? If he'd wanted to really hurt me, of course that's what he would've done.

'Everybody knows about that. Even my husband knows about *that*,' I said, with enough contempt to dismiss it as a negotiable item. 'The man practically issued press releases. He sold two of my shopping lists in a sealed envelope to a university; he swore they were love letters. He filched them from my purse. Didn't you know that?' Selling samples of my handwriting was something Chuck had often threatened to do – he needed the bread, as he put it – but as far as I knew he'd never done it.

Fraser Buchanan's face fell like a section of badly engineered land fill: if Arthur already knew, he could gain nothing by threatening to tell him.

'How did you get in?' I asked conversationally, to smooth over his confusion. I was interested, too: I'd met a lot of amateur conmen but never a professional. 'It couldn't have been the window over the fire escape.'

'No,' he said,'it was the one next to it. I swung myself across.'

'Really?' I said. 'That's quite a distance. And I suppose that was you phoning me and then not saying anything.'

'Well, I had to make sure you weren't there, so I could get in.'

'Sort of backfired though,' I said.

'Yes, but you would've found out sooner or later.'

He explained how he'd tracked down my maiden name, which

had never appeared in an interview, by combing the records of marriages. 'Were you really married by someone called Eunice P. Revele?' he said. Then he'd searched through high-school year-books until he'd found me. Matching me with Louisa K. Delacourt had been a guess, which he'd needed to substantiate by finding evidence. The Royal Porcupine had been the easiest; he'd also thought that was his ace in the hole, but to my relief he conceded it wasn't. 'Marriage isn't what it used to be,' he said with disgust. 'A few years ago that would've been worth a bundle. Now everybody tells everything, you'd think it was a competition.'

I asked him about the dead animals, also about the notes. 'Why would I do a think like that?' he asked with genuine surprise. 'There's no percentage in that. I'm a businessman.'

'Well, if you've been following me around, you might have seen who left them. The woodchucks and things.'

'I don't work in the mornings, love,' he said. 'Only at night, I'm a night person.'

We had another drink and then got down to brass tacks. 'What do you want out of all this?' I asked.

'Simple,' he said. 'Money and power.'

'Well, I don't have much money,' I said, 'and I don't have any power at all.'

But this he refused to believe. He hated celebrities, he felt they diminished him. All of them, however ephemeral, had money and power, according to him. Not only that, none of them had any talent really, at least not any more than the next fellow. Therefore they had got where they had through chicanery and fraud and they deserved to be relieved of some of their cash. He was especially contemptuous of *Lady Oracle* and of my publisher, and he was convinced that I'd got the book published by using my feminine wiles. 'He's always launching young unknown ladies, that man,' he said, during his fourth drink. 'With big pictures of them on the back of the book, just the face and neck and down to the tits. Flash in the bedpan, most of them. No talent.'

'You should take up literary criticism,' I said.

'What,' he said, 'and give up my practice? Doesn't pay enough.' He never used the word 'blackmail,' and he referred to the others he had the goodies on, as he put it, as his clients.

'Who else?' I said, my eyes wide and appreciative. I was letting him bask.

It was here that he made his mistake. He took out his black notebook, thereby letting me know of its existence. 'Of course, I can't tell you those things they'd rather people didn't know,' he said, 'same as I'll never tell yours. But just to give you an idea – ' He read out seven or eight names, and I was suitably impressed. 'Here's one, now,' he said. 'Clean as a whistle, you'd think. It took me six months on him. But it was worth it. Little boys' bottoms, that was his. All right if you like that sort of thing, I suppose. You can always find something if you keep at it long enough. Now, back to business.'

I had to have that notebook. My only hope was to keep him in the bar long enough to get him drunk and snitch it out of his jacket pocket. I'd noted which one it was in. Unfortunately, I was getting a little drunk myself.

After a long involved conversation, which got slower and more circuitous with every drink, we sawed off at twenty percent of my income. I'd have to send him duplicates of my royalty statements, he said, so he'd know I wasn't cheating. 'Think of me as a sort of agent,' he said. He had the same arrangement with several other authors.

As we got up to leave, he placed his hand discreetly on my ass. 'Your place or mine?' he said, lurching.

'Yours, by all means,' I said. 'I'm married, remember?'

It was a lot easier than I'd thought. I tripped him going up the steps to his fancy apartment building, and got the book while helping him up. I got into the elevator with him and waited till the door was closing. Then I slipped out and ran from the building. I fell down myself, once, ripping my hem, but it wasn't serious. I hopped into a taxi and that was that. Slick as television, almost.

Arthur was home when I got back. I could hear him typing away in his study, *rat-a-tat-tat*. I locked myself in the bathroom, took off my velvet dress, and went through Fraser Buchanan's notebook. Black leather binding, no name or title, gilt edges. The writing inside was tiny, like cockroach tracks. I scarcely bothered with the quite astonishing revelations he'd put down; I was looking, compulsively, for myself.

The book was organized like a diary, by dates. Useful items were starred; the rest was Buchanan's somewhat rambling notation. Most of the time he used only initials.

J.F. – 'celebrated' authoress of *Lady Oracle*. Met at party, pretentious artists. Built like a brick nuthouse. Red hair, dyed no doubt, big tits; kept pointing them at me. Played stupid, inane laugh, looked over her shoulder a lot. Underneath it a ball-stomper, could tell at once. Evasive about the book, should look into it. Married to Arthur Foster, writes for *Resurgence*. Pompous bugger.

And later:

Estimated income: ?? Not that much, but she can get some from Foster. *Check maiden name.

And later:

She's having it off with C. B. That's the most expensive fuck she'll ever have. The wages of sin is monthly installments to yours truly. *Hotel records. Get pictures if possible.

And even later:

*Louisa K. Delacourt.

He was systematic, all right. What did I ever say to offend him? I wondered. Was it hatred I was reading, or just hardheaded mercenary cynicism? Did I point my tits at him that night, or not? I supposed a short man would experience it that way. Was my laugh inane? He did hate me, I felt. I was a little hurt, as we'd just had a pleasant evening.

But it didn't matter, since I had the book and I intended to keep it. No doubt he would try to get it back; he'd be desperate, it was his living. It was also incriminating evidence: it was in his handwriting, it had his name on it, the address was inside the cover, it was undeniable. I was surprised no one had tried to steal it before. But then, he may not have told anyone else about it.

I tore out a choice page and sealed in into an envelope. I would send it to him in the morning, like the ear of a kidnap victim, just to let him know I had the book. I enclosed a note as well: *If anything happens to me the book is in good hands. One word from you and it goes to the police*. Stalemate, I felt.

I went to bed before Arthur did, but I lay awake long after he went to sleep, trying to undo the tangle that my life had become. At any moment Paul might swoop down on me, figurative sword in hand, and perpetrate some disastrous rescue that would ruin my life. Now Fraser Buchanan would be trying to get his book back. I'd have to think of a good place to hide it; a locker in the subway station, or maybe I could keep mailing it back and forth to myself ... no, that wouldn't do. I might get a safe-deposit box in a bank.

Malevolence was flowing towards me, around me, someone was sending me absurd but threatening notes, phoning me up and breathing; Fraser Buchanan accounted for only some of those calls. Someone was leaving dead animals on the doorstep, and if it wasn't the Royal Porcupine it was someone who knew about him. Who could possibly have found out? Perhaps one person was doing the animals, another the notes, a third the phone calls ... but I couldn't believe that. It had to be a single person, with a plan, a plot that had some end in view ...

Then all at once I knew. It was Arthur. The whole thing was Arthur. He'd found out about the Royal Porcupine, he must've known for some time. He'd been watching me all along, not saying anything; it would be like him not to say anything. But he'd made a decision about me finally, a pronouncement, thumbs down. I was unworthy, I would have to go, and this was his plan to get rid of me.

I thought about how he could have done it all. The anonymous letters would be easy. I could check our Yellow Pages to see if anything had been cut out, but he wouldn't be that careless. Most of the phone calls had been made when he wasn't home, though it was true that for some of them he'd been there. But he could have got a friend to help him. (Who?) The animals, anyone could find dead animals. Planting them on the doorstep would be more difficult, especially since I'd made a point of getting up first lately. But he could have put them there at night.

He was the one, he must be; he was working up to something and I didn't at all want to know what it was. The easy explanation would be that he'd gone crazy, in some very deep and undetectable way. But it didn't have to be that at all. Every man I'd ever been involved with, I realized, had had two selves: my father, healer and killer; the man in the tweed coat, my rescuer and possibly also a pervert; the Royal Porcupine and his double, Chuck Brewer; even

Paul, who I'd always believed had a sinister other life I couldn't penetrate. Why should Arthur be any exception? I'd known he had phases, but I hadn't suspected this completely different side to his personality; not until now. The fact that I'd taken so long to discover it made it all the more threatening.

Arthur was someone I didn't know at all. And he was right in the bed beside me. I was afraid now, almost afraid to move; what if he woke up, eyes glittering, and reached for me . . . ? For the rest of the night I listened to him breathe. He sounded so peaceful.

I had to get away, as quickly as possible. If I simply went to the airport and got on a plane, anyone at all would be able to trace me. My life was a snarl, a rat's nest of dangling threads and loose ends. I couldn't possibly have a happy ending, but I wanted a neat one. Something terminal, like scissors. I would have to die. But for this I needed help. Who could be trusted?

Chapter Twenty-nine

In the morning I waited till Arthur was out of the house.Then I phoned Sam.

'I have to see you,' I said, 'it's important.'

'What's up? he said. Marlene had answered the phone, and Sam sounded as if he was still asleep.

'I can't talk about it over the phone.' It was an article of faith with Sam that his phone was bugged by the CIA, or at the very least the Mounties, and he was probably right. Also, I wanted to sound paranoid enough from the very beginning to convince him.

'Should I come over?' he said, perking up.

'No,' I said. 'I'll meet you in front of Tie City on Bloor Street in half an hour.' Sam lived in the Annex, I knew he could make it if he rushed. I wanted him to rush; it would make him feel more urgent. Then I hung up, mysteriously.

'I'd thought very carefully about the story I was going to tell them, for of course it would be both of them; there was no chance that Marlene wouldn't come along too. The truth was out of the question, as usual. If I told them the truth they'd feel they couldn't help me, since according to the ideology merely personal problems weren't supposed to be very significant. If I could get each of them alone it would be different, but together they were each other's witnesses and potential accusers. I needed the right villains, persecuting me for a cause they'd consider important. I felt a little cheap about this. Sam, like most of the group members, was essentially honest, in a devious sort of way; whereas I was essentially devious, with a patina of honesty. But I was desperate.

I waited nervously in front of Tie City, looking at the ties in the window and glancing from time to time over my shoulder, until Sam and Marlene appeared. They'd actually taken a taxi, which gave me hope: ordinarily they never took taxis.

'Look normal,' I told them in a low, furtive voice. 'Pretend you're walking along the street.' We walked along the street, heading west, and I told them the place and time of the real meeting. 'I thought I saw one of them at the corner,' I said. 'Don't let yourself be followed.' Then we separated.

That afternoon at three-thirty we met in the Roy Rogers, the one on Bloor west of Yonge. I ordered a vanilla milk shake. Sam had a Roy with the works. Marlene ordered a Dale Evens.

We carried our trays to a round table beside a plate-glass window, through which we could see a small back yard with an enormous Coca-Cola billboard in it, boy and girl linking healthy eyes and swilling.

'You picked a great place,' Sam said. 'They'd never suspect this joint.'

'Did you know you can get authentic Trigger Shit by sending away for it?' Marlene asked.

'Authentic, balls,' Sam snorted. 'There's more of that around than pieces of the True Cross. Besides, the real Trigger was stuffed and mounted years ago.' Marlene looked put down.

I checked the underside of the table, as if for hidden mikes. Then I leaned toward them. 'They've found out about the dynamite.' I said.

Sam didn't say anything. Marlene rolled a cigarette. She'd taken to rolling them lately; the tobacco ends stuck out and flamed when she lit up, but she held the cigarette gamely in the corner of her mouth while she talked. 'Who has?' she said. 'How do you know?'

'I'm not sure,' I said. 'It could be the Ontario Provincial Police or the Mounties; maybe even the CIA. Anyway it's someone like that. When I went to move the car the day before yesterday I saw two men watching it. I didn't go near it, I just walked right by as though I had nothing to do with it. When I went back yesterday they were still there, or maybe it was two other men. That time I didn't even go down the street, I crossed over and went down a side street.'

'That means they haven't traced it to you yet.' Marlene said. 'Otherwise they wouldn't bother watching the car, they'd watch you instead.'

'They haven't *yet*,' I said. 'But they're going to. They'll trace me to the apartment; I gave that address when I bought the car. They'll get a description from the landlord. If they pick me up, they'll find out my real name and they'll get Arthur, and then they'll get you.'

Sam was shaken. His escape fantasy had come to life at last, and he didn't like it. Marlene, however, was very cool. Her eyes narrowed, partly because of the smoke. 'You think it's the Mounties?' she said.

'If we're lucky,' I said. 'If it is, they might never find me, and if they do at least we'd get a trial. But if it's the others, the CIA or maybe someone worse, they might just, you know, get rid of us. They always make it look like a suicide, or an accident.

'Holy shit,' Sam said. 'I'm sorry we got you into this. But it can't be the CIA, we're small potatoes.'

'I think you're wrong,' Marlene said. 'They hate nationalist organizations, they want to keep this country *down*.'

'Well, there's one good thing,' I said. 'Right now they can't trace it any further than that apartment, until they find out who I am.'

'We better get you out of the country,' Marlene said.

'Yes,' I said, perhaps a little too quickly. 'But I can't simply hop on a plane. If I disappear, they'll keep looking till they find me. I think we should arrange a sort of dead end for them.'

'What did you have in mind?' said Sam.

I gave it some thought. 'Well, I think we should stage my death; that way, when they start nosing around, they'll find out I'm dead and that will be that. There's not really anything to connect the rest of you with that car and the dynamite. We'll just leave it where it is and let them worry about it.'

They were both impressed by this idea, and we began discussing ways and means. Sam came up with a plan for a fake car accident, using a body mangled beyond recognition. He watched a lot of prime-time television.

'So where do we get the body?' Marlene asked, and that was the end of that.

Sam's face lit up. 'Hey ... what about a vat of lime sprinkled with your teeth? Nothing identifies you positively like your teeth. That's what they use in airplane crashes, to identify the victims. They'd think the rest of you was eaten away.'

'Where are we going to get my teeth?' I asked.

'You have them all pulled out, of course,' Sam said, a little hurt by my negative reaction. 'You can get a set of false ones, they're more hygienic anyway.'

'No,' I said. 'They'd torture the dentist. He'd tell them everything. I might consider one or two teeth,' I conceded.

Sam sulked. 'If you're serious about this, you have to do it right.'

'What I need is something very neat,' I said. 'What about this?' I pulled a newspaper clipping out of my purse. It was about a woman who had drowned in Lake Ontario, very simply, no frills. She had merely sunk like a stone, and her body had never been recovered. She'd made no attempt to catch the life preserver thrown to her. It was one of the first times, said the paper, that an inquest had been held and a death certificate issued with no corpse present. I sometimes clipped items like this out of the newspaper, thinking they might come in handy as plot elements. Luckily I'd saved this one.

'But it's been done already,' said Sam.

'They won't notice,' I said. 'At least I hope they won't notice. Anyway, it's my only chance.'

'What about Arthur?' Marlene asked. 'Shouldn't he know?'

'Absolutely not,' I said. 'Arthur can't act, you know that. He'll be interviewed by the police, he's sure to be, and if he knows I'm really alive he'll either be so phoney they'll know something's wrong or so calm and collected they'll think he did me in himself. He wouldn't convince anyone. We can tell him later, after it's all over. I know it's cruel, but it's the only way.' I went over this point with them several times; the last thing I wanted was Arthur on my trail.

Finally they agreed. In fact, they were flattered that I thought they'd be able to put on a much more convincing act than Arthur. 'Just don't overdo the grief,' I told them. 'Some guilt, but not too much grief.'

They thought I should have some forged documents to get out of the country with, but I said a friend of mine would take care of that, and the less they knew about it, the better. I was glad I'd kept my Louisa K. Delacourt passport and identification up to date.

Marlene said she had to go to a meeting, so Sam walked me to the subway. He was worried about something. Finally he said, 'Joan, are you sure about those men? Are you sure they were watching?'

'Yes, why?'

'They just aren't that inefficient. If they've been at it for two days, they'd have got to you by now.'

'Sam,' I said, 'I'm not really sure at all. Maybe it's them, maybe I'm mistaken. But that's not the only reason I want to get away.'

'What is it then?' said Sam.

'Promise you won't tell Marlene?' He promised. 'I'm being blackmailed.'

'You're kidding,' Sam said. 'What for?'

I wanted to tell him, I was about to tell him, but I thought better of it. 'It's not political,' I said. 'It's personal.'

Sam didn't push for details; he knew when to back off. 'I'm being blackmailed too,' he said. 'By Marlene. She wants to tell Don about us.'

'Sam, does she have to come along?'

'Yes,' he said. 'We need two witnesses. Anyway, she'll be terrific with the police. She's a terrific liar.'

'Sam, it's very good of you to do this for me,' I said. It was a lot to ask, I was beginning to see that. 'If you get into any real trouble, I'll come back and bail you out.'

He squeezed my hand reassuringly. 'It'll go like clockwork, you'll see,' he said.

'I didn't tell him about the other things, the dead animals and the phone calls and letters. That would be too complicated, I felt. Nor did I mention my suspicions about Arthur. Sam had known Arthur for a long time, and he wouldn't be able to believe he would do such things. He'd think I was imagining it.

The accident was to take place in two days, provided the weather held. I used the intervening time to make the arrangements. First I bought a skirt and blouse so I'd be wearing clothes on the plane that no one had ever seen me in. I went out to the airport, by subway and bus, and got a ticket to Rome, using my Lousia K. Delacourt identification. I said I was going on a four-week vacation. I bought the pink Mountie scarf and some dark glasses, changed into my new outfit in the ladies' can, covered up my hair, and got a Hertz Rent-A-Car, a bright-red Datsun. I said I'd be returning it to the airport in two days. I went to the ladies' can again, changed back to my old clothes and drove away.

I parked around the corner from our apartment, checked to make sure Arthur wasn't there, dug an old suitcase out of the cupboard, and packed a few essentials. I wrapped the suitcase up in brown paper and carried it like a parcel to the car, where I stowed it in the trunk.

The next morning I told Arthur I had a headache and was going to stay in bed for a while. I asked him to get me an aspirin and a glass of water. I thought he'd leave the house as soon as possible – he never liked it when I was sick – but to my surprise he hung around, brought me a cup of tea, and asked if he could do anything. I was touched: perhaps I'd misjudged him, perhaps I should tell him everything, it wasn't too late ... But he might be acting this way because he could tell I was up to something. I reminded him of the article he had to finish for *Resurgence,* and at last he left.

I jumped out of bed, put on a respectable dress, and stuffed my T-shirt and jeans into my oversized purse. Because of Arthur I was already three-quarters of an hour behind schedule. I drove the rented car east and went past the city and along the shore of Lake Ontario, looking for a spot where I could make a landing without running into a cliff or a crowd of people. I found a stretch of beach with some scrubby trees and a few picnic tables, which were empty. I hoped they'd stay empty; I thought they would, as it was a weekday in early June and the roadside families hadn't yet burst into full flower. I would leave the car here and rendezvous with it later. The trees would screen me as I washed ashore.

I drove back to the nearest pay phone, which was outside a service station, and called a taxi, explaining that my car had broken down and I was late for an appointment in the city. I described the spot and said I'd be standing beside a red Datsun. I drove back to my beach, locked the car, with my suitcase in the trunk and my ticket and Louisa K. identification in the glove compartment, and buried the car keys in the sand under the right front wheel. When the taxi came I took it to the Royal York Hotel, went in the front door and down to the lower level, changed into my T-shirt and jeans, crammed the dress I'd been wearing into my purse, and walked out the side door. The ferry dock was only a few blocks away. Sam and Marlene were already there.

'Were you followed?' Marlene asked.

'I don't think so,' I said. We rehearsed again the story they were to tell Arthur: they'd run into me on the street and on impulse we'd all decided to go sailing over at the Island. Sailing rather than canoeing, we felt: it was easier to fall off a sailboat, whereas if it was a canoe, we'd all have to tip into the lake, and I told them there was no reason for them to get wet, too.

We took the ferry to the Island. Marlene had brought a camera; she felt there should be a pictorial record showing me as happy and carefree, so I posed with Sam, then with Marlene, leaning against the railing of the ferry and grinning like a fool.

Once on the Island, we strolled up and down past the boat-rental places, trying to decide which outfit would be likely to be the least suspicious of us. we picked the most slovenly-looking one and were granted a boat without any trouble, five dollars down and the rest when we brought it back. It was quite small and the attendant said that really there should only be two people on it, but he'd stretch a point as long as we didn't take it out of the harbor.

'You know how to sail,' he said, more as a statement than a question.

'Of course,' I said quickly. The attendant went back inside his hutch and we were left alone with the boat.

Sam began to untie it briskly from the dock. We all got in and pushed out into the Toronto harbor, where other sailboats, their white wings flapping, were tacking competently back and forth.

'Now what?' I said.

'Now we just run up the sails,' Sam said. He undid various ropes and tugged at them, this way and that, until a sail began to move experimentally up the mast.

'You do know how to sail?' I asked him.

'Sure. I used to do it all the time, at summer camp.'

'How long ago was that?' Marlene asked.

'Well, I remember the basics,' he said defensively, 'but if you'd rather take over . . .'

'I've never been in a sailboat in my life,' Marlene said, with that shade of contempt women reserve for men who have been caught out in a fraudulent display of expertise. By this time we were moving steadily into the course of an island ferry.

'Maybe we should go back,' I said, 'and get a canoe.'

'We can't,' Sam said. 'I don't know how.'

We ended up with Marlene at the tiller, while Sam and I scrambled around, ducking the boom and trying to control the ropes which somehow in turn controlled the sails. This worked, after a fashion, but my spirits had plunged. Why had I concocted this trashy and essentially melodramatic script, which might end by getting us all killed in earnest? Meanwhile we wobbled across the Toronto harbour, past the causeway they seemed to be constructing out of dumped garbage, and out into the lake. With the boat more or less under control, I crouched on the deck, peering into my compact mirror and trying to cover my face with eye shadow from a pot of Midnight Blue. The blue face was Marlene's suggestion: that way, she said, my white face wouldn't be easily seen from the shore. It was for this reason too that I was wearing jeans and a blue T-shirt.

Outside the harbour it was windier, and there were real waves. We sped east with the wind behind us. My face was now blue enough, and I was scanning the shoreline, which looked quite different when seen from the water, trying to remember where I'd left the car.

'We're too far out,' I shouted to Sam, 'can't you get us farther in?' I could swim, but I was not a strong swimmer. I didn't want to have to float a mile on my back.

Marlene handed me Don's binoculars, which she'd thought to bring, that old Brownie training. She'd brought everything but semaphore flags. I scanned the shoreline with them and there were the sandbar and the picnic tables and, yes, the car, receding at a fast clip behind us.

'It's back there,' I called to Sam, pointing. 'How do we get back?'

'Tack,' Sam yelled, diving for a rope.

'What?'

'I'll have to take the tiller,' he screamed, and began to crawl back towards us.

'Oh, God, I just remembered something,' Marlene said; screeched rather, as otherwise we couldn't hear above the wind and the waves, which were beginning to look frightening. They had white foam streaks on them and were splashing over the sides of the boat.

'What?'

'Don . . . this will be all over the papers, and he'll know we were together.'

'Tell him you're just friends now!' I screamed.

'It won't work,' Marlene said, pleased that the thing she wanted revealed was going to be brought to light with no intervention by her; and in her despair or joy, she let go of the tiller. The boat swung, the sail collapsed, Sam ducked, and the flailing boom hit me in the small of the back and knocked me overboard.

I was unprepared and got a mouthful of unprocessed Lake Ontario water as I sank. It was much colder than I'd expected, and it tasted like stale fins and old diapers. I rose to the surface, coughing and gasping.

Sam had dropped the sails and the boat was wallowing uncertainly a little farther on. Marlene was yelling, 'Oh, my God,' very authentically, as if I really had fallen overboard and was drowning. She reached out her hands towards me, leaning dangerously, and called, 'Over here! Joan!' but Sam caught hold of her.

I couldn't climb back into the boat and do it again the right way; I would have to preceed from here. I made a feeble dive and attempted to swim under the boat, as we had planned. I was supposed to come up on the other side, where I would be out of sight from the shore in case anyone was watching, and this move was necessary as I'd spotted a family at one of the picnic tables. I made it on the second try, but Marlene and Sam were still looking on the side where I had disappeared: they seemed to have forgotten all about the plan. I tore the binoculars off my neck – they were weighing me down – and attempted to heave them into the boat, with no success; they sank forever. Then I remembered my dress, which was in my bag, stowed in the bow. 'My dress,' I yelled, 'remember to ditch it,' but they'd drifted downwind from me and didn't hear. They were trying to regain control of the boat.

I spat out more of the lake and lay back as flat as I could; if there's one thing I knew how to do it was float. I pointed myself towards the shore and kicked my feet under the water; I hoped I was wafting unobtrusively toward the sand spit, helped by the waves, which broke occasionally over my head. We had bungled, but that wasn't so bad. It would look better than if I had simply dived off the boat. I stared up at the blue sky with its white drifting clouds and concentrated on the next move.

Luckily I ran aground out of sight of the picnic tables, which were screened by the clump of bushes. I was only about five hundred yards from where I should have been. I pulled myself onto the shore and lay there, catching my breath, while orange peels, dead smelts and suspicious-looking brown lumps eddied around me, sucked in and out by the waves. My hair was full of sand and little pieces of seaweed. When I was ready I squelched as quietly as I could along the shore and crouched behind the bushes. My car was on the other side of them, I knew, but so was the picnicking family. I couldn't risk getting close enough to watch them, but I could hear the whining of the children and the grunts of the father.

I lurked in the underbrush for at least half an hour, dripping and shivering and avoiding the poison ivy and the drying mounds of human shit and melting toilet paper, the wads of crumpled sandwich wrap, bits of salami and old pop bottles, and wondering whether they were going to stay all day and if so whether I would miss my plane. Finally I heard the sound of a car motor and the crunch of wheels on gravel.

I gave them time to get away, then walked to the car, dug the keys out from where I'd buried them, took my suitcase from the trunk and changed into my skirt and blouse in the back seat, covering my wet hair with the Mountie scarf. My face in the rearview mirror looked startling; genuinely drowned, almost. I wiped the blue eye shadow off with Kleenex, which I threw into the bushes. I wrung out my jeans and T-shirt, rolled them into a ball, stuffed them into the green plastic Glad Bag which I'd brought for this, and packed the bag at the bottom of the suitcase. As I drove off I caught a glimpse of Marlene and Sam; they'd got the sail back up but hadn't managed to turn around, and they were scudding towards Kingston with all sails set.

I made it to the airport, returned the rent-a-car, and caught the plane with twenty minutes to spare. Sitting on the plane waiting for it to take off was the worst part; I couldn't quite believe that I hadn't been followed. But I was safe.

PART FIVE

Chapter Thirty

What price safety, I asked myself. I was sitting on the balcony in my underwear, covered with towels, taking a steamy sunbath in the middle of nowhere. The Other Side was no paradise, it was only a limbo. Now I knew why the dead came back to watch over the living: the Other Side was boring. There was no one to talk to and nothing to do.

Maybe I really did drown, I thought, and this whole thing, the hours on the plane – I'd watched *Young Winston*, without the earphones – the Hertz Rent-A-Car, the flat, my trip to Rome for the hair dye, was a kind of joke perpetrated by the afterlife. The soul sticks around the body for a while after death because it's confused, or that's what the Spiritualists said. In that case I should've been hovering somewhere near the oily surface of Lake Ontario, slightly east of Toronto Island, not allowing for the currents. Or they'd fished me out, I was unidentified, I was lying on a public slab; or I'd been cut up for spare parts and this panorama was going on because some other body got my eyes. My entire life didn't flash before me the way it was supposed to, but it would, I was always a late bloomer.

Learn to live in the present, take life as it comes, that's what they told you in the improve-your-head manuals. But what if the present was a washout and the life to come was a bog? I was feeling marooned; the impulse to send out messages, in bottles or not, grew every day. *I am still alive. Stuck here, have not sighted a ship for days. Am tired of talking to the local flora and fauna and the ants. Please rescue.* I was here, in a beautiful southern landscape, with breezes and old-world charm, but all the time my own country was embedded in my brain, like a metal plate left over from an operation; or rather, like one of those pellets you drop into bowls of water, which expand and turn into garish mineral flowers. If I let it get out of control it would take over my head. There was no sense trying to get away, I'd brought them all with me, I could still hear their voices, murmuring like a faraway but angry mob. It was too late to rearrange the furniture, I couldn't keep them out.

Where was the new life I'd intended to step into, easily as crossing a river? It hadn't materialized, and the old life went on without me, I was caged on my balcony waiting to change. I should take up a hobby, I thought, make quilts, grow plants, collect stamps. I should relax and be a tourist, a predatory female tourist, and take snapshots and pick up lovers with pink nylon ties and pointy shoes. I wanted to unclench myself, soak in the atmosphere, lie back and eat the flapdoodles off the tree of life, but somehow I couldn't do it. I was waiting for something to happen, the next turn of events (a circle? a spiral?). All my life I'd been hooked on plots.

I wondered whether Arthur had gotten my postcard yet. Would he join me, would we start again, would there be a fresh beginning, a new life? Or would he still be angry, had he really been the one ...? Perhaps I should never have sent that postcard. On the other hand, he might just tear it up, ignore my plea for rescue.

I lay back in my chair and closed my eyes. There was the vegetable man standing in the doorway, his arms full of, what else, vegetables; overgrown zucchinis, artichokes, onions, tomatoes. He smiled, I ran over to him, he crushed me in his shortsleeved olive arms, there was tomato juice all over the floor, we slipped in it and tumbled in a heap among the squashed zucchinis, it was like making love with a salad, crisp and smooth at the same time. But it wouldn't be like that, he'd appear in the doorway and instead of running over to him I'd remember my underwear draped on the chairback. 'Excuse me while I pick up a few things.' What would he think of me? I'd scuttle around the room, gathering, concealing. 'Won't you have a cup of tea?' Incomprehension. His smile would fade. What did I ask him here for anyway? And besides, he would tell everyone in the village, the men would leer and creep around my house at night, the children would throw stones.

I sat up in the plastic chair and opened my eyes. It was no use, I was jumpy as a flea on a skillet, I couldn't even have a sexual fantasy without anxiety. I needed a drink and I was out of Cinzano. And the children were already throwing stones; yesterday one had almost hit me.

I got up and wandered into the flat. I still had no routine, and there seemed less and less reason to do anything at any given time. I went into the kitchen, shedding towels along the way. I was hungry, but there was nothing to eat except some cooked pasta, drying out already, and a yellowing bunch of parsley in a glass of water on the windowsill. There was something to be said for refrigerators. Although they inspired waste, they created the illusion that there would always be a tomorrow, you could keep things in them forever. . . . Why had the media analysts never done any work on refrigerators? Those who had refrigerators surely perceived life differently from those who didn't. What the bank was to money, the refrigerator was to food. . . . As these thoughts dribbled through my head I began to feel that my whole life was a tangent.

I noticed that something was wrong with the ants. I examined their saucer of sugar-water: I'd forgotten to add water and the solution had thickened to a syrup.. Some of the ants were nibbling at the edges but others had ventured out onto the surface and were trapped, like saber-toothed tigers in the tar pits. Now they were dead or waving their antennae feebly. I tried to rescue the still-living ones with a matchstick, fishing them out and leaving them on the side of the saucer; but mostly it was no use, they were hopelessly glued. I was always bad with pets. *SOS*, I wrote in sugar-water. *Do something.*

I went back into the main room to put on one of my baggy dresses. I no longer needed the scarf with the pink Mounties: I'd dyed my hair the day after I'd gone to Rome, and it was now mud brown. It had none of the promised sparkling highlights. In fact it looked terrible. Why hadn't I bought a wig instead? I knew why not, they were too hot, I'd cook my head. But a nice grey wig would've looked better than the hair dye.

I walked up the hill to the market square. The road was scattered with handbills; perhaps there was an election going on, I'd heard sound trucks winding up to the square almost every day, playing catchy tunes and broadcasting slogans. I was outside it though, I was a foreigner, and there was something beyond that, something wrong. I was passing through a corridor of hostile eyes, the old black-draped women with their sausage legs no longer returned my *bongiorno*, they didn't even nod, they stared through me or averted their eyes. One put her hand over the eyes of the little girl sitting beside her and made the sign of the cross. What had I done, what taboo had I violated?

I went to the *macelleria* and pushed in through the many-colored plastic streamers that covered the entranceway like seaweed. The butcher and his wife were a comforting couple, round as dumplings, both of them, wrapped in big white aprons and smeared with blood. The trays in the glass display case weren't filled ostentatiously like those in the butcher shops in Toronto. What they sold was scarce enough: a few small pieces of veal-like beef, a lone organ: liver, a heart, a kidney or two; three or four oval white objects that I suspected of being testicles. Usually the butcher and his wife would lift, offer, suggest incomprehensible things, beaming all the while

But today they weren't beaming. When they saw me come in their faces went still and watchful. Was I making this up or did they seem a little afraid of me? They didn't help me out with the terminology the way they usually did, and I was reduced to pointing. Even though I bought five tiny squares of tissue-paper beef, an extravagant number, they weren't mollified. And I couldn't even ask them what I'd done to offend or frighten them like this. I didn't know the words.

To the bakery, the grocery store, the vegetable stand, money dripping from my wounded purse, and it was the same, something was wrong. Had I committed some crime? I scarcely had the courage to walk over to the post office, as I knew the policemen would be there. But I'd done nothing, I told myself, it must be a misunderstanding of some kind. It would be cleared up later. I would ask Mr Vitroni about it.

'Delacourt,' I shouted bravely at the post office. There was no change in the woman behind the counter, since she was never friendly anyway. Soundlessly she extended a fat envelope. Brown manilla, Sam's typewriter.

Outside I tore it open. It was stuffed with newspaper clippings, arranged neatly in order, the oldest one on top, and a typed note from Sam. 'Congratulations. You've become a death cult.' I thumbed quickly through the clippings. SUICIDE SUSPECTED IN AUTHORESS DEATH. INVESTIGATION CALLED FOR, the top one read, and it went on from there. Some had the photo off the back of *Lady Oracle*, some the grinning boatside snapshots Marlene had taken on the day of my death. There was a lot of talk about my morbid intensity, my doomed eyes, the fits of depression to which I was apparently subject (though not a word about the Royal Porcupine, nothing about Louisa Delacourt ... Fraser Buchanan was keeping a low profile). Sales of *Lady Oracle* were booming, every necrophiliac in the country was rushing to buy a copy.

I'd been shoved into the ranks of those other unhappy ladies, scores of them apparently, who'd been killed by a surfeit of words. There I was, on the bottom of the death barge where I'd once longed to be, my name on the prow, winding my way down the river. Several of the articles drew morals: you could sing and dance or you could be happy, but not both. Maybe they were right, you could stay in the tower for years, weaving away, looking in the mirror, but one glance out the window at real life and that was that. The curse, the doom. I began to feel that even though I hadn't committed suicide, perhaps I should have. They made it sound so plausible.

My next thought was: I can never go back now. Here were all these people spewing out words like flowers on a coffin, collecting their usual fee for doing so, and being very serious. If I rose from the dead, waltzed back and announced that it was all a deception, what were they supposed to do? They'd be stuck with egg on their faces, they'd hate me forever and make my life a nightmare. Women scorned to the contrary, nothing matched the fury of a deceived death cultist. It would be like the reappearance of James Dean, thirty years older and pot-bellied, or Marilyn walking down Yonge Street in curlers, having put on fifty pounds. All those who were expressing regret and remembering my ethereal beauty would be extremely upset if I were to materialize in the flesh. I'd have to stay safely buried on the Other Side, perhaps forever. In fact, my death was becoming so profitable to so many people that they'd probably have me bumped off and cemented and sunk in the Toronto harbour the moment I stuck my snout above water.

What had become of my neat, quiet, well-planned death by misadventure? Evidence had come to light – whose? how? – that I did not fall, but jumped. This was ridiculous. It *was* true I had meant to jump, but in fact I fell, prematurely. And some reporter got to Marlene, who overdid it. She said they threw me a life preserver but I made no attempt to reach it and went down with barely a struggle. Of course there wasn't any life preserver, she shouldn't have invented one. But who had interviewed my father, and why did he tell them I was a strong swimmer? He never saw me swim in his life. I wasn't a bad swimmer. I learned in high school gym class, it was one of the sports I didn't mind, because I was mostly out of sight. My specialty was floating on my back, that and the breast stroke. I wasn't much good at the crawl.

So they thought I jumped on purpose, refused the life preserver, and sank intentionally, and there was nothing I could do to prove them wrong, though an anonymous informant had volunteered the information that it wouldn't have been like me to commit suicide, I loved life. And it wasn't like me, at all.

Well, I thought, maybe I really did want to die or I wouldn't have pretended to do it. But that was wrong. I pretended to die so I could live, so I could have another life. They were being perverse and it made me angry.

I walked back down the hill, carrying my bundles. I loved life, it said this right in the newspaper. So why would I want to do a thing like that?

Chapter Thirty-one

I decided to ignore my suicide, since there was nothing I could do about it. For the next three days I tried to work. I sat in front of the typewriter with my eyes closed, waiting for the plot to unroll itself effortlessly behind my eyes, like a movie. But something was blocking it, there was static. I'd taken Charlotte through several narrow escapes: twice she'd been on the verge of rape, and she'd almost been murdered once (arsenic in the Spotted Dick pudding, causing severe vomiting). I knew what had to happen. Felicia, of course would have to die; such was the fate of wives. Charlotte would then be free to become a wife in her turn. But first she would have a final battle with Redmond and hit him with something (a candelabrum, a poker, a stone, any hard sharp object would do), knocking him out and inducing brain fever with hallucinations, during which his features and desires would be purified by suffering and he would murmur her name. She would nurse him with cold compresses and realize how deeply she loved him; then he would awaken in his right mind and propose. That was one course of action. The other would be a final attempt on her life, with a rescue by Redmond, after which he would reveal how deeply he loved her, with optional brain fever on her part. These were the desired goals, but I was having trouble reaching them.

For one thing, Felicia was still alive, and I couldn't seem to get rid of her. She was losing more and more of her radiant beauty; circles were appearing beneath her eyes, lines between her brows, she had a pimple on her neck, and her complexion was becoming sallow. Charlotte, on the other hand, had roses in her cheeks and a spring in her step, even though she was afraid to walk beneath the parapets because of the falling objects. The life of danger agreed with her; also, her sixth sense told her she would be awarded the prize, the prizes in fact, for in addition to Redmond she would get the emeralds, the family silver, deeds of land stowed away in attics, she would rearrange the furniture and give Felicia's clothes to the Crippled Civilians, she would sack the evil servants like Tom the coachman and reward the virtuous ones like Mrs Ryerson and generally throw her weight around. All she had to do was stick it out until the murderer's hands were actually around her throat.

Charlotte stood looking out the Library window. Two figures, a man's and a woman's were entering the maze. She was trying to see who they were; not that she was nosy, just inquisitive. It went along with her pluck. She heard a noise behind her, and turned. Redmond was standing in the doorway; his left eyebrow was lifting. The other one, the right, remained stationary, but the left eyebrow was definitely lifting, appraisingly, lustfully, ruthlessly, causing hot flushes to sweep over her, while the eye beneath it slid like a roving oyster over her blushing countenance. Did Redmond esteem her, or was he filled with a mere animal lust? She could not tell.

Meanwhile Felicia was lying in the shrubbery of the maze. She knew the maze was dangerous, but this very fact excited her. Her skirt was hiked to her waist, so was her petticoat, and her fichu was disarranged. She'd been making love with Otterly, who lay exhausted beside her, his left hand on her right breast, his nose against her ear, his ear in her long red hair. Redmond suspected nothing, which was fatiguing. Felicia wished he would suspect something; then he would realize how he'd been neglecting her. Although Otterly was ardent and inventive, he was also a bit of a fool. Felicia sighed and sat up, disengaging Otterly's hand, nose and ear.

Then she uttered a gasp of surprise. There was a hole in the shrubbery, and watching her through this hole was an eye. Beneath the eye was a ratlike smile, broadening into a soundless laugh.

'Master'll want to know about this, I'm thinking,' said the voice of Tom the coachman, gloatingly.

This had happened before, and Felicia knew it meant she would have to bribe him. But she no longer felt like it. She half hoped Redmond would find out; then at least she would know where things stood.

That night she sat in front of her vanity table, brushing her extravagant red waist-length hair and looking at her reflection in the mirror. She had dismissed her maid. She was very sad; she suspected Redmond no longer loved her. If he did, she would give up her present mode of life and go back to being a loving, conscientious wife. Charlotte would be dismissed and Felicia would stop having affairs with the neighboring gentry. 'Do you love me?' she asked him every evening when at last he entered the room, swaying slightly from the effects of too much port and brooding over the elusive Charlotte. She rubbed up against him like a jaguar. She was wearing only a chemise. She and Redmond had separate rooms, naturally; but Redmond hadn't yet given up his nightly visit to hers, he was not yet that blatant about his wish to be rid of her. Besides, he took a certain delight in tantalizing her.

'Do you love me?' she asked; she usually had to ask twice, because Redmond didn't hear her the first time, or would pretend he didn't. 'Of course,' he answered with a slightly bored drawl. He was familiar with her chemise, it no longer impressed him the way it used to. She smelled, these days, of wilted hyacinths, a smell of spring decay, not mellow like the decay of autumn but a smell like the edges of swamps. He preferred Charlotte's odor of faintly stale lavender.

'What would I do without you?' Felicia said adoringly.

'You'd inherit a lot of money,' Redmond replied with amusement. He was turned towards the window, raising his left eyebrow at himself in the reflection on the pane. An unkind observer might have said he was practicing. He was thinking of Charlotte. He liked making her blush. He'd become tired of the extravagance of Felicia: of her figure that spread like crabgrass, her hair that spread like fire, her mind that spread like cancer or pubic lice. 'Contain yourself,' he'd said to her, more than once, but she couldn't contain herself, she raged over him like a plague, leaving him withered. But Charlotte now, with

her stays and her particular ways, her white flannelette face, her blanched fingers . . . her coolness intrigued him.

Or so Felicia imagined, torturing herself, gnawing on her nether lip, that full, sensuous lip Redmond once loved to caress. Tonight he was later than usual. Felicia snuffled, wiping the tears with the back of her free hand. She was too distraught to bother with the niceties of a handkerchief. Perhaps she could foresee that life would be arranged for the convenience of Charlotte, after all, and that she herself would have to be disposed of. A tear rolled down her cheek, tiny electric sparks jumped from the ends of her hair. In the mirror there were flames, there was water, she was gazing up at herself from beneath the surface of a river. Whe was afraid of death. All she wanted was happiness with the man she loved. It was this one impossible wish that had ruined her life: she ought to have settled for contentment, for the usual lies.

I opened my eyes, got up from the typewriter, and went into the kitchen to make myself a cup of coffee. It was all wrong.

Sympathy for Felicia was out of the question, it was against the rules, it would foul up the plot completely. I was experienced enough to know that. If she'd only been a mistress instead of a wife, her life could have been spared; as it was, she had to die. In my books all wives were eventually either mad or dead, or both. But what had she ever done to deserve it? How could I sacrifice her for the sake of Charlotte? I was getting tired of Charlotte, with her intact virtue and her tidy ways. Wearing her was like wearing a hair shirt, she made me itchy, I wanted her to fall into a mud puddle, have menstrual cramps, sweat, burp, fart. Even her terrors were too pure, her faceless murderers, her corridors, her mazes and forbidden doors.

Perhaps in the new life, I thought, the life to come, I would be less impressed with capes and more with holes in stockings, hangnails, body odors and stomach problems. Maybe I should try to write a real novel, about someone who worked in an office and had tawdry, unsatisfying affairs. But that was impossible, it was against my nature. I longed for happy endings, I needed the feeling of release when everything turned out right and I could scatter joy like rice all over my characters and dismiss them into bliss. Redmond would kiss Charlotte so that her eyeballs rolled right back into her head, and then they could both vanish. When would they be joyful enough, when would my life be my own?

There was no coffee, so I made myself some tea. Then I gathered up my underwear from the places where it was growing, under the table, off the chairbacks, and put it all into the washbasin. I scrubbed it with a bar of stringy green soap in the reddish water, which had a faint odor of iron, an odor too of subterranean gas; the toilet was becoming more sluggish every day. Bad drains, bad dreams, maybe that was why I hadn't been sleeping well.

I wrung the underwear out; it felt gritty. There were no clothespins, so I draped it over the balcony railing. Then I took a bath, though the water was pink and unpleasantly like warm blood. I dried myself off, put on my last set of underwear, and wrapped myself in towels. I made another cup of tea and went out to the balcony. I sat in the plastic chair, head back, eyes closed behind my dark glasses, and tried to empty my mind. Brainwash. From the valley came a monotonous tinny sound, a boy banging on a metal plate to frighten birds. I grew sodden with light; my skin on the inside glowed a dull red.

Below me, in the foundations of the house, I could hear the clothes I had buried there growing themselves a body. It was almost completed; it was digging itself out, like a huge blind mole, slowly and painfully shambling up the hill to the balcony . . . a creature composed of all the flesh that used to be mine and which must have gone somewhere. It would have no features, it would be smooth as a potato, pale as starch, it would look like a big thigh, it would have a face like a breast minus the nipple. It was the Fat Lady. She rose into the air and descended on me as I lay stretched out in the chair. For a moment she hovered around me like ecto-plasm, like a gelatin shell, my ghost, my angel; then she settled and I was absorbed into her. Within my former body, I gasped for air. Disguised, concealed, white fur choking my nose and mouth. Obliterated.

Chapter Thirty-two

Redmond was pacing on the terrace. It was night; the wind was sighing through the shrubberies; Redmond was in mourning. He was relaxed, at peace with himself: now that Felicia was dead, drowned in an unfortunate accident when he surprised her fornicating in a punt with his half brother on the River Papple, his life would be quite different. He and Charlotte had secret plans to marry, though because of the possibility of gossip they would not make these public for some time. He gazed fondly up at her lighted window. Once they were married he would renounce his former wild and melancholy ways and settle down. She would play the piano and read the newspaper to him as he reclined beside a cheerful fire, wearing a pair of slippers embroidered by her own hand. They would have children, for now that his brothr was dead, struck on the head by the overturning punt, he needed a son and heir to succeed him as the rightful Earl of Otterly. It had all worked out rather well, really. Strange that they never recovered Felicia's body, though he had had the riverbed dragged.

The shrubberies stirred and a figure stepped out from them, blocking his path. It was an enormously fat woman dressed in a sopping-wet blue velvet gown, cut low on the bosom; her breasts rose from the bodice like two full moons. Damp strands of red hair straggled down her bloated face like trickles of blood.

'Redmond, don't you know me?' the woman said in a throaty voice which, he recognized with horror, was Felicia's

'Well,' he said with marked insincerity, 'I certainly am glad you didn't drown after all. But where have you been for thse last two months?'

She evaded this question. 'Kiss me,' she said, passionately. 'You don't know how much I've missed you.'

He gave her a perfunctory peck on her white, clammy brow. Her hair smelled of waterweed, of oil and decaying food and dead smelts. He wiped his lips surreptitiously on his shirt sleeve. Hope guttered out in his breast like an expiring candle: what would he do now?

He noted with repugnance that the woman who called herself Felicia was undoing the fastenings of her dress; her fingers fumbled at the hooks. 'Remember when we were first married?' she whispered. 'And we used to slip out here at night, an embrace by the light of the full moon. . . .' She looked at him with an inviting simper, which turned slowly to an expression of heartbreaking anguish as she read the disgust in his face.

'You don't want me,' she said brokenly. She began to cry, her large body shaken by uncontrollable sobs. What could he do? 'You didn't want me to come back at all,' she wept. 'You're happier without me . . . and it was such an effort, Arthur, to get out of that water and come all this way, just to be with you again. . . .'

Redmond drew back, puzzled. 'Who is Arthur?' he asked.

The woman began to fade, like mist, like invisible ink, like melting snow . . .

I could hear footsteps coming down the gravel path, at a great distance, as though through layers of cotton wool. I was still half asleep; I struggled out of the chair and all the towels fell off. I snatched one up, retreating toward the door, but it was too late, Mr Vitroni was coming around the corner, along the balcony. He had on all his felt pens; under his arm he carried a brown paper parcel.

I backed against the railing, holding the towel in front of me. His eye took in the line of dripping underwear. He gave his little bow.

'I wish I do not disturb?' he said.

'Not at all,' I said, smiling.

Your lightbulbs are shining?'

'Yes,' I said, nodding.

'The water is coming out?'

'The house is just fine,' I assured him, 'I'm having a wonderful time. A wonderful vacation. The peace and quiet is marvelous.' I wished very much that he would go away, but it looked as if he was going to sell me another painting. I would be powerless to resist it, I knew.

He looked over his shoulder, almost fearfully, as if he was afraid of being seen. 'We will go inside,' he said. Seeing me hesitate, he added, 'There is something I must tell you.'

I didn't want to sit at the table with him in a towel and my underwear; somehow it was more indecent inside than on the balcony. I asked him to wait, went into the bathroom, and put on one of my dresses.

When I came out he was sitting at the table with the paper parcel across his knees.

'You have been to Roma?' he asked. 'You like it?'

I began to feel exasperated. Surely he hadn't come here to ask about tourist sites. 'It's very nice,' I told him.

'Your husband, he likes it as well?'

'Yes, I guess so,' I said. 'He did like it a lot.'

'It is a city one must visit many times to know well, like a woman,' Mr Vitroni said. He took out some tobacco and began to roll himself a cigarette. 'He will come soon?'

'I certainly hope so,' I said with a hearty laugh.

'I as well wish that he will come soon. It is not good for a woman to be alone. Others will talk of it.' He lit his cigarette, brushed the unused shreds of tobacco back into the packet, and replaced it in his pocket. He'd been watching me carefully.

'This is for you,' he said. He handed me the package.

I was expecting another black velvet painting, but when I took off the string and unfolded the paper, there were my clothes, the jeans and T-shirt that I'd buried so carefully under the house. They were neatly washed and pressed.

'Where did you get these?' I asked. Maybe I could deny they were mine.

'My father, he has seen them in the earth, down there where are the *carciofi*. He has seen someone was digging. He thinks there is mistake, to bury such clothes, which are not old. He does not speak English, so he ask me to give them to you back. My wife washes them.'

'Tell him thank you very much,' I said. 'Thank your wife also.' There was no way I could explain, though he obviously wanted an explanation. He waited; we both looked at my folded clothes.

'People talk of this,' he said finally. 'They do not understand why you have put your clothes beneath the house. They know of this. They do not know why you have cut off your so beautiful hair, that everyone remembers from the time you are here before, with your husband; you wear always the dark glasses, like a bat, and you have taken another name. These are things nobody understands. They make the sign' – he extended two fingers – 'so the evil eye which you have will not make them sick or give them bad luck as well. I myself do not believe this,' he said apologetically, 'but the older ones. . . .'

So they knew me. Of course they knew me, they remembered everything for five thousand years. What stupidity, to have come back here.

'They ask me to tell you to leave,' he went on. 'They think your bad luck will come on me, my wife says that.'

'I suppose they think I'm a witch,' I said, laughing.

But Mr Vitroni didn't laugh; he was warning me, it wasn't funny.

'It would be better if your husband also would come,' he said gravely. 'Also, a man is here this morning. He asks for you. He does not know the name you gave me, but he says, a lady, so tall, with red hair, and I know it is you.'

'What?' I said, too quickly. 'Who was it?'

He shrugged, studying my face. 'I do not think it is your husband. Also he would know where you are living.' He could tell I was upset. If he was right and it wasn't Arthur, who was it?

'What did he look like?' I said. 'What did you tell him?'

'I think I should tell you first,' he said slowly. 'I tell him you are in Roma, you will come back after two days. At that time, I tell him, perhaps I can help him. But I say to him perhaps you are not the lady he searches.'

'Thank you,' I said. 'Thank you very much.'

After such kindness, I had to tell him something. I leaned toward him and lowered my voice. 'Mr Vitroni,' I said, 'I'm hiding. That's why I used a different name and cut off my hair. No one is supposed to know where I am. I think someone is trying to kill me.'

Mr Vitroni was not surprised. He nodded, as if he knew such things happened quite frequently. 'What have you done?' he said.

'Nothing,' I told him. 'I haven't done anything at all. It's very complicated, but it has to do with money. I'm quite rich, that's why this person, these people, want to kill me, so they will get the money.' He seemed to believe this, so I went on. 'This man who came, he may be one of my friends, or perhaps he's an enemy. What did he look like?'

Mr Vitroni spread his hands. 'It is hard for me to say. He had a red car, like yours,' He was holding out on me, what did he want? 'Perhaps the police should arrest this man,' he said.

'That's very good of you,' I said, 'but I couldn't do that. I'm still not sure who this man is, and besides I have no proof. What did he look like?'

'He was wearing a coat,' said Mr Vitroni helpfully. 'A dark coat, American. He was tall, yes, a young man, not old.'

'Did he have a beard?' I asked.

'No beard. A moustache, yes.'

None of this was any help. It didn't sound like Fraser Buchanan, though. 'He says he is a reporter, from a newspaper,' Mr. Vitroni said. 'I do not think he is a reporter. You are sure you do not wish him arrested? It could be arranged, I could arrange it with them.'

Was he asking for a bribe? It occurred to me that his visit was no friendly one. It was a negotiation, and no doubt a similar negotiation had gone on with the man. If I would pay, he would help me. Otherwise he would tell this man how to find me. Unfortunately I didn't have enough money. I decided quickly that I'd have to leave that evening, I'd drive to Rome.

'No, really,' I said. 'I'll handle it in my own way.'

I stood up and held out my hand to Mr. Vitroni. 'Thank you very much,' I said, 'it was very kind of you to tell me all this.'

He was puzzled; he must have been expecting me to make a deal with him. 'I could help you,' he said. 'There is a house, farther back, away from the town. You could stay there until this man goes away, we would bring you some food.'

'Thank you,' I said, 'perhaps I'll do that.'

As he left, he patted my shoulder.

'Do not worry,' he said, 'all will be happy.'

In the evening I packed my suitcase and carried it up to the car. But when I went to start it, the tank was empty. Stupidity, I thought, remembering it had been low on the trip back from Rome. But then I thought: It's been drained.

Chapter Thirty-three

I never should have told him I had money. I could see it all now, the plot was clear. They'd always intended it, from the very first. The old man of the artichokes was a spy, he was Mr Vitroni's father, he'd been sent to watch me, and as soon as he'd seen me ithout my disguise they'd consipired. If I agreed to hide in the secluded house I would become a prisoner. It would be folly to go to anyone and ask for gasoline. They would know then that I meant to leave. Also, no one in the town sold it, they would have to send out for it, and then Mr Vitroni would be sure to hear of it. He would come and tell me none could be had. I would beg, and he would say, 'Gasoline, that is very expensive.'

The soldiers or police were in on it, too, they would help him, and there would be no one to stop them. I'd virtually told him that no one knew where I was; it was an open invitation. When Arthur arrived they would tell him I'd gone away, they had no idea where. Meanwhile I'd be roped and helpless, they'd want me to send away for money, and when none arrived, what would they do then? Would they kill me and bury me in a gravelly grave among the olives? Or would they keep me in a cage and fatten me up as was done among primitive tribes in Africa, but with huge plates of pasta, would they make me wear black satin underwear like the kind advertised at the back of the *fotoromanzi* would they charge admission to the men of the town, would I become one of those Fellini whores, gigantic and shapeless?

This is serious. I told myself. *Pull yourself together.* Perhaps I was becoming hysterical. I didn't want to spend the rest of my life in a cage, as a fat whore, a captive Earth Mother for whom somebody else collected the admission tickets. I would have to think of some plan. I had two days though, so I went to bed. There was no use trying to run away in pitch darkness, I'd only get lost. Or caught: doubtless I was being watched.

I woke up in the middle of the night. I could hear footsteps outside my window, on the terrace down below. Now there was a scraping noise: someone was climbing the trellis! Had I locked the window or not? I didn't want to get out of bed to see. I backed against the wall, staring at the window where the outline of a head, then the shoulders, was looming into view. ... By the light of the moon I could see who it was, and I relaxed.

It was only my mother. She was dressed in her trim navy-blue suit with the tight waist and shoulder pads, and her white hat and gloves. Her face was made up, she'd drawn a bigger mouth around her mouth with lipstick, but the shape of her own mouth showed through. She was crying soundlessly, she pressed her face against the glass like a child, mascara ran from her eyes in black tears.

'What do you want?' I said, but she didn't answer. She stretched out her arms to me, she wanted me to come with her; she wanted us to be together.

I began to walk towards the door. She was smiling at me now, with her smudged face, could she see I loved her? I loved her but the glass was between us, I would have to go through it. I longed to console her. Together we would go down the corridor into the darkness. I would do what she wanted.

The door was locked. I shook at it and shook until it came open.

I was standing on the terrace in my torn nightgown, shivering in the wind. It was dark, there was no moon at all. I was awake now; my teeth were chattering, with fear as well as with cold. I went back into the flat and got into bed.

She'd come very close that time, she'd almost done it. She'd never really let go of me because I had never let her go. It had been she standing behind me in the mirror, she was the one who was waiting around each turn, her voice whispered the words. She had been the lady in the boat, the death barge, the tragic lady with flowing hair and stricken eyes, the lady in the tower. She couldn't stand the view from the window, life was her curse. How could I renounce her? She needed her freedom also; she had been my reflection too long. What was the charm, what would set her free?

If someone had to come back from the Other Side to haunt me, I thought, why couldn't it be Aunt Lou? I trusted her, we could have a good talk, she could give me some advice and tell me what to do.

But I couldn't imagine Aunt Lou doing this. 'You can handle it,' she'd say, no matter how much I protested that I couldn't. She would refuse to see my life as the disaster it was.

Whereas my mother. . . . Why did I have to dream about my mother, have nightmares about her, sleepwalk out to meet her? My mother was a vortex, a dark vacuum, I would never be able to make her happy. Or anyone else. Maybe it was time for me to stop trying.

Chapter Thirty-four

In the morning I had several cups of tea, to give me energy and calm me down. The trick was to be as calm as possible. I would act as though everything was normal, all was well, I would be unhurried; I'd do my shopping and visit the post office as usual, so they'd think I was cooperating. I might even seek out Mr Vitroni and ask about the house, so they'd think I was going along with everything. I would wait until the afternoon, when there were people around. Then I would simply stroll down the hill, carrying my handbag but not my suitcase, and hitch a ride to Rome. I wouldn't be able to take much with me, but I could get quite a lot into my handbag.

I went through the bureau drawers, deciding what I would have to leave behind. I packed three pairs of underpants. Nightgowns were not necessary; Fraser Buchanan's black notebook was. The typewriter would have to stay, but *Stalked by Love* I would take with me.

I picked up the manuscript, intending to roll it into a cylinder for easy packing. Then I sat down and started leafing through it. I saw now what was wrong, what I would have to do. Charlotte would have to go into the maze, there was no way out of it. She'd wanted to go in ever since reaching Redmond Grange, and nothing anyone could say, not all the hair-raising tales of the servants, not all the sneering hints of Felicia had been able to deter her. But her feelings were ambiguous: did the maze mean certain death, or did it contain the answer to a riddle, an answer she must learn in order to live? More important: would she marry Redmond only if she stayed out of the maze, or only if she went in? Possibly she would be able to win his love only by risking her life and allowing him to rescue her. He would unclench the hands from around her throat (whose hands would they be?) and tell her she was a silly little fool, though brave. She would become Mrs. Redmond, the fourth one.

Don't go into the maze, Charlotte, you'll be entering at your own risk, I told her. I've always got you out of it before but now I'm no longer dependable. She paid no attention to me, she never did; she stood up, put away her embroidery, and prepared to go outside. Don't say I didn't warn you. I told her. But I couldn't stop, I had to see it through to the end. I closed my eyes. . . .

It was noon when Charlotte entered the maze. She took the precaution of fastening one end of a ball of knitting wool, borrowed from Mrs. Ryerson on the pretext of mending her shawl, at the entrance; she did not intend to lose her way.

The walls of the maze, which were of some prickly evergreen shrub, were indeed sadly overgrown. Surely no one had been here for many years, Charlotte thought, as she pushed her way through the straggling branches, which caught on her gown as if to hold her back. She turned to the left, then to the right, unwinding her ball of wool as she went.

Outside, the sky had been overcast and a cold February wind had been blowing; but here, sheltered by the thick walls of leaves and branches, Charlotte felt quite warm. The sun had come out and the sky was clearing; nearby, a bird sang. She was losing track of time; it seemed as if hours had passed while she walked along the gravel path between the green, thorny walls. Was it her imagination, or had the maze become trimmer, better kept . . . and flowers had begun to appear. Surely it was too early for flowers. She had an odd sensation, as though unseen eyes were watching her. She remembered Mrs. Ryerson's stories about the Little Folk; then she laughed at herself for giving in, even momentarily, to superstition. It was just an ordinary maze, there was nothing unusual about it. Surely the two previous Lady Redmonds had met their fate in some other way.

She must be getting near the centre of the maze. She turned another corner, and sure enough it was there before her, an open gravelled oblong with a border of flowers, the daffodils already in bloom. Disappointingly, it was empty. Charlotte peered about looking for some clue to its evil reputation, but there was none. She started to walk back the way she had come. Suddenly it was frightening, she wanted to get out before it was too late. She didn't want to know any more, she'd been a fool ever to have come here. She began to run, but she made the mistake of trying to wind up the ball of knitting wool as she ran, and her feet became hopelessly entangled. As she fell, iron fingers closed around her throat . . . she tried to scream, she struggled, her eyes bulged, she looked wildly around for Redmond.

From behind her came a mocking laugh – Felicia's! 'There wasn't room for both of us,' she said, 'one of us had to die.'

Just as Charlotte was sinking into unconsciousness, Felicia was flung aside like a bundle of old clothes, and Charlotte was gazing up into the dark eyes of Redmond. 'My darling,' he breathed hoarsely. Strong arms lifted her, his warm lips pressed her own. . . .

That was the way it was supposed to go, that was the way it had always gone before, but somehow it no longer felt right. I'd taken a wrong turn somewhere; there was something, some fact or clue, that I had overlooked. I would have to walk it through, I would have to find a suitable locale and go through the motions. I thought of the Cardinal's garden in Tivoli, with its sphinxes and fountains and its many-breasted goddess. That would do, it had a lot of paths. I would go there this afternoon. . . .

But I was forgetting about the man, my car with its empty tank; I would have to leave the book for later and concentrate on my escape.

This time I really would disappear, without a trace. No one at all would know where I was, not even Sam, not even Arthur. This time I would be free completely; no shreds of the past would cling to me, no clutching fingers. I could do anything I wanted, I could be a hotess in a bar, I could return to Toronto and give body rubs, maybe that was what I should have done. Or I could merge into Italy, marry a vegetable man: we'd live in a little stone cottage, I'd have babies and fatten up, we'd eat steamy food and cover our bodies with oil, we'd laugh at death and live in the present, I'd wear my hair in a bun and grow a moustache, I'd have a bibbed apron, green, with flowers on it. Everything would be ordinary, I'd go to church on Sundays, we'd drink rough red wine, I'd become an aunt, a grandmother, everyone would respect me.

Somehow this was not convincing. Why did every one of my

fantasies turn into a trap? In this one I saw myself climbing out a window, in my bibbed apron and bun, oblivious to the cries of the children and grandchildren behind me. I might as well face it, I thought, I was an artist, an escape artist. I'd sometimes talked about love and commitment, but the real romance of my life was that between Houdini and his ropes and locked trunk; entering the embrace of bondage, slithering out again. What else had I ever done?

This thought did not depress me. In fact, although I was frightened, I was feeling curiously light-hearted. Danger, I realized, did this to me.

I washed my hair, humming, as if I were getting ready for a big evening. A lot of the brown came out, but I no longer cared.

I padded out onto the balcony on my wet bare feet to dry my hair. There was a beeze; far below in the valley I could hear gunshots, it must've been someone shooting at a bird. They'd shoot anything that moved here, almost, they ate the songbirds in pies. All that music devoured by mouths. Eyes and ears were also hungry, but not so obviously. From now on, I thought, I would dance for no one but myself. May I have this waltz? I whispered.

I raised myself onto my bare toes and twirled around, tentatively at first. The air filled with spangles. I lifted my arms and swayed them in time to the gentle music, I remembered the music, I remembered every step and gesture. It was a long way down to the ground from here; I was a little dizzy. I closed my eyes. Wings grew from my shoulders, an arm slid around my waist. . . .

Shit. I'd danced right through the broken glass, in my bare feet too. Some butterfly. I limped into the main room, trailing bloody footprints and looking for a towel. I washed my feet in the bathtub; the soles looked as if they'd been minced. The real red shoes, the feet punished for dancing. You could dance, or you could have the love of a good man. But you were afraid to dance, because you had this unnatural fear that if you danced they'd cut your feet off so you wouldn't be able to dance. Finally you overcame your fear and danced, and they cut your feet off. The good man went away too, because you wanted to dance.

But I chose the love, I wanted the good man; why wasn't that the right choice? I was never a dancing girl anyway. A bear in an arena only appears to dance, really it's on its hind legs trying to avoid the arrows. And now I didn't have any Band-aids. I sat on the edge of the bathtub, tears running helplessly from my eyes, blood running helplessly from the tiny cuts in my feet.

I went into the other room and lay down on the bed, feet raised on the pillow so the blood would run the other way. How could I escape now, on my cut feet?

Chapter Thirty-five

After a couple of hours I got up. My feet weren't as bad as I'd thought, I could still walk. I practiced limping, back and forth across the room. At every step I took, small pains shot through my feet. The Little Mermaid rides again, I thought, the big mermaid rides again.

I would have to walk up to town, hobbling through the gauntlet of old women, who would make horns with their hands, tell the children to throw stones, wish me bad luck. What did they see, the eyes behind those stone-wall windows? A female monster, larger than life, larger than most life around here anyway, striding down the hill, her hair standing on end with electrical force, volts of malevolent energy shooting from her fingers, her green eyes behind her dark tourist's glasses, her dark mafia glasses, lit up and glowing like a cat's. Look out, old black-stockinged sausage women, or I'll zap you, in spite of your evil-eye signs and muttered prayers to the saints. Did they think I flew around at night like a moth, drinking blood from their big toes? If I got a black dress and long black stockings, then would they like me?

Maybe my mother didn't name me after Joan Crawford after all, I thought, she just told me that to cover up. She named me after Joan of Arc, didn't she know what happened to women like that? They were accused of witchcraft, they were roped to the stake, they gave a lovely light; a star is a blob of burning gas. But I was a coward, I'd rather not win and not burn, I'd rather sit in the grandstand eating my bag of popcorn and watch along with everyone else. When you started hearing voices you were in trouble, especially if you believed them. The English cheered as Joan went up like a volcano, a rocket, like a plum pudding. They sprinkled the ashes on the river; only her heart remained.

I walked up the hill, past the black-dressed old women on the steps, ignoring their hostile eyes, and along the street that led to the post office. The policemen or soldiers were in their places; the massive woman behind the counter was there, too.

She knew who I was by now, I didn't have to ask. She handed me another of Sam's brown envelopes. It felt like more newspaper clippings, so I tore it open.

There were more clippings; but on top of them was a letter, on crisp law-office stationery:

> Dear Miss Delacourt:
>
> My client, Mr Sam Spinsky, has requested me to send you the enclosed. He feels there might be something you could do to help him in his present predicament. He had instructed me not to reveal your whereabouts until further notice.

The signature a scrawl; and underneath the letter,

> POETESS FEARED SLAIN IN TERRORIST PURGE!

Forgetting decorum, I sat down on the bench, right beside a policeman. This was terrible. Sam and Marlene had been arrested for murder, they'd been accused of murdering me, they were actually in jail. For a fleeting moment I thought how pleased Marlene would be; but then, she'd be quite cheesed off that I was the cause and not some strike or demonstration. Still, jail was jail. They hadn't told yet, that much was clear.

It was that family on the beach, the one having the picnic. They'd watched me thrashing around in the water, they'd seen me go under. They'd read the account in the paper, the interview with Marlene in which she said they'd thrown me a life preserver. But there was no life preserver, and when the police checked with the boat-rental place they admitted there hadn't even been one on the boat. They found my dress, though, in the bow; that made them suspicious. The family's name was Morgan. Mr Morgan said he heard a scream (he couldn't have, it was too far away, it was too windy) and looked up in time to see Sam and Marlene leaning over the side of the boat, just after pushing me in. There was a picture of Mr Morgan, as well as the picture of me, the smiling one taken on the day of my death. Mr Morgan looked serious and responsible; he was having the time of his life, he was important at last, he was acting out his own fantasy.

Poor Sam, By now he'd had his pockets emptied and his shoelaces taken away, he'd had louse-killer put on him and a finger stuck up his anus. He'd been grilled by two detectives, one acting kind and offering him cigarettes and coffee, the other bullying him, and all because of my stupidity, my cowardice. I should have stayed where I was and faced reality. Poor gentle Sam, with his violent theories; he wouldn't hurt a fly.

I was referred to as a 'key figure' in a mysterious dynamite plot. Marlene's father, apparently, had come forward with information about some missing dynamite, and Marlene had broken down and admitted to taking it. But she couldn't produce it. I'd been in charge of it, she told them; and she told them about the second-hand car too, but they hadn't been able to locate it. The police were assuming that what they referred to as Sam's 'cell' had liquidated me because I knew too much and was becoming traitorous. Arthur had been taken in for questioning, but later released. It was obvious he was both innocent and ignorant.

I'd have to go back and rescue them. I couldn't go back. Maybe I could send the police a token part of me, just to let them know I was still alive. A finger, an autograph, a tooth?

I got up off the bench, stuffing the clippings into my purse. I went outside and headed toward the hill Then I saw Mr Vitroni. He was sitting at an outdoor café table. There was another man with him. I couldn't see him clearly, his back was toward me, but surely this was the man. Come back a day too soon.

Mr Vitroni had seen me, he was looking straight at me. I hurried across the square, I was almost running. I made myself slow down. I looked behind only once, and Mr Vitroni was getting up, shaking hands with the man. . . .

I turned the corner and began to run in earnest. *I must be calm, I must be collected, I must collect myself.* My cut feet screamed as they hit the stones.

Chapter Thirty-six

I finally reached the balcony. The sun was sinking, the balcony was bright with sunlit glass, broken and sharp like fire. In the plate-glass window my reflection ran beside me, the face dark, the hair standing out around my head, a red nimbus.

I unlocked the door and went in. There was no one inside, not yet, I still had time. . . . I hadn't seen him clearly. Perhaps I could elude him. I'd wait until he was walking along the balcony; then I'd slip into the bathroom and bolt the door. While he was trying to get in, I could climb up on the toilet and squeeze through the tiny window.

I went into the bathroom to look at the window. It was too small, I'd get stuck. I didn't want to be either arrested or interviewed half way out a window. It was too undignified.

Perhaps I could hide among the artichokes. Perhaps I could run down the hill, perhaps I could disappear and never be found. But if I ran I would simply be caught, sooner or later. Instead I was going to defend myself. I refused to go back. I went into the kitchen and got the empty Cinzano bottle out of the garbage can, grasping it by the neck.

I crouched behind the door, out of sight of the window, and waited. Time passed; nothing happened. Perhaps I'd been wrong, perhaps that hadn't been the right man. Or maybe there was no man at all, Mr. Vitroni had made him up in order to frighten me. I began to be restless. It struck me that I'd spent too much of my life crouching behind closed doors, listening to the voices on the other side.

The door itself was ordinary enough. Through the glass pane at the top I could see a small piece of the outside world: blue sky, some grayish-pink clouds.

It was noon when she entered the maze. She was determined to penetrate its secret at last. It had been a hazard for too long. Several times she had requested Redmond to have it torn down, but he would not listen. It had been in his family for generations, he said. It did not seem to matter to him that so many had been lost in it.

She made several turnings without incident. It was necessary to remember the way she had come, and she attempted to do this, memorizing small details, the shape of a bush, the color of a flower. The pathway was freshly graveled; here and there daffodils were in bloom.

Suddenly she found herself in the central plot. A stone bench ran along one side, and on it were seated four women, Two of them looked a lot like her, with red hair and green eyes and small white teeth. The third was middle-aged, dressed in a strange garment that ended halfway up her calves, with a ratty piece of fur around her neck. The last was enormously fat. She was wearing a pair of pink tights and a short pink skirt covered with spangles. From her head sprouted two antennae, like a butterfly's, and a pair of obviously false wings was pinned to her back. Felicia was surprised at the appearance of the woman in pink, but was too well bred to show it.

The women murmured among themselves. 'We were expecting you,' they said; the first one shifted over, making room for her.

'We could tell it was your turn.'

'Who are you?' she asked.

'We are Lady Redmond,' said the middle-aged woman sadly, 'All of us,' the fat woman with the wings added.

'There must be some mistake,' Felicia protested. 'I myself am Lady Redmond.'

'Oh, yes, we know,' said the first woman. 'But every man has more than one wife. Sometimes all at once, sometimes one at a time, sometimes ones he doesn't even know about.'

'How did you get here?' Felicia asked. 'Why can't you go back to the outside world?'

'Back?' said the first woman. 'We have all tried to go back. That was our mistake,' Felicia looked behind her, and indeed the pathway by which she had entered was now overgrown with branches; she could not even tell where it had been. She was trapped here with these women. . . . And wasn't there something peculiar about them? Wasn't their skin too white, weren't their eyes too vague . . . ? She noticed that she could see the dim outline of the bench through their tenuous bodies.

'The only way out,' said the first woman, 'is through that door.'

She looked at the door. It was at the other side of the graveled plot, affixed to a door frame but otherwise unsupported. She walked all the way around it: it was the same from both sides. It had a plain surface and a doorknob; there was a small pane of glass at the top, through which she could see blue sky and some grayish-pink clouds.

She took hold of the doorknob and turned it. The door unlocked and swung outward. ... There, standing on the threshold, waiting for her, was Redmond. She was about to throw herself into his arms, weeping with relief, when she noticed an odd expression in his eyes. Then she knew. Redmond was the killer. He was a killer in disguise, he wanted to murder her as he had murdered his other wives. ... Then she would always have to stay here with them, at the center of the maze. ... He wanted to replace her with the other one, the next one, thin and flawless. ...

'Don't touch me,' she said, taking a step backward. She refused to be doomed. As long as she stayed on her side of the door she would be safe. Cunningly, he began his transformations, trying to lure her into his reach. His face grew a white gauze mask, then a pair of mauve-tinted spectacles, then a red beard and moustache, which faded, giving place to burning eyes and icicle teeth. Then his cloak vanished and he stood looking at her sadly; he was wearing a turtle-neck sweater.

'Arthur?' she said. Could he ever forgive her?

Redmond resumed his opera cloak. His mouth was hard and rapacious, his eyes smoldered. 'Let me take you away,' he whispered. 'Let me rescue you. We will dance together forever, always.'

'Always,' she said, almost yielding. 'Forever.' Once she had wanted these words, she had waited all her life for someone to say them. ... She pictured herself whirling slowly across a ballroom floor, a strong arm around her waist. ...

'No,' she said. 'I know who you are.'

The flesh fell away from his face, revealing the skull behind it; he stepped towards her reaching for her throat. ...

I opened my eyes. I could hear footsteps coming down the gravel path. They were real footsteps, they were on the balcony. They stopped outside the door. A hand knocked gently, once, twice.

I still had options. I could pretend I wasn't there. I could wait and do nothing. I could disguise my voice and say that I was someone else. But if I turned the handle the door would unlock and swing outward, and I would have to face the man who stood waiting for me, for my life.

I opened the door. I knew who it would be.

Chapter Thirty-seven

I didn't really mean to hit him with the Cinzano bottle. I mean, I meant to hit someone, but it wasn't personal. I'd never seen him before in my life, he was a complete stranger. I guess I just got carried away: he looked like someone else. ...

And I certainly didn't think I would knock him out like that; I suppose it's a case of not knowing your own strength. I felt terrible about it, especially when I saw the blood. I couldn't just leave him there, he might have had a concussion or bled to death, so I got Mr Vitroni to call a doctor. I said I thought this man was trying to break into the house. Luckily he was out cold, so he couldn't contradict me.

It was nice of him not to press charges when he came to. At first I thought it was only because he wanted the story: reporters are like that. I talked too much, of course, but I was feeling nervous. I guess it will make a pretty weird story, once he's written it; and the odd thing is that I didn't tell any lies. Well, not very many. Some of the names and a few other things, but nothing major. I suppose I could still have gotten out of it. I could have said I had amnesia or something. ... Or I could have escaped; he wouldn't have been able to trace me. I'm surprised I didn't do that, since I've always been terrified of being found out. But somehow I couldn't just run off and leave him all alone in the hospital with no one to talk to; not after I'd almost killed him by mistake.

It must have been a shock for him to wake up in bed with seven stitches, though. I felt quite guilty about that. His coat was a mess, too, but I told him it would come out in the dry cleaning. I offered to pay for it but he wouldn't let me. I took him some flowers instead; I couldn't find any roses so they were yellow things, sort of like sunflowers. They were a little wilted, I said maybe he could get the nurse to put them in water for him. He seemed pleased.

It was good of him to lend me the plane fare. I'll pay it back once I'm organized again. The first thing is to get Sam and Marlene out of jail, I owe it to them. It was Sam's lawyer that gave away the fact that I was still alive; I shouldn't hold it against him, he was just doing his job. And I'll have to see Arthur, though I'm not looking forward to it, all those explanations and his expression of silent outrage. After the story comes out he'll know the truth anyway. He loved me under false pretenses, so I shouldn't feel too rejected when he stops. I don't think he's even gotten my postcard yet, I forgot to send it air mail.

After that, well, I don't have any definite plans. I'll feel like an idiot with all the publicity, but that's nothing new. They'll probably say my disappearance was some kind of stunt, a trick. . . . I won't write any more Costume Gothics, though; I think they were bad for me. But maybe I'll try some science fiction. The future doesn't appeal to me as much as the past, but I'm sure it's better for you. I keep thinking I should learn some lesson from all of this, as my mother would have said.

Right now, though, it's easier just to stay here in Rome – I've found a cheap little *pensione* – and walk to the hospital for visiting hours. He hasn't told anyone where I am yet, he promised he wouldn't for a week. He's a nice man; he doesn't have a very interesting nose, but I have to admit that there is something about a man in a bandage. . . . Also I've begun to feel he's the only person who knows anything about me. Maybe because I've never hit anyone else with a bottle, so they never got to see that part of me. Neither did I, come to think of it.

It did make a mess; but then, I don't think I'll ever be a very tidy person.